NEW YORK REVIEW BOOKS
CLASSICS

ABEL AND CAIN

GREGOR VON REZZORI (1914–1998) was born in Bukovina, then part of the Austro-Hungarian Empire. He later described his childhood in a family of declining fortunes as one "spent among slightly mad and dislocated personalities in a period that also was mad and dislocated and filled with unrest." After studying at the University of Vienna, Rezzori moved to Bucharest and enlisted in the Romanian army. During World War II, he lived in Berlin, where he worked as a radio broadcaster and published his first novel. In West Germany after the war, he wrote for radio and film and began publishing books, including the four-volume *Idiot's Guide to German Society*. From the late 1950s on, Rezzori had parts in several French and West German films, including one directed by his friend Louis Malle. In 1967, after spending years classified as a stateless person, Rezzori settled in a fifteenth-century farmhouse outside of Florence. There he produced some of his best-known works, among them *Memoirs of an Anti-Semite* and the memoir *The Snows of Yesteryear*.

DAVID DOLLENMAYER has translated works by Bertolt Brecht, Elias and Veza Canetti, Martin Walser, and many others.

JOACHIM NEUGROSCHEL (1938–2011) translated works from the French, German, Italian, Russian, and Yiddish and was the editor of several anthologies of Yiddish literature.

MARSHALL YARBROUGH is a writer, translator, and musician. He has translated works by such authors as Wolf Wondratschek, Michae

JOSHU ... ding *Attention: Dispatc* ... *Moving Kings*. He is a

OTHER BOOKS BY GREGOR VON REZZORI
PUBLISHED BY NYRB CLASSICS

An Ermine in Czernopol
Translated by Philip Boehm
Introduction by Daniel Kehlmann

Memoirs of an Anti-Semite
Translated by Joachim Neugroschel
Introduction by Deborah Eisenberg

The Snows of Yesteryear
Translated by H. F. Broch de Rothermann
Introduction by John Banville

ABEL AND CAIN

GREGOR VON REZZORI

Translated from the German by

DAVID DOLLENMAYER, JOACHIM NEUGROSCHEL,

and **MARSHALL YARBROUGH**

Introduction by

JOSHUA COHEN

NEW YORK REVIEW BOOKS

New York

THIS IS A NEW YORK REVIEW BOOK
PUBLISHED BY THE NEW YORK REVIEW OF BOOKS
435 Hudson Street, New York, NY 10014
www.nyrb.com

The Death of My Brother Abel originally published in German under the title *Der Tod Meines Bruders Abel* by C. Bertelsmann/Mosaik Verlag. *Cain: The Last Manuscript* originally published in German under the title *Kain: Der letzte Manuskript* by C. Bertelsmann Verlag.

The translation of this work was supported by a grant from the Goethe-Institut.

Library of Congress Cataloging-in-Publication Data
Names: Rezzori, Gregor von, author. | Cohen, Joshua, 1980– writer of introduction.
Title: Abel and Cain / Gregor von Rezzori ; introduction by Joshua Cohen ; translated by David Dollenmayer ; translated by Joachim Neugroschel ; translated by Marshall Yarbrough.
Other titles: Cain. English.
Description: New York : NYRB Classics, 2019.
Identifiers: LCCN 2018029642 (print) | LCCN 2018031953 (ebook) | ISBN 9781681373263 (ebook) | ISBN 9781681373256 (paperback)
Subjects: | BISAC: FICTION / Literary.
Classification: LCC PT2635.E98 (ebook) | LCC PT2635.E98 A64 2019 (print) | DDC 833/.912—dc23
LC record available at https://lccn.loc.gov/2018029642

ISBN 978-1-68137-325-6
Available as an electronic book; ISBN 978-1-68137-326-3

Printed in the United States of America on acid-free paper.
10 9 8 7 6 5 4 3 2 1

CONTENTS

INTRODUCTION

I

IF YOU put a gun to my head and asked me to describe *Abel and Cain* in three sentences, this is what I would answer: Murder. Murder. Murder.

First-, second-, third-degree: premeditated, unpremeditated, involuntary.

Fratricide, sororicide, parricide.

Genocide, historicide, deicide.

Every *cide*, all the violence of the ides, suffuses every aspect of this grimly remarkable book, from its title that memorializes the victim and perpetrator of the first murder on biblical record, to its recurrent evocations of Nazi death camps and German cities under Allied bombardment. Then there are the book's myriad less literal killings, its *Gedankenmorde* or "thought murders," such as: the "murder" committed by writers when they write their family and friends into their books, and the "murder" of writers and books committed by their agents, editors, publishers, and introducers...

Not to forget the "murder" of books by their screen adaptations, and the "murder" of literature itself by film and television...

I could go on and on, but Gregor von Rezzori already has in this massive novel that might be two novels that contradict each other so brutally and so brilliantly that summarizing them should be a crime—or maybe it's just my punishment for loving them.

An attempt at summary, come to think of it, is what triggers the very existence of these pages:

At a Paris café on the eve of 1968, the *annus counterculturis*, a Galician Jew turned American literary agent named Brodny meets an initially unnamed German-language novelist and asks him for "his story," which the novelist takes to mean "the story of his life," but told in the Hollywood style: short enough to be sketched on a napkin, quick enough to be pitched in an elevator.

In the film business, the suggestively psychoanalytic term for this type of synopsis is a "treatment," and the writer is resistant, to say the least.

Meanwhile, the agent's not asking anymore, he's yelling, "Tell me the *story* in three sentences!"

The writer is so insulted by this demand for abbreviation, abridgement, encapsulation, etc., that he ditches the agent, dashes off to his hotel, and, forgetting his writer's block, dashes off this book, or books—in which he calls himself "Aristides Subicz," though it's unclear whether that name is his "real" name, or a pseudonym assumed for his scriptwriting hackwork, or a survival identity assumed during wartime.

(Aristides was an Athenian statesman. Subicz was the name of an ancient ruling house of Dalmatia, which spanned present-day Croatia and Bosnia.)

Of course, the more the writer Subicz explains to the agent Brodny why "his"—Subicz's—life can't be condensed for film, the more he ends up recounting that life itself: He narrates his birth in 1919 in Bessarabia, just after it had become annexed to Romania; his Austro-Dalmatian mother, who drags him around the Côte d'Azur as she flits between lovers, whom he calls "uncles" ("Bolivian tin-mine owners, Argentine cattle breeders, Irish beer kings, Dutch petroleum magnates," and a Romanian nobleman with Ottoman roots—Uncle Ferdinand—who might, but might not, be the boy's father); his mother's suicide and his subsequent adoption by his mother's estranged family in squalid, disembourgeoised interwar Vienna; his schooldays rivalry with chronic masturbator-cum-convinced Nazi Cousin Wolfgang; his affair with a Jewish woman named Stella and his friendship with her husband, John, a British diplomat and spy, who introduces him to haute society just as it's collapsing.

The anecdotes don't stop, not even for the Anschluss: Subicz keeps stuffing them in wherever he can—in body text, in dialogue, in parentheses—like he once had Aunt Selma stuff a cluster of oak leaves into the muzzle of Cousin Wolfgang's gun:

> 1939: I was already in Romania to be a soldier myself, thus could not say good-bye to [Cousin Wolfgang] when he was loaded onto a train to storm into the land of the Poles.... But I had asked Aunt Selma to put a cluster of oak leaves in his rifle barrel (as is customary in Germany in historic hours), and, touched by my tenderness, she had obediently done so. Cousin Wolfgang took the train straight into his baptism of fire. He had no time or chance to pull the oak leaves out of the rifle barrel. He probably didn't even recall they were there. All he knew was that the train stopped, out in the open somewhere, and he was surrounded by splintering and crashing. He thus realized he was being shot at and that it was his duty to shoot back at whatever he could see with his purblind eyes. So he shot back. And since my oak-leaf cluster was stopping up his rifle, the bullet flew back out and tore the bolt off the chamber and the thumb off his right hand....
>
> Cousin Wolfgang was sent back to Vienna with a transport of wounded soldiers on the very next train. En route, he was bitten by a rat, which had snuck (unscheduled) into the railroad car meant to hold eight horses or forty (damaged) men. By the time he arrived in Vienna several days later, Wolfgang was dying.

Subicz deserts the Romanian army fairly immediately after conscription and attempts a crazy reunion with Stella—who's found refuge in Switzerland—in Berlin. He waits for her, but she never comes; the SS has dragged her off to the gas and ovens.

The end of the war finds Subicz in Hamburg, a city that had just been leveled in what was then the heaviest assault in the history of aerial warfare.

In Hamburg, Subicz sets to work as a novelist, but with Reichsmarks worthless and Deutschmarks scarce—and a wife, and a son, and mistresses, and a prostitute habit—he takes on sideline gigs scribbling scripts for the "piglets" of the German film industry, eager to revive the glory, if not the aesthetics, of Weimar's Ufa.

2

How many Abels are we up to by now? Definitely Cousin Wolfgang, definitely Stella. Didn't Hollywood request a third sentence, though—a third death sentence?

Schwab.

The major postwar presence in Subicz's life is a man named Johannes Schwab, who like Subicz is a frustrated writer, but unlike Subicz isn't cheap enough for film, and so he goes to work as a book editor. Pity the earnest German, he thinks he's being honest.

Schwab, in fact, is Subicz's book editor—meaning that he vouched for Subicz's talent and got his author a series of advances. Needless to say, not a single page has ever come in.

Schwab, who also lives in Hamburg, though the name marks him as a Swabian, is the German "brother" to Subicz's errant "Austrian."

Schwab's first appearance is more like a diagnosis: "He was wearing a heavy turtleneck sweater (not a Hanseatic outfit but, with corduroy slacks and a beret, the guild costume of German intellectuals in the fifties, which costume he carried on into the sixties—typical of people who are behind the times but consider themselves avant-garde!)."

Two decades of waiting for Subicz's pages have taken their toll: Schwab arrives in Paris to meet Subicz (like the agent Brodny, earlier in the book, but years later in terms of chronology, meets Subicz) and Schwab confesses as much, between room-temperature gin and tonics, cigarettes, and pills: He's not on board with the *Wirtschaftswunder*, the Federal Republic's Economic Miracle, but he needs its salary and perks; neither is he down with the burgeoning student movements, but he needs their excesses and purpose. Subicz should be worried, but men who've survived mass slaughters tend not to worry too much about substance abuse and certainly don't stage interventions—at best, they get wasted themselves and pick up the tab, which is exactly what Subicz does. Schwab returns to Germany and binges to death. Subicz calls it a suicide, which is just the polite society term for another homicide he's gotten away with.

Indeed, in Subicz's narration, which takes up the two sections or folders labeled A and B, Schwab is presented as the Abel to Subicz's Cain: Subicz "kills" Schwab by abandoning him for the movies, or by failing to write a book that brings Schwab back into esteem at his publishing house, which is under increasing pressure to make profits as its media-conglomerate parent becomes a global hegemon. As folder C is approached, however, it becomes increasingly feasible that the roles can be reversed, and that Schwab might be the Cain to Subicz's Abel: Schwab "kills" Subicz by becoming too dissolute to edit him, or by having also championed Nagel, a famous but plodding German writer whose success has stymied Subicz (Nagel is a composite, but also the Nobel laureate and Waffen SS member Günter Wilhelm Grass). Another way to read the titular brothers is through nationality: Subicz's Austria-Hungary is Abel, murdered by Germany's Cain, which fostered Nazism and foisted it on Europe. Or else: Schwab's Germany is Abel, murdered by Austria-Hungary's Cain, Hitler's native land.

It doesn't ultimately matter which role any of them plays, however: At the end of the book, all of these characters, and all of these nations, are dead.

Schwab, as has been reported, dies of his habits, and Subicz dies in a car crash with a French starlet just outside Avignon, on the road from Paris to Cannes. Germany and Austria, meanwhile, have been reduced to mental habits, superstitions—because all of their cities have essentially become outposts of America, whose energy requires italics:

> *Already built into the trashy boxiness are the ruins of tomorrow, the tin-and-concrete wasteland of secondhand Americana, with*

> *mangebelts of rust and mortar, seething and teeming with ever-swelling, ever-swarming masses of more and more colorless more and more dissatisfied more and more demanding more and more hopeless more and more evil supermarket consumers in ever swifter, tinnier, more hastily glued-together, more and more perilous automobiles: highway rest stop eaters with empty gazes over munching chewing kneading swallowing mouths . . .*

As the folders unfold and Subicz's recounted conversations give way to dialogue from scenes from Subicz's abandoned novels, then give way to dialogue from scenes from Subicz's abandoned screenplays—all of which are interspersed with Schwab's own editorial notes—the border between the "brothers" is all but effaced, like the border between Austria and Hungary, whose wall came down half a year before the wall in Berlin, as if the grand old Empire were making one last bid to restore itself and reassert its standards before Coca-Cola and Levi's took over.

3

When Gregor von Rezzori died, in 1998, he still wasn't finished with this material. In 1976, he'd published what he called the introductory pneuma (which is framed by the two Paris meetings, the interview with Brodny and the bender with Schwab), and folders A and B, in a book called *Der Tod Meines Bruders Abel*, which was translated in 1985 as *The Death of My Brother Abel.* Folder C was published posthumously in 2000 as *Kain* (Cain) and never translated. Here, both volumes are together in English for the first time, and the effect is to make the give-and-take between Subicz and Schwab into something closer to a forking or branching: They're the two lives, or deaths, that might've been von Rezzori's.

Gregor Arnulph Hilarius d'Arezzo, known as Grisha, was born not after the First World War, like his two "brothers," but just at its start, in 1914—in Czernowitz, then the capital of the Duchy of Bukovina, later a major city in the Kingdom of Romania, and now a provincial city in Ukraine. His family were Sicilian aristocracy from Ragusa, who served as Habsburg officials. Grisha inherited their cosmopolitanism and became fluent in seven languages. His war was spent initially with the Romanian army, and then on false papers in Berlin, where he repeatedly tried to write about what he was witnessing. But every attempt at documenting his present led him to the past, and he eventually produced a distinguished oeuvre of cruel, beautiful autobiographical novels about his Empire childhood and teen years. Predictably, they were mostly ignored in Germany in favor of the lighter fare he wrote to pay the bills (his four-volume *Idiot's Guide to German Society*, and, yes, his scripts for film and television). German letters didn't know what to do with him: He wrote in German but wasn't German; not even the Austrians would claim him (not that he wanted to be claimed *by them*). His foreignness—indeed, his official statelessness, for a period—along with the *splendeurs* of his style alienated him from the *Trümmerliteratur* movement (Rubble Literature, the direct and even rudimentary immediately postwar German literature that tried to objectively describe, not subjectively evaluate, the contemporary scene, as a way, perversely, of mitigating its readership's war trauma), and he was too much of a nostalgist for the Vienna of Hermann Broch, Robert Musil, Joseph Roth, and Stefan Zweig to take part in the explicitly experimental Gruppe 47 (a group of novelists, poets, and playwrights that met between 1947 and '67, and included Ingeborg Bachmann, Heinrich Böll, Peter Handke, and Uwe Johnson).

It was a mixed blessing that Grisha's nostalgia—rather, his extreme alternation, or juxtaposition, of warm sentiment and violent incident—was most appreciated in America, which perhaps also appreciated how much he relished denigrating America, calling it stupid, crass, incurious, and puritanical. He enjoyed blaming the fact that he had to support himself with hackwork on the Americanization of postwar European culture; but then he always had a sly sadist's understanding of the American intellectual's appetite for masochism (perhaps because it was appropriated from the émigré Jewish intellectual's appetite for masochism). Almost all of his other books were set in memory, but this book—or books—is *about memory*, how it's made and remade, sequelized and enkitsched; how memory, as it passes out of the family, out of the community, out of the nation, and then finally out of the age, inevitably is generalized and broadened for mass consumption. He was a keen believer that the larger the audience for something, the dumber that something becomes—and the more ideologically correct it becomes too. Whether we believe that dictum or not, we keep proving it truer and truer in the third millennium of Christ—with our partisan "news" as much as with our anti-literary "media properties," and especially with our online interactions.

Abel and Cain is of a different tradition. It's one of those vast masterpieces for the chosen few, like *Journey to the End of the Night* and *Gravity's Rainbow*. Von Rezzori is a Céline with a conscience. He's a Pynchon who has outgrown the movies.

—Joshua Cohen

THE DEATH OF MY BROTHER ABEL

Translated by Joachim Neugroschel
Translation revised by Marshall Yarbrough

For whom else but you!

I RAN AFTER him. I caught up with him on the stairs. He turned to me and saw my face as I asked him, "You're coming back for sure? You promise?" He kissed me very tenderly on the forehead and on the eyes and on the mouth and took my hands and kissed one and then the other, saying, "I swear to you, my darling, of course I'm coming back." "Why don't you take me along right now?" I asked. "I can come with you right now." "Like that—naked as a jaybird?" he asked and kissed my breast. (I only had a towel wrapped around me.) I said, "I'll run and get dressed." I wanted him to come back to the room with me. "I'll wait for you here," he said. He was very sweet with me. He took my face in both his hands and pulled it close to his—and then tapped his finger on my nose. "Hurry up!" I ran back to the room to get dressed.

When he first tried to pick me up, I wanted to turn my back on him. A guy like him means trouble. Well into his forties and suspiciously elegant, with no real money behind him. But I'd had a bad day: two johns in the morning and then no one else until five. It was foggy all day. I noticed right off he'd been drinking, and he said, "You're very beautiful, my pet. We're going to have a good time. But would you mind waiting for one minute? I want to get an Alka-Seltzer at the drugstore. I've had quite a bit to drink and I haven't eaten all day." I thought to myself, Whatever you get at the drugstore, you can go fuck your mother with it, and your little sister too. But then I only walked a couple of steps away from him, up to the streetlamp and no farther, and I was too lazy to signal to Ginette, who probably was only half a block away in the fog. (She'd been standing out there all day long too.) Five minutes later, he was back, Alka-Seltzer in hand. (Whatever you really got at the drugstore, you can shove it up your mother's ass, I thought.) "Shall we go?" he said. "Or do you have other plans?"

Any other day, I wouldn't have taken him on. But the fog was getting on my nerves, I was tired of standing around, my feet hurt. I wanted to lie down for fifteen minutes, even with a guy on my stomach. Besides, something in his face made me feel I could deal with him easily if he tried any funny business: there was something soft and dreamy about him. Like Ginette's brother, who paints and bums around and is always wanting to kill himself. (All the same, you can really have a good laugh with him.) So I only said, "Do you even have a hundred francs on you?" And he said, "I thought children and soldiers paid half price. Why do I have to pay double?" I said, "Then take your tube of Alka-Seltzer and shove it up your mother. It's probably just the right size for her." But he laughed and said, "I think you're mistaken. My mother was very beautiful and knew some better sizes. Besides, that's how she made her living—like you." I thought to myself, You can talk all you want. Everyone makes up stories for us, and so do we, especially when someone asks What's a nice girl like you doing in this racket anyway. I've got six different versions in stock, all of them very believable. Anyhow, it doesn't matter much if a guy is bullshitting you or not when he tells you stuff, whether he wants you to believe he's a baker or a Rothschild. In fact, it doesn't matter at all. So long as he screws like a baker (fast and honest) and pays like a Rothschild, then everything's okay. But usually it's the other way around: they fuck you for hours and then they won't even treat you to a tisane over and above the fifty francs.

But anyway what he did was press two hundred francs into my hand—and now I was on the alert. 'Cause if a guy starts out like that, there's a catch somewhere. Then they've got some special kink—they want to spank you, or want you to spank them. But he wasn't English; he had a very slight Russian accent. Probably some Jew from Hungary or Romania—we'll see, I thought. Anyway, he took my arm like a fiancé, and I tried to shake him off, and he didn't say, "Ohlala! Are you ever touchy!" but instead held on and said, "Don't be afraid. I don't want anything from you that will humiliate you or make you feel ashamed. The first hundred is for the bed and the other one for friendliness, that's all."

I've heard that line too: "That's all." But no john ever thought of saying, "I don't want anything from you that will humiliate you or make you feel ashamed." I had to think about how that fitted in with him. Anyway, I let him take my arm, and we walked to the hotel like a married couple going home from a movie, warm and close together and in step.

When he paid Gaston for the room (without hiding the fact he had money in his pocket but without showing off about it either), he said, "And please leave us undisturbed for a good hour." I tried to give Gaston a look meaning I wasn't planning to waste the whole evening. But the bastard glanced away and said, "Certainly, sir. You've paid for twenty-four hours." So I thought Gaston knew him, and the guy was a cop. But then I realized it was only his tone of voice (and the tip too, of course). That prick Gaston simply caught on that this was one of those johns who feel at home in hotels (and much better ones than this). They instantly had that goddamn secret understanding between them, like all these asshole bourgeois types: bicyclists by nature, if you get what I mean; they bow upward and tread downward, and they'll all get strung up when the Red Internationale finally wins.

Anyway, I couldn't count on Gaston, and when we were up in the room, the usual stuff began. He wanted me to take everything off, including my panties ("Your feet will warm up faster without stockings," and all that shit), and when we were both finally lying in bed stark naked, he took me in his arms and lay back and said, "Let's smoke a cigarette."

I wanted to explain that he'd better not think he could play a joke on me for two hundred francs, and he ought to tell me what the hell he wanted or leave me be and go home. But when he lay there with his head on the pillow, staring up at the ceiling, I thought to myself, He's just impotent, or he's got problems getting it up—after all, he's not young anymore. I'm gonna have a lot of trouble with him; I'll probably have to take him in my mouth. Anyway, let's smoke a cigarette first, for Christ's sake. Maybe he'll doze off, and I can take off without him noticing.

So we watched the smoke going up to the ceiling and we didn't say a word, again like a married couple after a movie. Skin to skin under the blanket and head to head on the pillow. Except once, he asked, "Don't you recognize me? I was at the Madeleine once with a friend who had a quick number with you. Pretty much in broad daylight. A German. He couldn't speak a word of French. Of course, that was a while back, more than three years ago." And I just shook my head—who cares about his friends.

He went quiet again and kept on smoking. And once, he turned his face to me and kissed me on the temple. Strangely enough, he seemed like a kid when he did that, all dreamy. Then he carefully put out his cigarette in the ashtray and mine too and he uncovered my breasts and stroked and kissed them and said, "You're beautiful." And I thought to myself, If it's gonna be difficult, then let's get started at least. So I grabbed his dick to get it into shape, but he was stiff and ready to go. He started caressing me too, and so he wouldn't get me really excited I pretended I was; I put on a good act, like I couldn't wait for him to get inside me. But he held me close and he only kissed me—not on the mouth, of course (I don't want chancres on my lips), but everywhere else on my face, in a gentle rain of small tender kisses. Finally, I got so impatient I couldn't think of anything better to say than "You forgot to take your Alka-Seltzer." But of course he only laughed and said, "I don't even know where it is. In some pocket or other. No, wait: I think I left it downstairs on the clerk's desk." And when I quickly said, "I'll get it for you," he kissed me on the forehead again and said, "That's all right, my love. I don't need it now. I'm not drunk anymore."

It was like we actually had been married for ten years, and I decided to really bullshit, and I said emphatically, "Come to me now, but first you have to put on a rubber." But even that didn't faze him, even though usually johns give me the most long-winded arguments. He was as patient as a Franciscan and he smiled down at me (he was resting his head on his arm and looking into my face so kindly, it was like he was my aunt), and finally he just said, "Don't be difficult, dear. I'm not sick. If you like, you can examine me."

So that's the way it was. Fine then.

I looked him over and milked him and squeezed him so hard that I figured blood would come out. In any case, he was no Jew. And finally, he pulled me back on the pillow and said, "That's enough now, isn't it?" And he was already inside me; I don't even know how, but as skillful as a monkey and real deep right away. And he stayed like that for a while and just slowly moved around in me.

It wasn't the way it sometimes happens with a woman—a guy comes along and gets inside you, and suddenly you come, even though there's nothing special about him and you're not especially fond of him—it's simply that you're compatible in some way you can't explain. That wasn't it. I just started liking it. His tenderness, too. He wasn't excited the way men usually are. He could have gone outside on the street with the same expression on his face. Except that he looked happy. He closed his eyes whenever he gave me one of his soft, tender kisses.

I thought to myself, So that's what he's trying to pull, the bastard: he wants to drive you wild. When I acted like I couldn't wait anymore and wanted him to give it to me now, and began wiggling my ass and breathing heavily and rolling my eyes, he held me tight and said, "Shhh!" The way you shush a child. So finally I asked him, "Why don't you come? Is it hard for you?" And he said in the quietest voice in the world, "I like to have a little fun doing this. Don't you?"

Finally I told him he couldn't expect that from me. First I said, "I only come with my husband. You can understand. It's the one thing that only he gets from me." And I was about to think up a guy I lived with, who protected me and who I came with (even though that never happened with my Jules and was anyway very rare—once with Ginette, and with a man yes, but only once, a long, long time ago). But he must have smelled a rat. He said (still smiling and in his quiet voice), "Don't tell me fairy tales. You're just lazy, that's all. I understand that you can't come with every man if you don't want to ruin yourself. But

I'll give you another hundred francs, so you can take the rest of the night off."

If a woman doesn't want to come, then a guy can screw his cock to shreds, and with a guy in his forties it takes a while anyhow—and who wants to put up with that? If I hadn't been so tired and bored with standing around in the fog, I would have thought up something to get rid of him. Instead, I said to myself, Let him go on, he'll get horny enough to come before it gets tedious. So I shut my eyes and let him move around inside me. But soon it got weird: it was just too pleasant. He was incredibly skillful and lay on me without crushing me, and he was clean and he had no flab and his skin was smooth and he was well built. I thought to myself, Christine, my girl, if you get soft now, you might really come, and then you'll stay with him for a couple of hours and sleep till the day after tomorrow, and you may even fall in love with him, for Christ's sake, and then you'll be up to your ass in trouble. Pull yourself together, kid, and try to get rid of the guy as fast as possible and go out into the fog and earn an honest living. And at that same instant, he said to me (still in the same voice, as though we were sitting on a bench in the Jardin des Plantes), "Listen, my dear. You're very sweet. Let me make a suggestion. For a couple of days you try to get used to me and to living with me. I earn enough to spoil you a little. If it doesn't work out, we'll go our own separate ways as the best of friends, and I'll see to it that you won't have lost too much income. And if it works, we'll stay together for as long as it still works. I'm anything but rich, but I write for the movies, and there's always a nice payday waiting. With a woman with a good head on her shoulders to look after the money, one can live quite comfortably."

It wasn't my first offer of this kind, and what pissed me off most was the way he used the stuff about the movies as bait. You can fool some dime-store clerk that's still wetting her pants, but not a working girl like me. And besides, I thought, who does this bastard think you are anyway? Does he think maybe that because you've got a dick inside you, you can't think clearly? Why doesn't he just take a violin and fiddle a tango in your ear! And because I was mad, I did something dumb, and I thought to myself, If you tell me stories, buddy, then I'll tell you a couple too, and I said, "You're sweet, baby, and that's why I won't be nasty and lie to you. You see, I can't live with a man. I can't come with men—I don't know if I'm a lesbian, but in any case, I can't stand having a man around for more than half an hour."

Even as I was saying it, I realized how stupid it was to tell him that. Because it *is* true, sort of. The few times I've come in the last couple of years were with Ginette when a john took both of us on (which of course doesn't mean I'm really a lesbian). Anyway, you're always a sucker when you tell the truth. I was only hoping that if he thought about me and Ginette, he'd finally get going and I could get him off me. He instantly said, "If that's the only problem, darling, then we can take as many girls to bed as you can manage." And I didn't even have time to think, Of course, you pig! when he already had his hand on me, and I could barely say, "Take your hand away!" when he started to thrust into me very hard—and maybe I accidentally thought of Ginette and the way she comes when some guy fucks her and I play around with her—anyway, I didn't push his hand away—and all at once, I felt I was going to come, and I screamed, "What the hell are you doing to me!" and I felt him coming at the same time, and I came too and I didn't know what was going on, only that now he had his mouth on mine and was kissing me wildly, and that now I didn't even care that a stranger was kissing me on the mouth, because it was good and just like making love.

The worst part was that I dozed off right away. (I'm like a man that way.) But I can't have been sleeping for long, maybe fifteen minutes. And when I awoke, it was like when you're swimming in the ocean and a wave comes and lifts you up—and he was there and he caught me in his arms.

But that was only a dream. Actually I woke up because he was caressing me. He had uncovered me all the way and was kneeling over me and caressing my body, my shoulders, my arms, my breasts, my hips—and as though something exquisite remained in his hands, a fragrance or shimmer, some rare happiness in the feeling of warm fullness, he kept kissing his palms, the way an Arab or Hindu prays. It was very sweet, and I pretended I was still asleep so I could enjoy it, dope that I was. He wrapped me in his goddamn tenderness—I got so mad I nearly started to cry. "You lousy bastard," I said, "you pig, you sonofabitch!" I hit him, and he laughed, and so we scuffled around, almost tumbling out of bed, and then he was inside me again with his monkey skill, and this time he didn't need any help from his fingers, and I didn't think about Ginette, or anything else, I just came like in some dirty book, where they always come like it was as natural as pissing.

Afterward I was cheerful, like when I sometimes take the evening off and have a bit to drink, and me and Ginette's brother go to the booths behind the place Blanche and I try my luck in the shooting galleries. Christ, was I hungry! And for half an hour we tried to figure out what we wanted to eat and where, and he said he didn't know any of the bistros I knew and he had to get to know them. But then he said, "We're so close to Prunier, why don't we go there?" And I said to him, "I don't want to make trouble for you. They all know me here in the neighborhood and they won't let us in." And he said, "But, darling, they'll have to get used to seeing you in my bad company." And so we fooled around until we finally telephoned down to Gaston to send something up. I said, "Now we'll see how you're going to spoil me. I want champagne and caviar and oysters and lobster and a filet mignon. You're lucky the shops are closed now, else I'd have taken you shopping." And he said, "A couple of diamonds at Cartier, and Yves Saint Laurent's spring collection, is that it? I'm going to give you a good spanking and stick you in the kitchen and make you cook for both of us and spend no more than ten francs a day. You can go to the movies once a week and that's all."

And here a kiss and there a pinch and there a thump, so that we nearly started screwing all over again. But luckily, room service came up with the food, and boy was that ever a bullshit deal! I let the waiter know as much too. "Lemme see the bill!" I said. "They're ripping you off, these pigs," I said, and that was a stupid thing, which would cost me dearly. If I hadn't felt like I did, almost like I was drunk, I would have understood on the spot by the way the waiter looked at me.

But it was like I was crazy, I really didn't know why. We ate, and he fed me like a little girl and didn't want to have anything himself. He just watched me, and while he watched he became very melancholy. I think he'd been drinking all day and now he was having some more, and the sadness was breaking out. To get him to eat, I put pieces of food in my teeth and held out my mouth so that he'd kiss me and at least take a piece of bread. And to keep him from drinking too much, I drank the wine out of his mouth. And when he wanted to send for another bottle, I said, "You've had enough now and you're going beddy-bye. I'm so tired I can't keep my eyes open."

Once again, we lay side by side like a married couple, him on his back and me half-across him with my head on his shoulder. But neither of us could sleep, and finally I asked him, "Why aren't you sleeping?" "Why aren't you?" he asked. "I keep thinking," I said. "What about?" he asked. "About me and about you. About both of us." "Me too," he said. Then I thought he had really gone to sleep and I wanted to give him a goodnight kiss, and he gently pressed me to him. He wasn't asleep.

I was very happy and I said to him, "Do it again. Think about yourself, not me. I'm too tired to come again. But I want to feel you in me and feel that you're happy." And he must have understood that this was a present. He simply rolled me over and put his cheek on my breast, and then he was inside me. It was a quiet, enjoyable fuck, like between a couple that's had a lot of practice fucking together, and it was nice the way he came: with a moan of surrender. I couldn't see him in the dark (we'd put the light out so we could sleep), but I know how they come—they look so wild, as if they wanted to bite God in heaven, and yet it's their only human moment.

We fell asleep, and it was still dark when he woke me up. I sensed that he was dressed and I was scared to death and I said, "You're not leaving me!" And he caressed me and kissed me and calmed me. He would only be gone for a couple of hours, until I'd slept enough, then he'd come and pick me up, he said. He just had to put his things in order. "*Il faut que j'arrange ma maison*," he said. And I believed him and I kissed him and said, "Hurry up, I won't be able to sleep a wink till you come back."

But then, when he closed the door behind him, I got scared, and I jumped out of bed and grabbed a towel and wrapped it around me and ran after him into the corridor and only caught up with him on the stairs. And when he said, "I'll wait for you here, hurry up," I ran back into the room and just pulled on my shoes and skirt and sweater and coat. I stuffed the stockings and the garter belt and the bra into my handbag. I really hurried. But he was already gone.

It is night. In a shabby hotel on the place des Ternes, in a small room with flowery wallpaper, he sits at a dressing table with a covered mirror.

The room does not face the street, it faces an air shaft. It is now the only room in which a lamp is lit. He writes, *Il arrange sa maison*.

He has four folders in front of him. They are marked "Pneuma" and "A," "B," and "C." Two suitcases and several cartons of papers surround him on the floor. He occasionally rummages in one of them, takes out a sheet, and inserts it into one of the folders; then he busily continues writing.

The first folder is open. It says:

The most extreme language of madness is reason, but sheathed in the enchantment of the image, restricted to the phenomenal space that it defines—whereby both of them create, outside the totality of images and the universality of speech, a peculiar abusable organization, whose obstinate specificity constitutes madness.

—MICHEL FOUCAULT, *Madness and Society*

I

AS IF HE had been cast away among the lotus-eaters, he seemed to have forgotten his fatherland. He knew he was a stranger. The thin ocean wind told him so, tossed it into his face—the wind that blew, day in, day out, sweeping across bleak marshland and weed-choked rubble fields and straying into the gaps and ruins of meandering streets.

The heavy sky told him so, day in, day out, the dove-breast clouds, scraped by the broken rafters of gabled roofs; their shadows scoured the houses red and sore, water dripped from their feathers, till they dissolved in white; sometimes they perished from the arrows of a stinting and distant sun, brittle arrows that pierced them only to break against the struts of the loading cranes in the bombed-out harbor, where their splinters scattered over the wet stone jetties, palely brass-bright, cradled in the cold water, until new flocks of doves flew over, breast to breast, and quickly pecked them up.

The nights hushed it toward him, step-queens, no moon drifted through his blood, no dream-drunken bird measured the stillness of a black-and-silvery landscape with its warbling. Masses of cottony darkness pressed heaven and earth together, smothered the sparsely beaded streetlights and the pitiful contents of scrip-shabby department stores into pale fog-aureolas and let their oily shimmer ooze into the black canals.

The dropsical air carried it to him, in gull shrieks expelled wildly into nothingness, weaving the emptiness of eternity on gull wings—a nightmare carnival: Pierrots shooting clownishly to and fro and up and down, crossing, chasing one another, reeling, plunging, now surrounded by powdery whirls of snowflakes, now streaked obliquely with strands of rain. He could hear it in the city's din, which surged restlessly like the straying wind, now and again punctuated by the walrus bellow of a ship's siren, haunted by the ghost of the past. He heard it in the constricted voices, the faded intonations, the crumbling speech of the people he passed during his constant, futile walks: pale blond men and women who looked at him with eyes of faded blue in which blank uncomprehending amazement froze into the enigmatic gaze of nixies. Estrangement stood between him and them, and this strange place to which they were together condemned did not unite them.

Yes sir. That's how it ought to start. Orphically. The evocatively murmuring past tense. Rubble Age in Hamburg-on-the-Elbe, Germany, 1945–48. Enigmatic gaze of nixies (read: Hanseatic contrariness). Cast away among the lotus-eaters (read: displaced person). Sheer poetry, that's how I set it down. With a throbbing heart full of sacred hope: *As if he had been cast away among the lotus-eaters, he seemed to have forgotten his fatherland*—period. With a dying fall…

The first sentence has to ring like out bell metal:

> *Solidly immur'd in earth*
> *Stands the mold of hard-bak'd clay…*

Schiller, Mr. Brodny, in case your memory's failed you. You probably call him Skyler now. Well, we still call him Shillah. We are proud of him. Singing and ringing cherub's voice. Singing and ringing for a child's heart. Daddy, tell me a story. *Sissignore, subito!* The communication of fatefulness arouses our memory (or is it our morality?). Arouses our sensuality. Okay then, tell me a story, if possible in three short sentences. Of course this would require form. (Schwab would have said, "*Ni plus, ni moins.*")

That's not our strength, alas, us Germans. For the French, yes. Still Cartesians clear as crystal, these fellows. Infrastructural formalists each and every one of them—despite Vichy and Oradour, Algeria and Monsieur le Général de Gaulle. Despite the inundation of their intellectual world by Spaniards, Balkans, Russian Jews. A culturally homogeneous national style, you know. That's what Scherping says too, our mutual friend and missing link, big-time publisher, mass-culture maker, so he ought to know—perhaps not without a touch of nationalist envy, but no matter, the fellow is a masochist. Arouses our sensual memorality. In any case: the Frenchman's gift for form has always been apparent in his literature. First rate! Not a superfluous syllable. Every chef d'oeuvre its own table of contents, so to speak. Never a word too many. Exemplary. Yes, and their wines? You agree with our friend Schwab, right? And the women—let's not get into that. And the French cuisine—mmm, mmm. And the Impressionists too, logically; and of course Paris! Paris, man! The music, needless to say, comes from us. Offenbach (a Jew, but musically pure German). Wagner (first a scandal, but then acceptance). The only native a fellow who sounds like what French girls wash their pussies in: Bizet (highly esteemed by Nietzsche, to be sure).

As for my part, sir, I'll sing about Paris in any style you'd like—for instance art nouveau-ish waltz-wave-welling: *And if it weren't for Paree, then I might dream of you and mehehee* (whirl and hop) *in your most decent bed* (ramtata) . . . or else brisk, with marching brass blaring: *Oh come to the drum to Paree, old bum!!!* (thundering drums and clashing cymbals) . . . Life is a swallow's flight.

For the French, that is. For us, it's not so smooth and clear. We're known for being musical, but verbally we're rather cloudy, amorphous, nebulous. No wonder, what with all that hard-to-communicate fatefulness of ours. The conflict-ridden soul, you know. Too many, too vast, too stormy are the thoughts that circle our heads. The everlasting struggle between pure philosophy and great art. "*J'comprends jamais c'qu'tu veux dire, mon ours*"—Gaia's constant complaint. *Ours des Carpates*, mind you, not a German bear.

Actually, I'm no more German than you, Citizen Brodny, are American, no matter how set apart you may be, an ocean away, how clearly gone from one part of the world to another; no matter with what Anglo-Saxon pragmatism you can chatter on about the European nations' gift for form, their formal strength, their formal problems. (One man's meat is another man's poison, as they say—or do you prefer the equivalent in Yiddish? I can be of assistance either way, not just a professional literary flunky but also a polyglot *homme à tout faire*, a linguistic opportunist)...

But then, what difference does it make who is what? We are not simply and resolutely one thing or the other. Not in these dynamic times. Sometimes, a man is both and yet neither, a blend of nothing and everything. People like us, for instance. A refugee's fate. An émigré's lot. We lost our true fatherlands and then forgot them among the lotus-eaters. Or elsewhere, somewhere along the way.

What, by the way, was your fatherland, dear Mr. Jacob G. Brodny? Geographically, in any event, *Europe centrale*? Am I right? Just like mine, incidentally. One of those countries that were born with the peace treaties of Brest-Litovsk and Trianon and finally Versailles (and so about the same time as me). Back then, in the Käthe-Kollwitz-horror after the first blood-and-filth-and-iron chaos known as a world war, our continent was as fecund in giving birth to new fatherlands as darkest Africa is today.

Incidentally, both of them enjoying American midwifery in their difficult hour. Granted to them out of the loftiest moral principles, of course. Memorializing principles: the American notion of freedom and similar human rights tolerates no empires, hence no colonies either, whether black or white and no matter what continent they're on. Understandably so. If we are to believe Nagel (and why shouldn't we? He's a writer of international renown, a best-selling author, the sincerest bard of German domestic probity, Scherping's house star, the nail in Schwab's coffin, and presumably the supplier of some of your fattest commissions)—I say: if we share his opinion, arms should be given only to sovereign states.

Well, in adjusting the demand to this supply, I have stumbled into an *embarras du choix* (more poetic in German: *die Qual der Wahl*). For me, there are too many fatherlands, too many for me to opt for any single one.

Lack of character, I know. Like my stance in the war as a sort of draft dodger, not honorably mutilated, like Nagel. But mind you, I thought it gave me my only chance to achieve the dignity of a Nobel Prize (in literature, of course).

For doesn't this practice of anointing individuals with a knack for writing—systematically selected from just about every one of today's fatherlands, from Iceland to Ghana—doesn't it constitute a clear testimonial that each of the chosen nations has attained the cultural level that would permit it to fly national colors in full self-assurance and have an army equipped with automatic weapons? A few of them have even got the prize several times, and this so clearly a result of confusion that one suspects that once everybody had had his turn, they wouldn't know what to do next. Yet never has the Nobel Prize been awarded to a stateless writer. I thought it was about time. But I had to admit to an error, at least where I was concerned: the prize is never awarded for books that have not been written. Too bad. In certain cases it would come into more deserving hands.

But let us say no more. Nagel will get the prize. *Hail to him in victor's crown!* Had Schwab not been cremated, he would be turning over in his casket like Saint Lawrence on the grill.

Incidentally, this brings me to something I should have thought of earlier. Schwab, as Scherping's editor for so many years, must have crossed paths with you; after all, you're a great—what am I saying?—the greatest, or anyway the shrewdest of international literary agents. I'd give a lot to know what your meeting was like. As abortive as ours? Odd that he never mentioned it to me (but then, he was so tight-lipped). I, on the other hand, couldn't wait to set down the absurd story of our encounter. With the aim, naturally, of telling the whole world about it.

Che buffonata! You had the impression (to my keen regret, I assure you) that I was trying to make fun of you. I suppose you made the common mistake of misconstruing my ironic tone. Allow me to set matters straight: irony is not aggressive; it is the natural expression of a sad cur, not a biting cur. Especially when confronted with overweening self-assurance, if you get what I mean.

Granted, my reactions are neurasthenic. But I live among Frenchmen; I am overwrought. To be fair, I must confess I've probably been this way for some time. A decade and a half on German soil, two thirds of it on the Baltic coast—that's no bed of roses, either. But the French finished me off.

2

Now, what do you have to say, Jacob G. Brodny, full-fledged citizen of the U.S.A., with military and other honors in the European Theater of Operations, superman of the literary business in the finest neon-haloed American way—what do you have to say about this challengingly arrogant self-certainty of the French? Is it sclerosis? A sign of fossilization? Granted. Nevertheless: isn't it a thorn in your world-ruler side? You can't trust your senses anymore. Being French, as we are continually told here in Paris, is not simply having a nationality. Oh no: it is a divine right, a higher form of existence, sprung forth from a more valuable chthonic origin and precipitated from the mother liquor of a nobler national spirit. And this in your, in the American, century, Jaykob Gee!—when any form of existence other than the American form is scarcely possible in our part of the world! A phenomenal evolutionary obstinacy, don't you agree?

In the past, we were used to this sort of thing. The unpigmented, rabbit-toothed arrogance of the British, for example. Or the furious national consciousness of the Balkanese—say, the Serbs. Germans too could afford to be overtly German. That was simply normal in the waltz-wave-welling concert of nations, and it was part of the European panorama. A grand medley of peoples, and each individual a proud something: a Briton, Bulgarian, Bosnian, Dutchman, Helvetian, Hutsul. The Serbs as well, when they thought of themselves as Serbs, regarded themselves as something far more important than when they simply thought, I, Miloš, or I, Yanko. Miloš the Serb was virtually a Miloš squared, an intensified, elevated Miloš. The individual is not lost in the collective; on the contrary, he is transubstantiated into a clearer form with a higher specific gravity. Nagel writes, "To belong to a people in body and mind, to represent a people in language, in appearance, and in character, is a kind of nobility!" A cheap truism that we ought to bear in mind. Schwab, being German, found it a bit suspect—understandably. As a German, one attains one's best form by strictly disavowing Germanism (à la Goethe or Hölderlin). But that does not reduce the universal validity of Nagel's statement. Certainly not for the French.

And isn't it astounding in a time when there is scarcely a people, scarcely a nation that constitutes its own milieu, a product of which a member of that people might consider himself, so that now in fact no one can be a mold for national characteristics, no one can develop a specific style? Show me the stylistic difference between a Spanish and a Swedish gas pump. The scenic difference between a stretch of highway or an airport near Hamburg, Germany, or Rome, Italy, and Dallas, Texas. Today, all we have is a supranational style, and this style is American. A bit of highway near Pearris, Freanss, is already pretty American and thus no different from one near Tokyo, Jippan. Likewise the airports and gas pumps both here and there. Yet the French keep getting Frencher and Frencher. The Spaniards, the Swedes, the Japanese are visibly turning into gum-chewing, computer-trusting Americans. The French, however, have never been so intensely French as nowadays.

You will probably ask why this is weighing on my mind? Well, sir, it concerns a bizarre hobby (in the past, it would have been called *spleen*). I am seeking the other half of my life. Like Aristophanes's lovers, I am seeking a lost part of my own self, the other half of what was originally a pair. I lost it at some point or other—I suspect on an icy-clear day in Vienna, March 1938. I was barely nineteen innocent years old. Those years were amputated, removed from my existence, like Nagel's right arm. Since then, I have been on the trail of their feelings. For, like Nagel, who claims he can still feel the fingers of his missing hand move, I too can feel my then-self in an abstract way.

And so I am looking for that other part of my life wherever I might find it: in countries, landscapes, clouds, towns—yes indeed, especially cities, which, with their lights, fragrances, noises, colors, forms, moods, sometimes resurrect in me the totality of moods, forms, colors, noises, fragrances, light effects of an entire era (abruptly, with painful bliss and, alas, only for a fleeting microsecond).

In short, I am seeking the other half of my life in the vestiges—or rather in the echoes—of its time. A time that is growing more and more discernible as a style. To specify in fashionably art-historical terms: the era that developed art deco from art nouveau. The time of Europe's flirtation with America (I could attend the wedding only as an onlooker).

I am seeking a Europe that might still be European.

Actually, you ought to sympathize with this, Mr. Jacob G. Brodny. First, as a nostalgic Jew. Like every good American province, Europe today is fairly *judenrein*. But things were different once, weren't they? If not a promised land, Europe was at least a long-familiar and beloved land, a land in which you Jews saw fulfilled many of your boldest promises but, above all, found your most ruthless murderers. That makes for an unusually strong tie, doesn't it?...

But aside from that: as an ex-European—Eastern European, to be sure—you too presumably had half of your life sliced off. You may have no reason to mourn it, but be that as it may, you've gone with the times. Whether sadly or eagerly, you jettisoned anything about yourself that was a vestige and echo of a past form of life and vigorously settled into a new one: you became an American. In the great collective of the United States of our Western World, your halved self was transubstantiated into a new, bursting fullness. The American in you practically leaps out for all to see.

I for my half part have allowed myself to be guilty of the unfortunately widespread offence of being behind the times, and thus dragging the past into presence. I could not wholly renounce something that was somehow still alive within me, albeit in an abstract, ghostly way, like Nagel's shot-off arm.

Thus nothing newly whole, nothing newly full of life has become of me in the new (American) era. And of course I most certainly have not remained what I was. So kindly understand what I find so fascinating about the French. Not only have they remained what they were, they have even become more intensely what they had been. Schwab was filled with excited sympathy for this phenomenon.

Cast to and fro by the capricious fate that attends a filmmaker (I'm a screenwriter, as you know), I hang around the various mini-metropolises of Europe: Vienna, Madrid, Rome, Munich, Copenhagen, Milan, West Berlin. A Europe that is woefully shriveled, likewise mutilated by one half, ridiculously provincial, suburban, desolate. But for several years now (ever since a crazy romance with an American fashion model named Dawn, at least since Schwab's death), it's been safest to contact me here in Paris. No household of my own, of course. After my dismal experiences in an abortive marriage in Hamburg (with Christa), I tried to settle down here (with Gaia—chocolate-brown giantess, half-Afro-American, half-Romanian blood, Princess Jahovary—sounds like a freak show and looked like one, too). My attempt at domesticity failed, but you'll hear about that later.

Now, what so utterly frustrated me here is the unbelievable, downright incredible hard surface of the French. Cartesians clear as crystal, these fellows, and coalesced into a geode. It makes for a world that's not so easy to get into. At any rate, I haven't managed, even though I sense—good Lord! even though I *know* that it's my world. Yes sir, it is my world in almost every way, and I (or at least the I of the lost half of my life) am contained in it integrally (as you'd say in electricians' parlance, that of my Uncle Helmuth's former clan).

Here, nearly everything of the lost half of my life has been preserved: forms, colors, tones, fragrances galore, an entire language-world (which did a great deal to determine the style of that era), no end of art nouveau and art deco. And yet here I lose not only my sense of having once belonged to a world like this but any solid foothold in time, above all in the present.

The world is an event in which I do not participate, have never participated, and will never participate. The world is a French event, and I am not French. I am not even a *boche*, like Schwab—a potential killer of Frenchmen (I repeat: an intimate kinship, almost a kind of identification). Nor am I American, which would be a different form of killer of the French mode of being. I am nothing. Not only stateless in terms of citizenship but rootless by blood, *déraciné par excellence*: truly without a fatherland or a father, a man who doesn't know who spawned him, and whose mother deserted and betrayed her kin, her people; a man who belongs neither here nor there, unbaptized, with no religion, suspiciously polyglot, devoid of any tie to any tribe, to any flag... But of course in search of all those things.

The exceedingly lovely, the wondrously beautiful city of Paris, *la ville lumière*, gives me not the least bit of help in my search. On the contrary. The devastating presentness of its history excludes me as much as its historical presence does. In the uninterrupted continuity from Charlemagne to Charles de Gaulle there is not the tiniest gap for me to squeeze into. And yet the half of the life that I and my kind lost in that March of 1938 belongs far more here than anywhere else. I mean to say: The European Europe from which that half was born, in which it grew up, and whose colors, forms, sounds, fragrances, moods constituted its pattern, is far more present here than anywhere else. Where else might I seek it, if not here? Here, I am incessantly on its trail, on the trail of my self—but only ever on its trail, and sometimes, for auspicious, breathtaking micro-moments, I am even on my heels. But I will never reach my self completely. And this is all the more agonizing, as everywhere I go I am always on the verge of some kind of identification...

How can I make this clear to you, my esteemed Jaykob Gee? As a man who has traveled the world over, you must, of course, know Sneek, the Dutch Venice? There, you can punt along in a heavy boat, infinitely slowly, through leaden canals. To the left and the right, the banks drag by with such sluggish drowsiness that one expects the houses to topple forward like the heads of exhausted people, their eyelids shutting.

Well, in a movie script I once wrote, which like so many others will remain an unrealized pipe dream (none of my producer-piglets will ever want to actually film it), I set a chase scene in Sneek. A man has to catch up with another man at any cost, and the other is several boats ahead of him and flees . . . very slowly flees . . . infinitely slowly and always just beyond reach . . . and that other man is, of course, himself.

3

I assume that you too, sir, are not unfamiliar with such existential conditions, slipping off into the dream dimension of slow motion (with a resulting schizoid personality split). After all, this is a phenomenon of the times; I mean to say, a special perception or awareness of time that is inherent in our era (and also, by the way, the first step hashish eaters, opium smokers, et al., make into their psychedelic wonderlands).

I would not be amazed to experience this in Vienna. That is where I lost the first half of my life, and for consistency's sake I ought to look for it there—and never find it again. You will, I hope, understand me when I say that I lost it *precisely because that half is present there.* Like Vienna as a whole, it is there as part of a museum existence, and thus is thoroughly timeless, a dead thing in a dead city. On March 12 of the year 1938 Vienna died before my eyes and, with it, my then living and lived self. The two now belong together for all time—but no longer to me.

What I am seeking in the lost half of my life is not my *then* self but rather that within it that might connect in some way to my present self. Connect in such a way as to make me believe that it really was I and not just a legend, a literary invention, a fiction within me.

I am seeking *myself* in the European cities where I am cast away by my flimsy profession, as if they were not the cities and sites of my past but the cities and sites of my present. I seek my self in the airports, the highways, gas stations, Hilton hotels, supermarkets, movie studios, office high-rises of Madrid, Rome, Munich, Copenhagen, Milan, West Berlin, Paris. In seeking my self I seek a European continuity. This European continuity is to be found neither in the museum existence of these cities nor in my present self. Except, as I said, in an occasional split second of recognition which makes my search the more intense, and the more futile.

But in the airports, highways, gas stations, Hilton hotels, supermarkets, film sets, and office towers of the American province that Europe has become, I am nowhere to be found. I am nowhere whole, not in yesterday and not in this today, which is, however, an anticipated, fictitious tomorrow.

This has its consequences, of course. Split in two and equally far away from both past and future, I also have no true present. I am searching, my esteemed Mr. Brodny, for my identity, as you would call it. A typically American, a so to speak banally American phenomenon. However, as a hopeless European, I have cause to doubt my reality.

I am capable of illustrating this condition with several documents. Permit me to present you with two of them. Together, they should make the situation clear. The first is a sheet of paper, and unfortunately I can no longer say for sure whether it was part of a draft of a letter, in which I tried a while back (it was five, six years ago) to tease gently my late friend Schwab from afar, or whether it was one of the endless monologues that I delivered to him for the same reason when he came from Hamburg to visit me here in Paris, soliloquies intended to provoke a reaction from his dulled and yet at times doubly fine alcoholic's mind. But ultimately it makes no difference whether it's the one or the other. Let me give you the excerpt:

. . . You remember that passage in Nietzsche where he announces a coming artistic age? Well, that age has arrived. Today, everyone must realize his potential—to wit, by producing art. Be creative! Produce! Give

shape! Form! If you lack any distinct talent, make literature! One has the impression that for people like us, puberty drags on until the climacteric—and indeed beyond it. It is obvious that teenagers live with a sense of unreality and are looking for the meaning of life. But middle-aged bank directors collapse before me in sobs and confess, with their heads in my lap, that they would give all their wealth for my gift of literary self-expression. Every jackass feels the urge to realize his potential artistically. Statesmen like Winston Churchill and Amintore Fanfani find their true selves in painting. In Parisian society (which in my uncle Ferdinand's day was not afflicted by self-doubt, no, sir; it was a homogeneous conglomerate of Guermantes, Verdurins, and Rastaquères) every beautiful lady at least does interior decorating if she doesn't have her hands full being an archaeologist or running a gallery. You'd be amazed at what you can get into a film (and then into a bed) with a nod and a bit of celluloid. And if you expect a nineteen-year-old today not to find everything there is in life in throwing pottery (as I, incautiously, dared to expect with my son), you've got another thing coming.

Certainly, this is an encouraging sign of a general ennoblement of mankind. An upward development toward the spiritual realm, which one ought to welcome. As my uncle Helmuth, an electrical engineer and spiritualist, might have understood it, we are already living in a different vibrational state, dematerialized and spiritualized. We have ascended one level closer to God. But I don't feel quite right about it. I fear that we have once again failed to reckon with God's less spiritual other half—namely, with Mother Nature.

This powerful lady is always on the lookout to catch the flies that have all too ardently swarmed onto the honey of the mind because they are under the delusion that this is the true *reality. She will grab anybody by the scruff of the neck if he finds her rules too brutal, too monotonous, too idiotic and would rather ignore them. Anyone who prefers to follow laws other than those of the everlasting stupid cycle of procreation and annihilation is already playing on his own, and at his own risk. He should not be surprised if she raps him on the knuckles.*

Yes, indeed, I too bow respectfully to the beautiful courage of the human race, which keeps creating new fictions in order that it may confront the perpetual threat of cruelly productive-and-destructive nature and claim undaunted that existence must have some other purpose than merely eating and being eaten. I admire the insanely courageous way mankind lingers in the as-if, its insistence that we could have other aims than to breed and to kill. But not everyone is up to staying awake during such sleepwalking. Art is opium for today's people. Only a select few still consider it a vice, the hard lot of the damned.

Ask Nagel, he writes so nicely about it: "If any of the acrobats under the Big Top knows there is no net under him, he can still dare to try his stunt. But woe, woe unto him if he realizes it only when he is already on the tightrope..."

Here, I once again agree completely with our friend Nagel. A dangerously large number of dilettantes step out on the high wire nowadays. More and more of them, bolder and bolder. Everyone wants to get up there. This cannot end well. Certain experiences in Vienna make me feel that in the long run Mother Nature will not be content to watch this collective somnambulism and do nothing. I would not like to be called to account with the others when she intercedes to set things right.

My friend! I admire your courageous "Nevertheless!" I take my hat off to Nagel whenever another of his books appears on the market (as a best seller). I bow respectfully to you, Schwab, for still clinging to your intention, despite heartrending, soul-churning doubts, to write your book—even if you won't admit to it at any cost. But I, for my modest little part, no longer indulge in the lovely illusion that I might thereby succeed in pulling myself (like Münchhausen by his own pigtail) out of the knowledge of the total absurdity of existence.

No, no. I shall not step out on the tightrope. I shall remain pious. (Please tell this to dear Scherping, too) I shall remain an obedient servant of Mother Nature. Living against one's time—such has always been the attitude of the dandy. In this age of artists and self-realizers, I take the liberty of being a dandy in the purely biological form of existence. I run no risk. I perform my biological duties, nothing more. I realize my potential not in artistic creations like everyone else but rather in acts of destruction. Murder, though, is something I can do only in dreams. But for example I systematically lay waste to everything I have written over the past few years. Plus, incidentally, a lot of expensive food—come and join in! You can still eat well here in Paris—and you know how serious, yes downright fundamental my approach is to this activity. And of course in between I set my sights on even the tiniest possibility of a quick, pleasant act of copulation. On the off chance of procreating if my partner hasn't taken the right precautions.

So much for the first document. The second might be dated a few months later. I found it among the papers for my book where it had slipped in, by goodness knows what accident. A similar accident played it into my hands a few days ago. *Le voilà*:

> Paris in the blossoming of May. Printemps posters behind brightly greening plane trees. The first summer dresses. All the airy kitsch of Dufy.
>
> Schwab has arrived unexpectedly. During the day, we sit outdoors in front of the Flore, the Deux Magots, feast at Lapérouse or Chez Anne, shuffle through museums. At night we play Russian roulette.
>
> It doesn't take much psychological flair (as in Professor Hertzog's school) to guess why he sticks to my heels like that. My imperturbability is uncanny to him. He simply doesn't believe me. He thinks I'm dazed, in a kind of trance (like one of the mediums in my late uncle Helmuth's spiritist circle in Vienna: outside myself and somewhere in space, only loosely attached to my body by an astral umbilical cord, while the emptied shell of my body is open to any spirit that wishes to sojourn within it—in my case, needless to say, the demon of despair).
>
> He regards me as a character in a novel. Hence I have to act like one. A man who, after the end of a love affair in which he has carried on like a lunatic for three years, smiles and acts like nothing had happened—as if he had not personally experienced all the magic of insanity and happiness and misery and anxiety and senseless hope and foolish perseverance but had read about it in some pulp paperback, which he has only just put aside, or

seen it in a movie. Such a character is convincing only if, behind his feigned imperturbability, he nurtures the intention of killing himself. And that is what S. expects me to do.

After all, he ardently envied me for it. His rhetorical question: "Who is still capable of such a thing!"

(I see his face before me as he exclaimed it. It was raised heavenward, as during a hymn. Cousin Wolfgang up in the church choir: *"Queeheeheeheen of heaheaheaheaven, rejoice, Maa-haa-haa-rie-ha!. . ."*)

Who is still capable of such a thing at the age of forty-five? In 1964, the second half of the twentieth century, if you please—who can still fall in love like a schoolboy? At best, a department-store executive having a midlife crisis. But in people like us—inhabitants of a crater landscape, an emotional world that has been analyzed to atoms—if anything is still stirring then it's allergies . . .

So if someone like us kicks up such a splendid fuss, then there must be something exquisite behind it, don't you think? The intention to transvaluate that experience artistically into something exemplary. If you don't do that, you're cheating and you'll have to pay for it. You can't just escape it by producing psychosomatic sugar in your urine. Nowadays, neuroses are children's ailments. Anyone with any self-respect has to kill himself. *Ni plus, ni moins.*

Actually, S. has come to Paris because *he* has reached the end of his rope. Scherping finally went through with it and fired him. Fired him as well as his secretary, Fräulein Schmidschelm, which S. considers particularly insidious. But of course he has to admit that Schelmie is quite happy about it: now she's free of the burdensome job of alternately rescuing the publisher from the claws of Gisela or lovely Heli in the whorehouse or tracking the editor down during a boozing tour with his terrific *tante*. Schelmie has settled down on her regular stool at Lücke's Bar, clearing off only when the place is closed (all together six hours out of twenty-four).

He, meanwhile, has panicked. Not because he's worried about his further material existence (although in such cases, a thoroughbred bourgeois probably can't stop the involuntary tightening of his sphincter).

Of course, Scherping gave him—had to give him—a handsome amount of severance pay. Obviously he was forced to do so by a murderous contract (probably still fuming at the thought, grinding his teeth in woe and weal).

For now in any case, our friend S. is rolling in money. But fear is bubbling out of every pore. The "hour of truth" has come. He has no more excuses not to write his book.

And so first he came here. Hopelessly behind the times: still dreaming the dreams of the Futurists, the Constructivists. Sees their dreams as having come true here—in Paris of all places! Divine city of Reason on earth. This is where the human being first becomes human. Temple of the World. Ziggurat: hieratic tower connecting heaven and earth. Pure and simple: the City of Man: ANTHROPOLIS.

In truth it's me he's fled to. As usual, he wants to crib something from me. He's looking for my secret motor, my special driving force—something he thinks I've got over him. Some perfidious secret of existence. Some crafty, not quite permissible, ethically and aesthetically not quite unobjectionable but incredibly practical, exceedingly effective trick for living. That, at any rate, which makes me appear livelier, more present, downright *realer* in his eyes than the phonies all around (including Nagel, delusively spawning best sellers). Livelier than he himself, *en tout cas*.

He confesses this to me with a moan of beautiful, admiring envy. He calls it the thing about me that's "healthy as an ox." A "vitality that is not yet wholly dissipated." An "existence that has not yet become wholly abstract"—indeed, one with the possibility of acting like a department-store executive with December stirrings and falling in love with the most banal of all love objects, a fashion model!

Yet at times he regards my vacant-eyed and ingenious concordance with life as sheer flimflam. So much the worse! For then, you see, he becomes intrigued by the fact that my flimflam works. This too requires qualities and abilities whose nature and origin are puzzling to him.

He looks for them in my life story. Even though he all but knows it by heart, he listens to me more attentively, investigates more conscientiously, more methodically than ever. I supply him generously. (A Russian proverb says that you can choke a guest with cottage cheese.) He takes secret notes. Thinks I don't realize. (I take my own notes about him afterward, at home.) But biographical data are not enough for him. He rummages about in my present living circumstances. Paris, he feels, is a trump in my game. He combs the city for the secret nutritive powers with which it presumably nourishes me. He has come as a scientific Hercules, who, before the fight, begins by taking a tiny sample for chemical analysis from the soil from which Antaeus draws his rejuvenating strength. Of course, he also wants to be cradled a bit:

Fais dodo, Colin, mon petit frère,
fais dodo, t'auras du lolo . . .

My brother Schwab. My brother Abel.

Needless to say, I promptly told him about the grotesque way things ended with Dawn. I didn't spare the details that might excite him ("*Il n'y a pas de détail,*" says Valéry). Everything very literary, it goes without saying. Just as he expects of me.

First (in a gentlemanly, cultivated, discreet, tastefully allusive way, of course), I gave him a glimpse of my desperate financial situation: more debts than a village dog has fleas. Christa, my divorced spouse, now morally supported by Witte, has found a lawyer who would squeeze alimony for her and our son from my tombstone. Plus trouble galore with the producer-piglets: my latest screenplays are not being accepted. So I ought to have cut down to the bare bones in everything. Yet I live in *grand luxe*. I reside sumptuously at the George V. I still keep an apartment for my eccentric beloved, even though it has been empty for months now, awaiting her. (I used to go there daily to put fresh flowers in the vases and change the milk, the steaks, the salubrious vegetables, the eggs in the icebox; she eats everything raw; at the Marché Buci, they are ardently sympathetic and treat me like a worried father: "*Mademoiselle est votre fille, n'est-elle pas?*" Certainly. Humbert Humbert's the name. And *mademoiselle* is out of town? *Évidemment*. And Papa's watching her apartment for her while she's gone. Yes, that's what young people are like nowadays. They want to live independently but they can't really manage on their own.)

Mademoiselle was out of town a lot during the past few months, goddamn it! I couldn't get anything else done because I spent my days combing Paris for the bitch! Do you know how many lousy little hotels there are here where a silly American model can hide out? How many dirty family pensions? I tell you, it's just like the stars in the sky: God alone has counted them. I'd like to have His problems. He didn't have to comb through each and every one of them for a lunatic girl who might have snuck in to spend an entire week in a darkened room, consuming nothing but raw eggs from a plastic box, instant coffee from little packets, chain-smoking, pill-popping, afflicted by unnameable terrors, shaken by ineffable fears, in constant danger of falling asleep with the cigarette in her pretty kisser and burning up in bed. He didn't hang on the telephone for nights on end, waiting to get through because the night clerk had deserted his post and was screwing *madame la patronne* two flights up...

be that as it may, in that very spot, the sleazy, sordid hotel on the place des Ternes—which our friend Schwab knew well enough, didn't he?—she had found refuge with the handsome Pole and the breathtaking French madame. In the same room where the scene with the Indian doll had taken place two years earlier (S. blushes even now at the mere mention of it). Our first love nest. The setting for an unspeakably arduous, unspeakably joyless deflowering (at the mere thought of it, *I* blush). I don't understand why it didn't occur to me right away to look for her there (probably for that very reason).

In the end, that's where I found her. With great delight, I can report (relishing Schwab's round-eyed interest) on how I had to construct a whole set of fictions, a real house of cards, to lure her out of her hole: the past was snuffed out. Our relationship had never existed—that is to say, never reached a higher degree of intimacy than that of casual acquaintance. ("Oh, how nice to see you!") I called to ask if she would go out with me. (Her *date* for tonight.) Needless to say, I brought flowers, two dozen white roses. With scrupulous narrative precision I describe how she had once again kept me waiting for hours before she descended the stairs in a black Pola Negri gown, parodying herself with symptoms of daffy insanity: prancing toward me with the marionette gait of a mindless mannequin; her hands, in black elbow-length widow's gloves, dangling affectedly from bent arms; her head sporting a gigantic black mushroom-shaped stump of a hat, which cast its shadow over soup-plate-sized dark glasses sparkling with green and violet reflections, so that all one could see underneath was the mouth and chin and throat—very red, very white, perfectly beautiful: the tragic lips of Garbo, the tender and resolute chin of Ava Gardner, the stem-like throat of Audrey Hepburn, all the clichés of standardized female beauty in a halved head, as in a *Vogue* fashion photo.

My friend listens breathlessly as I describe with cruel precision the way she came along, sashaying and hip-wiggling, how she affected incredibly phony theatrical nonchalance as she called out "Hi!" in the guttural tone of her sophomore Americanese, with the jaw-dropping cheerleader smile that revealed all her immaculate glowing toothpaste-commercial teeth back to the molars. The way she didn't even bother holding out her cheek for a kiss (after all, I am her *date* tonight, am I not?) as she zoomed past, wantonly purposeful as a bumblebee in flight, and headed toward the handsome Pole's desk and instantly got on the telephone. The way I waited for her, holding my bridal bouquet of roses stiff in my lap, clumsy as a provincial beau at his first gallant rendezvous. The way I was forced to listen to her talking on the phone with somebody I didn't know, of whose existence I had had no inkling whatsoever until that moment. The way she said with desperate woe, "No, no! You can't leave me like that! You know I love you!" And the way I felt nothing, absolutely nothing, not the feeblest sting of jealousy, not even curiosity about whom she was saying it to (for at last it was not tormenting conjecture but certainty, *reality*)...

The way she then finally came to me, wordlessly taking the roses and following me out to the car—all this with the robotic motion and lifeless visage of a hypnotized woman. (I couldn't see her eyes behind the monstrous glasses under the brim of that blasted stump, but I knew every feature of hers so well that I could read the sorrow in the tip of her nose, beneath which incidentally was her mouth, now the mouth of a tired child made up for carnival: the festival had not been the expected happy delirium but, rather, wild and noisy and chaotic, full of crudeness, gloating malevolence; now, it's over, the dream is dreamed out.)

She did not reply when I asked whether I should take her to dinner, to the movies, or elsewhere. To a dance café perhaps? Home? Where was that? In our—in her apartment in the rue Jacob? Whom was I talking to? Whom was I thinking of? Did she want to go to bed perhaps? A tasteful idea... Finally, since I knew she enjoyed riding in an open car, I drove her to the Bois de Boulogne.

Ah, splendid! A starry sky over the rustling backdrop of black foliage, silhouettes that looked cut out of tin. In the daytime, it's probably bright and green during this season. Nature. Calms the nerves. Relax, my love.

Naturally the cars coming our way flashed their headlights at us. One even did a U-turn behind us, caught up, and cut us off, so that I had to slam on the brakes. Two guys got out, leaving their girls inside. But I knew what they wanted, so I waved them off and drove around them and on until we were off the main road. (One of the men, incidentally, had let out an appreciative whistle when he saw what was visible of Dawn under the black mushroom.)

In the side road where we finally halted, another car approached us. The driver stuck his head out the window and proposed a *partouse* somewhere in Neuilly. "*Non merci, mon vieux, nous avons des problèmes, tu vois.*" "*Oh là là!...*" Dawn remained wordless and motionless throughout. (Don't act so puritanical, I thought, you with your unknown lover!) But the night was soft, and naturally I couldn't help myself, I had to talk. Had to tell her what I felt for her. What I had suffered because of her. Suffered mainly because I had been forced to torment her (to my son: when Daddy spanks you, it hurts him more than you). That I had been forced to torment her, however, because I loved her so tremendously (just as Daddy loves his little boy). That she had never understood the full extent of the causal relationship (just like Daddy's little boy). How regrettable that was, though, what a waste of good time in our lives if one thought about it, wasn't it? Yet how beautiful, how wonderful it could be if...

Around us, the lovely city of Paris hummed and seethed (some fifteen million inhabitants when you include the suburbs: first-class nuclear target). And there I was, talking once again—oh shame! Once again spewing out the contents of my soul. *Vomitatio animae.* My inner life, fermented in its emotional essence ("a speciality of the bloody fucking middle classes," as John and Stella called it).

Thus did I talk, spitting forth a lover's verbal gruel. Nonstop and in detail. Soliloquizing. Laying my worldview at her feet. The ordeal of human life. God's coldheartedness. Needless to say, I did not make it sentimental (people like us avoid sentimentality like the plague). I said, "I'm sorry, my darling, I know it's not agreeable to be loved, but..." I spiced my verbal gruel with piquant little jests. ("What does Torquato Tasso say? Two souls, alas, are dwelling in my breast . . . That's not quite the case with me. Two breasts, alas, are dwelling in my soul, and they're yours!") In short, I did everything to make myself disagreeable.

Overhead, in the dark backdrop of branches, the stars were twinkling. Many, many. God alone has counted them. It must have taken Him His sweet time. Galactorrhea in the firmament. And it's big. If you imagined the sun (its diameter one hundred and nine times the size of the Earth's) as the head of a pin somewhere in West or East Berlin, then the next fixed star would be like a soccer ball in Hamburg. And here I was sitting and talking of my love. Pouring out verbal gruel.

Embarrassing. But—oh my goodness! What man hasn't been guilty of this sort of thing? And I of all people—how often, how many shameful times, had I not already done this! Talked away, tormented, pigheaded, and persistent, at some then-beloved female. Sputtering verbal figures wrung from necessity: aphorisms, sublimated from my spiritual ordeal. Sentences fraught with confession. Metaphysical knowledge. Blurted out to the beloved female body, to the sweet female flesh, to the soft skin, the fine, frail limbs, the tender curves, the airy, fragrant hair—oh misery! To a face that briefly epitomized all the sweetness of life, mother, sister, the regained half of the original pair, the fulfillment of the dream of being One, of blissfully entering, dissolving into, another human being. To eyes whose depths I filled with poetry and there found the answer to myself. (How did Scherping put it? "If only they couldn't speak. If they just barked or meowed, then we wouldn't expect them to react humanly like you and me . . .")

Oh well. In this case, this at that time beloved pair of eyes was now concealed by soup-plate-sized black glasses under the brim of the gigantic black hat-stump. I could just barely make out the tip of my present *adorata*'s nose, and under it the mouth: the beautiful mouth over the poignantly tender (and firm) chin over the stem-like girlish throat over the narrow shoulders and the beloved little breasts: two touchingly young, tender, bud-like handfuls of girlish breast (thoroughly art nouveau, but now covered by the black satin of the art deco dress—so let's stick to the mouth).

It hovered, blood-red, engraved in the dull white of the cheeks, chin, and throat, in the compact blacknesses of the hat and gown and car-seat leather and nocturnal foliage under the starry sky. It was a strangely isolated, a detached yet delicate piece of anatomy, with a mysterious life of its own. A mute mouth. A mouth without a face. And without an explicable expression, not cheerful and not dismal, not proud, not humble, not yearning, and not scornful, not smart, not stupid: just mouth. Beautiful, human (albeit human in a zoologically universalized manner: the mouth of mankind, of the species of man; and at the same time, something animallike in and of itself: a mouth-animal, shaped like a blossom for mimicry...). Where the lips swelled there was a wan, slightly greasy glow: reflection of starlight, sparkling too in the black glasses above and in the curve of the windshield in front and on the nickel fittings of the car door at the side.

And all this was embedded in white roses. For she had untied my bridegroom's bouquet and strewn the flowers in and around her lap. She sat in white roses, like a black swan. Her black torso loomed out of white rose blossoms into the black night. Above hovered the mouth.

I, however, sat next to her, talking. Talking my heart and soul out of my throat. And while I was talking and talking, about my tremendous love, about my misery and wretchedness, about my lofty goals and wishes—for both of us, to be sure, for both of us!—this mouth suddenly laughed. The red lips gaped, revealing two lines of white teeth, well formed and regular, two glistening rows. And while this mouth laughed, soundlessly and without the shaking of vulgar hilarity, her hand in the black widow-glove reached into the roses, drew out one of the blossoms, and put it to her lips, passing it over them as if to cool them... And suddenly, from between the bars of teeth, the tongue shot out and seized the blossom and yanked it into the teeth, which snapped shut and shredded it.

A fascinating spectacle. I depicted it vividly to Schwab. I let him take part in it, and he followed it spellbound, suffering with me as the red mouth devoured the white rose. The mouth kept laughing, soundlessly; small, white tatters of shredded petals stuck to the red lips. By the time the trimming and the stem were all that was left, I had stopped talking, switched on the engine, and was driving Dawn back to the hotel.

I had always captivated her with finely polished chivalry. ("We're not used to such nice manners anymore, you know.") And so this time too I did not hold back. I got out, walked around the vehicle, and held open the door, handing her out of the car. A ludicrous gesture of farewell, I admit (a movie script would have said here, on the left, "Musical leitmotif comes in softly"). She took two or three steps toward the hotel entrance, then wheeled around, came over to me, pressed her breasts, body, and thighs snugly against me, and whispered in a passionate, husky tone, "Darling, do you think you could spare another thousand francs? I need it to pay the bill here and some other things."

Her mouth laughed again when she put away the money and left. The white roses were scattered from the car seat across the sidewalk all the way over to the hotel entrance, like a strip of moonlight on a dark lake, with a black swan swimming away...

...and because of that, Schwab expects my heart to have burst in my chest!?... I peer into the round, gaping eyes behind his inch-thick bookworm's glasses. (Aunt Hertha rattling on the door to the shitter, behind which Cousin Wolfgang has locked himself in to read undisturbed: "You'll go blind someday!")

Well, what world-shaking event had occurred? I had lost Dawn. This time for good. Irrevocably. No, this time she wouldn't come back. To be sure, she wasn't just an extraordinarily beautiful but also an extraordinarily interesting girl, mad as a hatter, no doubt, but only sometimes, periodically. In between, she could be as smart, as merry, as full of wild joie de vivre as any thoughtless young thing...

A completely intimidated person, indeed, creature of a civilization of sheer collective madness, product of a civilization of money, dazzled by the myth of success, seduced by the rhetoric, the iconography of the commercialized love of life—a child still, barely twenty years old, I should really have borne a paternal responsibility, but the role doesn't seem to suit me; I failed shamefully even with my own son (probably by trying too hard, she would have said). And of course, the age gap was rather large for the glorious lover, I assume, even though there had been moments of incredible intimacy—we had plunged into one another with exuberant tenderness, a sudden profound union of souls and senses, of the kind that has been rather infrequent since the fashionable obsolescence of Rilke and D'Annunzio's emotional world. Ah! Her gigantic gray feline eyes close to mine (without the black glasses, of course), her mouth laughing happily (not scornfully), her beloved beautiful happy mouth...

and I had lost her. And the man reeling under the impact of this blow is not I: he is my friend Johannes Schwab. As though I had not personally experienced this whole foolish love story, which any sensible person would only shake his head at; as though I had experienced it vicariously for him, Schwab—what am I saying? For our entire generation, allegedly incapable of achieving much of a solid inner state, as though it were suffering from a kind of emotional scurvy. It was an act of salvation, in a word. From now on, people could point at me if anyone started in about the death of emotional life and the shift of feeling to collective experiences like soccer matches and politics. I was still different from the others; my emotional life was of prewar quality.

I was the exception that proved the rule, if you please. I

maintained the link with the emotional possibilities of our fathers, said Schwab. I was living proof that continuity had not been broken, at least in this respect—the "specifically European conception of love and capacity for love." That is to say, love as a revolutionary act, as the revolt of the individual against the strictures of society... and not as an adolescent, mind you, no, as a mature, reflective, much-tested adult. Granted, this too a way of dragging the past into presence—but not merely passive, not merely in the act of experiencing; rather inherited action...

And now what? Now that I had reached the head of the class and now that—as foreseen—the whole emotion business lay in pieces, now I refused to take the next logical step? I didn't despair, I didn't shoot a bullet into my head, I didn't join the Foreign Legion in order to vanish forever into the unknown? No. I was, I am, as cheerful and serene as ever.

It doesn't help to tell Schwab that I am in a certain respect only partially involved, insofar as it is not my entire self that lost Dawn. Only one of my two souls is concerned. Her loss, I say, is entirely the fault of those traits and qualities of mine that were stamped on me by my formative years in Vienna: the disgusting eagerness to take moral possession, the desire to improve and help, the need to educate and alter. As though it were one of the tasks of love to develop the other person toward so-called normality at any cost. (For instance: my persistent concern about Dawn's health, both physical and mental, my pampering and caring, my making sure that nothing happened to her, that she didn't do anything to herself. The picayune morality, the anxious conformism behind all that, and of course the cannibalism, the eating of human flesh in mental and physical ownership. In short, everything that made John and Stella so violently hate the *bloody fucking middle classes* and their shitty morality and that had, alas, partly become my nature during twelve Viennese years with Uncle Helmuth, Aunt Hertha, Aunt Selma, and Cousin Wolfgang.)

In contrast, however, I tell my friend, there is an entirely different side to me, namely, the side with which I won Dawn—in beautiful freedom: overlooking any craziness of hers, fulfilling every foolish wish, never correcting or criticizing her, approving of all her madcap ideas, even feeding her pills instead of *foie gras*, buying her mushroom-like hat-stumps instead of fancy hats, suffering with a smile when she dressed like a scarecrow... In other words, that in me which is of the artist, which tends toward the artistic, and on top of this the generosity, the elegant neutrality in handling human relationships that I had managed to copy from such outstanding personages as Uncle Ferdinand. The cautious live-and-let-live attitude of Uncle Agop Garabetian's extraordinary amiability. The imaginativeness, the delicious playfulness of a Bully Olivera, whose acquaintanceship had been one of the most fruitful gifts of my unbourgeois childhood before Vienna... Had any of the three of them, I said to Schwab, learned that someone wanted to kill himself, he unhesitatingly would have given that person the opportunity...

And this side of mine, I tell friend S., did not lose Dawn, can never lose Dawn. And most certainly not if the rubber collar around the other half of my soul was what made her leave me. "You understand what I mean," I say to him. "The very thing stated by Romano Guardini, whom you so highly esteem: 'The first step to the other is the movement that *takes away the hands* and clears the space in which the self-concerned quality of the person can come into action. This motion constitutes the first effect of *justice* and is the basis of all *love*.'"

He turns crimson. He thinks I'm trying to make fun of him. He regards my quoting (especially from Guardini!), my attack against the middle classes, and my ironical eulogy of the plutocrats Uncle Ferdinand, Sir Agop Garabetian, Bully Olivera, as a venomous personal jibe. "Don't act more cynical than you are," he says.

I say, "You misunderstand me. I'm quite serious. I'm talking about something that's very much on my mind: a sociology of emotional life, which I have been planning to work on for some time now. I maintain that the relative emotional frigidity of the uppermost (and lowermost) strata in any society is paired with a keener sense of reality than the sentimental romanticism of the *bloody fucking middle classes*. With the realism of a more thorough knowledge of life. Soul (I mean an especially passionate tension in one's nature that is designed for suffering) seems, as John and Stella always said, to be a prerogative of the middle strata. The bourgeois invents emotions that he can no longer draw from immediate contact with life. Ask Scherping, he knows a thing or two about it. He also knows what thrives especially well in these inner miasmas: a proclivity for the abstract, for the as-if, for the fictive, plus, of course, no shortage of art, especially literary art. Which you might consider an advantage—for a publisher. But interhuman relations are thereby unbearably complicated. I wish I had listened to Dawn's warnings in time. You know, she used to say, 'Most people fail because they try too hard.' It's really just like writing books, isn't it? If only we were more lighthearted, we'd be like Nagel and produce novels like cars on an assembly line. Dawn could be very shrewd sometimes."

Once again, I'm the one who's talking. But he doesn't laugh, and he doesn't eat any roses either. His upper lip (a bit long, and sensitive as a feeler, yet resolute above the severely retracted lower lip: the mouth of Paul Klee) trembles, as it usually does when he's very nervous. A couple of fine little drops of sweat hang above it. (Lately, he's been drinking oceans of rum and Coca-Cola, and he's always quite proud when he expertly orders, "*Un autre Cuba libre, s'il vous plaît!*") His eyes are bright and blank, like the eyes of a boiled fish.

And I am talking. Spouting confused verbal gruel. I say, "Why, on the other hand, were there so few neuropaths in Uncle Ferdinand's circle of friends, in the 'Middle Kingdom' of his playmates at the polo grounds and baccarat tables of Deauville and Monte Carlo? After all, their monstrous wealth and constant idleness ought to have created all kinds of neuroses and psychoses. But not a trace. On the contrary: the serenest rapport with life. Not a hint of communication problems or the like. Model sociability: Uncle Agop's parties were epoch-making. Bully Olivera had more friends the world over than Dr. Schweitzer. Plus the smoothest, most graceful love affairs with dozens of women. I remember what Uncle Ferdinand said to me about his relationship with my mother when I visited him for the last time, in Bessarabia, during the winter of 1939–40: 'She was an ideal mistress in the truest sense of the word—not only a great beauty but a great teacher of life. She used to say, "The entire secret of a harmonious mind lies in the ability to recognize the imminent formation of cramps and to prevent it in time. If you desire something that you can't get—then a cramp will form. You have to relax it before it distorts everything else. *Vous comprenez, mon ami?...*" I did understand her. She taught me that the encounter of two people is like the collision of two billiard balls: only *one* point of one touches *one* point of the other. Therefore we must never draw conclusions about the entire relationship. For only a moment later, some other point of mine meets another point of yours, changing the relationship entirely. The number of possibilities is infinite. Every instant is new and without precondition—that is to say, with no rights deriving from a previous moment. Hence, every instant of harmony is a gift. Every possible next instant of estrangement is due to a change of reciprocal position that must be respected.' That," I say to S., "is what I call realism. There's something really artistic about it. I wish our politicians had it, not to speak of the poets..."

Schwab doubles over as if he'd been punched in the stomach. He hears scorn and malice in every word. He believes I am out to torture him. His hand trembles so badly that his Cuba libre sloshes out of the glass before he can bring it to his lips. His sensitivity provokes me to bait him. I needn't think up anything. Whatever I say elicits something from him.

I say, "I don't quite know whether I should be flattered or

insulted by your suspicion that my equanimity about losing Dawn may not be genuine. That it is only feigned to camouflage wholly different and dramatic feelings." (I intentionally use the word "camouflage," which is bound to provoke him.) "How little you know me! I mean, how poorly you appreciate my literary *déformation professionelle*! Don't you notice? I'm so fascinated by myself *as a case* that I haven't got a scrap of attention left for my personal feelings. I must ask you to indulge me: regrettably, I cannot suffer, as you wish, after the loss of my beloved, because for the time being I am much too interested in what actually went on here. Something in any case that didn't simply happen to me. Rather something that, as you witnessed, I undertook of my own free will and with open eyes. After all, I dashed into this madness consciously and deliberately: I needed the experience. An experience, though, that was the very opposite of what you think.

"Possessed by my foolish love for a will-o'-the-wisp, an apparition of a human being—if we're being honest, right?—in any event, a sheer fiction of a woman, a fata morgana of a love object, I no doubt carried out something exemplary—I mean, something beautifully consistent with the zeitgeist. But why and to what extent? That it has something to do with *repetition*, that much is clear—Papa Kierkegaard would be thrilled. Once again rummaging for the lost half of my life, I was doing something in its style. In the style of the twenties and thirties, which quite commonly these days have come to trigger in just about everyone an ever more self-conscious nostalgia. Thus, not only did I repeat something, individually, but something repeated itself through me: the *it*, the *id* in me, part of the collective of my race, my civilization, my culture, and my time. It had me do what is due to be done in this time. Even in my extravagance, I was once again merely a leaf in the wind of the zeitgeist—isn't that a breathtaking thought? Everything that occurred, exactly as it occurred, is typical of the time—and that means: that from it we can draw conclusions about the quality and character of our time. For instance, the abstractness, the echo-like quality of the relationship between Dawn and myself, the experience detached from ourselves and all surrounding reality, not to mention the high symbolism of her farewell gesture, first eating the white rose and then making the sluttish request for money—simply glorious!! But you must understand that I now yearn for a less anemic reality. After so much abstraction, so much fiction, such a toying as-if, I would like to fortify myself with raw flesh and warm blood..."

I do so every evening at a cheap cabaret on the place Blanche, where a troupe of delicious negresses are making a guest appearance. They too perform in the Folies Bergères style of the Mistinguette and Josephine Baker era (ergo, they too drag the past into presence), with pistachio, violet, and flamingo-colored ostrich feathers foaming on their heads and from their tailbones, with sequined corsets, and stilettoes tall as their insteps and thin as a pencil under their sinewy feet. They hurl their wonderfully limber legs at the rotating colored lamps under the ceiling, as if they were trying to yank them out of their hip joints. They bend their pelvises forward and backward and around with such sharp, grotesque contortions that one involuntarily bends with them, vibrates with them as if in the back and forth of an erotic shadowboxing. Their solid, fine-tipped breasts jiggle like rubber, and the lianas of their arms intertwine and unravel to the intertwining and unraveling saxophone voices of the Dixieland band accompanying them. In short, they are worthy of admiration. I tell S., "Worthy of ad-miration. You have to come and see them, ab-solutely!"

He doesn't need to be asked, he clings to me anyway, never leaves me unguarded for even an instant. This suits me fine: I've already left a small fortune with the black beauties anyway; I've borrowed the money from the clerk at the George V. God's and the movie piglets' providence will see to it that he gets the money back. In any case, for now, Schwab has the honor of paying the bills.

He does so with obvious pleasure. After all, there's something for him here too. The spectacle boasts scenes that you won't catch anywhere else. For example, on the very first evening, the third from the right in the chorus line, a particularly sinewy and well-proportioned chorine, was irritated by her left-hand neighbor (softer, taller, more voluptuous), presumably because of the attention I paid the latter—an incessant torrent of flowers, a gigantic, sky-blue teddy bear, champagne between the numbers, whereby, needless to say, I drew the general attention of the audience to her. Finally, at the end of the performance, it was time for the curtain call and the artistes were presented by name, each one stepping forward and curtseying to our applause. The sinewy girl calmly waited for my favorite to bow and me to unleash universal jubilation (the pimps and beatniks and tourists attending the spectacle were amused by my clowning). Then, upon being called, the irritated chorine stepped forward very prettily, curtseyed, and sprang back with the agility of a monkey—planting the stiletto heel of her strapped shoe on the naked toes of her voluptuous colleague. The victim folded up in pain like a penknife.

Needless to say, it was the aggressor I took home that evening (to the apartment in the rue Jacob that I had been keeping for months to welcome the ruefully returning Dawn). I did not comfort the victim until the next evening. And needless to say, S., in his old rattletrap VW with double-H (Hanseatic Hamburg) license plates, tagged along both times. He pursued us straight across Paris to the Rive Gauche, even though I finally got sick of it and had fun steering my Ferrari very fast along the boulevards with lots of side streets, from which another car with the right of way could shoot out at any moment. But S. behaved courageously, downright heroically.

There was a third and fourth nocturnal drive (after all, the troupe had sixteen beautiful, coffee-brown girls), and we didn't have an accident until the fifth. I stopped and put the car in reverse. I had just barely squeaked through a traffic light when it changed from yellow to red. Schwab, not far behind me, lost his nerve and slammed his heavy Teutonic foot on the brakes. He failed to notice that some guy in an old 204 had been tailgating him—an atavistic hunting instinct, as we know, aroused by an apparently fleeing object. He smashed right into Schwab's rear.

Nothing much had happened, thank goodness. Just a lot of noise and banged-up metal. No one was hurt. Schwab complained about a whirring in his head, but then the old boy had been boozing rather heavily. It was a miracle he had been able to drive at all. The cars were wrecked, of course. The engine in Schwab's Beetle had been shoved into the back seat, the hood of the old 204 was arched up. But it was three a.m. and no one cared about precise details. So the matter was settled on the spot and without the police. The two drivers exchanged insurance numbers and encouraging pats on the back while I interpreted. Then I loaded Schwab into the (rather cramped) back seat of the Ferrari.

That evening, for variety, I had made my choice from the audience rather than the troupe: something uncommonly exotic, also coffee-brown but pure French (whereas the troupe came from Jamaica), extraordinarily elegant and expensively perfumed, luxuriously hung with real jewelry (discernible by the nasty flashing of the pure-water diamonds), yet quick, witty, obviously of above-average intelligence, yet also larger than life, with mammoth thighs and the gigantic face of a merry-go-round Moor—and she called herself Princess Jahovary! I found her fascinating. "Isn't she fas-cinating?" I said to S. after picking her up (she was with some suspiciously chic cocktail-party types, but I quickly maneuvered her away from them and to the bar). She obviously enjoyed me too. She said she was an agent for popular music, a record manufacturer. So not a kept woman then, as the diamonds had led me to think. We drank two or three whiskeys at the bar. Then it was time to go. I took her by the arm and waved good-bye to Schwab (as on the previous nights). And as on all previous nights, he hurriedly paid the check and plunged after us into the Russian roulette of side-street traffic. The fact that he was shot down from behind was (as John would say) tough luck. The one who really took it amiss, however, was the chocolate-colored Princess Jahovary. She wanted to get out when I wedged my dazed friend S. past her fullness into the back seat. She asked me to see her to the nearest taxi. When I told her we were only a few minutes from the rue Jacob, she acted as if this were the first she'd heard that I intended to bring her there, and she staunchly demanded that I drive her to the sixteenth arrondissement, where (typically) she resided. Nor would she hear of my first dropping S. at his hotel. So I drove her to the sixteenth arrondissement. Slowly and carefully, at her express wish. She wasn't just miffed, she was downright furious. "*Un bel caratteraccio!*" I mumbled to myself. She asked me where I had learned Italian. I said that knowing several languages wasn't always a sign of a good education but often merely the dregs leftover from a checkered career. And did she, as Princess Jahovary, speak Romanian? No, she said, her mother had never spoken it to her. And her father? "He was an American." Aha. No further comment.

But her anger had obviously cooled and she was cheery again. An Aries, no doubt? She cheerfully admitted it. Schwab had fallen asleep in the back. He had probably drunk a lot more than I realized. He was snoring and we laughed.

When we arrived at her building (a ponderous Second Empire façade, the thick leaded-glass panes of the entrance door safeguarded by numerous iron-rod flourishes crowned with brass buttons), she became affectionate but refused to ask me up. Nevertheless, there was some erotic grappling, and since Schwab appeared to be fast asleep in the back, we were not exactly cautious. I complimented her on her beautiful lips and said I'd love to give her a white rose to munch on—and she must have misunderstood, for she took me at my word, even though the bud was really cyclamen-colored.

I don't know what came over me. In any case, I felt myself veritably shuddering with lust for this mountain of chocolate-brown flesh in jingly jewelry and a Balenciaga *tailleur* and sporting the ridiculously arrogated name of a Romanian princess. Perhaps it was something utterly subliminal, the perverse notion that I was morally ravishing something abstruse, a sideshow curiosity like the Trunk Lady or Sheila the Elephant Girl. Whatever the case, I behaved quite uncontrolledly, moaning loudly and grinding my teeth. Finally, unable to hold back any longer, I bit her mahogany neck so that she too emitted a series of tiny, lustfully painful cries. Then, very confused, she fled into her mammoth bourgeois palace, and I drove Schwab to his hotel.

When we arrive, to my astonishment, he is sitting bolt upright in the back seat and his eyes are open. He doesn't say anything. Nor do I. Finally, not without effort, he creeps out of the car, trudges around it, sticks his head in at my window, takes my hand in his two hands, squeezes it ardently, and says emotionally, "Thank you! Oh thank you!" Shaking my hand, he keeps repeating, "Thank you! Oh thank you!"

Then he vanishes into the hotel entrance. I drive through the dead streets to the George V. It's four a.m. and the dawn is budding. At eleven, he rings me. He's made up his mind to fly back to Hamburg.

I drive him to the airport. He shows no sign of remembering anything. I have to give him a blow-by-blow description of his accident, though he's at least managed to understand that his car was wrecked and he did what was necessary to have it towed away.

We drink a farewell whiskey at the bar. When his flight is announced, his eyes fill with tears. He can barely speak. He holds my hand again and stammers, "Thank you! Thank you for everything!" Shortly before going through the gate, he turns back to me once more, reaches into his pockets, and hauls out fistfuls of bank notes, which he presses into my hand: "Adieu! And thank you! Farewell! Adieu!"

That's how *reality* presents itself to me.

4

So that was my friend S.'s last visit to Paris—in fact the last time I ever saw him. He flew back to Hamburg, where by means of a devious combination of alcohol and every kind of upper and downer he sought to inveigle Mother Nature into sparing him the embarrassing circumstance of a suicide. Within a few months he had succeeded. By the end of December of that same year (1964) he was dead.

You, Mr. Brodny, will probably fail to grant him your respect. Please bear in mind what a delicate case he was. Even when I first met him in Hamburg in 1948, he couldn't get over how unpredictable mankind was, and how confused the world. A Gottfried Benn fan, you see. A Benn reader believes in the power of the mind. Of course, he knew about the mind's vulnerability. I wonder how he would have endured the present (and with it the ever more clearly looming future). How would my image have changed in his eyes? I am not speaking about the curious fact that the easygoing chocolate-brown giantess was to be Dawn's successor in my heart and my ardent mistress for two years before she too passed away. By the way, her mother really was a Romanian princess and called Jahovary. But more about that later.

As for the confusion of the world: even the documentary value of notes like those presented above is questionable. I have in my possession certain others (along with many more, which were meant to serve literary purposes) concerning Schwab's visit to Paris a year before the visit just described. At that time, I made a point of opening his eyes a little to the childish expectations he came here with whenever he fled Hamburg and its philistinism (only to plunge into a spiritual low when he went back home, an abyss with an alcohol pond waiting for him at the bottom).

This was not an entirely pleasurable business. It really took it out of me, I can tell you. He was already rather ragged when he came from Hamburg—came looking for me: his chubby German hand reaching out for Mama's apron string. I picked him up at Orly. If a first glance was not enough to tell me what a state he was in, then he would have betrayed it on the ride to his hotel in the rue des Beaux Arts. (Though I was trying to drive at a snail's pace, as much as the curses and shaking fists from the vehicles around me permitted: Parisians prefer their traffic to flow smoothly.)

Schwab's baggage had been lost; it had been flown somewhere else—I believe to Caracas. Running around after it, waiting for hours and filling out lost baggage forms and insurance questionnaires, had reduced him to hysteria. I had to bombard him with nonstop gin and tonics to prevent an outburst. He was wearing a heavy turtleneck sweater (not a Hanseatic outfit but, with corduroy slacks and a beret, the guild costume of German intellectuals in the fifties, which costume he carried on into the sixties—typical of people who are behind the times but consider themselves avant-garde!). He was sweating like a cart horse; it was October, but as warm as summer. During the drive (his fingers clutching the edge of the dashboard, his nose pasted flat against the windshield, beads of sweat on his upper lip), he told me he had had a row with Scherping. About me, but originally about Nagel—an unspeakably ridiculous business:

He had had a few weeks of intense, highly stimulating work during which he hadn't touched a drop of alcohol (had even seriously thought of finally beginning his own book) when Nagel came along with something that caused him profound embarrassment. Nagel entrusted him with the first hundred and fifty pages of a new novel (the seventeenth in sixteen years) for a first reading, with an urgent request for absolute secrecy, especially in regard to Scherping. He, Nagel, was fed up with the renowned (Hemingway-like) directness of his narrative art and had tried a stylistic experiment that he wanted to present to Scherping only when he was sure his gamble had paid off. *Magari!*

In reading these pages, Schwab plunged into abysmal melancholy and hence into a battery of Saint-Émilion 1957, which I had once brought to him in Hamburg—two dozen bottles. It was a smooth, mannish wine, not all too heavy, yet full of strength, a true friend and comforter. Nevertheless, while making his way through the first dozen bottles, he did not dare venture out of the house, because he feared (correctly, no doubt) that Nagel was lying in wait to hear his verdict. He was living on old rolls and liverwurst and a tiny remnant of cheese, and he wouldn't answer the phone when it rang. Schelmie, his secretary, had been told to spread the news that he had gone to Bückeburg. (Why Bückeburg of all places is still unclear.)

By the time he came to the second case of wine, he was no longer able to leave the house. He lay on the sofa under a pile of rustling manuscript pages and had no intention of ever getting up again. But he had got up enough nerve to act—albeit not enough to look Nagel in the eye or even call him and tell him man to man what he thought of the form and content of his work in progress. (Even now, at my side, telling me the story, his goggle eyes widening in fear each time I innocently moved out of another car's way, he expressed himself rather evasively.) He did not want to write to Nagel; a letter would be too formal, too callously depersonalized, and also too blatant an admission of his cowardice (*déformation professionelle*: the written word is reduced to a sheer defense barricade and we withdraw behind it). So, in order to show that he was a warmhearted friend, a sympathetic human being, and even in need of sympathy himself, and also to demonstrate his fine detachment from the message itself, he selected the modern device of the tape recorder—a flight into abstraction for which he would pay dearly.

Ingenious man! With the timbre, the brio, the tremolo of his abstracted voice (a voice at anyone's disposal, so to speak), he hoped to express all the things that would excuse his lack of enthusiasm. Not the words but the voice alone was supposed to document his sincere interest, the honesty of his involvement, his conscientious perusal of the manuscript, the ordeal of reaching a verdict given the complex situation; likewise his admiration of the risk Nagel had taken, his hope that a second, carefully composed attempt might lead to eventual success . . . In words, this sounds quite discouraging, you know; but the voice ought to quiver in paschal promise, expressing everything that the meager word distorts . . .

and yet, forty-eight hours of isolation and the thirteenth bottle of wine gummed up his speech faculties rather badly. The first tape, he now surmised, must have sounded faltering. It probably consisted mostly of pauses, heavy breathing, tortuously begun and hastily concluded verbal digressions, frequent harrumphs, coughs, sudden spluttering assurances of sympathy—in short, everything that would try Nagel's patience and annoy him in the extreme when he heard it—all this interspersed with the annoyingly undefinable noises of a smoker, matches being struck and cigarettes being put out too energetically in an ashtray, new cigarette packs furiously ripped open (his fingers already trembling violently; this increased the softness, anxiety, femininity, sensitivity of his hands, which, by the way, were very beautiful), and of course the clinking of glasses and bottles, gurgling, splashing, swallowing. (And Nagel had been teetotal for years now, never even touched a woman anymore, in order to devote himself entirely to his art—like that little Algerian painter, late at night at the bistro counter behind the place Pigalle: "*Je donne tout cela à mon art!*")

For all that, the first tape was a highly interesting acoustic document. I proposed that he get it back from Nagel and send it as an experiment in avant-garde music to the Donaueschingen Festival. But my suggestion did not have the liberating effect that one hopes for from humor. Schwab remained despondent, distraught. He was brooding about what was to come.

He moaned. It must have been at around the fifteenth or sixteenth bottle (the fortieth minute on tape) that he finally got down to the nitty-gritty—namely, the difficulty, nay, virtual impossibility, of writing today. Writing in general and novels in particular. The insane presumptuousness of writing novels after Joyce. And certainly niting wrovels, hmm, excuse me, of, clink clink clink, blubblubblubblub clink swallow-swallow-swallow, heavy breathing, of writhing navels thorough-attack-of-whooping-cough clink clink in a totally sanforized pardon me standardized society. And at this point, he felt he had to come to Nagel's request. But now he feared he might have already pronounced a scathing condemnation of Nagel's experiment. (Indeed, Schelmie later claimed that it did sound like one.) And so he quickly began to flog his theme, but then he lost the thread of the argument as well as his temper, becoming very offensive, even insulting—but that, thank goodness, was articulated only to the extent that the seventeenth and eighteenth bottles permitted. Besides, he had already been in the dream dimension of slow motion for a long time.

Still, he had enough strength left to call up Schelmie and, in a slurred voice, to tell her to pick up the tape and deliver it to Nagel promptly, and not to listen to a word of it or breathe a syllable about it to Scherping. After that, he was unconscious for the subsequent forty-eight hours—he was a strong man.

Fortunately, I do not have to introduce Nagel or Scherping to you, honored Herr Doktor J. G. Brodny. (Doctorate from the University of Czernowitz? German department? Improbable; more likely Berlin, late twenties, nonracist intellectuals' paradise of the cursed *Systemzeit*; degenerate art; art deco. Fluorescence of the already rotten *Geist. Romanisches Café.* But that would require a whole biography, with the migration story, so let's omit the "Herr Doktor.")

In any case, you are familiar with both Nagel's irascibility and Scherping's vacillating hysteria. (After all, I had a carefully considered reason for imagining you as being partly clued in and familiar with the milieu—whereby it occurs to me that you may know about the incident I'm describing. But that wouldn't matter much.) Thus, I can save myself the trouble of depicting what happened to Nagel when he played the tape . . .

In our early period, during the Hamburg ice years right after 1945, when Nagel and I were still friends and he still drank our home-brewed turnip schnapps in manly nonchalance, he once, as impetuous as ever (a Sagittarian), almost swallowed an Alka-Seltzer tablet (black-market item) without water. I picture his reaction to Schwab's tape as rather similar. As Schwab remorsefully recalled, the foaming Nagel instantly hopped into the car (button gearshift for amputees) and drove to Scherping's, brakes screeching. Together with the chief bookkeeper, the head of production, and the sales manager—three solid German men with correct haircuts—and with Schelmie as a witness, they listened to Schwab's tape. Needless to say, Scherping swore on a stack of Bibles that he would finally can this editor, this increasingly uncontrollable drunkard; he would dismiss him on the spot without notice or severance pay; he would drive him in disgrace from the publishing house. (Nagel allegedly demanded this, and indeed it occurred seven months later.)

However, what occurred the next day was something that Schwab, in turn, did not have to depict for me—*conosco i miei polli*. When Schwab showed up at the publishing firm, he was *not* bewildered, crestfallen, intimidated—as he was now, here, at my side, in the Paris lunchtime rush hour (he did not know the meaning of fear, only fantastic anxieties, such as the anxiety of my killing him in my car). Towering upright and gazing straight ahead into space, disdainfully slamming doors with his provocatively pointed "Good morning!" he showed up at the office, still half-plastered and irritated by an acid stomach, angrily craving beer, his rumbling belly filled with leonine courage that recently (just when?) had spurred him to some daring deed he simply couldn't recollect no matter how hard he tried (a tape? but what had he done with it? he hadn't sung on it, had he?). At first, Scherping was speechless. Completely.

Completely speechless and filled with dark bliss, I assume. For that was exactly the situation he had been hoping for, had fantasized about time and time again. ("If you only knew to what far-fetched and insidious lengths we go to get our pleasure," he once confessed to me.) Finding himself powerless before an underling whom he intended to push around, being tormented, humiliated, treated like a little pile of shit by him—that was a night of love. And Schwab was the very man whom Scherping dreamed of for the part. Far more, oh, ineffably more sly, stealthy, secretive than even the most severe woman: he was the FATHER in his heavy demonic nature, the

Dostoevskian *starost* in his dark power (Schwab when the Slavic strain—his mother's maiden name was Mietschke—began to predominate in his bespectacled Luther-head. "A mountain with a stormy peak," Schelmie once said, frightened but poetic).

And if I knew my duck, he with his keen erotic instinct must have gone along with the part that was offered him, the old slut . . . In any case, he said it never came to an argument between him and Scherping about the Nagel affair. Before the subject could come up, he declared rather brusquely that he could no longer work for Scherping if he was not granted an appreciable sum to encourage the projects of certain authors. Scherping, who smelled a rat, asked, "Which authors?" pleasurably lying in wait. Schwab named not Nagel, as expected, but *me*. Scherping screeched out his fury into Hamburg's anemic autumn air. (It was the time of the asters, and Schelmie had opened the window on Rothenbaumchaussee to let in a bit of afternoon sun.) Now, his fury was vented against me. For fourteen years, raged the pain-tested, pain-loving publisher, he had been waiting for my manuscript. The multiple advances were reaching astronomical heights. Meanwhile, he raged on, I had absolutely no intention of writing even one more line of the novel, I was still prostituting myself disgracefully with the movies. If he, Scherping, took the bait and forked over a new advance, the recurrent and promising beginnings I kept sending in would cease altogether.

Well, and so forth. An old and—alas!—all too true tale, after whose telling a completely unleashed Scherping vanished for special treatment with Gisela, in Whores' Alley. Schwab, however, hopped the next plane to Paris.

And now here he was. In shock treatment because of my drag-race driving (yet I can swear I drove no faster than normal, even if S. maintained that the curses and shaken fists had been provoked by my inconsiderately cutting off, dangerously passing, and illegally squeezing into gaps in the lines of cars). He clutched the dashboard, longed for his baggage, and perspired.

I had to stop at the Deux Magots—one hundred and fifty yards from his hotel—because he needed another gin and tonic to moisten his glands. Before I could catch him again, he dashed across the boulevard to the nearest drugstore. Meanwhile I got entangled in an exceedingly unpleasant argument with a motorized policeman sporting an insect-head helmet (Death's messenger in Cocteau's *Orpheus*) who was trying to flush me out of my parking space. Then S. came back with a bulky armload of big and little boxes; generously littering the street with wrappers and bits of cardboard (and ignoring the now acute risk of becoming a traffic casualty), he pulled out vials, phials, and tubes and stowed them away in his baggy trouser pockets.

In the hotel, after demanding the room in which Oscar Wilde had died (it was a different one each time), he gobbled up pills from his bare palm the way insane Nebuchadnezzar devoured grass. Even before we went for breakfast in the Rose de France on the Île de la Cité (he loved the little square that opens up to the monument of Henry IV on the bridge), he quickly had to down yet another gin and tonic. Now he was staggering along in wavy lines, which he occasionally interrupted with a surprising side step. We ordered some *rosé d'oignon* for our meal, and he used it first to wash down another handful of very tiny, nasty-looking tablets. Then, as he told me with a sigh of relief and a bitterly twisted mouth, he was sufficiently fortified to let Paris collapse upon him.

This was my moment. This was what I had been waiting for. I affected a bored mien. I said indolently, almost casually, "It's chic to see you here—to welcome you in Pöseldorf parlance. (After all, stopping cold-turkey could lead to withdrawal symptoms, mightn't it, psychological disturbances due to a sudden change of environment.) Anyway, grand that you're here, as I said. But don't expect too much from the therapeutic effects of a sojourn in Paris. What you see before you here—this sun-dappled, life-teeming Paris, this energetic, challenging city with its tremendous traffic and busy crowds, a city of noble tradition, of course, a French reality beyond any doubt, this shiny world that allows you only to be a marveling, admiring spectator—is nothing but a myth you have brought with you. Imported from Hamburg-on-the-Elbe. Sheer deception. Dragging the past into presence. The truth these days looks slightly different.

"When they're making a movie and they want to give a modern cityscape a period character, they sometimes take small cardboard cutouts painted naturalistically—walls, merlons, gingerbread eaves, gables, oriels—and attach them to the camera lens, replacing or concealing whatever is missing in reality or destroys the illusion. That is, whatever does not fit in with the desired representation. Photographed together, the real city and the cutouts yield the intended image perfectly.

"I am expressing myself vividly enough, aren't I? I mean, it would be wrong if you had the idea that this is a solid, closed world, a world of Frenchmen, to which you find no entrée because you yourself, true to the cliché of a German, are too formless, too weightless, too nebulous. On the contrary, you have to realize that here, beyond the cutout of Paris that you carry before your eyes, evolution has taken a step into another aggregate state. This different state of things doesn't allow you to identify with it, because it's you—yes sir, you, yourself—who has too clear a form, is made of too solid material, flesh, bone, a turtleneck sweater, corduroy pants. In short, it's *you* who are too much alive. An act of dematerialization has taken place here, in Paris, which our kind still have left to us. A rarefaction of matter, as when water is transformed into steam. The molecules have moved apart, making contact and communication impossible—not really for psychological reasons but purely for physical reasons.

"I grant you, it's not easy to accept this. The city of Paris is constructed of hard stone. The French are a hard people. Their roots vein the rock beneath their soil—a fine soil, a rich earth that brings forth wheat and wine grapes in abundance, and, one would think, an earth whose children are cheery, sociable, bighearted. But no, they have stony faces, their souls are frozen in the glacial coldness of a national culture that produces instant classics, that emits each classic with a helmet, a shield, and a spear, like Pallas Athena springing full blown from the brow of Zeus. They still have the gift of form, these French. They think and speak nothing but beautiful petrifacts. When they laugh it sounds like pebbles clattering... And if one is not made of stone as they are (and is a pederast in the bargain, for along with a few exotics, a couple of Balkanese, and some Russian Jewesses, pederasts are the ones who make the stone circus here dance to their tune)—if someone does not belong to their stony world, he is simply ground down into sand. Soon he no longer exists, no longer finds himself present, finds only rubbish left over from himself, the *materia prima* of which he once was made, now pulverized, scattered. He is no more than a humming in his own skull; that's all that's left of him. Well, that is true, and yet it's still just another illusion. Reality is paradoxically the reverse. For all this is utterly abstract. It takes place in the concrete, but so entirely translated into the spiritual, so knowingly staged without any connection to the natural, that only lunatics can accept it as reality.

"Sure, you have problems with the language. This leads to even greater deceptions and misconceptions. Despite eight years of school French, eight years of studying this beautiful language that institutions of humanistic learning count among the living languages and that is no more alive than the grillwork on a Gothic church window—despite eight years of French, you, a highly educated man, can manage in this language to claim proudly that you are the state, and not much more. And there's little one can do with that nowadays, the state being the most controversial institution of the present age. Here, you are restricted to the purely optical; that is, so to speak, to the zoological.

"Here in Paris, you see mainly Frenchmen. Well, for all his national characteristics, a Frenchman looks as universally human as any other exemplar of the White Race. All in all, the French are an important, probably the most important, people in Europe. If one is struck dumb before the French, it is not just for reasons of linguistic ignorance—if you will forgive that expression—but out of admiration. Unfortunately, this obtains most of all for the French themselves. I swear to you: you could be as eloquent as Cyrano de Bergerac, but your chatter would never succeed in snapping the French out of their mania—the mania of their self-absorption. They live in a kind of trance—not merely a different state of consciousness but a different state of biological existence.

"Encounters such as you may have envisaged (Goethe runs into Lavater: "Tis thou?'—"Tis I!') no longer occur here, not even as a hostile collision. And it is no advantage to you that, forgive me for saying so, a Frenchman can identify you as a *boche* a kilometer away. It does not even bring you hatred, which, after all, would be a relationship of some kind, even if in the negative, so to speak. Not even the aggression normally and subconsciously released by the collective mind against old archenemies (I mean the aggression that once acted as Keeper of the Seal for such tensions in old Europe), not even this ancient human feature emerges here. This cannot be good in the long run, my friend. I worry about our dear old continent. You feel like a stranger here, all right. As if you had been cast ashore on a different star. Do you think you're the only person who feels like this? No, no, I tell you: the sense of being fundamentally alien here, of finding oneself on a different planet, among Martians, is not restricted to us non-Frenchmen, us foreigners, us transients in Paris. Some fifteen million native Parisians and purebred Frenchmen share that feeling with us. Just about everyone here lives on a different star. Simply through the abstraction of this French world, which immunizes the individual against the immediately human. Believe me, friend, it won't help you to truck through the streets in your still-earthly constitution, with good German fat on your belly and beer-thickened blood in your veins. One doesn't inveigle one's way into life here by being conspicuous. Take me, for instance: I am certainly anything but a run-of-the-mill type in these surroundings—true, I'm not exactly striking, but at least I can't be easily classified, readily placed in an ethnic category. I'm rather shapeless, amorphous. An ethnic jellyfish, as it were. A non-Frenchman with no pronounced racial characteristics or identifiable accent (since I don't give my diction the broadness of padded American shoulders, as certain other people can). Fitting in with no ethnological cliché and yet easily made to fit any at all. Whenever I find it too difficult to explain why I am not the child of any fatherland, too difficult to cite my confused background and the requisite facts about the ethnic, geographic, and historical conditions of Central Europe, then I can get away with calling myself a Russian,

Dutchman, Swiss, North Italian, or Irishman. But not a Frenchman, for God's sake. So one cannot deny there is something blatantly different about me.

"Now, one might think I could easily get lost in the crowd here, on the much-celebrated Paris boulevards, which, as we all know, sport the dregs of the melting pot like the head on a glass of pilsner beer. I don't stand out in any way, either in clothing or in conduct, I am not visibly stunted or crippled, not spastic or mongoloid, and I don't have an obvious nervous tic—an angular jerking of the head out of the shirt collar, or even a sneering sidelong twist of the mouth, tightening the nostrils and giving them a deathly pallor; in short, I am conspicuous by being inconspicuous, as it were. And still, the stares of all who come toward me tell me that I am a stranger, that I am essentially, substantially, and fundamentally foreign, and yet am nevertheless no more foreign than anyone else.

"The stares of the people coming toward me are neither curious nor disapproving nor even hostile, but certainly not pleasant or friendly. All they express is complete indifference. But they want me to feel this indifference. As if I were supposed to realize that I am not worth so much as a shrug, even as an alien. Just like any fellow Frenchman. *On se fout de vous, monsieur*, because it's intrinsic in the French national character. *On se fout de vous comme on se fout de tout le monde, mêmes de nous-mêmes.*

"But beyond that, I am devoid of a physiognomy, as far as they are concerned. I could run around without a face, as if painted by Magritte: a patch of blue sky with a cumulus cloudlet between hat and coat collar. But the French seem eager to make me aware of the abstract manner in which I exist here without existing for them, the abstract manner in which we all exist here without existing for one another: optically experienced not as human faces but as physiognomic splotches in the continuously and nervously altered, shifted, changing mosaic of the city; flesh-colored swabs in the torrent of hundreds of thousands of nonexistent coexisters on the streets, avenues, boulevards, and promenades; the flotsam of detached anatomical parts—a pair of eyes, an ear, a nose, a tuft of hair (lots of hair recently, long smooth curly kinky bushy shaggy matted hair), a bald pate, an extremely beautiful wart, the amazing craquelure of veins in a drunkard's cheeks, the scrotum-like bags under a rich dowager's Saint Bernard eyes, the ludicrous drama in an intellectual's knitted brow... drifting rubbish, as I said, lamentable testimonies to earlier human presence in a flooded area. The inundating element in which all these things float is the French national consciousness. And now I ask you: Is this a suitable price to pay for form?...

"You envy me for living here. But have you ever figured out how I really live here? Enviably naturalized, right? A true-blue Parisian. Chives in my soup. Greeted like a long-familiar person by the hotel clerk, by the concierge in the rue Jacob, by the waiters at the Flore and the Deux Magots, by the newsdealer at the corner stand, by the greengrocers in the Marché Buci. Granted, a long-familiar person with whom, for ten years now, they have never exchanged more than sporadic sentences about the weather and the lousy political situation. Of course, I also know a few Parisians who belong to a less accessible category. All kinds of movie people, not only the aloof creative ones but also the solid business kind: distributors, theater owners. I also know a lawyer, a banker, why, even pillars of culture, for instance a museum director. We call each other '*cher ami*,' we invite each other out for lunch or dinner, with the wives, if you please. My captivating way with the ladies even gets me invited to people's homes. I send flowers, exchange hugs, we drink aperitifs, I shine, I fondle the kids, the maid, I praise the food, admire the family porcelain, the wine, the elegant furnishings, I piss into the family bathroom sink, dry my hands on Monsieur's towel, brush my hair with Madame's brush—why, greater intimacy cannot be imagined, except of course the ultimate one. But that too has occurred, yes indeed. One has exchanged lewd tendernesses with the wives, *même dans le lit matrimonial*. The husbands were away. But even then, one parted with the feeling of having rid oneself of a burdensome obligation. At least with a sense of relief that one wouldn't have to go through the same thing again for another six months. The form is always maintained.

"I go out of town a lot, unfortunately. Still, I come back regularly, and then I may possibly have folkloristic experiences that make it seem as if some forgotten corners of existence still had the bright lively life that, before losing the first half of my life, I once assumed was naturally present and profuse everywhere, even if (and precisely because) I myself was for the moment not taking part. For instance, my aforementioned concierge in the rue Jacob evidently couldn't stand watching me suffer over Dawn, so she invited me to her niece's wedding in some almost rustic *banlieue* out near Le Bourget. And there I could sniff the warm, wine-soured, garlic-sharpened breath of the people. Since then, I say hello to every street cleaner I see because I imagine he might have been one of my fellow revelers. We ate and drank gargantuanly. We whirled in waltzes, swinging tubs of sweaty female flesh laced up to an ironclad roundness. We avowed our mutual friendship and thumped each other so hard on the back that our tonsils slid out through our teeth. Here too, of course, it came to lewd business with one of the bridesmaids, a girl in her thirties and hence short of breath during the inspection of erogenous zones. We made a date to get to the bottom of the matter, but naturally I didn't show up, and actually I'm sorry about it today, although one can't be too careful in such matters. The *animal triste post coitum*, you know, is especially dangerous here in Paris; one gets the craziest ideas.

"I remember a girl sitting at the next table in the Flore. I had been ogling her for a while, not only because her profile was vaguely reminiscent of Stella's (an Algerian Jew, presumably) but because everything about her—looks, eyes, mien—was simply screaming with loneliness. She sat there, crushed beneath the terrifying ordeal of being human, the curse that dooms us to live in an eternally irreconcilable dichotomy: on the one hand, we are herd animals who can't get along without one another and who are unhappy alone; and on the other hand, we are prisoners in the cage of the self, unable to escape, unable to reach the other, unable to find salvation from ourselves . . .

"This was so tremendously eloquent in the girl's wan face that I had to keep peeking at her. She couldn't ignore this in the long run, and when I stared very hard, she turned to me and our eyes met. At first, it was very beautiful—or it might be better to say, very pure—in a bleak way. We knew what we wanted from each other and what, in the best case, we could expect. We were agreed without having to pretend we had come even a millimeter closer together. I motioned to the waiter and paid for my Pernod and her coffee. It was only when we were on the street and trying to decide where we wanted to go that we first exchanged words.

"I could have taken her around the corner to the rue Jacob. The apartment was available. Dawn had taken flight again and I had temporarily given up looking for her. But she might return at any moment. So we went to the girl's place. It was far away, on the boulevard Extérieur.

"I don't have to describe what happened in that dump, which was unfit for human habitation. It was stereotypical, starting with the horror in her (and probably also my) eyes when we set about doing the dreadfully intimate initial manipulations of sexual intercourse, then, on top of that (registered, horridly enough, in full consciousness), the raging, one against the other, which in spite of everything did occur, and finally, the heartrending silence, which neither of us dared break, since a wrong syllable, a false tone, might have led to murder.

"Because she lived on a dead-end street, an absurd one-way street to boot, I had parked my car out in the boulevard. It was shortly before evening. The stores and offices had already closed, and even a nearby gas station was shut. Oddly enough, I can't remember the season. I know I didn't have a coat—but I seldom wear one, even in winter. You go from heated buildings to heated cars and then back again into heated buildings. So you don't really need a coat. But I believe it was the evening of a long summer's day. The precarious hour before darkness, when the Paris sky displays a full, an absolutely inexhaustible gamut of oppressive, heart-stopping stages of decay. The lava of cars flowed in two opposite torrents, roaring and glistening metallically along the boulevard. And there were swarms of pedestrians: the street teemed and crawled as with termites, pouring from all sides toward a black whirlpool, a vortex which, like a funnel, sucked in the thronging vermin, gulping it down in masses. The entrance to a Métro station, of course. Evening rush hour.

"This was fascinating to observe in my vulnerable spiritual state, removed from my everyday life. I stood in one spot for almost twenty minutes, watching the sidewalk shaft with its art nouveau frame as it sucked in humans swarming like insects. Gradually, the trickle thinned out, grew sparse, while the sky slowly receded, duller and duller, more and more spacious, backing away from the earth as though wanting nothing to do with it, until at last the final stragglers were sucked from the street.

"With the same mysterious immediacy of the first star of evening appearing in the sky all of a sudden, the streetlights went on, pallidly dotting the pigeon-blue, which darkened as it flowed out into the evening. And soon the torrent of cars on the boulevard exhausted itself too. All at once the city was utterly silent. I stood alone in an empty world.

"Believe it or not, I found this so beautiful that tears came to my eyes. I felt like the Prodigal Son who has found his way home. I understood how very much we really are the children of this world, this stony world of termites; children of the artificial rocky wastes, of twilight before nightfall... Oh God! the heart-gripping courage of the wan streetlamps...

"I went to my car. The street was completely lifeless. All except for one good housewife who had slipped out of a building to walk her dog. She had her back to me while the dog pulled her along, the leash taut as iron, and the dog's nose sniffed and scrubbed along the piss-black edge of the sidewalk. When she heard my footfall behind her, she was so startled that she jumped and let out a noise like a valve cap being sucked shut. A man on the street at this time of night could only be her murderer. Now let me ask you, Johannes Schwab, whether this isn't our real home. I mean, what are you actually looking for when you come fleeing here from Hamburg-on-the-Elbe? After all, you've got enough folklore there—at least in the philistines around you, those provincials who still in large part have been thought up by Wilhelm Raabe or Wilhelm Busch or formed after Wilhelm II and for the rest are merely insects. You don't mean to tell me that you come here from a world marked by the German soul in order to be uplifted by a Paris that begins as splendidly as the Eroica, with the beautiful notes of sky, Seine, and beautifully ordered city, and continues to build, soulful and stirring the spirit. No, no, my friend. The Paris of the Eiffel Tower and the Louvre, of the *bâteaux mouches* and alluring luxury garments in the shop windows along the Faubourg Saint-Honoré; the *bouquinistes* on the banks of the Seine, whose stalls, as we know, can be combed for bibliophilic *trouvailles* (for instance, a copy of Nagel's first novel, no?); the *ville lumière* of first-class whores and the charmingly authentic eateries in Montparnasse and around Les Halles, where one can feast on delicate (canned) snails dripping with garlic and all kinds of radioactive oysters—all this is not for our kind, it's for Americans: a larger-than-life Disneyland. People like us are looking here for something completely different: namely, THE CITY, the metropolis with all its perverse charms and exquisite terrors, above all the unreal and the surreal. The abstract and the fictitious. The as-if of the human in the inhuman. We are intoxicated by the loss of reality here, under the bombardment of tattered impressions, the drumfire of the fragmented, the disjointed. Nowhere can we become so urgently self-aware as here in the frazzling stream of the crowd. Nowhere is our self so fully shaped as in encapsulated anonymity. Only when the world dissolves into disconnected entities drifting by like flotsam in a flood—an ear, a wheel, an umbrella, a dog turd, a shop sign, a gaze—only then do we realize how grand we are. Only here can we understand that we carry the entire cosmos within ourselves, that we must become artists so as to express our inner wealth—and are even more majestic when we refuse to impart it . . . Here, in the torrent of the anonymous crowd that overflows all shores, every man is sovereign.

"Each plows his hard bow through the torrent, a figurehead of his loneliness, and gazes with stony eyes at whatever drifts past: that was you, that was what I was for you, a smashed bureau with gaping drawers between a hat and a collar, half a roof and perched upon it a cat that fled up the chimney between a shock of hair and an ascot, a mouth flitting past like a weary butterfly, unhappy, angry, obstinate, earnest, dreamy, disappointed, passionate, sensitive, whining, closed upon the soundless shriek for self-realization . . . And these too, as you see, are merely art-historical reminiscences.

"Let us pass them by. We are not attached to them, we are not sentimental—at least not in the long run. This too dissolves, everything dissolves into swatches, color strips, structures, patterns. It eventually turns monochrome: gray, the color of madness . . . And don't tell me it doesn't make you feel as happy as a pig in shit.

"But, of course, this is no vacation at a health spa to buoy up your soul so that you can go home to Hamburg fortified and endure life there for another six months. On the contrary: this place visibly sucks the marrow from your bones. It puts you into a different state of matter, as though you were still yourself but vaporized, as it were. Instead of being made of skin and fat and flesh and bones all welded into your Jockey shorts, you are just a tiny cloud, the astral phenomenon Schwab . . . But that is an elevation, believe me! The transubstantiation of ourselves into the abstract is an elevation. And how proud you should be that you, friend, are capable of such an elevation, such a transubstantiation of yourself—*without the aid of writing, without having to commit yourself to paper*! The others who write, and whom you so greatly admire—what are they if they do not realize themselves on paper? For example, your friend Nagel, *our* friend Nagel, if you insist. He's a delightful fellow, after all, and a great one, isn't he? But he's important only on paper. Tolstoy was a creep, Proust a fop, Joyce a stigmatized petit bourgeois—if you take off his glasses and comb his hair to the side, he looks like Hitler. But on paper, oh my! What demigods they are! Do you follow me? Or am I too muddled—this wine is far stronger than one thinks. Also, I'm alone so much here that I'm not used to talking, especially in German. If you think my words are swarming like flies on the dung heap of my thoughts, then please tell me so, I'll shut up . . . No? You're much too kind! Well, as I was saying—an abstruse notion, you will think: the crystalline hardness of the French, their quality of being formed, their capacity for form . . . all this must be due simply to this abstraction and transubstantiation into a different state of density... Perhaps a human being first truly realizes his potential in pure abstraction. After all, the most forceful human image is, no doubt, that of the man at Hiroshima whose silhouette was burned into the stone by the atomic flash...

"Be undaunted then! Walk on with your senses alert, wander with your senses open through this beautiful bright underworld that is Paris, or rather this overworld... You know, the thing that has always made photography (the invention most expressive of the zeitgeist) dear to me is the dialectics of the positive and negative image—don't you agree?—whereby the latter is surprisingly more informative. For instance, I heard a little story here that articulates the terror of a certain German past in the negative, so to speak. The story was told to me by a tiny homosexual Jew who managed to escape from Berlin in 1939 just before the war broke out. He was sixteen years old at the time. Well, just before he fled, he went into a pissoir in Charlottenburg with a big Jewish star on his jacket, which he tried to conceal, as best he could, beneath his lapel. A moment of twofold relief—gratefully enjoyed—but then a tremendous shadow suddenly falls on him. He looks up: next to him, a gigantic SS man in uniform was unbuttoning his fly. The SS man looks down at him and said: 'You're a Jew, huh?' Our little homosexual can only nod. The SS man: 'Well, then, c'mon, gimme a kiss!'... But I forget why I wanted to tell you the story—ah yes, of course: because you presumably wish to write about Paris; you have to make literary use of your Paris experience. Could you do so, *fairly and honestly*, knowing about such events and realities, as if the things you saw around you here were still real?..."

5

I am going into such detail about these not exactly edifying incidents because, as I have said, I am in possession of some notes about them. These notes were penned by S., whom you encounter in these pages as Schwab. This is not the place to explain how I obtained them, nor do I wish to go into the matter of which varying or even contradictory descriptions of particulars are closer to the truth. Likewise, I need not expatiate on my intentions in contrasting the two notes.

Paris, October 1964. Thanks to alcohol and H.'s new pills, rather blurry impressions. We walk past the Madeleine. We're no longer speaking. A day of agonizing tensions. I arrived by plane from Hamburg this morning. He didn't pick me up (even though Schelmie wired the arrival time). Supposedly the telegram reached his hotel too late. I'd like to believe him (but I don't). Trying to explain my embitterment to myself. Childish reason: I'd been looking forward to riding in his new car. Also, I lost my baggage. Tiresome, humiliating language difficulties (yet his fluent assistance would have embittered me even more).

The flight was very hard on me. Right at takeoff, heart problems, which kept on and then worsened unnervingly when the plane landed. Throughout the flight, the roaring PA system right by my left ear: "Ladies an' zhentlemen, Capitaine Malfichu and his crew welcome you aboar' our Caravelle Seine-et-Oise." PR vulgarity. The ass's language drill: "At your left an' below you, ladies an' zhentlemen, you may look now on ze town of Fulda" (pronounced Faldeh). And the icy droning of the turbine, which presses toward the bull's-eye, over the backs of the herding cloud lambs as one wing rises ominously... Fear, malaise, claustrophobia. I want to get up, and drop back in the seat, fettered: I forgot to unfasten the safety belt. All very ridiculous, very embarrassing. I couldn't get rid of the droning in my ears. It remained there all day long. (Hertzog is probably right; I take too many barbiturates and smoke too much; two and a half packs of Lucky Strikes yesterday—the pack I'd opened was empty by the time we landed. Didn't sleep last night, of course; tried to dope myself around three a.m. with a bottle of rotgut Algerian wine—no use, just a gush of stomach acid, so I doubled the dose. Only to hover among dreamy states of anxiousness and hallucinate along the brittle ridges of nightmares. Woke up around seven: Pervitin. Hertzog promised me new prescriptions, but he'll give them to me only if I come back to the clinic for two weeks.)

At Orly, my suitcase was nowhere to be found. After long, torturous fumbling in French, I understood: it had flown to Tangier. Since it had been uncomfortably cool in Hamburg, I'm wearing a thick turtleneck under my jacket. The welcome Paris gives me is still disconcertingly summery. I am sweating like a polar bear. I can't eat breakfast on the plane (the Montessori kindergarten spoons and the stewardesses' robust solicitude are too reminiscent of the psychiatric ward). So I have my first coffee at the Deux Magots. Then, parching thirst. The only way I can cope with it lately is a gin and tonic with lots and lots of ice (it doesn't agree with me, but the immediate effect is beneficial). I'm on my second drink and he's standing before me. His eyes only graze the glass, but he's too alert not to notice that I caught his lids narrowing. He therefore says casually, "Hey, that's a great idea, I'll have one too."

Elephant-taming methods. I sense that I'll have to arm myself with great patience just to endure twenty-four hours in this place. He tries to calm me down about my suitcase. "Are you invited to a reception at the Élysée? Well, then. It makes no difference at all what you run around in. I masquerade as a luxury gigolo just so that nobody will notice how broke I am. You can buy soap cheaply here, and I can lend you a razor. If it's absolutely necessary, we can stroll over to the boulevard Saint-Michel and spend fifty francs on three shirts and six pairs of catamite briefs."

I was irritated by his bogus linguistic nonchalance; the cheap freshness, preciously studded with the affectedly correct pronunciation of "boulevard Saint-Michel" (although I'm grateful to him for not saying "Boul' Mich'"). Also, I left two manuscripts on the plane, things I'm supposed to read. He doesn't find this so awful either: Schelmie must have copies she can send me. It makes me furious: Schelmie has no copies; I took the manuscripts precisely in order to spare her such measures of solicitude; now they're lost for good (this will lead to incalculably tiresome arguments with Scherping).

"Maiden efforts by promising young talents?" he asks, reaching for my cigarettes. "Or even one of yours?"

For an instant, I'm alert, eager, almost delighted. What is he after? Treating me with numb-fingered caution, the way you treat a paranoiac: you clear anything out of his way that you think might anger him. A moment later, he trips me up from behind. Yet inside, he is so nervous that he trembles. I catch myself thinking, irritatedly, So he's concerned about me. I make him uneasy. Why does he put up with me? He needs me. I'm necessary to him because I work for Scherping and I can turn the faucet on and off for his advances. His writhing helplessness is poignant. His scattered life grinds him down. One has to protect him.

I compliment him on his suit. I mean it honestly, but it sounds a bit venomous. (My exact words are: "Once again you look almost indecently elegant.") He smiles sneakily. It amuses me to see him wondering what he can get me with. (I anxiously await the outcome.)

We drink another gin and tonic (my third). Paris begins to collapse upon me. I've been here for three hours already and I still have the plane turbines droning in my ears. If I went to my hotel now, I'd tumble into bed and sleep the rest of the day away. So I drink another coffee (and take another Pervitin on the sly). He acts like he doesn't notice. For the moment (as if he realizes that I don't want him watching), he wraps himself up in a newspaper. I know that he scarcely ever reads the papers, that nothing in them interests him. So he is only pretending to read; he puts down the paper the instant I swallow the pill. In a chatty tone he asks me about Hamburg. But I interrupt and ask how he found me. A piece of cake: he asked for me in the hotel and was told that I went out right away; the most obvious thing was to check here.

This rankles me. I'm annoyed that I'm so predictable. An unimaginative provincial who arrives in Paris and can't think of anything better to do than sit on the terrace of the Deux Magots. He actually says as much quite brazenly:

"Nice sitting out here, isn't it? Especially on such a lovely day. One learns quickly that it doesn't get any better here in Paris. Nothing is quite what it is. But everything's bursting with clues to an artificial superreality. That guy over there, squinting so obstinately, is not Sartre, but he could be. And that gay Negro is not Baldwin, but he could be, and why shouldn't one take him for Baldwin? After all, the wild strawberries at Maxim's were grown in a hothouse, but that doesn't ruin the tarte aux fraises. *On the contrary, it's what guarantees perfection. It's as if the mixture of types here had been very skillfully prescribed by a public-relations firm working for the Ministry of the Interior: not inauthentic—that wouldn't seem Parisian—but simply artificial. Imagine how gladly you'd have stayed in Hamburg if there too the thugs and loiterers in the whores' alleys of the Reeperbahn were on fixed salaries, paid by Hamburg's Cultural Affairs Department."*

These are attempts at needling me—but they are too circuitous to penetrate my skin. I feel much more lucid now: the Pervitin is taking effect. But I can't stand it here anymore. I suggest a walk. The place de Furstenberg is a few yards away. ("Almost quite genuinely Parisian, especially if you bear in mind that a church tower designed by Buffet casts its shadow upon it..." He's bending over backward now and frazzling my nerves.)

I have to get some fresh air. I want to gaze along the Seine. We wander over to the Pont Neuf. The day is delicious; foggy this morning, it has brightened radiantly. But I'm sweating hard in my heavy clothes. I have to take off my jacket, but I'm so badly soaked that I'm immediately shivering. I get in a desperate rage about my body. I tell him more about my ailments and Hertzog's therapeutic method than I care to have revealed. I instantly regret it and ask him, more aggressively than I intended, why he's smiling. He asks me quite cheerfully to please excuse him. He says that our being on the Pont Neuf reminds him of a passage in Proust: Swann, deathly ill, goes out into society once more, knowing it's the last time. He runs into Guermantes and wistfully tells him that they probably won't see each other again. Guermantes, about to move on to another reception and only half listening, booms cheerily, "Vous! Vous nous survivrez tous! Vous êtes fort comme le Pont Neuf!"

I don't quite know how I'm supposed to take this anecdote, as pointed malice or as sovereign tactlessness. While I think about it, he himself realizes the ambivalence and turns it to his own advantage: he smiles shamelessly, as if he had deliberately led me up the garden path.

I sense that none of this is quite right, but I feel like an oaf. His unimpeachability humiliates me. He is healthy, alert, elegant. He speaks about Guermantes and Swann as if they were part of his daily circle of friends here. He reads his Proust in French. I snort in my bearskins and remember that only two hours ago at the airport, I was humiliated to learn how poor my French is.

My eyes swim as I gaze up the Seine. (I still have my reading glasses on, I couldn't find the other pair in my pockets, it's probably flown to Tangier with the suitcase.) His eyes are imperturbable. For him it's an everyday scene. But, as if to show me that he feels what it means for me to be here, he makes an ironically melancholy remark and then launches into his love story—with an aloofness that is sheer stratagem: he underplays it, reduces his chaotic existence to a microscope slide. It sounds written. The effects are precisely worked out. And with that he arouses my curiosity. I want to find out what the truth is. I offer to go with him to the hotel where he speculates the girl is hiding.

We walk halfway across Paris (but I can't think of any other way to tire him out). At the Madeleine, we wander into the stalking grounds of whores who roam the area in daylight. A redhead with provocative breasts sizes us up at a glance. She spots the john in me. It doesn't elude him. He jokes: "One can smell your solidity, and my disreputableness. I'm too mean for a big spender and not authentic enough for a good pimp."

This too makes me feel clumsy and awkward. I am moving crudely and ponderously through a light world. The air here is light; the people walk more lightly, speak more vivaciously; the colors shine effortlessly and lie upon things more lightly. I love this lightness, which I do not possess. (The remedy that Hertzog gave me, without letting on what it was, put me into this lightness. I have to get H. to at least give me a hint about the pharmacological, or rather toxological, makeup: I am well on the way to systematically poisoning myself.)

But the thought of it makes me light now too. My mood lightens. I feel hungry. He knows a restaurant not far from the hotel we are heading toward. A year ago, an extremely embarrassing scene with an Indian doll took place there. Incidentally, I think I remember the restaurant too: its name is Laget.

In half an hour, we are there. The food is marvelous though much too heavy. The wine is heavy too. I feel numb after the first glass. But I can still see well enough to observe how embarrassing it is that I slip off my jacket but refuse to let the hat-check girl take it. He says a few words to her that I don't understand, but she leaves with a smile. I have the impression it was a joke at my expense. He now quite bluntly makes fun of me; he quips his way through a distasteful tirade about his religious upbringing, full of allusions that again I don't understand. (Apparently he thinks I want to propose that he write his book about theodicy, even assumes I intend to write something similar myself.) Again, I drink more than I can take. And I have to pay the bill too. It's dismayingly high, and I have trouble concealing my shock. (I do so by announcing that I want to dine here every day; anyway, I'm in a very good mood; I order more wine and two framboises *with the coffee.)*

As we get up, an irritating mishap occurs. I want to say, jokingly, "Allons, enfants de la patrie!" *(one of the few French phrases I recall from school), but I bellow out the words. I'm so startled that I almost knock the table over. The wine bottle tumbles from its basket, the remaining wine spills across the tablecloth. We walk to the hotel. He shows me the room where he lived and wrote while waiting for the girl (in a different room, one flight up) to ask for him: three o'clock at night or seven in the morning, depending on her whim or mood. If he went out, he gave the porter the most detailed information for her on where she could reach him, when he planned to return, and when he'd be at her disposal again. (With a smile, he says, "Discreetly at your service any hour of the day or night, the perfect nurse," as if he wants to recommend himself to me.)*

He offers to drive me back to the Left Bank. His car is parked in a garage a few steps away on the place des Ternes. I beg off. I'm at the end of my tether. I want to be alone. But I tell him, "If you'd like to come with me, I'm going back on foot."

He cheerfully agrees. "I'd love to." And gently takes my arm because I am about to run down a baby carriage. All along the avenue des Ternes, he chats away at me (with constant gentle grabs at my arm to steer me past hindrances). But eventually he lapses into silence. He only asks once (when I stumble), "Shouldn't we really take a cab?" I retort that as a good German infantryman I marched from Ukraine to Mount Athos, but I get the words out only in fits and starts.

The redhead is still standing by the Madeleine. I shake him off. "Excuse me, but I think I'll go off with this girl now."

He says, "I'll be waiting for you in the café over there."

For a moment I feel like punching him in the nose. His eyes are as imperturbable as when he gazed along the Seine. But he gives the girl a small, encouraging smile. She makes a face at him: "Salaud!" *Then she takes me by the arm.*

Half an hour later I am standing on the street again, alone, a bit ransacked, humiliated. I am thirsty and, heedless of screeching brakes and invectives, I veer across the square to the café. He is sitting at one of the outside tables, waiting for me. I join him wordlessly. He doesn't speak either. I order a cognac (saying, with venomous pride in my French, "Une fine de la maison"*). He has a drink too. The jets droning in my ears are unendurable. I see his bright, imperturbable, alert eyes. "Ready?" he says in English. I stand up (not bumping the table this time, but the chair behind me topples over and he catches it). I say, "The perfect nurse." He* *does not answer. He picks up the bank note I threw on the table and presses it into my hand. It is the last one the girl left me.*

He heaves me into a cab. I say, "Leave me alone!" He tells the driver the address and gets in next to me. "You will sleep marvelously. Call me up whenever you like. After all, you know I'm waiting."

I hear myself say, "But not for my call."

He says, "For your call."

I bow and kiss his hand.

6

Et vous vous en foutez, monsieur. Lei se ne frega. You couldn't give a bloody fucking shit.

And of course you're perfectly right. You're in the business. It's your century. It's your world. And if I feel lost in it, that's my problem.

Only I would like to trouble you a bit with this problem, dear Mr. Brodny. Look: As an outsider by calling, predestination, and vocation, I am accustomed to running through the world in one abstracted way or another. The pretty prelude to my unfortunately still uncompleted book may have suggested as much.

But now I am speaking about Paris, dear friend—a city still at the heart of Western Civilization, one would think, and not at its extreme periphery. Yes, it may even be considered its throbbing heart; still the center of its cultural life, the termite queen of Europe. Yurop, sir. How do you spell it? Why-You-Are-Oh-Pee-period. Yurop—a remote American province, as we now all know, as everyone knows, down to the last sneering oil sheikh, but nevertheless a province that is said to have been the cradle of this renowned Western Civilization, the homeland of our fathers, mothers, all our blindly self-assured, dynamic, expansive forebears. Of course you and your fellow bearers of stars and stripes know it in another way. For you it became an integrating component of the world only recently, as the theater of WWII—a vile abbreviation for a collective suicide, by the way. A world the half of which always belongs to America: half of Korea, half of Vietnam, half of Germany... and believe me, it makes quite a difference if you think of a continent as homeland or as a theater of operations. The *European Theater*, as it is rather characteristically known in the (military) trade. Enter at your own risk, albeit with a guarantee of an honorable funeral—even if your body parts are scattered and far flung during the spectacle—on so-called V-Days (Vee for Victory, *mon cul*).

For you, sons of the New World in your youthful freshness, masters of one half of the globe—for you, the charm of this unhealthy, sporadically iron-filled part of the world probably consisted in the liberating dynamics of the landscape of catastrophe: the panorama in which fields and forests, marshes and meadows are wasted by storms of fire, battered by hailstones of iron; shacks and castles, churches and privies are equally smashed to rubble, and dead cattle and household goods drift in the yellow rivers—half a roof and perched on it a cat that fled up the chimney, for instance; and so it makes no difference whatsoever where you shit cook screw play with an orphaned puppy for a short while puke up your booze or kick the bucket.

But for us, if you please, this was once the sweet core of the world, a sturdy world, a world whose morbid charm and kitschy beauty you and your kind could scarcely have come to know in their juicy freshness, not after the steel tempest of WWII. Despite the efforts of people behind the times like Schwab and little old me, you could at best assimilate those values into Disneyland. Indeed, it was a wonderworld of many-towered cities, teeming with colorful people in colorful costumes (bourgeoises placidly strutting about among them, the biggest one a man with a skew nose, clipped mustache, polka-dot bow tie and dachshund: a man and his dog tried and tested in disorder and early sorrow). Our souls lived in that old world of faraway times, when Nuremberg was renowned for its *Lebkuchen* and its toy boxes, not for its trials and the subsequent gallows: the gingerbread houses crowded in intricate confusion around the cute dignity of the stepped town-hall gables, shadowed by the heavenward soaring of cathedrals. When the intimacy of town and country would be enjoyed in an Easter promenade along the city walls (with many-voiced bells ringing for Beethoven's deaf ears and the seductive devil playing around as Schopenhauer's black poodle). When the vast countryside was lovely with its silent lakes and ponds reflecting the cloud castles of the minnesingers and the poetic Wittelsbachs on the mountains. The lead-glistening light of storm-brewing, grain-ripening summer afternoons long ago; the murmuring of brooks under alders and hazelnut bushes, from which beautiful Melusina peers out, palely glimmering in the evening, when the birdsongs go silent and the wan sky over the forest has kindled the first star. Melusina, mind you, and not the radioactive refuse of the nearest chemical factory... And Alpine peaks, whose glaciers shine over King Laurin's rose garden and not over the Munich–Venice highway, which even South Tirolian separatists approve of. The fragrance of firs over Fontane's sandy marches and Stifter's timber forest of spruces, amidst the mourning torches of cypresses at Duino and on D'Annunzio's Versiglia shores. And Mozart, Bach, and Handel, and crisp golden-brown Viennese *Backhendl* with fresh green lettuce...

Right, Mr. Brodny, old pal? That was Europe for us. Or rather, that was *us*. *We* were Europe. We carried it within us, in our thoughts and feelings, in the self-assurance of everything we did, the way the French carry France and the hard city of Paris within themselves, though with the slight difference that we, at that time, were alive, were made of flesh and blood. Europe—that was the native soil of our *style*, continuously producing new forms, our always definite, specific essence, the this-and-no-other way of our existence.

And the many-domed, many-towered city of Paris, her roof slates glistening like dragon scales under the capricious sky: she was one of the constellations by which the course of that world was fixed. More than any other city, she was the spirit of our spirit. She came directly from our blood as almost no other city did. Yes, indeed, you heard correctly. I say: *we, us, our—our* spirit, *our* blood. For I include myself, despite all the snide hardness of the French today. I consider the city of Paris not only as a city of Frenchmen. It still belongs to me as well. I'm conceited enough to consider myself a child of Western Civilization, albeit a foundling, if you like, or a stepchild, since the lost half of my life belongs to the half of Europe that did not pass into American hands; still, women in Kishinev did not wear veils—Pushkin hated the place, but he occasionally visited it to see classics like Racine, Molière, and Scribe. It even had an electric trolley line (not in Pushkin's time, of course, but during my childhood). I may be wrong, though: the droshkies had the same foot bells as the streetcars elsewhere, and perhaps I'm even confusing this with my memory of Jassy or Czernowitz. You can certainly correct me here, Mr. Brodny... You see, I left Bessarabia at a tender age; I was brought up in Vienna—in less than ideal manner, admittedly, but still in European traditions, intellectual attitudes, emotional norms (intellectual errors and emotional failings, if you prefer). We never managed to establish with any certainty in which church of the Christian denominations, and indeed even whether, I was baptized. But anyway I'm not circumcised. Indeed, my Viennese relatives were out-and-out anti-Semites. If my cousin Wolfgang had not died a hero's death very early in WWII, he would most certainly have occupied a high office in the SA and, after denazification, in West Germany's judiciary... With a probability verging on certainty, I can claim to be pure Aryan, albeit not raised in the cult of Wotan. I was urged to fear God and love his sweet son—with a beard on the cross, and without a beard as dear baby Jesus. I speak four of the main European languages quite fluently, plus a few less important ones (for instance, Romanian and Yiddish) rather glibly. Not to mention my infamous talent for imitating any dialect in a highly entertaining fashion. I can sing songs from Hungarian, Romanian, and Greek operettas. My Balkan culture, which I sometimes even exploited professionally, was the true substance that I gave to my formative years in Vienna. Still and all, I have read around in seven literatures, I eat with a knife and fork, shave daily, suffer from the same tooth decay as Tintoretto, Blaise Pascal, and Oscar Wilde. I can't simply be dismissed without further ado as a Levantine stranded in the West, some member of an auxiliary nation, like a Volhynian German resettled in the Reich, a type having as great a right to asylum here as a Tartar abandoned by Barnum's International Show of Shows. I presume to be as much at home on this side of the

Elbe as on the other. By no means—I don't need to emphasize it—am I an American. I was, alas, not so consistent as you, Yankel Brodny. I did not become what our sort logically had to become after losing our other half. And yet fate would have it that I have to run around in Paris as a stranger, and, on the other hand, converse with you, J. G. the American, as if you were my brother Abel!

I am, evolutionarily speaking, just as obstinate, just as behind the times, just as anachronistic as the French. And yet, dwelling among them here, I feel as if I'd been cast away among the lotus-eaters. Here, Jaykob Gee, here in Paris, here in the brightest jewel in the diadem of cities that once crowned Europe, here in the one true metropolis left in Yurop, here I remain a stranger, and I become more and more of one the more I recognize it as spirit of my spirit, form of my blood, the more intimately I find it within me, the more ingrown every pissed-on cornerstone and little pile of garbage is in me. Homeland—its scent of exhaust fumes and empty vegetable baskets, its dove-blue and lemon-yellow light, the pale salamander bellies of its scrubby plane trees, its murderous car races in the streets, its witty sky above the dragon scales of roofs along the Seine... Under this sky, sir, in whose moods and whims I am greeted again by all the promise of my childhood, all the delights I expected of the world, all the yearning of my adolescence, all the urgent eroticism of my youth—under the sky of my life's other half, which I refuse to give up for lost—under this sky, I and everything around me become more and more abstract, more and more unreal, lose more and more density. As though the world were stretching out, spreading its material thin, flying apart in something like a universal molecular expansion. The things that were solid are starting to flow and the things that flowed are volatilizing in the ether. The boulevard Haussmann—a white stream, shoreless like the Rio de la Plata. The place de la Concorde—a Turner bay in which an obelisk is melting. Do you still consider this Paris, monsieur? Do you still believe this is Pearris, Freanss, a place in the core and heart of Yurop, our old quondam Europe? Geographically at least still on this continent, built on terra firma, and not an island floating in the unfathomable depths and distances of no-man's-sea?... I, for my half-part, am no longer certain. I cannot gain a foothold here. I'm lost here just as mindlessly as the German drunkard Schwab. His plight is my plight. I have nothing over him. True, I have lost half of my life, it was amputated. But I am lying when I say I have forgotten it among the lotus-eaters. It is a lovely phrase that is meant to be touching, the opening phrase of a book that has never been completed. In fact, I have forgotten nothing of the flesh-and-blood reality of the world of yesterday. I still carry my Europe within me. But a decade slips in between its image then and its image today—ten years that I likewise cannot forget, that afflict me in nightmares and daytime visions, all kinds of brutalities amid fantastic light effects, all kinds of incomprehensible events, which—alas! alas!—also belonged to the all too warm-blooded living reality of the world of the past. For instance:

Salzburg, November 1938. Sheets of rain.

We have come to town from our cuckoo-clock cottage on the Mondsee. Stella is preparing to return to Romania. John, entrusted with mysterious diplomatic missions, has left us to our own devices all summer. We have weathered the Sudeten crisis and the spectacular Munich Agreement with complete tranquillity. We learned of them from illustrated gazettes in which the grocer wrapped the cheese and from the mailman's political comments. ("You see? When they saw they couldn't put one over on our Führer, they dropped the Czechs, those bastards, those lousy sonsabitches . . .")

World events reach us here in late echoes, thinned by the mountain air and soothed by the indolent ringing of cowbells and the humming of flies in the summer heat above the lakeside meadows. World history hangs over us as remote as the thunderstorms that arise daily between the glacier peaks, rumble a bit, and then are dissolved by a dazzling sun back into the sheer washed-out blue of the Alpine sky. But were that history to take place over us, with us, we would pay as little heed. We do not exist in the world of others but only for each other. We have no eyes for what is happening around us, we see only each other. We have no wants, no wishes except for each other...

Nevertheless, Stella is wise enough to tell herself (and me) that our refuge from a reality that is gradually becoming ominous is due to John, and that it is advisable to follow John's directions.

These directions are very precise. In a letter from Warsaw (where he was transferred from Prague), John writes that it would be advantageous if Stella came to Bucharest. There it could be proved through my elective and nominal uncle Ferdinand (who had vanished from my life for twelve years) that I am a Romanian citizen. John feels it would not be advisable to come to Bucharest myself and take the matter in hand, for I would most likely be drafted on the spot. It would be better if I dealt in some other way with this irksome business—which can most likely be deferred but is unavoidable in the long run. I should approach it in such a manner as to leave myself elbow room later on. Uncle Ferdinand (who, incidentally, is delighted to hear from me), says John, will know how to settle this satisfactorily through his connections. In any case, given the circumstances, I would not be safer anywhere than as a friendly foreigner in Hitler's Greater Germany, so I am to stay where I am: on an Austrian lake that now is part of Greater Germany. However, says John, Stella's presence in Bucharest is imperative.

This means separating from Stella for a certain time, probably an unendurable period for both of us. But for me it means definitively cutting the umbilical cord to my Viennese relatives. (Uncle Helmuth—in high dudgeon because of my relationship with a Jewess and, through her, naturally, with all sorts of foreign plutocrats—has already cited his rights and duties as a guardian several times.) Meanwhile, we have packed our bags.

It is raining in Salzburg. We park the car at the Österreichischer Hof, where we plan to spend the night. There are almost no people about. I have trouble finding a porter at the hotel to carry our bags from the car. No one cares to show his face—and if he does so, then sullenly. Something is in the air.

Stella asks for a newspaper. We learn about the murder of the German official vom Rath in Paris and about the spontaneous reaction of the German people, who have avenged themselves on Jewish stores, homes, and synagogues.

On our way through town, we occasionally step on fragments of glass. The huge panes of a dress-shop window have been smashed. In the ruined display, a mannequin has been stood on its head, naked. Some wag has thrust a chicken-feather duster between the legs. An SA man, with a grim chin strap around his extortionist face, is guarding the artwork. His eyes follow us like those of a distrustful watchdog as we pass by so closely that we almost graze him. He gapes at the small blue-yellow-and-red Romanian flags in the buttonholes of our raincoats.

We are expected for dinner at the home of Stella's cousin, who has been living here for many years, married to an official in the provincial government. No one (least of all he) has any illusions that he will keep his job with a Jewish wife. She does not, incidentally, look at all Jewish. She has nothing of Stella's thoroughbred looks; she is blond and rather plain. What makes her attractive is a fine touch of sorrow, mildly set off by diligent kindness and friendliness ("an incredibly dear dumb goose," says Stella).

The husband is the prototype of the former Austro-Hungarian civil servant, the son of a privy councilor, the grandson of a department head, a man of jittery, almost servile politesse *behind which he absentmindedly thinks of something completely different. He is dry and yet no doubt profoundly sentimental, much more intelligent, much quicker, and also wittier than he cares to seem, likewise much more reserved and arrogant. (Stella says, "At first glance a milksop, but at second glance he's full of surprises.")*

They both adore Stella and treat her like a princess who occasionally deigns to step down to them from her grand world. They emphasize their modest provincialism with an insistence that is not without a certain irony, especially since their allegation so sharply contradicts the discreet refinement of their household, the exquisite food, which is limited to the most traditional dishes of the Viennese cuisine, the collection of choice and lovely peasant furniture and other folk art in their home, and their extraordinary musicality and knowledge of literature.

They have cooked up an explanation for my constantly being with Stella and whisper it to anyone who might be surprised at my hanging around her. They say that I am probably John's son; in any case, he was more than just close to my late mother. Of course, they do not hide the truth from themselves about the nature of my relationship with Stella and about the circumstance that John could not have been the only candidate for my beautiful mother's favor and thus for the possibility of fathering me—indeed, he would have to share his candidacy with a good dozen other gentlemen of his age group and financial position (including, last but not least, "Uncle" Ferdinand). However, Stella's kinfolk merely require an alibi to be as kind, as amiable, and as overpolite to me as to anyone whom convention does not force them to reject.

The maid opening the door for us, a middle-aged rustic innocent who has served them for a long time, is visibly abashed and embarrassed. When Stella asks after her health, she is taciturn, though she normally melts under Stella's sumptuous gratuities. To our astonishment, we find the parlor filled with people. A slightly awkward circle has formed; from its center, at our entrance, a count towers up. The bearer of a grand name closely identified with the most glorious defeats of the Austro-Hungarian army, he is the host's childhood friend and classmate from the Theresianium. He too admires Stella and has known John for ages. His handshake is warm. He is wonderfully elegant in his folk-costume suit, gigantic in his corpulence. An antediluvian breed of man.

We are introduced to the others. To judge by their names, noses, and accents, they are all undeniably Jewish. Berlin Jews, rich ones, who fled to Salzburg before the Anschluss *and are now trapped here. One exception is an extremely dapper, crisply stylish man in his mid-forties who must have come to Austria from*

Lemberg or Kecskemét. The host and hostess let on that these are not expected guests; the events of the previous night have brought together people who are more or less strangers, a sort of catacomb community.

The events are discussed in great detail, and the count is of the opinion that such outrageous vandalism would not have occurred without the annexation of Austria's much fiercer anti-Semitism to that of Germany. When contradicted, he heatedly insists upon his view, as though defending a privilege that may be taken away from Austria, which has already been shamefully pruned and now even incorporated into a despised Germany. But soon he lapses into silence, intimidated and visibly disgruntled, as the Berliners inundate him with a torrent of horrifying examples of pure-German cruelty, launching into a sort of contest as to who can come up with the most fearful atrocities. The elegant room, decorated with Alpine art objects, fills up with dreadful tableaux of gorilla-like SA men putting out their cigarettes on naked female breasts ("and such lousy brands too!" quips the Kecskemét dandy, who can barely stay in his chair, he's so eager to get a word in). They forget about His Lordship. This is private shop talk. We three Gentiles—the count, the host, and I—are soon excluded from the animated conversation about hair-raising cruelties. To be sure, it is not so easy to picture them in their full terrifying measure: the people who are narrating them (and who are also identifying with the victims) are physically intact, indeed obviously mindful of their bodily well-being; they are well groomed, luxuriously nourished, expensively dressed. It would take a very active imagination to visualize them cowering under riding-crop lashes in latrine ditches or kicked into bloody mush under boot heels. The host (quite reserved anyhow) occasionally ventures to ask, "Did this happen to you personally?" Or, "Did you witness it?" And each time, he is put in his place by an indignant retort in Berlinese: "Oh God no, but these are the facts mister, everybody back home knows all about it!"

Altogether, there is too much putting-in-place and impatient one-upmanship in this colorful Berlin speech, with its delicate undertone of Semitic singsong. These trapped émigrés are cultivating it with some verve, and eventually it becomes unbearable for Austrian ears. The increasingly irritated silence of the Aryans would have long since warned more keenly perceptive urbanites that a regrettable and perilous trade-off is in the making: namely, that a virtually physical repugnance toward anything Prussian is creating an alibi for a perhaps suppressed but no less ingrained hatred of anything Jewish. Stella is the only one who appears to sense this. She remains sovereignly neutral; and wherever she can, she mellows the fervor, which lets justified indignation degenerate all too often into tongue-lashing. She has skillful objections and intelligent arguments ready, but she makes no headway against the passionately concentrated Berlin snottiness and certainly not against the obnoxious wittiness of the élégant *from Lemberg or Kecskemét.*

He is a lawyer, he claims, and sees things as a professional who has given up wasting even one iota *of his intellect on the perversions of justice committed by a horde of savages (he calls them "Hitler's brown mob"). "So what d'you want, anyway?" he yiddles spiritedly. "When dey let the goyim go after us poor Jews, it's alvays de same thing, I tell you. Whether it's de Inqvisition in de thirteent' century—" "The fourteenth," the count corrects him. "I'm talking about the Spanish Inqvisition, but t'ank you anyway," the snappy dresser from Kecskemét parries. "Didn't it go on from around 1230 till 1834? A good six hundred years, if you please—even if it wasn't always against us Jews—de killers also went at each other's troats. And in our enlightened twentieth century, it's exactly the very same thing. De goyim like their blood, they relish it. So should we tear our hair out thinking whether things are a little smidgen less just here or a little crueler there than for de past two thousand years? I ask you."*

He, by the way, is the only one here who is personally acquainted with the Nazi authorities' rigorous methods. He was arrested right after the Anschluss *and held in custody until recently. His experiences have left him—to the general amusement—with a wealth of anecdotes, which he tells very wittily, leaving open the question of whether one should be enraged at the stupidity and inventive cruelty of the examining judges, guards, and attendants or follow his example in taking the whole thing stoically and ironically, as an absurd nightmare.*

"Yet still and all, you were *examined by judges?" the host throws in ambiguously. But the breezy lawyer crows proudly, amid universal jubilation, "What do you want from me, I'm no political prisoner, I'm a criminal!"*

One of the women from Berlin leaps up and kisses him spontaneously: "Darling, you're wonderful! You I love!"

This is the signal for the count to rise (his head almost bangs against the ceiling) and to beg the hostess (who is suddenly very embarrassed) to please excuse him: he must, alas, go on to a late meeting. "But we were expecting you to stay for dinner," she pleads helplessly, looking at her husband. But she gets no support from him, instead is tersely informed, "I suppose Max must have misunderstood. In any case, his meeting is more important."

The host reaps a thankful glance from the count, who now tremendously and corpulently bows over Stella's hand. With an emphatic amiability that excludes her from the others, he says, "I am inconsolable, my dear. I was so looking forward to seeing you. Please give my very best to dear John. And let's get together very, very soon!"

Pirouetting with elephantine grace, he spirals up from the hand kiss, managing as he twists to bid goodnight to the others with a gesture of apology, as though to indicate that his size prevents him, in this constricted space, from making an individual farewell to each person without greatly inconveniencing everyone else. Now, having turned his back to them, he leaves, throwing his tremendous arm around the narrow shoulders of the host, who sees him out of the room. We hear their muffled speech behind the door and their occasional bitter mirth.

The hostess desperately tries to catch Stella's eye, but Stella is gazing absently into space. The Berliners too have lapsed into dull silence, and not even the breezy lawyer from Kecskemét has a quip at hand to dissipate the general embarrassment. This awkward tension is further heightened when the returning host, instead of rejoining the group, peers rather ostentatiously at his watch and then goes into the next room to switch on the radio for the eight o'clock news.

But this exposes a pugnacious streak in the hostess. With a candor that almost makes her pretty, she declares that she was expecting only a few guests—namely, the count, Stella, and me—for supper. But if the others would be satisfied with something improvised, then they'd all be welcome. However, she says, she has to ask them to pitch in and help because her maid gave notice this morning—she need hardly explain why.

Her suggestion is accepted with enthusiasm all around. Everyone goes into the kitchen, where the Lemberger or Kecskeméter and the Berlin woman who declared her love for him prove to be proficient and inventive amateur chefs and have soon put us all to work. The atmosphere becomes downright boisterous, especially since the host, an old-time Austrian, is incapable of rudeness under any circumstances. Making the best of a bad situation, he serves an excellent Veltliner wine—but he turns away in disgust when one of the belatedly invited guests calls it "swell booze."

In the dining room, the table is quickly set for twelve instead of five, and naturally we do without being placed—everyone sits where he likes. The meal has the relaxed mood of one eaten in an Alpine hut, which leads some of the Berliners to shed their coarse Salzburg loden jackets, to which they are obviously unaccustomed. The wine connoisseur talks away at the host, who is seated rather far down the table; he assures him that there are two things he finds charming about Austrians, whom he does not exactly hold in high esteem otherwise: the Viennese Heurige *and the informal, natural ways of Alpine inhabitants, especially the Salzburgers and Tyrolians; he can't quite get along with Styrians and Carinthians.*

The host listens with the expression of a man suffering from a toothache. He also winces each time his Berlin neighbors bang a piece of cold meat or a dollop of potato salad onto his plate, telling him he's too skinny.

The meal drags on; more wine is brought. The Kecskeméter picks his teeth as his appraising eyes pass over the baroque treasures of the dining room. And needless to say, the general conversation soon swings back to current events. The focus is no longer the persecution of Jews but rather the figure of the archvillain and quintessential enemy of mankind: Adolf Hitler. One of the Berliners, dispossessed of his huge department store on the west side of Berlin ("I managed to scram in the nick of time—and now they've caught up with me here"), draws a disastrous picture of the German economy, a catastrophic situation that he blames solely on the stupid, obstinate, amateurish interference of the Führer (he calls him "Gröfaz," a traditionally Jewish-sounding portmanteau of "Größter Führer aller Zeiten"*): "Let's not kid ourselves: German thrift, German industry, German organization would make the economy work even with this top-heavy rearmament, if that swollen-headed Austrian peasant didn't stick his nose into everything..." Then comes example upon example.*

Similarly, the foreign-policy problems of the Third Reich are harshly criticized. No one makes any illusions whatsoever that the peace just saved by the Munich Agreement is anything but a delay of the moment when the "Gröfaz" will feel like starting his war. And finally, they get down to the personal and the private. They cite psychological data about the character of Adolf Hitler, speculate about his relationship to his parents and about his abnormal sex life. The woman who kissed the Kecskeméter claims that the Führer is a sadomasochist: he gets his satisfaction by finding some pure, blond female, scantily clad in velvety deerskin, and forcing her to confess that she wants to sleep with him; he then insults her in the most disgusting way and drives her out.

The hostess cannot refrain from saying, with an uneasy sigh, "What a dreadful man!" And oddly enough, it is this relatively tame comment that sends the host into an unbridled rage. Beside himself, trembling and foaming as if in an epileptic fit, banging his fists on the table, making the glasses and plates jump, he screams in a hoarse, breaking voice, "I won't tolerate this any longer! I won't allow such remarks made about this man in my home! This man is loved and honored by millions of people! He has restored human dignity to millions of people!" He shakes his fist at his wife. "To me this man is a saint, do you hear me? A saint!..."

Bessarabia, winter 1940.

This is an early winter of the Ice Age, which began one day in March 1938 and will last in two phases for the next ten years to come, until summer 1948.

The world is still full of beauty, albeit frozen. A blue-white-and-gold world. The deep-blue Romanian sky is as spotless as the snowy land beneath. There must be a powerfully shining sun, but I cannot place it in my memory. Its light is everywhere, dazzling from the great white waves of the swaying fields and from the twist in the river valley, from the furry hoar on twigs and boughs and on the crooked snowed-in fences of the village, where the house walls of old, weathered wood glow like gray silk under the snowy burden of the roofs—a light like molten brass and so cold as to be brittle and seem fragile.

I am a soldier: I am serving my country with a weapon in my fist, *as the national rhetoric puts it. We have ridden out on a drill, have stuffed newspapers under our greatcoats and into our boots, and still we writhe in the biting cold. Nevertheless, our spirits are almost recklessly high. We are serving our people rather comfortably. We play at being soldiers, whilst elsewhere the war has long since become deadly serious. We too are armed to the teeth and have live ammunition in our pouches, but we are not yet confronted with an enemy to measure ourselves against. We know that our Fatherland is threatened on many sides—and most directly here in Bessarabia. But this is cant, just as our willingness* to defend the Homeland with weapons in our fists *is still nothing but cant and posturing.*

We enjoy the sublimity of this cant, the nimbus of heroism it adorns us with. But even more, we enjoy our rough youth and, unconsciously, our blessed anonymity in the collective. In our uniforms we are Lieutenant Jonescu or Volunteer Popescu or Private First Class Petrescu only for the sake of functional differentiation. In reality, we are all young men doing military service with no responsibilities except toward certain cant. Serving in this way, however, we are sons of the people.

They creep from their huts, these people, swarming to greet us, bringing tzuika*—mild, oily plum brandy—and delicately rancid cakes: a people smelling rancid in their sheepskins, with deeply notched peasant faces, children peeping timidly from behind their mothers' aprons, silver-haired old men, trembling, dribbling, with broken voices, and here and there the cherry-dark eyes of a girl, the double humps of firm breasts under an embroidered blouse . . . We have dismounted and are chatting with the people, who have their hands in the sleeves of their sheepskins and are stamping from one foot to the other in this awful cold. War? Yes, soon there will be war here too. Those fellows over there, across the Dniester, don't want us to keep this good land. But we'll show them that it's our land, our Romanian earth. We, the sons of the people, will defend this soil with weapons in our fists . . . The cant comes trippingly over my lips, well drilled. I am so proud, so moved, so delighted to be a son of a people—whose language I hardly ever speak, whom I hardly know, whom I have hardly ever seen or experienced except in such a folkloristic genre picture as this one here: costumed farm laborers with backs crooked from bending over furrows and before all kinds of masters, servile people with friendly grins, people sprung directly from their soil, with hair like grass, with skin like bark, with hands like tree roots—and young girls plump as cherries.*

And we among them in our uniforms and helmets, warriors hung with sabers, lances, and carbines, with our hoary, steam-

breathing horses—it all looks like an opera set. The music is supplied by the dogs. There must be hundreds, to judge by the din. They are barking their lungs out. They are yanking so hard at their chains that they turn over in midair. They snap blindly, furiously, into the blue winter sky, drooling, foaming...

until someone finally notices that this raging is aimed not only at us and our horses. The dogs are pulling in another direction...

whence a boy comes running and screams, "Lupu! Lupu!"

He claims he's spotted a wolf.

This causes the genre picture to break into dramatic motion. All the men dash toward the end of the village where the boy came from. All the women scatter like chickens and chase their children to yank them into the huts. All these people are screaming as if impaled.

It being our duty to defend the Homeland against all enemies, with weapons in our fists, we have, needless to say, raced ahead of everyone else. Right behind the last of the handful of huts, we sight the wolf.

It could also be a very run-down dog—after all, it is quite improbable that a wolf would show itself so close to a settlement in broad daylight. But there is no time for such reflections now. We have already torn our carbines from our backs; rifle shots are already lashing the air, swirling up tiny fountains of snow around the "wolf"—I catch myself firing bullet after bullet without really aiming, much less hitting the mark.

Our yelling and surging at the end of the village has sent the "wolf" into swift flight. Then—presumably frightened by the shots all around him and perhaps even grazed or struck by one—he doubles back, and to his misfortune we have him as he flees broadside past us instead of sharply away from us. He is hit by a few bullets or bullet fragments. He bends to a bow, snapping at the bullet wounds, but an enormously powerful will to live pulls him forward. Only now he flees more slowly, more heavily, sits down crookedly on his hind legs when he is hit again. We naturally redouble our banging, and every time the wolf marks a new hit, the united peasantry around us howl triumphantly until their yowling is exceeded by a louder, more energetic one: the roaring of our officers, who command us to stop our senseless shooting on the spot.

It is as if we had suddenly awoken from a fit of possession. It's still on our faces; I see it in my comrades' wild eyes and uncontrolled mouths. It must be in mine too. The possession yields to the foolish insight that something inexplicable has happened to us, simple as it may be to explain. Our nerves got the better of us. The live ammunition in our pouches had to explode sooner or later.

We're in for it now. But who could have thought of that when the entire village was shouting and pointing to its archenemy...

The wolf—or stray dog—keeps twitching and then collapses. The bullets are in his flesh, he has fire in his bowels, he turns around in circles, biting his flanks, we can see him spraying blood. A few courageous peasants set out to club him to death with cudgels. But, incredibly tenacious, he gets to his feet and drags himself off. It is a triumph of the will to live, the will to survive at any price. It paralyzes our hands. My head is spinning, I've probably drunk too much tzuika *too fast. I feel sick.*

Berlin, 1941. Nighttime, total darkness.

I come out of the Jockey. I've been feasting. I've devoured Baltic lobster, Hamburg Stubenküken, omelet surprise*; I've boozed on gallons of Chablis, Mouton Rothschild 1935, port and Courvoisier and Heidsieck, danced the rumba and the samba, and whetted my member in my trousers on the pokey pubic bone of an East Prussian girl while dancing to "She wants no flowers, she wants no chocolate, she wants just me and only little me." And now it's time, now the thing's working on its own, "check, please," and out—and in...*

We're on the street now. It's pitch-dark. Berlin is blacked out because of air raids, so you can't see your hand before your face (but that's not at all where my hand is). A cab with narrow slits of light on its blackened headlights drives up (they know where to find the fares vital to the war effort), and I step into the meager glow, raise my hand—I have no right to use a taxi, I'm neither an armaments specialist nor in the Reich Food Estate nor in the Reich Security Service nor a doctor nor a diplomat nor an expectant mother, but my pockets are full of cash and cigarettes (there's a war on, you understand, we'll be honest again after the Final Victory). So I open the cab door and start pushing the girl in—when a figure leaps out of the dense blackness, shoves the girl and me away, and squeezes into the car. I reach in to haul the fellow out—after all, I *stopped the taxi, it's* mine, *first come, first served—but then I feel the leather of a uniform coat under my fingers. I get scared. I'm a foreigner, all I've got is a highly suspicious document that describes me as being "On a Special Mission"—obviously a draft-dodger, probably even a deserter. It's not advisable. I'm about to let go, to murmur an apology. But the man shrieks, "What! Grabbing an officer of the German* Luftwaffe!" *A fist smashes into my face. I'm scared. I've got to do something. I punch back blindly, strike too low, and bruise my knuckles on his collar. Something is dangling there, something with hard sharp edges: a Knight's Cross.*

I am terrified. I am scuffling in the darkness with an officer wearing a Knight's Cross. This is lèse-majesté, a desecration of the Third Reich, no mercy can be shown for this... Another car comes along, the narrow glow from the headlight combs the street. The Knight's Cross is lying on the asphalt—and the fellow is punching out wildly. But I've got him by the collar, I press him down, shove my knee between his legs, smash my fist into his kisser. The other car has driven past without stopping. I get a punch in the stomach—not very hard, he's no athlete. But I have to finish him off before he draws his pistol or his aviator's dagger and simply rubs me out. He can do it, he has to, he's a uniformed member of the armed forces, he's duty-bound... I smash my fist once more into his Adam's apple, he chokes noisily. He's young and rather thin, a kid, barely twenty-one, no doubt—like me.

Only I'm bigger and stronger. But if a patrol car comes, I'm done for. He's an officer of the most daring German service branch, highly decorated; he risks his life, whereas I...

I keep on pounding. They'll make short shrift of me, shoot me down on the spot like a mad dog. I bang his head against my raised knee; I hold the collar of his leather coat in my left hand and hit him with my right, knocking the edge of the collar out of my fingers. Somewhere, a flashlight beam starts to flit through the blackness. The air-raid warden from the next building, probably. I kick the leather sack, punch a mash of hair, blood, and flesh, he sinks to his knees, his head knocks against the fender of the taxi, I push the girl in, jump in after her. "Get going!" And the cabby hasn't stirred all this time, he probably hasn't even looked around. But then there's nothing to see, I can barely make out his silhouette before me in the darkness, in any case it's solid, no neck, he's probably well on in years. Thank God, all this was none of his business, the results were too uncertain, he doesn't get mixed up in things like this... And the flashlight beam dances closer. The cabby shifts the car into gear, the taxi starts off—slowly—much too slowly—the flashlight beam moves through the car window—I duck, pull the girl down next to me—now the cabby shifts into second and then to third—and I suck the blood from my smashed knuckles ("Watch it, kid, my dress!") and peer through the back window: I see the parabolic section of the flashlight beam whooshing across the asphalt and fishing, out of the blackness, the crumpled figure in the blue-gray leather coat, casting a flat atomizing shadow. Then, the beam swings up and after us—but its light atomizes too, before reaching us. I see only the round, white-yellow core of the flashlight... We arrive at my place, a highly respectable family boardinghouse in the Wielandstrasse. In front of the house a black Mercedes is parked, and behind it a military jeep. I am sick with fear: they've already come for me. My first impulse is to shout at the cabby to keep driving. But then I tell myself it won't do any good now. I calm the girl. I'll need her to testify that I was attacked and responded in self-defense.

The SS officer waiting for me in the parlor is extremely correct. After checking my papers, he returns them to me with a click of his heels, apologizes, saying he has to see the girl's papers too, reads a well-known name, bows with military terseness. "Excuse me for disturbing you."

He turns to me. "I was ordered to search your room. Could you please make sure that nothing is missing?" In my room, three men are rummaging through my closets and valises. One of them reports, "Nothing, Sturmführer!*"*

The SS officer waves them off. "Good, that's all." He says to me, "Would you please come to this office tomorrow morning at eleven." He hands me an address: Elsternplatz, in Grunewald. He gives me the Nazi salute and exits with his men.

For a while, I am breathless with terror, unable to grasp what all this means. Then it hits me, to my horror: Stella. She's tried to get to me again and they've caught her.

Near Stargard, Pomerania, 1942. In a manor house, evening, after a hunt.

The hostess: "... Well, the groom slipped right through her fingers just three weeks after the wedding... and then the business with the boy—why, it's horrible: during the Polish campaign, right in the first few days... it's hard to keep all your marbles after that... and then this all the time [drink gesture with her thumb sticking out of her fist], but otherwise a marvelous woman, manages on her own terrifically..."

the hostess lived in Argentina before the war—

"... Argentina? What do they eat there?" "Well, in the Pampas, they mainly eat asado." "What's that supposed to be?" "... Asado. You simply have to try it sometime, Schnipps. It's fantastic." "I just can't imagine it." "... fantastic, I tell you. A whole sheep roasted on an open fire..." "No! Outdoors, of course?" "Like the virgin of Orléans." "I thought she was the last in her line." "No, well, joking aside, it's really fantastic. And then when the

gauchos take their knives—" "But why knives? Vaseline does the job just fine!" "... our Henning's still the same old swine!" "But what do we need gauchos for, gang? We can make our own asado..." "You're not going to wake up everyone on the estate just for that!" "Why, it's almost midnight." "Is anyone still hungry?" "When I tell Stolze—Stolze, I say—third year of the war or not, it's all the same to me—Stolze, I tell you, will do it straightaway." "And outdoors, you say?" "Naturally. It's in the Pampas. Where else are you going to—?"

"Now listen, Stolze: we've got some foreign guests, and we want to show them that even in the third year of the war—by the way, would you like a schnapps? Well, let me introduce you. Overseer Stolze." "Why, you direct this estate, Stolze, eh? Don't be so modest!" "Stolze's fantastic. Nothing's impossible for him." "... Well, we shall try to catch one that's not too old. We'll do it in no time." "We can all pitch in to help with the fire. It's better if there aren't too many witnesses." "A little nocturnal exercise is good for you—right, Jutta?" "Why don't you ask your old lady?" "But put your rubber boots on, children." "Christ, is it ever cold!" "Someone bring the bottle—I mean, one for each of us, of course." "Of course, if the wood isn't dry..." "But you know, that she can pull that off—after all it's the third year of the war." "Why, Schnipps is out of his mind! Listen, cow pats are not peat." "What do you need a glass for?" "You're pouring the booze all over my dress, damn it." "Just pull your fur a little tighter around your modest charms." "Stolze is just fantastic." "He's absolutely reliable. He'll just report that the sheep died." "Hey, get your paws off me!" "Listen, that smoke is abominable! No, no, no! No Pampas for me..." "Stick in a good-sized piece." "I see what you mean by that—" "Henning, you old swine!" "My feet are soaked already." "Now, listen, a party pooper—" "Hey, look: the head's starting to brown!" "It's more natural in the rear." "If I catch cold and pass it on to the kids..." "You'll pour your workers a round, won't you, Stolze?" "Hey, that's enough wood now. The whole house'll go up in flames soon." "Actually, the dripping fat ought to be—" "Christ, I can't see a

thing because of this lousy smoke!" "Don't stand in the wind!" "You mean before you and not behind you?" "Well, even with that fire it's getting a bit nippy out here." "Stolze can tell us when it's ready." "Let the men—" "You can get drunk indoors too ..."

"You look like a chimney sweep." "Stolze said at least another half hour ..." "You know, life in the Pampas isn't my cup of tea ..." "My stockings are all screwed up in these rubber boots ..." "Someone put another record on." "You smell so nice—where do you live?" "Come on, I just scorched my hand. I've got to cool it off somewhere ..." "In his old age, Schnipps is having the best time of his life." "Of course, if the younger men are at the front—" "Who needs all that light for dancing?" "I hope you don't find this frivolous ..." "And the fire out there—it's just terrifyingly beautiful!" "Can you get any more liquid into you?" "Let me just go see if it's ready, this stuff—the lasso or chimborasso or whatever it's called ..." "Goodness, is that edible?"

"I feel like a cannibal." "Didn't I tell you? Charred on the outside and raw on the inside." "But we can't just throw it away—what a waste!" "Just imagine, a whole sheep. I could trade one for a crate of French—" "The wood is probably drier in the Pampas." "That filet steak with goose liver at Horcher's—well, you can just keep all your Pampas and your old gauchos ..." "Yes, but what are we going to do with the stuff now?" "Why don't you give it to the Russians?"

"Have you lost a lot of them too?" "If you want to split hairs, it's really not quite proper—after all, they're POWs." "Just another dumb idea. They're much too weak for farm labor." "Two-thirds of ours kicked the bucket the very first day." "The poor guys are so starved they eat grass like cattle!" "And you want to give them a whole sheep?" "They'll all croak on you." "That's what Udo said. If someone's starving, you don't just ..." "Well, none of our people are going to touch this. I know my Pomeranians all too well." "What the peasant don't know, he don't eat." "Stolze'll do something with it. He's fantastic." "Just dump it in the carp pond." "That's why the eels get so fat in the Baltic."

"When I picture the thing oven-roasted, golden-brown, and with nice green beans ..." "Anyway, put the fire out, Stolze. No enemy pilot has ever wandered this way—but you never can tell." "Goddamn it, Henning, if you don't keep your hands to yourself..."

1943, summer evening in the valley of the Unstrut, Thuringia.

We are drinking punch under a gigantic, night-black copper beech. Tiny fireflies are dancing over the cobalt-blue lawn around the black shadow of the bushes. The host: in his late forties, corpulent, rosy, his sparse hair almost totally white (you can't see much of him except, when he crosses his legs, you sometimes catch a dim reflection of his old patent-leather pumps, one of which is strangely inanimate, like the shoe on a wax figure). The hostess (on the narrow side of a white iron table, more speculative than visible): delicate, nimble, with huge, dreamy, hazel-brown eyes shimmering wet in the matte oval of her face. The son (first lieutenant in the Panzerjäger*): his uniform occasionally glitters with its German Cross in Gold, Iron Cross I and II, Close Combat Clasp (he calls them his "Christmas-tree decorations"); now on furlough from Münsterlager, where he is a drill instructor. "You can imagine what a load off our minds that was;* pourvu que cela dure, *of course." "... Possibly they'll grant me one more little outing to the front lines ..." "You see, he wants the Knight's Cross* à tout prix*—for the property's sake." "In the end it didn't help Horst any that he volunteered right off and went through the entire Polish campaign and lost a leg. Afterward, they fired him anyway ..." "And when Ottfried died in action ..." "And if you get killed, my boy, then the property won't be of much use to you ..." "Is that sheet lightning or a real thunderstorm—or what?" "Nope, the Leuna works." "It's a miracle anything's left of it. They're attacking twice a day now—" "That jasmine's delightful." "We've got all the time in the world to take care of the garden. We can't go out anyway." "Otherwise he's a very decent sort. He's the brother of the brother-in-law of our manager. He says, 'All I can do for you is simply* *have you stay inside your own four walls. If you leave the area of the house—that is to say, the grounds, you know—you have to wear the star. I would avoid doing that if I were you.' " "No, the kids are not really quarter Jews. Herbert and I are each half. According to the prevailing algebra, that equals more than half—morally, I mean." "It makes things a bit difficult with the help, of course. They hanged our old chambermaid because she had something going with a Pole here from the camp—" "We almost got mixed up in it ourselves—" "But ever since Jürgen got the German Cross in Gold—" "It does help, after all . . ."*

The new chambermaid emerges from the thick darkness around the jasmine bushes. "Dinner is served, if you please." The son gets to his feet. "Well, let's do something about our slender figures." "Please go ahead. We're not allowed to sit at the same table with you all—we're not Aryan enough . . ."

1944, Berlin.

Air-raid shelter. People thrown together. Ashen faces. The women dressed as if they were about to go sledding in the park: fur coats over coffee-brown track-suit pants; small plaid scarves wound around their curlers like a cross between a turban and a Phrygian cap. Whining kids groggy with sleep. The few men—aged, their faces notched and creased with hunger. The long-drawn-out howling of the all-clear signal releases some of the tension like a valve in a high-pressure boiler. Sighs of relief. People gather up the belongings they have dragged down here. Crawl out between damp walls and support beams. They're familiar with the whole business. These nighttime interruptions are part of daily life with its obnoxious routines. But still, it gets to you every time. Shouts from outside. A couple of people running along the street. When the basement door is opened, a smell of burning wafts in.

I find myself in a motley group who are viewed here with wry displeasure. It is a small party, given by a young councilor in the government dealing with the war economy. The scent of our cigarettes has drawn notice, but the real provocation is the cloud of good French perfume around the girls, plus the very hard accent of the little Brazilian attaché...Luckily, a few aerial mines exploding nearby diverted attention from us. There was pandemonium here for a good half hour. Only now do we feel our nerves quivering.

And the present mood is all the more euphoric. Not cheery, however, but coldly passionate, almost malevolent. We don't give a good goddamn now about the angry glares of the mothers, herding along their exhausted flocks of kids. We dash up the stairs, three or four steps at a time, to our host's apartment. Soon champagne corks are popping. And there are rolls with the finest Pomeranian sausage, and fantastic rumba records brought by the Brazilian. One of the girls is already dancing on the table, her skirt pulled up to her crotch. But she doesn't dance for long. Suddenly, she stops dead, gapes straight ahead, and cries, "My baby!"

It has just struck her that she left her child with her parents in the Motzstrasse. Where the aerial mines came down thickest.

She won't be held back. She doesn't even pull on her coat. She simply runs out into the night in her dress. Since I've got my eye on her and don't want her to just vanish into the night, I run after her.

We don't get far. At the second corner, where a building is on fire, we are thrust into a bucket brigade. An irate air-raid warden, obviously of great authority, waves a pistol in the air. He sticks it under the nose of a man who declares that he is a doctor and could probably be employed more usefully elsewhere rather than here, in this senseless attempt to pour bucketfuls of water on a blaze that no brigade can bring under control. "You will do your duty like everyone else!" screams the air-raid chief. "You know I have the right to shoot you if you resist my orders."

We take the opportunity to short-circuit the bucket brigade. We sheer out, passing a full bucket to the man in front and an empty bucket to the man in back. Pulling off this stupidly simple trick puts us in a good mood. We hold hands as we run through the smoking streets. But it's a long way to the Motzstrasse, and we probably won't get through anyhow. Flames are lighting up the sky over the ruins in the next few blocks.

The girl (she's so young you wouldn't guess she had a child; a minor accident, no doubt)—the girl gets tired. Tired and cranky, like the kids in the air-raid shelter. She launches into the same pouty Berlin jargon: "Hey, man, how're we ever gonna get to Motzstrasse if everything's cookin'? I'm wreckin' my shoes—just look!"

She has an insight of stoic grandeur: "Either they managed to get out alive and everything's fine and dandy or they're dead. Either way, I can't do anything."

We briefly reflect whether we should go back to the party. No, we can scarcely expect it to get any better. My apartment—in another highly respectable family rooming house, different from the one three years ago—is rather far away.

"Well, then, let's go to my place. It's right around the next corner." We hold hands again. You can say what you like, but it's good to survive.

1945, near Buchholz, on the Lüneburg Heath.

The dawn breaks over the black saw-teeth of the pines. The sky turns cold and smooth like polished stone. A hundred yards ahead, the freight cars that have toppled from the embankment are blazing. The air smells of burning rubber—or something of the kind; the smoky flames inundate the potato field with an eerie brownish red. In the ditch a few patches of March snow are melting rosily. A handful of men are working on the tracks—six or seven, guarded by three others. The workers are convicts from Altona who wear prison uniforms with round, rimless, visorless caps. The guards are policemen. In the cattle cars of the train, which is standing by the pines, mainly women are peering out—but in their condition it is hard to tell their sex; they could just as easily be half-starved men. For three days now, I'm told, such trains have been rolling through here nonstop, supposedly to a big camp near Belsen. The strafers have set a couple of trains on fire. Perhaps some of the people have managed to sneak into the bushes, but it doesn't matter—they won't get far. They're too feeble to survive outdoors, and no one will take them in and hide them—it's too risky. They're guarded by a single man here, an old geezer with a gigantic rifle—he looks like a home guardsman from the First World War. He carries the rifle on a strap across his back and he props his arm on the barrel like a huntsman. He only casually notices the few figures who have jumped out of the train to take a shit.

There is something macabre yet idyllic about this dotted line along the dark stretch of the waiting train: a foreshortened row of crouchers facing in different directions with dropped pants or hitched-up skirts revealing naked, lamentably bony behinds. Completely emaciated asses, so sharp they could shit into bottlenecks... And one of the men embraces his thin thighs under the knees and peeps back over his shoulder—like a faithful dog that has to shit but doesn't want to lose sight of its master. And he hops away from his pile, hops like a frog, glancing around with bulging eyes—does he have worms? In his nutritional state, he can't possibly be constipated—or is he embarrassed?... At any rate, he destroys the alignment, breaks out, disrupts the parallel—he is already close to the buffers between two cars, where he probably wants to hide—aha!—where he tries to creep through and vanish in the underwood of the pines on the other side... He has turned his skull ahead and peeps under the buffers and is about to take his final leap...

But the home guardsman has noticed something. There's something wrong. The alignment of shitters is untidily interrupted... The home guardsman slowly removes his left arm from the rifle barrel; his right arm reaches for the strap; he pulls the rifle from under his armpit, takes careful aim—he's probably taking fine sight, the target's not more than perhaps forty paces off—and the shot sings and lashes onto the train and then across and beyond to the jagged black wall of pines, which catches it and hurls it back, making it echo, across the potato field... and the shitting frog simply keels over on his nose; not even his arms let go, embracing his thighs as if they were his most precious possession on earth... he merely keels forward, and his naked white backside is turned toward the heavens like a moon howitzer; it suddenly seems tremendous, seems to swell, a gigantic, shiny egg, as in a Bosch painting; it lacks only a huge funnel stuck in it or a crane flying up from it...

1946, in a train compartment between Frankfurt and Würzburg.

I have a travel order from the British military government, and thus I have the right to take Allied trains. In scheduled German trains—that is, the ones hung with human clusters like bacchanal festoons—I may use the cars and compartments reserved for members of the occupation forces. In the British Zone, such compartments are nearly always empty. In the American Zone, they are moving brothels for GIs riding alone or in tiny groups. Between the main stations on a given stretch, a relay service of Fräuleins *has been set up. They climb in with a john at one station, screw all the way to the next station, and then pick up another client for the return trip. Commuter sex, paid for with PX commodities: cigarettes, chocolate, nylons, canned meat, coffee.*

I have come from Bad Hersfeld (from John) and am going to Nuremberg (to appear there as a witness). I have had to transfer several times: from a local to an express, from an Allied to a German train. The trip drags on and on. It is my first one after the war; I am seeing a wealth of medieval images: ruins, lunar landscapes, scattered beaten people. The Germans wear rags on their feet and coffee cozies on their heads. When they come to a railroad depot, they start out from far away, from their caves in the rubble fields. They swarm along like lines of ants, over trodden footpaths that wind through remnants of houses, right through the traces of former kitchens and parlors with nettles luxuriating in the corners.

I see many folk tableaux: the bare breasts of nursing mothers, grandfathers carried piggyback, silent gaping faces, trembling hands spooning out bread soups, sleepers piled up like logs, waiting rooms in which people cook and launder... The Germans are as human as in their fairy tales: a round-eyed, wonder-eyed, thunderstruck humanity, as if they had looked into the face of God.

The trip has been going on for days. I witness hordes of people swarming onto incoming trains, human surf breaking against the sides of railway cars, foaming up over the roofs and sticking there. Every train is crusted over with people like an old ship's hull with barnacles. When the train chugs out of each station, it drags along human seaweed, human sludge...

Over all this, there are yellow sunups and red sundowns, pale days, lulled by the rising and falling of telegraph wires. Fluffy, feathery skies. Landscapes screwing into and twisting out of the square of the train window. Furrows in the fields, breaking open with a hum, fanning open. Gliding mountain chains, approaching hills. Embankments that hurl the scent of hay in my face and then are torn away. Black nights, the sickle moon cutting its way through the darting clouds. Corpses of cities in the silver milk of starlight.

I begin to settle in to my trip as to a fate that had been dealt me; I learn to adjust, to orient myself, to seize my advantage: I have to find food, occasionally wash and shave, the toilets are stuffed with people, the station kiosks are looted bare, there are fistfights over a rationed herring sandwich. But I am alone in my Allied compartment—until Frankfurt. Then the German railroad service shoves an Eastern European in on me: a Ukrainian, a displaced person en route to Munich (that much is intelligible). We get along on the handful of Russian fragments I picked up in Bessarabia. Our communication remains rudimentary, and besides, he is not very sociable. He gazes out the window and sings, sings tender, preternaturally nostalgic songs in smoky vowels and melting labials: mnyesh-myets khroshtshuy svolyeshtschik, *what do I know. Songs about his little pony or his mother, in any case about deep homesickness and a long road . . . Meanwhile, the train lumbers off again, pulling out of the human ooze, out of the desperate tumult, away from the shouts, gliding out of the floury lamplight under the shot-up station roof, heading into the abstractly alive blackness of the switch yard: bars, twisted and torn, the skeletons of charred railroad coaches, engine wrecks magically present. The down-slanting shine of the illuminated train windows wanders on, a gliding chain of yellow rectangles: they tremble over black crushed stone. The first window leaps up a sooty wall and drops back, the others follow. Rectangle upon rectangle they repeat the leap and drop back, stretch, undulate, expand, shoot out into the darkness, contract, throw themselves like folded carpets over a ramp, lose one half of themselves in a pit and pull it out again. This becomes a dance, a grotesque geometrical dance of submission, a Constructivist parody of assiduity. Rectangles squeeze into squares, squares distort into trapezoids, constrict diagonally into isosceles triangles, straddle their legs and do splits, rip apart into hyperbolas and pour into the endless night. And the wheels grind in the tracks, rattling harder and harder, more and more noisily, crackling through switch clusters, shaking and jerking through the cars, wrenching them onto the predetermined track . . . a dinosaur leaps out of the darkness and attacks the train; he is smashed back; the mammoth proboscis of a water pump makes a grab for me, black and huge, run down by the pack of train-window lights; in back of it, red and green eyes flare up, move along, and are driven away, torn into, sucked up by the general falling, receding . . .*

and the Ukrainian sings. Sings mournfully, his head bobbing. His pony weaves a bassinet, his mother waits for him, he is very homesick, and the road is long . . . svysh yaaa schtschlik kasyateee, *or what do I know . . . His song has seven times seventy-seven stanzas, it is as endless as this journey, as endless as the night into which the beat of the wheels carries us, faster and faster, banging more and more breathlessly . . .*

I stand up, put out the light, and wrap myself in my coat. I want to sleep, lulled by the Ukrainian's singsong... But the compartment door is yanked open, a cold gust of air smashes in, a black hand switches on the light. A giant Moor in an olive-green uniform coat is standing there, a woolen cap on his woolly skull. "Get outta here, you fuckin' Germans!" "German yourself!" "I said, get outta here!" "I won't. I've got a travel order." "Shove it up your ass!" "All right. I'll call the MP." "But I got a girl." "Who cares?" "I wanna screw her." "Go ahead!"

He vanishes into the dark corridor. I pull the door shut, turn off the light. He yanks the door open again and pushes the girl inside. She sits down, a ruffled blackbird, her claws holding her handbag in her lap, her face a doughy splotch with two gigantic, dark, sunken eye sockets...

The Negro hangs his coat over the window to the corridor—the curtains were cut away in 1944, perhaps they were made into a child's dress, the child is probably moldering under ruins somewhere, perhaps a corpse was wrapped in them... "Get to the other side!" "You might say please."

He bares his white teeth at me, his unspeakably pure, tender-rosy gums. A strip of light from outside sweeps across his black face, he holds out a pack of cigarettes to me. I change from my window corner to the aisle seat of the bench opposite, wrap myself in my coat, pull up my legs, and push the Ukrainian snugly into his corner.

The Ukrainian keeps singing, unmoved, drawing the notes from his pumped-up chest, squeezing them through his larynx, mashing them into the ooze of the labials: shtcholoy vyzian beshnyevo-o-o-, *or something like that... His pony can kick the bucket, his mother can go screw the parson, Bessarabia is far away, and homesickness fills him with dismay, like the joy under the frock, and the song is as soft as the cock...*

The Negro tips the girl back onto the now empty seat. I pull my coat up over my head. I don't want to see what's happening, I can picture it: his black paw between her legs, burrowing through the panties (if she's wearing any), burrowing into the black fur, the middle finger groping for the wet slit, the other black paw kneading her breast . . .

I pull my coat tight over my face. There's a buttonhole I can peep through: monsieur le voyeur, le triste sire . . .

In the window, the dim reflection of the compartment door through gliding nightland, with telegraph poles whirring past; black agglomerations of bosky hills under the drama of the romantic German sky; shredding clouds, racing patches of mist; and pale and plump the girl's white thigh, rising, crooking at the knee, the stocking sliding down, the leg dangling, searching for a foothold, helpless, and behind it, in between, over it, under it, the dark mass of the Negro, his back slowly moving up and down, indolently palpitating, an olive-green torso with a black ass cut off by the white stripe of his lowered underwear, the girl's hand on the back of his neck, as if they were dancing . . .

Now and then, light flashes overhead: a lineman's house with a lamp whooshes by, the lanterns of an overpass . . . And the Ukrainian, with dangling head and, no doubt, watery gaze, seeks the moon in the apocalyptic clouds and finishes his song, swallows, begins a new one, even more mournful, more nostalgic. The road is long, the vowels draw the wanderer's weary feet from the ooze of mashed consonants: vshot-chokhoy kakda tsmyelyshnuyaaaa wayakhoy shtshaluuuy vsho-shoooo . . .

The air in the compartment thickens, I sweat in my corner, powerless, grim, monsieur le vivisecteur . . . *In his buttonhole, the dandy wears the orchid of a white female thigh with a Negro back wedged in . . .*

1946, Nuremberg.

A treatment to harden the soul. Pastor Kneipp's method. A ruthless alternating cure of impressions. Boiling baths and icy showers.

I take part (in a mess-alliance, *so to speak) in the glory of the victors, accusers, and judges. I am distinguished, I belong to the supermen. I eat with the Allies in the cafeteria of the Fürth courthouse. In the lascivious lard of shimmering canteen grub, six courses, splotched on a punched aluminum tray. In line. Queuing up with prison guards, tabloid reporters, file rummagers, gonorrheal secretaries—your turn, buddy. The ladle shits: brown cutlets—move along—puke of piercing green canned peas—move along—a pile of pus-yellow corn—move along—lymph of mashed potatoes—move along—a canned pineapple slice, canned condensed milk, coffee, Coca-Cola, a chocolate bar—move along—cookies, white bread, canned grapefruit juice, canned beer, cigarettes galore . . .*

Outside, the people are starving, selling their little sister or their dead son's Knight's Cross for a carton of Lucky Strikes. In here, we are showered with music from the loudspeaker can: "Blue moon, you saw me standing alone—without a dream in my heart—without a love of my own . . ."

Stella. She's the reason I'm here. Here, justice is being done before World History. Make sure you get a seat next to the black-haired girl with the pale cheeks and dark eyes. She survived the uprising in the Warsaw Ghetto. You just wouldn't believe how much knowledge goes into a pair of eyes, big and dark as they may be—she probably screws like an angel . . .

and while we stuff our faces here and work on the choreography of mating, somewhere off at an angle, upstairs, in one of the thousand honeycomb cells of the Fürth courthouse, the main defendants are being tried. When you've swallowed your canteen vittles, drunk your coffee and the rest of your canned beer, burped, put out your cigarette, wiped your kisser with the paper napkin, you can go upstairs and watch them being driven through a caged corridor like lions in a circus. The great figures of the crumbled Third Reich: Göring, Hess, Ribbentrop, Keitel, Kaltenbrunner, Frank—twenty-two men in all, accused of crimes against humanity, all kinds of war crimes, crimes against peace, conspiracy . . . Inside, they fill two rows of benches—twenty-two men of the white race, as pale as intestinal worms (they've been living under arti-

ficial light for nine months) but washed, clean-shaven, with clean hands and brushed suits. Göring in a kind of bridal silvery gray: double-breasted flannel jacket, marshal's piping on the breeches, Krakoviak boots on his short, fat legs. He's alert and lively, very interested in everything going on about him, slides around on the bench and peers everywhere. Next to him, Hess's saurian skull looks as if it had just clambered out of a diluvial ocean, sending a first bewildered glance into the prehistoric world from beneath its overhanging bushy eyebrows—when you encounter that gaze, you are peering down two gun barrels. Ribbentrop's bank-teller mug: empty, tight-lipped, arranged in dourly dignified wrinkles. Keitel's maître-d' skull. Kaltenbrunner's dripping Aztec profile. Frank's man-in-the-street mien puffed up with a convert's remorse. The homosexual scrotum in Funk's cheeks. Schacht's Punch-and-Judy head . . .

Outside, in the impoverished vending stalls of the bombed-out city, you can purchase them (with Hitler, Himmler, and Goebbels in the bargain) for a handful of marks: carved as ornamental corks for liquor bottles—bottles for liquor that can't be had anyway, that can be found only by Americans, Englishmen, Frenchmen, in the Arabian Nights bazaar of the PXs (the Russian, in any case, has no home) . . .

and here, on the witness stand, a man whose secrets are being wormed out of him—grave worms: "So you admit that you actively participated in the mass shootings of thirty thousand Polish citizens, most of them of the Mosaic faith? Fine—now who gave the orders for this action? . . ."

The grave worms creep through the tremendous Fürth courthouse, crawl through the labyrinth of its corridors, through the chasms of its stairwells, crawl in and out of its thousands of honeycomb cells, creep up the waxed lace-boots and into the machine-gun muzzles and under the grim chin straps and into the nostrils of the massive GIs standing guard at every corridor corner, outside every door, behind which something important might happen: "Our boys—we're so proud of them. American boys are not like others—only American boys have mothers—that's why they kicked the shit out of the goddamn Nazis . . ."

and that's why the Fräuleins *suck their cocks dry. When darkness comes, the streetwalkers ripple out from Fürth to Nuremberg, throng about the railroad station (which still reeks of fire and decay and wet rust), hurry around the old city wall, the garbage-filled moat. No poor lightbulb glows on the shredded ivy of the tumbledown stone wall. There's smooching and hootchy-kootching in the dark. Sometimes a match flares up and the night sends forth a Rembrandtesque blackamoor's skull with a Camel in his kisser. Then someone whispers in the dark: "Sir, sir, listen, sir. My sister—sixteen years old . . ."*

But we scoot past in beat-up jeeps, whoosh through the figures, our headlights hurling them into the background of the witch-hunt. The driver's silhouette is like cast iron, a black, helmet-crowned wedge pushing them apart. He steers the light beams with one finger, his right arm embracing the seat at his side, his left foot propped on the clapped-down windshield, his right foot pressing on the gas . . .

we streak with the gale toward sparkling lights, a Christmas wonder candle: in a flood of neon, the Grand Hotel Excelsior rises from the German rubble-night like a mescaline vision. In the lightbulb Alhambra of the entrance, the doorman, the big fat uncle of Papa Czar, in a sky-blue admiral's uniform, woven into the spaghetti tangle of his silver fourragères, assisted by iron men with machine guns, bayonets sticking out like flowers . . . They check the guests' passes; he pushes them through the revolving door, bowing and scraping. "Good evening, sir! How are you tonight, sir? . . ."

Inside, fashionable thronging and jostling at the bar. Athletic backs in olive-brown uniform jackets, rugby-player legs in officer's pinks, bare female shoulders, Chanel No. 5 from the PX in their armpits, Kleenex-cleansed necks under the touched-up hairlines: "I want you to promise me a job in Subsequent Procedures, darling—or where else should I go when this mess is over and they're all hanged? . . ."

Britons here and there: a Labour MP with a pimp's pompadour over the low furrowed forehead of a morning-gazette reader, surrounded by His Majesty's Own Hampstead Archers: Kitchener mustaches under Semitic noses, ringdove voices, Mayfair accents with a touch of Budapest, Honvéd elegance in khaki: shoulder straps waxed to a mirror shine, discreet little stars on the epaulets. A Foreign Office man: pinstriped suit, striped shirt, striped tie, ascetic scholar's head, boyish hair...

and Frenchmen: roundly shaped, with rattails under their noses, swift mouse eyes.

and Russians: in military tunics with board-like shoulder straps, shorn skulls, muzhik movements...

a Texas parrot shriek: "Aaoouuh! so you're a colonel—don't tell meee!" And whiskey, bourbon, vodka, dry martinis, Bloody Marys, bloody chips, and fucking salted almonds. "Come on, have one more on me!" and a fanfare from beneath: the floor show is surging, the rumba booming. "And now, ladies and gentlemen, our greatest hit, Miss Rachel Shefczuk of the Frankfurt Stork Club in her dance of the seven veils!" Tipped breasts brought into form by uplifted arms, Grete Wiesenthal leaps ending in a split, the white crotch cracks on the dance floor, a Stars and Stripes *reporter snaps flashbulb shots... a look around: journalist mugs in officer's uniforms, Jewish court stenographers, female interpreters, the black-haired girl from the ghetto doesn't seem to be here. Wonder if anything else is happening—but first something to eat...*

The snack bar is on the first floor, the big windows look out on the sidewalk, the room is filled with barrels of lemur food, just help yourself. Hamburgers, cheeseburgers, fuckburgers with mustard, with horseradish, with ketchup, with Tabasco sauce. Beer, tannic Chianti, Coca-Cola, orange juice, grapefruit juice, tomato juice. White bread, black bread, gray bread, milk for teetotalers, apples, pears, oranges, bananas, Japanese dwarf mandarins (canned), Chinese lichee nuts (canned)... Gray blobs in the blackness of the windowpanes: Nurembergers standing outside, staring in, hollow-cheeked, round eyed, wide-mouthed, gaping at this fairy-tale abundance. This can't be real, there's no such thing, this is verre eglomisé. *They stare without expression, without greed, without envy. This is so opulent that it's beyond their grasp. Movie splendor.* The Indian Tomb, The Treasure of the Silver Lake, Ali Baba and the Forty Thieves. *You can look at it and not even dream about it, there's no such thing, you can't believe that so much food can just be sitting there, all you have to do is dive in and stuff your mouth—it's humbug, a daydream . . .*

and every half hour, one of our boys comes along—oh aren't they wonderful—with a helmet and chin strap and chewing gum between his molars, he sticks his machine-gun muzzle into their backs and pushes them away—wiping the blackboard of the windows like a big, wet sponge.

The street is empty. Beyond it, shredded ivy hangs on the tumbledown city walls. Where do they go when they are shooed away from here? Not over there? Not in there, behind that wall? . . .

I've been there, I've ventured fifty or sixty feet into the necropolis of a smashed Nuremberg—and have fled back as though from a plunge into the deep, found refuge for my soul in the sparkling neon lighting of the Grand Hotel Excelsior, with whiskey, bourbon, floor shows, and Texas parrot shrieks . . .

never, not even in my most frightening dreams, have I experienced such solitude, such an abyss of desolation. This is no ruin of a city, this is the negative of the very notion of a city. The existential void par excellence. No, they can't possibly live there, not even a rat could live there now, it would become moonstruck, it would be frightened of ghosts, it would have to see a psychiatrist . . .

in the daytime, it's still bearable (although only just). A rubble field, yes indeed, but what a rubble field. Just let someone try to move freely through such a filthy anachronism: a medieval town of gingerbread houses shattered by high-powered bombs and razed to the very foundation walls. It's almost like a murder in a nursery. Incomprehensible, repulsively brutal. A child's hair and bloody brain-mush sticking to a smashed rocking horse . . .

and crickets are chirping from the steppe grass that has grown out of the crib . . .

you can spend hours here strolling through the brick dust without hearing any sound other than this ghostly summer chirping of crickets, without seeing anything stir. Aside from the ghostly chirping, everything is deathly silent here in Nuremberg's old city. You tower head and shoulders above the fragments of old houses and churches. Beyond the rubble cone that gently slopes up into a hill, the castle still hovers, as though placed there from a box of toys. And at its foot (better: at its roots), a few narrow-chested half-timbered walls remain upright, a quarter of a weary old gable roof hangs askew from a chimney pillar, and timberwork torn from the walls is still supporting half of a doll's room. It is as though in that terrible night when fire and explosives came pouring from the heavens, the tiny Gothic houses of this town tried to flee to the old stronghold to crowd, panicked, under its protection—and the destruction caught up with them before they could get even halfway there. And the ineffable, inconceivable horror ripped them apart, halving them, quartering them, mutilating them . . . Now they stand in shreds, rooted to the spot as if by some dreadful curse . . .

I sat down on the defense wall of the castle, letting my legs dangle, and gazing—gazing. It was a splendid day, a day in early autumn, full of misty light, and the demolished town of Nuremberg lay at my feet, flattened into its ground plan. The picturesque, medievally narrow world of nooks and crannies was vast and empty, topograpically marked off, abstractly drawn in two dimensions, like a blueprint. Only at the root of the castle trunk were those three or four ghosts of gingerbread houses still looming, caught by the spell as they fled . . .

and they set me to thinking: I had already seen them somewhere, once. I knew their contours, sharp as if etched in silverpoint, and this faded coloring, the watercolor in the dusty wall-yellows and old brick-reds of the rubble . . . I had once painfully absorbed all this—but when? where? . . .

When it came to me, it struck me so hard that I almost fell from my airy perch on the wall. They were the same contours, drawn with a hard pencil and sophomorically accurate, the same faded watercolors as the studies that Private First Class Adolf Hitler (at the time, more artistically than politically engaged) had doodled into his sketchbook in France during World War I: shot-up farms in September light... But this cannot be talked about here. Not even with the pretty survivor of the Warsaw Ghetto. This is not the time or place for cultivated salon chitchat. Important things are happening here. History has caught up with itself and is now taking place in the present, is even taking a step into the future. Here, a milestone is being placed in world history, casting a warning shadow into times to come.

Everybody says this to himself three times a day (at lunch in the cafeteria, at cocktails in the bar of the Grand Hotel Excelsior, at the slow waltz shortly after the floor show in the Excelsior souterrain*). Here too we live elevated by the magic of cant. We live in the nimbus of exceptionality. We are witnessing a historic expansion of international law. The Hague Convention of 1926 managed only to condemn war as a crime; it offered no legal sanctions against the perpetrators (much less defined the crime of conspiracy). Here they are now, the conspirators responsible for the last war, sitting as defendants in two fenced-in rows of benches, and we already know how this will end. The milestone in world history will once again be a gallows...*

They seem to know this themselves. They act stoic, sharply watched as they are by helmeted GIs, who, as a token of the solemnity of this historic moment, are wearing white cotton gloves on their dangling butcher paws. And across from them, raised up on a platform, enthroned at a long table, as in da Vinci's Last Supper, *sit their judges:*

in the middle looms OUR LORD JUSTICE Sir Geoffrey Lawrence, visible from the elbows to the head, an isosceles triangle (the acme pointing to God). Christian England, the bulwark of Western Civilization, invented by Dickens in his finest hour:

graying in the dust of files to abstract, patriarchal justice; learnedly sucking a pencil, discreet harrumphs purging the throat, mind, and conscience; and in the sea-blue eyes under the periwig (here set aside) the eternal boyishness of Britain . . .

and to his right and left, the apostles. (Not a zodiac describing twelve but one more than half, namely seven, the number of perfection and the completed action; the judges are arranged not dramatically in four trios, as seasonal constellations, but in the four-times-two-makes-eight of eternity.) At the left of OUR LORD's British colleague, two Frenchmen (their artistic tailor is Daumier) in bat cloaks, vain neck-bands, puffy lawyer-caps: the black brethren of the white cook and the red Communard, gazing with astute Cartesian eyes from behind their thriftily iron-framed glasses, and paper-flower bouquets of éloquence *proliferating from their narrow lips . . .*

and to the right, two Americans, Midwestern senator busts: square-shouldered, square-headed, square-faced, square-minded, craftiness in philistine droning, bull-like aggression in the pettifoggery of Civil Law, world potentates in cast-iron self-righteousness . . .

finally, farther to the right, two Russians in bombastic generals' uniforms belonging to the people (albeit without the full pomp of medals): over blood-red epaulets the size of meat platters, their stubble heads are as immovable as rocks on which the frail fuss and claptrap of the Capitalist Imperialists shatter . . .

one of them sheds an occasional Mongolian grin over a piece of paper, on which he doodles motionlessly. He is drawing caricatures of the people called to the witness stand, and whenever he pulls off an especially good one, he feels a childlike joy . . .

and there, on the witness stand, a man, become emotional in reliving the memory, tells about a mass shooting somewhere in Volhynia. His nerves can't take it, he weeps, although without tears: the sobbing shakes him dry, his shoulders heave, he can barely get the words out. He goes into agonizing detail about another man who was to be shot in a group. The mass grave was already dug, twenty yards by ten, several rows of corpses were already lying in it. And this man had a child at his side, his son, eight years old, a bright little boy—dry sobs, quaking shoulders... OUR LORD JUSTICE soothingly taps a sucked pencil. Would the witness kindly pull himself together and speak more succinctly, the Court's time is limited, this carrion-smelling nightmare is only supposed to take nine months, long enough to give birth to a legal changeling... So the witness pulls himself together and tells about how this child didn't quite understand what was going on, he spoke confidently to his father, but noticed, by the father's—how shall I put it?—absent, abstracted expression that something unusual, something ominous was afoot... the child suddenly became frightened and began to ask what was happening, why were there so many corpses lying in the ditch. And the father caressed his head and spoke calming words to the boy: It's not half so bad, my child, there is almost something good about dying young—And then the rattle of the machine guns or the automatic pistols or whatever they used—The witness can't speak, and OUR LORD JUSTICE clears his throat. This is a private digression, as it were; the witness should confine his testimony to the fact of the shooting alone (if possible with precise data on the number of shooters and victims)—harrumph, yes. The issue here is something more general, that is to say, human rights in the legal sense, i.e., we must accurately establish crimes of such magnitudinous planning and perpetration as to impinge upon international law...

and meanwhile: the voices of the simultaneous interpreters chirp away in four languages like twittering parakeets from the glass cage on the witness stand, secretaries for both prosecution and defense are walking up and down with copies of documents and affidavits for tomorrow and the day after and handing them from one table to another where the testy, frustrated lawyers sit. The court reporters, bored, bang away at their steno machines in a slow-motion estrangement from reality. Defense attorneys scribble away at objections for the day after tomorrow. Prominent guests with earphones in the spectators' section are deeply moved;

they take enjoyment in the drama of what is happening, take enjoyment in themselves, witnesses to an act of World History . . .

I too cannot escape the magical happening in the tiny courtroom. I have to come. These events are too interesting. I must not miss them. So long as I'm here I at least want to get something out of it . . . I've been listed as a witness, true. But I have every reason to doubt that I'll ever be called: I have only one murder to testify about, whereas here they are dealing with hecatombs. Stella's death is a private digression, so to speak, nothing to write home about: here you probably won't be questioned for fewer than ten thousand corpses. (John knew this, must have known it, but it was presumably his last good deed for me: to get me out of the German starvation world and shelter me in opulence among the grave worms.) The great moment will most likely not come: me on the witness stand eye to eye with Göring (after all, he's the one, the bastard)—me, an extra in World History . . . nevertheless, I have to be ready for it, I have to get my hair trimmed every week. After all, you can't enter World Events looking sloppy, with a gigolo's mane. (Plus the dark-haired girl from the Warsaw Ghetto said that long, neglected hair reminds her too much of old times—though wouldn't shaved heads be even worse?) Anyway, it's fun going to the barber. Way over there, in the farthest wing of the courthouse, I know a barbershop for guards—our boys so prim and proper, aren't they an example for everybody? Life in the jungle demands such knowledge. At the Excelsior I would have to spend good vouchers on a haircut, whereas here, for a couple of cigarettes, I can get shorn, shaved, powdered, massaged, and Brylcreemed. With the money I save I can buy the most wonderful things at the PX: nylons, for instance, for which certain girls will do certain things, or else quite simply cans: of corned beef, meat and vegetables, pork and beans: the last seven years have pretty much emaciated everybody, even with the Fräuleins *you're not always at the top of your game . . .*

Besides, the barbershop isn't far from the corridor where the black-haired girl is working on the statistical survey of the victims in the ghetto uprising. You might stick your fragrant and freshly Brylcreemed head in the door and casually ask how things are going (she's shown me the number tattooed on her arm, a barely legible blue spot on the very smooth skin with tender-blue veins; still and all, it's a sign of intimacy, an earnest of a burgeoning human relationship). Perhaps you can offer her the happiness of falling in love with her: Love bade me welcome, *and the dead soul lived again . . .*

perhaps she'll sing you something in Polish, something full of yearning, welling up out of mashed labials. Maybe even something in Yiddish (while my Brylcreem-smooth skull lies in her lap), tender Yiddish songs as in Bessarabia long ago. Di bist sheyn in maine oign, sheyner fin der velt—ikh hob on dir nisht kain khazuren, alles mir gefeit. Meyg zain tserrisn dus neyzale, meygst hubn seykhele vi an eyzele; Di bist sheyn in maine oign, sheyner fin der velt . . . *That would be nice, that would snuff out a lot, that would be balm for my heart, the old shard . . .*

you see, it's under great stress here, my heart. Pastor Kneipp's alternating baths make it pound in my tonsils a good dozen times a day. In the barbershop, for instance, they have a shoeshine boy and clown (as a back-court fool, so to speak, a caricature of all the postwar German lemur traits), a little boy they picked up somewhere: a wild, lice-ridden tatterdemalion, an unspeakably repulsive blob of slime, pesky as a blowfly, leechy as a crab louse, a microbe apprentice, pederastically fingered, pickled in gonococci like an eel in green— you must have seen with what democratic openness this basement rat throws himself at the victors—you must have watched it. It goes like this: The door opens, but not far enough for a chief of the Praetorian Guard. He does not merely enter, he towers his way in. Everyone in the barbershop is awestruck (especially me: I've been subpoenaed as a witness for the prosecution, but still and all, that's just a hairsbreadth away from being a defendant—and here I am, frivolously having my hair pomaded). The Praetorian bulks into the room. His skull is wedged in a helmet polished like plexiglass. A helmet of the avenging angels, it almost bangs against the ceiling. The barbers' razors tremble at the throats of the hygiene-deficient, who, choked by their white towels, peer up at the avenging angel...

and he, the avenging angel, stomps closer in waxed lace-up boots with thick rubber soles. Under his Grail-castle helmet, his kisser floats on the chin strap: T-bone-steak-fed America, sprouting from violent Lithuanian seed in Iowa, Irish madness in the brain, Dutch narrow-mindedness in the blood, Puritanical witch-burning fanaticism in the eyes, chewing gum between the crushing nutcracker jaws. He snorts from his nostrils like a bull of Colchis. His thorax, squeezed upward by a ten-inch-wide motorcyclist belt, is swollen like a barrage balloon over whose tip a truck is accidentally driving. A rubber club dangles from his wrist over the sausage-stuffed white cotton glove...

Yet, the basement rat is not intimidated. It scurries out of its corner and leaps at him, hurls itself at one of his leg columns and embraces it in a perfect tackle—straight out of Yale. A middle linebacker hit like that will shake Congress, will be discussed for decades at the White House... but the avenging angel isn't in the mood today (maybe his Fräulein *gave him a dose of the clap, or a superior chewed him out for having a hint of five o'clock shadow or not having the dewy scent of Mennen). He merely swings out his leg ("Fuck off, you bastard!")—and the rat flies through space with a whine, landing in its corner, crumpling in pain, wrapped up, burrowed up in its rags, and its face peeps up, that blob of slime, and it is the dismayed, deeply frightened face, marked by utter sorrow and utter injustice, of an abused child with huge injured eyes, which comprehend nothing and accuse the incomprehensible—*

and this child says, tonelessly, hopelessly, desperately, in a small, soft, child's voice, "But it's you who taught me to be a smart boy..."

1948, autumn, Munich-Geiselgasteig.

To get the feeling that I live in a dream world, I wouldn't need the junk and the false magic of this movie world: palaces consisting only of façades, rooms with only two walls, singers interrupted in their singing, dropping their arms in the middle of the most theatrical gesture, closing the mouths that had just been snapping at the air as though hunting an invisible fly—while their voices keep right on singing dulcetly in playback until the sound engineer interrupts and spools them back in a whistling monkey jibber for replay... I wouldn't need the suspension of logic in the lapse of time: the film stories narrated back and forth, a mishmash of events, the end filmed first and the beginning at the end. Or the lack of division between fiction and reality: Robinson Crusoe, Madame Dubarry, and Professor Dr. Sigmund Freud all joining me for lunch at my table in the canteen, each of them totally immersed in his part, whereas, in front of the camera, they are embarrassingly the disguised actors Meyer, Müller, and Lembke. Everyday life outside, beyond this world of shadow and folly, is no less a surrealistic dream.

The city of Munich is still lying in its mortar dust under the intact Bavarian postcard sky, with buildings broken out of the streets like teeth from a carious mouth. But the gaps now exert a magical lure. The rubble fields are gilded, they once again have a tangible realty value. New buildings are sure to proliferate shortly: business fortresses, office palaces, tenement barracks, twice, thrice, ten times bigger than the houses and buildings that used to stand here and have sunken into debris, ten times more efficient in their use of space, divided up like honeycombs, yielding ten times more rent, so that new capital is quickly created to tear down whatever still survives on either side and replace it with buildings that grow high, ten times, twenty times bigger, roomier...

All at once, we see department stores bursting with all kinds of wares, snazzy places. I can go in and buy an alligator handbag for Christa, or else a plush doe by Frau Käthe Kruse or the war regalia of a Sioux chief for our little son. I thus woefully redeem my guilty conscience for earning money sumptuously and spending it frivolously, indeed irresponsibly and heedlessly, for not husbanding, and certainly not saving, not gathering, but rather acting as if it were still the worthless old money, the trashy Reichsmark, instead of the sound and weighty Deutschmark with which we must shape our future, with which Germany, Europe, Western Civilization must rebuild from a rubble pile into a new efflorescence, with which we must create a new and this time permanent and definitive economic miracle.

But that's just it. It's all too miraculous for me. Too trusting is my belief in the fairy tale of it. Whatever money I earn runs through my fingers like water; for me it's movie money, dream currency from a dream reality. The very way I earn it is dreamlike and incredible. There's no fathoming what prompts Stoffel and Associates (my "producer piglets," as Christa calls them) to grab up every other, often maliciously ironic thought I come up with in order to create a simply great project, which most likely will never be filmed, but which, thanks to some technical bank and tax manipulations I've not entirely comprehended, will enable them, as producers, to create a different, even greater and more profitable project, and thus to acquire the capital for newer, bigger studios and even newer, technically ever more perfect cameras (the basis for even bigger projects, in which there'll be some pickings for me)...

I watch this chicanery and I imagine that things will keep on like this for me too, bigger and faster and more and more lavish. I place my naive confidence in a mysterious auto-functioning and parthenogenetic self-replication of prosperity. After all, that's what's happening all around me. The grocery stores are bursting with stuff to feed your face with. The hams, the sausages, the pâtés, meat salads, ragouts fins, *the cheeses, the primeurs, the fruits are doubling, tripling, decupling overnight. The shoe-store displays are collapsing under a plethora of shoes; never have there been so many shoes since people stopped going on foot—for hardly anyone walks now; people take cars. You can buy them again; they stand, shinily painted in venomously synthetic candy colors, behind mirror-glass panes at the dealers' showrooms, bigger and bigger, faster and faster, more and more cars . . .*

The miracle took place overnight. It was a new era, altering "reality" no less than that day in March 1938 that cut off the first half of my life and launched the ten-year Ice Age. This time too it's a solstice day, if I remember correctly: a bright day on which the sun stood still in the clear heavens (or never even made an appearance). Yesterday, the world was still a gray, wretched world—and a world of timid hope. Today, at one fell swoop, it was all there, everything you could have hoped for—only hope itself was no longer there; hope had become superfluous. Yesterday, people were skulking through the streets, gray-faced, dourly suffering, but occasionally envisioning utopias—futures that would be different from everything that had previously enslaved us and made us wicked, a human society in which at last, at last, the dichotomy between the individual and the herd animal in us would be harmonized. A fantastic expectation? But why not? All possibilities were open. That was one good thing about the last gray phase of the Ice Age: the total demolition, the annihilation of everything, of all cities, all so-called values, and most thoroughly the state, the social fictions, the image of mankind . . . Yesterday, we were still allowed to dream that we could reinvent everything . . .

that's what it was like yesterday. And then, overnight, everything essentially became what it had been before the Ice and Rubble Age, the same corrupt world, the same world of money—only in a cunningly new, brightly promising, insidiously abstract way.

The same people who were starving yesterday but willing to share a piece of bread were stuffing their guts today and gobbling up their neighbors' food. The same people who were thoughtful yesterday, willing to have certain embarrassing insights, critical more of themselves than of others, forgot all about yesterday—except for the things that gave them an advantage over the others. The same people who were full of ideas and plans yesterday, who sought new forms, new ways of living, wanting to set up kolkhozy for soil-tilling intellectual workers, wanting to exemplify a rediscovered human dignity—those same people now had no trouble resigning themselves to the perfidiously substituted spirit of possibility, were thoroughly imbued with its presentness, offered no resistance to it, were buoyed and borne by it, soon regarded it as a fresh element in which they could swim like trout in mountain water...

For it was a new promise of a long-promised world, a different Thousand-Year Reich—only this time from overseas. This time not primordially and mythically rooted in the dark precincts of a barbaric past but modern, bright, rationalist, and yet blessed with GOD's approval. You made a fool of yourself trying to warn against it, like a lay preacher crying apocalypse. It was a reality stuffed with all the values of Western Civilization. It had every kind of freedom and thus every possibility of human dignity. It was merely a question of choice, of the ability to go without. It resounded with lovely cant about democracy, progress, humanized technology that would serve man and not vice versa, fine phrases about racial equality, ecology, protection of animals... People could go right ahead and build cities again. Why, they were building the one grand City of Mankind: ANTHROPOLIS, the New Jerusalem, which the Bible-versed pioneers had sighted in the Golden West. The star-spangled banner waved over it...

but alas, the construction of this new promised world from the ruins of the old one came about too swiftly for us, too surprisingly, too much like a magic trick: you couldn't help suspecting some sleight of hand. You see, it really did occur in the twinkling of an eye, overnight: yesterday, people had been starving or profiteering, their only survival chances in the black market; today, everyone, without exception or distinction, held forty Deutschmarks in his hand and could buy anything he liked and anything he could afford or whatever his common sense bade or forbade. In any case it was all there in an instant, you could gorge yourself, fatten your body, buy new clothes, furnish your home, rebuild your house, found a business or an entire industry, drink as much champagne, whiskey, beer, wine, Coca-Cola as you liked or could stand; you no longer had to feel like a pariah, a subhuman, gleaning the cigarette butts of Allied occupation soldiers from the asphalt and picking through their garbage cans for no-longer-edibles; you now faced those soldiers on the same level, eye to eye, as it were, or at least gullet to gullet. And all this was extremely implausible, though factually documented reality—implausible, yet not to be denied.

Schwab had come to Munich on behalf of the Northwest German Radio Network (in cooperation with the Bavarian State Radio Network) to put together a nighttime program about the situation of writers in Germany in the first three years after the end of the war. Needless to say, these literati included people writing for the newly emerging film industry—hence, in Schwab's opinion, myself. We taped my contribution. Then came the day of the currency reform. The next day, I went to the cashier's office at the radio network to pick up my fee, which had been agreed upon in Reichsmarks but was given to me in Deutschmarks, five hundred Deutschmarks. Every other inhabitant of the three Western occupation zones had forty marks at his disposal. I was the richest man in the country.

Needless to say, we headed straight for Humpelmeyer's Restaurant. We couldn't get over the menu. We ordered brook trout, saddle of venison in cream with lingonberries, omelet surprise. *We washed it down with two excellent Franconian wines and a bottle of Châteauneuf-du-Pape. At the next table, a man who had eaten his way deep into a roast goose followed our mordant commentary: "It may interest you to know that I am looking for someone to bring charges against parties unknown for mass manslaughter and endangerment of health," he said fervently. "All this stuff"—he pointed his knife and fork at the filled dishes all around—"didn't tumble out of the clear blue sky yesterday. It must have been somewhere; people were hoarding it. For what reason, I ask you, for what purposes? Just go into any drugstore: you'll have no trouble whatsoever finding medicine that you couldn't get for love or money the day before yesterday. Where does it all come from? Something's wrong here. There's some vile swindle involved. Somebody must be doing a gigantic business. But tens of thousands had to starve to death. Mothers had to watch their children die because the same penicillin that you can get at any drugstore today for a couple of pennies couldn't be had for thousands of marks on the black market. We've got to get to the bottom of this."*

We agreed with him and asked why he didn't bring charges himself. He said, "If I did, it would be interpreted politically. I was Gauleiter of Linz for a while."

But it took only a few weeks to dispel any qualms about the new reality. Now it is overwhelmingly present. Like that twelfth of March, 1938, in Vienna, which separated the first half of my life from me, this new reality projects all previous experiences into the realm of dreams. But in this way, detached from the past and having, epiphany-like, virtually turned into its own realized future, this reality is itself becoming unreal.

*Supreme Movie Piglet Stoffel, who demonstrates his patronage by, inter alia, entrusting me with all sorts of missions he considers sensitive and that have nothing to do with my capacity as ideas man and potential screenwriter (he calls them "friendly favors" he "wouldn't ask of anyone else"), has "approached" me with a "request": a girl describing herself as an actress (she's taking lessons with some fluttery mime whose political past has damaged him) is on the cast list of the big new project of Astra Films (*A Woman Plays Foul*—a story of mine). Sure, it's a small part, but you've got to start somewhere, says Stoffel. ("The company has to think about the next generation. Otherwise, five or six years from now, we'll be screwed, our stars'll all be going through menopause.") Actually, the child (just nineteen) is a younger, wilder Astrid von Bürger: a dark-curled Brunhilde beauty, yet slender and firm. (I suspect it's not just a cinematic future Stoffel sees in her.) But,* *unfortunately, she's "strange," as Stoffel puts it. "Talk to the kid. I'd like to know what's with her. She's not off her rocker, but she's very weird. You'll notice it right away."*

After a dinner in Boettner's Oyster Rooms (three dozen Limfjord Colossal, with Chablis, black bread and cheddar cheese, then a two-inch-thick filet steak, a carafe of Chambertin, melon sherbet; six weeks ago, they served rationed herring paste and cabbage stew here), she reveals her secret. Her real name is Ernestine (Ernie) Rosenzweig (stage name: Gudrun Karst). Her father, pure Aryan despite the suspicious name, was a traveling salesman in the lovely land of Franconia, the Romantic Road. He was killed by some drunken rowdies (SA) owing to a misunderstanding caused by the unfortunate name. Fearing lest her daughter should fall victim to the same misunderstanding (the family lived in Dinkelsbühl), the mother put little Ernie into a Nazi nursery at the age of three. At fifteen she had a general's rank as leader in the League of German Maidens. At sixteen (1945) she was commanding a League of German Maidens camp in Allgäu, five thousand feet above sea level, three hundred and sixteen fourteen- to eighteen-year-olds who were being trained in close combat and the use of bazookas. She says she would have been willing to fight with a razor. Had anyone dared to tell her to her face that the war could not be won, the Russians were in Berlin, the English and the Americans outside Frankfurt and Hanover, she would have scratched out his eyes and torn his throat out with her teeth. But no one dared. Then next thing she knew there came a regiment of Moroccan spahis who, man for man, screwed their way through every last girl in the Maiden League.

Then Ernie wound up a lieutenant's prize. He was friendly to her and promised her a career as a nightclub dancer once the nonfraternization rules loosened up a bit. She can't remember how she lost him (or he her). At any rate, she got to Munich, using some food from the ravitaillement *of the French occupation to find shelter in a family rooming house run by an old-time screen star, Erna Morena. Having the same Christian name won the lady's maternal sympathy. Through her, she gained entry into the movie world. "But you can understand," she says, "that I usually feel as if I were in an aquarium, where things, people, and events swim every which way, like tenches."*

She is the right partner for me. (Christa obstinately refuses to leave Hamburg; and after our son's birth, she bluntly declared that she found conjugal duties more repulsive than pleasurable. But that shouldn't serve as a pretext for me; I promptly filled the gap in the mosaic of my sensual life.) In Gudrun Karst, I have found my spiritual complement. Together we swim through the aquarium of tenches.

I make sure that the underwater fauna surrounding her is tropically varied. I've rented a place for her with a countess to whom I had access by way of Christa's relatives. There, Gudrun is getting to know all of Bavarian nobility and the (likewise Catholic) Upper Silesian nobility who have fled here. She already shrugs scornfully at the mention of names from the odd years of the Almanach de Gotha.

I am wheeling and dealing to have her elected this year's Mardi Gras princess (it promises to be a scream). At the Astra Art Films ball, which will greatly overshadow that of Gloria Films, she cannot as yet play the starring role. This part is automatically awarded to Astrid von Bürger as a former Ufa star and Stoffel's spouse. But Gudrun Karst will lead the Pleiades, the group of seven up-and-coming starlets to be introduced to the public and the press. Bele Bachem is already designing the costumes with Bessie Becker.

The press (which is having a tremendous upswing in the new reality) is starting to get seriously interested in Gudrun Karst. To give her the status of a working student, I have registered her at the university (as a psychology and sociology major). Every morning when she is not shooting, I send her to school in a horse-drawn carriage (the last hackney cab in Munich). We have lunch at the Four Seasons, which is also the seat of the Montgolfier Club, an association of hot-air balloonists that Gudrun wishes to bring to life. In the evening, she plays Anouilh and Claudel under Schweikart's direction.

At night, in the rococo bed of the merely half-bombed-out home of the countess (I told her I have unfortunately drifted away from Christa—all too Protestant, alas—over questions of faith), I give Gudrun's mind the finishing touches. I explain the eschatological character of the time we are living through: the messianic promise of Americanism, the paradise of smart boys on earth that comes before doomsday. I tell her about the effect of atomic bombs and how the dollar got its name from the Thaler, *which in turn got its name from Joachimsthal, where uranium was first discovered in pitchblende. We chat about the German women who, like Scarlett O'Hara (like Christa), swore they would never go hungry again, and about the hazardous childhood of their sons, who, in the midst of bombings, gleaned pieces of fallen coal on railroad embankments from under passing freight trains; and about the later offspring, who are children today and whose every wish we fulfill (like me with my little boy) before they so much as sense the wish themselves.*

Even our erotic relationship has a spiritual element. When her senses gain the upper hand, I have her re-experience the spahis, man for man. She now quite regularly confesses to me when and under what special circumstances and conditions she felt desire against her will. Then, released and sobbing, she drifts off in my arms.

And all this for the sake of Astra Art Films and their reality.

Verily, I say unto you: The future lies in abstraction.

7

Such and similar things, my dear Mr. Brodny, stand between me and the image of the old Yurop, in which the other half of my life is lost, and are the reason I can't tell you the plot of my book in three sentences. The story proliferates with no help from me, quite on its own, in parthenogenetic self-propagation under my hands. Whatever I narrate breeds more narrative. Every tale hatches ten others: a hybrid cell growth that cannot be controlled by any form.

Around this and little else revolved my endless conversations with Schwab. Paris, city of dreams, gave us ample occasion to speak of it. Everything steered us to that cancerous proliferation. For instance (in connection with the definitive, I might almost say irredeemable, formed nature of the French): the curious fact that in our hemisphere one could obviously now create any number of fatherlands (along with Zaire, Uganda, and similar exotic ones elsewhere, there are now two in the German-speaking world alone, and with Austria and German-speaking Switzerland it would make four), but no new people, no new nation; while at the same time, you have the identity loss of most European nations and the sclerosis of the French.

Thus development of form as an evolutionary stage that has been outgrown, as Professor Leblanc maintains—but it would be too much trouble now to formally introduce the great physician and researcher; let's save that for later. Anyway, his views are not interesting in and of themselves but rather above all in regard to the situation in which he developed them—namely, at Gaia's deathbed, two years ago, during one of our hectic and boisterous chats, when my brave beloved, the chocolate-brown Princess Jahovary, laughing once again—(laughing with dreadful exaggeration, intoxicated in her more and more extravagant decay: all thirty-two horse-healthy mulatto teeth seemed to leap from her mouth, the lips could barely restrain them, the violet hue they had assumed in the past few weeks turned pale under the tension, like overly taut rubber bands—oh Lord! how often, how ardently, how voluptuously and pleasurably had I kissed them when they were still oxblood-red, those sucking soaking stamp-pad lips melting creamy-mild under mine! How tenderly I had marveled at them with my worshipful dwarf-gaze, my Lilliputian fingertips lusting for exploration, the hopping troll of my tongue running over the beeswax-warm mahogany of her cheek hills and slipping into the rococo pits of the corners of her mouth. There, with her fleshiness, voluptuously notched like a fruit bursting in sweet overripeness, the thread-fine bright line—the blemish of mixed blood—sprang forth;

as at the opening of the rock snail's shell, it accompanied her luxuriously curving contour, and there, where the soft, moist double hump of the lower lip, almost lascivious in its swelling, was delicately cocked over the chin recess, it was swallowed by deep cocoa tones covered with a down as delicate as mold... Oh Lord! to what foolish extremes did I not go in order to make them burst into a smile, those fat Negro lips, and to watch them rolling from the ivory of the teeth, brightly shining like hard-boiled egg white until, at the salmon-colored arcades of the gums, the ivory turned yellow, like translucent yolk, turned yellow into primordial cannibal strength which was now so protrudingly bared, so bitingly exposed... Ahh! but I loved her sword-swallowing, fire-eating laugh, I loved *nature* in it, crude, unadulterated nature, loved the laryngological glimpse into the yawning monster-throat, that multivaulted, hortensia-hued grotto, that lilacky Bomarzo, the art nouveau arches of pale-lilac lip-flesh, the Gaudí cornices of pale-pink gums, the purple cupola of the palate over the dragon's hump of the tongue, which knotted forward out of the rosy-fleshed gate of hell of the esophageal muscle with the bud-like flesh stalactite of the uvula—all this still ineffably fresh and clean, just scoured by surf on palm-fanned spice beaches, still incredibly healthy, full of animal vitality despite her lamentable condition; only, because she was emaciated, her face a skull, it now looked as if she had eaten her own tonsils and was offering them for one last inspection, awaiting an official go-ahead before swallowing them down. Oh, dear God, her torso was all skin and bones now, and I did not care to picture what she looked like farther below; but when she, half rising up, half sinking into the pillows, let her skeletal trunk, covered with a skin like saddle leather, rise out of her billowy nightgown, as frightening as one of the nightmare figures in Picasso's *Guernica*, and when she laughed and laughed, she really did look like a dying horse, a drowning horse, and I thought, She wants to carry them to shore, she wants to rescue them beyond death, these lovely, flawless teeth—and what a pity it was!...)—when she, laughing once again, complained, "*J'comprends jamais c'qu'il veut dire, cet ours—croyez-vous que c'est de ma faute?*" then Professor Leblanc, in the usual Cartesian crystal-clear way, developed his pertinent ideas. Bold, not only because they were articulated at the bedside of a cancer patient but of course especially piquant for that very reason: cancer as a universal phenomenon of the age; the inability to preserve form; hybrid growth of everything and everyone in accordance with the physicist's modern view of the world: the cosmos as a monstrous explosion. Form as antinature, in a word.

At any rate, it's an awful pity that Schwab died so early—I mean, alas, too early to hear my naive findings in this area being confirmed by a scholar of Leblanc's rank. I will not forget the pain around his mouth when once, on a similar occasion, he quoted Valéry's "*trouver avant de chercher*" (and I brutally remised, FOR UNTO EVERY ONE THAT HATH SHALL BE GIVEN . . . BUT FROM HIM THAT HATH NOT SHALL BE TAKEN AWAY THAT WHICH HE HATH . . . But all this later, later! . . .).

8

Meanwhile, you can glean from the foregoing, esteemed Mr. Brodny, how the dialogue with my dead friend continues. I mean how difficult—nay, impossible—it is for me to eliminate him from my thinking (so that in the end, you step up to take his place). Which, however, leads—on my part—to an unintentional, yet unavoidable, unbridled hybrid proliferation of everything I would like to narrate. Indeed, as you will hear, this was the dilemma of my book, which, thanks to an enlightening idea that occurred to me a few days ago on the road from Reims to Paris, was to become its theme. (After all, writing always means making virtues of necessity.)

For example, I just cannot do without Schwab when, as living proof of my (and Professor Leblanc's) views on the relationship between a people (as form) and individual character, I cite the handsome Pole, whom S., for some enigmatic reason, so violently hated (I surmise homoerotic impulses at the sight of the fellow's dreadfully muscular arms).

I am talking about the man who plays night clerk in this lousy hotel—he's probably perched down there now, at his desk, in front of the switchboard in the Rembrandtian light-space-darkness (a well-turned phrase devised especially for Schwab, which together with my superficial pretense to cultivation in describing such a trivial object would have been a tasty morsel of annoyance for him!), perched there in the meagerly shaded beam of the tiny night lamp, so deeply absorbed in one of his idiotic detective pulps that he does not hear the telephone...

well, this outstanding male, who looks like a holy dragon killer on a counterfeit icon—I mean, he's much too handsome, much too lewdly holy, with his egg-shaped face beyolked by archangel-golden curls, with black almond eyes and a straw whisk mustache (plus his ever-bared butcher arms)—this hormone-flaunting popinjay, I tell you, has obviously changed since he became a French citizen. You see, he wasn't naturalized during Schwab's lifetime (i.e., before five years ago). Back then, he was stateless, like me, but no one could doubt that he felt Polish, was Polish, and would always remain Polish—whatever that might do to a person. It was awe-inspiring. When he took my passport upon my first arrival here, he scrutinized the dubious document ("Alien's Passport of the Federal Republic of Germany... The bearer of this passport does not possess German citizenship"), then scrutinized me with undisguised disapproval (as though I had neglected to wipe my shoes on the mat when entering), and said insolently, "*En voici un autre!*"—as if he had had enough of this sort. And it was only upon my venomous question "*Quelque chose ne va pas?*" that he explained himself: "*Vous êtes apatride.*"

"What's his problem?" asked Schwab, who had come with me from his hotel on the Left Bank (he was his old self again, of course, namely drunk, and held his head, slack mouth half open, so far back that the eyelids had tilted over his carp-gaze behind the thick glasses, like the lids on a baby doll placed on its back; he looked as if he were asleep standing; nobody would have guessed that he was listening to my dialogue with the archangel by the key hooks).

"He's delighted that I'm stateless. '*Apatride*,' it's called in French,"

I said. "He probably thinks it's something mythological. A race that devours its children."

"*Ce n'est pas commode*," said the mustachioed angel-head over the rower's thorax. "*D'ailleurs, je le suis aussi, moi . . .*"

"What's that dialect he's speaking?" asked Schwab, his head raised toward the ceiling, like a blind seer.

"Not a dialect, an accent. Some Slavic snail's dish of labials and sibilants." "*Vous êtes polonais d'origine?*" I asked the holy athlete.

"*Oui, monsieur!*" he said, growing a foot taller: male beauty from a pulp romance, the far too short sleeves of his cotton T-shirt (Americans, as you ought to know, J. G., wear this as an undershirt) constricting his muscle-packed arms.

"There you have it," I said to Schwab. "Shove a national air pump up a man's asshole and see how it puffs out his chest. Enviable, eh? At least *one* thing is certain."

"Yes," said Schwab up to the ceiling (he was already having a hard time speaking). "The self-certainty of the stupid."

But it's really not so simple, I think. The issues require our careful attention. For instance (I still see this anthropologically, in terms of a people as a form), the relationship between aggression and form. Take the handsome Pole. Having ceased to be a Pole and become a French citizen (thus arriving in the refuse heap of the nationalized non-French, all those *bicots* and *pieds noirs* and so forth), he no longer swells up half so awe-inspiringly. Something gave him a fine pinprick; he no longer holds air. The perfect egg-shape of his apostle's head has become an angel hair-framed zero with a yellow mustache—a nothing, a child's drawing on a clouded windowpane; you can wipe it away with your hand. Honestly, I believe I could beat the hell out of him now. I could punch him straight in the mustachioed egg, *un direct en pleine gueule*, without having to fear his butcher-arms.

What's happened to him? He's lost his form and with it his self-assurance. Yet not his stupidity. Has he grown smarter as a Frenchman? Or by doubting whether he is really French and not still Polish? Are we, Yankel G. Brodny (*à propos*, what does the *G* stand for?

George? Gilbert? Ganef? or ultimately even Goy?), are you and I so unpleasantly smart because we are nothing and everything, because our heads hum with doubts as to what we truly are and where we belong? Have we in the course of one lifetime achieved something that took Signor Lombroso at least two generations to reach—genius (and madness)—by migrating and settling in a new environment? How is it in America, where such migrations are the rule? A people that originated with immigrants? Madness galore; and where is genius?...

But I'm already playing the Roman candle again, as Schwab ironically put it. I'm pulling your leg, sir. Still and all, you have to admit, it's an extraordinarily piquant theme: the sublime interrelationship between stupidity and form. The interrelationship between stupidity and self-certainty is far too obvious.

There's nothing interesting in the question of whether stupidity grants one certainty, but rather in its converse: does certainty make you stupid? (Is French self-certainty a sign that French intelligence is biologically a form of stupidity? The seal of a lethal factor?) And what about religious certainty? The assurance of a spiritual vanishing point that keeps the chaotic world in a manageable perspective? Or an intuitive certainty, a turn toward the feminine, as it were—female self-certainty, I'd say, is a form of intelligence more safe and secure in the lap of Mother Nature, more in harmony, in a sort of clinch with this dangerous lady. Madame, for example: the boss and owner of this hotel, the handsome Pole's employer.

9

Even while Schwab was alive, Madame played a key role in my reflections: the Platonic ideal of Frenchness, the image incarnate of the French Idea. Accordingly, Madame's self-certainty—for she is French in this especially—also has flagrantly physical causes: Madame was a beauty queen, Miss Nice of 1939, clearly a vintage that ages well.

Had I, dear Yankel Gilbert, earmarked you for the privilege of seeing Madame *à poil*, such as was granted Schwab and myself on one of those days five years ago—Oh, not amorously in a merry threesome, alas, but only with an indiscreet glimpse from an open window across a rather narrow airshaft into another window that likewise happened to be open. In the room beyond, Madame was stretching in front of the mirror in the wardrobe door, surveying her gorgeous nudity—oh, God! She too, I grant you, seemed to find the sight satisfying. She threw out her chest—and man, what a chest! Keeping her head high, with her henna-hair monster (known as a *boudin* hereabouts) at the back of her neck, and casting a proud look over her splendidly round shoulder at herself in the mirror, she propped her hand on her tightened waist over her plump behind—true bliss, that behind: her torso with its twin bounty of breasts fit into her hips like a wedge in a heart-shaped socle (Brancusi, Modigliani, art deco galore). And then did a tango step with a half twist in the mirror... then turned toward us full face—man!—and saw us, saw us in the window facing hers, saw us drooling, gasping, our eyes leaden-gray with lust, *les deux chleux*, the prematurely senile men watching Susannah bathing (I adapted the scene for one of my best movie scripts)... She fled from our field of vision and, invisible now and quite explicitly disgruntled, furiously slammed her window shut... I tell you, had I, in creative generosity, granted you too this feast for the eyes (but that wouldn't do: even we must obey certain laws), you would understand what I mean by the incarnation of the French Idea. This peony plumpness, this stretching sumptuousness—"as slim as a scepter and as mighty as a throne"—that's what their cathedrals are like: the black-haired aristocrat of Amiens, the ripe blond beauty of Madame de Chartres, the redhead of Reims with the jewels on her white skin, the arrogant patrician of Bourges, the incomparably elegant grace of the brunette of Coutances, the apple freshness of the Norman in a peasant girl's costume, the nixie Honfleur... and that's what their women are like: artworks with which a nation pays tribute to itself, in Delacroix, Ingres, Renoir, Maillol. And in Madame's case this was of special ripeness, man! Even rounder, even plumper, even tastier—plus the hard lithographic colors of Toulouse-Lautrec. You, being a connoisseur of women (I've pegged you), must know what I'm talking about: "*Vecchia gallina fa buon brodo,*" say your friends the witty Tuscans. *Madonna mia santa, che paio di poppe!* Does the handsome Pole get to play with them after hours? In German you could make a pun of it: Pole Poppenspeeler—who's that by, anyway? Theodor Storm, yes indeed. Nobody reads him anymore. Schwab—yes, Schwab loved Storm. Reread him regularly. Of course, he also loved Delacroix, Ingres, Renoir, Maillol, and all that crowd. A fount of culture—Schwab, I mean. An alcoholic too, alas. But the two often go hand in hand: a disturbed ego and an artistic sensibility. What do you think? Is he finally self-certain, my brother Schwab? Certain of himself in a definitive blissful state of stupidity, in a triumphal one-upmanship, over there, or up there—somewhere in the icy blue of the sky, in his Godly Fatherland, never to be lost again?...

But this is quite uninteresting. Back to Madame—the more edifying subject, God knows! Madame is, for me, France, even as France, for me, preserves the stylistic essence of the lost half of my life: erotically determined by the anima of the ripe woman. Don't be led astray by the ephebes of the fashion magazines. Those are ephemeral phenomena, fashions, reflections of the era. In its stony roots, France is still Motherland. A tiny Oedipal land of milk and honey, especially in Mama's severity... And now I want to tell you something that should make your eyes go round with amazement like Schwab's when I nattered on to him about my adventures hereabouts. So just listen closely now:

That Madame is of sovereign intelligence is something I need not emphasize: Madame is French. She displays this in the ineffably scornful hardness with which she keeps this crummy joint afloat. (Madame's *établissement*, called Hôtel Épicure without false modesty, is frequented, thanks to its half-peripheral, half-central location, by a very special kind of human refuse, a bourgeoisie of the marooned, so to speak, who have found a status of their own and even something like a special dignity in being failures, losers, hopeless beginners from the start. And they jealously preserve that status and dignity. Perhaps you know this genre from the petit bourgeois neighborhoods of

Warsaw or Budapest. Professions like that of a traveling salesman in colored fountain pens for first-graders; retired tax officials who become provincial tax advisers; unemployed theatrical hairdressers; an Algerian silversmith's family, eight or nine generations altogether, with a passion for sunflower seeds; on occasion a freestyle-wrestling manager with his warriors, "Haarmin Vichtonen the Finnish World Champion," "Costa Popovitch the Bulgarian Buffalo"; now and then, one of the old whores who have wafted around the place des Ternes like autumn leaves and whose ultimate lure is despair.)

Madame applies to everyone the cold neutrality of that ironclad law which says there's nothing free in life except death—and even death costs you your life. In pecuniary matters, Madame's severity has something sacerdotal about it. She is absolutely unyielding with dilatory debtors (including me, and I've managed to get credit at German post offices!) even if the poor devil, begging in vain for just a little more time, is losing his last chance for the business deal that will save him, or the toothless prostitute is losing her last client.

But then it may happen that Madame unexpectedly issues a merciful verdict, maintaining a desperate person in his desperation, pickling and preserving him in his hopelessness—as if to show the others, who believe they might escape their fate, that *their* fate is ineluctable. And in a miraculous way, these latter, floating belly-up and wriggling only every now and again, reflexively, are aroused by Madame's hardness to writhing life—like a pailful of whitefish that you dump back into the creek because they're not worth frying. They get together and bitch. Among Frenchmen, this is an act of communion—the only one they have left. There's no other way for them to find human contact with one another. By bitching, they fuse into a community, a community of select quality: Frenchmen.

This makes Madame's *établissement* an out-and-out national shrine. Every day, a handful of her clients get together and bitch in the furiously chopped-up cackling of French *éloquence*, in rising and falling and again rising and falling chains of words, tinkling without start or stop, like Czerny piano exercises. They bitch about Madame and about her inhuman unyieldingness, her shameless bamboozling and penny-pinching. Naturally, they also bitch about the defects of the hotel, the lousy beds and the rarely changed linen, the lack of service; aside from the night clerk, who never hears the telephone, there are a few cleaning women, mild loonies or alumnae of penal or drying-out institutions, who show up in the morning to do something or other with brooms, pails, and mops: that's the whole staff. This frightful French eloquence sweeps them up in its wake. Madame's clients even bitch at the disturbance caused by these more illusory than effective cleaning measures. They bitch at the universal mismanagement, politics, the world situation, existence, creation, God the Creator, and His Only Begotten Son, little *Jésu*. And lo and behold, their words visibly blossom. They want to say what they have to say in a better manner, and they always do say it better and better. Like strings of pearls their sentences intertwine and intertwist into arabesques, from which leaves break out and buds open up in resplendent, sensual fullness. The glory of language proliferates among them, a glassy rosebush, enclasping and fettering them, beguiling and bewitching them with its fragrance. They themselves grow into it, become part of it, like the human figures in the ensnarled illuminated initials in a medieval Bible: iterated and reiterated, their heads peep out of the rosebush's tangles, and its blossoms spring out of their mouths. And each of these blossoms is ennobled by literary usage, has at some point flowed into a sublime pen, has been purged by it, polished and artfully mounted to be presented to the Nation as a jewel for its treasury.

The speakers sound as if they know this and are proudly aware *that* they are quoting and *whom* they are quoting, and as if they are honoring the quoted by quoting him. Thereby and therewith, they themselves become taller, tauter, more dignified—*oui, on rouspète, mais on rouspète sur un niveau très élevé*... Their bitching has long since lost the hatefulness of anything personal. It sovereignly detaches itself, has turned into pure form, into Truth and Art. And thereby and therewith, they too, the bitchers, detach themselves from one another, become more and more impersonal, more and more formal, more and more stylized, more and more French.

There they stand, clustered in Callot grouplets on the dark landings or in the narrow, shabby stairwell corridors of the Hôtel Épicure, a third-class hostel for the homeless in one of those bog-like, stagnating corners of the city, whose maelstrom dumps out its slops here: a handful of castaways and failures, washed out by weather and life, wearing the rags of long-past prosperity, which was probably never theirs, the tatters of long-past fashions, hung with the improvised and converted implements of solitary existence, the seat-cane umbrellas, thermoses, the multifarious pouches and pockets: each man a Robinson Crusoe in the frightful desolation of the metropolis, Paris, isle of the marooned . . . For a few minutes, language has broken open the crusts of their isolation. They can speak with one another, communicate with one another. And now, this same language, in its refinement and perfection, is tearing them away from one another, pulling them apart in the same powerful flight that brought them together: the plunge and upswing of two hyperbolas arching toward, and then away from, one another.

And yet, among these castaways into, and castoffs from, life, something wonderful has happened—something that solidifies, edifies, and elevates them. The riffraff have become Frenchmen, self-certain children of the Nation until old age, worthily wrapped in the bunting of cant, swathed in it like mummies, isolated to a compulsively neurotic degree, stiff and proud. Proud of forming, along with millions of other isolated beings, the collective that bears the sublime name of *La Nation Française* and that, in an abstract yet effective way, gives their individual existence a dimension in which it is invulnerable, ordered, tested, and gloriously transfigured for all time, as pitiful as it may be in and of itself. Each individual is a choice blue-white-and-red morsel in the aspic of their National Culture (an image that would not have failed to arouse an involuntary snort from Schwab).

Like the crest of a municipal coat of arms—Marianne's Phrygian cap—Madame's burning red *boudin* hovers above all this. Below, in the white field: the blue shadows of her eyelids and the harsh lipstick of her Toulouse-Lautrec mouth. Man! . . .

Schwab was the first to pay his respects to the high rank of her intellect; this, in recognition of her keen discernment that he was a man of quality, even though the two of them never managed to exchange a word beyond a conventional "*Bonjour, madame*" and an icy "*Bonjour, m'sieur*" (the rest of Schwab's French vocabulary, including the singing of "*Allongs angfanz della patrieyeh,*" never found employment).

To be sure, he had every reason for thankful wonder at how sovereignly Madame ignored his drunkenness. Which is to say: she understood it. Once, after accompanying me here, when we were about to say good-bye at the entrance, he slipped out of my energetically supportive hand. Through the glass panes, he had spied the rubber tree in the vestibule and imagined he was inside and the plant outside. So he splintered through the door and staggered toward the tub unbuttoning his fly. Whereupon Madame said a brief word to the handsome Pole, who came from behind the desk, grabbed a chair, and shoved it (to my great surprise; I was just about to come to Schwab's defense) into the hollows at the back of S.'s knees. When S. crashed down on the chair, the Pole swiftly left, then returned with a bottle of calvados and a glass, which he filled and handed to S. Incidentally, Schwab's reaction was no less sensitive. He did not with gross familiarity raise a toast to Madame, as any other drunkard would have done. No, indeed. Schwab tipped the glass very elegantly and skillfully over his projecting lower lip, handed it back to the handsome Pole, rose to his feet, peered around, looked into the corner of the vestibule, spotted a broom placed there by the charwomen in preparation for the morning cleanup (it was well after midnight), grabbed the broom, and presented it to Madame, as he had learned to do in the army—ah! after a fashion, though not much of one, the hopeless Pfc. Dogface, four-eyes, the screwed-up, fucked-up intellectual—presented the broom, skewily, awkwardly, touchingly, and managed to blurt out, "*Madame . . . le boche . . . présente les armes . . . à vous . . .*" Sheer agony was glazed in his eyes.

I do not expect you to show emotion, Jacob G. I mention this minor incident simply to give you as graphic a picture as possible of Madame.

Rhetoric—especially national rhetoric!—creates reality, after all, creates its own flesh, which in turn creates its own mind. As for myself, I could prolong the list of unusual and intelligent things that Madame did in these years, starting with her surprising sympathy for Dawn, for the progressive abstraction afflicting the Daughter of the American Revolution, and the resolute way she took the soon batty girl into her maternal custody and ultimately into her arch-feminine, anti-male protection against me. ("But she must know that I'm ready to do anything for Dawn," I complained. And Schwab replied, "Yes. That's just it." "What?" I asked, obtusely. And S., "You're playing Ariosto. You're leading her into the Valley of the Moon, where they keep the time that is wasted in dreams. Madame realizes it. And that's what she wants to shield Dawn from.") But the list of Madame's wise and wonderful deeds would be incomplete if I neglected to mention that every so often, even now, she leaves her window open—of course, without standing naked at her mirror, but for occasional little glimpses of her physical merits all the same. As though she knew what delicious morsels are prepared from such inspirations in a writer's alchemical kitchen.

Back then, after our ignominious exposure as juicy voyeurs, leaden with lust for her gorgeous nakedness, Madame outdid herself and all expectations of her: like Bonaparte she crowned herself with her own hands...

I am speaking about her majestic assurance the next day, when returning our artificially unselfconscious salutes. Schwab had come over from the Left Bank to pick me up. As he came through the door, I arrived at the bottom of the stairs in the vestibule. Madame, as usual, was enthroned behind the desk, in front of the key hooks. (There is, as I have said, no clerk during the day; when the handsome Pole is off in some corner snoring out his fatigue after performing his multifarious duties, Madame receives and bullies her guests herself.) Both Schwab and I said, "*Bonjour, madame!*" at about the same time, and she replied with her icy "*Bonjour, m'sieurs!*" watching as we greeted one another. Her gaze was so clear and forthright that we realized she knew what made us boyishly self-conscious and, under her basilisk eyes, almost embarrassed. Namely, that the sight of her yesterday, her female body eavesdropped upon and lecherously felt and fingered by our desire and secretly enjoyed, had been an erotic catalyst, causing the essential core to emerge from the delicate saturated state of the friendship between S. and myself. As though in our shared lust for her we had in an abstract way consummated our wedding.

10

You shouldn't find anything strange, Mr. America, in my confessing these intimate events to you. The consensus, I know, is that Anglo-Saxons are easy to shock in erotic matters. The least protrusion of intimacy will elicit embarrassment—profound reddening of the face and rapid blinking of the eyes. But let me tell you this is true only of the social strata my paternal friend and patron John referred to as the "bloody fucking middle classes." Strata less caught up in their own shittiness appreciate candor (*désinvolture*, which Schwab used to talk about so much; tell me your ideals and I'll tell you what you're lacking).

John (later Sir John, after displaying a great deal of ambivalence at the Nuremberg trials and then being cold-storaged as His Britannic Majesty's ambassador in Manila, where he is probably still stranded today, God rest his soul! . . . but at that time, in our Nuremberg days, and before that in Vienna, simply the Right Honourable John William Robert Derek Russell Quincey Fogg)—well, John gave me an impressive object lesson in elegant unabashment. In regard to his deceased spouse Stella, for instance, with whom I, at nineteen, had maintained amorous relations, which I strove to conceal from him at any price, he expressed himself as follows: "An excellent poke, indeed, a most exquisite fuck—didn't you think so? Poor girl, what a shame she had to die so soon—though she too would today be fairly close to her forties. And you know, they don't age very well, those Bedouin Jewesses; they become skinny and grow mustaches—oh come on, you wouldn't roll her as eagerly now as you did back then, would you?"

Probably not. Though I had sworn back then I would always do it with her until the last breath I drew, with her alone, and never, no never, with anyone else. Stella was the first of my great, final, only, real and true loves, the latest for the moment having been Gaia, the black Princess Jahovary. To complete the list: Christa, my wife for a time; Dawn, the dervish; before, afterwards, and again and again in between: Nadine, the international star...

But Stella was actually more, was different, was more powerful, more divinely generous than any other woman after her. Christa, for instance (an experiment with inadequate means on an unsuitable object, to put it in legalese; to be a legitimate wife in an unconstrained legal position was ultimately the only demand she made on me). Or later, Dawn (likewise, an enterprise doomed from the start, albeit with more poetic, more hazardous, more insane, quixotic traits). Yes, even Gaia (sumptuous fulfillment unto death). And in between, before Dawn even, long before Gaia, and since then over and over again in almost dipsomaniacal repetition, Nadine: when I'm totally confused, estranged from myself, tangled up in hopeless movie projects, incapable of taking refuge in my book (the other act of insanity), close to the worst of despairs, apathy, when all my fuses have blown and my pity for her—for myself—becomes so ardent that it kindles a sort of passion in me... well, I don't want to exaggerate; a repeated flash in the pan, as Christa would have put it, and swiftly gone, granted: *tout de même*...

Stella was reality. She was the day. I wish I could have explained it to John—but what for? Besides, he probably knew anyway. He always knew more (true to the traditions of perfidious Albion) than he admitted or even hinted at. In every way, at every closer look, he was surprisingly denser, richer in dimension, and of course more inscrutable. (My ludicrous feelings of guilt toward him back then! The poignant conflicts with my boyish honor, despite Stella's semi-amused, semi-annoyed laughter, her impatient shrugging when I persisted... "*C'est jeune et ça ne sait pas*," Gaia would have said.)

Needless to say, I also loved him back then, and naturally John knew that too, as he knew everything else. Just as Stella knew that he knew everything and hence this too. It was a game I did not want to join, I was quite simply and foolishly young—and that means barbaric. I did not catch the essence of the situation. As a good philistine, I merely saw the scandalous surface: an elegant woman keeping a nineteen-year-old lover with her husband's sufferance. And since, according to convention, I was the most despicable of the partners, the gigolo, I refused to admit that our unconventional relations were lifted, so to speak, to an elevated moral plane by honest, noble, even passionate feelings. Hence, John was not a cuckold, Stella not Messalina, I not a kept stud but rather the love object of two beautiful souls, an ideal son and thereby a lucky fellow...

And I certainly didn't see what John and Stella presumably cared about most: *style*. The neat arrangement, the elegant and civilized behavior that puts such a triangle—forget about the feelings—beyond banality: art deco, lived, loved, lauded... Back then, in the lost first half of my life, even such matters had their form.

To say this to John later, in Nuremberg, where he was preoccupied with his poetic deed of madness in presenting to an astonished world Stella's death as a sacrifice of love, to make him somehow understand that now I finally knew how delicately we had danced, all the way to the threshold of the Third Reich, in step with the music of a cherished zeitgeist—well, my efforts would have been superfluous if not embarrassing. A characteristic of being German, he used to say, is to emphasize the obvious... And besides, how long ago it all was, faded, vanished, buried by the dust of the many, many years we have lived through since then!...

Only one other of my great, uniquely true, and final loves—told here for the sake of completeness—might possibly be compared to my love for Stella, I mean in the wealth of experience, in the grateful bliss with which I felt and practiced and ultimately buried it within myself as an undying memory, as the pretty expression goes. (Incidentally, it was for the longest time the only love without toil or suffering, the only love that poured out of me without being performed, without cerebral or—if you will—psychoanalytic help, without the Sisyphean labor of loving; the only love that flowed from me with the undemanding naturalness of a forest wellspring, watering my spirit as it bloomed.) My bliss lasted for fourteen years (a magic number for me in many ways: two times the evil seven makes a good number). But needless to say I destroyed this love—indeed, out of the need to achieve; out of an industrious desire to love.

It is a dramatic story, which I jotted down somewhere and then threw away. My interpretation did not fit; the reason I gave for the breakup (jealousy of the most abstract, artificial of my loves: Dawn) was quite unnecessary, could just as easily have been entirely different or altogether superfluous. It is nonetheless interesting that during this ideal love, I could still feel a need for that other, abstract, artificial love (for Dawn). Nature, esteemed Mr. Brodny, does not suffice for us, even in matters of love; here too we want to, must, achieve something artificial…

But I realize I could be suspected of playing a coy game of hide-and-seek. Nothing could be further from my mind. I am speaking of my love for my (and Christa's) son. He is now twenty years old. A hectically, indeed hysterically new generation. *Plus de pères, rien que des fils.* To play it safe, he no longer speaks to me, and he has taken his mother's name. I wish him love, beauty, the very best. There are moments, even now, when (with a pang in my heart) I understand him: during his first fourteen years, I must have been for him rather as my mother had been for me half a century ago or Stella almost thirty years ago, except that I was fortunate enough to lose both those figures at the right moment. I have been (biologically) preserved for him, and it must have been painful for him to learn something I didn't have to learn: that I was a human being, and that he was not exclusively the god next to whom there could be no other gods as I was for him. *The old, old trouble.* Always comes right before the natural end (of unstrenuous love).

But what good does it do us to be so wise, Mr. Brodny, my fellow sufferer? What good would it do if I told him that for fourteen years he was the dearest and most beautiful of my gods and closer to my heart than any of my goddesses?

However, Stella in those far-off days (1938 in Vienna, and then in the Salzkammergut, and then in Bucharest, and then here there and everywhere during the rat hunt of the early war years until her disappearance in a concentration camp) was quite simply everything for me. She was my life, the air I breathed, all the warmth and sweetness of this earth. She bore me anew. She nursed me with her milk. She liberated me from the dreadful confinement poverty stupidity dullness of my formative years in Vienna. Thanks to her, my "family" evaporated: my foster parents (Uncle Helmuth and Aunt Hertha—those names!), my actual foster mother (Aunt Selma, spellbound, and thus the only one truly related to me), and my cousin Wolfgang (my brother Abel, highly gifted, earnest, blond, youthfully robust, industrious, reliable, all the things that I'm not and wasn't, the born sacrificial animal, the smooth slaughter-sheep with the lovely, gentle eyes and the warm, meadow-scented breath). All those exemplary petit bourgeois people escaped from the narrator's box of toys, which had weighed on me like Fuseli's *Nightmare* after a bright, spoiled, suddenly and cruelly interrupted childhood with my beautiful mother (safe and secure in the sumptuous households of her Balkan-prince gallants; lovingly cared for and tended by my lavender-scented nanny Miss Fern—sounds good, doesn't it?), weighed on me through a dozen horrible years in Vienna, weighed on my so-called youth, my dully brooding puberty, my tormented, masturbatory, straying and strolling adolescence—all those petit bourgeois people disappeared into the fable land of memory, became the specters of a bad but happily concluded dream; at best, they were mere puppets from the trash bin of anecdote.

Stella liberated me from what she, in finest harmony with her husband, John (and perhaps because of my scruples concerning him), called the appalling hypocrisy of the bloody fucking middle classes. "Life in dark waters, fishing in them at second hand, a deceived hand, the pond already empty; life cowering under the whip of imperative *shall*'s and *must*'s that no one believes in but everyone clings to, because it gives a few not entirely stupid people the chance to do business and everyone hopes that some will fall his way; the ingrained dishonesty that tries to rig up a solace in every oppression and humiliation; the unnatural, invented, insane quality of existence in a constant as-if; the envious, mistrustful creature, concerned with and demanding rank and position . . ."

we know it all, don't we, know it by heart: all the qualities that make intellectuals and artists . . .

but let us not speak of that now. Stella, in any event, saved me from that petit bourgeois morality that turns everything sour; saved me from—even worse!—the insinuatingly intimate, pseudo-artistic sensibility of the philistines into whose hands I was delivered after my mother's death. She released me from the shameful ignorance into which my Viennese relatives had plunged me when they tried to pull me down to their level. To Stella, and to her alone, I owe my having lived the first half of my life consciously, with open eyes, as lived life and not just as a literary phenomenon, part fairy tale and part tenement story. She brought me to myself and brought me back to myself—myself as I had been meant to be, as God, the Creation, or Mother Nature, or whatever had originally designed me and meant me to become.

Stella revived in me the possibility of becoming that which should have become of me, the child graced with the gay, goodly, tender, and intelligent creature of my mother and the most beautiful conditions for growing up under the protection of my various nominal uncles and godfathers: a free self without bitterness, rancor, resentment (marvel at the result) . . . and at any rate: Stella opened my eyes to my time, too—the time that would soon form the last half of my life. Stella showed me not only that it was a gray, abject time, a dismal, impoverished time of wretched need and humiliating necessity, of social injustice, scarcity, envy, malice, anxiety, constraint, but also that one could still find, in this time, the "reality within reality," as she put it, the world that had made my childhood bright and brilliant and given me an inkling of what man is meant to be.

Stella aroused this vision of me, a vision horribly frustrated for twelve years, of my original destiny as the Son of Man (how appropriate! how true to the zeitgeist!), and she let me live that vision for a brief while. At the last minute, so to speak, before the era that could afford the luxury of such ideal notions went under in the icy blue-gold of a March day—or rather: froze at first…

For the moment, you see, it froze, congealed, became alien and distant, as if no longer belonging to us, as if it had never belonged to us nor we to it. We knew the era and recognized ourselves in it by hearsay, as it were. We experienced ourselves as history (which I had already experienced in my childhood). From then on, we lived with our past like Nagel with his shot-off arm—without it and yet with it in some abstract fashion. (Incidentally, to be precise: the day I am speaking of was March 12, 1938, in Vienna; the sky was Adriatically blue, the sunshine sparkling, and the temperature eleven degrees below zero Celsius.)

II

As for the phenomenology of that era, which has been preserved in me like an alien life: its light.

In my childhood: a bright, clear, wind-stirred, wide-open spring light. (Which signals a dragging of the past into presence, Jugendstil light dragged into art deco; our first impressions are not only our own: they are bathed in the light of our parents' heyday.) My mother sometimes sang, in her delightfully airy, sunlight-dappled mood (Bonnard), and I would ask her over and over again to sing the one that began

Mach mir kein bitteres Gesicht,
Es geht nicht, lieber Schatz,
Denn was dein Herr Papa verspricht,
Ist alles für die Katz!

A frivolous song. My mother sang it for fun. Of course, I took it very seriously; I suffered it, as I later suffered my Rilke. The stanza I loved most retains even now the entire mood of those happy days:

The poplars on the highway there
Sway in the wind of March.

That was it: the Jugendstil mood of my early days (1919–26). Still no end of nature: distance, urging, promise. And light, conjured up in another stanza:

The far blue distance calls for me
Pale-blue like your corset...

Pale-blue. Silk-blue. Intensifying in the yearning exultation:

And if it weren't for Paree
Then I might dream of you and me
In your most decent bed.

Do you hear it: Paris the yearning goal of migratory birds. The capital of Europe. But no matter: the wanderlust of those days. The lure of the horizon. And beyond it, yet another Beyond. The only anguish of my childhood: the pale-blue promise beyond the birches and beeches and alders and spruces and all the other dendrological bric-a-brac of the park in Bessarabia; there, way way beyond the fields, along the forest tracts and meadows of the river Pruth, where poplars, strung far across the land, lie westward on the great highway—*îți mai aduci aminte, domnule Brodny?...*

March-weather yearning. The land wide open in the fresh light. Spring once again lets its blue ribbon waft through the air. The threshing machine stands in the barn: be patient until autumn. The naked twigs still drip in the morning. The fields lie fallow. There is a powerful rush under the willows along the park wall. In the village, tiny brooks shoot along the paths. The village children send reed boats over their rapids, and I envy their freedom. Miss Fern tugs me past them. "Come on, you must not stare. It will embarrass them."

Uncle Ferdinand's bags are being packed, the servants drag them into his dressing room: huge calf-leather trunks fitted with brass latches, brass corners, buckled with straps, girded with the blue and gold ribbon of his armorial colors. Through the corridors the chambermaids cluck like big black-and-white brood hens, bearing piles of shirts ironed so smooth that they are slippery, balancing them firmly under their chins, the tissue paper crackling (a superfluous protection: Uncle Ferdinand will have his laundry rewashed and re-pressed in Paris anyway).

He struts enormously before us, up and down, past the open window, which contains treetops, bright spring breezes, and yearning. At regular intervals his shadow falls across the tea table where we are sitting. I in my Norfolk jacket with a bow under the broad, striped shirt collar, and I can't bear the bow because I find it girlish and it makes the village children laugh. My mother in a frock of light brocade as iridescent as snakeskin; her dress closes under the armpits in an intersecting line, leaving the throat and shoulders bare, as if placed there (this too is quite art nouveau—ivory inlaid in cloisonné, imitative of Luca della Robbia terra cottas; in art deco, the dress would be batiked, the superimposed bust would be plastic, the hair japanned).

When Uncle Ferdinand's large shadow falls across the tea table, the firmament of sunlight reflections on the silver—the samovar, the sugar bowl, the butter dishes and toast racks, the honey pot, and various containers in which tarts and pastries are kept warm—is for a moment snuffed out. My mother fiddles with the tea things, her movements uncommonly light. She is slender, erect, and wears a hothouse blossom in her hair: a Balinese gamelan player.

Uncle Ferdinand struts around us with solemn, almost ceremonial steps. He is celebrating himself. At each step, his powerfully vaulted torso—and his elegantly sloping bon-vivant shoulders, his alert head constantly turning to and fro, his sharply protruding nose and uncommonly powerful mustache, twirled thread-fine at each end—his torso nods, awe-inspiring, self-confident, self-certain, earnest: an immense rooster.

His eyes are rooster eyes: perfectly circular, light brown, with piercing black pupils. When he ogles at the cheese- or mushroom-patties, the currant tarts, he tilts his head as though taking aim, then stalks step by step to the tea table to seize the goodies with a nimble whisk of the hand. He balances the teacup very delicately before the vertical line of his vest buttons, then goes over to my mother to have her pour him more tea: "*Comme c'est dommage que vous n'ayez pas envie de venir à Paris, cette foi ici, mon ange. Vous nous manquerez à tous et surtout à Anne, qui vous aime si tendrement. D'ailleurs, autant que j'en sache, il y aura aussi John—cela ne vous ferait pas changer d'idée?...*"

He stands close to the tea table, arching his rooster chest toward the samovar; and the samovar belly, arching too (convex where he is concave, concave where he is convex), reflects him mockingly, caricatures him, distorts him grotesquely. He is suddenly drawn upward, as thin as thread, and then is collapsed into a broad sphere...

Fourteen years later, I was to see him like that again: in February 1940; I was a Romanian soldier, a defender of the Fatherland, a Fatherland in which I had become an alien; after returning home to Bessarabia from Vienna I was taken in again by the forgetful patron of my remote childhood as if I had been gone for only a school year: "*Ah, te voilà finalement. Il était grand temps qu'on te voie. Va vite te changer pour dîner. Ta chambre est celle sur la cour, comme d'habitude. C'est John, d'ailleurs, qui m'avait annoncé ton arrivée...*"

(*John, d'ailleurs... D'ailleurs, il y aura aussi John*... always John is in the background and guiding the course of my life...)

12

He is still Uncle Ferdinand the Magnificent. But something strange has happened to him; a bizarre retromorphosis has occurred, a development back into the species and genus, which makes the individual recede and the type come to the fore—and not the rooster type. He is no longer the giant cock-of-the-walk of yore.

God help me I was twenty-one years old then, and was still inexperienced in what age can do to a man—I mean, how much it brings him home, brings him back to his origins. Is it that my eyes, after fourteen years of Vienna, are unused to such immediate Balkanness and are more sensitive to it? I wondered, terrified. Uncle Ferdinand looks to me as if whole phalanxes of Levantine ancestors had marched right into him—all those Greeks from the phanar of Constantinople, who ruled for the Sublime Porte as princes over Moldavia and Wallachia, who married the daughters of the land, uncommonly black-haired daughters of boyars, with noses as sharply curved as their scimitars and the plumes of their otter caps. Uncle Ferdinand's nose is so crooked now that, like a parrot beak, it presses down on his (now yellowish white, now sparse) bristly mustache (as if the nose were devouring a narrow sheaf of bleached straw; similar tiny sheaves are proliferating in his nostrils and ears). This nose arches from its tip (overshadowing the chin and double chin) in a resolute curve right around the entire arc of the skull, between the eyes (now slightly bulging and mounted in reddened lids and pale lashes), seamlessly (with no notch in the root of the nose) into the receding forehead and then the dully shimmering parchment spheres of the cranium, over which a few damp, grayish-white strands are still combed (remnants of patent-leather-black hair, once brushed back from the forehead smooth as a mirror).

A balding old cockatoo, I would have been tempted to think, if Uncle Ferdinand's head alone had developed homeward into the Oriental and thereby into history. But the intrinsic, typical quality now coming to the fore, the element that makes a personal feature a revelatory mark not only of race and class but also of a specific human condition, the potentiality of man in a specific form—this quality has been elaborated (with admirable thrift in the use of artistic devices) by means of a contortion and distortion of the entire figure.

It is the same grotesque distortion that I saw in the fun-house mirror of the samovar belly during the remote childhood days of 1926: Uncle Ferdinand is both elongated and compressed at once. His stilt legs are drawn out; exceedingly long and skinny, they seem to go all the way up to his shoulders, on which his ears are set (with the yellowish gray-white sheaves of hair now sprouting from them). Once, his high rooster-chest was tremendously vaulted, and what a horned pearl-string of waistcoat buttons ran down it like a seam in a bold self-assured curve to his artificially tightened waist—like the trill that Miss Fern, a *Schnitzelpolka* piano virtuoso, fondled out of the keys at the end of the piece, her middle finger rigid, a trill like the energetic gondola arc in the emphatic underscrawl of a signature. But now, this conceitedly bloated, girdled, truffle-fed bon-vivant body is broadly squashed and billowed like a melon, precariously thrust on its spindly leg-trestle like a hunchback's torso.

There will soon be nothing human about this at all. It is merely a caricature now, and its essence has developed perfidiously. Uncle Ferdinand's personality has not been rendered harmless by the change, or banalized into cheerful reconciliation. On the contrary, it now emerges in all its sharp certainty. His incontestable authority has intensified, is now uncanny, but is no longer expressed by the complacent power of the rooster: it is as if the rooster's pomp has risen aloft and been suspended. Uncle Ferdinand is now devoid of pompous gravity, is virtually hovering in air, light, weightless...

In short: Uncle Ferdinand has not simply aged but taken a step beyond himself into the timelessness of symbolism. No, no: he is no longer the proud rooster on the hilltop who greets the radiant new day with the drawn scimitar of his crowing. He is something far older, more archaic, more archetypal; something has shifted him to the dawn of creation, as though he were perched at the beginning of time, still bringing his mythic influence to bear on Today, spinning threads of destiny...

of course—that's what he is: *Arachne*. He has become a spider. Uncle Ferdinand has turned into a gigantic, gray-yellow-white spider.

13

You understand my dilemma, Mr. Brodny. I am telling you stories not just for my personal pleasure. I am not letting my figures stroll across the page just for fun. No sooner have I drawn the picture of Uncle Ferdinand as a spider than I feel compelled to extend the metaphor wherever Uncle Ferdinand leads us—he too a phantom of the narrator, a tale about telling.

The figures have to work out—arithmetically. Otherwise, they will not be right—and do not seem right, at first glance. Uncle Ferdinand is an aristocrat, and the spider is no image for aristocracy. No one has a spider in his escutcheon. On a coat of arms, a spider would be the out-and-out negation of the knightly spirit: not just the symbol of treacherous ambush but a token of shameful languishing. Only old rubbish that's been stored away gets covered with cobwebs, dusty stuff now useless and worthless.

But as we know, life is a constant transvaluation of values. Something that may be old junk today, because it is useless, can be doubly precious tomorrow, because it evokes the mood of a yesterday that seems increasingly rich and pure, a life more pleasing to God

(presumably because we feel—through no special fault or guilt of today, simply the fault or guilt of existing—that we were more innocent yesterday than we are today and than we shall be tomorrow...)

True, in 1940 we were not so Americanized that we piously placed a cowbell of old-fashioned iron on the coffee table as an antiquarian relic, thereby marking ourselves as aesthetes and placing ourselves one rung higher in the cultural pecking order. But still, even then, aristocrats were understood as the aimless and useless, if quite evocative, remnants of a lost but all the same far more colorful world, closer to nature, less hectic, in short: a world altogether more pleasing to God—and thus fitted out with an antique value that was entirely fictive, to be sure, yet burdened with ethical demands that should not, in fairness, have been made on it. Throughout his life (he was born in 1872 and probably died soon after my coming home to him and the arrival of the Russians, to whom Bessarabia had been ceded;

i.e., roughly in September 1940), Uncle Ferdinand, who had a line of ancestors going back to the emperors of Byzantium, found himself in historical situations that made it impossible for him to exercise the virtues that troubadours and minnesingers idealized in the beautiful legend of King Arthur's Round Table as the Mount Olympus of chivalry.

You have to make allowances. In the capitalist era, the image of the aristocrat, even if he was one to let chivalrous notions of Honor, Truth, Courage, Sacrifice, and so on flutter over his head like banners, could no longer be that of Parsifal or Lancelot. The feudal lords of the epoch were really Napoleon III and Edward VII—sovereigns whose peers and paladins were the Rothschilds and Sassoons—no longer Gawain and the seneschal Kew.

My mother would accompany Uncle Ferdinand to the Riviera. That is to say, when we moved into the house at Antibes, which, as a matter of course, I regarded as one of *our* houses, intended solely for my mother and me, as well as Miss Fern and the rest of the staff (the maître d'hôtel, the housekeeper, the lady's maid, innumerable parlormaids, the chef, a few kitchen helpers, the chauffeur, the gardeners). There, after weathering the somewhat eerie merriment of the Mardi Gras, we looked forward more calmly to Uncle Ferdinand's regular visits from Monte Carlo, where he occupied an entire hotel floor. At that time, the Roaring Twenties, among the intimate friends who accompanied him, the percentage of names listed in the old *Almanach de Gotha* was almost infinitesimal compared with the names of Bolivian tin-mine owners, Argentine cattle breeders, Irish beer kings, Dutch petroleum magnates, and Levantine gunrunners. Not even the addition of a number of penniless Russian grand princes could even out this disparity.

We should probably renounce certain compulsive ideas in the concept of aristocracy; the intellect and nonintellect, virtues and vices, of the caste that had been manipulating the fate of Western Civilization for more than a millennium, especially its will to survive, to continue (like certain streams that suddenly vanish underground only to bubble up unexpectedly somewhere else, perhaps on the other side of a mountain range) in a new and entirely different form and manner, adjusted to a new and different zeitgeist.

In other words, though you might find all kinds of aristocrats and all sorts of odds and ends testifying to the legends of chivalrous origins—in Sleeping Beauty castles belonging to mediatized German princes; in baroque palaces flanked by black cypress torches and bombarded by sunlight, belonging to Spanish and Sicilian grandees; in the *manoirs* of certain deeply provincial French nobles, as solemn as though risen from the ancestral tomb; and, needless to say, on the poor farms both east and west of the Elbe belonging to Junkers in leather leggings—the aristocracy as a still-powerful upper class were now fraternizing with the "upper ten thousand" of the international business world and gathering at places that grossly contradicted the ethos of chivalry. They frequented the boardrooms of banks, industrial concerns, and insurance companies and, for relaxation, nightclubs and gambling casinos as well as yacht marinas on southern shores. These are the meeting places for the tiny group of men who manipulate not only movie starlets, playing cards, and polo mallets but also the fate of Western Civilization (and hence mankind).

So I need not cudgel my brain about the heraldic validity of the spider as a vision of Uncle Ferdinand's phase of completion. His aristocratic quality leaves every branch of zoology open to this possibility. Had not my fairy-tale childhood been suddenly aborted and had I not been cast out into the grayness of life as an eternally duped poor wretch, I would never have so much as dreamed of viewing Uncle Ferdinand as a standard-bearer of the chivalrous spirit, or his breeding as an ideologically acquired quality to be analyzed in the light of intellectual history. This was middle-class thinking, not only in its categories but also in its abstraction, in its remoteness from life. It wouldn't even have elicited a shrug from Uncle Ferdinand himself; he would merely have stared into space for a moment and then changed the subject.

Still, it is interesting to picture what might have happened if I hadn't retained any of the intellectual restraint acquired as part of a good upbringing, and it occurred to me to ask Uncle Ferdinand straight out (alluding, perhaps, to the similarity between certain notions of the ideology of chivalry—for instance, that a knight must always test his mettle anew; i.e., constantly realize himself anew—and analogous interpretations of existence in existential philosophy): the blank astonishment in the three circles of eyes and mouth in his countenance would be stupendous to behold. But this astonishment would promptly give way to an expression of great weariness and melancholy.

With the touching kindness he always demonstrates when he has to instruct youthful ignorance, Uncle Ferdinand would reply that human beings are not like our dear dogs: dogs, he would say, are developed into breeds having different functions, so that the physical and mental characteristics needed to perform those functions are passed down not only unadulterated but actually intensified—e.g., the pointer's and retriever's fine nose, the hound's stamina, the powerful fangs of the mastiff, and all the other useful and beneficial qualities of hunting dogs, as well as the extraordinary character traits of the various sheepdogs and watchdogs, and finally the droll, affectionate qualities of the breeds developed for playing, pleasure, and companionship... Rather, Uncle Ferdinand would say, man himself seems to be a breed with a highly developed specialty, a function that he probably does not yet understand but that is beginning, eerily, to crystallize: he is a kind of cosmic microbe, a bacillus or virus with the mission to destroy the planet Earth—and perhaps not just the planet Earth. But that's just by the by.

In any case, however, Uncle Ferdinand would continue, any further special function could probably no longer be bred. Every newborn baby has all the possibilities of human life available—some quite unexpected, even surprising, and some so amazingly pre-programmed that one is tempted to believe in transmigration (of a very desultory kind); however, any further shaping of these pre-programmed possibilities is left, Uncle Ferdinand would say, to environment and education... and, naturally, generations of belonging to a given milieu would also develop certain traits, features, and if not characteristics then certain tendencies that would, overall, identify the individual as belonging to this milieu. But nothing more than that.

Just as a peasant can be identified as a peasant, a seaman as a seaman, a boor as a boor, Uncle Ferdinand would say, each one of them—just like each of our beloved companions the dogs—has his specific character quite independent of that fact; that is, he may be either a very sweet or a very ferocious dog, a poor dog or a stupid dog.

Very few members of the two latter categories were to be found in Uncle Ferdinand's circle of friends—which was quite simply the world for him, the Middle Kingdom. Even rarer than a poor or stupid dog was a sweet dog. Most of them were ferocious dogs. Of course, Uncle Ferdinand and his friends knew how to make this ferocity seem innocent, yes, even lovable; namely, to seem fully and exclusively in service of the most gay enjoyment of life.

This was disarming, and would quite appropriately confirm John's statement that if everyone got to know the so-called exploiters of mankind personally, there would be no such thing as social envy and class struggle. These things really didn't exist, he said, when the common people had free access to the dining rooms and sleeping chambers of kings, and could gape to their heart's content at the great people of this world in their ordinary humanity (rather like the good citizens standing at the wolf cage in the zoo on a Sunday afternoon: "Just look at him scratching himself—just like Rover!").

And indeed, my memories of Uncle Ferdinand's friends (some of whom, incidentally, were as close to my much-beloved mother as he was) were heartwarming. Our spring sojourns on the Riviera—when Bessarabia still lay under snow but the small pond in the park was beginning to thaw—contributed in no small measure to the radiant effect that this entire lost half of my life had on me, not only the brilliance of those glorious early years but virtually the illumination of an era.

14

Never have I met anyone so effervescent, so funny, so eager for the craziest jokes and pranks as "Bully" Olivera, a tiny, roly-poly, mercurial South American who played outstanding polo and poker and, it was said, owed his immense fortune to the slave labor of entire tribes of half-starved, lice-ridden Indians. (One of his ideas, which would have delighted the pataphysicists, was to go to the Casino at Monte Carlo in the few hours between closing time and dawn—when you hear the shots of suicides—sugar-frost it, and then top it, at sunrise, with several tons of whipped cream and strawberries.) And never will I forget the kindness, the tireless concern, the unabating efforts for the welfare of his neighbors, the warm, active humanity of Sir Agop Garabetian (known in the financial world as "Mr. Choke" because of his cutthroat methods).

Aboard his steamer yacht *Nereide*, where Uncle Agop was the most solicitous of hosts at famous "little" dinners (which, needless to say, were far more intimate, more exclusive, and therefore more sought after than the great "galas"), he personified the highest degree of civilization a human being can possibly attain. Unforgettable to me are his charm, his tenderness, the cordial white-toothed smile in the pomaded, parted, twiddled coal-black beard that framed his Arabian Nights head like a rococo cartouche and gave him exaggerated pomp and *opera buffa* menace, heightened by a sparkling monocle wedged in his left eye socket and precariously clutched by the black caterpillar of an uncommonly mobile eyebrow. (Privately, my mother called him Monsieur Raminagrobis, which I, as an avid reader of Madame la Comtesse de Ségur, found quite accurate.) In contrast, the deep, Orientally wise melancholy of those almond-cut eyes whose pupils floated in the jaundiced whites of his eyes like black olives in oil. The blandishing melody of his voice, its sonorous strength nevertheless making the blood-red petals of the carnation quiver in the silk lapel of his white tuxedo. The gentle, skillful movements of his blue-flashing beringed *bayadère* hands when he placed a chinchilla around bare female shoulders that might shiver in the night wind; or when he raised a glass of wine to scrutinize it against the candle flames of a girandole (spiriting a ruby onto the diamond-sown indigo velvet of night over the forest of masts at the marina); or when, with positively scientific devotion, he helped a friend (and no less well-versed connoisseur) to select a cigar, or pushed over to him the crystal carafe of port that (according to those privileged to taste it) was in no way inferior to the magnificence of the Easter Mass in a Russian cathedral; when finally he stroked my head with fatherly solace because Miss Fern, to my ineffable regret, insisted on detaching me from my mother's arms (in which, ringleted and cherry-eyed, I lay like the daughter of Madame Vigée-Lebrun) to take me belowdecks to our cabin and get me into bed before the Charleston band began to play. This band, which along with the Venezuelan tango orchestra was a part of Uncle Agop's household, had several soloists who today are counted among the classical musicians of jazz: their art having been immortalized on records, they are the teachers of a generation of performers whom Gaia managed and commercially exploited; the money she earned was largely devoted to creating the atmosphere of suitable comfort and elegant freedom from care that I needed to write my book . . . yes, indeed, Brodny my friend, the world is small and round, one thing rolls into another. A whore's son simply can't become anything but a whore schnorrer; literary laws are more severe in this respect than life itself . . . But that should not prevent me from finishing the paragraph and returning to my reflections, to illustrate which I have invented Bully Olivera and Sir Agop Garabetian (and imbued them with such vim and vigor that their healthy appetite for life threatens to chew up the thread of my story) . . . I mean to say: Uncle Agop and all my other elective and nominal uncles and godfathers (and possible fathers) had a robust appetite for life during the era between WWI and WWII, when they lived in a reality within reality, and it was this that provided the brilliance that makes the lost half of my life seem illuminated as though by a promise of spring. Their irresistible charm and fascinating manners reveal not only that, as true masters of the art of living, they grasped the virtue of humanity as an aesthetic commandment but also that they were indeed great gentlemen.

They were the princes of their time, whether or not their names were listed in the *Almanach de Gotha*. Their courts were no less arabesquely and hieratically composed of officials, sycophants, favorites and minions with kith and kin, flatterers, jokesters, porters, couriers, stooges of all kinds, than any duodecimo court at the height of the Renaissance. And these courtiers were no less devoted to the enjoyment of life, albeit less ethically ideologized, than any court of love in the days of Chrétien de Troyes.

Only, in the year 1940, all this was no longer so concrete. It was its own self in a different state, so to speak: like ice thawed into water, or water boiled into steam. Even this world within the world and this reality within reality were subject to the process of rarefaction, of abstraction, which affected the entire world of humanity, as though its molecules were flying apart (just as, as we know, the whole universe is supposedly flying apart).

Likewise, Uncle Ferdinand's world of games and gamesters, the innermost circle of the shrewdest, hardest, most cynical possessors of reality, is on the verge of dematerializing. It would now take a Chosen Being to capture it in its new aggregate state and weave it together anew.

15

The vision of Uncle Ferdinand as a spider is thus perfectly valid as a symbol. Indeed, he is weaving the myth of his world. He is working on his Middle Kingdom, which needless to say is the middle of a pre-Copernican world; not a middle position between some higher and some lower world but a nuclear pole, from which the closer and farther circles of friends radiate and intersect and intertangle with the farther and closer circles of friends of other centers on the same social level. A kingdom of the extraordinarily wealthy, extending across many lands and girded by the Great Wall of Money, beyond which live those whom Destiny or Divine Providence or the random blindness of nature has denied the truly liberating, really propitious goods of this earth: teeming nations without money or happiness or names, without memorable faces, dwelling in areas that are unrecorded on the lovely maps and charts in the atlas of deluxe living—*on sait que cela existe et on s'en fout.*

This is the reason that Uncle Ferdinand does not even now (it is February 1940; the trees are covered in frost, the pond in the park is frozen, I could blissfully skate upon it like young Goethe on the Ilm, if I found pleasure in doing turns and waltz-wave-welling curves on my mother's deathbed)... I say, this is the reason that Uncle Ferdinand does not even now realize how abstract, how virile, how artificial is the activity on which he concentrates all his high intelligence, his energy, all the persistence of his domineering character—a princely character that is accustomed to giving orders, brooks no contradiction, and will not be discouraged by any obstacle. He authors the myth of his world and himself.

As if he had lived solely and exclusively for this "reality within reality," as if, like a character in a novel, he had been invented only for this particular one of the book's themes, existed only for, found his reality only in the world of the "upper ten thousand," as it was called in his day: the *beau monde* of the monstrously rich—whether they had always been rich, are rich still and now indeed are quite rich, or if they have only recently become rich and are newly settling into it—in any case, in the kingdom of the monstrously rich and their high life he finds himself realized, and among them especially the inner circle of dynamic enjoyers of life at Deauville, Biarritz, and the Côte d'Azur, with their many beautiful houses in all the most beautiful places on this wondrously beautiful earth; their parks and shooting grounds; their oceangoing yachts, polo ponies, Rolls-Royces, and Bugattis; their wondrously beautiful women, spoiled, sheathed in brocade and precious fur and hung with legendary jewelry; the expensive whims, jokes, flashes of inspiration; the captivating manners and the powerful carnivore teeth, in which (as Uncle Helmuth and Aunt Hertha alleged) the bones of the disinherited classes splintered so crunchingly (as I, in contrast, can assure you) that it was a delight to watch.

This is, probably, precisely one of the reasons Uncle Ferdinand hasn't given up this world of his for lost, even though one can hardly conceal that it is threatened in its core: his unbroken confidence in his strong-toothed playmates from the greens of polo fields and chemin-de-fer tables; these are people who will not easily give up the succulent morsels for which they waged such bloody battles, even if the devastations of WWII were to prove even more catastrophic than those of WWI. There is something like a quantum law even in times of danger, a law that those who have a great deal to lose will ultimately lose even less than those others who from the very start had little to lose—and men like Bully Olivera and Sir Agop Garabetian weren't exactly sleepy, even though dawn usually caught them in a swallow-tail or a tuxedo. Indeed, one could expect that, like most of the people in the inner circle, these men, thanks to markets made accessible again by the huge and general devastation, would simply seize even larger morsels in their teeth (as experience taught in WWI, to be confirmed after WWII by the various Economic Miracles of defeated fatherlands in Western Civilization and newly created fatherlands in Africa and Asia). But still: these men would most likely not be able to chew their morsels as unabashedly as before.

Meanwhile, however, these marvelously unchallenged consciences, with which my diverse nominal uncles and godfathers (and fellow travelers of Uncle Ferdinand's) managed to enjoy everything that their unscrupulous conception of the world permitted them, are probably the reason that Uncle Ferdinand appreciates them not only individually but all together, as a group, a troop, a swarm, a cheerfully baying, eagerly sniffing, keenly hunting pack, yes, presumably he even loves them, with the plainness of self-evident identification. Well, the sharp and shiny toothfulness of carnivore jaws is as old as mankind, as life itself, and will probably perish only when life itself does; yet in the unadorned fashion of the Bully Oliveras and Agop Garabetians, it belonged specifically to the most beautiful period in Uncle Ferdinand's life (a period whose late flowering coincided with my first flowering); and with it Uncle Ferdinand was always in agreement, he loves it effortlessly, self-evidently, with the surety of a profound inner correspondence.

He especially loves the era bestowed on him and his kind, the era of precarious armistice between two phases of a Hundred Years' War (for Uncle Ferdinand, just like John, sees WWI and WWII not as two distinct conflicts having distinct causes and goals and carried out with murderous weapons among European nations but as two skirmishes of one and the same European civil war, fought with all means and methods and bestowing on him and his kind a wonderful hybrid blossom during twenty-one years while the armies, aggressions, and weapons were renewed).

No doubt, the thing that Uncle Ferdinand most loves—as do I—about that era, the thing that gave its style that incomparably piquant mestizo character of refinement and violence, making it quite unforgettably vivid, charming, promising, the time of our lives, was: *the American touch*.

You may not believe it, Mr. Brodny, but that's what it was like. Uncle Agop's Venezuelan tango orchestra and nigger band as well as Dada and the Constructivist vision, bobbed hair and Expressionism as well as the conveyor-belt production of superfluous consumer goods and political street scuffles, transvestite nightclubs and the "simple life" reform movement, Einstein's theory of relativity and Fascism, Greta Garbo and Dr. Joseph Goebbels, Mistinguette and James Joyce, Mayakovski and various secret police (*et quelle est la différence entre le Négus et Léon Blum? Aucune: tous les deux ont une barbe, sauf Léon Blum*)—all the things that now make the years between WWI and WWII seem like a paradise lost we owe to the return of the prodigal daughter, America.

The delicious blend in that time of chaos and extreme stylization, of decadence and tempestuous promise; the suspenseful coexistence of gangster violence and pure, self-sacrificing faith in man and his right to light, beauty, happiness—the myriad contradictions, the perilous extremes, the explosiveness of all the legacies and tendencies of the zeitgeist made those years a time, a lifetime, more stimulating than could ever have been experienced before or after. It was most likely, as Stella maintained, Europe's most European hour. And just as she, Stella, realizes it, so too does Uncle Ferdinand realize (both of them, presumably, from the proclamations dropped by John at the ends of his sentences) that this historic hour of Europe could not have come without the return of Europe's prodigal child, America, without America's intervention in, its regress into European history. Be proud, sir. It's your century. It's your world.

Certainly, Uncle Ferdinand is an aristocrat and a European, a European's European, sated by the spirits not only of Roman civilization but also of Byzantium; were I to attempt to draw up his spiritual pedigree, I would have to show Irish apostles crossed with Moorish mathematicians, and Venetian seafarers with German philosophers. Nevertheless, or perhaps for that very reason, Uncle Ferdinand loves the American touch in the years of precarious armistice between WWI and WWII. He is delighted by the fedora's smart bootlegger look: the crease in the hat brim, so to speak, the brim clapped down at a slant over the brow of a killer's eyes. He enjoys the spirit of adventure that entered the remnants of a beau monde salvaged from WWI with the polo-playing tin-mine magnates and poker-playing oil tycoons and arms runners, a high society in which the coteries of the Guermantes had long since become intimately entangled with those of the Verdurins as well as those of the Astors and the Vanderbilts.

Uncle Ferdinand is neither a moralist nor a romantic. He is really an aesthete of a school for which antiquarian value per se does not exist. A man who has grown up among Gainsboroughs and lives with Roentgen furniture will appreciate a Sumerian cowbell or an iron spoon from the Fu-Ku or Shen-Si excavations only if it's an especially beautiful specimen. And he will, incidentally, always prefer the latest model of a first-class sports car.

16

Which, of course, does not explain why Uncle Ferdinand, now, in the heart of winter 1940, is still here in Bessarabia, no doubt in the most uncomfortable, most badly heated of his houses, and the one most remote from civilization. Only the bone-hard, frozen Dniester and thirty-five kilometers of land flat as the palm of your hand separate him from the Russians, who are just waiting to march in and clean house with his sort just as thoroughly as they did at home in 1917. In back of him lies a fatherland, Romania, which in 1919 welcomed Bessarabia's return to the Kingdom of Greater Romania by dispossessing my uncle of the best of his estates. Now, Romania will soon be blackmailed into putting up no resistance to the new invasion of the Russians; then, forcibly allied with her natural enemies, she will plunge into an escapade that can lead only to losses even greater than that of a single province.

Thus, Uncle Ferdinand would not need to stick his neck out for the heritage that his forefathers have left him here. This legacy is all too wretched compared with what these sage gentlemen have long since taken to more reliable countries like England, Holland, and Switzerland. And it is all too meager next to what he himself (vying here too with his friends from the polo greens and baccarat tables) has multiplied and invested in safe valuables and bank accounts throughout territories with a great future—like Brazil, South Africa, and Canada. Uncle Ferdinand certainly doesn't have to fear the emigrant's hard lot as I did or (initially, no doubt) you did as well, Mr. Brodny, my comrade in fate. If he wanted to sell just his coin collection (now in the vault of a private bank in New York belonging to one of his closest friends), the yield would allow him to live tolerably well till the end of his days (which end would no doubt be happily deferred by the necessary restriction of alcohol and luxury foods).

But, for the moment, there needn't be any talk of such an emergency measure. Even after the loss of his Bessarabian properties, Uncle Ferdinand would still be frightfully rich and could thus live carefree in California or the Bahamas, in Mexico City or Rio de Janeiro. Furthermore, he would be meeting a good number of the people about whose well-being he is occasionally anxious, cut off as he is from their cocktail and dinner parties and galas and often without even news of such events.

Meanwhile, Uncle Ferdinand is staying on in Bessarabia. He prefers it where he is, isolated and exposed, living in rustic simplicity—even without his French chef (who, as a defender of his fatherland, sulks in some bunker on the Maginot Line). The temperature here would freeze the radiator of his Cadillac and is even turning the shooting of wild geese into a dubious pleasure. Uncle Ferdinand holds out, even though without cheerful camaraderie or female companionship he is bored to tears every evening. His life is downright monastic—in a lovely, crazy, lordly gesture toward his friends, as though, by eschewing the chance to be safe with them, he could deny the very idea that for them, for their world, for his world, for their Middle Kingdom, a certain danger is now approaching: the terrible danger that henceforth they will have to camouflage themselves; they will no longer have the security of an unimpeached conscience in enjoying that they were what they are.

In the meantime, Uncle Ferdinand is doing what he would do if he were with them. By conjuring up his various friends and circles, he is weaving this world of his friends together, weaving away at its myth, re-creating it in a new dimension, perpetually resurrecting it. He takes it out of time, present as well as past, and places it in a sort of no-man's-land of time: makes it eternal. He lives through it once more, and all the more systematically for that. He pursues an enormously ramified, no doubt mostly one-sided correspondence with addressees in all countries still in postal communication with Romania. He instructs these people in minute detail about himself and his present circumstances, his social calendar as it would be if the circumstances were different, if things were as they once were—hunting, travel, and vacation plans in countries lying well out of harm's way. He reports on everything—no matter what—that he knows about his and their kind, and he requests equally detailed and precise answers. He has the caution, methodology, and pedantry of a general staff officer (which he was—in Russian uniform, intriguingly enough—during an after all halfway chivalrous WWI). And whatever information he picks up he tries to supplement out of his own (phenomenal) memory, photo albums, older correspondence, and newer memories and biographies, as well as items snipped out of society gazettes that manage to arrive every now and then. Moreover, he excerpts all pertinent notices from the most recent arrivals and departures in Lloyd's Insurance Register of Private Yachts, in the membership lists of the

Cresta Run Club, the Jockey Club, the Circolo della Caccia, the Royal English, Dutch, Spanish, Belgian, and Italian automobile clubs, the *Almanach de Gotha* of Princely Families, *Burke's*, the *Libro d'Oro*, and *Who's Who*. With the material thus gained (makeshift, to be sure, but as good as circumstances permit) he keeps his people up to date on the thing that bears the most infallible witness to the existence of a world of friends: the roster of their personnel.

Amusingly enough, the introverted quality of real aristocracy is thus more purely expressed in spiderlike Uncle Ferdinand than in the big extroverted rooster of his bon-vivant heyday. In high nobility, a more frequent type than this is the elderly gentleman absorbed in some kind of abstruse (even serious) research or collecting, and so neglectful of his obligation to present himself as a nobleman that only very sharp eyes can distinguish him from the next-best white-collar worker. And indeed, the intellectual disciplines in which aristocrats excel are the ordering, categorizing ones rather than the analytical, speculative ones. (Schwab tried to talk me into writing an essay on the difference between aristocratic and non-aristocratic intelligence.)

Uncle Ferdinand's close relations include ornithologists, shell collectors, and lepidopterists of the highest scientific rank, an important genealogist (important because he specialized in the multinational aristocracy of the former Ottoman Empire), and (lovingly esteemed by one and all) a princely cousin who had raised the aristocratic mastery of timetable perusal to such an art that he could reel off both the summer and the winter schedules of the entire national railroad network (*à propos*, as a true scientist, he was not content with this abstract lore: he traveled throughout the land, stationed himself on various overpasses, and, watch in hand, checked whether the timetable data corresponded to the facts).

In earlier years, Uncle Ferdinand made a nice name for himself as a numismatist. But what he is doing now is something more general, more profound, more fundamental. He is transcending into the metaphysical. Uncle Ferdinand makes the world he lived in eternal. Because he sees that it threatens to lose its self-evident quality (thus even were it to continue to exist, it would never be what it was), he captures it in the most beautiful blossom of its existence and transfers it from the transience of the timely to the timelessness of myth. He thus makes himself eternal, becomes an artist: the inventor, after the fact, of his own lifetime. He would never have existed if he did not exist in its chronicle.

The spider at the beginning of the world. Weaver of the world. Squatting in the no-man's-land of eternity and drawing its threads from time into timelessness, knotting them together there, weaving them back and forth and up and down, making sure that no tiny thread is disconnected from all the others. He has truly given himself over to his mission. (Naturally, he no longer reads any newspapers, no longer concerns himself with the administration of his estates, his foreign possessions, his business dealings; indeed, he no longer even entertains.) As narrow-minded as a spider that builds its web in a cranny where no fly would ever venture, Uncle Ferdinand has withdrawn here, to a remote, wintry, icy Bessarabia, in order to weave the myth of his radiant bon-vivant world, shone upon by an everlasting spring sun. It is an image of utmost faith in God: the spider hanging its web like a sail in the wind of destiny...

And lo and behold: against even the most visionary estimation, his web was well woven, and the wind of destiny bore me into it.

17

I repeat: It is the heart of winter in early 1940, toward the middle of February. Earth as hard as iron; one can scarcely believe that it will ever thaw again. No traces of spring breezes, of spring winds shaking the poplars, of pale-blue distances arousing yearning. True, the sky is silky blue now—the same Adriatically deep, spotless, ice-cold blue as over Vienna two years earlier, in March 1938. It is the sky under which the first half of my life froze, God alone may know how and why; I can't explain it, I can only tell about it... the fact is: this country, Bessarabia, the landscape of my childhood, has also frozen, a land of hoar and frost, with white foggy mornings before the icy blue of the sky stiffens the mist into feathery star crystals.

I am walking through an abstracted world, therefore, a world preserved under the glass bell of a well-nigh metaphysical coldness that I recognize and acknowledge as the world of my childhood. I am living again in my childhood home, from which I was torn away (virtually overnight, and not very considerately), from which I was driven for fourteen years (my entire youth, from the seventh to the twenty-first year of my life). Some of the domestics (a daffy lady's maid; a flatfooted footman, his head and body shaking; a gardener palsied with age) claim to recognize me. It's not true; they're just imagining things. One does not recognize the little boy who resembled the daughter of Madame Vigée-Lebrun in this cavalryman who screws the night away through all the hooker hangouts of Kishinev and spends a rueful morning scouring his pubic hair for crabs.

I stroll through the village, and I think I know every house, every crooked, willow-plaited fence, every mushroom-shaped, snow-laden, icicle-hung thatched roof, and also every face that gapes at me without knowing who I might be, and every eye, sparkling with curiosity, peering through the panes of the little windows:

but not a single eye can see me at one-third my present size, in a small gray coat with a tobacco-colored velvet collar, a round gray hat on my curly head, and the hated bow—enormous, spotted like a toadstool—under my chin; no one sees me holding Miss Fern's hand, nicely lifting my little legs in their buttoned leggings over the beer-colored puddles in the mire of the village street. No, I am no longer Christopher Robin.

I walk through rooms so musty, dusty, seedy that my heart contracts. I think I can still sense a breath of my mother's perfume—a sentimental delusion, of course. Only after a few days do I realize that some of the rooms have been completely repapered, refurbished, rearranged . . .

I listen to the huge, mysteriously chattering stillness of the park, whose floods of summery green were always filled with invisible life: busy birdsong and birds whooshing in the boughs, the needle-fine squealing of a dormouse in the foliage of the bushes, a rocking branch from which a squirrel, a marten, has leaped, an owl has soundlessly soared, bits of bark dropping down from heaven knows where, the soft gurgling of frog heads peeping out of the water and then vanishing in the reeds around the motionless water lilies on the pond, a rustling in the leaves, perhaps from a hedgehog or a ring snake . . .

I have always, all my life, carried it in my blood, this park. It was my Garden of Eden, my paradise promised and lost. Missing it was the bitterest part of my exile. I traveled toward it as toward a beloved, its image in my senses: the soughing of its treetops in the night wind, the sun-dappled coolness of its shade, the damp fresh moldy smell rising in autumn from the leopard skin of the forest floor, its mushroom taste of fern and moss and bark . . .

I regard myself as its creature. Whatever is in it I find also in myself: as the decor of my childhood legend, the proper grooming of its gravel paths, and the vain complacence of the Russian pavilion with the ornamental stained-glass lozenges in the birch woods; the Mondrian severity of the rolled, red, white-lined subdivisions of the tennis court, and the sumptuous flowering of the shrubs on the tall fence surrounding it . . .

and above and beyond this (always there, not simply aroused after years of exile in Vienna) the air of adventure: the sudden stench of carrion in the blackberry thicket of some remote unsupervised corner; the romanticism, true, of the huge cedars along the ramshackle wall crumbling under burdens of ivy, but also the sinister and disreputable quality of the black soil of the creek banks, hollowed out by rats and crayfish under the giant hairy umbrellas of the coltsfoot leaves . . .

I walk toward it, my park, and, within, toward all the vast, rich safety of my childhood:

the park receives me and has become abstract: white, rigid, transparent all the way to the far countryside, glassily sparkling under the silky deep-blue sky, tinkling in the frost as if transposed into another dimension, abstracted, its own myth and legend.

And for the first time I see it, see its framework, the way it is set in the countryside: a landscape garden, a piece of idealized nature within nature (*a reality within reality*), fanning out into the flatly troughed and then gently rolling and rising terrain, with the first signs of formal severity showing in the now-frosty snowed-in ornamental scrolls of the flower beds, between which the beeline central path leads to the gates with the snow-capped stone greyhounds on the pillars . . .

and directly beyond, in greater freedom: a spacious English park of goodly proportions between the open lawns and the dense foliage of the summertime trees. To one side, then, toward the dell, a peasant garden full of folk mock-heraldry in the ostrich tails of the black cabbage and the halberd leaves of artichokes, along the parallel rows of fruit trees, whose rounded tops are now dusted with snow and transparent, like the seed tops of dandelions (which my mother used to call "Larousses"). And on the other side, on the rising slope, a game preserve: the small herd of fallow deer that always stood there in the coppice are standing there now, finely drawn in the snow.

Signs in the snow: it's still alive, my park. Mystery is still stirring in it, making a frosted branch snap up so that its white fur drops off and sinks into the down of the snow bed, which receives it glitteringly, everywhere the snow bearing the fine script of life so quick and shy that it would almost not have been, but for these traces

(the most eloquent: a deathbed of powdery snow crystals, strewn with half a handful of downy feathers, three or four drops of blood, a yellowish spot . . . Chinese ideogram of a small catastrophe) . . .

It lives on unchallenged, my park. Everything in it is precisely as it always was, even twice seven years ago—except that I am no longer here.

Or rather: I am here in a dual, abstract way that can be mirrored back and forth at will: I as a child, and my own legend of myself as a child, and I now, likewise detached from myself. I gaze at both of them, first through one at the other, then through the other at the one. I gaze through my present self at the child who in his curly-haired, cherry-eyed charm, his well-bred, adorable moodiness and precociousness, was already, all too consciously, his own legend and probably deserved to be slapped. And I gaze through the child's eyes at the lightly built young man, scrawny, pale, shot up too fast, but visibly tough as a whip, wearing his uniform like borrowed clothing, with a strange watchfulness and, if you look him square in the face, something of Aunt Selma's enchantment in his eyes (and another, more modest garden in his mind).

I put my two selves side by side, testing them for this or that aspect, this or that value. I find that the twice seven years of exile, the hateful formative Viennese years with Uncle Helmuth, Aunt Hertha, Aunt Selma, and all their bloody fucking middle-class thinking and feeling and reasoning and arguing and praising and condemning and accusing, as well as the diabolically tempting Cain-like brotherhood with Cousin Wolfgang, were in many, many respects a wholesome testing, a hardening. And the no longer so finely groomed attitude, the no longer so sheltered and protected nature, the slight air of neglect—all these things they have so clearly left with me are balanced by a keener sight and a certain nobility in being able to hate.

But not even this has anything to do with me, really. This too is already a legend, which someday I may have to cultivate—like the other legend of myself in my childhood, the other myth with which I deliver myself into timelessness; I could not have existed otherwise...

Now, here, returning home to the land of my damnation to form myths of myself, I am once again new, different, something I have never been before:

A man who is everywhere a stranger, but most of all in his own home.

18

My book (which, as you know, was unfortunately never completed) was also supposed to describe a different cold world: the Ice Age five, six, seven (there we are again!) years later in Hamburg-on-the-Elbe, Germany: WWII's aftermath, known as the Age of Rubble, or the Age of Reichsmarks.

This period is experienced by the same person, an alien everywhere, soon at home everywhere, and most alien to himself in his own home—

experienced by a person who has virtually come out of himself and is beside himself, for whom, to be sure, this schizoid split became so much a part of his nature even then (1947) that it produced a peculiar, gleeful well-being,

a feeling of immunity, of invulnerability—not a resistance to surprises, which our cherished life always has in store for us, but an ultimate inviolability in regard to surprises (the result, of course, being a totally abstract relationship to existence, to the world, and, last but not least, to morality).

In my manuscripts, I have gone to great pains to explain and clarify how this trance-like state was induced by the experience of March 12, 1938—the day Adolf Hitler came home to his homeland, Austria, which German troops occupied amid the jubilant delirium of the people. But even the most conscientious analysis boils down to inexplicables. It was the day when one era ended and another began. A day of solstice, when the sun stood still in the heavens. It is easy to write this down, of course, but proving it will be far more difficult. However, that will be done elsewhere.

What I wish to say here can probably be best expressed in a description of the climatic conditions.

March 12, 1938, was, as we all know, an unusually cold day. Arctic iciness plunged like a guillotine blade into the loveliest and most promising spring. Yet the sky remained blank and blue, not a breeze was stirring. The sun's smile was caught, like that of a beheaded man. And because the saps of spring had begun to rise, buds and shoots and perhaps also hopeful hearts froze to ice so suddenly that they shone, the world looked as if it had been placed under a glass bell: extraordinarily smart and delicately pretty and well-nigh varnished all over. The springtime seething was cut off, naturally. And with it the mood of the first half of my life.

On that March 12, 1938, I was in Vienna with Stella. She had long since taken my destiny in hand and was already preparing my return to Romania, my call-up for military service there, and my visit to

Uncle Ferdinand in order to enter the sphere of influence of reliable friends; thus, she had already launched the entire intrigue that made me unreachable, lifted me over the coming events, kept me hovering, as it were, between heaven and earth throughout the war, but ultimately cost her her life.

We spent a summer of near-exemplary beauty in the Salzkammergut and managed to enjoy many more hectic days of sunshine in the following year, 1939, before the first shot was fired in September and Europe committed suicide for good. But, retrospectively, the iciness of March 1938 passed directly into that of February 1940 in Bessarabia, and then, fairly uninterrupted, into the diluvial period of Hamburg until 1947. And it goes on, visibly losing light, turning grayer and drearier, more and more wintry. I cannot recall a single bright day during the so-called Age of Rubble or of Reichsmarks from 1945 to 1948 in Hamburg-on-the-Elbe, Germany. Never did the sun shine but through aseptic gauze, even during the brief Arctic summers when trees and shrubs were greening amid the yellow tundra grass in Pöseldorf or Övelgönne.

At any rate, by February 1940, which I am now telling about, it has been going on for almost two years—this Ice Age that keeps getting grayer and grayer, perhaps because it keeps filling up with gray iron men and smoking, fire-spewing iron weapons, and more and more gray men keep dropping and turning into phantoms under the smoke-and-fire spewing of these weapons, many many hundreds of thousands of gray phantoms, flowing together in a denser and denser wintry fog that shrouds the world and veils the sun so thickly that it hangs as a small, pallid, powerless disk in the grayness, even after the thundering of the fires has been snuffed out.

I too, in my nettle-cloth uniform, yellow-green like dried peas, am now (in February 1940) one of the iron men. I too occasionally wear an iron helmet with a chin strap, and I handle iron weapons that are ready to spew fire. My regiment is ready for action. Each one of its four thousand young men secretly prays to God that, if it comes down to it, he will be among the few hundred survivors. We have sworn to serve our Fatherland unto death with our weapons in our fists, and the makers of this cant and these weapons are trying to harden our mood, our combative will, our readiness to die—harden them like iron. But nonetheless we are a rather sorry lot, shaking with fear whenever things look serious for us too, fatalistic whenever the immediate danger is merely put off until tomorrow. And terribly hopeful, by the way: that the Germans'll get it done.

The Germans. They've got a kind of warfare, called *Blitz*, that rips enemy armies open like a zipper. They spliced and crushed the Poles, they'll do the same to the French. And when the time comes—that is, when they can free their dreadful hands for the job—they'll work the Russians over in the same way. All we'll have to do is storm after them, spurt a little fire here and there, stick a couple of bayonets into anything that resists. Perhaps we, the cavalrymen, can even mount again and chase our fleeing foes, slicing and smashing them with lances and sabers, so that war will regain something of its old, colorful fun ... But the war hasn't reached us as yet. The war too is temporarily frozen; the adversaries are lying opposite each other like dragons, showing their fangs before charging and entangling themselves and tearing one another to shreds. Even the Russians are paralyzed in this hostile lockjaw, prevented from invading Romania by the Nonaggression Pact with Germany. Accordingly, the weather here is still bright and beautiful, almost festive. "Hitler weather," it has been called since March 1938: days pearling along crisp and cold under an azure sky, yet the woods and fields and meadows, the trees and bushes and groves are covered with a fur of frost, which shouldn't be mistaken for warmth ...

I, at any rate, can still play the peacetime soldier, the toy soldier. Uncle Ferdinand has gotten me an apparently unlimited furlough. Naturally, he knows the brigadier general. My regimental commander clicks his heels at the sound of his name. For his sake, I was simply shoved up the ladder from a one-year volunteer recruit to master-at-arms and finally second lieutenant. In his honor, instead of the dried-pea yellow-green uniform at dinner (we are a party of two, served by four footmen) I can wear the plum-blue, gold-frogged, red-braided officer's uniform, in which I feel like the lothario in a student performance of a classic Viennese operetta.

Uncle Ferdinand goes to bed very late. He finally has somebody to talk to about his Middle Kingdom, tell stories to, show letters, photo albums, and news clippings to. In short, he can now discuss the most urgent matters of the inner circle, the nucleus of this distant reality within reality. The discussion usually goes on until the gray hours of dawn. Finally, liberated at long last from my high boots and the throat-tightening collar of the hussar tunic, drugged with fatigue, numb with much-too-heavy food, far too much wine, coffee, kirsch, whiskey, my head spinning nonstop like a mill wheel, I tumble into the pillows of an English brass bed, which, I would swear, my mother ordered from London during my childhood. And now, the memories slosh over me, inundate me...

but the images, the scenes, the moods, colors, sounds, smells that I have carried about, as precise as if engraved in steel, that I have so poignantly preserved, like flowers pressed between book pages, like ribbons, locks of hair, and billets-doux stored through decades in splint boxes—now, all these things turn out to be inaccurate and deceptive; they tumble chaotically, dissolve, flow together and away...

I lie in the bed in which my mother (if memory serves me and this really is the extra-wide bed that she ordered from London before 1926) presumably received Uncle Ferdinand, the rooster... I am no longer a child and I can imagine what happened then. Nor do I have any illusions about my beautiful mother's professionalism in this respect: I can exchange Uncle Ferdinand at will with any of my numerous godfathers and nominal uncles and leave the scene unaltered. (Mama, after all, had ordered not just one of these brass beds but several, dispatching one to our house on the Côte d'Azur, one to Uncle Bully's house in Biarritz, one to Uncle Agop's house in Ireland, and God knows where else.)

Here, as everywhere, it was the same. A high-class courtesan (*poule de luxe*, as the term was in those days) always serves her present backer. My mother the trollop. I, the son of a whore. A suicide's bastard. Stella the Jewess's gigolo, kept by her husband, the spy...

I say this out loud to myself to test the effect that the echo of such disgraceful epithets might provoke in me. But there is no effect. Quite the contrary: It amuses me to imagine the irony with which my beautiful mother might have plied her loose trade and been ready to grant her sundry lovers' every desire. Thanks to her (and John and Stella and all my nominal uncles and godfathers) I am totally lacking in the sense of *shame* that my Viennese relatives tried to instill in me: Aunt Hertha occasionally at length and with insinuations about the past and my mother's end that were scarcely to be mistaken, Aunt Selma in spellbound silence, Uncle Helmuth with biting discretion, and Cousin Wolfgang generously not saying a word: the poor blind fools! The pitiful misled saps! The victims, constantly deceiving themselves, of the criminal narrowness of their reality within a reality! Martyrs of the falsity of their shittily vertical Middle Kingdom, who have no past and no trace of a future, but only a gray, cheerless present for all time: always reflected in themselves; seeing nothing before them but themselves, their eyes incapable of seeing anything else! . . . But what really torments me is the discovery that I know as good as nothing about my mother, don't at all know her as she really was; that I'm but a hypothesis of myself based on a hypothesis of her. The image of her that I have been carrying around might, on the whole, correspond only hazily and casually to her actual reality, despite the sharpness of countless details—like the images I preserved within myself of this house, the village, and even the park (images that here and now I find myself forced incessantly to correct). I have found photographs of her: they do not fit the legend of my sweet mother in any way, and yet they complement and complete it, as though I were now discovering an unknown dimension of her, of myself, that might conceal yet other dimensions . . .

I know and have always known that the radiant maternal goodness that I think I recall, the smiling-Madonna quality (without the crushed suffering of Our Lady of Sorrow), the lightness, the serenity that made me think I was a favorite of fortune—I know that all these were figments of my imagination, daydreams, retrospective projections of eternally unfulfilled wishes onto a concocted phantom. But that is not what unsettles me now.

Gazing at the extremely elegant, extremely fashionably stylized young woman on the (incidentally, masterful) photo portraits I have found here (they are signed: Bill Brandt), I cannot learn anything about myself. But I can learn a great deal about an era that haunts me like a ghost stalking a house.

To my small surprise (and secret satisfaction), it is not an era of mothers. The young woman embodying it is not a mother. With her steep, narrow shoulders from which the fur has slid, with her stem-like throat displaying the severe emerald necklace, with her shingled black hair like a patent-leather cap, her oval face with its small corrupt mouth, and her radiantly innocent eyes under her thin, high brows—this is the most feminine form conceivable of an ephebe. If someone like this bears a child, it must be either a demigod or a homunculus...

At first, however, this strange, beautiful creature in which I only very remotely discover familiar features similar to my own, as if in ironical reflection, is as desirable as a sister brought up somewhere else and entering my life as an adult: I know both everything and nothing about her, but I can vividly picture her as an excellent lover, with expert hands, like a Japanese flower arranger. What I see is the Eros of an era, and I—or perhaps that stratum of my existence that felt itself to be my self (and that I now feel *was* me at that time, as remote, to be sure, as abstract as Nagel's shot-off arm, my venerated Djakopp Djee)—this self is a child of that era and belongs to it more than my self of today does... and *is* no more and is merely an echo of something that has long since waned, just as tomorrow my self of today will belong to the echo of 1940 and will have waned and faded with it... if it does not emerge from me as an image and myth and live on as such.

And just as I am about to doze off with these thoughts, there is a banging in the big tiled stove, which is heated from the corridor. An old, familiar, deliciously cozy noise, announcing that Miss Fern is about to come in with a fresh, warmed-up bath towel in order to—but no. It means that fourteen years have passed; that my mother and ideal beloved is dead, drowned in the pond; and that I will now have to pull on my boots again, because Uncle Ferdinand, the spider, is waiting for me downstairs at the breakfast table (he hardly sleeps anymore) in order to weave me into his Middle Kingdom, so that it might live on as image and myth.

19

He waits for me with the cruelly loving patience of the spider waiting for the fly that strays into its web. He has long since had his tea, and his long, yellow teeth under the straw whisk of his mustache and the parrot beak of his nose are gnawing on a fragment of zwieback. Now he watches as I, with the ravenous hunger of an exhausted young man, wolf down bowls of oatmeal and milk (Miss Fern's long-missed porridge) and bacon and eggs and black bread and piles of toast with butter and honey and currant jam and orange marmalade. My exceedingly healthy appetite in my drowsiness, my visible freshening with the gradually rising day, the animal physicality of youth in me must repulse him, the rapidly aging man with the delicate stomach and weakened liver. But he doesn't show his disgust. His round eyes, still gazing sharply with piercing pupils from under their wrinkled, eggshell-thin lids, follow my every movement while his voice speaks to me: gently, in an elegant, tenderly ironic, lightly entertaining, conversational tone, changing language at whim or to fit the topic. Normally, he speaks a much-too-literary Balkan French, and pronounced with affected purity. But occasionally he uses the English of his generation, who, innocently believing that one must speak the King's English, mimicked Edward VII's German accent. At times, he lapses into his startlingly natural (albeit borderland-hard) Austrian aristocrat's German, or even Romanian, whereby an earthy, peasant-like vitality colors his diction.

I cannot escape him and his murmuring talk. He will follow me after breakfast when I stroll through the park, and the trees cover the tangerine-edged mother-of-pearl tones of the winter morning with the fine craquelure of frosted twigs and branches. He will have a servant help him into a fur coat that will enshroud him in otter from the ears to the ankles; the tremendous collar will prevent a heavy cap of the same otter skin from sliding over his eyes down to his nose. And he will walk along with me step for step and talk to me. He will accompany me when I take a shotgun and a couple of hounds and comb the river meadows for wild duck and hares. Why, he will even be at my side when I try to escape him on horseback: two stableboys will lift him into the saddle of an age-toughened, Roman-nosed hunter; his endless skinny legs with straightened locked knees will be rigid in the stirrups, and his globular spider body will still rise bolt upright on a steely spine. Clearly indifferent to the grim cold that brings tears to my eyes, he will stay at the right edge of my field of vision in the swiftly passing winter landscape. He will sway gently when walking his horse, seesaw up and down when trotting, and finally vibrate at a high frequency when galloping—and his voice will be unremittingly gentle, elegant, tenderly ironic, and casually conversational as it murmurs past my eardrum.

There is nothing thematically or even chronologically coherent in what he has to tell me. His talk does not follow the laws of axial structure as in a crystal; it has no beginning and no foreseeable end. This is life immediately rendered, illogical at a longer, wider range, randomly experienced in a fusillade of impressions, arbitrarily plucked out, reproduced in mental leaps and fragments. Yet all these things make for a full world and for reality, so fascinating that I am soon spellbound. I find myself woven into them, more and more densely, and paralyzed by them. I keep thinking of the flies that Stella and I tossed into the cobwebs of an old lakeside bathhouse a year and a half ago (summer 1938) in the Salzkammergut, and the loving and tender care with which the fat garden spiders wrapped them in their threads until they were swaddled like mummies...

Uncle Ferdinand reports on his Middle Kingdom even at lunchtime, when we eat a light repast of four courses and three wines, still in the bright breakfast room. But the age-palsied footman playing the maître d'hôtel here is already wearing his tails. (Is this the same man about whom my mother used to say, when talking about faraway

Bessarabia to the amusement of the entire Côte d'Azur, that it was easier to squeeze him into his tails than to teach him not to appear in them barefoot?)

And afterward, while we sip black coffee in the library, Uncle Ferdinand will open out the perspectives on what he told me during the morning. He will show me the albums, the photos of houses, yachts, hunts—the scenes where it all took place. We will contemplate various snapshots of the people involved and study their genealogy, their relatives in the *Almanach de Gotha*, in *Burke's*, in the *Libro d'Oro*, their business connections in *Who's Who*...

I soon know the personnel of the Middle Kingdom by heart. After all, I'm well prepared: I recall many of the names from my childhood; I know the personalities, characteristics, spleens, likes and dislikes, vices and virtues, thanks to the social chitchat that I snapped up as a child and that was recently brought *à la page* again in conversations between John and Stella. Why, I even know some of these people; I can quite vividly recollect them; I used to call them by their first names, address them as "Uncle Bully" or "Uncle Agop." Even if they only barely recognized me, they might still remember delightful Maud (my mother's stage name, her real name being Ilse; but I am convinced that she plied her loose trade with sufficient artistry to have a certain right to a *nom de plumeau*).

in short: I am predestined for the legacy that Uncle Ferdinand wishes to leave me. Not his name, his fortune, his position in the world, of course, but that which can remain of those things when all their earthliness has crumbled into dust that the wind carries away: the *myth* of his bon-vivant world.

For simplicity's sake, we also have tea in the library. The table is set with the same silver as it was in the days of my childhood. My mother loved the intricate and practical odds and ends: the toast racks and beehive-shaped honey pots, the hot-water-heated plates and bowls for pastries and canapés, the little silver muffin baskets. She was responsible for the English look of the tea table, while Russia and the Near East prevail in the huge samovar and the Sèvres porcelain fabricated *pour l'Orient*.

Aside from the chintz sofas and Queen Anne furniture (which I presume replaced the rug-covered divans and Boulle consoles that, before her time, adorned a country estate in the realm of the Sublime Porte), I wonder whether her taste has left its mark on other things in and around Uncle Ferdinand, starting with his tweed jackets, going on to his not really Eastern European passion for ocean sailing, and ending with his liberal choice of friends.

Incidentally, Uncle Ferdinand has an interesting cultural-historical explanation for the latter. He says, "We, the survivors of the cataclysm of the First World War, who were clever enough to amuse ourselves until the outbreak of this second one, have been accused of toppling the boundary stones of morality and opening our homes to people of questionable background and contestable reputation merely because they entertained us. By so doing, we supposedly undermined the foundations of society. But one can see this in a different light. Putzi Cottolenghi told me that when his grandfather was a young man, he called upon the Vicomtesse de Fegonzac in order to present himself to her. She was already eighty years old, and she received him with the words 'Don't you find, monsieur, that the nicest object on earth is a sturdy, erect penis?' That was still in the best eighteenth-century style, aristocratic through and through. *We* tried to win back the same freedom after middle-class Victorianism had so dreadfully strangled any natural expression of rapport with life. *Épater les bourgeois!* was *our* motto. And today, no one is grateful to us for our efforts..." And, having become truly pensive, Uncle Ferdinand adds, "A society preserves its ethical landmarks by ruthlessly expelling anyone who dares to transgress them. He is henceforth cut by one and all. But how can you do that in an era when people have taken up the American custom of drinking cocktails before meals, so that before dinner is even served, everyone is so drunk that no one recognizes anyone, or everyone is ready to hurl his arms around the nearest perfect stranger?..."

Uncle Ferdinand stares at me with his round, hazelnut-brown eyes nailed fast by the black pinheads of their pupils. His gaze does not plead for agreement; it is downright demanding. After all, he is presenting his Middle Kingdom not for my critique and analysis but as a costly gift, and despite the exposure of its internal dynamics, he is delivering it in its wholeness and unique givenness, as a *happening*, so to speak. I therefore abandon myself to the experience without offering resistance.

I gaze at the happy-go-lucky rich of the blissful years of truce between the two world wars. Not only do I peer into their lives, backgrounds, pasts, into their brains, their nooks and crannies, their bank accounts, their businesses and business methods; I am soon initiated into their games, with their often intricate rules, including those games that are not played at polo grounds, tennis courts, golf courses, or roulette and baccarat tables. I know the internal structure of this easygoing world of players, even the view from within this world to the world outside. (For instance, the geography that is a phenomenon of "seasons." "There are," says Uncle Ferdinand, "people whom you see on the Riviera in spring and then in London for the season, and afterward, of course, for grouse-shooting in Scotland in August. And in between, there are others whom you see in Biarritz or on the Lido or sailing in the Aegean or in Scandinavia—it all depends on whether someone prefers the sun or the rough sea. And then again, you see others in Deauville for polo or in Merano for the races, or at the autumn hunting in the Ardennes and in Hungary and God knows where else. And others in Egypt during the winter or for skiing in the Engadine. Yes, and then there are people whom you see all year long and everywhere—your friends, in short, the ones who really count...")

I am also familiarized with the secrets of those spherical hierarchies: the innermost circles from which the closer and farther circles of friends radiate, intersecting and intertwining with the closer and farther circles of other inner circles—I know them all as intimately as if I belonged to each circle right at the center and nucleus...

of course, I know them so intimately only from hearsay, albeit very thorough hearsay. After all, John and Stella talk about them constantly, naming, mentioning, quoting someone or other whose renown and guaranteed wealth plus no doubt quite reliably similar outlook on the world and on life would place him, as a matter of course, in some system of rings of friends in the Middle Kingdom (the manner in which they are named, mentioned, quoted, hints at differences in rank and degrees of intimacy down to the finest nuance)...

and this could mean that even John and Stella, incessantly and almost against their will, at any rate without the slightest intention, are weaving away at the myth of the Middle Kingdom—John and Stella, the independent ones, the completely unconcerned ones, without the slightest social ambition, who demonstrated ironic indulgence, at best, toward the conspiratorial innermost circle of Uncle Ferdinand's playboy world, and who do their assiduous best to avoid other, more rigorously closed systems of circles of friends of the upper ten thousand (for instance, with very few exceptions, the North German aristocracy)—even John and Stella, I say, did their bit in weaving away at the myth... and I can't believe they did this only because their wealth, background, and education automatically made them part of the cosmos of these rich, renowned, and influential people and sent them wandering like nomads through the closer and farther circles of their world within the world.

20

This makes me pensive, and I have the leisure to brood about it when I am permitted to retire for three quarters of an hour before dinner in order to bathe and change.

A guest of this reality, which seems more and more unreal (hostile armies are deploying behind each of the inner circles of Uncle Ferdinand's Middle Kingdom), I lie in the huge, old-fashioned tub in the middle of the bright, cheery, spacious room that my mother fixed up as a bathroom for me. In the fourteen years of my exile from the world of wealth, I never tired of describing it in detail to my cousin Wolfgang, because it was so utterly different from the damp, narrow hole in the wall, smelling of detergent, with its cold tiles and dripping, half-rusted water pipes, in the dark Viennese apartment where we bleakly vegetated through our dreary days (together with Cousin Wolfgang's parents, my foster parents—Uncle Helmuth and Aunt Hertha—as well as Aunt Selma, my real foster mother). There, the bathroom was a place in which those tasks necessary for physical hygiene and regarded as important in one's general philosophy of life had to be performed behind locked doors as an embarrassing necessity to be discharged quickly and prudishly. Here, it was an almost sensuously cozy room filled with comforts that pointed more to play and dawdling than to harsh cleansing, and you left as if you had just stepped out of a bandbox, with an aura of fragrant freshness, whereas there you came out steaming and scrubbed red but tired and tending to sweat. Chattering with Cousin Wolfgang, I gushed on about my childhood bathroom in Bessarabia. I was no less enthusiastic about it than about the park "in the faraway Balkan land," as Uncle Helmuth called it, sarcastically. I described the sumptuous delights of that bathroom: the huge, prewarmed bath towels, in which one could wrap oneself from head to toe; the gigantic sponges, feather light and crunchingly brittle when dry, heavily dripping when soaked in water; the fragrant soaps and pungently prickling colognes... but this, of course, elicited merely a disparaging shrug from Cousin Wolfgang, who was above such mollycoddling and used the toilet as a study where he could be relatively undisturbed.

Nevertheless, while cozily soaping my limbs in the perfumed water here, I cannot but be moved at the thought of my Viennese relatives. I think of the prophetic threats that Uncle Helmuth uttered—to Aunt Hertha's and Aunt Selma's chorus-like approval and even the tacit agreement of Cousin Wolfgang (who by now has, alas, perished as a hero)—ranting on against "plutocrats": those corrupt, degenerate exploiters of the have-nots, among whom he also counted John and Stella; those devils who pulled me back, despite all my enlightened upbringing with its sound views and true values, into the debauched world where my mother had gone astray and given birth to me, a fatherless child, and where, when she soon perished justly and shamefully, I would have been callously left to starve had not they, my Viennese relatives, taken me in.

In fact, there was little to say about this other than that it was correct. But it would never have induced me to hate that admittedly vile but nonetheless bright, cheery, spacious world of the rich, whose bathrooms I yearningly recalled, or to love the hard, confused, detergent-smelling uprightness of the benefactors forced upon me. Nor did it stop me from observing that Uncle Helmuth's upward tantrums, against the plutocrats, were no more violent than his downward ones, against the proletarians, and that we, the educated have-not bourgeoisie, were hated from below, in the concierge lodges and back courtyard pens of our apartment house, as much as Uncle Helmuth hated the *society people* still putting on a show of aristocracy, the "snobs," as he wrongly called them.

In this respect too I disappointed if not betrayed my foster parents. If they assumed that I, the bastard who had popped into their home from the taboo world of the rich, would become at least an ally in their even more violent dislike of the back courtyard proletarians, then their hope was lamentably misplaced. Aunt Hertha lamented this frequently and bitterly. How could she have known that Miss Fern had cautioned me to stay discreetly aloof from the "simple people" because I might otherwise embarrass them, and that these constant admonitions had aroused my burning curiosity to get to know these susceptible, hence obviously extremely sensitive people, get to know them as soon and as well as possible and find out what there was about me that could make them lose their composure, perhaps even assure them that there was no real cause for their response. Now that no visible social barriers separated me from them, I had the best chance to do so. So much childlike naiveté was bound to be beyond Aunt Hertha. And of course she could not know that the gray-faced men with collarless shirts, the haggard women in aprons, the snot-nosed children from the bedbug caves in the apartment house to which I was now exiled, were paradoxically the only people who had any sort of connection to my past life. Aside from the princely households of my mother's friends and patrons, I had known only such humble people. They were far more familiar to me, far more of a homeland, than the almost equally limited, equally gray-faced, grouchy but demanding and overpowering philistines with their baroque moral code and their egotism, who, arrogating the right to control my thoughts, feelings, and actions, styled themselves my benefactors and exacted gratitude from me.

I needn't bother saying that my actual attempts at openly approaching the *people* merely unleashed a fusillade of insults and vile imprecations. One of the mothers whose children I ventured to speak to pounced on me because their screams made her think I was trying to attack them. Furiously she grabbed my hand, yanked me up the stairs, and delivered me at our apartment door to Aunt Selma, paralyzed by such an affront to her, a lady. The mother poured out a verbal torrent, and since my German was lacking in those days and the barked-out Viennese dialect rendered it all the more unintelligible, I could only just make out that my relatives were well advised to keep this piss-elegant young dandy under control, otherwise there was no guaranteeing my safety.

Two or three years later, I did manage to break through after all. This happened in the course of a friendship I quickly formed at school with a boy who, to Cousin Wolfgang's endless and scornful delight, was the son of a trolley conductor and lived, not far from us, in the rear building of another tenement. By now I recollect very little about this friend; I can barely remember his face. I recall only that his features darkened sadly when Cousin Wolfgang, who, as a gymnasium student, also despised us for attending the much less highbrow realschule, shouted after us, "Next stop Wieden, transfer to the Circle Line, please don't push, keep the aisle clear!..." But I will never forget a summer Sunday that I was permitted to spend with the trolley conductor's family in a suburban garden near Mödling: a day of Maupassant-like nostalgia and enchantment, woven entirely of trivial things, with a picnic on the grass, during which the father's undershirt and the mother's stockings, rolled up under her fat knees, did not arouse any feelings of social repulsion. Rather, they made me forget about the bad clothes I had to wear after outgrowing the Little Lord Fauntleroy outfit I had arrived with from Bessarabia. We had a hearty sip of wine with our sausages and munched green apples from a tree and did airy gymnastics on a shed the roof of which Father Trolley Conductor had nailed down with fresh tarpaper. We spent hours fishing for tadpoles in a small brook and then drank a delicious glass of clotted milk in the evening, while Mother Trolley Conductor hollowed out a pumpkin for us, cutting eyes, a nose, and an enormous, toothy mouth, so that we could stick a candle inside and frighten the neighborhood children. First, however, to my great delight, Father Trolley Conductor gave an artistic performance. He placed the candle in front of the wall, and his hands created the most entertaining shadow pictures: barking dog heads and ear-wriggling bunnies and similar delightful things.

When I returned to my relatives, who excitedly recounted a hike through the woodlands of the Rax, I had my first fistfight with Cousin Wolfgang, which made Aunt Hertha say I had the makings of a criminal: all that had preceded it was a remark that Wolfgang had arrogantly tossed at me when I finished the blazing description of my day: "From a castle park to a garden plot—should this step be viewed as descent or progress?"

Cousin Wolfgang now lies in Vienna's Central Graveyard. I think of him often and with sincere affection. In those last few years, when it tortured him to see me reading Nietzsche as a matter of course while he wrestled with the same text like Jacob with the angel ("For you, it's a cowboys-and-Indians story!" he said angrily. "And for you?" I asked. "But this shakes your whole being! This bowls you over! It forces your inmost nature to make an ultimate decision . . ." And then his voice trailed off before my ironic look. Oh Schwab!)

in the last few years, I say, when he was standing up more and more resolutely for the worldview of the National Socialist German Workers Party, which was outlawed in Austria but was celebrating triumphs in the "Old Reich," he would speak starry-eyed about the *Volk*. We used to talk a lot in those days, just before and just after John and Stella entered my life (until his way of seeing the world no longer permitted him to watch unprotesting while I lived as the kept lover of a Jewess). This was the era when we had drawn so close through our fistfights as to recognize our brotherhood despite our incompatibility—good Lord in heaven! Fourteen years together in one room, at one table, in front of the same emaciated faces, in the same dripping, steaming bathroom . . . Too bad he departed from us so prematurely, my dear cousin Wolfgang! He has been lying in the ground for six months now (it's 1940)—a martyr to *his* "reality within reality," which he regarded as the only reality: as if its standards, its weights and laws, were valid for everyone . . . I should have done more to convince him of God's approval of better bathrooms . . .

21

Anyhow, there in Bessarabia I pleasurably prolong my bath. I feel it's important to mull these things over while I cover my chest and arms with the sumptuous, spicy foam. Despite the four-course lunch and the opulent afternoon tea, I feel hungry, which adds a degree of poignant warmth to my affection for Uncle Ferdinand, for I know how carefully he will have arranged the dinner and the accompanying wines. I am tense and overtired, but quite thoroughly happy. I feel as if once more I have escaped into another, new, unexpected state, a new, abstract reality. My frame of mind must be similar to that of the souls who, at the Last Judgment, have managed just barely to slip under the angel's dividing hand to the right side of God—only to realize that they are floating in space because they have lost the ground under their feet.

I would have liked to chat with Cousin Wolfgang now. I enjoy picturing him seated here on the edge of the bathtub as he so often did on Sundays in the bathroom of the apartment in the Twelfth District, when Uncle Helmuth and Aunt Hertha and Aunt Selma had gone off to the woodlands of the Rax, and he and I, claiming we had to study, enjoyed a quiet day of ample loafing and undisturbed bathing joys. Our brotherhood was unclouded at such times.

Now, here, I could talk to him "fairly"—as we said—about John and Stella: with more thorough knowledge and greater insight into the ways and dynamics of their world. I could explain to him why it made no difference at all whether they were the exploiters and oppressors that Uncle Helmuth made them out to be (and that he, Wolfgang, agreeing with his father for once, saw them as): John, the second son of the second son of some high-ranking peer, who went through the typical education process at Eton and Cambridge, who, casually and peripherally, as it were, became a linguist, highly esteemed in that field for his knowledge of Sanskrit and ancient Persian and for his translations and editions of rare manuscripts from the early Sufi period, but who one day chucked his bookworm life and entered the British diplomatic service, where his duties were of a very special sort; and Stella, the daughter of a Bucharest department-store millionaire, a woman for whom squandering money was an inner compulsion, a redemption of her socialist conscience from the guilt of being a capitalist's child. Stella, who, in Berlin—the legendary Berlin of the late twenties!—had been friends with Paul Flechtheim, Gottfried Benn, Max Reinhardt, George Grosz; who had studied sociology in Heidelberg, psychology at the Sorbonne, art history in Florence and Freiburg, and was as well known in Prague as in Madrid. Stella, who had her winter chalet at Saint Moritz, her summer villas in Saint-Jean-Cap-Ferrat and Biarritz, and regularly won the prize for being the most elegant "Lady in Her Car" at the autumn races in Baden-Baden as well as first prize in the golf tournament. Stella, the indefatigable nightclub denizen, the chain-smoker whose collection of lovers was as significant as her collection of Futurist art. Stella, who had read her Marx as passionately as *The Divine Comedy*, who knew her Einstein as thoroughly as the writings of Lilly Braun... Whether it was correct to call these two people plutocrats, cynically knowing participants in and promoters of an inhumane system, even its parasites—this made no difference whatsoever;

it wasn't the issue, any more than to what extent and in what manner they would have been able to open new horizons for Cousin Wolfgang too, to have done for him what they did for me: expand the world by adding a different world, freer, roomier, airier than the petit bourgeois confinement in which we spitefully crammed our Plutarch and Hölderlin in order to be *something better* than the uneducated in the back courtyards. They could have opened up to him a world that was cheerier, brighter, more humane than our sweaty, anxiety-damp probity made insipid by hopes that were never fulfilled, the philistine probity about which we boasted because it cost so many sacrifices, though it brought us nothing that did not feed our arrogance; in any case, a world in which the bathroom pipes weren't rusty from the wet laundry always hanging from them.

He hated all these things as much as I did, my brother Cousin Wolfgang. He suffered as much as I did from the stench of cabbage and watery soup in the stairwell of No. 14 in a long line of tenements built in the same ugly way, dilapidated in the same grease-smeared, gray, filthy decay. He felt as much as I did how our vitality was suffocated under all sorts of lamentable restrictions and shameful renunciations. He felt as much as I did—like a lead band around the mind—the eternal anxiety about that cherished bit of breathing space beyond sheer existence, threatened daily by higher rents, potato prices, job dismissals, forced evictions...

he was as ashamed as I was of the rigid demand for recognition, the jealously alert, distrustful class arrogance and cultural *hauteur* with which we looked down on the "trash," the "little people," the proletarians and semi-proletarians from the back courtyard and basement holes. We, the educated ones, strictly brought up with so-called good manners ("Would you please stand up, you ass, when a lady enters the room!"), as poor as church mice but clean ("Did you wash your neck? Show me your fingernails!"), bypassed by Fortune, stepchildren of life, scared of a hundred taboos but proud. Uncle Helmuth, a native of Thuringia, the son of a pastor with innumerable children, respectably starving as he worked his way through college, getting his degree in electrical engineering and occupying a low industrial position only because research was paid even more poorly. And Aunt Hertha and Aunt Selma, the stiff-necked soldier's children, born somewhere between Przemyśl and Udine, the daughters of a Lieutenant Colonel Subicz, who (successfully emulated by Cousin Wolfgang a quarter century later) promptly died in action in Galicia in November 1914 and strangely enough also turned into a myth. A myth, to be sure, that no one beyond our four walls cared a fig about and of which no other token was left but a yellow photograph showing a waxed mustache over a uniform collar, a saber with a thickly knitted gold-thread sword knot, and a medal earned by a legendary saber scar across the forehead. That was all that remained, or could be learned, of Lieutenant Colonel Subicz. But his spouse, who likewise had died prematurely, was a *von* Jaentsch, and that sufficed to give Cousin Wolfgang his rigid spine and his scorn for trolley conductors, and Aunt Hertha her occasionally breezy but normally wry and caustic complacence, and Aunt Selma the bewitchment in her old-maid boniness; and it never let any of them forget what a disgrace it was that the third daughter, born in Dornbirn of Lieutenant Colonel Subicz and his spouse née von Jaentsch, beautiful Ilse (who characteristically called herself Maud!), went astray and perished by her own hand, leaving behind a bastard as a stain on their clan: humble me.

My brother Cousin Wolfgang had all these things in his blood just as I did—like a disease, a wasting toxin (which, however, if you overcame it, made you especially robust and immune to susceptibilities). For him too, it would have meant salvation to leave all these things behind and manage to forget them. For him too, then, the temptation to switch his world out for another must have been irresistible. But no: Cousin Wolfgang was one of those people who prefer to *change* the world—lock, stock, and barrel. He did not live in life, he lived in ideas and convictions. And suffered because a sharp-toothed doubt gnawed on the most sublime ideas, the firmest of his convictions—

and it would be idle, invalid, to perceive in this doubt some possibility of hauling him into my camp: for the camps are long since indeterminable, the fronts vague, shifting; everyone is entangled in everyone else, no matter what ideas or convictions a person was once moved by—

and thus it is also idle to brood about the philosophy underlying the subtle distinctions in John and Stella's social likes and dislikes. The resulting valuation seems strange. For instance, they take a lively interest in the fates and concerns of the working classes, and not just theoretically, they naturally *adore* their chef, spoil their caretaker's wife, treat their chauffeur, John's butler, and Stella's chambermaids with patriarchal care and kindness, heartily shake hands with their dentist when encountering him in the lobby of the opera, greet his wife with explosive recognition whether meeting her for the first or the tenth time; however, they display ethereally remote *politesse* toward the wife of a bank director, because the borders are so fine here as to be all too easily crossed; and with vigorous cordiality they are icily neutral toward the wives of those of John's diplomatic colleagues who cannot deny a background that is, no doubt, highly respectable but simply not quite to be counted as part of Society.

a year and a half ago, I recall, all this was terribly interesting to me. I felt the bliss of a butterfly hunter who has caught an especially rare and beautiful specimen when, for instance, I discovered that it is always the wives who determine the final place in the social hierarchy; for the time being, bachelors are uncategorized, with every opportunity open . . .

but it is winter 1940, the first Ice Age commenced two years ago and is about to climax, the butterflies are dead on their pins in the glass cases, my passion for lepidoptera has deepened into a passion for deeper biological dynamics: now, for instance, I would like to open Cousin Wolfgang's eyes to what the stylistic difference between John and Stella's informational conversations and Uncle Ferdinand's overflowing chitchat signifies for their joint world. When John and Stella exchange information about the *beau monde* they belong to, they do so in a businesslike way, which is cool, terse, and precise. Their membership is presumed by their social prestige and their financial standing, matters that must be administered both cautiously and soberly if they are to be well administered. John and Stella, in the web of the higher and highest circles, hang on the threads of innumerable commercial, social, familial, and, last but not least, simply human interests. Unavoidably, they talk about their world. But only privately. They leave no doubt that it is a closed world. They even lower their voices as though fearing that outsiders might be eavesdropping. Even when they are alone—or privately with me—they speak quickly, in shorthand and ciphers: they refer to people either by nicknames and pet names (Maxi, Bully, Manetti, Coco, Toto, Cloclo) or by titles that reveal nothing to the uninitiated about family connections and that conceal degrees of kinship like that between the Baron Charlus and the Duke of Guermantes. Or else they speak about their friends by using—even more mysteriously—the names of their estates, which are not always identical to their family names. John and Stella practice the utmost discretion. Even when directly asked, they avoid exposing all too intimate facts. And they handle anything beyond the sparest information with a certain blurry sketchiness, which one can follow only with precise and comprehensive knowledge and which is therefore accessible only to true initiates (even though the subject matter is usually something that anyone might just as well know). Even I, who live with them in a way that one could—God knows!—call intimate, am sometimes afflicted by a vexed impatience at this hush-hush business over banalities. And though Coco's wheelings and Cloclo's dealings are largely matters of indifference to me, I do find that when John and Stella exchange their quick and quiet seals and ciphers, I am as spellbound as someone trying to divine the hushed cooperation of face and gesture between two deaf-mutes.

Still, this never happens without John and Stella's instantly apologizing and hinting that these are matters that could not possibly be of general interest but that must, alas, be briefly discussed (by them). They leave no doubt that only one part of their existence belongs to this world within the world—the worldly part—and that neither their egos nor their true interests have settled there. John and Stella wish very much to be treated as individuals and persons, quite independent of membership in the *grand world* of society (which is actually a very small world)—even if they can't deny that, within this particular world within the world and its reality, they live in an ever more abstract and unreal reality. Still and all, they *live* in it; they speak of something that is *alive*.

Uncle Ferdinand is altogether different. He identifies fully with his Middle Kingdom. Never for a moment does Uncle Ferdinand think of himself as outside it, for he is intergrown with it in every fiber of his being. And yet he speaks of it with utmost indiscretion. He exposes the most humiliating facts, reveals the most compromising circumstances, does not spare the most personal and intimate details; but he does all this with a reporter's sobriety, which is disarming. He narrates even the worst scandals in a matter-of-fact way that allows any judgment, makes no moral or aesthetic evaluation, but simply testifies to something that exists, like life itself.

Above all, Uncle Ferdinand speaks with this relentless scientific detachment to me—an outsider. True, he pretends to take me for granted as one of his own kind, to whom he may assume that his world is not alien and whom his tales would not strike dumb, like the fables of Sinbad the Sailor of the copper city to which the roc carried him. But the thoroughness with which Uncle Ferdinand exposes each bit of trash (Toto's wheelings and Cloclo's dealings) in every kind of connection with other bits of information both trivial and significant—demonstrating, explicating, dissecting—merely betrays how well aware he is of dealing with a nonmember who must be taught the rudiments.

Uncle Ferdinand is deliberately telling tales out of school because he wants to transmit what went on *in* school. He wants to instruct me about his Middle Kingdom as minutely and precisely as possible. Whether he seeks to understand his aims and motives is debatable. He probably never asks himself. Something urges him to it. It might be his loneliness and nearly monkish isolation from the world here in threatened, wintry Bessarabia, his yearning for his friends, the other paladins of the Middle Kingdom, his homesickness for them. But his exile here is voluntary. And so it is to be assumed then that something urges him to it as well: perhaps the clear insight into the nature of the time, perhaps an instinctive sense for it. When Uncle Ferdinand feels the urge to talk about the Middle Kingdom, then it is not really *he* who is speaking—something speaks out of him. *The Middle Kingdom wants to speak through him*. Uncle Ferdinand must *speak* his world, for otherwise it no longer is and will never have been.

True, the kingdom of the rich and richly influential has not gone under. WWII, expanding more and more icily, more and more lethally, in this heart of winter 1940, may have disrupted the overlappings of the circles of friends. But Maxi, Bully, Mutzi, Putzi, Manetti, Coco, Toto, Cloclo, or whatever their names are, they're all still getting by. Restricted perhaps, cut off from their own kind, without galas, dinner parties, cocktail parties, treasure hunts, but certainly not in dire straits. Some of them may even die, but they have heirs to their wealth and spirit. The carnivore's teeth have not been blunted. Once the deluge is past, they will weave themselves together again, probably tighter, tauter, finer-meshed, and richer in booty than before, with threads of interests more mercantile, more *mondaine*, more tightly connected and in the end more quintessentially human. Nevertheless—or rather, for that very reason—their world will never again be what it was in Uncle Ferdinand's time. For it is already a world of shadows and will remain a world of shadows, albeit occasionally moved to become lifelike by a shadow player and evoked for the glory of the shadows' magic.

22

That is what I would like to explain to my dead cousin Wolfgang: Uncle Ferdinand's innocence. His eminently creative inability to act otherwise. The way he is woven into his time, his unity with the spirit of his time—an involvement so intimate that he will pass away with it, but singing of it, telling of it, like a dying swan.

My cousin Wolfgang, who as a boy once sang so charmingly in the church choir, so angel-precious, that in listening Aunt Hertha's eyes brimmed with tears, wouldn't be able to close his ears when he heard Uncle Ferdinand say: "When I think back over my life, naturally my youth at the imperial courts in St. Petersburg and Vienna and London was incomparably more brilliant than the period after the first great war. However, life was almost more entertaining after the war. It was like going to bed with a duchess: God knows what discretion it required, what complicated preparations you had to go through, and then all kinds of obstacles and dangers, with her having pangs of conscience that in the end she'd have to confess it all, and then when it happened it wasn't much different than normal. That was the old world. The new world was like hopping on the Orient Express in Paris and looking around to see who else is on board and spotting a fiery female and not knowing whether she's a *cocotte* or your cousin, but either way you make up your mind to spend the night in her sleeping compartment: it's a lot more fun, a lot more adventurous, don't you think, even if she turns out to be married to your dentist, even if you've once again hung around with people with whom you really shouldn't have any personal relations; it's irksome enough to endure her husband's fingers in your mouth. However, this became unavoidable after the war; I mean, associating with such people. They were suddenly there like flies in summer—the snobs, you understand—and I must say, a new tone came into the world with them, of course, and thereby a new taste into life. I don't even mean a bad taste, although this goes without saying. Yet it was somehow more enticing, more *piquant*... Now, there are two kinds of snobs, after all: one kind is sometimes even simpatico, and quite useful too—like courtiers. In our day, these are courtiers *sans* courts, alas, but with the same qualities: pushy and bootlicking, ambitious and groveling with their superiors and snappish with their inferiors, but always so poignantly helpful, so pleasantly assiduous... These are simply people who always want to be included but don't quite have the grit for it, nor can they be alone. They're dependent on you; you have the impression that they look up to you, like children to grown-ups; it breaks your heart when you have to send them off to bed... However, there are also very unappealing people among them; that's the second category. You have the impression that they clamber up to you like mountain climbers, sweating terribly all the while, and so you are cold to them and treat them badly, thus taking on snobbish manners yourself without meaning to do so. Or else you feel involuntarily tickled by the thought of being something like the north face of the Eiger, you feel flattered that they would risk their necks to climb up to you, you recognize the athletic ambition. So you tolerate them. A kind of mutual complaisance develops: while they ecstatically inhale the ambrosia of their gods, one of whom is you, your nostrils suck in the sweat of their brows like a sacrificial smoke. And in this way, too, all sorts of bad manners evolve, don't you agree? When one is with one's own kind, one would never dream of thinking oneself better than anyone else. But if you're incessantly surrounded by people who suck up to one person and snub another and make someone else realize that he is more than someone else or less than someone else or is doing something or other that is better or worse than what someone else is doing, or that he has more than other people or less than other people—yes indeed, then you too involuntarily start thinking about what you really are and do and have. And then it occurs to you that someone or other may be more or have more or do better things than you. He can be anyone and anything, a scientist or a *nouveau riche* or a film star... And then, of course, the whole thing blows up; you no longer have a society in which rank and fortune and kindred opinions and manners go hand in hand, you've got a motley crew consisting purely of people with nothing in common except that one talks about them, no matter why or in what terms, whether it's because a man may be a prince or a jockey or an adventurer who hopes to break the bank at Monte Carlo—so long as people notice him. For, after all, that's what snobs are all about: they want to be seen moving about quite casually among the noblest, the richest and the brightest and the best. And for this reason, of course, everyone has to know who they are. The snobs then make sure that the group keeps getting smaller and smaller and more and more exclusive. And anyone who doesn't get fed up with taking part in this everlasting exhibition, or who doesn't suddenly feel ashamed of having so much more than the others, and doesn't withdraw, will, of course, do his best to belong to the select few and will show the others that he is and knows and has more than they—and thus the world will ultimately consist of nothing but snobs. But you know, when they first started hanging around us, the snobs, it was often very entertaining..."

23

Uncle Helmuth too is innocent in his fashion—namely, in the fashion of the damned. He is condemned to hate himself. He doesn't realize it, of course. He thinks he hates others.

Uncle Helmuth feels challenged day in, day out, from above and from below and from all sides. He sings the loudest part in the chorus of those who have been given a dirty deal. Above him stand the rich, the plutocrats, the undeserving happy, free, frivolous. For them he doesn't count; they look down their noses at him. He wants to hate them, but actually he gazes up at them in worship. He nurtures a childlike admiration for his factory director, who, until March 1938, played not only a leading role in Austrian industry but an even greater one in preparing the annexation of Austria to the Third Reich of our compatriot Adolf Hitler, and then of course vanished from the scene. (John and Stella once met him somewhere and called him "a stupid arsehole.") And as for a certain Countess Kannwitz, who was interested in spiritualism, Uncle Helmuth absolutely gushes about her, calling her "one of the most important women of the century, probably the reincarnation of a very high luminary of mankind, like Buddha, or Madame Blavatsky." She was an old fool who used to run after girls in high heels, bang her umbrella on their shoes, and rant, "Don't wear high heels, they're only for whores!" Which regularly led to highly unpleasant scenes.

Uncle Helmuth's hatred is even purer downward, toward the "undisciplined riffraff" of the "proletarians." Granted, they are poor and ought really to be his allies against their mutual "exploiters" and "slave drivers." But Uncle Helmuth feels separated from them by a class barrier. He is an "academic"; he attended university (making sacrifices that he talks about like his wounds in WWI). Uncle Helmuth wears a collar and tie; he has a doctorate in engineering and is married to the second daughter of the late Lieutenant Colonel Subicz and Frau Lieutenant Colonel Subicz née von Jaentsch. This separates him everlastingly from the ignorant and dirty rabble in the back courtyards. And yet he has to admit to himself that, unlike him, this ragtag mob have no prejudices, are not ruled by fictions, and thus in many respects live more freely, happily, frivolously than he.

Since it is basically the envy of the unredeemed that makes Uncle Helmuth hate both upward and downward, one might think that he would see redemption in America. The United States appears to be a society that has succeeded in making social envy the driving element of the national dynamic. In a land where every shoeshine boy is a potential millionaire, one had better not treat him scornfully. And if his road to riches is a little longer than Mr. Rockefeller's, then the distance serves his self-respect as a measure, even if he breaks down en route.

But no: Uncle Helmuth does not feel challenged by American competitiveness. He says too many "values" are lost in it. Americans are "uncultured materialists" with no respect for the "spiritual side of life" and its values—so bitterly hard for him, the eleventh son of a destitute Thuringian pastor, to secure.

In reality, Uncle Helmuth embodies the spirit of "uncritical social criticism," as John calls it—and in this respect, he is a potential Nazi. Criticism, says John, was the intrinsic forte of the Nazi movement. In criticizing, the Nazis were always right. But, like the criticism voiced by the German National Socialists of that time, Uncle Helmuth's is too general, too universal, and thus ultimately not maneuverable, an overcanvased ship. His criticism comes not from sober analysis but from resentment, from a general sulkiness about life, an ill humor that only imagines most of the insults and injuries that nourish him, and thus has no solid goal, no concrete object. Uncle Helmuth reacts instinctively against any stimulus that he views as characteristic of something opposing him. It may be a lady in sable or a whistling tramp, a speeding car, a silly advertising slogan on a poster, a kiss on some woman's hand, a certain way of donning a hat—particularly anything testifying to a way of life that strikes him as freer, lighter, cheerier than his own, thereby putting his own in doubt.

And because he feels like a victim of a worldwide conspiracy against him, he stuffs everything possible into this hate: blame for the whole dreary monotony of his existence; the probable disappointment in his thwarted professional ambitions (he really wanted to go into research and not industry); his concern about the state of the world, which his newspaper makes him worry about every morning, reminding him how helpless he is, how much at the mercy of the powers working their influence therein. Perhaps he also tosses into this garbage can of his choleric emotions the sexual frustration of a man who has Aunt Hertha for a wife and in adjacent rooms Aunt Selma on one side and Cousin Wolfgang and me on the other, all as possible eavesdroppers; and certainly he adds his spiritualist notion that there is a true, non-earthly hierarchy of nearness to God, or rather farness from God, in which he occupies a totally different, much loftier rank, roughly at the level of Buddha or Madame Blavatsky, with no one realizing this at all...

He has a collective name for everything he hates. The species that he imagines as enjoying a more carefree way of life than his own (and thus ruining it—and this comprises proletarians as well as plutocrats, also "society people," and "snobs" like John and Stella) is summarily known as "they." "They" are the people responsible for (or rather guilty of) the fate of mankind—the powerful (oppressors), the rich (exploiters), the undisciplined uneducated (anarchists)—and are pilloried in sentences beginning "*They*'ve got us in another mess..." or "*They*'re grabbing the lion's share, of course..." or "*They* can't bear seeing something in order..." The obvious flippancy, frivolity, unscrupulousness, inconsiderateness of these plainly well known but unnameable anonymouses inspire such rhetoric as "*They*'re amused... *they* skim off the cream and relish it... *they* laugh up their sleeves, of course... *they* just let you kick the bucket..."

And this *they* is elastic enough to cover whole strata; nay, whole peoples: the British, for instance ("*They* imagine they're superior"). It extends to writers of popular songs ("*They* give people highfalutin ideas") and to Jews ("*They*'ve known how to cheat our kind for two thousand years now"). In addition, there is room for the traditional whipping-boys of middle-class resentment: *they* (aristocrats), *they* (Reds), *they* (priests), *they* (Freemasons), *they* (journalists)...

Thus, we can hardly assume that Uncle Helmuth has Uncle Ferdinand's Middle Kingdom in mind in particular when he says, with specific emphasis and an indignation-bloated ring in his voice, "They"—meaning "plutocrats," "society people," "snobs." I remember when I first moved into his home. In those days, the smart set of the upper ten thousand did not have the publicity they enjoy today as the so-called Jet Set (or Café Society)—an unwanted publicity that was to be so prophetically foreseen by Uncle Ferdinand. Uncle Helmuth could at best get some impression of it from my childish blather. (Incidentally, I soon stopped the blathering once I noticed the frosty rejection concealed beneath the artificial irony with which my stories were received.) Perhaps Uncle Helmuth's imagination was assisted by the fashion magazines and society gazettes that Aunt Selma sometimes bought on the sly; she dreamed whole afternoons away with them in her darkened room, but somehow or other they came to light and were then devoured by Aunt Hertha and Uncle Helmuth (albeit more hastily, more sketchily, more nervously). This wholly inadequate reportage presented yearning eyes with the dream life of the happy rich at the North Sea, Mediterranean, and Alpine resorts of high-society geography—a life lived in the chandelier brilliance of casinos, at racetracks, on the decks of huge white yachts, on the lawns of birthday-cake-like country villas and bougainvillea-flooded terraces on sepia-blue, pine-shielded shores—yet could only give a hint that this was where the true focus of his social hatred might be found: the nucleus, the axial pole of that other, blissful way of life that was so sneeringly opposed to his own, which made his own seem less worth living.

The images that Uncle Helmuth saw in those smart-set periodicals traitorously smuggled into his four-room household were, at worst, the listing sails of an oceangoing regatta and, mounted like medallions in the sky overhead, the not very informative portraits of the ship owners in breezy skipper's caps, white turtlenecks, and stylish navy-blue blazers; racetrack bleachers crowded with ladies in flimsy frocks and enormous heron-feather hats, and gentlemen in gray toppers and polished leather binocular cases hanging sprucely from narrow straps on their chests; or else a snapshot series of men and women standing in the same cataleptic convulsion, the right leg twisted and the knee turned in, the left knee bent, toes pointed inward, the arms yanked over the right shoulder, head stretched to the left, eyes peering down toward the feet at a small white ball that is to be struck by a golf club that is swung against the backdrop of a cascading weeping-willow branch; or else a saber-legged grouplet of four, each man wearing spurred boots and a cork helmet that casts a shadow like a mask over his suntanned face, in the sportily gloved left hand the grip of a casually shouldered polo stick, and in the right a silver cup—Messrs. Bully Olivera, Putzi Cottolenghi-Strazza, Bruce Spencer-Fox, and Jean de Fegonzac (grandson of the beauty-loving vicomtesse)—and below, perhaps, a close-up of Sir Agop Garabetian, who donated the cup and whose monocle, in his Arabian Nights face with its twirling black beard, flashes sheer benevolence toward all mankind.

Such photographic documentation preceded detailed descriptions of the subsequent soirées, with exhaustive lists of names. But when it came to precise particulars of the ladies' toilettes and jewels, the reporting was taken over by draftsmen who knew how to render the essential better than any writers or photographers. Now, it may be astonishing to realize how much (thanks to a perceptiveness that should be of interest to novelists) can be deduced from even the meagerest external signs of a human being's condition, yet such vision-restricting peeps into the world of "the beautiful people" could not possibly have permitted the insights that empowered Uncle Helmuth to snort, "*They* are to blame for everything! *They* have all mankind on their consciences! People like us have to drudge for *them*!"

Or: "It's for *them* that people like us had to risk our necks for four years! . . . Bu-u-u-t"—his voice trembling in the bombast of indignation, giving the ominously drawled vowel a wavy, swinging staccato—"bu-u-u-t, if the whole business starts up again, then it will go against *them*!"

24

There is no denying that now, in February 1940, it looks as if Uncle Helmuth will turn out to be right. Of course, at first blush, such a positioning of fronts is not clear-cut. One has to see the situation with John's eyes, too: agreeing on this point, as on so many, with Uncle Ferdinand, he regarded the First World War as a class war and views the Second as merely and certainly an intensified continuation of the First, with a more decisive focus on the true goal.

According to John, it is both a tragic and a grotesque (i.e., tragicomical) error that WWII is likewise being waged among nations, peoples, states, rather than, by unanimous international consent, between the representatives of a coming new world and those of a dying old world (among whose representatives John certainly counts himself). With incomparably fewer losses, he feels, they could achieve the same end that will ultimately come out of the slaughter and that (with the exception of Russia) did not emerge fully from WWI: namely, the extermination of the old upper crust and the takeover by the bloody fucking middle classes. Not by the proletarians, mind you, as the latter have always been promised, but by Uncle Helmuth and his kind.

This notion has been haunting me for some time now (namely, since the post-March days of 1938 in Vienna, in their abstract vacuum). The gray iron men who came to us down the Nibelungen river, pouring into a human sea that surged with enthusiasm, these young men with the heavy, stomping boots, the wonder-craving eyes under gray helmets, and the gentle names (Adolf Emil Wolfgang Helmuth), were soldiers in a civil war. And though it never came to a German civil war at that time, and for the moment brothers and sisters embraced jubilantly, people soon realized that once again an hour of vast collective bloodshed had come.

You didn't have to hear the Führer's speeches on the radio or to read the newspapers. You sensed it, the way animals whiff a storm, a flood, a fire. It surfaced when the intoxication, the delirium, the yowling, howling ecstasy of the first few days (or rather, the three-day-long day) subsided. The roar, in that steel blue Ice Age coldness, was followed by a sudden, huge silence. In this silence, you sensed it. You sensed it the way a murder victim senses his murderer's breath on the back of his neck even though the murderer is still far away, not yet visible: when you turn your head, the street is empty, he is still skulking along somewhere far behind you, around a corner, hugging the walls, but he is coming, he is coming, he is drawing closer to you and closer... Thus, too, the hour of vast collective bloodshed. No drums were booming or trumpets blaring when the hour finally came on September 1, 1939; it came as if it had been sneaking up for a long time and had finally arrived. And no matter how hard you tried and how willing you were to find some historically meaningful necessity, you couldn't come up with an obvious one. Unless you sensed that the Adolfs Emils Wolfgangs Helmuths had made up their minds to exterminate anything that was not of their kind. And, indeed, you sensed it. It was *their* turn.

Thus, the fronts seem clear. Clearer, at any rate, than in WWI. But not completely clear. For instance, Uncle Helmuth's comments since March 1938 revealed that not all of *them* emigrated when the brown brothers of the Reich marched into Vienna, not all of *them* fled like bats from a cave when a light is carried in. He had always called *them* "shady elements," alluding to *their* "obscure machinations." Now, evidently, a certain portion of *them* who were not so allergic to light had remained, and they occupied his imagination more keenly and more intensely than ever. They were now personally closer to him, so to speak, were more of his ilk, and in donning brown uniforms had changed their identities but not their power and arbitrariness, not the infinitely freer existential form that towered over his own and made it appear subordinate. But because they were of his stamp, for the moment he looked up at them kindly, yes reverently. He knew them individually, knew their names (Reich Field Marshal Hermann Göring, Reich Propaganda Minister Dr. Joseph Goebbels, Reich Labor Leader Ley). But in general they were still (albeit now in a positive sense) *they*. At first he spoke their names in a different tone, of course (as Cousin Wolfgang did about the "New Human Being," the "People"). With stars in his eyes and the booming of unconditional trust in his breast, he would say, "You don't have to worry about a thing; *they*'ll take care of it properly!" But this gradually changed again. The intonation became flatter, more sober. Soon the individuals melted back into the old collective term; the names gave way to the anonymous expression his powerlessness used for those in possession of power: *they*.

The more the days plunged, light and blue, into the great icy vacuum from which an ever-greater past promised to emerge from an abstract present—very much the right basis, then, for a great future—the more taciturn Uncle Helmuth became. I saw very little of him then; I had already moved out of the apartment and was chicly installed in a *garçonnière* (paid for by Stella) in the center, so I saw Uncle Helmuth only when I visited Aunt Selma or Cousin Wolfgang, who refused to meet me anywhere but in the "joint parental home" ("If you want to see me, then the place that was your home for twelve years ought to be good enough, right?"). But by early 1939, one could catch the irked overtones whenever Uncle Helmuth mentioned *them*. ("*They* seem to be forgetting that we people of the Ostmark are Germans too, after all.") And then the hour of vast collective bloodshed began palpably to advance on him too. It must have been around this time that I last saw him, but I can imagine that by September 1939 everything was back to normal: "*They*'ve put us in a fine mess!"

25

For Uncle Helmuth and his iron men, I am now in the enemy camp, even though I too am standing as an iron man to fight side by side with millions like me against some kind of "*them*." This is paradoxical, but I enjoy every moment of it.

Having bathed nicely and rubbed Geo. F. Trumper's West Indian Extract of Lime into my skin, having slipped into my exquisite, freshly ironed linen after sprinkling it with a few drops of Knize Polo, and having donned my plum-blue gold-frogged-and-braided operetta-hero uniform, I will go downstairs. Uncle Ferdinand will be waiting for me in the drawing room. He will be wearing pumps and black trousers, a starched shirt with a tuxedo tie, and a velvet jacket, in prince-of-the-Church violet, that is no less imaginatively frogged than my uniform. His Russian greyhounds will be lying next to him on the sofa, and when I enter, they will raise their bored lady-in-waiting heads and graciously bang their tails twice. On the low Chinese enamel table in front of him, there will be a large silver tray with a battery of bottles and carafes and all sorts of high and low, smooth and bellied, stemmed and flat-bottomed glasses. And he will brusquely tell me to have a drink, for he will be impatient to talk about his Middle Kingdom, against which the iron men have taken up arms.

Outside, the world is at war. Two hours ago, we were having tea in the library (Indian tea, not Chinese, like Mama), and for a few minutes it looked as if a huge, soundless battle were being fought in the west. The acanthus jungle of frost flowers on the windowpanes was blossoming as if on fire. The ribs of the leaf plumage were going up in yellow flames. But it was only the sun in a flawless heaven, at sixteen degrees below zero Celsius, gliding into its molten-iron bed.

Now, it has long been dark behind the frosted windows. A cold, heavy, ruthless darkness, such as one learned to fear in childhood when hearing about death and graves and tombs in horror stories. (Miss Fern didn't want these servants' stories told to me, and it was all the more sinister when the servants whispered them into my ear when she wasn't around; I was scared numb, and yet happy to belong with them by sharing their terrors.)

The cold, heavy darkness must be in people's hearts, for the night is pure. Surely the sky is filled with high stars. The knotty acacias by the courtyard gates are throwing their naked branches up to them. The village lies hunched in the blue snow. The yellow squares of windows are carved out of a few of the houses' black walls under their snowy bonnets, pricked by icicles hanging from the edges of roofs. It is so cold that all the dogs have crept away, silent. And perhaps, from the dark thicket of sloe bushes along the cemetery wall, where the three birches loom, a slim figure swathed from head to toe in a black cape will now emerge and come up the village road without visibly moving its feet and float to the pond in the park, where it will vanish...

I have to think about Aunt Selma, my dead mother's sister. There is little likelihood that she ever told me horror stories, but she has their romantic poetry within herself. In all her being is the tomb-like darkness of a well shaft. Deep down lies a pure surface, dark and round, a hare's eye staring at the heavens. Of course, you have to catch her off guard. This is not easy, considering her harshness. The image of her afternoon nap blots out any other image that I have of Aunt Selma. There was no way of talking her into lying down. As if to demonstrate that it was her accursed destiny to *slave away* for us and allow herself scant relaxation and no full rest, she took her nap sitting on a kitchen chair. Seldom did she really sleep. She dozed like a horse in its harness. Her head jerked forward, eventually swaying back and forth as though to a mute internal singsong. Earlier, we were told, her hair had been extraordinarily rich and lovely. She had cut it off because "it got in the way during housework." The part in it, dividing the ashen strands down the middle, expressed a harsh humility. If you touched her shoulder to suggest that she lie down on the living-room sofa or the bed in her own room, the weary draft-horse head yanked up and murmured with closed eyes, "Just wait—I'm coming. I'm just going to rest for a minute."

If she intended to arouse our sympathy, then it was only to reject it gruffly. Fate had decreed that she be our servant. She used up her life for us in a feeling, rooted deep in peasant blood, of responsibility for her clan: for her sister Hertha, whom she really didn't care for that much and toward whom she acted as a quarrelsome older sister; for her brother-in-law, whom she despised; for Cousin Wolfgang, whom she felt indifferent towards even though she thought he had all the qualities of a "dear, well-behaved, hardworking boy"; for me, whom she regarded as her booty, something of her own, the sole property ever granted her. She worked her fingers to the bone for us in stolidly monotonous housework, performed with an anger that was more or less part of the routine and that she put on with her kitchen apron, laboring with tooth-gnashing gee-up, with the cumbersome creaking and obstinate squeaking of wheels on the cart she dragged over her life's stony paths.

It was, as she revealingly put it, a "cherished ordeal." She rose "with the chickens" at dawn, got us all up, prepared our breakfasts, made sure we left the house on time. And then, all alone and probably with odd bits of incoherent monologue, she "slaved" the morning away, airing the beds hanging out the rugs washing the breakfast dishes sweeping the floors straightening up making the beds re-placing the rugs peeling potatoes scrubbing vegetables slicing onions and wiping the tears from her eyes with her apron putting water on handling pots pans plates left and right up and down like a percussionist dropping the gas ring swearing at the gas cursing the gas company accusing life wiping the hair out of her face tearing the lid from the pot that had boiled over sucking her scorched finger—that was how she spent the morning until lunchtime, when Cousin Wolfgang and I came back from school, I from the realschule, he from his stuck-up humanistic gymnasium, Uncle Helmuth from the plant, and Aunt Hertha from the office (she was bookkeeper in an ancient, oddball, lopsided little music-publishing firm). Aunt Selma set the table and served the loveless food, cooked from thrifty recipes. She hardly allowed herself time for even a bite: every day for twelve years I heard the sentence "Selma, would you please finally sit down!" alternately from Uncle Helmuth's and Aunt Hertha's lips. No sooner were we fed and the table cleared than she began to do the dishes, and at times it almost came to fisticuffs when Aunt Hertha tried to help her. "No, I simply won't hear of it—please! You're tired and overworked yourself; you're in the office all day long; please let me do it!"

Uncle Helmuth and Aunt Hertha caught the trolley back to the plant and the office, and Cousin Wolfgang and I started our homework (but only during my boyhood and early adolescence; later, I broke out, ignoring threats and rebukes, playing hooky and strolling through the adventure of Vienna). Meanwhile, Aunt Selma spent the afternoon waxing the floors watering the flowers polishing the silver doing the major laundry the minor laundry patching linen sewing ironing darning, until Uncle Helmuth and Aunt Hertha came home for supper (always cold: usually sliced cold cuts with mustard pickles, a hard-boiled egg, kippers, vegetables left over from lunch). Her years thus passed, like the potatoes with which she prepared

Bohemian dumplings (Cousin Wolfgang's favorite dish), vanishing between her fingers on the grater. And it was "just for fifteen minutes now" after lunch, when she had cleared and washed and put everything in order, that she permitted herself some rest in the harness. Seldom did she let herself go so far as to put her folded arms on the table and drop her head on them like a sobbing woman. I was the only one who knew that she was different than this: that she was really indolent, work-shy, and moony. I was her property, the fatherless orphan-boy of her dead sister, placed under her guardianship by the court, her booty; but that was not the only reason she favored me wherever and however she could, sacrificing herself for me even more thoroughly than for *the others*. Whenever she winked, luring me into the kitchen to slip a penny into my pocket or spirit a piece of cake topped with whipped cream into my outstretched hand, I would sense that this was also a bribe. She knew that I saw through her. We were the same sort.

More than once, I managed to catch her unawares, but each time, it was as if she were catching me. I recall the first time precisely. We were alone in the apartment, a delicious silence. I lay in bed with one of those marvelous childhood diseases that are painless but that keep you out of school and free from responsibility. The adults are full of loving care; they don't criticize, threaten, or demand. Moreover, the fever gives your thoughts a gliding lightness, as if in slow motion, and the least exertion changes them, like images in a kaleidoscope, into something totally different. Words are transformed into numbers, just as they are in the minutes before you drop off to sleep, or into images, entire sentences standing there abruptly, like totem poles looming out of slow waters, while at the back of your neck, at the base of your skull, a small, sticky knob like a medlar fills your mouth with a lukewarm taste of brass. I was thirsty and I wanted to pee too. So instead of calling Aunt Selma, I got up and went to the bathroom. And that was when I saw her through the open kitchen door. She was standing at the window, gazing out into the courtyard; or rather, she had been gazing at the courtyard (or the sky above it), but, upon hearing me, she shifted her eyes to me. And even though there was absolutely nothing to see outside but the ugly wall of the left wing of the apartment building and a patch of indifferent sky overhead, her gaze was full of something very definite, something she had seen with great clarity, with a hungry, wolf-like sharpness, even. And she was smiling. Of course, it was just the vague start of a smile, its tenderness contrasting poetically with the danger in her gaze. Since then, I have often thought that La Gioconda's smile, which people make such a fuss over, can be understood only if one imagines that she was peering into the distance a millisecond earlier and the smile remains as she looks over toward us.

Later, I often lurked about to see this distant gaze of Aunt Selma's. It was never in her eyes when she *slaved away*. Her entire nature was confused at such times, bewildered and jittery, quarrelsome and vehement. She had a way of wiping her forehead with the back of her hand as if she had run into a cobweb and was whisking it out of her face. But no sooner did she drop her arms than that gaze came into her eyes. Her truer being now seemed to be flooding over and into her, and it was silent and listening. Neither Aunt Hertha nor Uncle Helmuth nor even Cousin Wolfgang noticed this strange presence of Aunt Selma when her mind was absent. (Even though, for Uncle Helmuth, this must have been one of the most ordinary circumstances of his weekly spiritist séances. But, of course, when Aunt Selma's spirit was absent, no spirit of a departed man or woman entered the momentarily vacant shell of her body; it was *she herself* who entered it—and that should have provided the mathematician in Uncle Helmuth with food for thought.)

Aunt Selma darns stockings, bowed over a darning egg. (It was incredible to see her achievements: there were holes that had ripped into the darned areas and been redarned again and again, so that archaeological strata of darning work covered our toes and heels.) She sits and holds her head at a slight angle, and I know: she is now listening to *herself*. She hears herself like a faraway melody. I think, Now that strange, almost Gioconda smile is budding in her. But she senses that I have caught her unawares, and she turns her head to me. And no matter how quickly I look away, she catches me lurking. (I once heard her saying to Aunt Hertha in the kitchen, "The boy has something shifty about him; he's not open and straightforward, like yours. Sometimes I find him downright sinister.") The *others* live in the empty rooms of their terribly lonesome indifference. Even Cousin Wolfgang. My brother Wolfgang. The open, honest, dear boy, already reading his classics at twelve and thirteen (while I was struggling to understand what logarithms were, and, because I didn't believe I would ever succeed, perusing penny dreadfuls under my school desk, fleeing into a world of wholesome archetypes, instead of consulting Mocznik-Zahradniczek's *Mathematical Textbook for Realschule*); Cousin Wolfgang, who at sixteen began his enterprise of absorbing all the great thoughts recorded during six thousand years of history (which barely allowed him to have a single thought of his own but which did not prevent him from exhausting the prime of his mental energy in the dissolute fantasies of masturbation); my brother Wolfgang, with whom I had grown up in the hellish intimacy of a room shared day and night for twelve years, in the brotherliness of mutually smelled farts and mutually knocked-out teeth, in the shared torment inflicted by adults and parents and guardians, in the agony of our impotent and useless hatred of them . . . even he never lost his gaze into nothingness.

Sure, he daydreamed sometimes too, he said when I asked him. About what? Oh, you know. You imagine you're going to do something important (a gymnast's dreams, so to speak): contribute to the welfare of mankind (the gigantic swing on the horizontal bar), become famous, respected, loved . . . Rich, too? Sure, if possible, rich too. But that's not the most important thing (leaping from the horizontal bar, elegant knee bend with arms stretched level, straightening up elastically; the palms slap against the thighs; body frozen at rigid attention: Bravo! *Mens sana in corpore sano!*). What do *I* dream about? he returns the question. What do I mean—nothing? You can't dream about nothing. A mood—eh? Okay, then, not a mood, but what? A sensation with no object, a listening out into the stillness, a peering into nothingness, that's not a dream . . . Fine, I'll spare you the quotations, but even the contemplation of the mystics . . .

It was after this conversation that he began to treat me a bit condescendingly, my brother Cousin Wolfgang. Every so often, I saw that his high forehead under the blond German adolescent's shock of hair (the steeple head that he had inherited from Uncle Helmuth along with his slightly short legs) had become more arrogant by a few dozen important books, his eyes more and more bewildered, more and more tormented. At such times, I felt sorry for him in his emptiness, in his terrible indifference, which was filled only with himself and the great thoughts from six thousand years of history. My pity was so deep that I yelled at him, shouted some obscenity at him, which provoked him into pouncing on me. He was a lot stronger than I, with his gymnast's muscles, but I always managed to get the better of him with cunning tricks and dodges. And I was anything but a generous victor, thrashing him without mercy and then being treated accordingly by the rest of the family ("He shows an outright sadistic vengefulness against anything better than him; it would be no surprise if this soon turned into genuine criminality!"). But why didn't he too occasionally stare into space, my brother Cousin Wolfgang? Why did he always have the rim of a helmet shadowing his helpless gaze?...

Whenever he realized that along with all the great thoughts of six millennia he had also absorbed all the great doubts, he would get nervous ("jumpy," Miss Fern would have said). Something of the bewildered fidgitiness of Aunt Selma the cart horse came over him. He made faces as if cobwebs were sticking to his nose... granted, that too reveals a kind of inner life: the inner life of people with shining, watchful eyes that never deviate from the object and the purpose and the meaning. A truly lovable, fabulously decent, warmhearted, magnanimous, even intelligent fellow, my cousin Wolfgang, God rest his soul! He lies in the Central Graveyard in Vienna. Not exactly a soldier's grave, but the stone says that he died a "Hero for the Führer and the Fatherland." (Aunt Hertha, who "isn't as quick to switch sides" as Uncle Helmuth—he inadvertently sobbed, "*They*'ve got my boy on their conscience"—was supposedly the one who insisted on this inscription. But then he did himself believe so strongly in what was written.)

26

So that was what we had been living toward, as things turned out historically. The five of us penned up in a four-room apartment on the fourth floor of a tenement in the Twelfth District (Schönbrunn in its abstract glory before our noses). Each of us in his enormously empty space, casting a long shadow, a monument to his own lonesomeness and indifference. Around us roared the city of Vienna—it too an empty space, its roaring similar to the kind one hears in an empty seashell. To be sure, each of us filled his space with some kind of activity, fiction, illusion, even with ghosts. Not just Cousin Wolfgang, who sought out the plaster busts in the corridor of his humanistic gymnasium for this purpose: . . . Uncle Helmuth, for instance, had real phantoms. Every Saturday evening, he would frequent them in his spiritist circle, the way other people went bowling or to a tarot game. When the medium went into a trance, her eyes rolled back and the whites peered out like the ones the good soldier faces when his bayonet plunges into the body of his enemy. From her lips (she normally stammered, heavy-tongued, and in shredded sentences), Uncle Helmuth had relayed many an interesting tiding from the beyond, which he repeated to us. As early as 1937, when nothing as yet hinted that he would one day tend in this direction (although he often remarked upon the miraculous doings in the Reich, as opposed to the slovenliness here in Austria), he announced something to us in conspiratorial secrecy. He had received a revelation from *over there* (the beyond, I mean, not the Reich). He had learned that *there*, in the immaterial and actual Reality and Truth beyond ours, Adolf Hitler occupied a much higher rank than here on earth, higher even than Buddha's and Helena Blavatsky's and his, Uncle Helmuth's, as well. And he, the Führer, had taken the ordeal and degradation of an earthly, material existence upon himself willingly, like Jesus Christ, in order to bring mankind one level closer to God.

(Of course, Uncle Helmuth asked us to keep this to ourselves for the time being. The spirits, he said, pursued their goals in a very complex manner, which we earthlings could scarcely comprehend.

Their intentions could be discerned by us only after they were carried out and on the basis of the results. We therefore had to be careful not to interfere rashly in this delicate spinning and weaving... Incidentally, Uncle Helmuth was extremely annoyed upon learning that Wolfgang had joined the illegal Nazi movement, and he declared Wolfgang's membership null and void since he was still underage.)

I say: That was how we lived back then (three years before this winter of 1940, but far away, before the start of the Ice Age). Each of us lived his dreary days in his own emptiness and either stared into nothingness or filled the terrible hollow of our existence with frail actions, fictions, fancies, yes, even with ghosts. Aunt Hertha (to remember her too with piety) filled her emptiness (and, one hopes, other of her hollow spaces) entirely with Uncle Helmuth. She worshiped him, but not for himself. She worshiped him as her counterpart.

For, you see, Aunt Hertha too had relations with superreality. She had heard from *over there*, an indisputable source, that every self materializing here on earth is merely one half of a spiritual unity whose other half is embodied in a different self, usually of the opposite sex. Every self seeks this other half, and when it has found it, then there is no end to bliss. Such was the case with her. She had found her counterpart in Uncle Helmuth and henceforth lived only for him.

It didn't bother her that Aunt Selma despised her for it ("Why, you're in bondage to the man!") or that Cousin Wolfgang visibly suffered from it. Her mind was fixed on the sublime. A person who has found his counterpart has not automatically arrived in the Nirvana of bliss. On the contrary, he (or she) is chosen for special tasks. For when such a unity is completed, then in its fully restored spiritual capacity it naturally understands the mission it must carry out through its materialization. By means of brotherly love and the proclamation of the True Doctrine, it must build the ever more spiritual, dematerialized City of God on Earth. Superfluous to mention that she, Aunt Hertha, as the female (i.e., more tested, more earthbound, hence doomed to greater suffering in material existence, and thus, of course, more sublime) half of the Helmuth/Hertha duo, believed in Adolf Hitler's mission of salvation long before Uncle Helmuth did.

Now, Cousin Wolfgang believed the same thing more and more resolutely and was more and more ready for action. In the evening he would disappear without saying where he was going. I alone saw him in our room girding himself up and pulling on shoulder straps. I also found brass knuckles and rubber clubs and once even a pistol on our bookshelf—behind the Spinoza, comically enough, which he must have felt was secure from me. But even though my brother Cousin Wolfgang now daily armed himself to flee the emptiness of the house and submerge himself in the bliss of Nazi comradeship, he could only shrug at his mother's ravings. He believed that if she had read her Plato, she would know that with her—or rather, Uncle Helmuth's—silly notion of a counterpart, she was making a gospel out of the joke of a drunken comedy writer—the dumb cow!

Still, Cousin Wolfgang was fair enough ("intellectually honest," he called it) to admit that the reason his parents' no doubt basically harmless spiritualism enraged him so much was that he was jealous of his father to the point of occasionally murderous hatred. This realization (especially the insight that his own spiritual ambitions sprang from the desire to expose the knuckleheadedness of this "cross between a mechanic and an Anabaptist" whom to his great disgust he had to acknowledge as his procreator) annoyed him doubly because it required him to recognize a so-called Oedipus complex, thereby corroborating the obscene theories of the Jew Freud. Although, to be sure, Germanic mythology also had . . .

Thus we lived, with our spooks in our heads and our webs across our eyes. Or with eyes that saw through them, and thus stared into space, into sheer nothingness.

Twice a day, the dining table united us in a group of five, and not even quarreling could lure us out of the terrible indifference and solitude within which each of us kept his league-long shadow. When we had been fed lunch, the table cleared and the dishes washed, and the Helmuth/Hertha duality was happily gone, then Aunt Selma would grant herself her cart-horse snooze in harness (hardly ever more than twenty minutes). Next, while Cousin Wolfgang and I got down to our homework, she would go back to her drudging. Usually, but not always. And I caught her unawares one last time.

It was one of those wasting, silent afternoons that only a large, teeming city can produce (according to the stereotype, I should have someone practicing the piano on another floor of the building). Once again, I had failed to understand something (let's say it was differential and integral calculus this time), and I wanted to pee, or drink a glass of milk in the kitchen. Cousin Wolfgang, in order to be completely undisturbed, was probably cramming in the shitter. I did not hear Aunt Selma drudging anywhere, but the door to her room was ajar, and I peered inside. She was sitting on her bed, looking through a couple of magazines. This time, she did not sense my eavesdropping, so I found her fully emerged from her well, so to speak. She was slowly turning a page. I could see by the covers of the other magazines strewn across her bed that these were fashion and society magazines ("smart-set gazettes," Uncle Helmuth would have said indignantly; she had probably pinched and scraped to save up the pennies to buy them). As she sat there on the edge of the bed, very straight, her legs in front of her and her knees scarcely bent, her posture very noble, I saw for the first time that she was tall and slender and had full, firm, high breasts. Her throat, her neck, which I had always seen in the draft-horse collar, was now free and lithe, and her slightly bowed head perched on it gracefully. I saw that she must have been very attractive as a young girl, equal in beauty to her frivolous sister. But I saw this well nigh at the edge of my gaze. What my eyes grasped fully was that she was dematerialized and thereby entirely her true self.

Again she had the vague Gioconda smile hovering around her lips, but now it showed no cruelty, it was gentle, shadowy, charmingly dreamy. She turned a page and, before looking down, lifted her head and stared out the window with her distant gaze, as if her eyes were holding their breath. She seemed to be listening for something, something that was not sound and certainly not speech, notion, or thought. The smile stirred her lips to the bare extent that the surface of the well water is ruffled when, from above, from the small blue disk of sky at the end of the shaft, a voice calls.

I thought to myself, She's a nixie. Some terrible curse forces her to dream that she is a household cart horse, and only when she's completely oblivious of herself, and is no longer trapped in the nightmare of herself as a draft horse, only then can she emerge from her well shaft, can her nixie eyes look upon the alien world of human beings, can she see the faces and visions of her dream and brood about what they might signify. I said this to myself thus, poetically, because I saw how profoundly her Dalmatian-hill-girl head, in this moment of objectless dreaming over some banal object, had been transformed into something that struck me as the epitome of the German. And already in winter 1940, in the tub of my bathroom in faraway Bessarabia, I knew that a further precious element from the lost half of my life was thereby irretrievably lost in an icy, sinking Europe.

27

I hope it does not irritate you too much, esteemed Mr. Jay Gee Brodny, if I do not unravel the thread of my narrative chronologically but instead, in order to proffer you an insight into the various paleontological layers of my existence, draw it back and forth, pulling out a piece now here, now there, in order to revive some significant moment or other, some informative situation or episode, and thus perhaps to display something that strikes me as worth narrating for a very specific reason. What I envisage is a self that keeps emerging out of itself in constant regeneration, like horse willow, yet becomes more and more self-alien, more and more self-inscrutable in this phased growth, so that ultimately the time experienced and the world experienced seem to it like a theatrical stage during the continual set changes and scene changes in a play whose author has in no way adhered to the classical rules of unity of time and place—whereby, of course, the protagonist of this tragicomedy is always a different person, although spectrally the same, as it were. This can hardly be depicted except as a literary equivalent of looking at raw footage for a film, but I admit that this unsteadiness in storytelling is, no doubt, due to many years of watching movie editors at work and witnessing their laudable persistence, the way they scour through the provisionally stitched together takes, the way they comb through the wealth of filmed events, forming a new series that is often the opposite of the original outline, until the intended meaning of the whole becomes acutely evident. For, as Nagel has his leading character, the narrator, say in his latest (rather plainly autobiographical) best seller, "What we imagine we are expressing is not always what we are actually urged to express. That is why the writer's labor commences beyond language, where one confronts oneself eye to eye..."

And here lies the reason I am telling you so much, so meticulously, about myself, sir. In fact, it's the reason that I, unfortunately, cannot tell you my story in three sentences. After all, that *was* what you asked me to do, wasn't it?

Needless to say, you did not expect to hear my life story. You had learned that I was writing a novel. A book for which Big-Time Publisher Scherping (heeding the literarily expert but commercially catastrophic advice of his editor Schwab) had paid considerable advances over the course of fourteen years (until he fired S.). That much money invested in one author brings commitment. The man becomes more and more valuable, more and more desirable. If the chance arises to foist him off on some other sucker, then he advances to the status of genius and potential Nobel laureate. I assume that Scherping deployed all his eloquence when he told you about me. But you, Mr. Brodny, are too much of an old fox in this business not to smell the rot in the overly fat bait. When you invited me to tell you my "story" in three sentences, you weren't only asking about the commercial value of what I wanted to tell, nor yet whether I had it in me to write a good book, you were plainly asking whether this book *can ever even be completed*.

One could not ask in a more intelligent way. *Chapeau, monsieur:* if I were wearing a hat, I would doff it to you. For you, Great Brodny, are not just a pike, a shark, but an *Orcinus orca*, a killer whale, in the carp pond of international publishing; you know all too well the kind of writer you have before you. You recognized at first glance the fateful personality split that took place within me—back then, during a different paleontological era. It actually took place in 1949, at the end of the second Ice Age in Hamburg-on-the-Elbe, Joimanny, when I felt as if I had been cast away among the lotus-eaters, and Big-Time Publisher Scherping, in the bosom of maternally strict whores, chanced upon a movie treatment left in the brothel and sent his blessed editor Johannes S. to seek out the author and talk him into writing a novel—*the* novel of the era, of course, the masterpiece of the century. Since that time—a period now of nineteen years of my life—the screenwriter who works his fingers to the bone for the piglets of the postwar German movie industry (as Aunt Selma, RIP, used to slave in the household during my formative years in Vienna) has existed alongside the dreamer in me with lurking eyes lost in the distance, and he, the dreamer, has been working on a book. On *his* book: *the* novel of the era, the masterpiece of the century. And while the screenwriter, the assiduous servant of the lively producer-piglets, keeps pouring more and more stories into the feeding trough (stories that can indeed be told in three sentences, goddammit, and occasionally even made into cinematic works of art, which may even win a gilded palm frond at the next festival on some sunny coast, but will, alas, in spite of everything, never become a box-office smash)—while the screenwriter humbly works in the sweat of his brow, the other one, the brilliant novelist and potential Nobel laureate, is chasing after his *fata morgana* and dreaming of writing the masterpiece of the century, and writing his fingers to the bone and going blind and turning his mind into sauerkraut, in vain, in vain, because his work begins *beyond language*, as Nagel says: "*There, where one confronts oneself eye to eye.*" . . . And over there, friend Brodny, no story can be told in three sentences. There you merely unearth black bugs, fruitful as termite queens; they give birth incessantly to many, many other stories, which give birth to new stories, which, in turn, give birth to new stories, so that they teem and swarm. Their narrator drowns, suffocates in stories, and every single story wants to be told, has to be told, if (as Cousin Wolfgang demanded in his gymnasium ethos and Schwab, moved, repeated twelve years later) he wishes to speak *fairly* and *honestly* about an era and its people . . . and if the writer wishes to write all his stories down and put them into a form, it will lead to the madness of the *chef-d'oeuvre inconnu*, to total chaos, to a progressive division of cells proliferating in more and more metastases.

Tell me a secret, dear Yankel Brodny. How does Nagel do it? Confront himself eye to eye while writing and tell a story whose essence can be summed up in three sentences? I don't doubt his fairness and honesty for even an instant. I know the man; he was my friend. But he's fooling someone: either himself or us, his readers. There is something shady somewhere in the way he lays the eggs of his stories and hatches every one of them into a novel. To his credit, I have to say that he is less infected than anyone else by the narcissism of the time, less spellbound by the utterly amazing mystery of existence, even when confronting himself eye to eye. Thus, he appears to succeed in peering through and beyond himself and perceiving his fellow men and neighbors Tom, Dick, and Harry. Okay. No one is saying that novels have to be ineluctably autobiographical. On the contrary: there is a widespread opinion that there is no such thing as a true autobiography. Even more unavoidable in literature than in everyday life is the con of the as-if. Fiction, Mr. Brodny. *Nagel iz a firstrayt fikshin-riter. I am an even better fikshin-riter. But Nagel has the colder heart.* He does not sufficiently love his fellow men and neighbors Tom, Dick, and Harry. Otherwise, he would commit to them more fully and turn them into human beings, not marionettes. As he presents them they function purely to present the events of which "reality"—according to his steadfast troglodyte opinion—is woven. Sure, this method produces stories that can be told in three sentences, but one wonders why he bothered to use more than three.

And that is Nagel's con, Mr. Brodny. For reality does not consist of events. It consists of existences. Believe Uncle Ferdinand. In his Middle Kingdom, only the same things keep happening: champagne breakfasts lunches polo games golf tournaments hunting parties Mediterranean cruises cocktail parties intimate dinners galas poker chemin-de-fer roulette movie stars duchesses and other whores. These things keep repeating themselves from here to eternity—and thus, nothing happens. However, Bully Olivera and Agop Garabetian—what full existences they have! Tom, Dick, and Harry, if one takes them lovingly and thoroughly in hand—what miracles of creation! If Nagel succeeds in letting Tom stroll through a novel without supplying the total content of his skull, the myrmidon teeming of Dick's thoughts ideas impressions experiences reflections, the entire meteorology of Harry's spiritual life, then I can only repeat: *Chapeau, monsieur!* This strikes me as neither fair nor honest. I for my part love people; I encounter them wherever I go. All I have to do is stick my nose out the door and I run with the pack. There are crowds of people around. They populate the towns, the highways...

But I see I am boring you. You've scarcely got a shrug for my problems. As far as my novel and I are concerned, you knew at first glance: this guy is cradling a dead child. You don't want to squander your time on my adolescent writing problems. Please, however, permit me to take the matter seriously. These were the problems that caused the death of my friend S., my brother Schwab.

28

Five years ago, shortly before I saw a white rose eaten from its stem and before I was smart enough to view this sight as symbolic of the fact that my romance with Dawn had no future (I am speaking of a past that seems more remote, more past, more legendary to me than any other, even more alien than the present), I had pretty much finished dreaming my dream of myself as the author of the literary masterpiece of the era and future Nobel laureate. This was the time of my increasingly hectic dashes from Hamburg to Paris (via Holland, where my son attended boarding school, and where I would hurriedly insert a visit that was probably disappointing to him). I dashed back and forth until I finally stopped going back to Hamburg. Except one last time, in early 1965, for Schwab's funeral. And, oddly enough, I retain the memory of those days as a happy period, despite all the ordeals that Dawn inflicted on me. I served my piglets fairly and honestly, was, with my nationless language skills, even more useful to them here in Paris than in their country, but of course was not fairly and honestly rewarded for my services, though I lived well on their expense accounts. Paris, the bright and beautiful underworld, into which I had descended like Orpheus to bring Dawn/Eurydice back to the light of day, turned out to be a rather comfortable place to live. I enjoyed the renown of a man having a romance with a setting star, Nadine Carrier, to whom I ran back after sporadic abstinence like a dipsomaniac to his bottle. My name haunted the gossip sheets ("Will Nadine be unlucky in love with her screenscripter?"). Whenever I visited my son at his Dutch school, his classmates asked me for autographs, and here in Paris the newsdealer in the stand outside the Deux Magots treated me like a familiar and intimate friend. My cases, crates, and cartons were crammed with the starts, the commenced and uncompleted chapters, the drafts, notes, and all the possible sketches for my book that I had carried through life for fourteen years, and now I was about to dump them into the nearest dustbin and finally be liberated from my obsession. It was only with Schwab that I kept up the fiction that I was still writing, and I construed his farewell gesture, when I last saw him, in October 1964, as a desperate request to keep going, undaunted. After being fired by Scherping, Schwab could no longer get me advances for my book, but he urgently wanted me to finish writing it. He stuffed into my pockets the money that was bursting out of his, in order to obligate me to write, the bastard...

A little later I didn't need him, for Gaia had entered my life, the chocolate-brown Princess Jahovary, God bless her in her vanilla-scented weightiness. It was she who from then on identified with my masterpiece, and since my need for love had not been fulfilled by all the previous one great only and exclusive loves, I loved her ardently and did whatever she wanted. Thus did my suffering begin anew.

At this time, Nagel was at the height of his fame, and, with the nasty alertness of a rival secretly arming himself, I studied his lean style, which was itself learned from Hemingway. Next to it, anything I wrote seemed like Gaudí's Sagrada Familia next to a utilitarian building by Adolf Loos. I was green with envy. I would tell myself, every morning, noon, and evening, "Save! Pinch! Scrape! Be picky, like an old maid. From all you've imagined, envisioned, the same as from all you've lived, experienced, select only what contains and renders the essential. Nothing superfluous! A book is a masterpiece if it contains not one syllable more than its table of contents!" However, I probably had a different notion of the contents of a book than did Nagel. Which was what I told Schwab. I said, "One has to make up one's mind; you too have to make up your mind, dammit; after all, you too are thinking about writing a book. Don't deny it! I planted the idea in you, just as you planted the idea in me: like a parasitic ichneumon wasp's egg that hatches and eats up its host. Well, stick to business. No more excuses. Don't be an alarmist—especially with yourself. Even if you tell yourself that everything around us is totally chaotic and that chaos can't be turned into form, your heart is still tormented by a nagging feeling: the feeling that it would be your human duty to arrange chaos in your way. Didn't the notes of a flute build the walls of Thebes? Or was it singing? Words? . . . My cousin Wolfgang would know. He was a humanist like yourself—and you don't remember? Regrettable, but of no importance, for the moment. What I want to say is that even if your pride commands you to claim that only silence is possible against the wealth of absurdity around us, your noble insatiability will demand that you find the word to *name* such a stance. *It* will force you to do so—the *IT* that also urges Nagel to express himself. Even though his banalities, puffed up as literature, do not quite express what *it* urges him toward. Do not try to hide how greatly *it* urges you, dear friend; one can tell by the tip of your nose. Of course, not to tell some trivial story artistically, as Nagel does, but to create a reality out of existence, a reality reflecting the reality we live in and through—to a frightening degree—that's what *it* urges you to. You do understand me, don't you, as a humanist? Perseus had to look at *a reflection* of the Gorgon in order to slice off her head; the direct sight of her would have turned him to stone . . .

and isn't it wonderful that Pegasus sprang forth from her dripping blood? Climb on, friend! Undaunted! Do tricks on horseback! You are of the fearless breed who never hesitate to keep their eyes open. Staring into nothingness, like my aunt Selma. You are not of the bluffers and barkers who lull us to sleep with fairy tales, as nannies do to little tots. And do not be discouraged if you can wrest the word from yourself only in tortured efforts: your stammering will be all the more poignant..."

and while I chattered on, friend Brodny, filtering such shallow tidbits through the dull eardrums of an alcoholic into his extremely sensitive soul, I myself was afflicted with the most absurd anxieties about how I would never finish my book, and I invented a new reason every day to tell myself that I couldn't possibly write it. No, it couldn't be written—not as I wanted to write it.

In Gaia's time, when I was living a luxurious life at her expense (I was used to it from Stella, of course), I had again hit upon the amusing idea that the novel of the era, in which everyone was to recognize himself, recognize his era, his destiny, was something I couldn't write because I lacked the essential experience of my generation: the war. Yes, you heard me correctly, sir: I lack the experience of war. As far forward and as close to the whites of the enemy's eyes as possible. An experience that had, after all, been granted to my colleagues Nagel and Schwab. Nothing of the sort had been allotted to me. I had laid down my arms when Bessarabia was peacefully handed to the Russians. While Nagel was gathering material for his *stories*, losing his arm in the process, and meeting God, I was carrying out the struggle as an interior experience in the beds of the homebound wives of warriors. The steel storms came down as aerial bombs upon a man with the most peaceful of intentions. Of course, Schwab (to whom I once indicated my qualms in this respect; to be sure, only in order to explain to Scherping why my book was making such little progress)—Schwab argued that this inexperience should have made me even more aware of the essence of that event of war, the hole that that suicidal madness had torn into the world, the corruption into which the time had decayed, that enormous void whose suction had demolished the entire past and driven apart the very molecules of the entire present and future, thus dematerializing them, making them unreal, implausible. But Schwab's argument was, of course, merely one of his charming civilities, inspired on such occasions by his lovely envy. I rejected his amiability. Apperceptive occurrences that had to be explained with the aid of epistemological metaphysics were too abstract for me, I said tersely.

I also had fun refuting my own theories. By trying to show that it was madness to invent a reality out of causal connections in order to have it mirror a reality determined solely by chance, I set up a collection of crazy causes with completely nonsensical effects. I also looked for them in my own background and found a good number—for instance, my marriage to Christa, which had come about because her devouring mouth had so tormentingly drawn my notice in Nuremberg, in the canteen for German attorneys and witnesses at the Fürth Court of Law. This then led to fourteen years of mutual torture and a son who hates his father. Still, it led to "multiplying" me, to fulfilling my biological duty. From this too metaphysical connections can be deduced: a devouring mouth, the symbol of Great Mother Nature...

29

And thus the years wore by, highly esteemed Mr. Brodny; autumn leaves and calendar leaves flit through the images left in my memory. Soon those leaves will be as dense as the leaves of the countless manuscripts I have gathered for my book, rejected and abandoned, ripped up and patched together, shredded and stored away for later use in folders, cartons, and cases—for nineteen years, to be precise. And meanwhile, the other half of my split personality served the movie piglets and snickered derisively whenever the future author of *the* novel of the era, the potential Nobel laureate, gnashed his teeth in envy at the expressive devices of cinema, its immediate visuality, its freedom from place and time, its multidimensionality... and all these things merely to present pulp novels and granny fairy tales!...

Pop art indeed, governor... but what inexhaustibility in raw material, in the immediately pictographic, vivid... while our sort are supposed to depict the most sublime, the most complex, the most multivocal, the most fragile things in pale words within the rail network of grammar. (A snort of protest from Schwab. He turns red with anger at such statements; the blood drains from his cheeks as, in annoyance, the thrust of air driven from his nostrils loses strength, eventually being taken back in a ponderous sigh.)

In those days, when brooding on the problems of writing novels, even far below the intellectual stratosphere of Messrs. Lukács and Robbe-Grillet, I (and my brother Schwab) did not find those problems as childish as perhaps you do, esteemed Djakopp Djee. Being fed up with theory and ideology, we did not tackle the issue on the soaring level of the essayists but rather on the pedestrian level of the pragmatic writer, usually ending up at the dead point where the psychology of the writer coincides with the question of the significance of what is to be written. Why bother with a novel today? What else remained to be said? And was it of any importance how it was to be said? The aesthetic was indisputably of secondary interest.

There was one thing we did agree on, though, Schwab and I: it was no longer possible not to include the author when writing. Even in scientific experiments, after all, the person of the experimenter is largely taken into account nowadays. Intensifying our self-observation, we soon realized that it was probably this *it* (Nagel's *it*, presumably borrowed from Freud's *It*, or Id) that urged us to write. To put it in plain terms: what *it* urges a fair and honest writer to write is *himself.*

This conclusion instantly stirred up a whole swarm of further questions, and I had a devil of a time luring poor Schwab into their midst and watching him flail about with them. I did it with vile pleasure. After all, he was acting as if the business concerned him purely in theory and for my sake. He was professionally interested only insofar as he was an editor for my publisher, Scherping, and thus obligated to dispel my doubts in myself and my work. Dispel them so thoroughly that I would speedily finish that book and earn back my advances. The fair man! The honest man! Yet he never concealed his distress when noticing how utterly I saw through him. He never resented me for using the grossest con man tricks (always pretending I had something far more profound in mind) to lead him to some relevant theme and snidely wait and see how long it took him to realize that he was dealing with some commonplace—after all, he was usually quite liquored up. For it must not be forgotten that in those days I was at the peak of my dichotomous existence. The potential author of *the* novel of the era and the future Nobel laureate—incessantly constructing new arguments for why it was superfluous, impossible, sheerly arrogant, and hubristic to want to write and yet never ceasing work on his book in his mind and on any available scrap of paper, nourishing his parasite's egg with himself—this author lived in the most intimate symbiosis with the eager servant of the movie piglets, and each of the two personalities within myself kept an eagle eye on the other, each slyly learning useful things from the other—

and thus, in my existential form as a servant of swine, it warmed my heart to watch what happened to certain scenes of a script I had written, scenes written in the sweat of my intellectual's brow and fixed on celluloid after murderous financial sacrifices, scenes tugged back and forth, back and forth on the editing table, and then, after a quick snip of the scissors, twisting and hissing into a wastebasket... scenes for which I had struggled with my producer piglets in the thick blue cigar smoke of all-night script conferences, had wrestled over like Jacob with the angel; takes for which directors had suffered heart attacks and world-famous actresses fits of hysteria; image sequences in which cameramen of international renown had seen the crowning of their careers; shots in which lighting artists had expected the final recognition of their earlier, so wretchedly neglected work... and snip! It was as if they had never been, like so many important, significant, decisive moments, episodes, situations in our lives. With no harm to the plot and no damage to the film's artistic value...

When I told Schwab about this, he got very excited, and it was child's play to lead him to the idiotic question of whether and to what degree people like us can rely on our apperception. Could we really trust our conscious minds to make the proper selection from what they perceive seamlessly and to retain whatever is worth remembering, to forget trivia and only trivia? . . . In what way, then, was that ominous *it* involved in this process, the *it* that urges us to express things we may not have had the wish to express at all? No doubt it is a demon pledged to the zeitgeist, determining our ideas in a manner that *happens* to us, so to speak, and leads us, much to our own amazement, to make statements revealing thoughts that are peculiar to the present era, thoughts of the zeitgeist, notions, insights, intentions, in the style of the era—

in a word: something latent in the zeitgeist wants to be said and pushes out from the lips, pens, and typewriters of those who feel impelled to speak, even if it's not what they originally wanted to say at all; forces them to say it in Pearris, Freanss only minutes earlier or later than in Hamburg-on-the-Elbe, Joimanny or Athens, Wyoming—that is to say, simultaneously—so that someone who has an idea that is extraordinarily interesting, because it is new and previously unuttered, that someone can be certain that at the same moment several dozen equally clever men all around the globe are having the same idea. And when you are about to write a particularly original and topical book, you can go right ahead and prematurely bet your probably meager income that at the same moment a good dozen other authors of the masterpiece of the era and future Nobel laureates are about to set down an almost identical book . . .

and by saying all this I had gotten Schwab to the point of letting the *it* in him, the demon urging him to do something different from what he was planning, drag him into the next bar in order to work out his spiritual equilibrium with as even a number of glasses as possible. While I, with innocent eyes, set about offering him various examples of the scurvy, often tasteless pranks played on me by my memory (so often admired by him).

30

Indeed, my esteemed patron Brodny, I cannot bank on any sort of selection being made here. I distrust my subconscious. My treasure chest of memories is filled by sheer chance. I have an excellent example of this, an example I held up to Schwab with great effect. An impression taken up quite by chance but, inexplicably, with extreme keenness, and preserved down to the last detail—I am haunted by it even today. It is the image of a family filling their faces at a highway rest stop, something I saw during one of my dashes to Dawn in Paris, accompanied by Schwab. The scene is branded in my memory. Quite ineffably horrible contemporaries they were. Schwab, needless to say, did not perceive them, happy man. (Or else his subconscious functions more selectively. I suggested this to him when he showed some anxiety about his forgetful ways; however, his answer was a desperately derisive snort.)

I, for my part, see them even now: informally grouped around the adjacent table among vegetable fritters, sandwich wrappings, plastic bags full of orange peels, beer glasses, and Coke bottles. Dortmunders on a weekend outing or something of the sort. (John would have said "white trash.") They were eating. Wildly relishing whatever it was they were feeding on ... and they clung to me like burrs; I couldn't get rid of them, people who didn't mean a thing to me, unable to arouse the slightest interest on my part: a paterfamilias with a beefy neck, chewing disgustingly, in a Lacoste shirt with a crocodile logo; a materfamilias, shoveling repulsively, with curlers under a kerchief turban; an aunt or housemate or friend, crocheting with a knife and fork, sporting pubic hair under her hat; four children like organ pipes, chomping dreadfully: in short, highway rest stop people, humdrum faces taking nourishment, the kind of people that pass us daily, hourly, by the tens of thousands, sucking on the caries in their teeth. People that one looks at without seeing, hence that one has never seen before and, if God be gracious, will never see again—

and these people were photographed by my memory, which obviously functions of its own accord. Photographed more sharply than any other face ever stamped on my mind; not the face of a beloved, not the face of my little boy, not Schwab's face ... and I don't know why, I still don't know why today.

All I know is that I carry the image of these feeding anthropoids around in me like the Zadir. I could have committed a murder and forgotten it, but I can't get *them* out of my brain. My head could be chopped off—*they* could be detected in some sediment in my blood, my tissue... For God's sake! A man sees a few things in his forty-nine (going on fifty!) years of life, especially since these years span the core of the twentieth century, from WWI through WWII and on up to today: forty-nine years, up and down and back and forth through Yurop, the heartland of our civilization, from the meadows of the Dniester to Pearris, Freanss, from Scandinavia to Syracuse, Sicily, yes sir... Years in which a great deal has happened. Admit it, Djay Djee: a thing or two has happened between 1919 and 1968, hasn't it? Now, if a man didn't make a ruthless selection from among the accumulated material, what would become of him?

It simply can't be summed up in three sentences. Believe me! Not in our time. Not since everything has been growing frighteningly, running rampant, running riot, devouring the people, the cities, the objects, the events, the stimuli. Hybrid cell growth is also an explosion, after all, isn't it? To be sure, a slow-motion explosion. Describing this sort of thing requires details. *Abbia pazienza!*

Needless to say, one strives to restrict oneself to the essential. One sticks to the tersest, most economical outline. One focuses on what one would like to say, as transparently and graphically as possible, and so one plies one's craft decently and honestly, until—well, yes: until it suddenly urges you to say something that was not even foreseen in this outline, that does not even go into it, that has nothing to do with it, and that no amount of effort can visibly connect with it... yet *it* has to be said and it drives you until you finally say it.

One can only hope that the *it* is wiser than we are. That it says something more essential than what we are trying to say—or even: than what we have yet been capable of saying. Something we did not realize, whose meaning we did not grasp but which is instantly grasped by everybody once it is said because it is in the zeitgeist and was as yet unborn—and if you hadn't said it, then someone else would have done so a moment later.

"I hope I don't have to spell out for you what consequences this has for the nervous system," I said to Schwab. "People like us live like someone who's hard of hearing, always tormented by the fear of missing something. The fear that something may be spoken of that we don't know or aren't supposed to hear. I tell you: Our eyes aren't red just from scribbling by lamplight. Mainly they're red because we keep peering around mistrustfully to see whether something is being scribbled behind our backs. Imagine what I am going to have to endure until I figure out why those chewing *horlàs*, those anthropoids who must have already anticipated the posthuman evolutionary stage—why they've stuck with me so solidly that I can't get rid of them! All because you, of course, had been without alcohol for two hours and had to have a drink; otherwise the withdrawal symptoms would have hit you like epilepsy. It was *you* who lured me into that bloody roadhouse, man. It will probably take years now for this crop to grow before I can harvest its meaning. And until then that little group of highway people will stay with me: father, mother, aunt, four children, shoveling, chomping, chewing, swallowing—making me wonder what they signify. One has to be prudent as a writer. Live cautiously. A poet, as we know, is a mouthpiece through which a god speaks (mainly to tell what he is suffering). But even simple people like us are chosen to speak and at the same time frail, vulnerable, easily exasperated. After all, our kind too lead lives of devotion: we are tense strings over which the zeitgeist passes, making us quiver. And the zeitgeist strums quite vehemently, does it not? *Il nous joue de la belle musique;* we do not even know where to flee. However, the intrinsic feature of the zeitgeist, its exclusive peculiarity, which determines its style (and thereby ours), is something we do not hear so long as we remain in its tempestuous contractions; this is recognized only by those who come after us. Even we who are chosen to speak know it at best after *it* has urged us to express this knowledge. And he who wishes to hear the mystery of the zeitgeist, that which says itself through us but is not yet named—he who wishes to *name* it must make himself so taut that sooner or later he will snap. For the zeitgeist only whispers it; you have to filch it from its breath... Yet when we ultimately reach the point of jumping out of our skins at every fart because we mistake it for a breath of the zeitgeist, thinking we can hear something in it that no one else can hear, and when we absolutely want to be the first to express it . . . when our throats tighten with fear lest we are late with everything, forgotten by our zeitgeist, never its mouthpiece, when we are *epigoni* after all, adding only frills, unable to say anything fundamental to our era, then our situation will affect our souls, dear friend. No one could be more aware of this than you."

31

No one knew this better than he, my brother Schwab, and he accepted the consequences and kicked the bucket. I, however, have survived.

Even though the parasitic egg of having to write was laid in me and has been devouring me for nearly two decades, I have survived. I have survived him just as, to his consternation, I survived my romance with Dawn and, two years later, with Gaia. Just as I survived Cousin Wolfgang and Uncle Helmuth and Aunt Hertha and Aunt Selma. And presumably Uncle Ferdinand and ultimately John too. Just as I had survived Stella, although surviving her was the most shameful of all.

That is what prompts me to think back so often to the winter of 1940 in Uncle Ferdinand's home: my innocence back then! The fullness of a world that had not yet gone under in the Ice Ages. The world of the first half of my life, which I had not yet survived.

Uncle Ferdinand is still alive.

I sit across from him at a long table. I am wearing the uniform of a good regiment, which may not be the same one in which he once served his old Fatherland—a Fatherland that is no longer his and indeed is hostilely facing his (and thus my) present Fatherland—but no matter! Uncle Ferdinand's real Fatherland is the Middle Kingdom, and he counts me as part of it. He treats me with the paternal camaraderie that the commander of the Imperial Russian *garde à cheval* would show toward a cadet who had just been promoted to cornet.

I am grateful to him, with mixed feelings. True, I am sitting at a table at which I sat as a child, waited on by servants some of whom claim they knew me back then. I sit beneath ancestral portraits that in depicting Uncle Ferdinand's forebears may possibly be depicting mine—but none of this matters. We haven't seen each other for fourteen years. Uncle Ferdinand is certainly enough a man of the world to see right off how much or how little is left of Miss Fern's upbringing, but he cannot really know who I am. Anything might have become of the child that was once troublesome enough as a hanger-on (or even worse: a charitable gift) of a delightful mistress. The child that once annoyingly ran underfoot and has now surfaced again, a young blade sent to his home by his old friend and confrere John, to whom he is deeply attached, whose father he once knew and on whose estate he, Uncle Ferdinand, shot the most unforgettable grouse of his life, but a man whose diplomatic missions have always been rather obscure, suspect particularly now that he is married to this bluestocking Bucharest Jewess. Pretty, yes, spirited, and to be seen everywhere, elegant, witty, quick, but—well, you know.

I wonder if Uncle Ferdinand knows that I am Stella's lover. I wish he did. I have a guilty conscience toward John, but I'm proud nevertheless. I love Stella. Love her intelligence, her wit, her maternal tenderness, her unerring frankness, her fairness and honesty. I love her with all my senses. I love her taut body, the dull-shimmering olive tone of her skin. She is fourteen years older than I, and I love her ripeness, her experience, the mellowness of her beauty, her sharp spiritedness, the first gray threads in her black thick-stranded desert-Jewish hair. (Absalom supposedly was blond, but one of my most beautiful erotic fantasies is to see Stella dangling from a branch by this black shock and to ride toward her to bore through her with my lance.)

I was just thinking of her, in the bathtub. I was looking down at my thin, tough body, still tan from the summer. It lay in the water covered by a floating galaxy of dissolving soapsuds. But from a dark moss bed in the sepia skin, a sturdy stalagmite grew through the greenish transparency of the water. Stella, my star (indeed, that was her maiden name: Stella Stern).

It would not surprise, much less scandalize, Uncle Ferdinand if he knew that I was Stella's kept lover. Along with the glue of gossip, of the ceaseless informing by everyone on everyone, the unflagging mutual mentioning, naming, citing of all by all, the Middle Kingdom is held together by two further glues: money and a sperm thread industriously spun by everyone, everywhere, up and down, back and forth, in and out. Every man has slept with every man and every woman. Everyone, thank goodness, is rich enough to think of money as a means to the most exciting, most amusing games, and to leave moral considerations out altogether. Every man and every woman have satellites, escorts, parasites, flatterers, whores, floozies, gigolos, catamites, henchmen. Everyone has his little court, and it's in a courtier's power to be treated as a lackey or to command respect (yes, experience teaches that members of the Middle Kingdom at some point like being treated rather insolently by some such creatures).

Uncle Ferdinand could not treat me with more exquisite charm and paternal kindness if the ancestral portraits along the walls, the pale Fanariots with the saber-crooked noses and the fiery-eyed boyars with the crooked feathers on otterskin caps, were truly my forebears too and he really were the commander of the *garde à cheval* in which I had been freshly promoted to cornet. He sits opposite me, watching me dine. He himself eats almost nothing anymore; he briefly pokes his fork into the meager food on his plate and then leaves it untouched. His yellowish-gray spider head over his stiff white shirtfront, which has pushed his bow tie all the way up to his earlobes, is mystically transfigured in the glow of the table candles, like the head of a pagan priest. The glasses of wine before him sparkle like test tubes containing reagent fluids of different colors. He does not touch them, either. His round, thin-lidded eyes are nailed to me. And I sit opposite him, bolt upright, in my operetta uniform, striving to appear as relaxed and casual as possible. I use elegant John as my model—he is a model for me in many respects—and I deceive him.

Yes indeed, Mr. Brodny: such is my innocence back then, twenty-eight years ago. Stella is still alive, and I love her. I don't as yet know that I shall never see her again. She is with John in Bucharest, and I delude myself into thinking I can hurry into her arms at my next furlough (which Uncle Ferdinand effortlessly obtains for me by way of my regimental commander). Stella, my star! . . .

and all the while, I also love John. I measure myself against John; I compare myself with him. I know that of all the countless lovers of my mother, he was the only one whom she loved passionately. I would like to be like him. He is more plain: his profile and his hands are finer, more cultivated, his eyes are brighter, larger, more sincere, less shifty than mine—yes, it is that shiftiness which reveals Subicz's lineage from a tribe of mountain Dalmatians. John has smoother, less unruly hair, which lies more naturally on his head—the hair of a model child, the kind of hair Miss Fern tried to make mine be with furious strokes of the brush. John must have been an exemplary child from a splendid home, *un ragazzino molto fine, elegante, intelligente, perbenino* (I am grateful to Lieutenant Colonel Subicz that I am not such a brat).

John has the best manners a person could possibly have. I am fascinated with the way he takes me for granted; that is, the way he, almost thirty years my senior, treats me as a perfect equal in every respect (in contrast to Uncle Helmuth's Fafnir-like, menacing demand that we *respect our elders*). I was delighted with the way John took me for granted from the very beginning—or new beginning—when I met him again after twelve years: no longer Miss Fern's spick-and-span, combed-and-brushed, piss-elegant little boy, the bastard of sweet little Maud; now a scrawny, towering youngster, wretchedly dressed, aureoled with the odor of a tenement apartment, dissipated because of certain back-courtyard experiences, with a dreamy and unreliable lurking in his eyes. I am enchanted by the way John took me for granted then, welcoming me as though not a single day had waned since last he saw me with my hand in Miss Fern's; "Hello, dear boy, awfully glad to see you. Let's have some booze." (Two years before Uncle Ferdinand's "*Ah, te voilà, finalement. Il était grand temps qu'on te voie*": chips off the same block.)

John's cordiality toward me has not diminished for an instant. I know that he is too rich to worry about the tailor bills that Stella pays for me (especially since he can tell himself that Stella, who is even richer than he, probably pays them out of her own pocket). Not the slightest shadow of a smile, not even a millimeter-high twitch of his eyebrows, an involuntarily accelerated blink, ever betrays his thoughts when he suddenly sees me all spruced up as if I had stepped forth from the latest issue of *Adam*. I virtually live in his home. Although my official place of residence since I left my relatives is the *garconnière* in the middle of Vienna (my rent paid by Stella), I am at John and Stella's house in the Rennweg from dawn to dusk. I drive his car, drink his whiskey, screw his wife; his chambermaid washes my shirts, his valet presses my trousers—and John treats me as politely as if I were His Britannic Majesty's ambassador. His savoir faire is enthralling; he is indefatigably attentive, obliging, friendly—and completely invulnerable to intimacy. I am in awe of his tact (and almost incapable of looking him in the eye ever since Stella told me that he is delighted with my tact). We are such an exemplary, civilized trio that I often cramp up and hold my breath to keep from throwing up.

32

All that I have survived. And not only that but also the farewell from the park of my childhood, when the Russians came to Bessarabia with the summer. A little later I survived the bombs on Berlin when, on a highly suspicious pseudodiplomatic mission, I avoided a heroic death on the front. I survived Stella's disappearance when she—the Jewess, the wife of an Englishman in a position both important and mysterious—hit on the insane idea of trying to enter Germany unrecognized from Switzerland in order to see me once again...

and I also survived the shameful rat-flight the length and breadth of the German lands, the ludicrous game of hide-and-seek with the authorities and draft-dodger hunters: I survived the second Ice Age in Hamburg-on-the-Elbe and Nuremberg, where John hit on the insane idea of calling me as a witness to Stella's murder...

and in Schwab's eyes all these things were a remarkable wealth of enviable experience, which I absolutely had to get down on paper. I began to believe him and divided myself (already reduced by half a life) into two further halves, of which one half, the potential author of the masterpiece novel of the era and future Nobel laureate, set about systematically to undermine the life of the other self-half, a pioneer in the reconstruction of the postwar West German film industry. I undauntedly survived the marriage to Christa and an affair (which rocked the worldwide public) with the fading movie star Nadine Carrier (including several relapses); and I survived my son's scorn. (A young man a father could be proud of, by the way: *un ragazzino molto fine, elegante, intelligente, perbenino.* The Dalmatians have Mendeled out. Christa's clear, corn-blond brightness. Her better-bred hands. Her small mouth. Her eyes, brighter, larger, more sincere than mine. No cunning in them. Her hair, smooth under the brush stroke.)

No use imagining that if Uncle Ferdinand were still alive, he might be interested in meeting my son, grandson of beautiful Maud. Except for the data in the *Almanach de Gotha*, the only genealogies that interested Uncle Ferdinand were those of horses and dogs. And even they did not interest him anymore during that faraway February 1940 when I saw him for the last time. The only thing that interested him then was the *act of handing down*.

I still sense the unerring gaze with which he watches over my table manners. In them, he does not read my aptitude for someday entering the ranks of the Middle Kingdom but only my polite willingness to listen to him. My powerful appetite evidently pleases him; I won't tire easily. His fatherly concern, his elegant, seemingly unconditional familiarity and comradely intimacy, should not deceive me. I would make an embarrassing mistake if I presumed to derive any privileges from them. "I like to treat everyone as my equal," says Uncle Ferdinand. "But that doesn't mean that he may treat me as his equal."

The elegant as-if of our equality is quite naturally due to his not asking me anything. He does not wish to know why I am not seen in the right places at the right time through the annual course of the "seasons." Why I do not play polo near the Pyramids in January, zoom down the Cresta run on my knees, belly, and elbows in Saint Moritz in February, play in tennis tournaments on the Riviera in March, sail near Ragusa in April, dine with Lady Diana Duff-Cooper in London in May, attend the night races at Auteuil in June, waltz with Geraldine Apponyi on Budapest's Margaret Island in July—and so on through the moons until the graceful cycle concludes and recommences. It is tacitly assumed that only private reasons are holding me back. In case of doubt, at my age, a romance that must be discreetly handled (and then indiscreetly gossiped about). Otherwise I would quite obviously be doing all those things, though to be sure WWII is, to some extent, a hindrance.

Nor does Uncle Ferdinand ask to hear where and how I have spent the almost one and one half decades since my short pants and long, buttoned gaiters and little Norfolk jacket with the tremendous navy-blue-and-white polka-dotted bow under the Eton collar, and Miss Fern's admonishing English dove-cooing in my ear. And even if he became absentminded and let the question slip out, he would not wait for my answer. For if he doesn't know the answer, then the events must have taken place outside his world, and anything happening beyond Uncle Ferdinand's world has but remote significance for him. There is no room in the Middle Kingdom for the people, things, circumstances, incidents I could tell him about—except, at best, Uncle Helmuth's spiritist séances. And Uncle Ferdinand would know about them from Countess Kannwitz without Uncle Helmuth's making an appearance.

But perhaps Uncle Ferdinand himself does not even wish to hear anything about his Middle Kingdom. If he wants to keep informed and up to date, it is probably only for the sake of inventory. Like the task of the ornithologists and shell collectors among his princely cousins, his true chore is to sift, count, arrange, and name, not to analyze and observe. The world is as God the Almighty has created it: *è così perchè è così*. Uncle Ferdinand has already told me basically everything worth knowing about his Middle Kingdom—its structure, its mechanics, its functioning. Only seldom do I hear something more, lessons about habits and conduct—say, that the toughest hunts are ridden not in England in red nor in France in green but in Ireland in glen check and brown boots. I am told of Count Dankelmann's famous five driven partridges in Upper Silesia: two shots at the approaching covey, change guns, shoot only *one* barrel, change guns again lightning quick and take the last two shots at the flushed fowl... Anecdotes likewise recede into the background. (For instance: "She was terrified of having a baby, but she didn't want to do anything to protect herself because she was afraid that some birth-control device might injure her and then she couldn't have the child that she wanted someday from a man she really loved. And that was why—" I understand. Expressed in the floweriness of folk poetry:

And there you see the reason why
it's only through the asshole by
which narrow passage for the fart
he finds the entrance to her heart.

Although Uncle Ferdinand is so prudish that he freezes at the slightest obscenity, he now has a good laugh. If an off-color joke is heartily ribald, he appreciates it as he would a hearty peasant dish that occasionally interrupts the monotony of his daily *haute cuisine*. He has me repeat it twice: "How did that go again? 'And there you see the way—' Oh yes, of course, 'the reason *why*'—otherwise it won't rhyme. It's only through the asshole by—well, well, very funny indeed—she lets him find his way to her heart. Very funny, really very funny!")

but this is only a short digression, after which we return all the more assiduously to the business at hand. He rapidly becomes impatient whenever I show lacunae in my education. He is slowed down by having to localize every last detail and connect it to the others: "Well, naturally, they got to know each other better at Titi's wedding, because he's a cousin of Mutzi's—in Rome, of course, where else!" An intake of breath, with which he controls unruly stirrings. Then relief, because he thinks of something that excuses me: "But I keep forgetting how young you are. *J'ai une mémoire admirable, tu sais: j'oublie tout...*"

Which, needless to say, is pure *coquetterie*. In fact, his memory is fabulous, worthy of a cabaret act. It enables him to focus on the titanic chore of keeping the inventory of the Middle Kingdom. The material is gigantic: "*une mer à boire*," as he himself admits. Scientific meticulousness requires that every detail be recorded of the happy inhabitants of that reality vanishing into legend: the tonnage of their yachts and the horsepower of their sports cars; the names of their horses and dogs, their pedigrees; the jewelry, hair color, and liver spots of the women; the cock sizes of the men; the quality of the silver used at this or that gala dinner; the names and vintages of the wines that were drunk; the bizarre wanderings of the jewels important enough to have destinies of their own ("Well, first Toto inherited it from his mother, an Aldobrandoni, and he gave it to his wife, Nini, and then she gave it to Lazzi when she had an affair with him, because he had gambling debts, and that was why Lazzi sold it to Joshi for a song, and then Joshi gave it to a Parisian dancer at the Lido; he was madly in love with her, a girl named Yvonne; and then she . . .").

The catalogue of the Middle Kingdom is like the Marquis de Sade's *120 Days of Sodom*, and, like this key opus of modern literature, it is bound to end in sheer mathematics. Uncle Ferdinand's reports grow more and more abstract. The Middle Kingdom is dematerializing. It makes no difference that its de facto survival is endangered. Uncle Ferdinand appears less disturbed by the realization that Poland is lost once again ("despite the stubborn assurance to the contrary in her national anthem") and that he will probably have to write off Stash and Wanda, Kotja and Olga, once and for all, and with them the fantastic wild boar hunts in Volhynia. He is much more worried about whether roulette and other games of chance are really still elegant. Who is still playing them? Of the friends in the innermost circles, only the Greeks and a couple of Sicilians and Spaniards (he lists them by name).

The tide of gray iron men, rising all around Europe, is of no concern to Uncle Ferdinand. He knows that they have massed just a few miles across the Dniester and are menacing him directly and personally, but he doesn't care. Nor does it matter to him whether others are about to blow up the Maginot Line before pitching into one another. Nothing, incidentally, says that they won't make a detour and invade France via Belgium (as a former member of the general staff, Uncle Ferdinand thinks of General Schlieffen with great respect). In other words: Jacqueline and Guy and Alain and Marie-Jeanne and with them the stag hunts in the Île-de-France and the pheasant shoots in the Ardennes and in Sologne are as much at the mercy of providence as, perhaps, Ian and Daisy, Hugh and Elizabeth-Anne, in their splendid country houses and play parks full of first-class horses, dogs, sailboats, on the other side of the Channel. But more than anything, Uncle Ferdinand is haunted by the observation that for some time now—that is to say, increasingly since the last decade, from the end of the delightful twenties till today—more and more friends of the innermost circles have been complaining of boredom or (usually this goes hand in hand) have become boring themselves. ("If you can still remember good old Nicki—he was absolutely mad about your mother, and she liked him because he was so entertaining—I'll never forget what he said at Stefanie's funeral: '*C'est commode, un enterrement, tu sais: on peut avoir l'air moussade avec les gens, ils prennent cela pour de la tristesse...*'"—Stella calls this kind of *esprit* provincial.—"And then he married that person, that former actress. There was nothing to say about it. After all, in our day, the king of England stepped down from the throne because of a love affair, but he didn't become more boring because of it, on the contrary. But poor Nicki, he was a completely different man. And when that person died in the bargain, he never stopped talking about her. He was unbearable. No matter where you ran into him, he talked about her. Eventually, nobody wanted to have anything to do with him. Who wants to hear about such matters all the time? People have enough problems of their own. If everybody carried on like that, that would be the end of it. And so ultimately we quite abandoned poor Nicki. Sandro as much as said so in his eulogy when Nicki died. And he talked about what a valuable person Nicki had been. Oh, well? *Éloge funèbre. La moitié de tout ça lui aurait suffi de son vivant.* But poor Nicki had really become unendurably boring..." This reminiscence has unforeseeably arisen during the recitation of a long list of cocaine sniffers among his friends, and he terminates it with a necrologue: "I can understand old Silvio Francalanza. When he turned ninety-five, he simply shot himself. Things had gotten too boring for him. *Basta, fini*, goodnight, everybody. I can understand him perfectly.")

33

It is midnight. The witching hour, Mr. Brodny. Back in Vienna, at twelve midnight, Uncle Helmuth and Aunt Hertha would exchange intimate glances at every creaking of an ancient and decrepit piece of furniture (almost pure Biedermeier, a *von* Jaentsch heirloom). They knew what was happening: visitors from the beyond. The departed were going about. Uncle Helmuth even knew them by name. During the séances of his spiritist circle, they would materialize in the temporarily emptied physical shells of the mediums, identifying themselves and revealing from which sofa nook or dresser corner they were creaking. You should not be surprised, sir, that I, familiar at an early age with such occult phenomena, have gotten into the habit of summoning ghosts. We live in the era of historicism, obsessed with the notion of rationally comprehensible causal connections; they alone guarantee our reality. I, for my part, am haunted by the loss of a full half of my life. I would like to conjure up the vanished reality of that half. I have to do so. I ask for your sympathy: it's not pleasant living amid the realities in the no-man's-land of time. To feel comfortable here, one must be dead, like Uncle Ferdinand, like Cousin Wolfgang, like Schwab and all my other loves. They still exist marvelously as heroes of their myths. Which, of course, also means that they have to put up with being summoned forth by shamans like me. People like us have the power to call them from their shadowy existence into time's no-man's-land and to materialize them in the magical element of *writing*. Just look: all I have to do is use my quill, my ballpoint pen, the keys of my typewriter, to place a few hundred letters on this sheet of paper, and Uncle Ferdinand—the Uncle Ferdinand of winter

1940—will live before our eyes. His yellowish-white spider-head is wedged deep between his high-thrust shoulders. The straw whisk of his mustache bristles out horizontally on either side under the parrot's beak of his nose. The skin on his forehead is so smooth that it rosily mirrors the glow from the fireplace. I sit opposite him, listening attentively. The reflection of the fire's glow is fitful in my boot shafts; the boot tips are in a pool of red light. Uncle Ferdinand is also staring at this. Though physically still very much alive in that winter of 1940, he is no longer of this world. He already belongs to another dimension. He now belongs to the marvelous no-man's-land of space and time in which history and stories exist.

He is already with his ancestors, whose pictures gaze down at him from the high walls of the dining room. His faith in immortality has placed him among them. Perhaps Uncle Ferdinand does not really believe in the immortality of the soul in God, even though he has been brought up in this faith and would regard it as poor taste to doubt it. But he does believe in the immortality of fame. His ancestors did not die because they entered history. He too will not die, for he will become history. Stella says that he is one of the modern princes who do not determine the fate of the nations with an open vizor but manipulate it surreptitiously, rather in the way a man rummages under a girl's skirt. Hence, says Stella, his proper place is not in the history of the world but in the history of manners. Nevertheless, when you consider the people in the highway rest stop, this is still the history of the manners of gods: mythology. Meanwhile, he thus placed himself in my shaman power. I need only a few dozen letters again, and he scurries over the glossy curvature of the samovar, withdraws into the constriction under his belly, telescopes into his spindly legs, is caught by the ring over the samovar foot and is dreadfully flattened out; then, extended into a serpent, he slithers around the base of the cone over the heater flame and, as though liquefied, pours into it—

and he steps back from the tea table. He has gotten hold of his watercress sandwich mushroom patty currant tart or cucumber sandwich, and struts once again as a giant rooster through my childhood day—

and in the silver on the tea table, as his shadow moves away, the springtime rises again, a hundred times in a hundred radiant stars. Spring, outside the window, wafts through the air, blue and full of distressing promise. It is the springtime light, the sweet core, of the lost half of my life. It has not even been snuffed out by the years of my Viennese upbringing with Uncle Helmuth Aunt Hertha Aunt Selma plus Cousin Wolfgang as a dowry of the spiritualized philistine world. The dismal gray of those fourteen years was still lined with that light—as was yesterday's fog (the day before yesterday's fog? or that of how many nights and days ago?), through which I walked from the place des Ternes to Calvet's on the boulevard Saint-Germain in order to meet you, Mr. Brodny. Don't think me certifiably mad if I repeat that this was the light of the old Europe—behind the fog even here, in Pearris, Freanss, in the year 1968. It froze on a solstice day thirty years ago, in March 1938, in Vienna, Austria. The first phase of the Ice Age then commenced. Now, the second age is already long since past. But the ice doesn't seem to have thawed completely. The gray mist is still hiding that golden light. How long will it take the mists to dispel altogether? And will the light that finally breaks through be the old light again? What do you think?

34

How regrettable, dear Mr. Brodny, that our meeting yesterday (the day before yesterday? the day before that? I can't remember which day it was; since then, I've been living behind closed shutters and without a timepiece; I write; now and again I sleep for a few hours and then continue writing, and I shall not stop until I have explained to you why what I have to say cannot be said in three sentences)—how frightful, I repeat, that our meeting was so inauspicious! I would very much have liked to talk with you. As a compatriot, so to speak—former compatriot, for now of course you're an American through and through, while I, hopelessly behind the times, have remained a European. You see, I insist on imagining that you too originally came from Bessarabia. I insist that I saw you when I was a child there. You were one of the men who purchased Uncle Ferdinand's harvest. We had gone on a carriage ride. It was still very warm; my mother held a white parasol over us. Uncle Ferdinand told the coachman to turn into a field. There you were, standing by a fiery-red thresher that puffed small white clouds of steam into the spotless sky. You were wearing a linen jacket and leather gaiters, and you greeted us—my beautiful mother, Uncle Ferdinand, Miss Fern, and me—with such forceful verve that Uncle Ferdinand automatically and irritatedly waved you off, telling the driver to keep going. Thus, our first meeting was unconsummated, Mr. Jacob G. Brodny. And, at the second meeting, it should not have surprised me to discover features in you that I had not reckoned with—for instance, the dismayingly clear singsong of your angelic voice. I was quite taken off guard by this cantorial tenor.

But all this is nonsense, of course. Sheer fantasy. A fancy of my overstimulated imagination. If it were true, then you would have to be over ninety years old today, in 1968. And besides—why? There is no reason to assume it. Not the slightest thing to go by. At best, some sort of manipulation by my subconscious. The foggy day outside, from which I came, was edged with a light that reminded me of autumn days in Romania. Autumn and also spring days. (I myself begin to fear for my mind. *Abbia pazienza!*)

And you greeted me so dashingly, with such forcefulness. Without having ever seen me before. As if you had known me for years. I found this heartwarmingly pleasant. It led me to joke on the spot. I could not guess that you expected more ceremony from me. After all, you are a mighty man on the literary scene and I am nothing but a writer.

But no matter. Right after our first exchange went awry, everything else went awry. But you should not therefore believe, Jaykob Gee, that I didn't like you. On the contrary. I liked you very much: the way you sat there, enjoying a thrush pâté on small pieces of white bread. From the mashing masticatory movements of no doubt perfectly filled molars, your cherubic voice asked what I was writing. Could I tell you the plot in three sentences?

Try putting yourself in my place. I had come from the fog outside, as I have said. From a white-surging ocean. A bright, splendid blue-gold autumn day could be divined at the bottom. The fog was lined with gold. The dove-blue and lemon-yellow city of Paris was completely dissolved. It had turned into gray-whitish steam suffused with gold.

I had walked all the way from my hotel near the place des Ternes to the boulevard Saint-Germain. Or rather: I had swum. Along streets that had turned into white-surging riverbeds. Across squares like vast bays. Through the great flood areas of the Tuileries, where tree stumps, planted in the steam, loomed into the air. Across the Pont Neuf, which had turned into a cloud bridge over a steam-filled chasm. As I walked, I was overcome, of course, by all sorts of memories. Thanks to my drifting through the fog, they too were detached from any context. As if moving through fitful half sleep, full of exchangeable and exchanged meanings. They came floating from every place that hovered between Bessarabia and Paris in the torrent of time. They were not in me—I was in them. Dissolved and disoriented. The thing bearing my name was not a person. I was a surging flood of memories.

I should have explained this to you, Mr. Brodny. I should have told you that the contrast was too abrupt, too enormous, when I entered Calvet's. There you sat, so unbelievably concrete, so utterly self-assured and American, so—how shall I put it?—so formed, so solidly immured... Yes indeed, in my disheveled mental state, I involuntarily thought of Schiller. I said with boyish zeal:

> Solidly immur'd in earth
> Stands the mold of hard-bak'd clay...

Yes indeed. There you sat, Jacob G. Brodny, the world's most efficient, the globe's most important literary agent, square-shouldered, square-faced, with iron-gray woolly hair in an angular crew cut and heavy dark eyes under heavy thick lids in your striking Jewish head. You sat there like a solidly cast iron cube between the wall and the table. And before you there was something that seemed to come from a German fairy tale, all those things straight out of Red Riding Hood's little basket, spread out before you on the neatly folded red-and-white-checkered tablecloth: little plates and little forks and little knives and little spoons and sparkling little glasses. And in a pleasingly shaped little pot of fired clay, half-covered by a layer of white fat half-scratched away by your knife, the thrush pâté gave off a spicy aroma. And in a little basket next to it lay the wine, half-swathed in a snowy napkin, like a dusty, ruby-red-capped and white-bibbed child-mummy: a bottle of blood-red Château Margaux. You, Mr. Brodny, were sitting there, breaking pieces off a stick of fine white bread, smearing them with clay-colored pâté, and inserting them between your greasy satrap lips. You were chewing very pleasurably, earnestly, eagerly, washing down the food mush every so often with a sip of the dark wine. And where your form-fitting, albumen-bluish nylon shirt was wrinkled by your chest hair, a black bug ate at your heart.

I should have taken that into consideration. Likewise, the clear bell tone of your voice. But I was so thrown off by your request to tell you my *story* in three sentences that I forgot the black bug in your heart and did not even perceive your voice. This may be pardonable. Going by the purely optical effect of your utterly American appearance, Jay Gee, one expects the usual mixture of senatorial potato-mouthing and lay-preacher sanctimony, squooshed out in chewing-gum cow pats. But not that heavenly milk of a voice. That voice does not fit under a Stetson hat. It doesn't even go with the Cosa Nostra boss's cigar jutting up toward the brim of his fedora. I should have noticed that voice. But I was bowled over, *bouleversé*. Once again: *Abbia pazienza!* Forgive me!

35

Certainly: I have spent nineteen years of my life pouring the bell metal of my memories into the mold of a *story*. I was, I am, ready to explain in detail how and why. Nevertheless, nineteen years is a considerable stretch of time. It adds up to—I've figured it out—six thousand nine hundred thirty-five days (plus five days for leap years) that I have spent as attendant to my own lunatic self. Six thousand nine hundred forty days and nights of which not a single one has passed without doubt assailing me, paralyzing me at some point or other: doubt in myself, in my strengths, in my gifts, my intelligence, my knowledge, my memory, my perspicacity, my honesty, my character, my calling, my good fortune, and everything else one needs in order to write. And even doubt in what I was doing... Good God, how often was this not discussed with Brother Schwab! How often was it not discussed in the intellectual chitchat of the feuilletons! The doubt in the necessity of writing, if you please, or in its effectiveness. Why write at all, nowadays? Don't the highway rest stop people have their fill? Aren't they crammed up to their eyebrows with newspapers, movies, television, comic strips? And let's not even talk about the craftman's doubts in the rightness of a conceived form, the possibility of carrying it through... You yawn, dearest friend? I couldn't agree more. Nevertheless, our sort take our profession seriously to the point of self-destruction. Just imagine: six thousand nine hundred forty days, of which perhaps a dozen may have been completely happy, because I didn't think about writing—and afterward they struck me as sinful, as licentiously wasted time.

I can also tell you that, of course, there have been days of fulfillment. Days of euphoria, of creative ecstasy. The bliss of procreation, you know. When nuptially white paper is irrigated by myrmidons of script and becomes gravid with significance. A magical act of creation (which can bring forth not only literature but also newspaper articles, film scripts, cutthroat publishing contracts, love letters, death sentences, declarations of war). Here, however, under my pen, the book of my generation is emerging. Indited by the conscience of our race, Jacob. It is emerging out of such states of self-intoxication. The writing days... But these blissful moments are buried in weeks, months, seasons, years of weary indolence, incapability, irresolution, dullness. In days so sluggish as to make the daily life of Oblomov's footman seem Stakhanovite. And he, Oblomov's footman, has a totally unburdened conscience about his indolence. People like us wouldn't. For us, an unburdened conscience is theft of our own work. A carefree spirit is embezzlement. The man who works away toward a quick end is a saboteur.

You can, of course (like beautiful Maud), reply that the art of life consists in relaxing ever-new cramps before they actually appear. The same holds for the art of writing. Golden words, assuming that one lived a self-determining life and wasn't in fact for the most part passively lived. It is not I who write, Brodny-*leben*: *it* writes out of me. Ask Uncle Helmuth about the torments that a medium suffers before the vessel of her physis is so utterly purified by her that an otherworldly spirit can slip into it and use it for a while as an earthly instrument of expression. But I do not wish to lament. Though hopelessly behind the times, I live the destiny of my era. Anyone who is not a performer in it will, presumably, have an even worse time.

However, you must understand that your blithe request for me to tell you my story in three sentences touched on things deep within me. It was as if you had met a mother who devotes everything to keeping her child alive despite its simultaneous malignant tumors, scrofula, and consumption, and you asked her how many seconds the child does the hundred-meter sprint in. I found you a bit tactless. A bit too forceful, Yankele Brodny. I approved of Uncle Ferdinand's slightly vexed gesture of dismissal in Bessarabia. You were obviously buying too well, too cheaply, from the peasants. We were not certain whether you, clapping us on the shoulder, might not claim that the grain on the stalk was half-rotten. I felt you lacked savoir faire in dealing with *grands seigneurs*. In six thousand nine hundred forty days of alternating between compulsive expression and juvenile ink-retention—one hundred sixty-six thousand five hundred and sixty hours of testing and rejecting, of anxieties, flickering hopes, blazing certitudes, and ashen disappointments, as well as faith and courage—people like us achieve a certain dignity. After which you don't squander your grain anymore. Just a few days ago—about a week before I received the message that you, the powerful literary agent Jacob G. Brodny, wished to see me and would be delighted to dine with me chez Calvet—a few days earlier, I tell you (I had just barely arrived here from Munich via Reims), I fancied I had something to say in my book. Despite all theoretical and particular doubts. During my drive here from Reims, it had suddenly emerged before me quite clearly. I had only to cheat my producer-piglets, who had ordered me to Paris, of a few short weeks; I had only to sneak off for a while, to some place where no one would suspect me of staying. I had only to unpack my papers there and launch into my shaman arts: with the anthracite-gray magic conjuring up spirits by means of black letters on virgin-white paper...

Unfortunately, something interfered with my plans.

However, bullheaded as a human being is (behind the times not only in the flight of years but also the flight of days), I was still not ready to admit final defeat. I became aware of my failure only when you asked me to tell you my story in three sentences.

36

And since things deep within me were touched by your Mephistophelian demand, I had a vision. I saw with what appetite you ate your thrush pâté. I scrutinized your mouth. I was fascinated by the dumb show it was performing with no spiritual effort on your part. You were relishing the taste with such gusto; one could see that your entire essence was sublimated into the fine-tasting food mush. After each morsel, your lips closed solidly, like rubber cushions lying snugly on top of each other, and while your jaws were crushing, your lips kneaded along, stretching and twisting as they assumed an expression now of bitterness and indignation, now of insult, hatred, baseness, and finally of almost majestic scorn. Scornfully, with sneeringly pulled-down corners, your lips suffered a swallowing hop of your Adam's apple; they waited for the rather choky slide of the delicacy down your gullet; then they opened, contorting into a gorgon's grimace in order to give a pale-violet tongue tip a chance to cleanse any pâté remnants from suspiciously perfect jacket crowns.

Please don't misunderstand me. I am not a neurotic aesthete. Business breakfasts in gourmet restaurants with producer-piglets are part of my professional routine. I know the expression of involuntary disgust that one sees in people eating sumptuously. Their autonomously working mouths. Incidentally, as you know, I once wed such a mouth. It was in Nuremberg, at the canteen for German attorneys and witnesses in the gigantic Fürth courthouse. You got the same food as in the Allied cafeteria, but here it was poured out for you like swill. It looked half-fermented and maggoty. Still, it had nutritional value, vitamins. Germans were not picky in 1946. That mouth too was detached from the human being it belonged to. It too remained closed while the human being chewed. It too worked valiantly, albeit with the most peculiar clowneries for itself, just like yours. And the chewing, swallowing human being to whom it belonged and about whom it was completely unconcerned, and who was likewise unconcerned about it, was entirely sublimated into the taking in of nutrients. It was a young girl, corn-blond, with lovely posture, like someone who knows how to ride well. Over the capering mouth hovered a pair of aquamarine-clear fairy-tale eyes, seeing nothing. They were switched off, so to speak, or were listening (so far as eyes can listen), likewise into themselves, to the intake of vitamins from the disgusting canteen grub.

A burning pity overcame me at this sight, a pity not for the girl but for the *condition humaine* in general: for the human creature and the tragicomedy of its existence. Outside, the city of Nuremberg lay in rubble, as did the rest of Europe. The mass graves from the Don to the Pyramids, from Andalsnes to Salonika, were barely covered. The land was still full of iron men, and children ate from their garbage cans as from troughs. Here in Nuremberg, judgment was to be pronounced on WWII: the crime of war, war crimes; crimes against humanity, the crimes of conspiracy for all these things—twenty million victims. The self-assured zeal with which the gallows were constructed for several of the accused did not permit the hope that the twenty million victims would be the last. And amidst these atrocities sat a foolish, lovely young girl, eating with ardor and physical devotion, as though she were eating the flesh of the LORD. Ate with utter creaturely devotion. Sated herself, provided her body with nutrients. Had turned all her senses to this act of providing nutrients... this too a kind of gratitude: indeed, that of the flesh. I began to love her.

But that was in my mind when I saw you eating, Mr. Brodny. The year 1962 was also in my mind, the year when I was at the peak of my fame as the writer of shitty movie stories and completely at a standstill with the work on my book, on which I pegged hopes of my salvation from screenplays. It was the year I finally got divorced from Christa and soon didn't even have a place to live. I moved from hotel to boardinghouse and from boardinghouse to hotel, while people in the street pointed their fingers at me because I was the lover of a world-famous star, Nadine Carrier. The escape from Nadine to the crazy love for Dawn was also in my mind—Dawn and the abstract existence I entered into because of her: the growing unbelievability, unreality, of my existence (which so fascinated Schwab), while all around me lay a world of tormentingly immutable facticity: millions of people teeming over highways, hundreds of thousands eating at rest stops. Everyone, it appeared, knew what he was doing, how much he was earning by doing it, what he could afford with it, what things cost. The supply of purchasable goods was overwhelming, the choice soon imprisoned the entire individual. Everything was getting better, more perfect, more obligating; you had to have it, otherwise you didn't count... And I sleepwalked through the sorrows of a lover whose beloved has been abducted to Hades like Eurydice (I still remember very precisely a conversation with Schwab on the Pont Neuf)—sleepwalked through Paris, the bright and beautiful underworld...

all these things were in my mind, as well as Bessarabia and Uncle Ferdinand. And then I heard you speak (without, of course, noticing your angelic voice). Aside from the free and easy "Hi," which, I must confess, got on my nerves, you very soon said, "I've heard about you, young man." (Why so young? At worst, you're only five or six years older than I.) "You're writing a book." (Indeed.) "Tell me the *story* in three sentences!" This was said by your hardworking mouth, which lent such original expression to feelings, sentiments, moods that you did not even have, while you consumed pieces of white bread, mashed in Margaux and sputum, with *pâté de grives*. And quite to my surprise, I heard familiar sounds in your diction. Neither your bellowed *r* in "story" nor the thick *l* of the recent immigrant conceals the slightly nasal Viennese *Kaffeehaus* yiddle of your speech pattern, Jaykopp Gee.

And with that the lid was off my memories. There was no stopping now, and I was not solidly immur'd in earth, I was floating away from myself, floating through the catastrophe-land of Europe, back to the lost half of my life. There was too much of my past in your tender yiddling cadence, from Ostbahnhof to Hofmannsthal, I couldn't pull myself away.

And yet there you sat and were everything that Europe no longer was, everything that it had meanwhile become, to my sorrow: the same Hilton Hotel from Madrid to Oslo, the same service-station diner, the same airport, the same jukebox from Bückeburg to Calabria, the same supermarket, the same T-shirt on girlish tits, the same hard neon light on evenings when the sky turns to stone over the phallic cities.

And there I had a vision all at once. You, Mr. Brodny, were the model American (hadn't gone over on the *Mayflower*, to be sure, but all the more militant in New World spirit for that: a pogrom-tested Babbitt from Galicia), and as the personification of that spirit you were devouring not *pâté de grives* but a dish named Yurop. The thing you smeared so thickly on your little pieces of white bread and inserted between your perfectly serviced teeth, the thing on which you closed your lips, leaving them to their so original play of expressions while you were totally sublimated to being a chewer and swallower—that thing was not thrush pâté, it was Europe. Her spirit, her soul, her dream of herself, her self-illusion. Her old skillfulness, her inexhaustible wealth of forms, all her many forms so thoroughly imbued with her spirit, with the essence of her being. You devoured her, perfected by Walt Disney and frozen and packed in nylon, in the candy color of a *Time* & *Life* magazine insert. Indeed, that *was* a feast! I saw palaces and cathedrals vanishing into your mouth, which closed over them, contorting—either disdainful or offended, mocking or arrogant—while your teeth chewed. Entire cities, lovelier than Nuremberg, were gobbled up by you, for instance Bruges or Siena or Prague. With you, I tasted Paestum still in swampland and a tangle of wild roses, I saw a spring morning in Brabant melting on your tongue. You forked up the Lübeck *Dance of Death* and chewed it with delight; you then inserted Michelangelo's *David* with its oversize head and fists (but what a head, what fists!), promptly followed by a Klimt portrait of a lady. Shakespeare's sonnets tickled your palate. You swallowed the façade of Chartres with all the mysterious queens and angels and granted yourself, last but not least, the concluding chapter of Proust's *Du côté de chez Swann*. And you washed all this down with a wine that got its color from Giordano Bruno's blood and its charmingly virile spirit from Spinoza. And on top of this your angelic voice now clambered over the threshold of my consciousness...

I had to hold my breath and writhe and squirm to keep from throwing up.

37

I ought to have been overcome by the same pity that I once felt for Christa in Nuremberg. Or rather for the *condition humaine* in general: for the human creature and the tragicomedy of its existence. But this would have led only to my suffering, and I have avoided suffering as best I could ever since I lost the first half of my life. There has been too much cause for pity since then; one simply can't manage it.

Do credit me, however, with not dragging the past into presence at least on this occasion. Imagine how simplifying and abbreviating it would have been had I been able to give vent to my dichotomous feelings with a nice hearty "Kike!" What a lovely tension, with the possibility of release granted by such short circuits, has been lost to us because of German immoderation! Europe without hatred of Jews—why, that's like faith in God without the devil. The loss of a metaphysical dimension. Naturally we've subbed in something else in its place: irony. As time goes by it gets ever more bloody. I, however, become more of a coward accordingly.

It was sheer cowardice that prevented me from confronting you, Mr. Brodny. I was afraid of the black bug on your heart. Your bug and mine might have pounced on each other. We would have had to become brothers, like Schwab and me. Even without the clarion fanfare of your voice, I would have recognized God's angel in you, J. G. And I did not want to wrestle with the angel. Not after what I'd encountered in the past days and nights.

Out of cowardice I have armed myself with irony. The rest was simple and logical. I dropped into a couple of bistros and drank. I did not feel like eating (which you may understand). I even went to the Crillon and asked for Nadine. Luckily, she wasn't in. A couple of Americans at the bar tempted me to bait them. But they noticed I was drunk and good-naturedly gave me the brush-off. I could have gotten pushy and provoked them into a fistfight, but I didn't want the bartender to tell Nadine, because then she'd know I was in Paris. This way, he'd take it for granted that I was with her in the Crillon and find it superfluous to talk about me.

I wanted to walk across town again. The fog had lightened, but the golden day underneath had vanished. It was already getting toward evening; I don't know what time it was. At the Madeleine, I ran into a streetwalker and unloaded my grief on her. I didn't get home till late at night.

"Home," as you know, is at present the Hôtel Épicure by the place des Ternes. I owe it to Dawn. This is where I tracked her down in 1963 the first time she disappeared. This is where the scene with the Indian doll (and Schwab) took place, and this is where she became my mistress. This is where I deposited her for good after her mouth had eaten the white rose in the Bois de Boulogne.

Since then, I've been returning here regularly: whenever I'm fed up with the true-blue folkloristically preserved greasiness of the deluxe tourist hostels on the Left Bank; whenever the movie piglets won't foot the bill for the George V; whenever I want to write undisturbed for a couple of days or read Nagel's latest best-selling novel; sometimes simply because I want to be as alone as I truly am; sometimes, in Gaia's days, whenever we had fought or I was overcome with a surfeit of my luxury-consumer existence; and over and over again when I have the compulsive thought that I might be pounced on in some hour of grace by the vision of a form for my book (as occurred during my drive here from Reims, as has occurred all too often throughout the last nineteen years; for the *IT*, which wants to be spoken through this book, constantly prowls after me; I can sense it at the back of my neck—only whenever I try to make a swift grab at it, it evaporates)...

in short: I return to this lousy dump like a murderer to the scene of his crime.

You know the details of my stay this time: I spent over a week here (one day more or less makes no difference) as a voluntary inmate (solitary confinement). The cause, as indicated several times, was an illumination during the drive here from Reims: I finally had collared my pursuer. The *it* that wanted to be spoken through me had revealed itself. The parasitic egg that Schwab had once (nineteen years ago!) planted in me had hatched, had gotten through its caterpillar stage, and was now floating before my eyes as a richly colored butterfly. All I had to do was grab him. Only—since we're dealing with such pretty metaphors—I had reckoned without zoology and without the relationship between the guest and the host.

The eggs of the parasitic ichneumon wasp, Mr. Brodny, never become butterflies; they are placed in caterpillars which, in turn, nurture the hope of becoming butterflies. The evil guests eat up their hosts from the inside; no beautiful metamorphosis ever comes about. All that remains is an empty shell into which (as into Uncle Helmuth's mediums when they stepped out in a trance) an astral being, freely floating in the beyond, can take up residence and materialize at will. Should your kind interest in me go so far that you muster enough patience to skim through the papers I am sending you with this (far too lengthy, far too prolix—forgive me) epistle, then you will find the faithful notation of such an occurrence.

Any utilization for book dealers—as the first glance will reveal—is, to be sure, out of the question. The three folders, A, B, C, contain dismally fragmentary material. Needless to say, you have long since divined that these fragments are pieces, patches, sketches, notes for my book (the masterpiece of the era, right? the lifework of a potential Nobel laureate). May I take the liberty of leaving them with you as a legacy, not with a thought to any possible publication but as reparation for my regrettably poor behavior chez Calvet—

and with the hope that you may find someone to tell you the *story* in three sentences.

A

You must realize that writing is one of the most lamentable roads, leading to anything and everything.

—André Breton, *First Manifesto of Surrealism*

The limits of my language stand for the limits of my world.

—Ludwig Wittgenstein, *Notebooks, 1914–1916*

> Why did I write? What sin to me unknown
> Dipp'd me in ink? My parents' or my own?
>
> —ALEXANDER POPE, *Epistle to Dr. Arbuthnot*

> Fear is a female faint in which freedom loses consciousness; speaking psychologically, the Fall of Man always takes place in a faint.
>
> —SØREN KIERKEGAARD, *Fear and Trembling*

I sort through my papers with a restlessness that nests deeper, closer to the breeding grounds of fear than the fidgety impatience I've retained from my damned formative years in Vienna, a restlessness like a nervous tic, the involuntary closing of an eyelid or the annoyingly recurring, dribbling twitch of a tiny muscle in a nostril, as if a tiny alarm clock there were ringing at unpredictable intervals. Those were the "years of my deepest humiliation." At least that's what I used to call them when I told my friend S. about them, quoting a once current phrase of Hitler's—ironically, of course, but without any joy. Even today I see that time, in which those charged with raising me discharged their duties upon me like acts of revenge, trying to make me "get my head out of the clouds," to teach me to "take life seriously," as an attack (albeit one presumably undertaken with the best of intentions) on everything bright and true in my being (see notes on Cousin Wolfgang: my two-pronged relationship with him, my feelings of guilt towards him—and not just after his death).

It is night. The eighth since I have locked myself in this room. Eight nights and a goodly portion of the days (during which I prefer to get some sleep; the nights are quieter) I have spent rummaging through my papers. These are the notes for my book (though not all, sadly; I feel the absence of some with such agitation that I break into a sweat). What is here is chaos: countless beginnings, chapters worked out or drafts of outlines, fragments, the remnants of discarded drafts, attempts, outlines, studies, essays, ideas, thoughts—in short, all that piles up over nineteen years of, alas, all too frequently interrupted—but always with manic persistence recommenced—labor on a book: two suitcases and a few large cardboard boxes full of wastepaper, from memo pad paper with microscopic scrawls to sheets of A4 paper with lines of text crisscrossing them like saber strokes; from newspaper clippings to book pages filled with handwritten glosses on the margins of the printed text (there's even a beer coaster among them, a few yellowed comments written on it that today are wholly detached from any conceivable context and thus unintelligible).

This is not the first time I've undertaken such a sifting. I'd say it occurs with periodic regularity. Whenever I delude myself into thinking I might yield to the hope that I could finally find enough time, concentration, leisure (or rather: freedom from pressing necessities) to produce something conclusive and whole out of this welter of eruptively hurled-out literary production, the compulsion to create order overcomes me. Needless to say that each time I have had occasion to lament how thoroughly I had acted in prior cullings. In the past I have destroyed the irreplaceable—in all likelihood this time as well. And not once have I managed to advance the new conception, for whose sake I so horribly mangled the old one, far enough that my manuscript found a clearly defined form.

Not this time either. Although this last attempt (and failure) was undertaken with a clearer notion than ever before, and, unlike the previous ones, was not stymied by some unforeseen and unavoidable obstacle. What prevented achievement was something completely unforeseen, something that lay not in the thing itself, in the conception of the book or in my shortcomings as its author. It came from *outside* (I emphasize this word in order to indicate that I mean something that in fact came from *outside normal reality*: see the notes on Uncle Helmuth's spiritualist circles; also Gaia's mother—in Folder C).

Its way was prepared in me by a state of unusual exaltation, likely as a result of my heightened state of expectation. Eight days (and nights) ago I set to working in a state of excitement such as had overcome me before now only in the most humiliating moments of love. (The same foolishly intensified existential awareness; the same heedless fixation: nothing matters anymore that isn't connected to this one, this only true, this all-excluding love: the same *immediate presentness.*) Incidentally, en route here, in Reims, where I had spent the night, I had dreamed my dream.

It is an evil dream, which has haunted me for several years. Nineteen years, to be exact. Not regularly, of course, but at various short and long intervals. I can never figure out what triggers it. This time too there was no apparent cause. It ambushed me like a highwayman. (The element of surprise is its most effective feature.)

The dream was in most of its features the same as always. I commit my murder for no other reason than a vile *cover-up*. Covering up some shameful crime that would come to light if I didn't murder the old cleaning woman. Like a coward, I kill this lamentable creature of mislived life—mistreated, humiliated humanity, foul flesh and rags—in the most brutal way. And as I go to bury the corpse, I realize with increasing certainty that nothing can help me, that I have murdered in vain and that I will be found out—worse, I will be found out along with the deeply disgraceful reason for my committing such a dreadful crime...

As usual, this dream haunted me in the daytime, too—an insidious pursuer that follows me step by step and disappears around corners when I try to confront it. For, as usual, everything I did during those days was aimed at luring out the terror of the night in me.

An unclean game. In the end it takes on a nearly erotic aspect (our friend Scherping would find it blissful). But I do not play it for pleasure.

It inveigles and hoaxes me with the promise that I'm on the verge of some kind of revelation. The paralyzing horror at my deed has a moment of utmost intensity—in the moment in which I awake. I think I recognize in it something that is at the core of my being, or at least the key to it—and which I lose by waking up.

This goes on for a few days. I act as if nothing had happened, go about my customary business. I see this person, speak to that one, settle my accounts with yesterday and make my plans for tomorrow. But secretly I wait for the terror of my dream to ambush me again.

For it is always near—and yet I can never conjure it up. If I think of it, it fades away. If, seemingly unconcerned, I busy myself with something different, it skulks after me. If I glance around (so to speak), then the street is empty... But I sense it hiding somewhere behind me. It lies in wait for me, as I for it. Only it is incomparably more skillful, more nimble, more agile. At times, I feel the horror very close. The expectation that it will assault me again makes my knees go weak and the hair stand up on the back of my neck. But I am too impatient, I anticipate its desire. Even before the blow occurs—the terrible blow with which it might enter me and descend to the refuse heaps of consciousness in which the key to myself is lost—I already want to relish the rending that would pass through me if finally I were to lay hands on it—

And thus, everything dissolves into nothing again—as in awakening. There it was, the massive rending—but before I could see what was opening with it, I lost its pain. I can still feel its far-off echo. This too vanishes.

Should I then try to summon up the individual events of my dream, it is to find it completely empty. What had been image has become *verbal*. I can say in words: that I have dreamed this or that—but it has lost all reality. My attempt to grasp it has robbed it of its magic. There I stand, empty-handed, a swindled swindler.

I then try to deceive myself with all sorts of childish maneuvers.

I fake guilelessness. I pretend to focus my interest on something else, something peripheral, innocuous—for instance, I count up the women I have slept with in any seven fat or lean years—

> *for even our wealth of amorous adventures (as shown by the Leporello lists we secretly kept up in triumph and humiliation) is not due to skill* in eroticis *but occurs or fails as naturally as good or bad harvests (of course, the soil must be conscientiously tilled). And just as our fate, according to the mood or grace of the weather and the ripening, sometimes brings a shortage and other times leads us to abundance, and perhaps from prosperity soon back again to meagerness, so too we are granted a fixed quota of erotic success, inscribed in us, readable in our faces, so to speak, which, with its clear benchmark, ensures that it is neither exceeded nor unfulfilled. And you cannot trump it with any effort or skill, with any physical, much less mental, quality or quantity. Neither the beguiling eloquence of Cyrano de Bergerac will help you nor his long nose (or whatever other lengths or sizes can be brought to bear), because Nature has created poor and rich in every respect—and hence in this respect too . . .*

Such are the things I busy myself with and write down, and thus end up among my papers again; that is, lying in wait for myself

and yet I know that I cannot escape my destiny; I am pressured by time: I'll soon be fifty, I could be dead tomorrow, and I haven't done my work! Here's my book, proliferating before my very eyes, in horrible hybrid cell growth, turning into a monstrosity—hence, I yearn for the dreadful, pleasurable *recognition* to fall upon me just once more, one single and lucid last time, the recognition with which (albeit for only a fleeting moment) I can be certain that *it is true*, that old nightmare: that I *have in fact murdered*, shamefully and for no other reason than to conceal some baseness deeply rooted in me—

but when? how? where? and whom? That's what I can't grasp. I've repressed it.

Even without consulting Dr. Sigmund Freud, I realized long ago that my forgetfulness suggests disreputable sediment in the dark depths of my soul, and I wisely make a point of not trying to fish it out with what that great son of the literary nineteenth century recommends as a fishing rod: the biographical. My horror, which I fear to the point of lust and then desire again, is of the sort that cannot be pursued back to my parents' bedroom. It springs from the sheer terror of existence itself. Such a momentary revelation of the totally *unknown* that lies behind and beyond all that can be known is what the primitive man calls GOD.

How fine I'd have it if it were just a matter of biography (something like the early experiences of Freud's Wolf-Man). A street ditty in a movie. Perfect pap for my piglets. The stuff writes itself, in contemporary style, which, in its love of atmosphere—oozing quotations of style—betrays its attraction to the past:

POSTER

(in psychedelically dynamized Jugendstil *graphics: the linear flow narrowing to a cascade, the spectrum sprouting teeth, a buzz saw of nerves—rose-madder, sulfur-yellow, leek-green, violet . . . with interspersed boutique heraldry: two male hands, hacked off at the gentlemanly cuffs, with forefingers stretching like pistol barrels, point from either side at the name)*

ARISTIDES

Chief Mechanic for the Western Union Tunnel of Love

(collage: model of an early locomotive from pioneer days, its cathedral-bell smokestack sending up as a cloud of steam a distilling flask with alchemical stuff in it—toads, snakes, embryos, homunculi; in the engineer's cab, his booted foot on a female body with a bald head, General Custer with a drawn sword, his left hand waving a fresh scalp)

invites you
on a
TRIP TO HADES
into the
SPIRITUAL INNARDS
of the
CONSUMER SOCIETY TROGLODYTES

(newspaper advertisement praises a method for treating clubfeet and ears that stick out; likewise nose-shapers, body-hair removers, wart, blackhead, and goiter remedies)

Idea:
!A MIDDLE-AGED MAN COMES TO REALIZE
THAT HE IS REPRESSING GUILT!

God grant that I could come up with such a thing: I could sell it instantly to my piglets.

the peppy little producers, co-producers, copro-producers *who teem and crowd wherever the milk of financial assistance, government grants, and development prizes pours from the overlapping folds of showbiz and the culture industry*:

the bright, alert magician's apprentices, soon outstripping the great film sorcerers—*and the hatchlings of the movie business, living it up on expense accounts; rosily fattening on petits fours, foie gras, crab claws, slices of Nova Scotia, caviar dollops at the press conference buffets (with champagne, of course!), their tiny eyes sated and wearied by young starlet flesh—*

yet physically in top shape—*supremely fit, swept along by the process of beauty-construction in the studio and location wardrobes—groomed and spruced up, their little fingernails pared, filed, and polished between the motherly breasts of staff manicurists, their cheek skin smoothed and salved by epidermically solicitous makeup men, their intervertebral disks loosened and their bodies shaken aright by studio chiropractors, kneaded and massaged to firm up their tissue by junior-star gym teachers, their blood circulation refreshed in stars' genuine Finnish saunas in the bungalows of leading men, their flesh treated to ultraviolet rays even in the winter months and then tanned to a crisp by the spring sun over the beach promenades of Mediterranean festival settings—*

men of the world, of course: *well traveled, as they go about preparing big unrealizable projects, and thus surefooted on the parquet floors of Hilton hotel banquet rooms—*

hence mentally too at the highest attainable peak: *shrewd, crafty, brazen, hard-boiled—and infernally clever at wielding the magic wand that every moviemaker carries in his old kit bag and that opens wide all doors, hearts, female legs—yes, even bank accounts:*

so that over and over again by the fictions of uncovered checks and uncashed allowances they manage to keep shooting off a firework of verisimilitude, of adventurously colorful and dynamic, lightly pulsating life; and with swindling promises and dishonest assurances they determine destinies (and not even necessarily for the worse) without ever being troubled by the law: for they do nothing but add more and more possibilities to the everlasting game of the exchange of fiction and reality...

For two decades now, I have been their partner in this game, their stooge and assistant, their officious servant and loyal stable boy. I know them and their keen instincts. I know how eagerly their little ears perk up to the whisper of movie ideas, wriggle with every flash and trash therein; and I know that this particular thought-trash would most blissfully tickle their little piglet ears.

It would be best to funnel it in through the telephone receiver early in the morning.

Special priority call, Paris–Munich: Hello? Intercosmic Art Films? Hi there. May I speak to Herr Wohlfahrt.—Ah, it's you! I didn't *recognize your voice.—What? All night? Who with? hahaha!—Who'd've guessed!—What? What project? Man, you're obsessed! But listen, I've got a new one for you. No, not a package, for now. But it would be a piece of cake making one out of it.—Anyway, that'll be your problem.—What? Imagine, well just let it . . . by the way, you really put one over on me with the last contract.—You certainly did! But, okay, that's water under the bridge. Listen: just picture it, right?—so, a middle-aged man—okay?—let's say early to midforties, close to fifty—so precisely the generation that's now stepping up to the plate.—What?—That's right, our generation, right on the nose. It'd be ridiculous if it weren't, right? Anyway, a man in his best years, something for the female audience, okay?—No, I really mean it. Something a woman can identify with. Her guy, right? Postwar reconstruction man, head of the family, divorced, with a kid and so on, irreproachable life so far, right? Well, one fine day, let's say on a business trip abroad—quite by chance, you see, this man suddenly comes to realize HE IS REPRESSING GUILT! He has COMMITTED MURDER AND KNOWS IT! But he doesn't know who the victim was. Or how it happened. And—*Ne coupez-pas, mademoiselle! Ah, merde!!—*Hello.—Intercosmic.—Hello! . . . ah, there you are. Did you get it all? Well: HE NO LONGER KNOWS when and how and where. Suspenseful, right? But that's only the beginning. I mean, the opening situation.—What? No, no! You know me. I don't like flashbacks either. You know that. No way! Anyhow, that's just the basic idea. Now, the point is: do you want the rest of it to be a genuine German problem film?—What?—Well, so who cares? No, no, don't just wave it off as old hat. The times are changing again. Back in 1958 I wrote down something that says:*

Highway rest stop near Karlsruhe. At the next table, they're overcoming the past: "Oh, you people are always saying Hitler did this wrong and that wrong and so on. But I say: just try to do it yourselves!"

Slice of life, sir. Highly topical not just in Germany, but overseas too... By the way, murder isn't just a political phenomenon—but as you like! The good thing about this material is that it's flexible. We can leave it open as far as the distributor is concerned: Scientifically psychological à la Tennessee Williams—what?—Esther's husband, right—or espionage à la Bond, all kinds of thriller-type stuff. And if all else fails, you can always make it a social satire—No, not a screwball comedy, damn it, a satire, topical, realistic. With a KNOCKOUT part for Nadine...

Okay, agreed. You'll have the treatment in four weeks. In two languages. German and also French for the worthy Mr. Coproproducer. Do you want it in English too? It makes no difference to me. My kind are as fluent in the main European languages as a grand-hotel clerk. We speak them, write them, sing them in the morning while shaving. At your service, my dear piglets. Naturally, I'll keep Nadine informed.—What? Of course not. I certainly won't let her interfere too much. What do you think! We want to get the work done. I mean: complete the project. Okay then. If necessary, I'll go to bed with her. It won't satisfy the lady's need for literary expression, but it'll calm her down for a while. Anyway, as I was saying, I'll get back to you in four weeks—

with empty hands, needless to say (my name guarantees quality and absolute unreliability). With empty hands stretching out, demonstratively, to receive another advance:

for Nature creates rich and poor in the movie business too. With the vast amount of beauty and talent on offer, the rise of a star, for instance, can always be explained by many factors; but the ultimate reasons are always a very special aptitude and predestination for SUCCESS. Likewise, any reward is left to the workings of an Eros unique to the cinema: either you never get your money or you're inundated with it like Danaë... And this cornucopia shower has nothing to do with quality or punctual delivery. It may be deserved or undeserved, but it's never hit or miss, like in a game of chance, rather it always favors only the person of means, film-erotically preordained.

Here too we would have to apply the harsh biblical verse: FOR UNTO EVERY ONE THAT HATH SHALL BE GIVEN, AND HE SHALL HAVE ABUNDANCE, BUT FROM HIM THAT HATH NOT SHALL BE TAKEN EVEN THAT WHICH HE HATH...

Just as for more than two decades I have been fishing in the brackish waters of postwar German film (with little more than the bait of promise and God's blessing), so would my outstretched hands be filled up again this time too—

and I would end up right back where I am now.

For this is precisely my situation. A screenplay is expected of me in eight weeks: a screenplay after a treatment that I delivered six months ago and that since then has been reworked by me and other screenwriters seven and seventy times. Waiting for it are not only my producer piglets, but also (hired by them and ready to start filming) an entire staff in Cannes. Chief among them, in the Negresco hotel, Nadine Carrier, an international star in the waning phase that is transfigured, if not completely lost from sight, by the nimbus of outstanding thespian ability.

Madame Carrier is already waiting for me here and now, in Paris, at the Hôtel de Crillon. Ready to participate in the treatment. Not only artistically (may the LORD preserve me!) but also personally: with an open Thou-soul striving toward my own self (and, needless to add, with the attendant hospitably open thighs). She's already been waiting for eight days. That's how long I've been lost to the movie world.

I'm playing a risky game. Of the eight weeks I've got for the treatment, I'm trying to use four for different ends. If nothing else it would mean twenty-eight days of peace and quiet. I'd live in a hotel (expensed, naturally): ideal conditions for a writer. The advance I've drawn is enough to cover Christa's alimony and my son's monthly allowance (my two most ruthless creditors). The piglets have to leave me in peace, it's in my contract. It's only Nadine I have to keep at a distance—both physically and, sadly, emotionally as well. But I'd have twenty-eight whole days and nights for my book! . . .

—My book—

That sounds as if I were carrying it within me like Nagel carries one of his: like a divine mission . . .

as if, in the flood of printer's ink inundating us, I were chosen to create the maelstrom that could stir up the human race; I, the *conscience of our race* (as if this race still existed as a race and as if yet another pang of conscience might help it):

the book that bears witness to man in the second half of the twentieth century and to his heroic effort to save himself from himself:

—Prometheus as fire captain: using the brittle hose of humanity to put out the fire the spark for which he stole in its, humanity's, name;

Daedalus astray in his own labyrinth: shouting warnings to others not to follow him;

Noah in the deluge of overpopulation: doubting whether he is truly the only righteous man to choose from,

the tragicomical hero at the end of a civilization, who (in order to carry out his mission with clean hands, hands that violence has not desecrated) has no way out other than literature—

literature, which has slid below the mark: the feuilleton amidst the mixed news items on the development of the cobalt bomb, the strategic importance of space travel, speculations on the outcome of the Korean conflict, the state of arms negotiations in the Congo and Indochina, the Vietnam War, the failure of disarmament negotiations, the fruitless conclusion of this or that world summit.

Stephen Dedalus would have had to be a reporter to make the front page. Otherwise, his self-realization as the "conscience of our race" remains a thoroughly private matter.

My book is a thoroughly private matter. Professor Hertzog (of Hamburg: Schwab's psychopompous) would say it is the wish-fulfillment of my guilt complex

> *—final justification of an existence which isolated itself with nothing but a promise (which referred to nothing but itself): And* sundering *and* sin *are cognates. Hence (just as sinfulness contains an obligation to do penance and can escape itself only by willingly accepting its punishment) the arrogance of such an isolation, such a sundering, can be atoned for only with the arduous demonstration that it was justified—*

My book is a promise that I've never made in words (not even to Gaia—and she certainly paid enough for it!) and that anyone who's been blown into the birdcage of my existence and soon back out the other side (lovers within and without the bounds of law; growing and still unconceived sons; well-meaning people of all sorts, chief among them my friend Schwab) thinks he can demand from me like overdue rent. All because, while I never promised it in words, I have presumably pledged it with each of my bizarre actions, with each of my peculiar character traits, each of my far-fetched qualities—in short, with my alienating and rebellious way of being this-way-and-not-like-the-others:

> *—afflicted with the most annoying of all birth defects, which arouses no pity like other strokes of a stepmotherly Nature, such as a cleft palate, for instance, or a harelip, or other bizarre deformations and malformations: a hump, a hydrocephalus, all kinds of nervous and mental ailments, cretinism, falling sickness, and the like. No indeed. This is a far more repulsive handicap, which summons an arbitrary hatred against the altogether different, the fundamentally alien:*
>
> *THE CAIN'S MARK OF EXISTENTIAL CONSCIOUSNESS*

stamped on those who are condemned to recognize in themselves not just any human being but humankind itself:

as if the capsule of their individuality had a crack through which the individual leaked out into the teeming of his species, and further out into the swarming of past generations, along the entire family tree to the root ends at the origins of the genus, and then right into the cosmos: so that every experience has an echo from the universe . . .

but instead of a human specimen of salient character emerging from such profound depths, all that comes out is an uncertain, unsteady, unsettled seeker, who listens beyond things and cannot accept empirical reality in its givenness and its causality as a complete world, and who keeps countering it with skulking nonconformity, a pigheaded if-and-but, which in an insidious way dislocates and unmoors all that is conventionally established, generally believed and determined through unanimous agreement, until eventually nothing is reliable anymore, and reality knows as many redirections, subterfuges, and loopholes as a lawyer; and thus it is only fair that such a misbegotten troublemaker (if he does not wish to be counted among the dangerous fools and recalcitrant villains and be truly isolated behind bars) must ultimately accomplish something that will turn his stated ideas of interpreting the world and life into a model for a new kind of life, expanded by a new dimension

whereby, of course, my book might not have remained a private matter—and this is the dilemma that can destroy a conscientious man (for instance, Schwab).

I have been working on this book for nineteen years. Sometimes it blazes out of me. Then I can't do or think of anything else. I drop everything else, I ignore what's happening around me. Everything gets delayed and disorderly. Important deadlines are forgotten, excellent opportunities are lost. I fail to deliver promised work, I neglect bills, I'm sued, creditors beat down my doors. I won't see anyone, I open no mail, I disguise my voice on the telephone. I barely sleep, I eat standing up or at my desk, I stop shaving, I don't even scratch out the dirt from under my fingernails. I'm in a trance, the hours fly... until my writing stalls, until eventually I can't go on, and my doubts about the whole thing return, and fear, rebellion, surfeit, and finally all sacred enthusiasm is snuffed out.

Sometimes, the flame is steadier. For a happy span of time I work a few hours every day with a clear mind. I don't have to strain my mind, there's nothing for me to invent. There's material galore, in heaps, in piles of paper covered with writing. I link up fragments, fill out joints, smooth over bumps. The sober craft of working and reworking makes me feel my growing abilities and capabilities. I am pumped so full of faith and confidence that I soon burden myself with other work—work that brings in cash. I then spend the money right and left: it is a light currency and I'm on top. I feel I can do the impossible, I dare to make all sorts of ambitious plans, I accept obligations I cannot honor—and I soon find myself so entangled in promises and agreements, contracts, coercions, warnings, dunnings, final notices, that I have to apply all my time and energy somehow to complete things I have hastily begun, finally to tackle things that are long overdue, further to delay things I have frivolously promised...

most of these matters drag on forever; I dare not even think about my book. And the weeks wear on, the months, the years...

There are also periods when I am incapable of anything. I brood obtusely and stupidly over empty pages. I am unable to form a sentence out of a subject, verb, object. Nothing comes to me. Even my worst spirits abandon me: my impudence, my wittiness. Doubt in myself, in what I have to say and in my ability to express it, sucks up what little energy drove me to the desk to at least make a stab at it. Discouragement assails me, impairs my other work along with it. Even (and especially) the movie scripting, long since a cynical routine, is now impossible. I dawdle through the days, grow restless, swell with impatience, long for action, want to be among people and thus avoid them. So I leap over not only my own inhibitions but all sustainting distances as well, smash the neutrality of noncommittal relationships and make them personal: I soon find myself entangled in disagreeable friendships and useless love affairs from which I can extricate myself only in the most brutal fashion. I get lazy, I can't get out of bed in the morning or into it at night (at least not my own). Suspicious passions break out: I collect all kinds of superfluous stuff (deluxe editions of books I won't read, sinfully expensive objects I don't know what to do with and soon give away). I tend to my appearance with the vain punctiliousness of an aging pederast, I shower my tailor, my shoemaker, my shirtmaker with orders, I spend a fortune on neckties, ascots, dressing gowns, slippers, soaps, toilet water, brushes, files, and I reach under every skirt I can find. I feel time flying by, and I run a race with it: no car is fast enough for me, I drive heedlessly at breakneck speed, I invent the necessity of dashing from place to place: the experience of speed both calms me and tires me, both whips me up and wipes me out, leaves me unfeeling and unthinking.

But my book still glows in me. It has burnt to ashes nearly a third of my life.

It screwed up my marriage with Christa and drove Dawn to the madhouse. It was the lie (never fully exposed, yet shining through everywhere and soon filtering into everything) that kept Gaia from trusting me (which then caused her death). It turned my son (a child with eyes like well water in which I was reflected as a star) into a bitter little bookkeeper of my unkept promises and unfulfilled assurances—hence turned me into an ever shrewder swindler, an ever craftier liar and counterfeiter. It turned my existence into a more and more threadbare as-if.

For whatever I write, it ultimately writes *me*. Whatever I narrate, *it ultimately narrates me*. In other words, it is not *I* who live my life, *my book lives me*. And what I live and how I live are determined by the success or failure of my book.

So I live my life dissolutely, banking on the fact that my book (should it succeed) might not rectify things but will in any case justify them (and that it doesn't matter anyway if the book doesn't succeed). I live into the notebook of botched attempts, so to speak: toward a still-incomplete final draft. I can allow myself to drift along however chance determines, whatever circumstances dictate. Even in a no-exit situation, when all bridges are burned, I am exempt from decision, because decision comes not with what immediately happens but on the pages of my books.

Thus my book lives me, over and beyond the dramatic high points of my existence, from which peaks I may survey a battlefield—not necessarily a field of honor, for the time being; on which (for the time being) only others are killed in action. I myself tarry outside the events until the decision has been made, has fallen, with my book. Reality presents itself to me in two alienated ways; on the one hand, delayed in the weightlessly weighty movement of slow motion, in which my seeing eyes perceive "reality"; on the other hand (experienced by me as lived) as arbitrarily swift, uninfluenceable, and inevitable as if filmed in fast motion.

And all this has the ineluctabilty with which, terrorized until I scream in primal horror, and yet voluptuously paralyzed by curiosity about the foreknown, I dream that I am luring the old crone across the threshold of my cellar in order to murder her brutally.

I have not left this room for eight days and nights. Madame gets me wine, bread, cold meat, and eggs (which I drink raw from the shell). The handsome Pole brings the food to my room, sets it down at the door, knocks, and is usually gone by the time I open. The chambermaid comes every morning, makes the bed, and finds little else to tidy up. I don't let her touch my papers.

These papers drive me to despair. Each one directs me to another, which it refers to, which it adds to or is added to by—and which is not at hand. Because, with some other junk that I have left behind, it lies in some trunk in Hamburg, Munich, Barcelona, or Rome, or wherever else it was my movie-parasitical hotel-lobby-loafing life cast me away. Or even worse, it has been destroyed in some auto-da-fé like the one I have instituted here.

I find chapters that I am sure I have written down in a tighter, clearer version. But that version is lost: entire folders are missing.

I am often so sharply beset by impatience that I rip up wads of papers: sketches that strike me as totally absurd, first drafts that demonstrate my most lamentably unimaginative, inexpressive periods, unrelated notes—whatever they refer to is lost. A bric-a-brac of documents testifying to practically anything—but not the definitive shape of the book, crackpot structural designs, dozens of beginnings... It all strikes me as crazy, chaotic, erroneous, and useless. I regret the time, energy, ink, and paper that I've squandered. I destroy it like something very shameful, like the traces of a scandalous past. A few hours later, I stick my head in the wastebasket, rummage around, pull out the crumpled tatters, smooth them, and arduously glue them together again.

Once, I almost beat up the chambermaid (a half-dotty, gentle-eyed old woman from Brittany with the dreamy name of Monique) because she emptied the wastebasket before I could salvage a couple of irreplaceable notes.

Sometimes, I write. I often toss out pages with rough sketches I think I have already completed. But they also contain drafts for later sections, notions, discoveries, comments, the order of the subsequent chapters—and only when I reach them do I realize what is lost.

Thus do the days go by. At night, I murder.

Yet I could have a marvelously simple time of it. Put my book aside, as I've done so often in the past, and serve my piglets. Not just four weeks but a full eight (of which still seven are left)—seven fat expense-account weeks in Paris.

(To Schwab, in the style of a music-hall ditty:

Oh come to the drum
To Paree, old bum!

and his face: the twisted, tortured smile and the abrupt, simultaneous bloating of the cheek skin in disgust—)

Fifty-six late-summerish early-autumn days in Paris:

Had a nice sleep, well into the morning, had a nice bath, cleaned up nice: not in the usual mobster outfit filmmakers wear—turtleneck sweater, sailor's trousers, tam-o'-shanter, cowboy boots—but as a gent with a cineastic note:

Douglas Fairbanks Jr. style: just in town for the game, café-society denizen on studio lots; a gentleman with graying temples but crisply suntanned, racing driver and record-album expert, Playboy Club member and St. Tropez yachtsman: elk-leather coat and gold-buttoned Dunhill blazer, Battistoni shirt, Hermès necktie, Gucci shoes.

Dressed like a hack and writing like a hack.

A stroll through the Faubourg Saint-Honoré: swimming through display windows: the smoky reflection of the sentries at the Élysée:

(*Petit Larousse* heroism: in the *rouge et noir* of the uniforms the symbol of the *hasard* of politics.)

Viewed through their transparent astral phenomena in a different dimension (permeating theirs), the harvest festival of *de luxe* clothing:

feuilles d'automne in silk and velvet; over the hair-tips of fair mink the brilliance of ripe grain; bucolics in the tortoiseshell inlays of Boulle furniture; abundance of fruit petrified in rock crystal and rose quartz; oxblood in the gold-embossed leather of old bookbindings (and everything else besides) . . .

Interspersed: the bright, smoky-marbled evergreen of malachite: *La vieille Russie:* hunted around for Fabergé writing paraphernalia: Monsieur collects.

(to Schwab, in a parody of Nagel:

> "*—in the insatiable hamster-bustling of the battened and fattened, whose hunger grows as their larders fill, as though they knew instinctively that soon they will face a winter that knows no mercy . . .*")

Next: lunch at Prunier's:

surrealist food (the corpse flesh and vaginal forms of mollusks; the barbed armors, nippers, pincers, antennae of crustaceans: horror-movie material) . . .

the afternoon outdoors, to mull over the treatment.

Versailles (the castle in the glass coffin of autumn air: Disneyland)

or Fontainebleau (park landscape in Technicolor: the foliage colorfully discolored—pretty much the only thing that, along with the breasts of aging international stars, still fills the word "resplendent" with substance);

occasionally, a quick and useless visit to the Boulogne studios to view the newcomers: new faces inspire new ideas...

sometimes, scribbling a few notes on some café terrace, for instance Fouquet's—for sentimental reasons—if the tables are still out. (I don't know if they really are. I've been locked up here too long, and it's October);

once, at most twice, a week, dinner with Nadine, a chat and some fornication to avoid creative differences about the movie;

and in the very last week, a week of unleashed, unreflected writing (it wouldn't be the first time, God knows);

in short, living the life.

After which, to be sure, I would reach the far end of never-never land: where you have to eat your way out through the enclosing mountain, and it's not made of rice:

for six solid weeks: critical objections from the piglets (compared with whose artistic empathy Nadine's is a gift of the Muses); at least six more weeks: changes from the distributor (it is not true that man is descended from the ape: the ape is a man who has imagined himself returned to nature out of shame of his humanity);

another six weeks: changes from the director (who, soon united with Nadine in spirit and in bed, has a dreadful say in the matter)—

summa summarum: four and a half months of coprophagia.

But that's the normal steep cost of doing business: I have to take it into account.

I had taken it into account when planning to do what I had originally intended to do: misappropriate four of the eight weeks from the movies (and from cineastic existence) and write in monastic isolation through the blue-gold days and the quietly misty evenings—

not the agreed-upon screenplay, but my book . . .

I had pegged all my hopes on being able to do it. Finally to put together a part of this book large and lucid enough to convince Scherping that I was still worth another advance. That way I could have sent the piglets and their goddamn cinema to hell and I'd have been free for my book—

if my dream had not come to haunt me—and with it Schwab. I've squandered the last seven days and nights with the two of them—and thereby all the hope I set in my book.

My rotten experience in these past few days and nights (a morass of one hundred and ninety-two dream- and trauma-choked hours of powerless fury, disappointment, and despair over the contents of a half dozen suitcases, bags, and cardboard boxes full of disordered papers) teaches me that I cannot be precise enough in my notes:

I write this in Room 26 of the Hôtel Épicure on the rue du Roi Philibert, a filthy little side street off the avenue des Ternes, veering acutely from the end of the last line of houses on the avenue and forming a sharp angle with the place des Ternes.

At the point where it crosses the avenue, a couple of vegetable carts supply Parisian coloring: the color splotches that we (not unversed in art history) experience as *Impressionistic*; and, in the spider-legged spokes of the cartwheels, that *certain French filminess* of all kitsch practitioners since Dufy:

—a piece of so-called genuine and typical Paris, which, in folkloristic sentimentality, we ramble after, seeking it in more and more hidden, more and more remote corners, in order to feel the melancholy of watching it disappear here too—whereas it is no longer so much Parisian as just suburbanly colorful and provincially contemplative and characteristic of a vanished era that has produced a similar atmosphere everywhere in the once not yet metastatically proliferating metropoles and that survives most

> *tenaciously where the dreadful development is slower, so that sporadic impressions caught today in Copenhagen or Turino often seem more Parisian than Paris itself—*

A so-called *picturesque* nook, then. During the day, garbage is dumped on the sidewalk. Once in a blue week, a pack of Chaplinesque slap-stickers in baggy overalls shows up, municipal street cleaner's caps on their curly hair, cigarette butts behind their ears, and gigantic, cumbersome brooms like halberds under their arms. They turn the hydrant on at one corner of the street and send the filth swimming to the other corner. At night, a couple of cheap whores come roaming around from the place des Ternes, withdrawing into doorways at any sign of police. After midnight (like now: it must be close to one a.m.), the area is perilously quiet and empty except for occasional car tires whimpering around the dead square—spookily, as though ghosts were having a drag race.

I'm well concealed here from my piglets and Nadine: isolated in the dense, close square of the walls of this room, deep in the narrow-chested, box-like structure of the shabby hotel, whose fire walls stick to the half-timber gables of the houses behind: former stables converted into petit bourgeois homes, presumably; their yards—with mangy geranium window boxes, atrophying jasmine bushes, and oleander saplings in weathered tubs—preserve the defoliating poetry of the horse-and-buggy world, the autumn efflorescence of mankind, already preparing for its journey of no return.

From the wallpaper's sharp floral pattern (once a playground for bedbugs, repeated in the bedcover and the slipcover of the upholstered chair), a thousand round eyes peer at me—wondering whether I can muster the patience to remain by myself... they too steal away when I glance up to catch them unawares, and all I see are insignificant roses badly printed on bad paper and cheap cretonne in the tight-meshed tangle of their thorny twigs. (And no prince will break through them to stagger back in disappointment upon finding me here instead of Sleeping Beauty.)

Here, I am finally at home: nestling in my murderer's den like a fetus in its swollen womb, lovingly depicted by Professor Leblanc's freckled hand: a ghastly little creature cozily curled up for the somersault of life from the mouth of the womb into the crouched burial position of Stone Age people, woeful little legs drawn up to its blistered forehead, webbed little fists furiously clenched against its blind pug face...

In general, there's a lot of homey secrecy here, in Leblanc's terms: the brutal iron coat hook on the door (clinical white enamel) is waiting for cattle to slaughter, as if a halved woman were hanging from it, meticulously prepared by the professor's artistic, carrot-haired hand:

Gaia's splendidly fleshy, exotic leg (slightly bent at the knee, the foot in the high-heeled shoe of society whores), testifying to the humanity of the fallow anatomy above it:

over the massive thigh (in the evening-shadow tones of the shiny mulatto skin, pouring, as if smoked, from the tender, mucus-glistening constriction of the silk stocking), the elegant arc of the abdominal-wall cross section curves into the intensely downy parabola summit of the vagina, tipping inwardly into the blossom pistil of the uterus—

"*Et je vous assure, mon cher ami: c'est pareil chez les noires comme chez les blanches—d'ailleurs, ne me dites pas que vous avez senti la moindre différence*"—

over it, the concave red-white-red stripes of the rib cage—

"*Et voyez-vous: l'intérieur du thorax est tout à fait—mais tout à fait égal chez les unes comme chez les autres: bien entendu à l'extérieur il y a quand même des variantes...*"

and from the throat, as if blown by the pipe of an art-glass blower: a wolf-toothed grin, forcing its way like cigarette smoke through the labyrinth of the frontal sinus and nasal cavity.

"*C'est ça, mon cher: ce que vous avez aimé!*"

I sit here like a maggot in the heart of night.

The glow of the lamp on the dresser where I write (I've covered the mirror) peels a slanting hollow cone of yellow light from the darkness:

in it, I huddle over my papers (caught in my own web).

The light gathers around my feet in an elliptical puddle; in it, I suck in my shadow.

Here I dwell in the core of nocturnal stillness. The telephone at the switchboard (two floors below me) futilely bores into the stillness with its dull buzzing. It is doomed to be ignored. The handsome Pole is asleep, or reads, with world-remote ardor, one of his detective stories. (Or is he with some woman somewhere in one of these rooms stacked like boxes one atop the other? It doesn't concern me anymore.) The silence is too thick for this buzzing thread to penetrate. The sound merely sews it thicker, a small-stitch quivering of desperate patience, pausing only to resume, like the stickily entangled murmur of a fly on sized paper:

(the buzzing fly is surrounded by the cringing black corpses of its fellow flies that have buzzed away their lives into the unrepentant nights of the Hôtel Épicure:

corpses of souls: when I was a child, I thought of flypaper whenever I saw the glow of candles in the old honey-gold of the effigies of saints: it had grown black with the souls that stuck to it—)

And I try to picture the nights when it was *my* patience that let the buzzing of the switchboard telephone bore across a thousand leagues into the night stillness of the sleepers here and vainly shrill away against the vicious despotism of their dreams.

Back then, I was assaulted by a different madness from my present one: love.

I loved Dawn.

I was far away from her: in Hamburg, in the apartment I had set up *for us* in a lover's petit bourgeois world-embracing yearning for happiness—

at number 9 Heilwigstrasse:

—as if the address were an incantation conjuring up that

self-effacing bourgeois happiness that both of us knew would never be granted us—could never be granted us, because of fate: not admitted by the story set down for us: because we would thus have lost what had driven us to each other: the other yearning inside us, unresponsive, without a model, making us susceptible to any insanity, a yearning beyond ourselves, steering our lives toward each other in a different way: like two parallel lines meeting at infinity, in the beyond of a story worth telling—

I loved—and as if in this state not only did the primal motifs of nature have to keep sounding but also, along with the leitmotif of personal fate, its full theme, so in this love story there was a cool-jazz repetition of what had been a trumpeted marching song of my love for Christa (and was to be an atonal *valse musette* with Gaia): from building the nest to devouring the mate, from the blissful isolation *à deux* to the desperate effort to reattain someone who had become unattainable.

THE APARTMENT

(this time):

*A model shell of insulated coupledom in the immediate nearness of the present, a spaceship for the icy spheres of absolute earthly happiness. We live in style, the ordinary style of the era: in splendid isolation, which screams to be published in all the relevant widely circulated magazines on the arts of living and interior decoration (*Oeil, House and Garden, House Beautiful, Schöner Wohnen*): the home of the successful screenwriter and his enchanting companion on this stretch-of-the-road-of-life (a star model from New England, to be seen repeatedly in* Vogue, Harper's Bazaar, Elle, Grazia*). Hence, the fragrance of the great big world even in the space-saving kitchenette: Chinese spices, hand-forged iron pots for Indonesian rice specialties, shashlik skewers, Swedish designer flatware, health foods (Bauhaus style of nutrition culture: purely functional wheat germ, soybean extract, sea salt, brown sugar). A yoga board for bathroom gymnastics. The house bar is* *a Hammond organ of luxury consumption: Drambuie and Izarra, Passover wine, tequila, raki. A record collection with early English church music, Vivaldi, Earl Garner, Strauss (*Ariadne*), Boulez. The furniture (two rooms plus sleeping alcove) showing cultural growth in fast motion: English walnut (Queen Anne) combined with Finnish pieces (mass-produced). The knickknacks: pre-Columbian, Gold Coast, Tang Dynasty, Dada. On the walls: samples of Arabic script, ancient Coptic woven fragments, and the works of masters in whose names Tarzan's gurgling jungle shriek is abstracted into the flashing, smashing, crashing of the spaceship when it shatters against the satellite: BRAQUE! ARP! WOLS!...*

I lay in the Le Corbusier armchair (an abstract warrior of steel, fur, and leather), holding the telephone (enameled in clinical white) to my ear:

from it I was drinking in the vast space of night: mythical: like a man who has to drink the ocean in order to reach an island where his happiness is exiled:

the space of night that separated me from Dawn.

She was in Paris in the Hôtel Épicure. Why didn't she answer? Was she ill? Cheating on me? Was she wandering in a daze through the streets of the *bright underworld?* I believed that my voice had the power to call her back to me—*Orpheus* (Schwab had found this image; and I reveled in the way he flinched when I then quoted that line from Cocteau's *Orpheus* with which the lovers are sent back to their lives:

"Go on! Go back home to your mud!")

During the day, it was easy to get through on the telephone. I was then told: "*Mademoiselle vient de sortir. Non, m'sieur, elle n'a pas laissé de message*" (the hated snail-fed indifference in Madame's voice). "*Et vous-même? Vous allez bien?... Non, j'en sais rien, m'sieur. D'habitude, elle rentre assez tard*" (*d'habitude* a syntactical formation of perfidious smugness). "*Non, m'sieur, elle était à la maison hier... Oui, elle a passé toute la journée dans sa chambre*" (and wouldn't take my calls... and why this gloating note in Madame's thick throaty voice? Is she, too, jealous of the handsome Pole? Her hatred of Dawn is obvious).

"Certainement, m'sieur: le moment où elle rentrera… Oui, oui, j'ai votre numéro. Non, je n'y manquerai pas. À bientôt, m—"

I waited until midnight. Then I couldn't stand it anymore. I grabbed the phone like an alcoholic grabbing a bottle. (Schwab: how greedily he interrogated me about my futile attempts to resist.

> *"You seriously mean"—a puff on the cigarette in his trembling fingers, smoked to a dark brown like an old meerschaum pipe—"you seriously mean that these are self-imposed drills? Compulsory soul-testing exercises, as it were—to test our powerlessness? Do we not know it precisely enough already?")*

I was practicing (so to speak anthracite-gray) magic:

By combining letters and numbers in a circle of mysterious correspondences, I summoned into the telephone receiver the voice of a servant of the spirits:

"Hello, this is long-distance operator four."

Language of pure poetry: a code word for the universe—

I uttered a magic formula of words and numbers, and the locks to astral space burst open:

The rustle of the vast expanse of night

In its echo the world was dissolved. Like charring paper, the shadows crackled across the earth, melting in the smoke of sounds. Mystery flew in flitting signals from continent to continent: sounds flashed like quick silverfish swallowed by the leviathan of darkness. Twittering voices slipped like white mice into the enormous hole of the darkness…

Then, far, far away, the broken line of a repeated fluting came filtering through: flickering and fading like a will-o'-the-wisp, flickering and fading, it sewed the tiny stitches of its seam into the moor of the celestial expanses:

—ancient yearning prophecy of doom—tadpole of the Word:
in the embryonic liquid of the umlaut to the unborn consonants—
In the great maternal belly of night, *space-time* was conceived
—tape measure of my patiently stretched impatience—

The voices of spirits were startled. They fluttered in chaos like pale birds (the powdering of gulls in the headlight beams when I drove through the night to my son in Holland):

One voice close by:

"Are you still speaking?"

Another, half-remote:

"You still don't have a connection?"

One very far:

"Paris, hello, Paris?"

Far, far away, another coming toward me:

"Le numéro ne répond pas, m'sieur."

Again, the half-remote one:

"Hamburg, can you hear me? The party in Paris is not answering!"

The close voice, lunging:

"The party in Paris is not picking up."

I said, "Please keep trying. Someone has to answer. It's a hotel."

The last sentence stood like a mountain: planted there by faith.

I listened to my own voice passing through the cosmos. (My breath had thrust its way between me and the echoing expanses. It perched on my chest like a beloved cat: *a purring of the secret of myself.*)

I was no longer a magician. I no longer conjured up lower, subservient spirits in order to awaken a slumbering corpse and have her follow me, sleepwalking from the underworld into life. Something more powerful had emerged from me, walking through the night with my voice, like the word of an archangel:

It announced to the anguished waker the tiding of *patience.*

Beneath it, the earth had gone wintry and rigid: *a poor people's land in the broken poetry of a collage*: snowy expanses of paper, forests scattered like shreds of felt; the rusty wire ribbing of the plowland in the stringwork of roads, glass shards, glittering like ponds—and settlements like Bethlehem: humble earth-stars, sheltered from burning out by God's hollow hand.

My voice passed over them, across a thousand leagues, to arouse again the sparse rippling of the strand of pearls, the monosyllabic flute tones:

Tracer trajectory fading in its goal—

the tiding of PATIENCE cleaved to the telephone switchboard in the Hôtel Épicure.

Here, it was transformed into a desperately malicious buzzing, and it feebly sawed away at the trunk of the stillness

—which had grown into the stairway chasms with crooked roots and sprouted its branches into the corridors and rustled its dark foliage in the rooms over the gaping mouths of the sleepers—

sawed away and dulled its teeth with each of its powerless strokes.

This went on night after night from twelve to four. If I then fell asleep, I dreamed and committed my murder.

The jittery disquiet of love. That beatific state of being beside oneself. High frequency of existence in full, immediate presentness. A sporadic condition, announced by a preliminary stage of amorous inclination; until chance selects a specific woman, every female is a potential love object—which may explain some of my relapses with Nadine.

Meanwhile, the pure gifts of God: effortless, cheerful, uncomplicated, noncommittal bedroom affairs (similar to periods of effortless success when writing: gambler's luck: being in harmony with the cosmos: FOR UNTO EVERY ONE THAT HATH SHALL BE GIVEN...)

what is spared in such encounters? What remains untouched, unstirred? Does so-called love dig deeper into the mire at the bottom of our souls? Does it unearth things more deeply hidden there—more essential, more fundamental things? And what is it that makes one encounter cheerful, well tempered, pleasant, enriching, carefree, while another, equally random, initially perhaps even more trivial, crashes into our lives with the full force of destiny?

Christa's devouring mouth in the canteen of the Nuremberg law court... and years of our tortured efforts to reach each other, of my tormented attempts to reach her, like a deaf-mute trying to recite a poem taking shape within him...

and in contrast: Gisela, whom I first see as she crosses the bombed-out railroad terminal in Hamburg, her head high, her figure tall, slender, unapproachable—a queen. She strides through the mouse-gray teeming of refugees and belated homecomers, the war-damaged and the war-dazed, looking neither to the right nor to the left. More vision than tangible reality, she passes through the medieval misery of this crowded humanity of mislived lives, through the mob of rags and worm-eaten flesh, like a beautiful ship through brackish water, *le beau navire* of eternal boyhood dreams, a ship's figurehead of possibilities of experience, scarcely believed anymore but now, with her, surging up again, new and powerful—

and I dare not follow her; I want to keep her as a vision, reserved for all possibilities of experience. Nor would it make sense to follow her, accost her: as wild, as adventurous as the time may be, this woman is beyond the vulgarity of such adventure.

It is futile to hope that I will ever see her again: the age is medieval, whole peoples are on the move, the wind of our time is driving them along like chaff, God alone may know where they come from, where they are going... only her majestic stride, long, swift, and light, is purposeful; even though her purpose and her destination may be unnameable and far away from here, she bears the certainty of reaching her goal—

and then, several weeks later (it is the year of OUR LORD 1947, the Ice Age is approaching its bitter end; before passing into the new phase of the world, it sinks its teeth one last time into the survivors' rubble cities, coating their makeshift lodgings and their woeful rags and trash with ice, their hunger swellings and reconstruction dreams, the final hopes of the timid, the finest intentions of the valiant...

but the tougher souls will survive this too, will live to see the approaching year of OUR LORD 1948 and thereby the impure miracle of the new epoch:

the pitiless, the greedier and greedier souls, survive ever and always;

and with them, those who are eternally outside reality, the eternal dreamers;

the former and the latter are destined to become the founding fathers of the mankind of tomorrow; fools and somnambulists, criminals and monks:

this is the stuff with which—on which—they will create the tremendous conjuring trick of the currency cut, the sinister prestidigitation of the onsetting economic efflorescence and thus the new reality:

the abstract world of the prosperity-termites in the baleful profiteering, proliferating administration of deranged production and demented consumption: the horrible, abortive total of identical life-drained days in the nightmare geometry of cities of utilitarian buildings, shooting up like crystals in some nasty mother liquid:

Already built into the trashy boxiness are the ruins of tomorrow, the tin-and-concrete wasteland of secondhand Americana, with mangebelts of rust and mortar, seething and teeming with ever-swelling, ever-swarming masses of more and more colorless more and more dissatisfied more and more demanding more and more hopeless more and more evil supermarket consumers in ever swifter, tinnier, more hastily glued-together, more and more perilous automobiles: highway rest stop eaters with empty gazes over munching chewing kneading swallowing mouths...

Christa's empty, inward gaze into the emptiness beyond the wall of the Fürth law court, while the kneading, munching, chewing swallowing of her thrifty lips betrayed the secret—guarded by good breeding—of wanton voraciousness: a vision of the future, a blueprint of the world our son was to be born into:

the emptiness in the gaze of the innocent culprits, having lost the wonderful possibilities that were soon to be forfeited forever, with that final start of the new era in 1948.)

the time I'm telling you about is still 1947; the Ice Age, which has lasted ten years, is clamping down one last time: one evening, a day drawing to a close as the future dawns (the food rations are approaching those of Buchenwald, but the film industry is already back in bloom), during one of my aimless strolls through the world of the lotus-eaters (the first star is already sharply needled into the turnip-water-stained sky over a starving Hamburg), I wandered into the red-light district of the Gänsemarkt

(long since vanished, this ultimate remnant of the old walkway district, now replaced by the Axel Springer building with its utilitarian geometry towering into emptiness—

but at that time, it was a place of profound Christmastide expectations, a stronghold of seething, sap-driving, vital warmth and the seashell-carbolic-acid smell of whore cunts, an El Dorado of sexual plight and the torment of erotic fantasies,

in the honey light of dim bulbs in windows at the base of the swiftly darkening shafts between half-timber gables on bowing gingerbread houses, the sparkle of promises shimmers like a treasure half buried in a dark riverbed: the Rhine gold of rubble-dwellers, the abstract fabled wealth of association

> *nixie-bright female flesh bursting through the fish baskets of bodices, caught smooth as eels in the black nets of cancan stockings; lascivious gaping coral lips millipedes of false eyelashes peacock-blue-green mother-o'-pearl of mascaraed eyelids; blond hair like beer foam, black hair grease-enameled in piglet-tail whorls, painted on floury-powdered skin; cartwheel hats the plunder of ostrich plumes the impudent fire of crab-red wigs over violet feather boas the pale medusas of tremendous breasts fat arms like dragon bodies guarding the grottos of acrid-smelling shaven armpits the lacing of hams of tremendous matron-thighs high-heeled champagne-bottle-shaped boots tightly buttoned up to the jellied-meat of old knees emaciation-larvae of weak sweaty cellar-child-skinniness back-courtyard-vileness of eyes and words knife-sharp voices and the clatter of keys on the salon windowpanes)*

and there—I cannot believe my eyes, but there she is: the same woman; the woman I saw just a few short weeks ago, striding as proud as a queen through the tattered railroad terminal.

She sits with her back beautifully straight, gazing imperturbably out into the street. Her full, rusty-brown hair is swept up; she wears nothing but a lightweight sleeveless sweater with a narrow turtleneck and very short velvet pants (years later, they would be all the rage as so-called hot pants); her wonderful long legs are bare; her feet are in flat suede pumps.

I purchase a quick trick; she handles it with sovereign and businesslike dispatch, merely stripping off her hotpants; only after I put a bonus on the table is she willing to pull the sweater over her head. She is not wearing a bra, her breasts are magnificent. She knows how beautiful she is, and she is intelligent enough to know that such beauty counts for little here; the important things here are stylization, alienation from reality, denial of reality, which the imagination puts, unrestrictedly, into the splendors of its creations. This doesn't bother her; nothing fazes her: she is sovereign, utterly sure of herself.

Our coupling takes place on a narrow, greasy sofa; the room is tiny and messy, repugnantly appointed with teasing effects in the worst petit bourgeois taste; one can smell the bedbugs in every nook and cranny. The thin door cannot be locked, it opens onto a stairway that creaks continually under footsteps, voices speak, as loud and as close as if they were with us in the room. The whole place smells of chamber pots and disinfectants.

I have to overcome an instant of panic, which ambushes me with a memory

a similarly horrible room in an ill-famed hotel in Vienna: Cousin Wolfgang and I have saved up enough from our laughably meager allowance to pay for a cheap streetwalker. The instant we approach her, our nerves flutter: we are still in school and are tormented with the fear of being caught, of not having enough money, of getting into an ugly scene with her pimp, of getting the clap. When we are asked which of us is to go first, Wolfgang takes off: he can't bring himself to find the lamentable creature desirable: everything disgusts him: the place, the circumstances, the thought of himself in these lower depths. I am no less repulsed, but more resolute. He remains outside the door, waiting for me. But I too fail. I too am incapable of letting natural drives prevail over upbringing: the girl's Zille face, her limp little breasts and

> *pointed shoulders both move and repel me, the bushy triangle of her colorless pubic hair fills me with horror. I stick out my hand, think I'm touching something like a big boil, and pull back. Since I offer no sign of being ready, she becomes impatient, milking and tugging me, and finally she lets out a string of curses, but I am stubborn, I have to show Wolfgang I am man enough to overcome the sentimental philistine in me. What I now undertake is a symbolic act of protest: my defiant renunciation of the spirit of my formative years in Vienna and their bogus aesthetics as I undergo this test to show I am capable of striding unfazed through such filth, freeing myself of Uncle Helmuth Aunt Hertha Aunt Selma and everything they are and feel, think and represent. I would like to penetrate the girl as if I were boring a knife into Cousin Wolfgang's heart . . .*

Here it's different: I am free to the point of weightlessness, as if I were on a different star with a weaker force of gravity. The failure of my efforts to get close to Christa has released me from my last tie. Now there is nothing left for me to rebel against. My soul is calm. I can have pure enjoyment; the shining slice of little windows under the Biedermeier gable on the house opposite is beautiful in the reflected golden light from below in the street. The young woman is beautiful. Her soul too is calm. Neither of us feels much pleasure, it is a business transaction. In order to reach orgasm, I have to shut my eyes and imagine following her after seeing her stride through the tattered train station, approaching her and properly seducing her, contrary to her actual intentions, she being overpowered by the eroticism of adventure, swept away, giving in . . . I am grateful to her for this dream.

We talk afterward for the length of a cigarette. Her German has an eastern tinge: she is from Upper Silesia, probably the daughter of Germanized Poles: Gisela—she does not tell me her last name. I ask her whether she would care to have a cognac with me; her answer is clear, resolute, and scrupulous: her percentage of the overcharge on a mere two glasses of cognac will not make up for the loss of possible business during the time we would spend drinking them, but if I ordered a whole bottle, she would be willing to chat with me for an hour.

She smiles. Her whore's profession, she says, consists mainly of such chiseling. Contrary to the popular conception, there is a great deal more talking and boozing in a whorehouse than there is sex. As for the latter, her life here is presumably calmer than that of many a decent Hamburg housewife.

The cognac is wretched and many times more expensive than a select one would be today at Maxim's in Paris, but that doesn't bother me; my pockets are stuffed with money: movie money—an inflationary currency, especially when handed out in one as worthless as the Reichsmark. My delight with the girl increases. She merely sips, but tells me with her open, comradely smile that I can imagine she knows all sorts of tricks to make believe she is drinking like a lord while actually pouring the cognac away; so, for my own sake, I shouldn't insist that she keep up with me. Nor can she drink, she adds: alcohol is one of the narcotics that wreck the lives of most of the girls in the whorehouses along this street.

I ask her if she has been plying her trade for a long time. No, she says, only a few months. But you can work your way in very quickly, if you're not stupid. Unfortunately, most of the girls are. Practically any girl who winds up on the street owes it to stupidity or laziness.

And what about her? How did she wind up here? I ask, ready for some tale of high drama.

She came to Hamburg as a refugee, she says obligingly and without pathos, and then she found herself on the street. Her parents had insisted that she get out of Upper Silesia when the Russians came, with the first wave. They themselves were supposed to come later, but they didn't make it; they are still there or else they've vanished; she hasn't heard from them. "But they wanted to get me out," she says, and laughs, "so that the Russians wouldn't rape me." The Russians caught up with her and rolled over her before she was even halfway to Berlin. The combat troops barely had time for raping; that came only with the stragglers, in Berlin.

The early days were bitter in every way: hunger, cold, and pretty much constant menace. Still, people were as helpful as they could be. There was something like an "emergency humanity." (I ask her where she got that phrase; she says she made it up, just now.) She took off for western Germany in fairly hazardous circumstances, but she doesn't go into detail (she doesn't give me the particulars until a later time). At first, she moved in temporarily with distant relatives in Schleswig-Holstein (in a one-horse town near Preetz: later on we went there to delight in the good people's astonishment at her elegance). But the narrow-minded, intimidated philistines, in a fever of concern about their meager property (they ran a grocery; at night, behind tightly closed shutters, they devoured the sausages they kept hidden during the day), had been so reluctant to take her in that she left after a short time—all the more hastily since the father had, of course, made a pass at her. She went to Hamburg.

"Within a week, I realized I'd have to wind up in some bed or die in the street," she tells me calmly. "I've never done so much walking in my life—and never in such thin clothes and on such an empty stomach. One day, I ended up on this street. At first, I didn't know what it was, but the penny dropped soon enough. It was morning, scarcely any clientele. I got to talking to the girls, and they were friendly and nice and understanding. After my country relatives and the railroad policemen who kicked me out of the waiting room when, like hundreds of other people, I tried to warm up there, except that I came several days in a row—after all that, I felt at home here. I asked the girls what things were like for them here, and what you had to do to get into one of the houses, and they all told me to do it; they said I should go to the police and register."

She explains that the whorehouses are city-owned. They are run like rooming houses, leased as concessions to veterans of the trade who have saved enough money and have impeccable police records. The girls pay rent and get a percentage of the receipts, plus any personal bonuses from the johns. "But most of the girls fritter away their money and start boozing, or else they play cards or snort cocaine or do lesbian stuff and ruin themselves that way—they're always very over-excited, and they can't come with the johns . . . The worst thing here is the boredom."

What does she do about it? I ask.

"I observe," she says. "I never get bored. Although I used to."

When was that?

At school, and then later, when she worked for a photographer.

"If you ever want to get out of this someday," I say, "maybe I can help you find a job. I've got movie connections. For a girl with experience in photography, there must be work in the movies: maybe editing; that's not so boring."

She muses for a while, her elbow propped up, her hand, holding a cigarette, on her temple. "I want to stay here until I've saved up a nice tidy sum. I'm in no danger of going to ruin here. I'm not interested in alcohol or drugs or other girls. I want to be a first-class whore—one who gets top money. To do that, I have to specialize in something. S and M is a pretty sure gimmick. You wouldn't believe it, but most of these guys come here for some crazy thing like that. They can fuck all they like anywhere else without paying. We make our money off guys with fantasies in their heads and their crotches. And homeless guys like you."

I toast her. The stuff she's told me so far is small talk, so to speak. But the last sentence establishes a personal relationship. I desire her intensely. I suggest going to the sofa again. Any time, she says, without batting an eye; naturally, I have to pay for the second time just as for the first. "Even after the bottle of cognac?" I protest. Even after the bottle of cognac, she replies, unruffled. "But you'll have most of it left." Not even jokes can soften her heart. I shell out the bills on the table, and she instantly rises, pulling her sweater up over her head and the velvet hotpants down.

During the year we were friendly (until the birth of Christa's and my son, when a fit of philistine morality persuaded me to break off these friendly, intimate relations with a brothel whore: after all, our son was a born Hamburger; his respectability was paramount)—during that full year granted to us by our cheerfully carefree, often exuberantly fun, always stimulating, high-spirited friendship, I never once succeeded in sleeping with her without first paying the set fee. No matter what I did to try to change her mind—cunning, tenderness, violence, surprise—she was adamant, as if she would be violating an oath by giving herself just once without payment, and as if it would bring the entire structure of her goals and plans crashing about her ears…

and I insisted on it stubbornly, obsessively, as if my fate hinged on a victory over her, over her implacable refusal—my entire fate, the realization or failure not only of my personality but of all my goals and plans…

for it was then, during the early weeks of my tempestuously erupting friendship with Gisela the whore (the Ice Age was clamping down one last time, and the teeth of the winter of 1947 cracked and splintered: I can recall sudden puffs of soft spring wind wafting unexpectedly through the days)—it was then that it happened, that I left something behind in her room, the copy of my treatment for a big movie project at Astra Art Films, commissioned by my primordial piglets Stoffel and Associates; and one of her clients, the then rather small-scale but later big-time publisher Scherping, found the manuscript and read it and excitedly passed it on to his editor J. S., ordering him to track down its author immediately, so that this genius, evidently as yet undiscovered for *belles lettres* and hence lying fallow, might instantly write a book (to wit, about wartime experiences, which I did not have, to be sure, but which were dealt with in the film treatment) and thus give mankind the masterpiece of the era, the great novel of the waning century…

and how we laughed at this, my accomplice, the whore Gisela, and I! How amused we were when she first described Scherping to me, with his quaint *bonhomie* and transparent slyness, his yokelish cunning when he got her to impose and inflict punishments on him, as if he himself had not invented the reason for them, had not begged to be punished (for Gisela now specialized in discipline, and word of that sort of thing gets around quickly in the appropriate circles)… our bliss when she told me about his blubbering ("If only just once I could be beaten, whipped, tormented for something I really had done"—for Nagel's best sellers, for instance)…

and Schwab, Scherping's emissary, striding through the red-light district "like a blind seer," head thrown back, fish-blue eyes looking neither to the right nor to the left, pride in his high thinker's brow, humility about the mouth twisted in disgust, slippery desire in the soft, moist flesh of his twitching lips. Later he would become my friend and fellow sufferer in literary limbo, Johannes Schwab, whose mighty appearance I did not tire of describing. (Oh, but during those last months of the Ice Age, he was as Reichsmark-lean as anyone else: truly, it was a slender nation of Germans in the year 1947!) Schwab, I say, with his large, clumsy frame and ungainly Martin Luther head, with the wind of culture blowing in his luxuriant (still flaxen) hair, his Coke-bottle eyeglasses and ill-fitting baggy-seated tweed suit. He was such a model of the world's idea of a German intellectual that when he first appeared in Whores' Alley, the cry "Herr Professor!" leaped from window to window along the entire street, from one thickly reddened whore's mouth to the next...

and one of the girls, lovely Heli, still young and warmhearted as freshly baked bread, trustingly dedicated to the foolish faith that the world contains a God-willed, occasionally disturbed, but always gloriously restored order, in which a small, well-to-do portion of mankind, better instructed in the spoken, written, and printed word, is, in moral terms, superior to the larger, poorer, less educated portion and determines which among the lower born it will raise to its level—lovely Heli fell hopelessly in love with Schwab: the "educated man," happily able to read and write...

(what a blessing: to be loved by a whore, who submits to anyone, whom anyone uses unhesitatingly, and to be loved by her because of your superior dealings with language, which is similarly a whore, whom everyone (aside from a chosen few) uses unhesitatingly; to be loved by her unreservedly, giving herself with all the power and powerlessness of feeling, beyond the never wholly dissolved remnant of hatred and disgust that lurks in every love, beyond the struggle between the sexes, a battle never waged to the point of purification... how greatly I envied him, Johannes Schwab, the Scherping Publishers editor, sent to me with the evil angelic tidings of literary conception, and how often and how excitedly we spoke of it, Gisela and I . . .)

for what we had—no: it couldn't be called love. It would never have occurred to us, Gisela and me, to call it that. Mutual attraction, affection, great liking—yes: all that. But not the mawkishness of love. Not its moistening need for tenderness. No suffering whatsoever at the withdrawal of that tenderness. No urging and shaking and quaking to find entry into the soul of the other (who doesn't even know what you're talking about). No metaphysics, but all the brisker, all the more pleasurable copulation: the fixed advance payment eliminated any possibility of misunderstanding even here; it was sexual intercourse without dross or sediment, an art form with itself as its own subject, so to speak, not "*it means*" but "*it is.*"

No: it was not love, thank goodness, that made Gisela a pure joy for me (and perhaps me for her), more cherished in memory than some of my great passions. We were quite in control of our well-tempered, well-balanced, well-wishing and -meaning emotions. Between our brain glands and our reproductive glands (both delightfully animated), our metabolisms functioned perfectly: no increased blood pressure because of spiritual exuberance, no diaphragm flickering from psychic interference with our calm metabolic rhythms. Our mutual affection was as cool and deep as a well, and we didn't even try to wage the battle of the sexes; we confronted each other in an armed-to-the-teeth armistice in which sex did not interfere but ran conflict-free on the ball bearings of financial arrangement, ruffled neither by the transcendent nor certainly by the transcendental.

So we were also spared the torments of jealousy; our friendship was purged of this mire. Moreover, the idea that she slept with other men or helped them to achieve pleasure in a different way (always pasteurized by financial arrangement) did not deflate my ego; instead, it inflated and expanded my experience, for the ones she found worth mentioning were not lovers glued to her by the mucous filaments of sentiment but interesting cases of sexual psychology.

(*Cousin Wolfgang, taking the volume of Krafft-Ebing from*

my hand and thoughtfully weighing it, says: "For me, dear cousin, this is nothing but the grossest obscenity," and I, quoting my favorite verse from Romeo and Juliet, *"Call me but love, and I'll be new baptiz'd..."*)

sometimes those lovers were authors of felicitous linguistic creations, which we preserved like objects found on a stroll along the beach, seashells and colored pebbles (the dockworker, a heavy man, who as he ejaculated cried out, "Trials and tribulations!" or the retired cavalry officer expressing his delight at the fullness of her breasts with the words "If a flea galloped over those things, it would split a hoof!")

and the endless fun of wandering through Hamburg in quest of adventure. It was summer (it seemed like the first summer in decades), and the miracle of the currency cut had taken place, the shops were beginning to fill up; production was not yet going full blast, spewing out junk, like today, so there was still prewar merchandise from secret warehouses, handmade things, "one-hundred-percent" genuine; and she went shopping with me. She had astonishing amounts of money and she spent it judiciously on top-drawer, durable goods chosen to last: leather coats, fine furs, handmade shoes, silk stockings (not by the dozen but by the gross), cosmetics by the carload, jewelry (completely flawless one-carat diamonds); she paid cash for everything and was treated like a princess—

and the shock, the terror, the stupid confusion in the eyes of a salesman or store manager who recognized her, who might have been her customer the day before; the inner struggle in the decent, law-abiding citizen, for whom business interests won out to the exclusion of all else...

We rented a car, and I taught her how to drive. We motored deep into the Holstein countryside and the Lüneburg Heath, fetched up at rustic inns, lay under firs in the sandy grass (yes, indeed; even when I was overcome by libidinous stirrings there, I had to pay in advance), hiked barefoot through the silt of Baltic beaches, danced at farmers' festivals and on the casino terrace in Timmendorf—

and the incessant awareness in our conversations, in our laughter, in our delightful mutual silence, in our thoughts of one another when we were apart—the heart-lifting awareness of an extraordinarily sovereign, utterly unassailable situation

("What can happen to me now?" she used to say. "Disease, death—fine, that's nature. But otherwise? So what if the Russians come. I'll receive them like anyone else. With champagne, if they want it—and pay me for it.")

the ether-clear awareness of living at the extreme boundary of existence, on the razor's edge, in perfect freedom—this intoxicated us like a drug.

I was giving her a driving lesson along a country road, and we stopped at the entrance to the highway, where I was to take the wheel. It was late afternoon, and she had to return "to work." We had had fun and were in a good mood. We liked the open car; she wanted to buy one just like it—if she ever needed a car. Before changing seats, we smoked a cigarette. With her head tilted back, so that her full hair dropped over the back of the seat, she blew the smoke into the air. "You once told me that if ever I got fed up and didn't want to work in a whorehouse anymore, I ought to tell you, and you would try to get me an editing job in the movies. I've done a lot of thinking about what I would really like to do; I've thought about what would be fun and what would be sensible. You know what it is? I'd like to have my own brothel."

Happy days before the Fall of Man; before I was stricken with the passion for writing. Happy days in the Eden of immediately lived reality, of firsthand experiences that were real, even if these concrete experiences were merely a threadbare pretext for the more powerful abstractedness behind them. Days of innocence, before the vice of writing abstracted even the abstractness into material that could be experienced at second and third hand: into book-page reality, in which the pseudologic of art forges the infinitely multidimensional logic of nature into the theatrical metal of arbitrary, confected artifice. God-affirmed days, in which the world still fell into the self like a summer morning through a window, not mirrored out of the self as a multiply broken reflection of self, a spectacle making its own producer and lead actor and sole subject, performer and stage all at once and all in one: the world and the self were identical to the point of loss of the world, worldlessness of the totally isolated self lost to itself beyond measure . . .

I loved Christa then.

I loved her even though our marriage had become as bleak, as dreary, as hopeless as the ice-gray diurnal life in the rubble fields around us—which for me, however, for Nagel and our kind, and even for that fussy man Schwab, was a constant adventure, a frontier existence in a no-man's-land to which we could lay claim, a deeper and deeper daily penetration into a state of unconditionality, which seemed precious to us because in its desert emptiness, open to all winds, it was full of possibility, hence full of promise, an undaunted Promised Land that we would build into a new Garden of Eden once we had fully reconnoitered it, once its borders were established and the claims were staked . . . but for others, of course, for Christa and her kind, it was damnation in limbo, an everlasting routine of poverty, joyless, colorless, with the ever same nagging necessities and miserable chores, a trudging on the treadmill of hopelessness, merely to deal with the same lamentable troubles and the same woeful needs.

It certainly saddened me that I had to count Christa among those others—the poor by nature, so entangled in their woeful needs and lamentable troubles, so doomed to the wretched daily routine that, as Nagel was to write later in one of his best sellers, "They could not brace their spirits for a festive tomorrow . . ." Nagel, the flatfooted poet! Christa appreciated him for that, had to admire him for his wonderful verbal power; it was part of her cleaving to workaday routine that she loved craftmanship; it was the only thing that took her out of it, the poor thing . . .

Sometimes I was overcome with a hot wave of pity when I saw the despair in her eyes—in the radiant aquamarine of her childlike eyes!—because, of the four pounds of potatoes she had managed to scrounge somewhere, three pounds had been frozen and were half-rotten, or because the fuel for our alcohol burner was used up, or because the wall of the room we lived in at the bisected villa on the Elbchaussee was sporting a new crack, and dampness was seeping through. Granted, things like that can be awful, but looking closer they didn't seem so bad; almost everything was ruined anyway; we could just as easily have laughed about it, especially since I knew that Christa would waste no time routing me out of a wonderful conversation with Nagel (precisely at the point when our spirits were "ardently bracing themselves for a festive tomorrow," of course, a tomorrow that would be hers too, after all!) in order to get more potatoes or fuel, never mind where or how; or, ruthlessly stubborn, demand that I do something about the damp wall; remove the crate of ludicrously useless slipcovers and damask curtains from her family's home in East Prussia—treasures that some fool of a fleeing relative had rescued from a fire and proudly dragged west—and replace it with my books and watch *them* molder.

"If you could at least make something pretty from these pieces—an evening gown, for instance..."

"An evening gown?"

"Well, okay—some clever housedress..."

"A housedress? To wear in this creaky dump? I'm already freezing to death in ski pants and a sailor's sweater."

"Then throw the junk away!"

"I wouldn't dream of it! Somebody will take the slipcovers in exchange for beans, peas, turnips, cabbage..."

Ah, no, my pity never lasted long, even though it had been the origin of my love for her: the sudden yearning and understanding of human weakness and humility in a fellow creature and spontaneous identification with it, the physical commiseration of my tenderness when I had seen her chewing and swallowing the American Army chow in the canteen for German witnesses and defense attorneys at the court in Nuremberg—chewing and swallowing with a dedication that was so totally, so unconditionally, so definitively and finally only physical as to leave not a sliver of space for any lofty inner life, for the mind or soul, for the enjoyment of the "bread one doth not eat."

In Nuremberg the sight had moved me to tears, as I've said. I felt I was watching the basic truth of the *condition humaine*. The dreadful existential plight and exposure, the heartrending destitution, of the zoological species *Homo sapiens*, everything this naked and exposed creature undertakes beyond coping with the immediate existential necessities of finding food and shelter, mating, raising offspring, all its grotesque spiritual leaping into the metaphysical realm together with the proliferating madness of its artistry and intellectuality—all these things seemed futile and therefore poignant.

Such an insight (I had discussed it with Christa often enough!) should have brought us together all the more humbly. It should have made us love and protect each other in this state of exposure, aid and assist each other as much as we could. At those times, people truly met at point zero, as the term goes; thus they could have easily laid down arms, formed an alliance, jointly confronted *an existence under spiteful conditions*. But precisely because we were—albeit only legally—joined in matrimony, the knowledge remained one-sided and hence ineffective. Right after the passage from bridehood into matrimony, that is, right after the legalized transformation of favors into actionable duties, Christa saw me no longer as a fellow traveller through the earthly vale of tears but simply as the archenemy of women, a failure on all fronts, a man who with others of his kind had started a war and shamefully lost it; and now, in this devastation, instead of putting a decent roof over our heads, he was nattering on about a beautiful future—and, to make matters worse, had gotten her pregnant, thereby adding one more extortionate, helpless mouth to the existing hungry ones.

Nevertheless, I loved her very much. Only I saw, alas, that I could not count on her as I could count on, say, Nagel. I could not count on the same understanding, at least. It should be said that not only was she of that order of women who on principle try to tie us down to accursed earthliness, she was of a different race entirely: despite her good background, she was one of the poor in blood, the gray-faced, rummaging through the rubble fields, looking for the remnants of their property, instead of being delighted to be rid of it and able to begin a new, unencumbered existence. I had no sympathy with these people, though day in day out they were a vivid reminder of the *condition humaine*. They did not rebel against it. To use a literary expression that does not come from Nagel, they ate the flour even after they themselves were put through the mill. Rather than react with sovereign scorn towards the tremendous injustice of life, they strained and made the harness all the tighter; they moaned under the lashes of real and imaginary ordeals, but put their heads in the yoke.

They were our natural enemies, Nagel's and mine, as it struck me at the time, and they hated us as profoundly as we hated them. It was a time of promise, in which (as Nagel was later to write) "we readied ourselves for the adventure of renewal," and they turned it into a workaday grayness, which ultimately nipped our confidence in the bud. We lived in the frivolity of the saints, like the lilies of the field—for "whatever one may say about the ludicrous weakness of the human spirit when confronted with the relentless conditions of nature, that weakness does give us the strength to transcend our plight, even if only temporarily and with fictions" (Nagel)...

So, we lived like the lilies of the field, Nagel and I, and they, the flatfooted race, heaped shit over our loveliest blossoms. For us they were what *they* had been for Uncle Helmuth: the wicked OTHERS. They spoiled the dreams of the dreamers, the fictive happiness of the enraptured. Even before, when they had been so well housed and sated that the fat on the backs of their necks burst their rubber collars, they had lived shabby, workaday lives, and they would go on like that once they were sated and well housed again. Even now, with their world shattered, they did not face what had happened as a challenge. They took everything as a stroke of fate, which for better or worse had to be weathered with heads bowed. Whatever was to come—even if it wasn't worse but, unexpectedly, better—theirs would be the same maggot's existence in the same roll of neck fat. They could not picture, hence could not bring about, anything better. Unlike us, they lived without the Easter promise, lived instead with the tenacity of termites, which was far superior to our childlike-fantasy ways. For them, the future was not a sublime vision, its rays transfiguring even the gray present, but something they trudged toward; it could bring them at best a more sated, more corpulent, more stably housed, although equally dismal present—and yet still they were certain it was theirs, no matter whether the terrors lurking in it were the same old terrors or even worse.

Incidentally, I do not know where we overexcited windbags, we visionaries around Nagel—or rather around the homemade turnip schnapps in Nagel's garden flat—got the idea that we'd been given a mission. We truly believed we were meant to find the solution to any conflict, plight, evil, stroke of fate in human existence (we called them "problems"). We played ourselves up as if we and no one else had to find the key to the future of Germany and thereby, per Major General Baron von Neunteuffel, to the destiny of the entire world. We searched for the "spiritual foundations of a new humanity," even before Professor Hertzog supplied us with this rousing formulation. Meanwhile, the other race, Christa and her ilk, concerned themselves with the rationing stamps for a special allocation of barley. They did not think beyond the next day, but, petty, sullen, and tenacious, they spared no effort to ensure that the next day would at least be no worse than today. We dreamers and windbags viewed this narrow-minded scorn of the spirit as a danger for the day after tomorrow. But while we were talking about how to stave off that danger, they kept puttering and pottering on in their obligatory dreariness, creating the foundations for their world—and the day after tomorrow was then as empty of hope as today and tomorrow.

Thus time passed. Time passed over all of us, utterly sovereign. It didn't give a whit about our conflicts, our different opinions and ways of life. Time did the only thing it is supposed to do: it passed, and made everything that lived in it pass as well. As usual, it did not do so in a steady series of developments but was seemingly inconsistent, leaping unexpectedly, tarrying whimsically now and then, sometimes even taking a step backward after two steps forward, as in a dancing procession, and eluded precise observation as it whizzed along.

In those postwar Ice Age years, time seemed to have made up its mind to tarry, and whether a man brooded dully on his hunger or drew from it the fanatical fire to blather on about the spiritual foundations for a festive day after tomorrow, the harsh time lost nothing of its grimness. Whether we lived through a morose daily round of petty, sullen, and tenacious efforts or in the Easter expectation of a new humanity, we all lived in an odd state of waiting. Even the most hopeless gray faces in the Quonset huts, for whom tracking down potatoes was a fairy tale and gleaning coals on railroad embankments a quixotic quest—even they were waiting for something, whatever it might be, good or bad. We all were waiting just outside reality, waiting as if we weren't really living but were being lived by someone or something—or better yet: dreamed of by something or someone, nightmarishly dreamed of by some mysterious "it": destiny or divine providence or whatever one might call it, or merely a collective spirit that shaped the era—in any case, something from somewhere outside of us and our realm of perception.

And all the while, time was dribbling away from us without our noticing it. We breathed out our existence, day in day out, and the days, objectively speaking, truly were gray and grim and cold and clammy, like the watery puddles in the bomb craters, whose dead surfaces shuddered and raised goose bumps under the raindrops during the so-called mild seasons and, during the biting icy winters of those legendary years, froze into blind eyes that gaped sightlessly into the stony sky over the city ruins.

And all the while I loved Christa. I loved her body, even though she let me have it only as if it weren't worth the trouble to refuse me. She developed a new habit: no sooner did I slip into bed with her than she would raise her arms to her face, her right hand clutching her left shoulder and her left hand her right shoulder, so that her elbows stood before her mouth like two bastions in the wall of a fortress: she did not want to be kissed by me anymore. A kiss demands emotional connection or, conventionally, presumes it. This, as she would have put it, was "not in the cards anymore." But I was allowed to luxuriate all I liked in her full breasts and further downward. It wasn't even worth the trouble for her to deny her senses an involuntary participation in my passion, and she permitted herself an occasional thrill, sometimes even the churning up of an outright orgasm; thus my nightly masturbation with my spouse often achieved a perfection that almost amounted to a true act of love.

But afterwards, of course, there was a certain emptiness which after a while made me turn spiteful. It seemed like the most sublime kind of castration, the way she made me so acutely aware of how abstract the role of us men is in a process that, presumably, constitutes the only, or at least the quintessential, meaning and purpose of our existence: the preservation of life by means of the preservation of the species. In zoology, of course, this is known as mating—what mockery! It is actually the separation of *Homo sapiens* into two utterly different species. The fruit that our first parents picked in the Garden of Eden gave them the knowledge of their separation into two total strangers. In the moment of utmost bliss, Christa was as remote from me as Saturn. She let me know what tremendous spaces I was trying to bridge with my ridiculous striving for spiritual union.

Very well: I learned my lesson. Soon—we hadn't been married for a year—I scarcely dared approach her, lest I alarm her with my warmth, annoy her with my tenderness, my need for some token of her affection, understanding, indulgence, some small gesture that would let me feel that I was more to her than merely the man whose task it was to ensure her physical well-being, to which end after all it was not entirely insignificant that I had something dangling between my legs that relieved the occasional itch between hers more effectively than her own middle finger or the candles of her teenage years.

It could hardly be denied that, as a provider, I was a nothing. As for my ability to ensure the rest of her well-being, I soon no longer even dared wonder about it. One way or another: I was put in my place. My ego shrank to the measure of what I was biologically: a seed carrier, a drone, nothing more. It struck me as presumptuous on my part to have any other claims and to seek any but a purely physical union with a daughter of the Great Mother, a world-bearer, able to resurrect mankind from within her body—to reduce, inside her belly, millions of years of protozoan-to-primate development to three-quarters of a solar revolution, to mold a human being perfect in all faculties of body, mind, and soul, and to release him into life, letting him become Messalina or Saint Cecilia or Adolf Hitler or Jesus Christ or anything in between.

My goodness, what a difference in realities! How unreal, in contrast, was our male contribution to this extension and continuation of the world, of life! . . . How meager, what a wretched crumb from the table: a few angry minutes of dark sweet pleasure, a few moments of effacement, of cramped discharge, while, in several ejaculatory thrusts, that wonderful, for us ever-incomprehensible, ever-mysterious, essential, actual something took place—beyond our awareness, snuffed out in a few instants of blissful near-death, in the dazzling of utterly sweetened pain . . . and then basta, finito, done! Well, that was that again, thanks a lot, don't worry about the rest, *ci penso io, dottò* . . .

After that, our hunger for reality ought to be comprehensible: the insatiable hunger for immediate realization, for tangible proof that we men, too, are real, that we, too, can achieve reality, actuality, with our own actions—

". . . but you *can*," said Christa, with her sapphire-blue, round, childlike eyes. "All you have to do is go and find a little wood to chop."

"*Saw*, sweetheart, *saw!* You're misquoting. The original goes: 'Men saw wood—one pulls, the other pushes, but they're both doing the same work; by decreasing, they increase.' Granted, a rather silly image from the *Corpus Hippocrates* for the identity of creation and disintegration. But what can you do: statements about the *archai* can't be worded in rational terms, because they are ir-rational and prim-ordial; such statements can only be figurative, isn't that so? . . . But I for my part would like to take part in creation, and in a less destructive way than I am allowed by this so illustrative image, do you understand me? I do not care to limit myself to the male work of destruction in order to contribute to creation. At the risk of sounding like a screaming queen, I'll say it loud and clear: I would like to give birth. Freud gave you women dick envy to explain your inconsistencies. Allow us men to envy your uterus. I do not wish to have to reinvent, reconstruct reality in order to experience it: I want it to be immediate . . ."

It was love's labor lost. She understood every word, but not the meaning of what I was saying; she simply thought I was crazy. And I must admit, those were muddled thoughts I was voicing—voicing in my way, furthermore, which was an intellectual patchwork, figuratively speaking, stitched together from age-old commonplaces; I am almost ashamed to be writing this down now.

Meanwhile, indulge me: That was not yet a time like today when people can draw ready-to-use intellectual material from paperbacks and cultural radio and television programs. We were troglodytes. Those who—like myself, like Nagel and our buddies around the bottle of turnip schnapps in Nagel's garden flat (later, the nuclear group around Professor Hertzog; I shall give a detailed account of this elsewhere)—those, I say, like us, from the juiciest generation of cannon fodder for WWII, whose best years of learning and education were suddenly interrupted by that historic event and who were left behind with the always insatiable hunger of the half-educated and the autodidactic—such people, in their poignant attempts to analyze the spiritual bases for yesterday's catastrophe in order to destroy the seed of evil and perhaps eliminate it from the spiritual foundation of tomorrow and the day after tomorrow, felt like pioneers and rubble-rummagers and refuse-recyclers. We continued to feel the naive need to explain everything *ex ovo*—even age-old commonplaces and platitudes—to ourselves as well as everyone else. For not only had the commonplaces and platitudes become extremely questionable but also we could no longer count on understanding them without an *ex ovo* explanation—or on being understood when we did explain them. We were troglodytes and lived among troglodytes—not like the spoiled youth of today, in an environment that obtains its well-founded knowledge and reliable intellectual depth in oversize paperbacks and educational TV channels with all the paraphernalia of prefaces, forewords, and introductions, notes, addenda, and bibliographical data (home delivery free of charge). Far off still lay the present day, in which the satisfied highway rest stop person might, figuratively speaking, transpose the elegant atmosphere of the champagne advertisement into cerebral experience and—in fashionable comfort, aristocratically leaning back in his plastic-bolster sofa, clutching a beer can, listening to the cultivated voice of a moderator—mentally follow the most exciting philosophical paper chase (forgive the shallow metaphor; it forces itself on me!) with a cheerful Husserl, behind the pack of yapping Jasperses, cross-country over Heidegger and Wittgenstein; for him, the sovereign self-servicer in all other situations of life except for the unacknowledged intellectual situation, our lederhosen-boy-scout ponderings in the prehistorical year of 1947 must seem like a quaint folksong.

But, as I have said, time only appeared to be stagnating in those days. What lay ahead moved one hour closer to us with every revolution of the clock's hand. Of course, the star of Bethlehem was in the winter sky of 1946–47—thanks to a need, intensified by the lack of real bread, for the "bread one doth not eat." But as the winter of 1947–48 drew to a close, one could tell that this bread had no hope of keeping up in the race with the bread one *doth* eat, as soon as this last appeared in sufficient quantities and thickly stacked with cold cuts. Soon the black market was running smoothly, new democratic parties were a reality, the press and the publishing world were flourishing, and instead of the star of Bethlehem the star of Astra Films had risen over Hamburg. The interregnum of the Quonset-hut intellectuals ended without anyone's noticing.

Only a very few, who were fervently seized with the spirit, as if they were making amends for something—a remnant of the nuclear group around Professor Hertzog and, needless to say, the psychopomp himself—kept on, although now they had company pension plans; they were working in radio or in the new magazines, newspapers, publishing houses; intellectual subhumans like your humble servant wound up in the movie business. Only the uniquely bold and intellectually pure, like Nagel, raised the lance of the free intellectual creator and ran boldly henceforth against the windmills churning for future highway rest stop people.

And in keeping with this pregnant age, all my lamentable attempts to explain myself to Christa were doomed. To be sure, I tried with what I thought was a great deal of tender care. After all, I loved

Christa: I took her in my arms and cradled her like a child. At times, I even thought of interpreting our disturbed or, rather, never properly established relationship not only philosophically, as a symptom of the zeitgeist, but also as a personal failure on my part, admitting that although my stoic attitude toward the general situation in the rubble landscape might be to my credit, it left those who had bound their destiny to mine rather on their own, and that this might have contributed to the misery that had developed in our love relationship, which Christa too had originally seen as promising the realization of certain atavistic ideals and expectations: a lifetime alliance of deep mutual affection, kindness, understanding, of unconditional belonging and security, of appeasement in and with each other, hence, a harmonious home, a sunny bearing-and-breeding place for happy offspring, the nuclear cell and fundamental element of future society, a freer, happier, more just, more humane society...

I was speaking not only to Christa but also to our child within her, to our future in her body, which had swollen up with that future, turning white like a fat maggot, but which I loved nevertheless and would always love, even though my love soon threatened to become incestuous—"You're molesting a child, and your own flesh and blood at that," she said, but she let me be, so long as I didn't try to get pushy, emotionally speaking, and urge her into anything more than lazily letting me be. My God, there was even a certain kindness in it, in her swinish, lethargic letting me be, and maybe all my blathering on was actually the cause...

she probably didn't think it annoying at all, my blathering—as I stammered into her flaxen hair, pathetically wanting help, a blather zooming into flimsy universals, preposterous metaphysics, verbal gruel of spiritual distress; as I held her in my arms, warming and protecting her—I, who was writhing in pain, I who was flayed, I who had nothing to hold on to, the ground gone from beneath me... I held her protectively, cradled her, with my arms crossed over her belly and my hands placed gently on her heavy breasts, cradled her and her child within her and in this child myself... and she didn't think it was annoying at all, she let my splashing verbal gruel trickle down her; phlegmatic by nature and nourished with nothing more fortifying than turnip juice, she endured my monologues with the same dull equanimity with which the Germans, believers in the spirit, listened into the ether to hear the hissing and honking of educational radio broadcasts or read the Cassandra-like articles promising disaster in the feuilleton, as if all these things were part of the background noise of everyday life, like the clapping wheel of a brookside mill where one has grown up and still lives or, on a more contemporary level, like the traffic din in city streets before a few carefully laid carpet bombs brought silence. Since she left the lower reaches of her body to me, together with the supply of oxytocin occasionally flowing, upon certain stimulations, into the muscle fibers of her uterus, it no longer mattered if I also profited from the patience of her eardrums in the upper reaches—

and I spoke and said (said the same thing over and over, in all sorts of verbal combinations, spoke of the same thing incessantly): "You know, darling, you've got to understand me when I tell you that your only duty as my wife and beloved is to keep allowing me to experience afresh that I am a man—only please, don't let me experience it to the point of despair. I want to be *your* man, for you! More than anything, I want to be your *man*! I am proud to be your man—but I am afraid of the curse of being a man. I am afraid of being made all too conscious of my utterly male condemnation to unreality, to invention, to feigned reality, to the reality of fictions: in short, to the creation of the world as an as-if. I'm completely in your hands. It's up to you whether I experience myself as a real man: strong, courageous, reliable, above all: overwhelmingly erotic, irresistibly virile . . . I have to believe this, even if I know it's not actually true: I have to think it, in order not to doubt myself when I go about my man's work of reinventing and rebuilding the world. I need faith in it, in order to endure the fact that even as the strongest, most courageous, most reliable, most manly man, I am nevertheless merely a manikin of life, a tiny means to an end, a tool. I must delude myself, in order to pretend that I do not have what I am now holding in my arms: the life-reality in you with our child in your belly. I share in that life-reality only in the unconscious moment when you and, inside you, the Great Cosmic Mother Nature use me as a tool—an indispensable tool in the process of creating life, for the moment, but still of secondary necessity... *I* as such am abstract and with no true reality... can you follow me? Can you understand how important it is for me to be strengthened in my self-confidence by your love, your longing, your trust?... Granted, I cannot be denied as a part of the world, as a tool in the tremendous process of creating and perishing; but as a tool, I naturally view the world as a workpiece, something that must be worked on, altered, and re-created by myself. Created on my terms—for you, for all of you: for us and our children. It is my intrinsically male mission to work on the world *as if* it had an order. Unordered Nature at all times threatens us with annihilation. We cannot exist in chaos; we must oppose it with the as-if of an order. To deck out Nature with the fictions that enable us to exist in it—that is men's work. But it is work that must be done in the security of absolute self-confidence. We sleepwalk across the chasms of insight into our true nothingness, into our fission-fungus role in the events of life: splitting reality into truth and fictions, we deceive ourselves about it with our fragile visions and illusions; but the least appeal can terrifyingly rouse us out of our life-delusion, and we then plunge into despair; we then find our reality and realization only in destruction, because destruction too is a reshaping, a reinventing of the world: an enactment of our own transience, only not abstract, not merely feigned, but undeniably real, at last... Do you understand, my darling?"

She was silent, and I knew she had only a fragmentary and incoherent grasp of a sentence or two of all I had said to her, but she did listen to the singsong of my voice and heard from my finely ground shriek of distress that which was hers, and presumably that which was actual (that was what later made me so impatient with Schwab: that he always took me at my word)... and perhaps she caught the madness woven into the monomania of my endlessly reiterated melody, the gentle eeriness in the obsessive idées fixes, all of which was not without its peculiar enchantment and could be, in the compulsive recurrence of motifs amid the overall confusion, as insistently fascinating as drawings done by madmen.

But perhaps she felt and thought something entirely different or was even about to fall asleep in my arms; it didn't matter, I was talking to myself and, over myself, into the world, the world in which our son when he grew up would experience the same distress and, presumably, be thwarted by the same eternally anxious questions. I said, "The awful thing is that we men cannot escape despair, even if we recognize the dreadful illusion and fiction of our men's work or perform that labor unswervingly under the constraint of somnambulism. Because we have to reinvent the world in order to experience it in our reality, we also have to reinvent and reenact the destruction in it: ourselves in the destruction... We have to become murderers in order to experience ourselves as real... isn't that horrible? This comes out in even the most beautiful of our myths. Do you remember the story of Daedalus? Hertzog called him the 'compulsive inventor.' Daedalus built the labyrinth, a symbol of the world: the artistic copy of confusion, in which, as the epitome of the dark and dreadful forces of Nature, the minotaur dwells, half animal, half human, full of demonic might, devouring human beings... Daedalus banished it into his image of the world, and now he, the compulsive inventor, must also invent an image of his own spirit, the spirit of human beings, of men, which aims beyond itself, eternally insatiable, into infinity, heedless of the sacrifices... so he makes wings for his son Icarus to fly to the sun, and when Icarus comes close to the sun, it melts his wings, and the boy plunges to his death. Daedalus sacrificed his beloved son because of the compulsion to reenact, as an image, the manliest of male deeds: the action of getting beyond oneself to the point of atrocity."

I cradled her gently in my arms, for now she really *was* about to fall asleep, and that made me feel tender in a suffering kind of way, like that day in the canteen of the Nuremberg court, when I saw the embodiment, the incarnation, of creaturely indigence and human neediness in her chewing, chomping, kneading little mouth, in its bitter heartiness when she swallowed one of the chewed-up, chomped-up bites, in her utter forlornness, her removal from the world, her absorption in her bodily self, her *physis*, the sheer biological functioning of her anatomy. I realized that she had to pay her dues for the intrinsically female ownership of reality, and that the price was no smaller than what we men paid in our longing for it.

I said, "I know, my poor darling, that all my blathering is no excuse for my inability to get you the herring paste that would make the frozen potatoes fit for us to eat." (There you are: I said "us": I was identifying with her; I was generously hiding the fact that I didn't care about herring paste in the least, and if I did have to eat frozen potatoes, I would prefer eating them without herring paste: out of love of the unadulterated, or rather out of a delight in alchemistic transubstantiations of things, in order to turn lead into gold and derive enjoyment even from the unenjoyable.)

I said, "I know: other men bring their wives butter and nylon stockings, even egg-yolk liqueur, like your cousin Hatzdorff. That doesn't make him any less manly, of course; no, no, that's not what I was saying; on the contrary, he is the truly strong, courageous, reliable one; and your cousin Jutta must appreciate these qualities in him, despite her teenage swooning over Nagel, who, aside from the liqueur of the eggs that one doth not eat, has little to offer her... yes, indeed, I know I'm tasteless, but you could overlook a bit of silliness on my part now and then; Nagel would have laughed heartily for at least thirty minutes over my pun... Seriously, though, darling," I said, kissing her hair and caressing her thick stomach, and thought myself repeated inside there as my son, "if there is one thing I know for certain, it is that several decisions are being reached here and now in our misery, and that it is important to know where one belongs. I admit it is more difficult and more courageous to get hold of butter than dreamily to give in to the chimerical idea that now, here, in this ice-wind-whistling rubble wasteland of a shattered world, it must at least be possible to lay the cornerstone for the future kingdom of God on earth, but I think one might nevertheless find some sense in the butchery we have miraculously survived (albeit more vegetating than alive); we might at least assume that it has purged the world and that the enemies, who bled each other white, have now realized how insane they were and will join together as brethren so that, united, they can transform the remnants of a devastated civilization into fair conditions for a humane existence on earth... and not recommence at a point from which the new bad end can be instantly foreseen: a world of profiteers and racketeers, of the horribly shortsighted and blindered, of the fanatics of abstract ideologies and the fanatics of materialism... What I fear, my darling, are the dangers that come with people who are all too efficient in getting hold of butter. They are the human type to whom we owe the most exquisite terrors brought to the utmost perfection of destructiveness: the engineers and electricians of my uncle Helmuth's ilk, the professional termites with slide rules, who, in carrying out their male mission of reinventing and reworking the world, are all too crazy about reality. More than anything else, I fear what stands behind them, driving them to self-oblivious work: money, which Nagel so poetically calls the 'idol and Moloch of this godless time.'... Today, we must decide where we belong if Gottfried Benn's prophecy comes true and, one hundred years from now, the world consists exclusively of monks and criminals."

And Christa spoke, in words that were, to my utter amazement, intellectually not at all simple, albeit grammatically correct, fluent, and elegant: "If I had a pound of butter now, I wouldn't doubt for even an instant that a hundred years from now I would want to belong among the monks."

She was brilliant. She would always speak illuminating truth whenever—seldom enough!—she was willing to open her disdainful little mouth and say anything at all. Once again, she was speaking nothing but the terrifyingly pure truth—the very thing that everyone was thinking and feeling. For we dreamers and blatherers, we illusionists, we utopians, we intellectuals (already we were being derided as such), were by no means the only ones to perceive the dangers inherent in the way people were preparing for reconstruction. Soon it was possible to turn the act of prophesying a new and final cataclysm into a profession, as a newspaper editor, or as an educational-network director, or even as a novelist; and this was possible because one had only to say what everyone knew anyway; one had only to say it so that it did not stand out as too importunate a sound amid the usual background noise. After all, everyone had made up his mind to do good, and he would have been even more mindful of doing so if the circumstances of life had not forced him to take into account things that were less than good. The reconstruction, especially after the memorable act of the currency reform, had its pleasant sides—this was undeniable—and for the time being, people, as consumers, avoided the alternative of "monks or criminals."

No, no: we were not the only seers who could read the future and foretell to what extent they would have to cut their ideals to the cloth with which time had graciously covered the past. Even they, the people of the other race, the stone-hearted bourgeoises whipped by anxiety about life and therefore occasionally irritated, and concerned only with their narrowest interests—even they realized that something was sprouting in our Ice Age winters, something beyond their immediate present. Today's time was pregnant with tomorrow's time, and our universal mission was to make sure that this tomorrow would not be a changeling, as yesterday had been. They nodded when they read such things in the new newspapers, whose pulpy paper lent a touching purity to their contents, as if the words, arriving in hair shirts, could do nothing but tell the truth . . . and the monstrous birth of the future took place beyond or below the threshold of the collective consciousness, virtually on its own, with no visible help from individuals and yet with the admirable assistance of everyone and completely unmolested by the admonishing and warning and morally armoring claptrap of the pseudo-intellectual philistines, who were soon well paid again for making the tiny celluloid balls of their intellectual elitism dance on the pitter-pattering fountain of their eloquent pessimism.

It was given to Christa to sum up this complicated and dismal state of affairs in a single sentence, and I loved her for it, even when this sentence passed an annihilating judgment on us and our impulses for a happy humanity. It was a rather sordid attempt at justification when I told her, "I admit that even we, who do nothing but speak of the devil, know only what must *not* happen so that the devil won't get us, but do not know how to stave this off—much less what should be done instead. We talk about the new spirit that should inspire us, yet even if we spoke about it with nightingale tongues, we would be incapable of inspiring anyone with it. It is as if no one would have it, unless everyone did. Either the new spirit is part of the time and is pouring into everyone or it is not part of the time, and then it is idle to preach the new spirit: the seed of the word will not sprout..."

I could have added, "It is like our situation, yours and mine: I can speak to you with the tongue of an angel, and because you are not imbued with the same spirit, my words will be empty sounds for you"—but I did not have to say it; she knew that everything I said referred profoundly to us. It was from the noise of my words, not from the words themselves, that she knew what I meant when I spoke of the plight of those who felt called to speak: "Those people who are trapped ecstatically in their dreams, the people you call intellectuals, it's true they do nothing but talk; and if it becomes practicable, they will have to clear out and give way to the professional termites with slide rules and, behind them, the profiteers and shamans of money idolatry... and yet the idle talk of the visionaries is the salt of reality—how can I make it clear to you?—it is the herring paste without which you people could not eat your frozen potatoes because they would stick in your craw... Please try to understand what I mean: The movers and shakers depend on the visions of the dreamers: those for whom the world is real are nothing without the others for whom the world is an idea; the two have to work together to reshape the chaos into a world we can live in: it is an act of procreation, in which both participate, just like you as a woman and me as a man, the sons of the mothers and the daughters of the fathers..."

It was truly heart-wrenching! I might have added that it was for the sake of this cooperation that people *spoke to each other*, but then I would also have had to say that this very thing was the most deceptive of our illusions, we dreamers and visionaries, for not only was it a dreadful proof of the fallacy of this statement that I had to repeat it to her here, even though it had been iterated and reiterated for thousands of years and already wore a yard-long beard, like all my other philosophemes, but, above all, we could immediately experience how unreal, how purely theoretical, such basic philanthropic statements were. Did not Christa and I bear the most eloquent witness to the human distress of being unable to speak to each other, the horrible plight of always speaking past one another, of using words that signified something quite different from what was meant, words filled to bursting with affects, emotions, resentments, hence achieving something quite different from what they aimed at—semantic explosives, so to speak...

but nevertheless, I persisted in my monkey chatter, held firm to the proposition concerning the necessity of speech and the delusion that speech was a means of fostering understanding. I believed in the curative power of the word and in the high priesthood of those who force it to produce the clearest expression of its most profound content; and I bombarded Christa in a way that not only made it impossible for her to understand me but was also bound to incense her, turn her against what was said and against me for saying it. I said, "You know, darling, every sentence we speak reveals something, and the revealed can signify the most sublime thing—salvation in the crucial sense, as Kierkegaard says—or the most insignificant thing—the articulation of something random. 'We should not allow it to confuse us; the category is the same; phenomena have this in common: they are demonic, even if the differences are otherwise dizzying. The act of being revealed is the good thing here; for revelation is the first expression of liberation. That is why we have that old saying: If one dares to speak the word, the mirage of enchantment will vanish, and that is why the sleepwalker wakens when his name is spoken.'"

I kept my voice low, as a precaution, for by now she had already fallen asleep in my arms, and I was afraid of waking her by talking loudly—even more however by ceasing to talk: a sudden stop to my stream of words might unbalance the gentle transformation of her dozing off into deep sleep. So I kept talking, and I secretly kept hoping that she was still listening, or, even better (like the hope that sustains lazy schoolchildren when they take a book whose lesson they have not learned and put it under their pillow for the night), that her subconscious, by a sort of intellectual osmosis, would absorb the substance of my monologues; and even though her all too human sleepiness made me feel tender, I nevertheless began to feel bitter that she so mercilessly left me writhing in the plight of my compulsion to express myself, she, cruel in the superiority of silence, making the speaker appear an idiot, so that ultimately there was only one way to interpret her hard-heartedness: she simply didn't love me, had probably never loved me, or at best only in her meager way, which I did not regard as "true" love, even though, for all its meagerness, it struck me as far more reliable and far more pregnant with reality than my importunate and possessive "true" love. In any case, I suffered, because I could not avert my eyes from the fact that my loving had turned into a steady and annoying pursuit of a word of love, of a revelatory gesture from her; had turned into an incessant jolting and jouncing in order to get something out of her, something that (as she put it) was "not in the cards anymore"; and thus, I was eventually seized with a hate-filled self-scorn, which I—a true intellectual!—projected onto the state of the world and a vision of its imminent destruction. Naturally, I also knew how ridiculous this was; I knew that I would someday take bitter revenge for it. "Don't forget," I told Nagel, "the reason why Robespierre became a mass murderer!"

But Nagel, who had only a rather nebulous idea of Robespierre and the circumstances that had made him a mass murderer, assumed I meant the class struggle, whereas I had meant "excessive virtue and an excessive sense of order."

And yet Nagel was right in a way, with his class struggle—although then again he wasn't—because Christa was so extremely highborn, virtually from a gold vein in the bedrock of East Prussian aristocracy, while I was a bastard from a remote Balkan land. I could not have more successfully invented a hero's wife in a novel, the servile relationship that exists between a husband and a wife (especially a wife who is loved hopelessly). It was not only the humility of the hopelessly loving husband but above all the dog-like devotion and uxorious worship, the impotently indignant dependence with which the husband looks up to the totem pole of the "wife" and "mother of his children" while he may hate and despise her with all his heart, the wife whom he has raised to that level—these things often made me gnash my teeth like a serf in bondage. I said to Nagel, "Don't believe for a second that the institution of marriage, which has been raised to a sacrament, has its origin in a biologically reliable guarantee of the legitimacy of the offspring. The roots lie much deeper. They go back to prehistoric times, when hunters and gatherers started to farm and store grain. The underlying goal is to cope with times of dearth, to get through the winter, so to speak. If a man doesn't hunt and gather sex from dawn to dusk, then one day he will come back empty-handed; the fat times are followed by lean times. Might not then one of our early forebears, upon contemplating the imperishability of a bear haunch smoked by chance and recognizing the advantages of preservation, hit upon the idea of dealing with sex in the same way: I mean, legally preserving the steady playmate; the wife as a preserved cunt, to be consumed at any time of the day, the night, the year, even though nowadays, thanks to the increased use of deep freezing, it might lose a bit of its flavor...

but while speaking so heretically to Nagel, I had the audacity to continue my boundless monologues for Christa's ears, downy with tingling blond hairs, in order to stammer out in entangled circumlocutions things that millions of husbands have been saying to their wives for countless generations: "Darling, if only you knew how easy I am. A little affection, a little tolerance and understanding, a little friendliness and good cheer..." and I instantly choked on my own stupidity, terror took my breath away, for I could picture her jumping and showing her small, sharp teeth; in dreadful shame, I heard her asking if I had taken leave of my senses, expected her to bubble over in good cheer—with three frozen potatoes and my bastard in her belly and the room temperature a few degrees above freezing. She was right, she was right!... So I instantly corrected myself: "Of course, dearest, you have no reason to throw your arms around me like an exuberant debutante in a novel when her fiancé comes to her laden with gifts—but now and then, let me feel that I'm not the sole cause of your ill humor. Just a small gesture—anything, you understand. The shadow of a smile, a touch of your hand on mine, a glance of sympathy. That would be more than enough, it would work wonders..."

Yes indeed, it was because of such modest, undemanding wishful thinking that I performed before my wife Christa like a St. Vitus dancer for hire. With an almost cultic thoroughness, I stylized the male dance before merciless female supremacy (a dance as old as mankind) into philosophical reflections on civilization; and Christa's unshakeable silence seemed to take on a sacred sublimity. When I discussed it with Nagel, I naturally used modern-day metaphors for my crazy actions. I said, "Damn it, there are people who play chess with themselves—isn't that so? But I for my part am playing something a lot more exciting. I'm playing soccer with myself; I'm a whole team, so to speak, with a goalie and defense and forwards, and with the concentrated energy of eleven professional players, I dribble and kick the ball of responsibility into my wife's half field—I mean the responsibility for our misery, for our unintended but ineluctable mutual torment... I play it into her heart, you know, the responsibility for our terrible incapacity to understand each other, the responsibility for our bleak loneliness living at cross-purposes... and my playing is masterful in both tactics and technique: Posipal to Spundflasche, Spundflasche to Stuhlfauth, Stuhlfauth shoots—GOAOAOAL!!!... But, unfortunately, my wife's half of the field is a wall, a solid wall on which I have only painted her players, and the better I play against them, the more sharply I shoot, the more violently the ball bounces off the wall and back into my kisser. There ought to be a penalty for a thing like that, don't you think? Or at least satisfaction for me: there must be such a thing as justice, even here on earth. Sooner or later, the ball has to smash into the face of the woman behind the wall, and smash her good and hard!... I mean, sooner or later, the woman has to realize that I want only what's best for both of us!"

But this, unfortunately, was not the case for the time being, and so no little gesture was shown. Christa couldn't understand that I had only pedagogical reasons for playing off on her the responsibility for our mutual failure: I was only trying to arouse understanding in her conscience and, with that understanding, her feeling for me. She was unable to realize that I did so in order to create *order* between us, to close a life cycle, in which affection gave birth to kindness, and kindness gave birth to deeper and deeper, more and more ardent affection. To be sure, whenever I was completely honest with myself (and I was, at times), I did not set much store by whether she loved me still or a little less, or whether she had ever really loved me with "true" love; granted, I did love her, but more as my wife, the mother of my son, than as the girl, the woman Christa—oh my goodness! My eyes had long since been drawn to other women—what am I saying? Not just my eyes (and she should have understood this, too: after all, the adulterer is homeless, all too willing to return to his own hearth). But that didn't matter: the important thing was our *case*, so to speak: two people with a foundation of positive feelings for one another, right? In any case, two people who did not have it in for each other, who were actually seeking each other—and yet they did not understand each other, spoke past each other as if speaking different languages, soliloquizing into the isolation, the torture of an inability to express themselves, fell silent with each other... Obviously it was not a unique case; nothing special about it; on the contrary: a rather run-of-the-mill condition for many people, but that was the very reason I didn't want to throw in the towel; I wanted to force her to understand that the soccer ball I wanted to smash into her face was, so to speak, the eternal *ballon d'essai* from the depth of the deepest human misery: the attempt to break out of the imprisonment, the entanglement in one's own self... "I speak to you because I love you," I wanted to say to her, "and even if it sounds as if I wanted to blame you because we are two human beings and not one, because I am I and you are you and each of us is in solitary confinement in his own self, eternally separated from the other; even if we are banished into two cells from which we cannot communicate with knock signals because neither knows the key to the other's code... even if it sounds as if I were reproaching you for being blind and deaf to all that, listen to me anyway, listen to me: for whatever I say, it means only that I love you, and even if the word turns over in my mouth in the bitterness of not being understood, I mean only that one thing... and no one should ever say anything else, for whenever there is no love, demons prevail and speech produces nothing but confusion; no one should ever want to say anything else; all speaking should mean only that one thing..."

and whether she was listening or had fallen into a deep sleep, she was silent. And what should she have said anyway, since she did not mean that one thing?

The disquiet that I want to keep dammed up and imprisoned in this room until it surrenders and dissolves into the blissful torrent of *speaking*—the speaking of everything caused by disquiet—often becomes so powerful that it constricts my throat, making the blood pound in my temples and the sweat bead on my forehead: the urging of a reversed eroticism, as it were, an eroticism turned against myself. I crave a woman, yet I am not my SELF; I am a SELF detached from myself; I do not actually exist; I am merely a notion of myself, a projection of myself. And I crave the chimera of a woman, a notion of woman, which corresponds to my notion of myself. My imagination makes an effort for these two: it wanders through the numbered cave dwellings of this rundown hotel for stranded beings; it pictures a woman inside each cave, on her own, forlorn, helpless. A half-crazy American fashion model, for instance, who similarly exists in the bright and beautiful underworld, like a tench in the aquarium of a pederasts' bar—was it really possible that the handsome Pole snuck up to join her at night? Or is he really sleeping with Madame instead of guarding the telephone behind the hotel desk? Is that why Madame is being deliberately cold to me? That would mean that she is playing my game...

For four years now, I've been a regular customer in this lousy hotel; and one would think that by now me and Madame la Patronne, in the splendor of her full-blown tits and her blazing red *boudin*, would have developed if not out-and-out intimacy then at least a certain familiarity. Parisian shopkeepers, flower vendors, newsdealers, waitresses have cultivated such impersonally personal relations into a cordial art—the only and final manifestation of something that has otherwise vanished (if not turned into its opposite): *la courtoisie française.*

But not Madame. Gravel-hard *politesse,* that's all. When I arrive, a nasal "*Bonjour, m'sieur, vous allez bien, m'sieur?*" without a further glance at me while she writes my name in the guestbook. She hands me the key: "*Je vous donne la vingt-six comme d'habitude*"—the room with the windows facing hers. And not the softest flicker in her eyes. (I too occasionally leave my window open, sometimes even when I'm not alone.) We maintain form—and form is abstraction, hence immediately erotic. It's gotten to the point where I wonder whether I am in love with her.

I need not say that Madame has not only kept all her charms but even quite uncommonly increased them. Scarcely four years, as I said, have passed since Schwab and I were able to feast our eyes on her. The peony freshness of her cheeks is barely assailed by an autumnal breath, by the frost of the first cold night. The black roots of her strong hair, when it has not been freshly dyed fox-red, reveals two or three white threads at most. The glimpses that Madame occasionally grants me through the window do not permit any precise examination; but according to an established cavalier saying, a woman's body ages more slowly than her face. Her body must therefore now—now, man, at this hour, in this night—be bursting with ripeness (a notion to which Schwab would no doubt have gladly drunk a beer)... Madame must sense what effect she has on me (in me). But no: we do not smile when facing each other. Our gazes meet frankly and coolly and do not slide down to cleavage or fly level. If our fingers touch when I receive the key from her hand, this touch is unheeded, even when one of her nails, lacquered bone-splinter hard, scratches the back of my hand. Once, I came in after a rather lengthy drive from Reims, wearing a cashmere sweater and soft rubber-soled shoes; the friction of the leather car seat must have made me as electrically charged as a Leyden jar, and a spark leaped between our hands with a perceptible shock. We pretended not to notice. A pleonasm to mention something that was by no means unexpected. We wish each other Merry Christmas and Happy Easter and also exchange inner feelings through the usual reflections on the situation of the world and the weather: "*Et qu'est-ce qu'il est devenu, vot' gros ami allemand?... Il est mort? Tiens, je l'aimais bien . . .*" Sometimes, I am seized with the desire to do something unreflected, even violent: hit her in the face, *une bonne paire de claques dans la gueule*, or else clasp a Cartier bracelet on her wrist without a word of explanation. But I know: If I hold my ground and keep as gravel-hard and impersonal as she, then her window will stay open.

Scherping once told me a pretty art nouveau story—a childhood trauma of his. His mother was beautiful and used to punish him cruelly for the slightest offense. Once, when he had done some misdeed for which he must have expected worse punishment than normal, she summoned him. She was sitting at the mirror, brushing her hair—very beautiful hair that flowed richly over her shoulders and back. He had stepped in and paused at the door, not daring to take a step toward her, so fearing her punishment that he trembled. She gazed at him in the mirror and did not say a word. She kept brushing her hair, never taking her eyes off him. This went on for a while, which seemed like an eternity to him—an eternity in limbo. Hell, by comparison, was redemption. He could stand it no longer and asked her to hit him. He sobbed and begged her for it. She still said nothing and continued brushing her beautiful hair. And gazing at him in the mirror . . .

Scherping says that his expectation that she might turn to him, open her arms, and cry "Come! I forgive you!" has stayed with him all his life. He will torment every person who loves him until that person stands before him with the same harshness—just so that someday someone will nevertheless open their arms and say to him, "Come! All is forgiven!" He will demean himself with everyone until he is hated: in order that someone someday will tell him he is forgiven. He despises the women who love him. He worships the unyielding ones.

I write. I love reality as an unyielding lover. Realizations for me can occur only in abstract. I despise cheap fulfillment. I need Madame's never-kept promise. God forbid I finally did land in bed with her—or on the divan behind the clerk's desk, on the pool table in the lounge, on a pile of rolled-up carpets in the stairwell. An assault, wordless, brutal, a willingly granted rape, my fists clawed in her arse, my bared teeth foaming between her wonderful tits, the backs of her knees hooked over my shoulders, expertly bestial, in keeping with her voluptuous, sweaty, hennaed female ripeness—

even if we vented our rage on each other, if I made her fizz, burst like a geyser, if she brought me to a snarling frenzy of destruction and then gasping exhaustion, my back crooked as though whipped, my head dangling between her knees, blind and drooling, we would not forget for even a moment that we were merely playacting, playing ourselves in the scene, a performance, inauthentic, rehearsed, put on. We would be playing nature but we would no longer *be* nature. And we would know it in every moment, know that it wasn't us at all who had hammered themselves into one another, balled up together into something "that was hatred and that rolled on the floor like an animal with wounded legs": nothing at all original in us, no urge, not the faintest remnant of primordial man, but rather the opposite: only something learned, inherited, uncritically acquired: conventions of a collective lifestyle. Traditions even of the senses. This would be *the reality* that we produced.

I lust for Madame. A rammer grows from my groin to smash through the fictions separating us: to smash *it*, the fiction of the *other*, which throws me back upon myself and isolates me in myself; smash the fiction of bodies that imprison us and keep us locked apart; smash the fiction of *woman* that makes me the fiction of *man*; smash the fictions of solitude, uniqueness, and unrepeatability, which exclude me from the world, splice me away from oneness with *God* and His cosmos . . . Assuming I were to meet Madame in some dark corner of the hotel—there are so many! Madame all alone and lusting as much for me as I for her (or even merely guileless, unprepared, so that I could succeed in catching her off guard): I pounce upon her, yank her skirt high and her underwear off, and thrust my rammer into the blackness between her white hams, bore into her with all my might . . . for all the pleasurable yelping, all the snarling and gasping, the two-backed animal we would form (in the bed or on the sofa, on the pool table or on a carpet roll in the stairwell), the epileptically twitching package of human limbs human clothes human hair and human flesh would remain unaltered: Madame and I, each of us hermetically encased in his or her story and because of it hopelessly different from the other. Each one a tissue of his or her memories, a product of the specific, manifold, complex fictions that he or she has lived, is still living, and will continue to live. None of this, nothing, could be shaken off, not even with the wildest fucking. Nothing could be changed, nothing overcome, not even with the fiction of love. After all, everything would still stand between us, keeping us remote from each other...

we couldn't even deny the national dimension of our existence (or the lack thereof, depending): Madame would still bear in mind that she is a Frenchwoman, and she would feel sublimely superior, even though she was receiving a non-Frenchman into her. *One* form of pride would still be with her. Dutifully she would place my carefully emptied testicles on the altar of the *Patrie: "Voici! N'y a qu'une française qui baise comme ça! Qu'il s'en rende compte, le pauvre bougre!"*

And I, for my part, would fuck Madame-to-the-second-power, *the Frenchwoman!* I would fuck Marianne with her banner waving, fuck her so that the blue-white-and-red cockade would fly out of the Phrygian blood sausage; I would get my revenge on her. I would humiliate, besmirch the superiority, unflappability, enormity of their national fictions, the legendary, the nonpareil, the incomparable self-assurance of the French. I'd pay them back in full here: *Je baiserais leur Liberté, je fouterais leur Égalité, j'enculerais leur Fraternité* and all their *gloire* and *culture*, all their shitty sense of family, chamomile tea...

and thus, this would most certainly not be an individual act but rather all the more a collective act: a vengeance in the name of all those who, like me, nurturing hope for Europe, have lost hope because of the French: because of their fossilization, their cataleptic stylization, their utterly inalterable *form*.

The sexual act too is tradition, is form. Our very drives are secondary and artificial. Even before we hit on the idea of using our thumbs as pacifiers to drive away the boredom of our baby existence, we are products of civilization, prisoners of our inevitable fictions, mewed up in the cage of our traditions, in the straitjacket of our conventions. In vain do we yearn for a transcendence into the natural. We mime originality because we want so badly to believe we are real; and all we find over and over again are fictions. No matter how deep we tumble into the chasms of our animal nature, we encounter cultural goods: our shrieks of pleasure, however guttural, sound like opera; the obscenities we stoke our fires with are, at best, a weak copy of Rabelais; the mendacious words of tenderness that we murmur at each other to benumb our despair are as classic as Rostand; and our imaginations, which are supposed to pull us toward unification with the universe, are ruled by the most artistic, the most stylized Frenchman: the Marquis de Sade...

and Madame would actually be proud of this. Being a Frenchwoman means carrying French cultural awareness between your legs too. *Kalokagathia* is attained when the *culture du moi* matches the *moiteur du cul*...

Thus, if we forgot ourselves with each other, we would be doing nothing but constantly quoting, citing, reciting. We would be declaiming a rutting fuck by all the fine, grand, good rules of the Comédie Française, and that brief moment of snuffing out, toward which we would thereby be whipping ourselves so fiercely, would distort our faces into the two masks that hang over every provincial theater.

And the horrifying aftermath is, at its best, cinematic art.

We've met the quota of obligatory biological performances. Now there's nothing left to depict; that's the final take. With the last quiver of our orgasm, the scene fades, we are no longer in the frame, we have played our cameo parts: the well-rehearsed roles we have prepared for since we first heard about sex, with curiosity, anxiety, and yearning; that we have never tired of rehearsing and reiterating; that we have memorized more and more perfectly, more and more adroitly, an imperceptible flicker, a mere grain of light in a movie that has been repeating the same event millions of times for millions of years now, performed in every waning instant—now in the just now beginning, just now passing, just now passed second—by millions of performers in precious few, pathetically unimaginative variations: in beds and on sofas, on pool tables and carpet rolls or on the bare ground, in haylofts, forests, roadside ditches, railroad compartments, lying, standing, squatting, in clay huts or igloos, under starlight and in the darkness of caves, in the palm shade of oases, camping tents, canopied beach chairs, and by the thousands in the roaring wastelands of big cities, from in front, from behind, sometimes with him on top and her underneath, sometimes with her on top and him underneath, or *à l'amazone*, sideways, with the lady crooking her leg. The possibilities are soon exhausted; at best, there are still a few acrobatic improvements, like those of a horse of the *haute école*, between the pillars. I personally find this extremely uncomfortable, at times even annoyingly comical, but that is a private view; it doesn't count on the global scale; in any case you always take part in a collective enterprise even with the most peculiar contortion. Every individual act of coitus is merely a partial action in a steady mass course of events, whether or not the participants realize it. Still and all, the theatrical passion deployed is astonishing: every actor or actress devotes *élan vital* and every power of expression—most of all, the pent-up ones, the trembling, bashful ones whose palms break out in a sweat before their other glands open. The less naturally gifted ones simply make up for it with artificial means: panting, gasping, rattling, laughing half-crazily, sobbing, murmuring sweet nothings or slobbering obscenities, raging fiercely, in ecstasy, in murderous delusion, or fading with the slaughter-victim look of lovers...

all in all, carried out by the millions, as mentioned, recorded over millions of years, the result is a highly interesting, significant, with-it, modern film. The title, needless to say, is *Reality:* Mr. Warhol's undisputed masterpiece if he'd let me write the script: the history of mankind subsumed as a continuous act of mass procreation.

For we are born for nothing else than to cooperate in the preservation of the human race. To eat in order to procreate and to die in order to be eaten by worms so that the worms may procreate. We occur on this shitty planet for no other purpose than to let the same thing occur over and over again. We exist for no other purpose than simply to cooperate in life—in life, which is lived by eating life in order to create life. Life that procreates by eating life. And having done this, having played out our tiny parts in this huge, in this sublime play of Mother Nature's, we are kindly furloughed from reality for a while. We can go and play our own little games. We can whip up our own reality, some gaudy figment, a merry or dreary as-if. Our private or collective little fiction. For instance, that we are writers and have to write our books. Or readers who have to read these books. Or great actresses, like Nadine Carrier, who gives so ineffably much to millions of people with her mature art of portraying human beings. Or literary agents... Some gracious or ungracious delusion, according to our taste. It does not count, it is not essential, *it is not real*. The real thing is our biological existence as a minute particle, as a mini-micro-function in the sublimely stolid play of Mama Nature.

For whether we pray or kill one another, argue with joke with or gyp one another, kick one another in the balls deliver weighty thoughts or wet clay for kneading fetishes, whether we laugh weep twist in pain or leap for joy, whether we are awake or dreaming, dancing or sleeping—everything is aimed at only *this one thing*, means only *this one thing*, is concerned with only *this one thing*, leads to *this one thing*: to procreate in order to create procreators. It all has only this one purpose: to preserve life. It has only one reality: the reality of being created in order to create life-devouring life and to be devoured by life. A perfectly meaningful playing together, in order to produce an inherently meaningless duration: the duration of life from here to eternity. Achieved by a gigantic squandering, a continual immense lavishing of myriads and myriads of individual lives. An insane wasting of tens of thousands of genera, species, breeds: the game of a certifiably mad demiurge.

Thus would we have performed our mini-parts, Madame and I—a micro-role, an imperceptible flicker of a grain of light in a film hundreds of thousands of billions of feet long—and now we'd find ourselves on the shadowy line between horror at the nothingness of this reality and terror of the fictions that fill time for us between two such acts of biological realization: so-called everyday life and its reality, which everyone takes for granted as reality...

the very thing that drives Nadine into her dressing room after every completed take in order to exult in having some guy (in an emergency: me) between her legs...

(then, afterward, the other horror in her eyes, when the veils of orgasm dissolve and those eyes are forced to recognize the fellow lying on her, heavy, as if dead, and are forced to recognize that she too has been expelled from this reality of being and has been cast back into her nothingness: the immense terror in it, as if she had looked right in the face of the whole swindle, the sheer madness of Creation)

Nagel once told me a story from his seafaring days. Leaning indolently over the railing of some ship he'd signed on with, he watched a pair of mice that had fallen into a vat of syrup on a wharf and had been able to clamber out. It was the image of pure love. The two little mice licked each other with heartrending, nauseating fervor. They clutched at each other with their little paws, slopping and lapping; they drew their little tails through their little mouths; they bored their rosy little tongues into each other's little ears; they kissed the little drops of syrup from each other's every little finger—and for a moment, they stood nose to nose, peering into the black pinheads of each other's eyes, and then sprang apart as if the devil had leaped between then. They had forgotten all about each other, said Nagel; had completely forgotten they were mice, with good reason to be frightened of any other animal, even another mouse; and so they were both frightened to death when they saw each other so close up...

But I believe that Nagel does not have the full image of reality. From my own experience, I believe I can say: Each little mouse saw itself in the other's eyes—and behind, the cat.

Yesterday, late at night, in a fit of irrepressible contrition, I began a letter to Christa, intending to explain, far too long after the fact, my inner turmoil. (What for?)

Fortunately, I didn't get past the beginning. Not only was I embarrassed about making such an apology in confessional form but I was overcome by pure fear: I caught myself writing like Nagel: the closer to self-confession I got, the more dithyrambic I became... yet stylistically all the more restrained. The beautiful soul that does not wish to say outright how beautiful it is—you're supposed to notice by its quivering. The poet as a taut string, which resounds splendidly even when he scratches his ass—

And even this style is smugly abandoned with an ironic stylistic cover: a wink to the reader, making quotation marks unnecessary—

and this to Christa (whom I could best approach spiritually in a street song, if not with Rilke):

You to whom I never say
That I lie awake at night
Weeping...

at any rate, did I squander an entire night trying to fathom what the devil it was that kept urging me to make confessions in the first place?

(To continue in Nagel's style:

—as if my accusers were drawing nearer and nearer to me, about to confront and unmask me—and I were futilely hurling new masks of me at them, each closer to the truth than the last and yet not the truth, but only an image with whose delusion my guilt only worsened—

whereby the most deceptive of these images would emerge with the confession of the whole truth.)

As always when in the mood for parodies, I was desperate, restless, jittery, mordant particularly toward myself—and this naturally ended once again with my clumsy attempt to stumble across the threshold of consciousness behind which my murder lies in darkness.

It was almost morning by now. I had switched off the light and thrown myself onto the bed, and once again I recapitulated the image of my dream in every detail. I set up each one in front of me, sneaked around it, tried to attack it from the rear, as it were, to take it by surprise and thereby force it to surrender the truth that it was mirroring to bits—but something came at me from behind: a horror at myself, which made the marrow freeze in my bones.

I spent the day destroying everything that was literature in my book. Everything that did not reflect the purest verifiable truth. Any figment, fiction, fancy, fantasy that could disguise or falsify truth. I thus destroyed my book for good; but I wanted things to be clean and orderly at last.

It is now long after midnight again (I heard twelve strokes from somewhere a while ago; that's beside the point anyway; I feel utterly fresh; I am writing easily again—only I feel a cramp burgeoning in my hand—poor Nagel!)—

I wrote down what happened yesterday and (together with a few jottings I fished out of the garbage with Monique's help—I believe she has become shrewd and stores my refuse in some broom closet) put it into a folder of its own (everything else into Folder C).

To supplement the above, I must add: If my reckoning of time is correct, then it has been exactly one week since I went back to the Épicure. I'd come from Reims, as I've said, spending the night there while en route from Munich. There wasn't much traffic on the roads, and I made rapid headway. The day was high and bright and clear, the sky blue, the fields golden. I drove through the Frenchest France, toward Paris. Hamlets lay there like primer pictures, small toy towns, and everything about them was utterly French. *La douce France*. The heartland of Europe.

I had it in my blood. It had been in me since my childhood, implanted in me at the same time that Miss Fern's gentle firmness and strict moderation, the scent of Pear's soap, the sharp stroke of a scrubbing brush, and the burning of Geo. F. Trumper's West Indian Extract of Lime on my shivering skin breathed the breath of Great Britain into me. It belonged to me like my fingers or my voice or the tip of my nose. Just as, presumably, rock 'n' roll rhythms or Donald Duck (and with them New York and the Rocky Mountains, and with them, America) belong to my son. It was an element in my chemical makeup, and I wondered if I was capable of *speaking it*.

Let's assume, I told myself, that you had to explain what France is to your son, who has never heard of it and doesn't know the usual illustrative material. Or even better: to the wolf boy—one of the outcasts who has grown up among animals in the wild and scurries around on all fours. You've caught him and you're supposed to teach him about the human world. How will you tell him about France? Her essence: her fragrance, her sounds, her colors, her light, her mood, her unmistakable style?...

What is this—France? You carry it within yourself as the impression of a very definite azure density of air, golden fields, a little blue-white-and-red flag on neatly banal municipal buildings, tin soldiers in red trousers, buttoned-back jacket tails, and front-squashed shakos or gray-green WWI *poilus* in steel helmets with a middle rib, high coat collars, and puttees, such as you scissored out of sheets of pictures by the dozens when you were a child in Cannes. You carry it within yourself in the *maquis* on the rugged coasts of the Corniche and in the pictures of particolored marketplaces where old gentlemen, wearing berets and carrying poles of white bread under their arms, browse around for the fleshiest eggplants, the ripest tomatoes, the plumpest mushrooms. It speaks to you in the airy lattice of the Eiffel Tower, in the tiny, sharply etched illustrations of Larousse, the classicism of Corneille and Racine, of course, in Impressionist paintings, and so forth up to *La Reine Pedauque* and *Cousin Pons* (to spare ourselves the banality of the classics) and the sublime spirituality of Paul Valéry... But *what can you say about all this?* How can you crystallize the common essence, the—well, unmistakable Frenchness? How can it be said? Oh Lord! *What can be said?*...

And just what did I have to say? Myself—certainly. But wasn't France in me too? It was part of the light that illuminated the first half of my life. It was one of the elements in the spectral composition of its light, as specific, intrinsic, and irremovable as the greenish-golden flickering of the German nixie-world or the full yellow wine light over the sepia and cypress darkness of the Mediterranean coasts, the glacier blueness and trumpet flashes of Old Austria in a dying Vienna or the melancholy under the brooding sun of Eastern Europe. I had to be able to *say* these things. I had to be able to say what the light had been like when a spring wind full of urgent promise, the wind of a new era, had blown through it before the great Ice Age—and then, from one day to the next, as if the pendulum of time had swung back, the light had tipped over into a different state.

For it had been at the center of my days then, this light, even when they were bleak and gray. It shone even on the dreary tenement apartment of my Viennese youth, padded it with confidence: that beyond, past the houses across the way, which may have blocked our view but could not totally extinguish the brighter, airier vastness of the sky overhead, lay Schönbrunn. It had been my comfort in the bitter early years of my exile from the vast stretches of Bessarabia and the light-and-color intoxications of the Côte d'Azur, and I went to the park there as often as I could. Sat on a bench, breathed, gazed. Did not know, of course, what it was that calmed me. Only sensed that the vast layout of these imperial grounds and the little garden of the trolley conductor's family, which I had visited one Maupassant-like Sunday, had something in common, which I carried within myself along with my yearning for the park in Bessarabia: a piece of orderly nature—the European legacy, which we were squandering. Here in France, there was something left of that legacy, and *this* was what I had to say in my book.

After nineteen years, I still did not know what it wanted to be, this book of mine. It had always been clear that it would have to be an autobiographical novel. A novel because its subject was a continent: the period of a lifetime. Autobiographical because this necessarily had to be the lifetime of the person telling it. "It's gotten around that the world cannot be experienced objectively," I said to Schwab. "The titans in the early years of our century knew that one can no longer reflect reality without showing the person who experiences it. Where the eyes through which they had the reader experience such a world-within-the-world weren't exactly those of a narrator in whom the reader unerringly recognized the author himself (as in Proust's *Remembrance of Things Past*). They belonged to a potential narrator, who to some extent was a projection of the novelist into the plot: a character placed in the midst of the events and trying to unravel what was problematic in them, because he will presumably have to tell about it all someday (like Joyce's Stephen Dedalus and even Musil's Ulrich)."

Thus, I felt, in literature that is more than broadsheets and street ballads (a possibility that must be accorded even to us dwarfish epigones), the world is the experience of a character who is, only fictitiously, *not* the same person as the author himself. The first-person narrative blossoms. But for the cunning reader, this zealously confessional anonymous narrator, this *I*, is transparent enough to reveal the *writer* of the story. The reader follows the con of fiction up to a point, but no further. Fiction is possible only with the reader's tacit consent. A complicity that should not be overtaxed.

I blathered on endlessly with Schwab about all this. "We are in a dilemma," I kept on saying. "Especially you—if you really intend to write your book one day. *You* would truly have something to say. Come now: such a valuable, massively earnest man—a top student, completed doctoral dissertation lying in his drawer, not handed in because of his elegant discretion (spiritual hygiene to the point of near-sterility)—and what is expected of him but an act of self-exposure or, worse, a glimpse into his spiritual digestive processes? This is sure to be embarrassing. Insuperable for an aristocratic character such as yours. I, on the other hand, am an entirely different type. I have always been narcissistic, exhibitionistic. But let us not talk about me and my effronteries. Let us take Nagel—a model of the contemporary man of letters. He is not without his discretion either, no, no. Yet he is incomparably more democratic. In a dignified way, even: deliberately run of the mill. Highly simpatico. You are disgusted at the thought of being in bed with the reader, but it's only half so difficult for Nagel, because he lets it happen on the basis of the universally human.

"Needless to say, he's honest enough to admit that he too has no *message* to convey. Even the best-selling author Nagel does not give us beautiful images, lofty thoughts, or soul-expanding emotions anymore; he only hands us problems. Like everyone nowadays, he is nothing but a pile of completely unanswered questions. Like every upright writer, he too stammers on about himself. But he stammers only the stammerings of everyman. He stammers of the questions that every moment of existence holds under his nose, everyday problems. He circumspectly chooses those that haunt everyman. Thus he can honestly go halves with the reader. He truthfully admits that the questions concern primarily him, the writer Nagel. In exchange, the reader accepts his disguise as a character in a novel. Naturally, it must not be too exotic. For example, Nagel puts his own writerly head on Bookkeeper Müller's shoulders. The reader accepts this, especially when Bookkeeper Müller admits that he spends part of his leisure aspiring to higher things by writing short stories. That's a good deal. The reader gladly identifies with Müller because he too doesn't want to spend twenty-four hours a day trudging through his daily round and would love to write short stories himself. That's why he reads books, after all. What makes him a reader is the escape from and beyond his shitty workaday life. Thus, with Nagel's book, in which he identifies with Müller, he can tackle the problems of existence arm in arm with the writer Nagel and, together with him, fail to solve them. But I ask you: Does our friend Nagel realize how clownish that is? When the whole fiction of Bookkeeper Müller, without Nagel added in, is an imposition one can't expect the shrewd reader to accept, then half of it is actually ironic. Do you believe Nagel gives this any thought?..."

I was driving with Schwab back then on a day like this. A day in autumn 1964. Panic-stricken, I had set out from Hamburg, for Dawn had vanished once again in Paris. Untraceable, no matter how much I telephoned after her. So I had to go back to haul her, in a state of total bewilderment, out of some Épicure-like dump and calm her down until she had pulled herself together enough to endure a few more weeks of existence. Schwab had insisted on coming along. At the time, I was busy with one of the movie piglets' usual big projects, so I wanted to get to Paris as fast as I could but have the car handy because I knew it soothed Dawn when I chauffeured her around, with her precious hair in the wind. And so I didn't hop a plane; I didn't go by way of Holland, where my son probably spent a whole melancholy-heavy Sunday waiting for me in vain; instead I took the Autobahn to Baden-Baden, and, with my then still alive German friend Schwab, slipped into France via Strasbourg. Because I hadn't managed to leave Hamburg until late, we spent the night in Reims, going on to Paris the next morning.

"There's something else that good old Nagel doesn't seem to see," I blathered on during the drive, "namely, that with his silly bookkeeper who writes short stories, he throws away the very thing he would like to write himself: a novel. If he wrote about himself, the writer Nagel, who writes not only short stories but whole books, and indeed so incessantly and uninterruptedly as to make you think that he can't live without writing, *then* he would have a novel! A writer who writes about writing will reveal the world in a new way. A lost possibility will open up to him: the very possibility of showing a human being in a world with which he has a living relationship. Hence, a world in which one *lives* and not just exists in isolation. We are told on all sides that the novel is dead, and that's because its last great theme is exhausted—the incompatibility of man's inner world with his outer world, the individual's forlornness in society, the unreality of the world man has created. But these are simply the problems of novel characters, not novel writers. These are the troubles of Bookkeeper Müller, whom Nagel has disguised himself as. They concern the writer Nagel only because he falls for his own trick and identifies with Müller the bookkeeper, not with Müller the short-story writer. Okay, through Müller he identifies with the reader—but by way of Müller's intention to write short stories. The reader is totally uninterested in Müller in his workaday existence. He's enough of a bookkeeper himself and has enough everyday problems of his own; he doesn't need Nagel for that. In order to escape, he reads books and wants to write short stories. So why doesn't Nagel go all the way and let the reader identify fully with *him*, the writer Nagel? With a writer not only of short stories but also of books, day in day out, year in year out. Someone who lives from and for writing books. For whom writing is life. Who can experience the world only by writing. That way he'd pull off the trick of a symbolic existence. A writer interiorizes the outer world. The more incompatible he finds the existence of man as an individual in a world that cares not a rotten fig for him, the more the world becomes an immediate, burning, living issue for him, and he for it. And the more subjectively he makes an issue of it, the more objectively he grasps it and the more objectively he renders it. The world becomes an object again. One not only swims in it, as among fish in an aquarium, but confronts it, simply by writing, by *describing* it. Admittedly, the writer who sees the world only from his special vantage point circumvents the problem of society. *Il s'en fout totalement*. He has an easy time of it, after all. He is in the enviable position of getting along marvelously without society. The more isolated he is, the better he works. Cervantes, as you as a top student must surely know, wrote *Don Quixote* in a prison cell. Fine: In the prison cell of your existence, you, as a writer, will find your great theme today: yourself. The self as reality—in German, *Wirklichkeit*, from *wirken*, to work, act, operate... working: writing. Acting by writing. Become real by writing. By describing, writing about, how you want to describe the world and in doing so experiencing defeat, you draw out the world as reality. You become a defeated Don Quixote, who, being entangled in his inner world and thwarted by it, achieves experience of the outer world. In this way, the reader Müller, staring bewildered into nothingness, is shown the road to the interior and then out of it into the exterior. You present the world to him. For the writer who writes about himself writing, the world becomes once again a means of experiencing the world—and thus, for the reader, once again a means of experiencing himself. Heed these golden words, dearest friend, for they may contain salvation for you too. No more roguish acts of lightning-swift exposure. No more brief liftings of the costume so that the reader can see the naked author underneath—the flasher author, the bashful exhibitionist. Rather a grand act of submission. Hara-kiri. Offer yourself freshly butchered on a platter to your fellow man, Bookkeeper Reader Müller. No more machinations, no more going halves. You need not borrow Bookkeeper Müller's costume from Reader Müller in order to hide your nakedness. You don't have to wink at him from that costume: 'Look at me; I know that you know that I, naked underneath, am the author; but a very tiny little thing that wishes to write short stories is dangling between your legs too.'

"Show Müller what you really think of him. Smash all your innards, smoking, into his face. Show him what you think of his fifty-fifty partners; for instance, Nagel. But no! Nagel is an upright fellow: a Sancho Panza, who, for sheer love of being a lackey, continues Don Quixote's heroic struggle. This is not for you, no, no: Show Reader Müller what you think of the great writer Thomas Mann sitting at his desk and giggling into his *fist* because he, who has just Wagnered *Faustus* out of that selfsame *fist*, is now masquerading as *Felix Krull, Confidence Man*, and cutting capers for us. Pull down those borrowed pants! The Mardi Gras is over. Today, even a child knows that existence can be endured only if existence describes itself. Ask any modern-day child the old, idiotic question, What does he want to be when he grows up? Not a fireman or train engineer, as in our day. No, he wants to become an artist. A circus performer if he is especially talented and in the best of health. But if his gifts are average, then a sculptor, actor, painter, moviemaker. In delicate cases, the brat is already writing. He's had the outline for his novel lying in his little desk since long before puberty, since the age of six or seven. And his enraptured parents are encouraging him. Just imagine how proud I am of my son's ceramics..."

I waited for his reaction, a sign of agreement or rejection, or else simply amusement or boredom; but Schwab, at my side, remained wordless and gazed unswervingly forward into the road flying toward us. It was a straight-as-an-arrow road through land that surged toward us in a vast breath; intoxicatingly set between the round tops of apple trees, the road dipped steeply into the depressions, like a roller coaster in an amusement park, and then up the other side, straight as an arrow, and the apple trees, dense green spheres, continued to accompany it. *La douce France* flew past Schwab's profile, which was strangely delicate for such a massive Martin Luther head (a silverpoint drawing,

I thought to myself); every acre of soil had been fertilized with French and German blood. I knew his father had died in action here, just before the end of Doubleyou Doubleyou One, in 1918. Schwab had never known his father, but he piously nurtured his memory: German Professor Anselm Schwab (no relation to Gustav).

In those days, one of my delights was to let the landscapes of Europe fly past Dawn's profile. She loved an open car and was very beautiful when she closed her eyes and held her face with its blowing hair into the headwind. I thought of the cruel game I had played with Christa: "If there were two people you loved equally, and you had to sacrifice one of them so that you and the other could survive, which would it be?" I loved Dawn. But I never doubted for an instant which of the two I would sacrifice if I were forced to choose between her and Schwab. I sensed I was becoming irritable, and I stepped harder on the gas pedal. I had been driving rather fast anyhow. Now things began to get interesting.

"You may have goodness knows how high an opinion of Nagel," I said (and knew I was hitting a raw nerve, for Schwab held Nagel in very high esteem and regularly despaired when Nagel failed once again to achieve what Scherping ingeniously called the "breakthrough to himself"). "But so long as Nagel does not realize that he is always deceiving himself, that most honest of all men, he will never become a first-class writer. And that's very much your concern, honored friend. You and no one else are called on to tell him that. After all, Scherping pays you to administer pastoral care to his authors. Not that there aren't purely ethical motives as well. When a man like you is too prim and proper to contribute a work to literature, then he at least has the damned duty to make sure the general level of culture is raised by the works of other people. A self-abnegatory task, I'll admit, but as we all know, it is always the best who fall in war, likewise the best who perish in the culture business. The survivors write, there's nothing we can do about it. They write to survive, and they survive because they write. But they shouldn't make it too easy on themselves, right? I know you'll have Scherping to deal with if you convince Best-selling Author Nagel that what he writes is shit. But after a dozen best sellers, even his publisher ought to allow him an excursion into literature. Naturally, that sort of thing might mess up the Complete Works. The Oeuvre. Without failed attempts, it will be more homogeneous, of course. Twelve gentle street ballads by Bookkeeper Müller, who wants to write short stories. Twelve illustrated broadsheet tales, striding like valiant hikers toward their noble goal of assuring us that, despite all the murky confusion, the world is ultimately an orderly structure. It may not be obvious why this is true, but it is comforting to believe it. It could be an orderly structure at least. It should be in any case. *Per aspera ad astra* even for the potential short-story writer Müller. After all, it's always the same story with the same character, and the same destiny, simple and obvious as a child's mechanical toy. The coil-spring tension of some tiny man-in-the-street problem, some common, current conflict—for instance, in the potential short-story-writing Bookkeeper Müller, the bad conscience caused by belonging to an elite—transferred to the gear transmission of our theoretically humanitarian and in fact misanthropic social conditions; and the thing is already purring along its path, joining with others of its kind, creating a tiny world, a tiny as-if, which, minute and simplified, is nevertheless a fair image of the big, bad world, as though it were our dear, bad, workaday life itself. Meant merely to be wound up, reduced to the simplest term, deciphered with a pocket multiplication table. A tiny fiction, sharply true to life but so remote in its own reality that if you look at it, your gaze is lost in dreams as in the glass-encapsulated oceanic vastness surrounding a meticulously rigged ship inside a bottle. Happily, you add it to other bric-a-brac in your home, in the culture cupboard, where next to the dictionary you use for your short-story writing stand a dozen contemporary novels like peas in a pod. In terms of its skill, this belongs with the little Calderesque mobile whirling overhead. But imagine Nagel understanding that his Bookkeeper Müller, who wants to write short stories, is *not* material for a novel, no matter how tragicomically he has Müller struggle through to the light or be doomed with all the powers of earth and heaven. Still, it's an excellent topic for an essay: 'Imagination as a Gamble.' For once, a sober posing of the question whether the courage for this should not be reserved for an elite of more or less violent lunatics. Can it be consistent with order if the gamble of imagination is also granted to Bookkeeper Müller? And what damage is thereby done to his soul? You see, if this is accorded to just anyone, then it would leave the door open for such questions as well... Oh, come on, you don't have to snort so indignantly, I'm quite serious. One is confronted with the question of a sound relationship between fiction and reality. We realized long ago that this relationship is out of kilter among people like us. The psychologist piglets didn't have to demonstrate the close connection between writing and masturbation. That has always been a source of our arrogance. The onanist is a sovereign. He has the biggest harem on earth, and no woman can resist him. Above all, however, he eludes Mother Nature's dirty game. Who wants reality anyway? Don't we do everything we can to flee it? For instance, by reading books. And certainly by writing books! Even Short-Story Writer Müller knows that. It is simply human. What gives us a special place in zoology is the fact that we cannot endure reality and incessantly oppose it with fictions. Mother Nature's monotonous game made us sick to our stomachs long ago. We refuse to admit that only one single reality can dominate: the sheer, brutal, infinitely unimaginative reality of being born in order to create life-devouring life, and to be devoured for the procreation of other life. We push this reality into the background and cover it up with a camouflage backdrop of fiction. All well and good. But the problem is the mixture: too much fiction blinds us to Nature, while a man is devoured before he knows what hit him; too little fiction renders Mama Nature's unendurable cruelty too evident. Here too we lunatics with too much imagination are nicely left out of the game. We know we'll be devoured; in the meantime, we send up the balloons of our fictions, create a reality within reality, valid for us alone, a world within the world, in which we can be happy-go-lucky, a Middle Kingdom in which we are sovereign. If everyone thought and acted along those lines, obviously things would become chaotic. The man in the street must be allowed to go halves with reality and veil it agreeably, and he must be permitted enough consciousness that it not catch him at unawares."

Schwab continued not to show any interest, and I laughed.

"Perhaps there is a possibility here to save you too," I said. "I mean: the essay. If I were you, I would write an essay that would be a consequence and heightening of the essay on 'Imagination as a Gamble' and also a genuine German contribution: namely, 'On Causality and Necessity.' The German contribution would come directly from the German genius: its language. No other language more blatantly expresses the predicament of having to stave off necessity: *Notwendigkeit*: having to *die Not wenden*: see the translation of *Not*: need, want, privation, indigence; care, sorrow, misery, affliction; trouble, difficulty, plight, predicament, emergency, extremity; danger, peril, distress; necessity, exigency, urgency... and all this wants to be *gewendet:* turned away from us, take a turn for the better, turn out for the best... Incidentally, a theological theme. I can sniff the LORD Zebaoth. Our most reliable camouflage backdrop. No, no, I've been talking nonsense again: Nagel knows what he's doing. When he feels like philosophical profundity, he merely sticks a steel helmet on his Bookkeeper Müller: not only does this make Müller totally universal and humanly akin to everyone, even without the urge to write short stories, but also thrusts him into the midst of the realest events, and Mother Nature laughs at the human beings dancing to her pipe in the name of the most astonishing fictions. Yet for Nagel, going halves with Reader Müller, all that has its own necessity. Whenever Nagel opens the little treasure chest of his wartime experiences (for which I envy him more and more hungrily), something else emerges in the glow of the German Cross in Gold, the Iron Cross First Class and Iron Cross Second Class, the Close Combat Clasp, and medals for being wounded: that something else is the Lord God. From out of the gunfire, HIS eye gives us an encouraging wink, indicating that the whole hullaballoo has been put on in order to help Private First Class Müller find his identity. On a literary level, a hail of steel is just sufficient to forge a young man into a self whose inner wealth (of doubt, of course, but now also self-confidence, thank goodness) will supply an entire generation with a basis for seeing its own portrait in that self. The fact that the riflemen Neumann, Lehrmann, Meier, and Kunze, all the same age as he, are shot to bits is significant only in that it displays the harshness of this test of destiny. It is part of the drama's background dynamics. Chiaroscuro flatters. Nitpickers are referred to the irrational fraction that remains when we try to divide life by reason. But for the Bros. Nagelmüller, what results is *necessity—Notwendigkeit*—and with it, subsequently, alleged causality. This is then known as: history. *Bravo!* A final European attempt to insert an orderly structure into the absurdity of existence, to make it into a meaningful structure. Does Nagel know this—Nagel, whose intellectual lodestar is Mr. Hemingway? Does he know how much he, in his Europeanized Hemingway imitations, is still rebelling involuntarily against America's message that life is, more than anything else, irrational and subject to violence? For wasn't that what the New World pioneers brought home to us from the harshness of their wide-open spaces? Dealing the coup de grâce to millennia of frail efforts to put Nature in order? Just what is our culture, our civilization? The tradition that our origin and ultimate bliss are *in a garden*. That unordered Nature can have an order and thereby a meaning and purpose. This is the message of Western Civilization from the Bible to Nagel. True, Mother Nature is not overlooked, especially in certain gory and decay-green depictions of man as the Son of God nailed to a cross. It's odd, though, that despite their spectacular evocation of anxiety, these often sincere, even unsparing likenesses of everyday human life have something comforting and morally edifying about them, don't you think? This depicted world is no less dreadful, monstrous, devastating than the real world at our fingertips. However, the artist's depicting hand has also gotten himself, man, into the picture, has brushed and stylused him in. This makes it a human world, a world with the dimension of its echo in the human soul. It keeps it in suspense, as it were, hanging from the conceptual balloon like the Saviour on the cross. The image of horror contains horror, spellbinds it. The image of terror includes terror, canceling it somewhat, offering only its outline and not its weight, only the reflection of its harshness and not the harshness itself. Disorder, so represented, has been sifted by him who has ordered its elements in his representation. Meaninglessness fills up with the intent, the meaning, of the person who recognized it as meaningless . . . Yes, we know this: The image of reality is a magic formula that casts a spell on reality itself, in a dialectical equilibrium that gives it a logic in itself, the analogic of representation. And that's what we're charmed by. We've been charmed by this since our very first primer picture and nursery story—what am I saying: since the Cro-Magnon cave drawings . . ."

Four years had passed between then and my latest trip from Reims to here. I drove along the same French highway, cutting straight across the land over hill and dale; the day was as bright as the day when Schwab had sat next to me in the car. I remembered adding: "Fine, I've sensed for a while now that I'm getting on your nerves. But I'm antsy, I can't get along without the usual *Kultur* gallop. In fast motion, I promise you! I promise you I am heading straight for something that is certain not to bore you. As Uncle Ferdinand used to sing: *Parlez-moi de moi, et exclusivement de moi-même, et je vous aime . . .* Now where were we? With the shamans. Ever since the Cro-Magnon cave ceremonies, man has been—(à propos, back then people must have been a more likable bunch than the riffraff we saw at the rest stop yesterday)—anyway, for millennia now, man has been charmed by the same old con and the same old con men. He's been getting his eyes rubbed by the spell of image, in which man and the world are united as one, fiction and reality in a magic equilibrium. Still the same old devices: drums, geometric figures, mutterings of conjurers, lightning-swift casting of runic staffs—*our* devices, dear sir: the devices of the *Kultur* Association for Art and Literature (a chartered and incorporated club), lyre, quill, chisel, and palette embroidered on the banners by the ladies' auxiliary. And, if you please, we also have to sing the old ditty. The Song of God: *Oh, you beauteous forest you, / Who built you so lofty, who?* Well, who? The Parks Department? No. Ask Nagel, he knows. He'll even tell you. Cryptically, to be sure, and bashfully—a Hemingway disciple in hairy-chested sentimentality—but unmistakably. And he's right. What can we do: like it or not, we are serving God. Working on the most sublime of all fictions.

Since the immemorial beginnings of language, we have been filling the names of things with our exultations and lamentations, and we have been speaking of them as if they had found a response within us. Millennia before the chanting of the pre-Homeric rhapsodists, an orderly image of the world had already been conjured up, because the rhythm of ordered words had brought that image into the world. What does a man do if he closes his eyes in a state of idiotic rapture in order to hark within himself to the responses of things to themselves? Or to rivet his eyes on them until, forgetting himself, their images rise up again within him, forcing him to render them with an added human dimension? Am I then being indiscreet if I ask again whether it is the right honorable intellectual timidity in the face of this that will ultimately prevent you from writing your book? I am being presumptuous, but after all, you did talk *me* into writing *my* book—good heavens, fifteen years ago! that's how long it's been!—and I want to get a little revenge. So, tell me, am I wrong in assuming that you are revolted at the thought of dealing with devices that enable all intellectual fraud? I mean, the suspect ingredients that turn a sentence into a fetish and a stanza into a revelation of the numinous, a formation of ABC's into a Gospel—let alone a crappy best seller? But you're not answering me, you're leaving me in eternal uncertainty as to whether I should join the lousy game of asking, once again in my own way, the question about the meaning of existence—a question that, even if I don't find an answer, I will nevertheless have already answered with my own way of asking, with the originality and passion of my asking... Come on, bestow a comforting word! Just say that creation fulfills its meaning in man, and that his existence contains a premeditated plan and an ultimate goal of salvation. Just convince me that the dreadfulness of the world is matched by so-and-so many sublimities, which cancel the dreadfulness out. Persuade me that anyone who cannot recognize this in Alpine peaks, in sunsets reflected in the Mediterranean and in autumnal landscapes, will find it all the more cogently in the *Gilgamesh*, Beethoven's Ninth, or the Angel of Reims... Tell me all these things, I need them as backup. I'm driving to Paris to pull a twenty-two-year-old American girl out of some dump she's holed up in, because her beautiful eyes are still full of the terror of the wide-open wastes in the New World from which she comes, where an arrow can come whizzing out at any moment from behind the rock outcroppings, and Grandma wears an Indian scalp on her belt; where the pistols in thigh holsters are still as loose as in the days of Billy the Kid; where the ears of sleeping Negro children are devoured by slum rats in the huge stone wastes of the cities... in short, images for people for whom the pretense of GOD is an absolute necessity for enduring the thought of the world; eyes, alas, that did not try to recognize HIS revelation through European culture, certainly not in the cancerous proliferation of the Old World, in the horrible teeming of the motorized army ants, the chewing *horlàs* who chomp on their morsels, zealously insalivating them, washing them down with a swig of beer wine Coca-Cola apple juice milk booze mead lemonade club soda—swallowing, jerking-up of the Adam's apple, parting of the lips, tongue-dragon rolling forward and flicking a few food-gruel remnants from the teeth, a slight burp—excuse me, it's just my stomach—and then the next morsel is shoved in... and behind it lurks the big cat NATURE, ready to devour them all. *Against this* I have to tell my disturbed young beloved, make her believe, that this ceaseless gruesome production and destruction of living creatures is made up for by a heartful of love (isn't that so?), and, in case of doubt, by such verses as, Springtime drops her azure ribbon, or Peace lies on all the mountaintops, or a few bars of Vivaldi, or a Cézanne landscape... I have to tell her this convincingly, so that she will come to her senses and allow herself to be photographed for the spring collections of Coco Chanel and Monsieur de Givenchy and Yves Saint Laurent for *Vogue* and *Harper's Bazaar* and *Elle* and *Marie Claire*..."

That was fifteen hundred days ago. I survived them, writing and undauntedly loving: loving Dawn loving Gaia loving Nadine still loving Christa—always ready to flee from the terror of life into the gracious madness of love, or rather, from the ungracious hallucination of having to write into the not much more gracious delusion of having to love. Schwab had chastely withdrawn from this neurotherapoetic bathing cure: he was dead, was now next to me only in spirit. The little pile of earthly substance to which his large body had been reduced was probably well preserved in some urn. I still don't know where that urn wound up—at the Ohlsdorf graveyard or in a display cabinet with his Hamburg relatives. Perhaps Schelmie got hold of it and put it on the shelf behind the bar at Lücke's. I couldn't quite tell whether I was sad about it. I certainly must have been in a way, for I was sorry not to see him. But on the other hand, now I had him around more comfortably, especially when traveling. I didn't have to get fidgety with nervous expectation that he might again be overcome at any moment by some irresistible desire for whiskey or beer or a hedge to piss behind or matches for his innumerable cigarettes after burning his fingers on the last one and absentmindedly tossing the dashboard lighter out the window. True, he had always been at the mercy of my chitchat (and was a man who loved to suffer, as I well knew); but now I had him unresistingly at my disposal, and he could never again escape my convulsive monologues. It crossed my mind that a witty Frenchman (I don't know who; anyway one of the luminaries whom Stella called "provincial") described writing as a welcome opportunity to talk without being interrupted—

And in the enigmatic way in which seeming trivia spark the revelation of something fundamental, it came to me with an illuminating bang: I suddenly had my book very clearly before me. It loomed before my mind's eyes in flawless architecture: a glass cathedral, whose symbolic formula, like the axial system of a crystal, could be read from all relationships of the lines and masses. A House of God to celebrate myself—Hosannah! At last, I had the blueprint within me.

Naturally, it had to be a book by a writer about writing. "Here we have it at last, our spiritual child!" my spirit called to Schwab's spirit. "But it's too bad that you're pulling it out of me posthumously. When you were alive, it would have aroused your keenest envy: a book about the very writer of this very book. This, of course, completely involves the author.

"And this means that everything that comes up in it has to refer to writing. Of course, it's necessarily an autobiography. However, for such a confession to be of interest beyond its confessional aspect, it has to tell a life story that is typical of the era. It must be proven that and why and how the life story of someone who writes is typical of the era. It must become evident that a man of this particular era has no choice but to write—and thus to write this life confession of someone who writes.

"But if this is to deal with writing in a truly transcendental way, then every situation of the confessed life—that is, every situation that necessarily leads to writing—must simultaneously be a metaphor for a corresponding situation *in* writing. This can hardly be achieved with such a thoroughly banal biography as mine, dear friend, muddled as mine may be. Once again, art will have to lend life a helping hand. Instead of bare, complex, and paradoxical reality, this too will require an agreeable, plainly simple, and logically flawless as-if. We resort to the expedient of a *hypothetical autobiography*, dear friend. In a word: we must not be as honest as we would like to be. We shall have to cheat. In the language of art, you have to say, we must *invent*. Very well then! Let me worry about that. For the moment, I'm delighted. My book—or shall I rather say *our* book?—has finally found its form!

"The situation of the writer in the process and experience of writing is archetypal. His intimate incorporation of the world; his absorption in things in order to suck out their articulable essence; his wholehearted devotion to what wants to express itself through him—all these things correspond to the embryo listening to its own growth. Aren't we cozy in the warm black womb!...

"The writer, in the mother liquid of his desire to write, his urge to write, is budding. What he writes has to bud. Has to develop out of itself. There mustn't be any plot barreling ahead. The story grows statically out of itself, adding stratum after stratum by wearing out stratum after stratum.

"This assumes the condition: *I accumulate in order to have something to lose.*

"There's nothing to add about the time and the place of the plot. All pastness of the described (and describing) existence is telescoped in the presentness of narrative. The entire story of the person who narrates himself is present in that person's here and now. But the story refuses to be told in chronological sequence; it has to be told as the ever-present historical content of his presentness: he contains himself in all phases of his story, confronts us in any phase and is all phases at once.

"The style too results from this accordingly. A life in the steadily changing multitude of its moods demands the totality of possible forms of expression. First of all: the half-light of the cell situation, of the budding person, his isolation from the world, flight from the world, search for the world, in the light beam of the desk lamp—these subjects require a chronicler's diction that conjures up the atmosphere of the remote past, and this must be artificial in order to always keep alive the awareness that we're dealing with an as-if: an allegorical story that tries to illustrate a universal truth in a chain of symbolically transparent situations. Just as I must use archetypal imagery in the story without being inhibited by fear of the occasional banality, so too my language must risk walking the line between genuine poetry and occasional kitsch, the contemporary and the antiquated. A tightrope of language, yet a catalogue of style: from characterizing jargon to the icy neutrality of standard language, from trivial chitchat to intellectual argot, from the perfidious mendacity of a salesman's eloquence to the poetry of a pimp—nothing can be left out. Finally my movie piglets get a word in. Finally Scherping becomes a bard. In short: a style of barbaric *haut goût*, like the decadent Latin texts in the centuries during and after the migrations of the peoples, a style that has something nervous and spasmodic in its incessant changes of milieux and moods.

"What did you always say about the novel? It is in its space-time a continent unto itself. This cannot be unspooled linearly on the thread of a simple life story, not unless you section it out, cut it into little pieces, scatter it, so to speak, across the entire landscape. Especially if what is described is to be described in the very state of being described—that is, the describing is the actual subject—then nothing may, nothing can be achieved chronologically: everything has to be ready at all times to be in the present. As a writer, I do not speak about writing as about something that has taken place; I keep on writing by writing it down. I keep living my writing the way I live my life. I must tell about it the way I would tell about my life to someone who lives with me: Living on. My continent in its space-time is an island in the ocean of time. My reader is with me on this island, which for him still lies in darkness. He wants to get to know it—by all means. My story sweeps across it like the beam of a lighthouse. It sweeps along the horizon all around my island, always sweeping across the same areas; but each time the light beam hits them, they reveal something previously unknown, until eventually the entire topography is experienced.

"I know: I will have to exercise caution—for instance, the balance of intellectual and emotional stimulations. A delicate matter, eh? But these are secondary matters, matters of execution. Generally speaking, all I have to do now is rummage through the jumble of papers in the trunk and pick out the ones that fit in with this new plan. And I'll have my book, damn it—I'LL HAVE MY BOOK! What do you say? HE WHO HATH WILL BE GIVEN . . . Why the hell don't you say something? It's a bad joke on your part to have been dead for four years now."

Then, suddenly, everything was gray all around me, like the densest fog. I heard a brief, hard bang, and all at once, I didn't know where I was, I got scared, I slammed on the brakes and the car almost whirled on its own axis, with crushed stone spraying up around me.

I stood up. I opened the door. On a stretch of freshly rebuilt, still unasphalted road, I had come close—not too fast, luckily—to a truck. When I went around to pass it, he had stepped on the gas. His back tires kicked up a stone, which flew into my windshield. It was like an opaque stroke of lightning that totally blocked my view.

I should have taken this as a warning. But people like us, heroic as we are, we do not do such things. I dug a hole in the debris on the windshield so that I could see, and then on I drove to Paris. I was absolutely determined to start work immediately.

This was—let me repeat it once again—eight days ago. I did not hesitate for an instant. I drove straight to the Épicure, unloaded my suitcases, cartons, and boxes, parked the car in the garage, bought myself a big jar of instant coffee, went up to my room (number 26 as usual; it's always free, seems to wait for me), and got down to my papers. The first slip I took hold of said, in red letters, SCHWAB. That same moment, the horror of my dream attacked me with such power and present reality that I thought someone was actually standing behind me, catching me in the abominable act of murder.

And while I tried to hold on to the flash of recognition that made me realize that my dream was true, that I had really murdered someone (and that I would soon also know whom and how and when and where), I was overcome with a sense of profound shame:

the con artistry of my actions became so horrifyingly blatant to me, just as a lunatic may realize in a lucid moment that he is a lunatic—

the incredible con artistry of a writer's existence—a fiction inventor, a man playing his game like an unsophisticated child, in an utterly menacing world—composing his as-if like a moron who accumulates pebbles and who, babbling and drooling, watches them dribble apart as he tries all the harder to build up the same pile again . . .

What was I doing here? What was I working on?

Schwab—who *is* he?

It is the name of a character I have sketched for a novel, for whom my (now deceased) friend S. was the model. The invented name for one of the many figures (freely drawn from life) in the untold (never fully drafted and ultimately rejected) drafts of my book.

Originally, S. had not been given a significant part. To be sure, I had toyed with the thought of letting him stroll across the stage; after all, he was important in my life story, and hypothetical as my projected autobiographies may have been, I nevertheless took from the one reality whatever served me for the truth of the other reality.

But still, the Johannes Schwab character was merely one of the tinier pebbles from my idiots' game, a so-called *supernumerary*—

so that was what had become of the living man, the human being, my friend and spiritual brother J. S . . . I still know rather precisely when I had begun to jot down utterances, habits, particular features of his: here, in Paris, one morning on the Île de la Cité, when we were on the Pont Neuf, gazing up the Seine, and he made a remark implying that he was planning to write about me. I wanted to beat him to the punch. Surprise him one day with a portrait that would completely scuttle his plans. But never had I seriously planned to use him as a main figure in any of the countless drafts for my book.

Yet now a certain Johannes Schwab was erupting from every even halfway intelligible sheet of paper. He clung to me like a shadow—and placed me under him. He was not to be shaken off. He was simply everywhere. He dominated everything. He squeezed into the new draft of my book and did not look all that bad in it. But he made it burst: he enlarged it, made it boundless. If I gave in to his pushiness and took the character of Johannes Schwab into the story, then he pushed the events in a different direction, way beyond the plot line. With him, the story proliferated all over the place, beyond its original shape, metastasizing in new and entirely unforeseen dimensions. It could scarcely be kept under control; it demanded a thorough rethinking; it required a plot ten times longer; it opened new paths for invention. But without him, the story now seemed lifeless, artificial, too obviously contrived, too literary to be believed, too private to be interesting. My dead friend S. suddenly seemed to contain all the life of my book.

For eight full nights and fitfully dozed days, I sought a way out of this grotesque dilemma (always pursued by my lurking dream), until finally I realized that my resistance was futile. Either I had to take Schwab into my book (which meant that I would have to rewrite it; that is, again put it off indefinitely) or else, for the time being, I would once more have to fling my outline to the wind.

That's bad enough. The thing that has been agitating me so profoundly since then is the discovery of such a blatant, absolutely undeniable, inexplicable, and effective magic.

At some point when S. was still alive and kicking, I found and wrote down a name: Johannes Schwab...

and thus a human being is put on paper and is *alive*...

he has the features of my friend S. (who is no longer alive), he moves, he carries himself like my friend, he talks like him, he articulates thoughts that *he* could have uttered, he behaves like him, he has his unhappy genius, his standoffish character, his forcefulness and his weakness, his whims, crotchets, and eccentricities—and in the end his destiny as well. *The demonic power of words on the page has awakened a dead man.*

Now I have him around me day and night. Since the baneful hour when I re-exhumed him (in his role as a character in a novel), he has been my worst tormentor, the most sublime, the most murderous instrument of self-destruction.

He peers over my shoulder when I rummage through my papers; he watches my fingers when I write (yes even as I write this down). It was he who drove me to destroy entire sections of the book. Because of him, I ripped up and threw out the tangle of beginnings, finished and still unfinished chapters, drafts, outlines. Because of him, whenever I continued working on something these past few days and nights, I eventually dropped the pen in disgust, and furiously and desperately tore my scribblings to shreds.

He has infiltrated my thoughts, my soliloquies; he comments on them sneeringly (for instance, now); he encourages my most abstruse plans, praising them only to undermine them. He sabotages my best ideas; he presumes to judge my abilities, my intentions, my resolutions, my decisions (it's beyond my strength to carry them out, right?); he scorns, mocks, warns, proves, convicts, and shames me—in short, Schwab conducts himself with extraordinary willfulness (probably infected by my own worst manners). What his model (friend S. the graceful: in his lifetime the finest standard-bearer of the freedom that is granted everyone; the sovereign appreciator of any spiritual form or utterance so long as it was at least halfway equal or even superior to his; the proud and happy discoverer of my literary talent and its most ardent defender against infidels and doubters, a man who always practiced the tenderest admiration for me, an admiration deftly concealed and hence all the more flatteringly manifested)—I say, what friend S. would never have dared to do Schwab does unsparingly: he delivers the most annihilating criticism, offers the most cutting, most destructive analysis, paragraph for paragraph, line for line, word for word, expresses fundamental doubt in both the mission itself and the calling of the man who has undertaken it: your humble servant.

The creature from my pen, whom I have called Schwab, carries on like a literary tax investigator, so to speak, an unrelenting snooper who quickly spots the finagling in a balance sheet, ferrets out any evasion, tracks down any unlisted source of income—

and, unfortunately, he does not limit himself to that. He uses the literary as a pretext to burrow into my private life, and there he really throws his weight around, demands absolutely accurate data on incidents that I would much rather have let lie, confronts me about things I may have once, foolishly blinded, viewed as vile and concerning but on which I might now blissfully look down, like a martyr at his battered body—if the former vileness had not been restored, thanks to his pastoral activity, drilling down into the bottom of everything—

as if even the most false, stupid, nay inhumane commandment still contained something ethically valuable in essence, not forfeited with the Expulsion of the Idols, and which even with the establishment of a new and more radiant God cannot be completely banished from the world—

Thanks to Schwab, I am surrounded again by a forest of those formerly worshiped totems and feared taboos, with all their terrifying grimaces: I experience the most absurd incidents of my formative years in Vienna under the same moral pressure that made them traumas in the past, not to mention later events. In short: My dead friend S. (*le pudique*, who blushed furiously at the slightest indiscretion, so that his lips turned pale and began to tremble; S. the broad-mindedly playful man, *passionné des cascadeurs*, enraptured gaper at my feats in the art of life, who released an orgiastic "Ah!" at every vault, every *salto mortale* with which I managed to twist out of the allegedly fateful alternatives of existence; S., who was in love, the fiery head of a claque in a small but select audience, endlessly delighted by my adventures, my gambles, and their stunning peripeties, as well as my ether-clear somnambulism)—this friend S. was replaced by a man named Schwab: an unpleasant zealot and tough-as-leather moralist, a boorish second-guesser and nitpicking examiner, who continues to live the life of tactful, sensitive, generous S. but in a puritanically narrow-minded and aggressive manner, in annoying, obtrusive, uncanny ubiquity—

and I, for my part, find myself embarrassingly obsequious to him. I am at his mercy. I am as submissive to this changeling of fantasy and reality as I was to the "protective spirit" that my foster parents invented to keep me on a string during my formative years in Vienna. (This was allegedly one of the spirits that joined the séances of Uncle Helmuth's spiritist community, the New Star, every Saturday evening: a lofty gentleman in the beyond, I was told, taking care of my dead mother there, hence astrally, they were to her what my various uncles had been when she was alive; however, he was far more severe, more serious-minded, more draconian. With faces stricken lifeless by shock, Uncle Helmuth and Aunt Hertha informed me of his disappointment at my conduct, which he observed very carefully; they scarcely dared hint at his threats of punishment—just the usual, terse "You'll see . . .")—

The pen-and-paper homunculus whom I had given the name Schwab has taken possession of not only my conscience but also, thereby, my book—

but not quite without a deeper meaning. That is: not just for art's sake: Schwab is not merely a personification of my literary conscience: he *is*. He *is* S., my dead friend. J. S. wants to materialize through him, in him. Fine! I am supposed to write J. S. into life as Johannes Schwab. Of course, I must warn you, my honored dead friend J. S., this is no longer you: *Schwab* is here on the paper. *He* is living his own life here. I cannot do anything for you now. *He* will have your features, your powerful body; *he* will move like you, carry himself like you, speak like you, speak thoughts you could have uttered, reveal feelings you could have felt; *he* will act like you, for he has, I repeat, your unhappy genius, your standoffish character, your forcefulness and your weakness, your whims, crotchets and eccentricities, and ultimately your destiny as well: *he* will have died *because he could not write his book.* But he will be *he*, not you.

Nothing can be done about it, alas. He is already here, on these pages, already living in them—and in a sharply outlined figure at that. If I had written down nothing but his name, *Johannes Schwab,* he would already be quite unmistakably himself. He no longer escapes himself—and I could not help him escape. No man escapes himself if he has forfeited himself to the demonic world of words on the page, whether alive or deceased.

I do not doubt that you, friend S., in that world beyond where you are now, are among the free, the mighty, the illuminated (although it strikes me as a bit suspicious that you feel such a vehement urge to cross back over the threshold, so vehement that already you virtually have a foot in the door, so that I cannot shut you out). But there's not much left for you to do here. Someone else has taken your place. And here (I am obliged to point this out to you), here we must apply the harsh biblical verse: FOR UNTO EVERY ONE THAT HATH SHALL BE GIVEN... BUT FROM HIM THAT HATH NOT SHALL BE TAKEN EVEN THAT WHICH HE HATH.

So I ask your forgiveness. I, for my part, must now join Schwab. For I too am in these pages: I am already placed upon them, pasted on them, and will appear all the more vivid and diversely colored the more I pull away from them—*into One who writes me...*

Here too I wish to be of assistance. My wanted poster is quickly written.

I write. But I lack the so-called demonic element one expects of a writer. I am (despite Aunt Selma's occasional doubts) a good, softhearted, anyway banal person. I love children, dogs, cats, fresh milk, the moon in the evening sky, my friends (Schwab and Nagel). I of course do not love myself. I find myself extremely suspect.

I hate my lie of a life. The grand hopes and good intentions I left unrealized because I was supposedly summoned to some greater fulfillment—I would have left them unrealized anyway. I'm a miserable screenwriter, not because I have the zeitgeistian task of writing the great novel of the twentieth century but simply because I am indolent, negligent, apathetic, easily bought. My book is an excuse. The years I have squandered on it—I would have squandered them anyway. The people I have disappointed because of it, the women I have exploited, deceiving and deserting them, my son whom I have frustrated—I would have exploited, disappointed, deceived, deserted, and frustrated them anyway. The shameful junk I have written for my piglets to scrape out a meager living with partridge and Mouton Rothschild—I would have written it anyway.

For I have this phlegm in me and I would have coughed it out in one way or another—if possible ardently believing that it was a message of salvation.

Nevertheless, I'm no monster, no freak. No splendid malformation like a medieval curse. Nothing to put me on the level of dwarfs, bearded ladies, Siamese twins in a sideshow. I am simply weak flesh. An average child of mankind. Though a retarded child: a child of almost fifty, constantly playing with the detritus of his life while daydreaming that one day it might be used to create a literary masterpiece.

That is what I daydream about every moment in which I'm not pursued by the nightmare of my sleep, dream it blasphemously, almost sinfully ignoring the sober experience of here and now. I sneak away from the full reality of Here and Now so as to skulk back along a stretch of the path of life and pick out a tiny, colorfully glittering splinter out of the past from the detritus, turning it back and forth in sheer delight before my inner eye: to see whether it contains the secret that is called SELF and that eludes me when I think of my SELF. Whether it isn't a piece of reality from me?...

I embrace a woman, am one with her—her mouth tastes sweetly of my saliva, I feel the warmth of my skin on her smooth limbs, I feel sensual pleasure, physical happiness concentrated to the point of painfulness—

and my thoughts wander through a day of my childhood: what was it that I lost (or won) back then? What might it mean in my book?

I sit, leaning back in the leather easy chair of an executive office, portentously splaying my cigar between my index and my sexually experienced middle finger, cognac in a snifter, leg over leg (my comically abbreviated reflection in the deep brilliance of my polished shoe tip: a towering microcephalic with elephantiasis of the outer extremities: knees like a mammoth, hands like barn doors, a newspaper advertisement of the man of success: a caricature of five-and-dime splendor). I witness another act of modern magic: the breathless voodoo rite of conjuring up money. One speaks of a film project, talks about art and means profit. A shaman's dance: The counterfeiters drum out their cant. Language foams under the strokes of their witches' brooms, sentences tangle up into serpents' nests, numbers are encrusted with the lecherous spawn of zeros, individual words bubble out from the sputum of mouths, float through the room, the air delicately traced with cigarette smoke and fragrant with secretarial secretions (a hazy stretch of surf coast: on the ribbed sand in the crumbling foam, the purple-fish aperture of a vagina), and strike out in vicious pursuit of one another: the iridescent bubble of "cultural mission" hits "box-office receipts" and both burst in a soapy flash; the "level of quality," which "absolutely must be maintained" (how? where? by whom? for what?), collides with "production costs," which tear the skin off the nothing that they and it are made of; "artistic creation," "universal human problem," and "topical issue" concatenate in a mucous cluster—and furiously the "co-production considerations" pounce upon them and shatter with them ... and all this floats over a roaring surf of blathering, waves cresting, agitating, foaming, only to vanish in the sand: a crumbling squandering of words, hissing and seething foam, seeping of mirages and phantoms ...

nevertheless, the surging, heaving emptiness brings something forth, for, mightily and magically, the totem of the Project grows, and it will both create and determine lived reality...

and meanwhile, I walk up a mountain slope near Lake Zurich, hand in hand with Dawn, and brood about what makes the nervous texture of this hour as heavy as a honeycomb—Dawn's profile against the sparse backdrop of the firs (trunks as rusty as her hair)—or the constrictions of Nature, which painfully jerks up the memory of a late-summer park somewhere between the Pruth and Dniester rivers: a park with a little pond where a frail old-fashioned boat is rotting:

Si je désire une eau d'Europe, c'est la flache
noire et froide où vers le crépuscule embaumé
un enfant accroupi plein de tristesses, lâche
un bateau frêle comme un papillon de mai—

(And Schwab, dismayed, pausing at the little Sisley in Hamburg's Kunsthalle, the almost foolishly poignant expression with which he looked at me in order to say, "There really was such a thing once: such a summer garden")

There really was. It belonged to very simple people. The man was a trolley conductor, the woman carved a lantern for us from a pumpkin, the son was my friend in times that have wafted away. There really was such a thing, this little garden, a piece of orderly nature. And I find myself in it again, the way I may have once been and no longer am (even though, or rather because, I now am only in such pictures).

I seek myself in it, madly in love with the various images of myself, a mythological caricature (damnable expression of misanthropy in the great Daumier): Narcissus as archaeologist, mirroring myself in the shards unearthed from various strata of my prehistory (when I had not yet begun to think about my book) and, in bewilderment, comparing them with the images of my later existence:

—in search of the innocence of a time when my life was still a first draft of a life, dreamed within the myth of its time—

I see my Fall and Original Sin in the reality that has sprung up around me—a betrayal of the myth of my time. I am a foundling of this myth, a latecomer to an era that had set out to dream the dream of man as a blissful inhabitant of ANTHROPOLIS but was born into the age of maggots teeming in the carcasses of cities. Through my veins runs the nostalgia for the promise of that time of beginning, and from it I draw a majesty I feel guilty about—

and that is why I have to believe I can write my book. In it, I hope to find what I no longer am and no longer have. I know I'm thereby robbing myself of the present, destroying it, so that it can become only a rotten future. The past lies before me as my future. This is no mere wordplay: it is my last innocence, and I do not want to lose it.

My book is my chaste vice. Whenever I think of it, I blush like a whore in love. When I sit down to work on my book, I don wedding garments. I slip into a different, a purer, existence. I become timid and high-strung (like Schwab, my dead friend).

In my book, I stop deceiving. I renounce my cheap (and sturdy) irony, all my tricks. I jettison my imaginative faculties (become almost proverbial in the movie business). I put aside my shrewd way of combining an accursed knack for the "depth effect" in "the art of spinning a yarn," the "interesting yet lucid architecture," and all the other legerdemain, for whose sake even so-called serious producers (not to mention the piglets) overlook my breaches of contract, my failure to meet deadlines, my constant revision of outlines, and instead go on paying me (as they say) "top fees."

Here I am humble and confess my poverty. I have nothing to offer but my bare self. And this self becomes more and more wretched with each passing day. I am no longer who I was when I began to write my book. At that time, I was rich: I lived on the dividends from my innocence. Today, I live guiltily, hand to mouth. At that time, I was able to dream, and I fed from the honey pots of fantasy. Now, I gnaw on the bare bone of reality. Whatever I suck from it merely increases my hunger.

Never in the preceding days and nights did I so ardently long for reality as at this moment. Somewhere in the marsh of my consciousness, a drifting memory had sunk to the bottom, and every so often (in the fidgety daze of overexhaustion, or after an evening of stuffing my belly, or under the new moon, or the devil knows when), the wraith-like, dissolving image of that memory rose to the surface—and it looked damn near like a corpse—

and I screamed with longing to recognize that memory. As on my first day here, in the terror that befell me when I reread the notes on Schwab, I yearned for this recognition. I wanted to have committed this murder, no matter how dreadful, cowardly, and contemptible, and no matter how shameful the reason—so long as it was true, and real. I knew I had the possibility within me. Everyone has the possibility of murder within him. But I needed reality. I needed it for my absolution. A deed, no matter how cruel and vile, can be acknowledged and admitted as a misdeed, can be regretted and expiated. But there is no absolution for the mental predisposition to be a murderer.

I needed something solid as testimony for myself. I had to be able to grasp who I was. I could no longer be merely a possibility of myself. Schwab had put a bug in my ear when he said that if he were really going to write his book, he would begin with my eyes gazing up the Seine.

He had wanted to write me before I did so myself—my cunning friend. He had wanted to beat me to the punch with *his* book, as much as he allegedly wished that I should write *my* book. But *what* had he wanted to write about me? What could he write about me? My story—what was that? The story of a checkered life. Was that my SELF? A chain of more or less loosely connected incidents. A pattern of circumstances that had produced their consequences in me. A cooperation of more or less causal processes that had led to me. What did that mean to him? What did I—my SELF—mean to him? Just what can anyone mean to anyone? He can be his brother or opponent, friend or foe, his slave or his master, his model or his horror... but those are projections, self-relations, metaphorical assimilations of the other into one's own self. In other words: fancies, figments, fictions. How does one break through the web of deceptions and truly reach the other person? Only by murdering him (or being murdered by him)? With what can one really still identify? Only with a murderer or with his victim?

It was ridiculous. Probably the closest I ever got to murdering someone was my last good-bye to Cousin Wolfgang. 1939: I was already in Romania to be a soldier myself, thus could not say good-bye to him when he was loaded onto a train to storm into the land of the Poles. In military gray, in which he had appeared a few weeks earlier, poignantly planting himself in front of me ("Well, what do you have to say now?"). But I had asked Aunt Selma to put a cluster of oak leaves in his rifle barrel (as is customary in Germany in historic hours), and, touched by my tenderness, she had obediently done so. Cousin Wolfgang took the train straight into his baptism of fire. He had no time or chance to pull the oak leaves out of the rifle barrel. He probably didn't even recall they were there. All he knew was that the train stopped, out in the open somewhere, and he was surrounded by splintering and crashing. He thus realized he was being shot at and that it was his duty to shoot back at whatever he could see with his purblind eyes. So he shot back. And since my oak-leaf cluster was stopping up his rifle, the bullet flew back out and tore the bolt off the chamber and the thumb off his right hand. A million-dollar wound. Nagel, with the sacrifice of his entire right arm, was not more thoroughly exempted from further military service.

Cousin Wolfgang was sent back to Vienna with a transport of wounded soldiers on the very next train. En route, he was bitten by a rat, which had snuck (unscheduled) into the railroad car meant to hold eight horses or forty (damaged) men. By the time he arrived in Vienna several days later, Wolfgang was dying. It was tragic, if you overlooked the comic part. But you couldn't make a murder of it.

I never told you this, I said in spirit to Schwab's spirit. Out of tact, of course. And naturally also to avoid revealing all my professional secrets. Now that you're over there in the beyond and know everything that goes on in my mind, it's no use my concealing anything. So, then, listen: I didn't want to confess to you that I wanted to keep the idea of myself as a murderer, albeit such a pathetic one, for myself. I didn't want to grant you the possibility of expanding me on a literary level. If you were to write me, then it would have to be my SELF whom you drew, not some literary fiction of me. I refused to give you this possibility of myself—like the Dollar Princess of operetta fame, who reveals nothing of her riches because she wants to be loved for her own sake and not for her money. I wanted to experience myself through you as a pure SELF—which, needless to say, is sheer nonsense, or, even worse, self-deception. The feeblemindedness of vanity. I wanted to see a representation of myself, mirrored in your beautiful envy. The admiring envy of the happily unchallenged invulnerability and sovereign frivolity of the foster child of Sir Agop Garabetian, Bully Olivera, and Uncle Ferdinand, embellished with the listening, spellbound eyes of Aunt Selma's adopted child. And my disappointment was consistent with this when I learned that the first of your notes about me used me only to describe Paris.

> *Very intense blue, now lightened by the reflection of the extraordinarily dramatic sky: announcement of the Last Judgment (describe the scale of cloud formations & illumination effects in the Paris sky: from the most transparent aquamarine—"pale-blue like your corset"—to lead-blue and lemon-yellow as in Seurat, and so forth up to the color violences of the Apocalypse). Eyes that have gazed until aching at what he sees: the river now reflecting as if polished and notched hard-edged along the quais, where the roaring lava of the cars rolls in a swift, tenacious, compact torrent that is skin-covered and streaked by a metal virtually oxidizing with spectral colors; the torrent stops at the traffic light at regular intervals, damming up there for minutes at a time, and then roaring loose again in a metallurgic vomitatio. The rows of buildings along the riverbanks have become the real quai walls, a*

makeshift dike for these evil flows which the mirroring ribbon of the river divides into two crosscurrent beds. The rows of buildings, against the catastrophic sky, seem broken, like teeth, streets of ruins; in the garrets a Golgotha of window crosses.

You see that this note is in my possession. And I am quite capable of reading it as a literary metaphor—now that I, thanks to the folder Schelmie tactfully turned over to me after your death, have been able to peer into your professional secrets; now that, thanks to your occult return, the crumbling masonry of my self-confidence has been dismantled stone by stone, and I dare not set pen to paper without first permitting you to test me, punctiliously and painstakingly. With self-tormenting pleasure, I assist you in this game. Enjoy it when you hurl my visions, intentions, ideas, emotions, into your mortar, pound them into powder, weigh them on your apothecary's scales and then drown them in aquafortis, only to shrug off coldly the result of the examination and ask me, with a disparaging wave of your hand, to get rid of the residuum:

—as if writing were primarily an act of conscience, and every sentence a touchstone of the moral person of the writer who undertakes to write that sentence down:

so that, with every line, the author's responsibility increases—not only toward the reader (whose fragile salvation might be imperiled by the slightest dishonesty of literary intention, the least impurity of form), but also toward himself:

because dealing with the magic device of words on the page unleashes not only the demons, who seize other people's lives, but also the devil, who carries off the inattentive writer himself—

The results of the self-investigation in which you so kindly help me are not encouraging. My dream is my last hope. Kindly understand this. If my dream is not telling the truth, then I am done for. I, my SELF, would not really exist. I would be in no way essentially different from any *horlà* maggot, any highway rest stop person. I would then no longer be your brother, dear Schwab. If this dream (and its dark echo during the days) is nothing but a dream, then I, my SELF, am nothing but the cluster of concepts to which so-called science wishes to reduce man, nothing but a banal object of town-and-country psychology. A man-in-the-street type, who can at best lay claim to being haunted occasionally by a man-in-the-street trauma, the ordinary aftereffect of some even more ordinary early experience, some silly, deep-seated shock from the piss-sphere. For the scientifically enlightened, of course, a keyhole to the soul, into which every degree-holding underpants inspector can insert his skeleton key in order to snap open the mechanism of the causal relationship between dick length, frustration, and manifested ideals, and to ascertain a quite normal, meaningless deformation of the psyche, which should not occasion any serious concern.

If that was the case, friend Schwab, then I could just as well lower my flag. Then I could give the chambermaid a fat tip for taking my garbage heap of papers down to the furnace. I could pack up the rest of my belongings and go to Nadine at the Crillon.

She is waiting for me there anyhow. We meet again after a year apart. "Don't say a word! I told you so, didn't I? One day, you'll vanish from my life the same way you dropped into it. No explanation is needed. It's a character trait. It was just as assured that you would come back. Sooner or later, you all disappear, and sooner or later, you all come back to me."

Tant pis pour toi, mon ange.

Incidentally, she didn't have to put this into words. She would come toward me and *offer me her lips*, un-made-up and weary with kissing—the lips of the great tragedienne in a housedress. Wordlessly, she would then walk past the splendid floral arrangements to the folding table with the Second Empire silver tray, which she drags along to every hotel and every location. There, without asking, she would mix my margarita just the way I like it (smokingly cold and strong, with a furry crust of cryptocrystalline salt around the edge of the glass). Then (without the least triumph at the feat of memory gleaming in the spiritual bath of her dark-ringed eyes) with a smile she would *offer* me the drink: the grande dame, voice muffled to boudoir level, relaxed, loftily sophisticated: "I never forget that I grew up in a slum. The important thing is that other people forget it..."

This is stated so casually, as something so plainy self-evident (or expressed mutely with the eyes, mimicry, gestures) that the knot it ties in your bowels relaxes instantly. The evocation of a child sketched by Käthe Kollwitz gracefully withdraws to the wings, clearing the stage for the present figure: the delicate woman who, by dint of unsuspected strength (and high intelligence), has managed to overcome social inequity and establish her talent—and thus her ripely mellow humanity—in a halo of radiant light bulbs.

She knows all this. She would smile knowingly. It was the prelude to what she loved most: sibling togetherness. And if this softly mournful yet courageously hopeful chamber-music prelude to intimate sibling togetherness had sounded thirty-seven times during the previous twelve months in exactly the same way (although not with a margarita but with a whiskey and soda or whiskey on the rocks, a martini, a gin and tonic, or a bullshot), with thirty-seven men who, like me, had sooner or later disappeared only to come back again after one, two, seven, ten, or eighteen years; and if it turned out the most recent guest in her life was on the stairs about to disappear or waiting in the next room in order to take off either tomorrow or the day after tomorrow or in two weeks—none of it mattered in the least:

she lived for the moment, detached from its historical context. She playacted in life as little as she did in front of the movie camera (or, earlier, on stage). She was always completely herself. In full intensity. She lived only the present situation—which was fixed in space, isolated even from the next room. She lived it whether as Mary Stuart or Phaedra, the madwoman of Chaillot, Fräulein Elsa, Ninon de Lenclos, Mother Courage, or simply Nadine Carrier, the much-tried, much-tested woman: the great tragedienne, the lover, the intellectual, the bravely enduring, the nevertheless impish.

It did not matter what author had invented the situation; it did not matter if the creator of the moment was named Racine or Kleist, Ibsen, Shaw, Anouilh, Arthur Miller, or the Good Lord, Providence or Chance. She cozied up to the scene, filled out the moment and imbued it with her presence, raising it from the stream of events, incidents, occurrences, and nailing it fast to its unique, unrepeatable presentness.

This was certainly not alien to my nature. Oh, no. If ever there was a man who saw the past as a tangle of happenings more familiar from hearsay than from personal experience, more ghostly and spectrally illusory than real, if ever there was a man who viewed the future as an ocean of vague possibilities for such happenings (and thus regarded the present as a free-floating, pliant dimension open to any myth), if ever there was such a man, then it was I. Never was I so distinctly aware of this as when faced with Nadine's highly cultivated, disarming naturalness. Thus, while I sipped my margarita (and she went to the record player to put on *our* record, the Beatles' "And I Love Her"—her memory was really fabulous!), I would have the chance to mull over the notion that every intensely lived life is veined with *betrayal:* the blood path of reality. The Arabs, in their profound way, see things rightly when they say that memory is sin.

Who is not familiar with that? Who has not held his beloved in his arms and told her in ardent or entrancedly stammering words something that, regrettably, he once (if not more often) said to someone else (and will presumably say again to a third, fourth, or fifth person): that this moment is the fulfillment of his being, and he would rather die than ever betray this uniqueness... Now, whether ten years or ten minutes lie between the confession and its repetitions alters nothing fundamental in the contradiction—nor, paradoxically, nothing in the possible (even probable) truth of this and all other assurances. Only in connection with one another will one or all the others seem like a lie. And who, if you please, will dare to make this connection? The continuity of the personality?... It was Nadine's profession to change her personality as often as her costume, and mine (when I saw myself chiefly as a writer) to carry within myself the entire gamut of possible personalities between Jesus Christ and Adolf Hitler. This was not the difficult part of the matter. The sibling intimacy of our togetherness was thoroughly genuine. ("All I want is to be close to you—do you understand?") Yes, indeed. Sure. Me too. I do by the way want something else as well, but first let's be close to each other.

It wouldn't even get on my nerves. Nadine was an artist. The gently spontaneous way she would sit down on the farthest corner of the sofa (armed with a glass: I must confess I don't know what mixed drink is her favorite), pull up her feet, and slip them into the folds of her dress (I have long since accepted circulatory deficiencies in the extremities as a hallmark of sublime femininity) would certainly have nothing aggressive about it. *Being close to each other* really meant nothing but making the moment last as long and undisturbed as possible. This was to be understood in terms of time and space, and thereby metaphysically too...

In support of the metaphysical, "our" record would be playing. Its melody, so often hummed back and forth between us in the past, was as insinuating as a suppository, and the straightforward suggestiveness of the lyrics (*she gives me everything—and tenderlihy*) would relieve us of the strain of having to bridge our closeness with spiritual emanations (technology had for once achieved its purpose!).

I could hold the glass, meanwhile drained of the margarita and licked free of its salt-crystal boa, and turn it back and forth in front of my right eye while keeping the left one shut, and I could mix my memories with the delicate rainbow waves in which the colors of Nadine's flowers dissolved behind the glass:

Memories of situations that, by means of arbitrarily drawn connections between the foregoing and the following, expose what is lived, said, and done moment by moment in the most sincere veracity as lies, deceit, betrayal. For instance:

I stand stark naked on the scrubbed planks of a grooved and dented floor in a schoolroom in Berlin-Charlottenburg, March 1942. One year earlier, with Stella's help, I slipped out of Romania (and its army). Brilliantly grasping the situation (before Stalingrad, before sacrificing her life for me), Stella advised me to volunteer for the German army, so that I would no longer be regarded as a Romanian deserter. Bureaucracy took its sweet time (a breathing spell for me). But now the time has come. A notice fluttered into my hands from the military commission, I dutifully reported, presented my papers, and was told to strip to the skin—among a pack of glum, monosyllabic, already graying draftees. They peel themselves out of gray clothes, the bloated bodies of Hans Baldung Grien, the crooked hip bones, shoulder blades, the battered, constricted rib cages of Egon Schiele. Among them, my nakedness radiates like an Apollo's. A coarse person in a veterinarian's smock has placed me against a rod with centimeter notches, screwed a sliding peg hard against my skull, measured my height, peered at my soles, into my throat and larynx, as well as deep into my anus, tugged up the foreskin from my glans, questioned me about diseases and possible complaints, then pushed me in front of a long table, where the members of the Conscription Commission sit before heaps of papers and a collective ashtray filled to the brim (with the butts of collective cigarettes that are handed from man to man like a calumet). At their center, Chief White Horse, a hoary colonel, who (if he weren't sitting) could presumably keep himself erect only with the help of his high riding boots. A terse, uncommonly snappy dialogue unfolds between him and me:

Colonel, turning to the puffy medical corps captain, who, it is painfully obvious, has been dispatched here from the reserve post in Berlin-Wedding: "... Except for a couple of fillings in the teeth, he's perfectly intact... Something you don't find anymore nowadays..." To me: "A born infantryman, my lad!..."

I, blushing: "If you will permit me, Herr Colonel..."

Colonel, unpleasantly impressed; White Horse pricks up his ears: "Yes?"

I, modest, but firm: "In Romania, I was trained as a cavalryman."

Colonel, paternally clearing his throat à la Papa Wrangel, his ears now alertly playing forward: "Oh, yes... I understand... But then the cavalry dismounted, unfortunately—"

I, trumpeting a confession: "I would like to request permission to join the paratroopers!"

Colonel White Horse, raising his head, his eyes shining, his mane waving in the wind: "Good lad; yes... officer's child, eh?"

I, simply, but loud and proud: "Yes sir, Herr Oberst. My grandfather."

Colonel, spotting a mental obstacle: "Hmmm—yes. Training takes a long time." Accepting the obstacle, increasing his tempo, intensifying his volume: "We don't want to wait that long till the Final Victory, do we?" Emphatically digging in his spurs: "And you want to be there when it comes, don't you?!"

I, wildly enthusiastic, helping with a crack of the whip: "Before then, Herr Oberst!"

Colonel (yohoho!): "Well, then, how about the tank gunners—bravest lads on God's earth!"

A splendid leap: the horse and the rider snort blithely.

I, radiant: "Thank you very much, Herr Oberst, sir!" My naked arm jerks out, exposing my underarm hair, its manliness so poignant on my adolescent body: "Heil Hitler, Herr Oberst!"

My about-face is so snappy that a thick splinter from the cauterized floor shoots into the ball of my foot. Ignoring it, I stomp smartly, back stiff and tin-soldier chest rounded and vaulting, into the next room, where, after receiving my papers, I pull the splinter out and my clothes on. I am blissfully certain that it will now take at least seven weeks for the certificate of qualification to produce its results and for the official order to be issued, and for me to submit it to the Reich Ministry of the Interior together with the other documents required for attaining citizenship in the Third Reich. My papers will then be handed to me by the postman against a receipt at my apartment (subleased) at 14 Wielandstrasse, Berlin. Whence, unfortunately, I will have moved in due order to Klein-Klützow on Lake Papenzien, in the district of Deutsch-Krone, Pomerania. Whence, after a sojourn of thirteen weeks, I will move once again, this time to Stedlinger in the Franconian Jura. Now the precarious document might have to take a further detour by way of Kienberg on the Erlaf, in the region of Scheibbs in former Lower Austria (now the Danube Gau in the Ostmark) and Illerstein near Crossen, in Neumark, Prussian Silesia. And if it then circuitously catches up with me back on Wielandstrasse before the Final Victory is won (without me), a further delay will be open to me (and this was what Stella farsightedly foresaw): in order to enter the German Wehrmacht honorably, I had to be a full-fledged citizen of Greater Germany, and in order to become one, I had to prove my pure Aryan extraction—certainly an extremely time-consuming enterprise considering that I, regrettably, cannot state for certain who my father was. Meanwhile, however, my already invalid Romanian service pass (which Stella also procured for me) certifies my voluntary registration with the German tank gunners: proof of a commitment to the German Victory, which will make everyone who checks my papers click his heels automatically and send his hand racing up to his cap visor...

"You're smiling? What's so funny?"

The wide sleeves of the dress have glided away and now she places her folded arm on the back of the sofa, propping her temple on three fingers of her hand. Her hair splendidly ruffled: light, soft, fiery (her stylist spends two hours a day on it). Her dark eyes with their blackish blue circles *rest* moistly on me.

"Nothing, darling—something silly. It has nothing to do with us." (This "us" is a hand reaching out to her, a deathbed for the small, cold bird of her own hand, mercifully arching towards her. Soon the bird will lie in it with tiny, rigid, fragile claws.) "Well, no. It does have something to do with us, insofar as we're brother and sister..." Only we can't stay that chaste, goddammit! ("*Whatever you do, don't forget that if Madame Carrier doesn't bite then we're screwed—okay?*")

Okay. That was the difficult part of the matter. For what Nadine esteemed more than anything else was sibling love. ("Why do you want to destroy that? The bond between us is so much more than sexual, isn't it?")

Exactly. If only she knew how passionately I'd love to keep things between siblings! But, alas, as a little sister, she had a penchant for precocious sophistication. The effect was humanly delightful but scarcely conducive to the smooth development of movie projects (many a poor fellow screenwriter could tell you a thing or two about that). However, if the relationship was not purely one of brother and sister, then, as they say in the business, you could get down to the nitty-gritty with Nadine Carrier. If she waxed poetic, then you had to hop into the sack without further ado. If she wanted to hop into the sack, then you could beg off, pleading work on the script. But it was I, alas, who had to make the first move.

The first move was to convince her about the material for the screenplay. It's easiest to talk about it in bed. You had no choice: the orphic melos of artistic inspiration (which would soon permeate her entire being, swell up in her into a dithyramb and become a hymn) was commenced in her uterus. And this uterus was temporarily blocked by elements alien to art. ("I have to tell you that there is someone in my life who means almost as much to me as you once did.")

This didn't necessarily mean very much; I had been permitted to learn it, and I would soon have it reconfirmed. Still, one had to be considerate of her notions of order in these matters. (Please don't push! Everyone'll get his chance! Everyone in his time! An orderly line makes it easier to take care of everyone, so if you've had your turn, then please go to the end of the line!)

The trouble was that I quite sincerely liked her. I suffered with my little sister when I raped her. The very thought of it tormented me. Her face torn back into the crackling, spraying fox hair, the face staring with large, childlike eyes into the dreadful resolution of my face, trying to understand what brought this wild, sudden change over me ("Is that really you? Tell me it isn't you!")—

the thin eyebrows rise into a gable of terror as though under a threatened whiplash, and amid unuttered words ("You can't really want *that?!*") the mouth tries to bring out a "No!" from the fear-choked throat, a "No!" that finally, since it is not granted verbal expression, forces a prematurely aged shaking of her head. The face—still anxiously investigating, the circumflex of the eyebrows awaiting a blow—begins to turn back and forth in front of me, gently and swiftly at first, like the mechanism of a fine clock, then swings out farther and farther, more and more unsteadily, teetering more and more, thereby coming closer and closer to me (hobbling on its knees, so to speak) until, rolling under a wild and desperate kiss, it suddenly buries what the lips do not wish to say ("Why do you torture me?! You know I can't refuse you!")—

a kiss with which negation virtually tries to burrow into me, whereby our lips curl over our teeth in all kinds of overlapping folds, like blotting paper loosely drawn over a roller, a kiss with which negation is minced as fine as chives under a chef's knife...

but then her head just as suddenly tilts back again, as though a karate chop had cracked it at the cervical vertebra. Her splendidly trained hair now flies out from the lunar arch of her forehead. Her mouth stays open. From her eyes, an Edvard Munch gaze breaks like a final shriek. Then the eggshell-thin, bluish-brown lids drop, form two moist, narrow slits that shimmer lasciviously from the thicket of lashes, while an unusually skillful shift of the pelvis receives the inevitable, point-blank, and her legs fold in surrender over my back...

This I had to contend with, it was part of the emotional ceremony. You don't just throw an international star over your shoulder like a shopgirl. But I couldn't suppress a certain annoyance. I was born under the sign of the Ram, my impatience is cosmically determined, given the slightest resistance I immediately turn stubborn, I have to put my skull through the wall.

(Besides, in the end it's almost ridiculous: here you are, you're staying in the same hotel—am I supposed to sit at the bar and smile at the slut who works evenings? The last time it was a girl from Würzburg who made a go of it at the Crazy Horse with a Hitler parody: pubic hair shaved to a toothbrush shape, a steel helmet perched on her bottom and finally used as a chamber pot—or something like that, anyway: she couldn't be prevailed upon to say exactly how she'd imagined it. Whatever the case, the act wasn't a success, so she went looking for her daily bread here and in the course of this search ended up in my room at three a.m. drinking whiskey, speaking to me extensively of her fatherless child, who lived with distant relatives in Rothenburg ob der Tauber, I've kept the address somewhere ...)

Maybe, I tell myself finally, Nadine is right. We struggle for equilibrium between fiction and reality. It's well known that there are situations that prove from the first glance to be inevitable. Nadine knows me well enough. She isn't so dumb that she doesn't know what is blossoming between us from the moment I called to tell her I was coming (*"Oui, c'est moi! ... bonjour, mon ange ... écoute: Serras-tu à Paris le douze?—oui, c'est un mardi—bon, j'arrive de Munich—oui, en voiture ...* will you be home that evening? Shall we say around seven o'clock? ...) If she were for any reason indisposed or if there were actually someone in her life who meant almost as much to her as I once did and wasn't yet on the verge of disappearing, then all she had to do was say so. But a "yes" to the question "Will you be home that evening?" meant "yes!", that much was indisputable.

But unfortunately with her too (even she is still very much a woman!) I had to account for the usual womanly margins. They're cut down with chitchat: "All right then—granted: I hurt you—no, of course not an abandoned lover and all that—that much is clear—All I mean is: objectively, on a personal level, I might have ... but you see, that's precisely where the misunderstanding is—I know: a year might be extreme, but I just needed to get some distance, try to understand: twelve months for a new run at things—after all, we had hit a dead end (*cul de sac*), so to speak—or rather I had, I mean: emotionally—I'm sure this is all inordinately complicated, you know me, probably a lot better than I do myself, I don't need to explain anything to you, doll ... I mean I've got Sagittarius in the ascendant, this figure aiming off into the distance, right? A lot of times you miss the tree for the forest ... plus the centaur aspect, the wanderer—no, no: it's not that you willfully wanted to bind me to you, definitely not, what frightened me far more was just this underlying—yes, sure, I'll have another if you're having one: with a touch more lime juice, please—you see, that's just it: this incredible wealth of empathy you have—it's like a creeping poison, and plus I have, if you will, trouble surrendering myself—completely, I mean ..."

But no. One shouldn't start out envisioning the worst. I wouldn't have to go so far, I hope. Everything would play out a lot more casually—maybe actually coming right out with the transparently emotionally packed cinematic offer ("It was clear you wouldn't let go of me: and so I spent twelve months with you on my mind. Here: the result is a screenplay...")

But that again meant putting the cart before the horse—with the most undesirable result. The bluestocking wouldn't have drowned in the churn of emotions, and I wouldn't be spared the rest ("I can't at all imagine how artistic collaboration is meant to be achieved without Eros.") Anyway, whatever the case: there would end up being a few hours of sweaty acrobatics before (as Wohlfart said) "the thing was in the bag"...

Hours for which I (knowing myself) would one day have to take bitter revenge...

and in spite of all that, I really did like her! I could have beaten her up. Why all this fuss?! Her performance needed no fancy dramaturgical contrivances. It played out quite like an epiphany. The effect was already in her physicality alone: her child's body, at thirty-three, not much more lacking in vigor than it might have been at thirteen. She could grow as old as a tortoise with it; she had been born as old as a stone—two or three hundred years would scarcely make any difference. With her infantile leptosomia she was just made to lie there like a drowned woman cast up on the beach, with waves smashing over her, man for man...

No, no—this was no violation. It was the ocean of eroticism in which she drowned, and which bore her light burden ashore, in order to go *beyond* her—

She could not sink into it, of course. Orgasms were denied her. But she could not help being moved, carried, will-lessly washed back and forth. She was meant to embody the female destiny, and this gave her a tragic sublimity pleasantly reduced for clever domestic use—and I could look and look until my eyes ached and see what I had done again:

The gigantic eyes in the small, wan face, blurring black on the edges, like coals in the head of a melting snowman, eyes that were so eloquent in expressing the variations on the basic anxious question ("Is that you?" "Is that really you?" "Who are you?"); the aureola of her hair, ruffling lightly yet flowing, peacefully sunset-like yet blazing ("Don't forget, I'm a witch!")...

her thin, fragile neck; the even flute melody of her clavicles; her disarmingly adolescent arms, hanging childlike from her thin shoulders (one was involuntarily tempted to see whether a pair of dragonfly wings had not grown from the shoulder blades)...

the movingly yielding melancholy of her tiny breasts like bloodhound whelps—and with them the quite powerfully forested triangle above her crotch...

then again, the parenthesis of her thighs now so poignantly clasping nothing (often, when lying on her bath towel in the swarthy sand of the Dalmatian coast while she came striding toward me after a shoot, I had seen the prettiest landscapes in the bronze-sword-shaped air space between her thighs: a clump of black cypresses over a fragment of fieldstone wall; an upside-down blue triangle of Adriatic Sea with the right-side-up white triangle of a sail; the smoke-colored silhouette of the isle of Rab)...

her dance-of-death knees; the calfless shinbones, then the surprisingly large, broad feet—bone cartilage and strings of sinews red and prominent through the white skin, so very much a déjà vu of some other pair humbly folded together under a nail—just where was that?...when was it?...That's it! An alabaster insect with yawning wing covers, skewered in an insect cabinet, lifeless in its terrible liveliness. One would have to consult Uncle Vladimir to pinpoint it zoologically...

Truly! My Supreme Piglet Wohlfahrt hit the nail on the head when he said of her: "What does she have to act for? The woman's a natural."

She was a natural at making me suffer, even her evocation of the early part of the lost half of my life (which made her a sort of mother for me), even its tasteless facsimile, produced according to the banal law of stylistic repetition. It was certainly no accident that this daughter of Pre-Raphaelites, who had ascended from a manger in Belgian coal country, rose as a star of the cinema at the very apex of the new era, when the sensitive vanguard of art consumers began to sniff out the triumphal rebirth of art nouveau. (This certainly had not been the crowning of a thespian career but an epiphanal consummation. With gentle abruptness, like the evening star, she was there, in the firmament of the screen, surrounded by the dancing and flickering of sparks. But alas, she also shared the uneasy destiny of the evening star, which soon gets lost in the magnificence of astral space...

Logically then she was also true to form from a career standpoint: always striding, ever more ethereally, over fields of asphodel towards the river Lethe... which, again, particularly suited the taste of cinema zealots whose aesthetic sense had been fashioned from the filigreed lilies and water lilies of stained glass windows in Berlin's back courtyard tenements)...

But there was no helping it. This all had to be overcome. It was part of my arrangement with the producer piglets "to be carried out at the place of destination." *The Prodigal Daughter*, a Wohlfahrt Production of Intercosmic Art Films, was at stake.

("Well, you can take my word for it, maestro, the material as such isn't at all bad—right? Of course. We still have to talk about the ending, it's not convincing, we've gotta come up with something, but I will, I will, you can count on it. Anyway, where would you be if it weren't for your pal Wohlfahrt, who had the brilliant idea of getting Nadine Carrier (though it didn't hurt that the treatment was tailored to her to the point of tactlessness), where would you artists be, I ask you, without the lightning-fast mind and vigor of the entrepreneur, the manager, the producer—if you want to be ruthless enough to use those words, I don't have anything against being called that, at any rate being called a businessman, I admit I'm one, whom you so greatly despise, not you personally, I know, you're an old hand in the business, you know the responsibility weighing on our shoulders. I'm talking about intellectuals in general. Why, they wouldn't even know where to steal their pens from if it weren't for us, with our all-inclusive production organization. And yet they imagine that we, the people who make their brainstorms

come true and also let them get a nice fat share of the money—why, they imagine that we brazenly exploit them! Let them think what they like for all I care—forget it, I don't want to discuss it anymore. But there's one thing you can't say. You can't say Wohlfahrt does not respect the mind. Please, be my witness. When the mind creates something that can be realized as something beautiful, making not only an economically important industry like the cinema blossom—have you ever looked at the statistics?—yes?—you haven't? then I advise you to do so, it will open your eyes to the situation. And with all this we independent producers give the masses the possibility to escape their dreary existence by enjoying first-class quality entertainment. That is our cultural mission, which people always use to put a noose around our necks. And yet all you have to do is mention the present case: here is a subject that's fairly alien to the general public, but it's got possibilities for artistic development. For this kind of thing, we're always here, we hold our own, which you can see once again with this project of ours, The Profitable Daughter. *Here we have a treatment that, among so many hollow nuts, makes me, Wohlfahrt, realize right away, damn it, Wohlfahrt, you can make something out of this! Put it together with some concrete possibilities, and I'm already surveying the field: who're the good distributors? which performers are great box office draws? which popularity poll do theater owners send me? Market research is the name of the game—who reacts to it like a seismograph at the slightest tremor? Wohlfahrt! Let's get cracking! Here's my offer, I say to the money guys: a subject—right?—not ideal as yet, but it's sort of got the makings of an interesting screenplay. So that's why we two are sitting here together, to develop it. Movies are teamwork. In you, we've got a writer who knows the business, your name is not unknown to the public, no one remembers the old flops, and if the distributors start bitching, I'll tell them, Let the dead bury the dead. I, Wohlfahrt, will vouch for the man and for his total cooperation with the production. In life, you've got to be able to make decisions. I'm known as a man who's willing to gamble—always on a solid artistic foundation, needless to say, that's the opening move, now we're gonna play our trump card: a lead actress who's all the rage, a European star. If you read 'Nadine Carrier' in the movie ads, then you know nothing can go wrong here. The screenplay may be pure shit, like so many of her movies, but the audiences will flock to the theater anyway. The next step is to hire the up-and-coming young director. Who's got him if not Wohlfahrt? Dennis Kopenko created a sensation in the industry with his first opus. This isn't your Grandpa's cinema. This is avant-garde. And it's not kid stuff either, with bedwetting leftist ideals. This is solid work, I can market it as a commodity. Two or three big names in the featured roles—and you've got a first-class package. Now that's a reality, not a pipe dream. The moviegoers will bite, and coproduction with a foreign country—France at the top, as usual—makes the enterprise foolproof. And if we can talk the Americans into it, then the project will gain a global dimension. The ruble has to roll, my friend, what else can it do! We all wanna live, and so do you, after all. Don't act as if the financial part of the affair doesn't concern you. I've seen your new car—damn it, you won't get that with pure intellect. I for example only spring for something like that to make the right impression. Nowadays, people like us have to know how to present ourselves—if for no other reason than to avoid intimidating those little bureaucratic shits in the government-subsidy office. Those guys wanna see prosperity, the economy's gotta advance, especially when our industry goes through hard times. The thing that convinces them is the courage of the entrepreneur. Don't give in. Attack the enemy resolutely. That's my motto. People today don't want a depression. People today want the welfare state. Make a note of it: Wohlfahrt knows his onions. The main thing is for you to know your onions too. We're fast workers. That's why I'm assigning you the job of going to Paris and convincing Madame Carrier that you've written the role of a lifetime for her. The end, as I've said, will be taken care of as soon as possible. It's got the right makings, as I've said. The woman'll see it at first sight. She wasn't born yesterday. But it's your job to make sure she doesn't turn everything upside down. The methods you use are your business. I'm just telling you not to waste even half a day. You've got to have a treatment in four weeks, ready for a screenplay, something I can hand in for a government prize. Without the 200,000 subsidy, we're screwed. I've already got Kopenko and the other artists under contract. Wohlfahrt works fast and resolute, before anyone else can grab anything. I'm no dream dancer, and I don't expect my team members to be dream dancers. The responsibility is yours. The Paris co-producers have been notified, they're not forking over one red cent without Carrier. So everything depends on your script. I've told them: What's today? Today's October 11, I said. My author's got exactly four weeks to put a first-class treatment on its feet and four more weeks for a first-class screenplay—something with which Madame Carrier can expect the hit she hasn't had for a long time and urgently needs. I'll be working here parallel with you. On November 11, my writer will deliver. It'll take the prize commission another six weeks to decide. Meanwhile, I've set up the shooting staff, the assistant director and the cameraman are already out scouting locations. I'll take care of the sets and so on right here. The studios are ready for February. The trailers'll hit smack dab into the Christmas market, and by January 1, at the latest, the first shutter on the outside shots will come down in Cannes. So get to work, comrade. I'm counting on you. Our project will rise and fall with you. You know what it'll mean—especially for you in your financial state. I don't have to point that out. I'm just reminding you that according to the contract you've just signed, your expense account is also limited to four weeks . . .*")

There was nothing I could do, alas. I had to take up the burden: along with the slow awakening of the woman drowned in the sea of senses—even though she had remained wide awake between the crescent line of her torrential hair and her eyebrows painfully drawn into a pointed bracket . . . I, my SELF, who was actually the shattered castaway on the beach—I, my SELF, the somersaulting breaker, hurled into shallow water, feebly running off her childlike body, the reflecting trail drying in the sand . . . I had to overcome it along with the gaze coming sore and dark from the wet thicket of her lashes: the gaze first seeking a hold on the ceiling and then, as though involuntarily following a transparent fiber on the retina, sliding down to me in a slanting arc and clinging to me with the anxious question "Who are you? Is that *you?*"—

together with the awful silence with which we would both reply to that question...

and finally with her kiss of reconciliation, chastely offered with corrupted lips.

I would respond to the kiss warmly and gently, humbly knowing that this moment, bursting with betrayal, would later be recognized in connection with the past and the future and might thereby become one of those rare moments of reality possessed, the memory of which inveigles us into continuing to endure life.

Still and all, this would enable me to withdraw from an ever more painful affair. I would not need to occupy myself with my book—which means, with myself or, worse, with Schwab. I wouldn't have to hide here in the Épicure any longer, could step out into the day, into the open air with an open expression, wouldn't have to wonder whether my nightmares were true or not, but rather would know that I'm not capable of murder.

But, on the other hand, if that weren't the case (and I wished with all the ardor of despair that it were not)—if it were true, and the *recognition* on the first day here when I saw the name Johannes *Schwab* in my papers delivered on what it had promised me (not just like a conjurer, who draws gold pieces from one's nose and triumphantly displays them only to make them vanish again)—if my old nightmare, last dreamed in Reims, was indeed the horrifyingly and essentially truthful reflection of a murder that I, my SELF, had undertaken and committed to the very last gasping and twitching of my victim, then I could still hope. For then I had something to tell, after all, something concerning not only me and my psychotherapist. I would have something to write about that wasn't of interest only to literati and consumers of literature deeply schooled in psychology, but absolutely everyone.

A murder, no matter how vile its motive, no matter how despicably committed, no matter with how much literary hedonism it may be grasped, goes beyond, must go beyond the private and the literary sphere. A murder (and presumably only a murder), despite all modern-day problems of interpersonal communication, establishes a relationship with the other—and indeed one that instantly becomes transcendental:

> *—for everyone carries the murderer inside himself and is simultaneously a murderer's victim. And thus the terror aroused by a murder is a primal terror, the immediate realization of the Evil that dwells in us—more fundamental, more essential, more arbitrary than all drives (and, incidentally, contained in all drives). And such a confrontation with this terrible thing in us, bloodily witnessed by a martyred victim, who I, my SELF, am, and a murderer, who I, my SELF, am, instantly raises the question of the why and the wherefore and thus of the how of creation. Why is man born with this terrible thing in him? Who created him in this way and for what purpose?*
>
> *For this reason, every street ballad about murder is actually primal history, and even the most inane crime novel (beyond the silly hunt for the murderer, who could be anyone, and not just for the sake of suspense) is a circuitous search for God, a search left to the acumen of the reader (who can draw his ultimate conclusion from the struggle between good and evil in the intellectual dual between the detective and the criminal)—*

I had dreamed my dream in Reims, on my way from Munich to Paris. For a couple of days, I tried to tell myself that I had interrupted my trip in Reims because of exhaustion. That's not true. *It* lured me there.

I like driving long stretches at night. The roads are emptier, and I'm more lonesome, more intimate with myself. I love being encapsulated in the spaceship of the car, which hums and zooms like a hornet into the glare the headlights cast ahead. This has something of the boyhood delight in concealment, in caves and grottoes—I love my cozy isolation in the big womb of night. Nowhere else—not even here, in the glow of the lamp over my papers, while Paris snores all around me—am I so autocratically isolated. In my car, I am a sovereign who detaches himself from the profane bustle of the surrounding world with a few moves of the gearshift. A bold isolationist who holds his fate in his hand and races toward it, tracking down the etiological secret of the aleatory. Anything chance may hurl at me has the character of necessity.

And I don't have to be alone if I don't want to. Sometimes, with the press of a few buttons, I invite abstract guests in: voices that speak to me in many languages, music whose sounds I pull along with me over windswept hilltops, through the ravines of black forests, past dead villages with their rows of houses that fall back as though mown down. I press another button, which cuts off my visitors, denying them entry into my spaceship. While the world around me is as silent as in the Carboniferous, I fly, I dash through its blackness: hovering in the shimmer of the dashboard lights as though I were lying in the sickle moon that cuts through the rushing clouds of an autumn night.

No, no, it certainly wasn't exhaustion that made me strike the sails of my flagship (the Dutch *Schout bij Nacht*) in Reims. Quite the contrary. The truth is so trivial that Kapudan Paschà is ashamed to write it down here: I was lusting after a woman.

I had already been in Munich. During my Hamburg days, at the start of my ignominious career as a screenwriter, after the endless, confused, sometimes dreamily bizarre, always traumatically reverberating script discussions with Stoffel & Associates, I would flee to Gisela in Whores' Alley. And now, during the last eight days of daily hot air talked away amidst cognac and cigarettes in the leather armchairs of the Intercosmic Art Films office (the piglets called such meetings "conferences"), between a thinker's brow, a smoker's cough, heartburn, and my trouser fly, I had only one wish: to lie with a woman, not to think, to feel only female skin, to smell a female, to knead female flesh; briefly and brutally to unleash latent atavisms (murder instinct, anthropophagia) and then to sink into beneficent stupor (the postcoital numbness of certain species of mice). The Chinese definition of happiness: warm, sated, dark, and sweetly drained.

Naturally, I had tried to satisfy this need. I got plastered in

Schwabing's abstract cellar gloom, in vain. I'm too alientated from the local customs; I used the wrong semaphore: my British necktie and the wretched shoulders of my jacket look antiquated, miserly, devoid of department-store reality; they serve to repel rather than attract, elicit distrust and mutual clumsiness. Language too no longer obeys me. Not even liquor can reduce it to simple communication, much less to conveying my physiological desires. Either it falls short of the target ("All I want to do is screw you, kid") or overshoots it ("You probably aren't even capable of loving").

Only once did I get my hands on something. After the bar closed and I paid a tourist-trap bill, after shouting in the street and an unpleasant scene with a policeman ("I insist on having your badge number! I'm a foreigner and I will not be spoken to in this way!"), after a bone-quaking cab ride and then a wild *Weisswurst* gorging in the din of Donisl and another taxi trip, she turned out to be a kind of biting albino rat. We wound up in a room in Harlaching that looked as if a tornado had whirled through it. She was equipped with the clitoris of a hyena, which, however, hysterically yelling, she wouldn't let anyone approach—and certainly not me. Despite a numbing quantity of whiskey from a bottle acquired at a brothel price, and despite a tumultuous rolling around in bed—which woke up the next-door neighbors and made them bang their protests against the door and the walls—any peace-bringing discharge of my neuromuscular tensions was out of the question, not to mention any appeasement of that erotic urge that wants to absorb the feminine and make it an integral component of one's own being, like the wonderful *Schistosoma haematobium*, which, a velvet-lined casket, carries its beloved all its life within itself and releases it only temporarily, to lay eggs.

The matter ended badly, of course, with a couple of resounding slaps, which did not produce any meliorating effect. On the contrary: now the neighbors were properly mobilized, and they did not take my side at all... It took me several days to repress the incident.

On the evening of the tormentingly long day that the piglets required for what they term "executing the contract"—drawing up and finally signing a document that reduces by half the agreed-upon honorarium and stipulates all kinds of loophole contingencies for further reductions—I left Munich. My car had been waiting since noon with freshly changed oil, a grease job, a full tank of gas, and the tire pressure carefully checked. Packed with my suitcases, briefcases, portfolios, and the cartons of papers for my book (I dragged them everywhere, as Nadine did her deluxe tray), the car stood ready in front of the hotel. It was a flat, low monster, like a predatory bug, and a small pack of more or less expert observers was always gathered around it. In the grouplet of scraggly-dressed young Germans (even in Gypsy garb, they manage to have something stiffly awkward about them), I was struck by the gaze of a girl: dark, beautiful, relaxed, open wide in the eternal, primal question: "*Is that you?*"

I took this gaze with me into the smoky turquoise into which the blue of the Bavarian sky had faded on this October day, gilded with autumn foliage. And now the turquoise also filled the roads with magic spaciousness. It hinted at a night frost; pale, wan, and hazy, it shimmered around the dividing and hardening contours of the neo-Gothic gables and neoclassical moldings and the baroque-capped twin church towers. My curved windshield sucked in pallid strings of light and scattered them. To the left, the massif of the railroad station, star-studded red and green, accompanied me for a while. White-waving columns of steam with capitals edged in a dawn-red blaze tumbled up into the blue, rolling with a fiery glow—technology's romantic early period, when it still had a volcanic character. On the right, tooth gaps in the line of buildings recalled the bad wartime and worse postwar time; architectural horrors of the Wilhelmine and Reconstruction eras glided past, then, while the rail strings frazzled out under black Egyptian tau symbols with emerald and ruby eyes, flattened out into suburban beer halls. A square, with a trolley shelter painted Josephine-yellow and decorated with peeling geraniums, evoked a children's-book illustration of garrison bandstand concerts. One breath farther and the *Spiegelfuge* of a church façade, carved of plaster, sprang back into the lilac-blue of shadows. On the left again, a landscape-shaping dimension of depth yawned open for an instant: a perspective bordered in black-silver-black by two canals between tree-lined avenues, shooting out straight as an arrow toward the façade of Nymphenburg Castle at its focal point, as if carried off at the wrong end of a telescope. Next, housing-development row houses and crumbling suburban villas hid behind front-yard thickets—a couple of big Technicolor gas stations . . . I turned onto the Autobahn—and the gaze of the girl whom I would never again meet hung over me like the Star of Bethlehem. But I hurried away from it.

I did it without melancholy. I was even exhilarated: faithless by blood. I love to leave cities in gathering twilight. Then I don't have to say farewell to them. I just wait for the moment when the broken light disintegrates their density, pulling them apart as though with a magical molecular expansion and thus canceling their gravity. I drive for a while into the darkening countryside. The evening is a sigh of relief. The earth is liberated of the bad dream of another wildly marauding human day. The city falls back. Gradually, the mange that it spreads along its outskirts is healed. Once I'm beyond it, the city's magnetism lets go of me; I too can breathe more freely again. Behind me, the descending night swallows up the city. It no longer exists; it was never real, only a dream: the echo of an existence I attempt to escape.

Soon, I had uncoupled myself from the evening suburban homecomers on the Autobahn, dived beneath overpasses that hissed away above me, and plunged into the denser and denser texture of evening, which, after a few precarious minutes of sharply dividing sky and land, caught them both in its veil and let them blur into each other. The huge deep-sea eyes of my diving bell were switched on. In its interior, the lights on the instrument panel were already glowing. The speedometer needle had quickly scaled past the apex of the dial and scurried down its right half now; reeling slightly, it hung over the final marks. The tachometer needle hovered calmly beyond the border span that a red segment ordered it not to cross. To my right, in the scattered, powdery glow of my lights, fields and meadows flickered like the blue-gray checkered backs of cards fanned out in the hand of a nimble-fingered player, then were swiftly raked in by the edge of my side window. To my left, like bristles under a sharp stroke, the trunks of a forest bent toward me... All this broke off, changed, jumped back and forth and up to hilly terrain in cringing, hunchbacked leaps, and then out into uncertainty; came soaring down, leveled off again, smoothed out. The sagging darkness trussed up the scattered beams of my headlights, squeezed them into two intersecting cones in the hose of the road, ripped out a hollow space, at the end of which they were swallowed by the pent-up blackness. I was hurled into the dark space and toward that place of uncertain encounters dashing ahead of me. Its harbingers were the pale tracer bullets of the dividing line, sometimes the red-glowing rectal eyes of a truck, which I signaled to before the shadowy monster loomed and towered to my right and whooshed past me... I was warned. I was holding my destiny in my hand. I was sovereign.

But I was not alone. I had invited a friend in: Schwab, who was dead now. And I chatted with him, in the manner that had always irritated him the most: in the parodying patter of cultural chitchat, into which I could insert the barbs of my malice, which had to lodge in the matters he took seriously—"—for instance, European heritage. Can you tell me why you take it so seriously? It's a sackful of fictions, that's all. With some mental hygiene, one should be able to shake it off. Sentimental values at bargain prices. Nowadays, any self-respecting person has a Biedermeier dresser in his assembly-line bungalow. Even in America. There, it's Colonial Style, of course. Very popular lately. Those fellows used to be way ahead of us, lacking a past as they did. But now they're spending their advantage on dubious antique furniture. They too are discovering their history. Not as a lived myth, you understand, as a Western, but dragging the past into presence as a sentimental recapitulation. The Western is timeless. The eternal song of civilizing man facing off against nature. The Biedermeier dresser in a vacation bungalow is barbaric booty: a souvenir plucked out of Civilization's refuse.

"The Western is life; the Biedermeier dresser a genre picture. The only use the hero in the Western has for the Biedermeier dresser is as something to block the bullets from the bad guy's revolver—that kick of his boot heel that knocked the dresser on its side is what gave the American myth its strength, its persuasive strength. Could people like us do that? What would you do if bullets started flying? You would spread out your arms and throw yourself in front of the Biedermeier dresser. Shall I confess something to you? I disgust myself. I'm sickened by the evasive way I sneak out of cities at nightfall as if from the scene of a collective infamy which I have taken part in only as an observer. As an observer and occasional thief. For I carry off a small prize. I've spirited away something of the museum exhibit, and with it I slip into the black sack of night, which draws tighter and tighter around me. I steal away with a voluptuously tickling fear in the back of my neck, a fear that may drive the sentimental value away again. I carry the city along, virtually purged of artistic invalidity: for instance, a Munich consisting of nothing but spice-card cottages, gingerbread palaces, wax-dip churches, crowding around color-splotched squares on which mushroom-cultures of parasols proliferate, among which rustic market women peddle their tiny witch brooms of soup greens. A Munich of jovial, house-proud streets, which lead to the water-lily tangles of Schwabing's art nouveau landscape garden jungle. A Munich, then, that doesn't at all exist outside my imagination, which utilizes old postcards and fairy-tale illustrations as cutouts placed in front of a totally different reality. But I imagine I have taken along its soul, the soul of a bourgeois city aired by mountain breezes and set with Hellenistic serenity in pleasing farmland, which the yellowed autumnal pages of a fin-de-siècle calendar have lent the friendly spaciousness of time of a summer resort, in the not at all petty tranquility of which the arts abound in fruitful liberty. I envisage this under the glass bell of a delicately fleecy sky, powerfully blue, with the lace of snow-covered Alpine peaks along its brim. And I visualize it for solace, when I realize I am breathing a sigh of relief to leave Munich, the real, present one, which transmits entirely different, nightmarish impressions: an unreality confusedly spun into the steel-brace network of high-rises, the display-window unreality of department stores, an unreality that, from behind the reflections of swarms of contemporaries and torrents of traffic-lava—reflections insanely reiterated as in a fly's faceted eye—offers the instrumentarium of a modern-day deification of nature: the tents, raincoats, hiking boots, sleeping bags, folding boats, snowshoes, loden coats, felt hats of the bawling backpackers:

> *Oh, just see the archer stride*
> *Over hill and dale,*
> *Bow and arrow at his side...*

"We suffer, we sensitive people, because our history runs counter to our culture... Do you see the difference between us and the Americans? I mean the difference in rank, which gave any gum-chewing GI the right to kick us in the ass with the heel of his boot when we bent over to pick up his cigarette butt? Not because we were beaten but because we had given ourselves up. Because we betrayed our dream of ANTHROPOLIS. We slip like marauders from the cities, where bulldozers are still digging out the last bombs of WWII. With full camping gear, we throw ourselves on the bosom of Mother Nature. The hero of the Western rides toward the city—the city he wants to help build, to cleanse of all evil, to turn into ANTHROPOLIS, city of mankind. These are two entirely different attitudes in the world. No wonder our city gnaws at our hearts like a black bug... We woeful heirs! We need nature in order to recover from the horror of a geometry withdrawn from life that surrounds our cultural rubble heaps. If we have sighed with relief in her bosom, if we have so rightly thrived there in the blackest night in which she has made a small feast of a few million dead, then we think again on our ancestral inheritance, on our old-fashioned heritage, on the wonders of our history. Slightly irritated because such and such of lesser artistic value has been handed down along with them. Come now: What would you think of a small act of cleansing in this regard as well: the wealth of culture straitified into art-historical eras and cleansed of all that is stylistically alien, purged of all that is stylistically held over. Thus correcting nature as well, making her developmental tendencies clearly visible, and perfecting them.

"Just think, for instance, what incredible clumsiness it took for life to alter, diminish, or add even the slightest thing in Tuscany after the blessed moment of two and a half centuries from the birth of Cimabue (c. 1240) to the death of Piero della Francesca (1492: also the year of Lorenzo the Magnificent's death). The very idea! What was historical development thinking in continuing to concern itself with it? Here, it had produced a masterpiece. Couldn't it leave it alone and turn to another region that had not yet fully flourished? Michelangelo—fine. But in Florence, he was already stylistically out of place. Far too baroque, that man, far too lush, too un-Tuscan. Rome, all right. That's his home. That was his true hometown. There he could go wild. Even at the risk of depriving Florence and the world of a wonderful tomb, he should have limited himself to Rome. It would have spared us some of the worst horrors of the nineteenth century. But certainly after him: from the seicento to the settecento (which had quite delightful results elsewhere, for example in the Veneto) they should have simply prohibited any artistic attempt in Florence. Just imagine if we had gotten control of the matter in time. What a Disneyland of cultural history Europe would have become! An Italy without the Risorgimento. The Netherlands, where after Vermeer anyone who touches a brush has his right hand chopped off. In Germany, the natural development would have been halted shortly before the Thirty Years' War (although I have to admit: Grimmelshausen was worth it). And of course, without this barbarity, all those highly gifted pastors' sons would never have turned up, those to whom your Fatherland owes such an intellectual debt—as I do my Uncle Helmuth. True, the private tutor trade would have blossomed, flourished even, it might even have produced important pupils and not just poetry and philosophy. But I am speaking of the truly plastic arts, the formative arts, pleasant to our senses and therefore truly civilizing, arts that, unlike literature, do not stir up our brains. Intellect is a precarious thing, after all. It testifies to a high aesthetic sensibility, that the old aristocracy had domestics to do their thinking for them. Be that as it may: you would know how to present this Wonderland of Europe, varnished like the color prints in the Propyläen History of

Art, neatly cleared of the refuse of cultural decline here and there, the corners swept clean of the feces of epigoni. In short, an Americanly perfected Europe: a gigantic museum, splendidly lucid in its arrangement, its inscriptions intelligible even to the semiliterate, purged of the stylistic anachronisms committed by those who are behind the times, the latecomers. Just think of the treasures of Europe's landscapes as designed here by Lorenzetti, there by Altdorfer, there again by Breughel, there by Le Lorrain, here by Caspar David Friedrich, there by Constable and Turner, here by Courbet, Corot, and Cézanne! Imagine this pleasure adorned with Piranesi ruins and crowned with hilltop towns à la Matthäus Merian, towns by Paolo Ucello, by Dürer, by Canaletto, on whose squares we are greeted by Praxiteles and Brancusi, and whose halls relieve us with frescoes by Giotto and Picasso. Gardens by Lenôtre, where we ensconce ourselves with Hanau porcelain and Gothic two-pronged forks to feast on nightingale tongues prepared according to Lucullan recipes, and to sip at our Mouton Rothschild from Cellini's crystal goblets, while behind the ornamental shrubbery, following a libretto by Herr von Hofmannsthal, a Klimt-costumed lady of the Viennese haute volée surrenders to a Böcklin faun. Is this not precisely the conception of Europe that you carry within yourself? Admit it: cultural history—that's as surprising, as frightening, as the garden of Bomarzo. No matter where you go, no matter where you turn, the monsters of arts and artists come toward you, insanely multifarious, and drive you from reality into nightmarish unreality. Perhaps you now understand what makes my film piglets so dear to me. Too much culture is harmful to mental health. Just think of the sad fate of Huysmans's des Esseintes. I, for my modest part (born under the sign of the Ram, with the Archer in my ascendant and half a dozen sputniks in my first house)—I was not made to live *à rebours*. I cannot exist in a world that I might continue rebuilding from the models salvaged from the rubble. I would rather do without the models. Probably I'm not schizophrenic enough for my cultural level. Either way I agree with Wohlfahrt: one must be able to decide in life. I don't want to sneak out of the cities of my ancestral homeland Yuropp like a marauder in a disaster zone.

Nor do I want to enter them like someone who doesn't want to see what he must be ashamed of. I don't want to shut my eyes in the suburbs, in the residential districts and principal avenues, only to open them at the Renaissance town hall, the Gothic cathedral, and the cement-propped remnants of the Roman walls. Memory is sin, you understand! Our kind are already sufficiently afflicted as it is. There are things I haven't told even you. For instance: the way the trauma of art worship was inflicted upon me at an early age, thanks to my beautiful mother, whose life was so brief, and to my aristocratic uncles, so well versed in many kinds of splendors. Starting with Uncle Ferdinand's coin collection and the countless pilgrimages to historic monuments in the hinterland of the Côte d'Azur, which at the time got me excited mainly because I was allowed to sit next to the chauffeur in Uncle Agop's Isotta Fraschini or in Uncle John's Rolls-Royce (Mama herself drove a Stutz). I would wear a little raccoon coat, a leather auto helmet, and far too large, simply enormous goggles, in which my head looked like a horsefly. But then of course came the art books lying around everywhere—of which Gobineau's *Renaissance*, in a deluxe folio edition with tissue-covered illustrations, has remained vivid in my memory. Then the magazines—including one named *La gazette du bon ton* and published by a M. de Brunhoff, the same man whose *King Babar* was to elicit my three-year-old son's first aesthetic judgment twenty-seven years later: 'It's so pretty, Daddy!'...

"By the way, the volumes of the *Gazette du bon ton* I saw as a six-year-old must have been old issues. The magazine no longer appeared in the time I am speaking of—1926. It had ceased publication in Paris in 1916 and was continued, strangely enough, in Berlin until 1919 by Flechtheim. I once found an issue in Aunt Selma's room. Thus does the cultural heritage intertwine generation with generation. It was only natural that I should fall in love with a *Vogue* fashion model...

"Last but not least, certain austere bell tones in Miss Fern's voice transmitted culture, especially when she spoke of Florence, rolling her *r* in a way that sounded like a muted drumroll. Before the war, she had looked after a little girl 'of a very noble family' there, and she always held up her charge's exemplary breeding to me. In a strange blend of desire, envy, and hatred, I was secretly and hopelessly in love with the little girl: my future anima, Dame Cultura personified.

"But things got dark after that, my friend. I spent the years of my Viennese upbringing in preparation for the raw power at the breast of Mother Nature. Twelve long years. The first four in a totally idiotic school in the Twelfth District, then eight in the dreadful obtuseness of a high school in the Thirteenth. Until Stella rescued me: taking me to the commencing summer-solstice festival of the year 1938.

"And you know: what kept me from going completely obtuse during the twelve bitter years of this apprenticeship in triviality, mere usefulness, or pure decoration (culture as a status symbol), what protected me from becoming a will-less instrument of the zeitgeist, chaff in the wind of time—it was the CITY. The city as a promise, you understand: the Jerusalem still to be built: ANTHROPOLIS...

"The promise of the city comforted me first for the loss of my mother and all the luxurious circumstances and happenstances of my previous life. Of course, I was despairing, disturbed, disoriented. But even as a child, I wasn't exactly sentimental. Despite any disquiet, I did find the change extremely interesting. I lived in a twofold awareness, a dichotomy at least as exciting as the wonderfully scary and shivery moments at home in the evening before my leap into the crib: when I eerily imagined that the wolf would now come shooting out from underneath to grab my bare legs, even though I knew there was no wolf under there.

"This, of course, with effectively exchanged emotional values. I convinced myself that the things I was told were true, and that my mother really had just gone off on a long trip from which one fine day she would return and take me home again—yet I simultaneously knew that this was nonsense: that my mother had died and the truth of her death was merely lying in wait in order to shoot out from its hiding place and pounce on me, as the paralyzing terror of reality pure and simple. But in the meantime, there were so many new and exciting things to see and to experience.

"Incidentally, I must say to their credit that my Viennese relatives made an honest effort to ease my adjustment. Uncle Helmuth very plausibly explained to me the principle of the steam engine and (I suppose because he was taken in by my precocious powers of apprehension) recommended that I read Helena Blavatsky's *Isis Unveiled*. Unfortunately, the text was beyond me; aside from a few descriptions of occult phenomena that terrified me to the marrow of my bones, it left no trace in my mind. Aunt Selma, ranging hungrily about, seized hold of my need for affection. Despite Aunt Hertha's nagging, her sour philistine lectures (prompted by a certain insecurity towards me), the liberation from Miss Fern's discipline was at first agreeable, even though I vaguely missed the support, however unjustly, like someone accustomed to a tight corset and now released from it. And Cousin Wolfgang was simply a gift from heaven: my first buddy and accomplice—also my first audience, breathlessly listening, in the dense blackness of the room we now shared; as we whispered from bed to bed, I would tell him of the glittering tumult of the carnival in Nice: the staggering, shaking, hopping, reeling, whirling dance of the giant puppets through flurries of confetti, explosions of paper streamers, and crazily screaming, teeming, frolicking masses around the slowly moving caterpillar procession of floats. Or else about the very gently swaying maze of sailboat masts in the harbor at Monte Carlo. Or the automobiles gliding along like state carriages, heavy and majestic, their wheels rolling over the Promenade des Anglais with the sound of a bandage being slowly pulled off your skin. The purple bougainvillea cascading over white terrace balustrades. The green, white, and red of the tennis court in Cap d'Antibes, feathered in palms and embedded deep in the intense blue of sky and sea, behind the magnolia boulevards and laurel hedges. And naturally also our park, in the distant land of Bessarabia (whose name sounded dappled, like a guinea hen) and the pond in the park...

"whereby I was already, if you please, animating my accounts with experiences that were not necessarily always mine (Typical! Christa would think). Besides, please do not forget: the dark bedroom that we shared for twelve years, Cousin Wolfgang and I, may have been uniformly murky at first, but on closer view, once the eyes had adjusted to the finer light values in the darkness, something shimmered through the narrow cracks between the blades of the window blinds, shimmered regularly, now brighter, now darker, now more reddish, now more bluish, casting a dim reflection on the linoleum-covered floor. This shimmer was Vienna, one of the legendary big cities (ineffably more adventurous, more variegated in its population, more confusingly tumultuous than a Mardi Gras with its frivolous fireworks), whose name had echoed in the conversations of my divers uncles whenever they brought my beautiful young mother all manner of splendors (returning conquistadors, laying gifts at the feet of their empress): dresses crustily embroidered in castle-garden-bed patterns and glittering with diamond clasps, gigantic circular boxes containing hats adorned with feathers (I believe they were called aigrettes) from ospreys and birds of paradise, diadems from Cartier, red-white-and-green eardrops (baked out of rubies, diamonds, and emeralds) from Buccellati, furs from Revillon, deliciously soft, tenderly flattering the cheeks, still dimly redolent of a sweet little animal through the hint of lily of the valley, greasily polished heavy leather bolsters from Brigg, filled with clattering, from whose throats (opened by a sensationally modern zipper) the steel-and-ivory heads of golf clubs stretched like starving nestlings, umbrellas from Hermès (their slender handles: a small forest of miniature totem poles with dog and parrot heads); simply all manner of cunning barbarities: crocodile-leather vanity case from Hies, for instance: marvelously space-efficient, filled with a multitude of objects (doubled by the mirror inside the open lid) fitting precisely into the furrows of the chamois lining and crowned with monogrammed ivory tops: perfume vials, powder boxes, cold-cream jars, soap dishes, ivory combs and brush handles, and the inevitable, never utilized manicure set, which could not lack the tiny obstetrical hook of a shoe-buttoner;

"in a word: luxury articles. I do not wish to irritate Christa with them, her aquamarine gaze is already deeply sunk in the trout-blue of your gaze in order to find out whether you share her thought: namely, that I mythologize my background as a whore's child... What I meant to say was simply this: I had been able to witness the ambassadors of the great cities lay their patterned splendors before my mother. (There was usually something for me too: a dearly loved stuffed dog named Bonzo, for instance—but let us forget these details, our chat is already overladen with them—yet on the other hand shouldn't a good novel also be a cultural-historical catalogue?) In any case, for me it had been only a matter of a time before I would visit these cities and probably even live in them. Soon, I would drive through teeming streets in Uncle Bully's Delage, be led by Miss Fern through vast parks to fountains spraying their water up to the clouds—so close that a puff of air, bewitchingly redolent of autumn leaves, fresh garden soil, gasoline, and roasted chestnuts, would carry a fine shower of the rainbow-flickering spray over me—and soon, one night, I would be in one of the luxury hotels of these cities, and could listen to the roaring surf of the streets while, with a beating heart, I tried to envision the images that would be unfurled tomorrow...

"Previously, I had, so to speak, viewed only the covers of their paperback editions, and very casually at that: with a glance, say, through a sleeping cabin window into the sooty pigeon-blue of a railroad station where, under the title (Bucharest, Budapest, Belgrade, Trieste, and so forth: *édition spéciale, bonne pour les Balkans*), red-capped (incidentally, extremely ragged) porters dragged baggage around, and the little wagon of oranges, chocolate bars, and lemonade bottles was always too far away for someone to call it over...

"and sometimes, as under a thumb cropping over the edge of a book, a brief glimpse of an open page: seen through a dueling network of struts and stays (while the train lumbered dully across a bridge), a street filled with bug-like vehicles and teeming ant-like people... and even this image had been alive with anxious promise...

"Now I was actually in one of the truly big representatives of those big cities. I had not yet penetrated to where its heart, beating red and blue, seemed to glow in a melting pot—but it was really just a matter of days. I had only to step out the door (I eventually did just that, but that's another story)... in any case, I hope you understand that for the time being, I had no time to take precise stock of my losses. The world that I'd lost was still lying about me (if no longer quite intact, it could at least be found with relatively little effort)...

"But one day I would find myself walled out from that world by a neighing collective laughter. For it happened, you see, that at the local school of our district (when I was still in the same class as my Cousin Wolfgang, who was only a few months older than I and slow in his intellectual development) I was led astray by the Tempter. In contrast to Cousin Wolfgang, I was not shy. Miss Fern had taught me a kind of trusting frankness that made me unsuspicious of, albeit reserved toward, strangers. I did not hide the fact that I knew all sorts of things, that I could read and write and even chat in dainty childhood French and fluent nursery English. Vast amazement on all sides; a few of my schoolmates quickly moved away from me, while the teacher (who smelled dreadfully of old clothes), with a self-conscious grin, pressed his scraggly chin into his collar, as an intention warmly fermented beneath the Adam's apple and the diaphragm to cozen me into becoming an instrument of humiliation for my coarse schoolmates.

"It was not yet in my nature to see through such political maneuvers—that was to be the first fruit of my education—and after calling attention to myself by boldly letting the small, naked worm of my finger push out from the compost that was the mass of pupils, I presumed to announce that I could even recite a few stanzas of a rather difficult and very beautiful English poem. Very well! Permission granted. I was planted in front of the blackboard. The teacher stood by his desk with a squashed smile, embarrassed, twisting his brownish-yellow cuff. Hurling out my arm toward him, raising an accusing finger against him, I commenced:

Has God, thou fool! work'd solely for thy good,
Thy joy, thy pastime, thy attire, thy food
(now, as Miss Fern taught me, face the audience!)
Who for thy table feeds the wanton fawn,
From him has kindly spread the flow'ry lawn:
(arm and finger thrust toward the ceiling)
Is it for thee the lark ascends and sings?
(shaking my head in ecstasy)

Joy tunes his voice, joy elevates his wings.
(taking a small step forward; then somewhat softer, more intimate)
Is it for thee the linnet pours his throat?
Loves of his own and raptures swell the note.
(again addressing the teacher, firm)
The bounding steed you pompously bestride
Shares with his lord the pleasure and the pride.
(thundering)
Is thine alone the seed that strews the plain?
The birds of heaven shall vindicate their grain.
(again to the audience)
Thine the full harvest of the golden year?
Pars pays, and justly, the deserving steer:
(proclaiming)
The hog that ploughs not, nor obeys thy call
Lives on the labours of this lord of all.

"Well, that was it. As I stood there, highly satisfied—Miss Fern would have praised me for an excellent recitation—there was silence. But then it broke loose. It began with one of the little friends with whom I was destined to sail out into the blue ocean of cheerful knowledge: an uncontrollable splutter emerged from his snot-clogged nostrils—and that was the signal for a collective discharge. They erupted. They howled and bawled with laughter. They doubled up, rolled over one another, curled up and through one another, pissed in their pants in fits of vulgar orgasm... and here I must try to be very clear in describing what this laughter produced in me. It will instantly put you on the wrong track if I tell you that my first emotion was erotic pleasure—yes indeed; I made the acquaintance of a feeling I had never known before, something that I now can name: mortification.

"And this was also (aside, naturally, from my Freudian lascivity as an infant, and so on) my first erotic stirring; more precisely: it intimately involved my first conscious erotic stirring... but don't be so foolish as to let out an 'Aha!' (uttered with pleasurably closed eyes and leaving an aftertaste)—This delight, I tell you, was transcendental...

You can believe me: I have since relived those moments thousands of times: I have had every chance for conscientious analysis. In the foreground—inundating me with a hot wave of blood—was: mortification. Behind it, something else opened up, and there the erotic budded. But needless to say, at the time I did not realize what it was. I merely sensed it. From then on, it was to remain in me as a certain urge, however ineffable.

"The connection between it and the yowling and neighing of my little schoolmates was as distant as that between, say, a cyclone and a solar flare. Sure, it had an immediate and painful effect. I saw the shaking and rolling of the little shorn skulls, the obscenely gaping mouth-caverns and red ears dissolving into a rainbow-sparkling radiance in a monstrance of tears, heard their roar through a sharp droning in my ears, tickled by a sobbing from my throat. Nevertheless, this was, so to speak, a straightforward matter: it erected the wall that separated me once and for all from any kind of fellowship, barricaded me outside the much-lauded community in which the others lived so well, so self-complacently. I, for my little part, was now assigned my destined place. I felt as lonesome and abandoned as the ace of spades in the hollow of a not yet apperceived recognition. And I was mockingly watched by the eyes of that model Florentine girl whom Miss Fern had planted as an anima in my soul... and my hatred of her moved into my dear endocrine glands and settled there for all time. Hatred: the "measuring emotion," as Stella so accurately put it. I knew that I would get my revenge. Understand me: Not on the dolts who laughed at me. They were already forgiven, for they knew not what they did. I wanted to take revenge on myself—revenge for the unforgiveable foolishness of my innocence.

"And that is why, dearest friend, this humiliating early experience regrettably did not have an edifying poetic consequence. I did not tarry in majestic isolation, filling the hollow of a not yet apperceived recognition with zealous study, safeguarding the dangerous terrain of the emotional world with solid knowledge—like for example you, honored friend, or like Cousin Wolfgang surprisingly enough on one fine day (which sadly Providence didn't allow him to survive long either).

"No, for me that Arcadian land of culture has always been a steppe, in which I roam hungrily amidst the rubble of lost realities and howl at the moon in the cold leftover fire pits of departed nomads: still in the hollow of a not apperceived recognition, do you understand?... And even that just the core hidden in my being (but then I don't have to tell you that): My vital self deserted with flying colors and joined the ruffians. For even though the laughter of my tormentors had irrevocably barred me from their community, I became the leader of their brutality. For twelve long years, I was the conductor of their collective baseness. Whenever anyone more finely textured, helpless, apparently awkward wandered into the common lowlands and stimulated the collective mirth, it was I who sounded the alarm with a first splutter from snot-clogged nostrils and thus gave the signal for a frenetic collective invitation.

"Only once did I reveal on what side I really stood. I have to beg for your kindly patience in this trial too, or my early experience will not enjoy the counterpoint that life manages to arrange so well. I'll keep it brief: A few years later, Cousin Wolfgang's educational path had already separated from mine. Uncle Helmuth's explanation of the principle of the steam engine had not found the same swift grasp in him as in me; he was considered backward in many respects, anyhow, and so they decided to give him a humanistic education and me a more scientific one. I was thus well on my way towards the intellectual uniformity of Keyserling's *Chauffeurmensch* and my only cultural accomplishments were occasional cartoons (drawn clandestinely under my desk, unnoticed by the teachers). They were accurate, mordant caricatures, and so successful that the fame of my genius reached the upperclassmen.

"A pupil named Czerwenka (isn't it odd what trivial details stick in the mind?) was having certain difficulties in keeping up with his class and lacked even halfway decent marks in just about every subject. He turned to me with a request initiated with a poke in the ribs: Could I prepare a drawing on the theme of "summer," a homework assignment, which he could hand in as his own?

"Why not? I even enjoyed the idea. Asking a few questions off the point, I took Czerwenka's intellectual measurements and gazed at his thick face and ink-stained (incidentally, conspicuously small, effeminate) hands in order to fathom his psychology. In the very next class (descriptive geometry), I drew a picture of Summer such as might presumably be reflected in Czerwenka's innermost being: a canal shore with the exposed innards of a gas plant in the background—everything shaped roller-like, a kind of cyclopean cylinderism—and in the foreground, a group of sphere-headed bathers, sinking elephant legs and barrel torsos into the sluggish water. Thick, sure contours—you would have recognized a talented imitation of Léger.

"Czerwenka was most satisfied. This was precisely what he wanted and would have put on paper, but, alas, he had no knack for expressing himself with a pencil. The drawing teacher seemed to know this too. He told Czerwenka point-blank that the drawing could not be his. Who had done it for him? Czerwenka, cornered, gave him my name. 'I don't believe you!' said the drawing teacher and sent for me. The drawing teacher was a gangly, jittery, rather young man who, it was rumored, had an artistic private life: he was counted among the talents of the Viennese Secession, was honorably represented with dynamic pen-and-ink drawings in its annual exhibits, and taught at our school only out of sheer artistic destitution. His indifference to our achievements seemed to confirm this gossip about him. As for me, I had always used his classes to do my homework for the next few classes, where, in turn, I pursued my drawing activities. He had noticed this and had shrugged, with that scornful disgust that is the final weapon of an impotent teacher against the ringleader of class perfidy.

"For the first time, I stood before him face to face. 'Did you draw this?' he asked, holding the drawing out to me amid the tense silence of the upperclassmen. Czerwenka morosely nodded toward me, his eyes downcast. So I said, 'Yes.' The drawing teacher pushed a piece of chalk into my hand, pointed first at the plaster model of a flayed muscleman bending an imaginary bow in an unrealistic lunge, then at the chalkboard, and said, 'Copy that!'

"I began at the nape of the skinned bow-bender and with one stroke drew the S of the back line down to the corded nodules of his buttock musculature and along the thigh, the back of the knee, the calf, to the heel—I got no farther. For the drawing teacher ripped the chalk out of my hand, peered at me wildly under the tangled shock of hair on his forehead, sized me up and down, and said, 'You bastard!' Stomping back to his desk and tossing the chalk into the dusty cardboard box at the blackboard, he muttered, as though to himself (but so loudly that everyone could hear), 'And someone like this is vegetating in this idiotic school!' Before reaching his desk, he turned back to me and shouted, 'Tell your parents they're morons—morons and criminals! Tell them that I said so. My name is Weidenreich—Leopold Weidenreich. Go on—get the hell back to your class!'

"An artistic temperament. Imagine the difficulties I would have caused him had I actually delivered his message to my foster parents. He seemed, incidentally, to have realized as much himself. Thereafter he never even deigned to glance at me, the striking Herr Weidenreich, and I remained untroubled by any effort on his part to cultivate my gift, the efflorescence of which promised so much that he could go off the deep end at the mere thought of its remaining undeveloped.

"The incident might have had no aftermath if I—yes, you see—if I had not been surrounded henceforth by an enigmatic aura—how shall I put it?—as though stamped with a mark of Cain that separated me from my classmates far more than my obscure background, my (now rather rusty) knowledge of languages, my hysterical clowning, and my bellicose quarrelsomeness. This aura rather annoyed them and turned them against me, and yet it had definite authority. A short time later, Czerwenka (six foot three and three years my senior, but now only one class away from me) advanced toward me to deliver the punches he had planned for me. I checked him with a single glance that blended grandeur and malice; in hunter's parlance, the mere glance of my eyes drew an opaque veil over his. He took off with his tail between his legs.

"Incidentally, it would be appropriate to point out here that this aura of malicious grandeur was certainly not restricted to the milieu of my school in Hietzing. For example, I can recall with clarity the time when Cousin Wolfgang (who knew nothing about this incident with the art teacher) hissed at me in venom-bloated despair, 'You and your arrogant ways—UNTO EVERY ONE THAT HATH SHALL BE GIVEN, AND HE SHALL HAVE ABUNDANCE!!!' This could have been a proud moment in my young existence—just like that other moment, when you imparted the same words to me, your mouth aglow with loving envy... It could have been one of my great moments, except that (here, as with you, and also as with Weidenreich) the mere glance from the eyes of my anima (which eyes I had meanwhile removed from Miss Fern's fading Florentine charge and inserted in various other heads attached to riper bodies) pulled an opaque veil over mine.

"But something else occurred after my being pilloried as a ridiculous bearer of culture and a somber member of the elect: I began wandering around the city. I sought the city. I played hooky, and rambled. I went on exploratory journeys through the streets of Vienna for days on end. I would come home in the evening, then, next morning, start where I had left off the previous day. My more than measly allowance went for trolley tickets. My scholastic performance declined accordingly. There were torturous scenes with Uncle Helmuth, and also with Aunt Selma, who could not bear having "her" child compare so shamefully with Hertha's child. For Cousin Wolfgang was a marvel of scholastic triumph. He was soon wearing thicker and thicker glasses, in which you saw either a gigantically magnified pupil or yourself dwarfed and topsy-turvy. The fuzz of manliness erupted prematurely on his upper lip, pimply chin, and calves. His cowhide schoolbag, with its bleak barracks aroma of cheese sandwiches and wet bathing suits, a smell that announced his return when he came up the stairs, weighed a ton from all the books he carried—pure, sheer intellect in old, thick, musty tomes. But I was roaming about Vienna. With drawn flanks and Aunt Selma's bewitched gaze. I was seeking the city in the city. With the drawn flanks of a stray cat and Aunt Selma's spell in my eyes, I sought, in Vienna, the city of humanity: ANTHROPOLIS—

"and I knew I wouldn't find it, because I was isolated from the others and I hated them. Always and everywhere, I found only the past, life already lived, striking me as livelier than present-day life. Cultural refuse. Testifying to a history that had become fiction. I sought Paradise and found that I had lost it. Eventually, I gave up running through the city and I went only to museums. Hence the bit of culture that I can display."

Chatting thus with my dead friend, I had soon covered the distance to Kehl and driven across the Rhine—once again Germany's border, not its river, as a couple of disagreeable nightwatch policemen and customs inspectors, of the "We're not really like this, we're just doing our jobs" sort, so vividly forced me to realize. I left Strasbourg and its cathedral tower rammed like a thorn in the flesh of the night as it veered to my right in the blackness behind the blue-tinged halos of arc lamps; then I once again slit open the wind-blasted nightland with the beams of my headlights.

By the time I neared Reims, the gaze of the Munich girl had bored so deep into me that I sprang a leak. I yearned for human contact.

I had driven into a rainstorm. The windshield wipers cut two tiny shiny segments out of the night, now interwoven with silver threads of rain that shot through the headlights and scattered on the hood. Watery veils enshrouded me. Beyond the roadside trees, whose branches rattled against the darkness, the landscape tossed and turned in a nightmare. Every clod of earth here was fertilized with the bone meal of two nations.

Claustrophobia overwhelmed me in my bathysphere. I wanted to feel people around me. Even if it were just through a warmly lit windowpane or through the brittle wall of artificial non-acknowledgement that diners in a restaurant raise against other diners. And so I turned off toward Reims, toward the halo over the city where the city's heart seemed to glow white as in a crucible.

But it was a cold heart. Obliquely illuminated by spotlights fixed on the surrounding houses, the cathedral stood cadaverously mute in the deserted square, wanly scattering the reflection of its charnel-house yellow into the darkness behind the shivers of rain, which had now become misty and fine. I knew a hotel somewhere close by—the one where I had once spent the night with Schwab—but I also wanted to stretch my legs after several hours of hard driving. So I parked the car, took out the essentials for overnight, locked up, and walked across the square—

and above me floated a great angel, smiling blindly into the night.

The city was dead, except for a group of three men and two women about to climb into a car at the end of a line parked along the curb. One of the men was unlocking the car door; one of the women wore a hat that recalled the style of the 1920s; its narrow brim cast a shadow over her eyes; the nose and lips underneath were well shaped. Walking past, I tried to drill my gaze into her eyes, but they were undiscernible beneath the shadow, which lay upon them like a domino mask. She turned away, saying, "*... et si tu penses qu'ils te font payer trente mille balles pour une nuit, tandis que dans le Midi tu as une très belle chambre pour quinze mille maximum ...*" (Beloved! And together we could've counted up the stars! ...)

In the hotel, which reeked of wine, like an old barrel, from basement to roof (the restaurant was already closed), I took a room, fell into bed, and dropped off instantly.

I awoke from my dream at dawn. As usual when it had taunted me, I lay paralyzed for a while until its images drifted away, one after the other. Having sucked their fill of my marrow, they slipped back into the unwatched world whence they had crept up. What lay here now was like a negative of myself: it bared black teeth at me from between white lips. I had devoured the ashes of my confidence in life. For a fragment of the instant that shattered on the threshold between dreaming and awakening (when I realized with holy terror that I had dreamed the truth and had indeed truly killed someone), I was—without illusion or delusion, without guile or ruse—*myself.* I was, in an innocent, childlike way, ME. But with the next splinter of this instant, my certainty (and ME with it) was already dissolving, and what was left of my dream was merely an echo and eventually merely the memory of an echo, like the empty after-feeling of pleasure following a night of love. And I was again what I usually am: an echo of the SELF that I had been at some time or other (a time untraceably lost in oblivion, and perhaps even then only an instant).

I wasn't awake yet, merely on the verge—that is to say, exchanging the immediate for the mediate, exchanging lived reality for words. The more consciously I awoke, the more verbal I became. Images were replaced by vocabulary. What I—my SELF—had been waned. The remaining vacuum filled up with the gruel of the effable. Filled up and became the bit player who, each morning, under my name, tackled the daily existence of a forty-nine-year-old with literary ambitions:

—in the daily betrayal of the genius in us, who is at home in the fable world of dreams: where fish have voices to speak to us, and flowers eyes to look at us, and where we, passionately open like listening children, experience ourselves in inconceivable anxiety and bliss, suffocating because of nameless guilt or fleeing from unnameable threats, rooted in the ground and turned to stone, or lightly floating over smiling lands and domed cities… and unamazed, because all wonders are natural here: the immaculate conception is taken for granted, as is the resurrection of the body after death; of all possibilities (which are realities gravid with the miracle of life here), only one never fully comes true: falsehood, because, encapsulated in itself like a glass vessel, it is always transparent as illusion, always appears as itself, simply as falsehood—until, in my awakening, the images are replaced by words, which force us into grammar and thereby back into time: where, in the unceasing decay of the present into the never-again of the past and the not-yet of the future, we become victims of a self-imposed illusion, an abstract reality that we have created and in which we soon yield, even with our souls, to the necessities enjoined upon our bodies—

and thus, pedestrians instead of flyers, girded with cant, hiking boots laced with locutions, and knapsacks full of commonplaces, we march, supposedly rational, towards our lightless destiny—

The night's poetic expression. But I was soon awake. The reality of October 12th was ready to receive me as though it were the first day of Creation.

I surprised this day when it was still embryonic. The light still had something of the sap-milk of buds. The night had not entirely defoliated; its colors had not yet fully emerged and its contours were only just becoming firm. But day's capsule was already breaking open. The objects around me celebrated their rebirth into the visible. Over the small, worn carpet in front of the bed, the lightly flowing sunshine of a French autumn day poured more and more amply, insinuating a shadow into the *sérail* motifs of the pattern, the shadow of an obscenely bent chair leg in Louis Philippe style, the chestnut-brown wood absorbing the rays and letting them blaze up on its embossments.

This, and the tenacious smell of wine, which the sharp air, penetrating through the open window, could not completely drive out from the discolored crimson rep of the curtain, sufficed to place me immediately in the here and now and to conjure up the things around me: the well-worn plush-cushion luxury of the provincial hotel room, the bright street with the two rows of (now leafless) lindens from which the first sounds of car engines would soon come, the cozy old town behind them, laced tighter and tighter in the corset of iron-concrete construction (hence shorter and shorter of breath), the still vast and broadly rolling, now autumnally fire-red wine-grape-land in which it lay... and above all this, the hard dome of a sky that grew more and more spiritual the closer I came to Paris—

Paris, damn it, Schwab!...

and instead of putting up with this as if my dream had merely changed its theme and motive (once, ages ago, this was how I had known how to live: effortlessly gliding from the reality of dreams into the unreality of days), I now frantically tried to hold on to the terror of my dream in order to wrest from it the key to the incomprehensibility of my waking existence, and in so doing, I plunged more and more hopelessly into the vortex of the verbal; I transformed image substances into notions, which instantly hijacked those images from their magical realm into logical connections, in which they lost all meaning; I got tangled up in word structures that shredded conscious experience into temporal and spatial processes; I used the polished and prepared surgical kit of concepts (*murder, disgrace, conscience*) to shoo away the reflections of what I had felt and with which it had provoked the echo of meaning.

Thus I lay awhile, immobile, enfeebled, and discouraged, still throbbing from an assault by deep fright against the center of my essence—and I was already mentally wandering again down side streets and dead ends, after myself—

I thought, for instance, Just what am I? Am I what just now so dreadfully afflicted me in my dreams? This caricature of Raskolnikov: the craven murderer who kills an old crone because she sees through his baseness? Or am I in reality not that... not completely at least... or but then again am I what is lying here and thinking about itself? The body, which is self-familiar to me with its needs and urges, its gradually commencing disintegration (which makes me love it all the more tenderly), the brain—this clown!—whose monkeyshines and escapades, conjuring tricks and acrobatic feats, I know so well, no willing, reliable, systematic worker like Cousin Wolfgang—like you, dear Schwab!—but a skillful climber of smooth walls, a nimble jumper, a good, swift diver, a fearless reconnoiterer and fabulously cunning thief?...

Naturally, I am both the one and the other and all this at once; and, beyond this, a wealth of other possibilities that could take form in certain situations... But whatever I may be, it can be uttered, it is articulable: it congeals as something shapable—

except for an ineffable remnant, which is *really* I—my SELF.

and now I ask: how much textual material does it take to select any one of the human possibilities and present it in words, clear-cut and unmistakable?

It is obvious that the tens of thousands of words in a language allow for an infinitude of combinations, enough to revive even the very finest nuance of a human existence. The great literature of the world has proven it without a doubt. So it is better to ask: *How little does it take?* If we focus on the gospels individually, we can see that each is barely the length of a brochure. Hence, for young Werther, an almost luxurious extravagance was deployed. Yet King Lear, for example: he's there in just a few dozen lines. And besides: who wants to go that high? For a normal case, all we need is a brief excerpt from Lao Tzu, and editorials, Art Buchwald, *Bambi*, and a biblical verse... What am I saying! All it takes is simply the utterance of a name or simply and plainly the little word *I*...

Thus I lay there and was soon reconstituted from chatter with myself into that which I really am.

Besides, now the day arrived in earnest. I had to go to Paris. I got out of bed and went over to the washstand to look at my face in the mirror above it. The more thoroughly I nailed down my stare, the more vacant my face became. I was able to confirm that my eyes are an intense blue (I have been told so repeatedly, and I ought to resign myself to sharing my outstanding physiognomic feature with popular depictions of the Mater Dolorosa and the Hitler Youth). But despite utmost concentration, nothing else about myself came to mind. The scouting trip through clefts and fissures left by life in my epidermis proved as abstract and fruitless as a theoretical promenade along the footpaths shown on a landscape relief map in a spa pavilion. If absolutely necessary, this man could be expected to kill, to murder, but the likelihood was neither revealed by a special sign nor excluded. I soon gave up on myself and began to shave.

The day was as bright as it had promised to be. The sidewalk glistened metallically with rainwater that had not yet evaporated, and oval drops glittered on the roofs and hoods of parked cars. The cathedral looked like an art-historical disabled veteran that Professor Sauerbruch had patched together from several disabled veterans. I went to my car and unlocked it—

and above me floated a great angel, smiling a Mona Lisa smile into the autumnal sky blue.

During the drive to Paris, I examined my dream systematically.

Earlier, whenever that nightmare had ambushed me, such efforts had proved fruitless, and this was the case again. The images could be summoned, but not the terror. I know the sequence by heart. I can run it forward and backward like a film at the editing table and linger on any detail: It is always the same giant office building, with empty corridors leading to empty hive cells, and elevators whose empty cages float up and down like bubbles in slowly boiling test tubes. Somewhere high up under the roof and deep in the basement, they change their minds and directions, rattling and rumbling through cyclopean cogwheel innards. The risen ones now sink downward, the sunken ones rise up again, and so on for all eternity: even in my dreams, I'm a shabby symbolist. It is night. I have let myself be locked in, unnoticed by the building guards, and I am lying in wait for the cleaning woman. She is gray and worn out with slaving, an old woman. I can picture her body: worm-eaten flesh hanging in four skin pouches from the leather-covered skeleton; two of the pouches dangle in front, on the monkey bars of her rib cage, two in back under the primeval pelvic bone-butterfly—a beggar costume of a body, as in medieval *danses macabres*. She covers it with slovenly old-crone clothing: coarse, urine-stained underwear beneath strata of sweat-yellowed smocks and aprons whose color has been leached out by laundry water and caustic detergents. All this fills me with violent disgust. Nausea chokes me. But I wait for her, smiling. It is a murderer's smile, *sharpened like a pencil*... And while I try to lure her to the basement under some flimsy pretext, I realize that she sees through me. She knows what I am planning to do to her. Knows that I want to silence her. Knows that I know that she was the witness to an unspeakable baseness, and that I am going to murder her for that reason.

She knows then what will happen when she steps across the threshold to the cellar into which I force her. By entering, she is the one who lures me to my crime.

So she wants to convict me: I still haven't revealed my intention and yet I am already in her hands.

Panic seizes me: only now does my vileness become manifest and grow in enormity...

I hold a coal shovel in my fist. It bears dreadful witness against me; I see it in her eyes, see *myself* in her eyes. By showing me myself, like a mirror, she forces me to admit to what I am. I have to murder her *because I am a murderer.*

I lift the shovel. I could put it down again, I could pretend I was indulging in a gross practical joke—but her eyes are relentless, they shriek out my condemnation. If I let her escape now, then I'll be done for. The first stroke hits her across the skull and smears her gray old-crone hair with brains and teeth, but does not snuff out her eyes. Now no amends can be made. Now she will merely testify the more dreadfully against me... I smash away at her in an impotent chaos of shame and pleasure and disgust. The more surely her bones break and her abominable and atrocious flesh becomes one with the tatters of her clothes, the more irrevocably I become one with myself; the more terrible is the truth that she has recognized in me...

And here my horror bursts through the dream. I know that I am just dreaming all this—and when I flee into awakening, I am attacked by *recognition:* I know that this once really happened.

And I have thereby lost it. Only its echo resounds in me.

I drove through one of those blue-and-gold autumn days that make us believe that the world of children's picture books still exists. That we are capable of restoring this world. Somewhere in the countryside, where the high trees are reflected in a small pond at the edge of the fields, beyond which distant mountains stand blue, and where we shall all settle someday when we have had success in life and the condition of our coronary arteries has not yet forced us to live near a hospital: in some village that has remained as true to nature as possible, and that the influx of movie people and hit songwriters has preserved from violation by modern barbarity and refurbished with rustic authenticity...where the world shall once again be as it was in our childhood, though autumnally mellowed, wisely purged, days following one another as full and pure as the vesper bell tolling.

Days of the harvest of life, in which the plain and simple things are gathered in, the things we take for granted. In the morning, the rooster on his command hill of dung greets the sun with the saber blade of his crowing, the barnyard dog stretches with a wagging tail, the ducks quack their way to the pond with wiggling asses. Noon light dapples the fieldstone pavement under the lime trees by the barn, the windowpanes reflect the rusty foliage of the walnut tree in the blue of the sky with its cumulus cloudlets, and the silvery threads of Indian summer drift over the fields. Behind the violet of the faraway mountain range, the evening kindles a cold glow, over which the bell of heaven tolls sootily. The lime trees swish, the cows moo in the byre, the farmhand leads Farmer Brown's horse to the blacksmith—

Whose cock was all rectangular,
But love showed him a guile.
He stuck it in a vise to file
It smooth into a cylinder.

That is the goal of our hard labor. This beckons as a reward for an upright life of crookedness—it already beckons to me; I feel I can grasp it. A movie starring Nadine Carrier could not possibly fail. A movie that has not bombed is bound to pull the next one after it. So: three solid scripts for Madame Carrier (if possible with a percentage of the gross), and everything would be hunky-dory. You can get a small farm in cider country: very easy what with the rural exodus; they're a dime a dozen. And all my sins would be forgiven. There'd be a house for my son, and he could say, "This is *our* house." Maybe Christa would come back to us. The old woman of my dreams would be killed off and all the dead would stay dead. I'd finally have peace and quiet to write my book—

MY BOOK

the book that bears witness to being a human being in this era—a breathtaking success!!!

the highest-sales-storming, best-seller-list-peak-surpassing sensation!!!

A BOOK WRITTEN BY THE CONSCIENCE
OF OUR RACE!!!
FANFARE!!!

and the smashing of cymbals sends a powdering of ten thousand white doves like confetti into the air—

and rolling and foaming out of the seething of the boundless crowd emerges the mighty back of the whale

EXCITEMENT

and sends after the swarming of the doves the skyward fountain of

JUBILATION

the upward proliferating atomic mushroom which tears out its stem together with the root fibers of uptossed

caps coifs papakhas
hats shakos
bonnets képis
hoods
berets

while the whale EXCITEMENT powerfully rolls over on the ball bearings of its back, into the deep again

so that the whirlpool crater of its suction
wreathes into

APPLAUSE

in a swelling surge that sends the phonometer into the high numbers way over the red borderline of frequencies audible to the human ear

and the crowd gapes open in the wedge-blare of trumpets

!!!CLEAR THE WAY!!!

for
in the surging of red flags
it comes zooming along,
the troika
of the

ZEITGEIST

drawn by the three stallions

ALBERT EINSTEIN
SIGMUND FREUD
and
KARL MARX
!!!THREE GERMANS!!!

who have carried the mind of the West beyond the Gobi Desert all the way to the Middle Kingdom—

The children's choirs sing:

Lao-tse
Mao-tse
sock them in the snout-tse
smash them in their kissers free
give it to them one two three!

!!!THREE GERMAN JEWS!!!

so that the Protocols of the Elders of Zion may be realized by the chosen people within the chosen people

The Kyffhäuser a cappella chorus sings:

Yankee doodle
Flirty Gerty
sighing for a Jewish noodle
Gerty is a pastor's daughter,
never does the things she oughter.

and over all their silver-haired evangelist heads (Einstein silver above; Freud below; Marx all around), they wield a banner saying

ARISTIDES

—an evening star in the firmament of the waning novel—

!!! !!! !!! !!! !!!

(in the microphone, the breathless voice of the blurb writer: "... with his brilliant style, which reflects reality in a thousand facets, a style oscillating between crystalline hardness and rubbery flexibility, ironical, often even parodistic, then again as simple as biblical prose, yet utterly precise, always superbly precise, this panchaotic synoptist grasps the panorama of the present day as Bismarck once grabbed his king by the scabbard, virtually clutching, as it were, the reader's sense of human responsibility by the moral balls...")

and

SILENCE

so that you can hear a pin drop: the one with which the President of the Republic of VIELLE FRANCE is about to stick the Grand Cross of the Legion of Honor on the brilliant publisher's breast (the pin has slipped against the hard-currency-filled wallet in the pocket of his philistine lounge suit: M. Malraux hands him another)—

while the honorary members of the Comédie Française playing the roles of the latest Nobel Prize laureates (Ghana, Lapland, Monaco, San Salvador, Central Vietnam, Honduras, German Democratic Republic, Holland, Tibet, Indonesia, Panama, Switzerland) spray a triple salvo of ink with their Parker fountain pens

in honor of the first

STATELESS MAN

ever to be accepted into the Olympus of moralistically vitamin-rich, socially redeeming, full-calorie literature (whispering in the audience: "*Mais qu'est-ce-que c'est qu'un apatride?*"—"*Quoi? Tu connais pas ta mythologie? Ce que tu peux être con! Ce sont eux qui bouffent leurs enfants. Tu n'en as pas entendu parler?*")

but then

a bard's mane swings:

SIR JOHN LENNON

of the

BEATLES

and the eardrum-splitting whistling of bats originates with the sulfur-yellow hell of epoch-making puberty—

and while it is filled with thrills from the first zap of an electric guitar

the white elephant comes swaying along on pneumatically pounding rubber soles

his name is

BALLYHOO

and the question mark of his trunk carries a board on which is written:

QUO VADIS WESTERN WORLD?

and he rolls along in the guitar's sweet vibes (which are followed by the shrill voices of a hundred thousand bats) and he is fantastically beautiful:

In each of his rubber joints, stamped into his bark-skin-like thumb prints of titan gangsters, ten times a hundred Negro boxers roll their shoulders;

in each of his steps, shuffling with the sole-pressure of ten times a thousand atmospheres, ten thousand Puerto Rican boogie-woogie dancers swing their chicks so hard that they petrify into body-halos like the divine whores of Angkor Wat;

in the swaying of his fullness, directed by the Cuban cigars of five times fifty-five Wall Street tycoons, the opulent hips of ten times a thousand batter-battened Aunt Jemimas—

we now all sing:

bigbig is BALLYHOO and beautiful:

his toenails, elegantly clipped like the gateway arches of Kairoan and as red as the flesh of the Persian Revlon Melon, are the shields behind which thousands of wishful fantasies feel safe; his forehead, wisdom-buckling up to the bare skull, like that of Socrates, but flat, narrow, and domineering beneath it, like a Florentine coat of arms, is, like the southern firmament, strewn with myriads of pearls of the HONDA breed; from the meager wreath of his white eyelashes, TWIGGY'S peacock eyes peer, gold dust–powdered; of his mighty tusks (their ivory is milky like DAUM glass, they are curved into lunar sickles like the papyrus barks in which the pharaohs had themselves rowed through the indigo velvet of nights in the Valley of the Nile), the left one is encrusted with amaranths and is known as LIBERTY, the right one inlaid with an ivy tangle of green copper and known as TIFFANY: they carry us through the fragrances of NEWMOWNHAY; the gentle palm-frond fanning of his ears blows ten times ten million posters into the pagoda of the sails of the fully rigged ship VOGUE; on his back, as tremendous as the snowy flanks of the Himalayas, tassled like a cardinal's hat in the red braid of the fashion fiber COCO CHANEL, sways the all-purpose object

PANDORA

(a female torso in segments made of LALIQUE that can contract telescopically and may be used as a dresser, a dummy, or an anima)

and around him the mannequins stand like coral branches from whose twigs chains hang like spider webs in which the gold beetles of the jewels are caught; dreamy, the tenches of the most delicate lingerie swim back and forth among them; like frost, like mold, elegant furs are draped over them; in the breathing of beauty sleep, their shampooed hair floods in slow-motion rhythm...

and BALLYHOO hurls the sign that says:

QUO VADIS WESTERN WORLD?

far behind himself into the ecstatically yelling mob (whoever catches it can soon wed the giant SUCCESS) and stretches his trunk out into a greeting, blessing, trailblazing erection

and lifts it steep and shoots out from the gigantic exhaust pipe, high into the sky (where even the lightning rod of the Empire State Building no longer scrapes them), the stream of

PAPER

with which ten thousand breathlessly chaff-chopping rotary presses incessantly feed him:

shoots their roaring torrent all the way up to the cirrus cloudlets sailing in the icy wind of the stratosphere, so as to fan out featherily with them over the continents

and descend like manna over Manhattan
and Adelaide, Athara, and Agrigento
and Bissau, Berne, and Basra
and Chuch'i, Charleroi, and Coventry
and Delhi, Diredawa, and Dar es Salaam
and Elk Point, Etumba, and Elberfeld
and Florence, Fukushima, and Fort Knox
and Gombe, Galveston, and Georgetown
and Hebron, Hoboken, and Hyderabad
and Inverness, Isalmi, and Izmir

and Jawhar, Jiggalong, and Jurf ed Deraswish
and Korsör, Kimberley, and Keflavik
and London, Linz, and Little Rock
and Madras, Montevideo, and Mandalay
and Natal, Nashville, and New Orleans
and Oklahoma, Olasvik, and Oallam
and Penang, Pittsburgh, and Pucallpa
and Quebec and there aren't many more Q's
and Reggane, and Rome, and Riobamba
and Surabaya, Salem, Sfax, St. Pölten, and St. Louis,
Tampico, Tocca, and Tamalameque
Ulm, Udine, and Ullapool,
Vancouver, Västmanland, and Viroflay,
Waipio, Westchester, and Winnipeg,
Xanthi, Xique-Xique, Xaparais
Ypern, which just about does it,
and Zofingen, Zenit, and Zaragoza—

—read it today in the *Times Literary Supplement*, the sensational computer prediction of the unique success of the book!!!!

The machine, data-fed by a committee of market researchers under the supervision of Mary McCarthy, draws the ascending curve of the dizzying edition-record-breaker

seventy-seven times at the top of the Book-of-the-Month Club;

the stage version running on Broadway for two years; eleven months at London's Aldwych Theatre; seventeen full weeks at the Comédie Française; Felsenstein is planning a production in East Berlin;

the TV version beamed by satellite *Xenia 29* from all stations in the Western hemisphere; presumably crowned by a

MAMMOTH MOVIE

A Wohlfahrt Production
of

INTERCOSMIC ART FILMS

absolutely superstar cast:
Marlene Dietrich at the soda fountain;
Frank Sinatra as caddie;

Richard Burton and Liz Taylor as Philemon and Baucis;

in all other parts:

Peter Sellers

The net receipts of the world premiere, with the presence of Princess Margaret, Lord Snowdon, Igor Stravinsky, and Jacqueline Kennedy Onassis, will go to charity (despite the thirty-six-million-dollar budget of the film);

a dance performed by the Mongoloid Ballet of the United Insane Asylums of New Jersey;

plus, as already agreed, the publisher has announced a

Comic Strip Version

even for the further diffusion of this monumental intellectual work, which is not easily accessible to people of all educational backgrounds (to be syndicated in more than one hundred and seventy-six leading dailies in fifty-eight countries simultaneously)—

!!!ATTENTION!!!

fan clubs, autograph collectors, organizers of culture conventions, cocktail-party hostesses, advertising specialists!!!

As is well known, the author, who lives in extreme isolation on his mountain farm near Gstaad (and is now on safari in East Africa), avoids any kind of publicity; requests for social events, television appearances, round-table discussions, and commercials are to be directed to the publisher. For information on background and foreground, physical statistics, skull formation, palm lines, sexual habits and proclivities, horoscope, hobbies, etc., please consult the life story penned by Bill Pepper with the personal cooperation of the author:

The Working Beast

(airtight information on all the links between biography and fiction!! The complete key to the characters, places, episodes!!! Also see the in-depth psychological study by Dr. Hertzog!!! As well as the monograph put out by the same publisher: *Aristides par lui-même! A Portrait in His Own Words*, profusely illustrated with previously unpublished material, including rare photographs of the author with Louis Armstrong, Gina Lollobrigida, Dr. Barnard of the Groote

Schur Hospital, Moshe Dayan, and many others. In paperback for only five ninety-five!!!)—

but until then, we'll live on advances, comrade! Both financially and morally (as if this weren't the same thing for Christa and associates). We are living toward a promise—

living as sheer abstractions: anticipating a future that hovers before us like the proverbial carrot before the donkey's mouth—

and thus the procession winds up without much ado. *Ferme le pot de confiture*, as Gaia would say; the audience disperses—

only you and I, brother Life-Dreamer, jog along undaunted behind ourselves: always on the same gray mount of a present that will be no different tomorrow from today; always a new day in which we await ourselves the next day; always a new loan of twenty-four hours on a property that may contain only twenty-three—

hours that we let wane by serving the piglets, pouring swill into their troughs and then consuming what they leave over for us; hours of frittering and, of course, also hours of desperate wishful thinking: fallen angels from imagination's realm—

which make the mark of Cain on our foreheads light up when the urgent pleading appears in our eyes:

> You who are entangled in the chaos of our life and fear being throttled in it—be patient for just a bit longer: we are not lying when we say:
>
> *I have only to doff my gray coat in order to be king.*
>
> And you who think you have seen through our con, you who hate us, despise us, want to shrug us off, ignore us contemptuously—just wait:
>
> *The day will come!*
>
> And you who love us—oh, do not torture us. The day will come, it will come for sure, it may come tomorrow—

End of transmission.

I drove very fast. It was a precarious morning, and my mood was as fragile as the glass-spun light in which autumn lavishly wastes its colors: postdiluvial, a rainbow across gurgling water. I floated above it, kept my sensoria under a steady, gentle pressure like that of my sole on the gas pedal, the quivering of the speedometer needle, and the dials of the tachometer and the oil gauge.

Like these, my sensoria were, of course, ready to drop to zero as soon as I let up. I had to keep them at full speed, even if it became dangerous. Life is just a risky business; I don't cudgel my brain about what could happen if I'm doing a hundred ten and a tire bursts or a piston jams because of some worn-out valve in the bowels of my car. The results wouldn't exactly be edifying, but that's life, things like that happen, not all miracles have ceased...

Incidentally, that was an amusing notion. It could really happen—and what if it did? What if my car flew from the road at this speed, caroming back and forth like a billiard ball between the boulevard trees, and eventually boring into the plowland beyond? Wouldn't that be a godsend for my son? He could turn me into his myth (which, if I went on living, he could not, presumably, do: "My father died before he could finish his work"—that sounds nice when the father is twenty-four, less nice when he's seventy; forty-nine is the outer limit anyway)... In any case, the idea was pleasurable because of its novel-like dramatics. I saw the ruins of my vehicle, a wheel ripped from its axle, springing far into the field, reeling and fluttering around its tire like a decelerating top. The metal casing was squooshed up like a discarded piece of tinfoil (candy bar wrapper), the engine block had been shoved in, blood was oozing underneath into the peacock-blue, iridescent oil... perhaps my hand was dangling slackly from the half-shredded door, with the frame bent in like an hourglass (a jewel from Gaia's stories about the youth of her mother, the alleged Princess Jahovary: the hand she had to suspend in morbid grace over the balustrade of the box when she was taken to the opera as a girl; her governess whispering to her, "*Gabrielle, n'oubliez pas la main morte!*" and the totally different meaning of *la mano morta* in Italian: a lecherous paw in a crowd, wedging, as though accidentally, between a girl's thighs—fine: it boiled down to the same thing).

At any rate, what I imagined could actually occur a few miles down the road. Would probably occur someday, if I kept driving through the countryside in my foolish fashion. It was even bound to come; I have known my death for a long time—now I suddenly felt it very close.

I am not timorous, which is why I drove no slower than before—in fact, even faster, more daringly, passing other cars more heedlessly, taking curves more ruthlessly—but my throat did tighten:

if I died (not necessarily today or tomorrow or the day after but perhaps in a couple of weeks, in six months, in a year), then I would be dead *without having written my book*—and that seemed like eternal damnation to me—

All at once, I knew what dying meant. This was no ineluctable biological phenomenon, no final decay of an organism, its dissolution and transformation into other kinds of matter; this was the death of my soul:

my book would never exist; it would be snuffed out with me, as though it had never existed (which indeed in an absurd way might be true: it didn't in fact exist yet, of course, at least not in reality, but still actually did within me—but it would with my death lose even this actuality, not to mention its factual reality)—

And that would be as though I—my SELF—had never existed.

The evidence that I had ever been alive would forever be hidden in a dream.

Incidentally it was in my Hamburg days that I began dreaming the dream of my murder—in the first few years of my marriage to Christa at least, though it seems to me it started when I first started thinking about my book. Occasionally, the dream varied in structure. Sometimes, I had already killed the old witch, was about to bury her, and was trembling with fear at being caught; drenched with sweat, I was drudging away at forcing her unexpectedly bulky old-crone bones, and the tatters and tangle of poor woman's clothing, misbegotten flesh, brains, and blood-smeared hair, into the narrow pit I had dug with the shovel—I know they're on my trail, they're about to look for me here, they're already coming down the steps of the basement, whence I can no longer escape... Or else I had already buried the corpse; I was no longer in the basement but knew they were finding it there; she has moldered upward to bear witness against me, her carcass will expose me as her murderer—that's what she wanted, she wanted me to murder her, she descended to the basement with me wittingly, intentionally, in order to become one with my murder, instantly, at the first stroke (with which I had by no means wanted to kill her)...

I learned all this by heart long ago. I knew the consequences: the taste left in my mouth for days, the enjoyment left in my mind for days—

I have grown accustomed to living with it. It has not recurred that often—perhaps four or five times during the past nineteen years (enough for domestic use). A few days later, the hunt (for big game, so to speak) ends, making room for the everyday snares and traps: the bird-catching of lived moments (sometimes there's a parti-colored goldfinch; sometimes one begins singing; sometimes one even speaks: if I close my eyes, they whir about in my head—but the cage has holes: the ones I want to keep fly out and the others stay, even when they have died: decay with dusty plumage in the corners, piles of fusty tatters...).

for a while, something archetypal lingers marvelously within me: large, silent, indecipherable, like the stone faces on Easter Island—

then, diurnal drudgery carries me off.

Now and then, I tried to track down the origin of this dream in myself. I visualized the time, the days, that preceded it. For instance, a humdrum day one and a half or two years ago here in Paris (in the constellation of Gaia, whom I loved at that time, Venus ascending, Mercury in the first house): we lived sumptuously and with costly joys, spent our days sybaritically; bought our salmon and caviar (as well as vodka) at Petrossian, venison and fowl at Fouchon, cheeses at Marboeuf; the only arguments were about things like whether we preferred the *vins des Côtes* (Ausone) or the *vins des Graves* (Cheval

Blanc) to Saint-Émilion (and which vintage, needless to say); we agreed about Chablis (Blanchots, Les Clots, Grenouilles, and Vendésis); with trout, we particularly esteemed a Pouilly-Fumé. We drank Burgundy less often (and if so, it was Clos de la Ferrière or Clos de Bèze-Chambertin); our selection of calvados, marc, kirsch, poire, framboise, cassis, as well as cognac and Armagnac, was considerable. In short, the days began with sensual joys, sensual feasts, and ended with sensual intoxications. Our wakening in the blond pear-wood Second Empire bed was a dove-like billing and cooing (which, to be sure, usually degenerated into a wildcat mating). Then we bathed amply, voluptuously. Floris of London supplied us with bath oils, bath salts, soaps, toilet waters, potpourris; otherwise, Madame remained true to the products of the House of Guerlain; I for my part held steadfast to Knize Ten and Knize Polo; in summer, however, I loved the somewhat vulgar freshness of Tilleul from d'Orsay. Eventually, we harnessed up: *Madame très chic, très simple, assez sportive* in her Balenciaga *tailleur*, a delightful little hat, long gloves of course (in this respect, one can always rely on Hermès), the pocketbook, however, from Germaine Guérin—everything we owned, everything we used, everything we surrounded ourselves with was exquisite, unique, at least top quality (although we often came across simply enchanting finds at the Prisunic). The Rothschilds served as our model for the soundest, most unimportunately luxurious lifestyle. Madame herself is something unheard of, inimitable, *un vrai objet:* a Creole (to put it delicately), super-life-sized in every respect, especially in the physical: chocolate colored, over six feet, a live weight of one hundred fifty-two pounds. Dame Africa from the Gobelin cycle *The Continents:* tropical, fruit-proliferating, leopard-spitting Louis XIV sumptuousness. Yet Madame had the affectionate tenderness, the lily of the valley–delicate intimacy, the entrancingly alert coquetterie of the *midinette.* At the same time, she was a tremendously capable businesswoman (record industry). A lady with an executive's vitality, the precision brain of a nuclear physicist. Being a Frenchwoman, Madame was naturally a housewife in the best sense of the word, an outstanding *maîtresse de maison.* (Only the footwear left something to be desired: this was where *le côté noir* revealed itself. The niggers in Madame's family tree expressed themselves more eloquently here than in her radiant corn-golden mulatto skin.) It was sensual bliss to dress this mountain of smoked flesh in *haute couture*. Furs, for instance, came to true life on her: when she donned her sporty lynx, the packs of hounds started to bark in Rambouillet, the huntsmen blasted a view-halloo; when she wore her autumnal chinchilla, the leaves of Fontainebleau turned golden yellow; in her sable, she dashed about like a troika team. Certainly I helped Madame with her toilette. I loved this tributary rite of dressing, I loved my adoring lady's maid service (who else was supposed to do it? The cook went shopping, the chambermaid went to take a few of Madame's things to the cleaners). With transfigured eyes, I hold out Madame's lingerie (lemon-yellow frothinesses, with umbra darkening behind them). I gather up hastily scattered brassieres and laddered stockings, tuck them away out of Madame's sight. I help her into her petticoat (taking great care with the lacquered pagoda of her hair); Madame is impatient—you understand, we stayed in bed too long. As usual, Madame has precise appointments to keep; her time is money, on which I live, with the help of which I will complete my book, write a masterpiece. So we do not tarry over breakfast; I'll munch a slice of ham from the icebox later on, drink the tea she has left standing. I quickly fill her handbag—compact, lipstick, checkbook, purse, driver's license, address book, house keys, cigarette case (Fabergé), lighter (Dunhill), a small shopping list (on which I have quickly and secretly scribbled "*Je t'adore!*")—Madame is practically out of the house, I run after her, helping her into the ocelot (it'll bite me any second), I race ahead into the hallway to buzz the elevator, a kiss—"*À tout à l'heure, mon ange!*"—the scissor gate moves past her Three Magi Moor's face, closing across it like a coarse-meshed veil, then she sinks to my feet, sinks to the floor, is swallowed up; I peer into the shaft, which deepens before me, then breathing a sigh of relief I return to the apartment (it looks as though a robbery-homicide has taken place), I'm still in my bathrobe, still unshaven, from the bathroom window I can see into the courtyard, where the small fiery-red Morris reverses in an arc and then moves forward again, swings in to the *porte cochère*, and she looks up to me, waves from the car window, *très jeune, très dynamique—ah, ce que je l'aime!* (she'll soon be thirty-four, looks twenty-nine, if not younger). Filled with happiness as never before in my inconstant existence I get down to my day's work—that is, I get myself in shape for it, the important thing is to keep in the mood. If I wish to write a topical book, I must do so with sovereign composure, ironic distance, lucid insight. The dark passion of the hunger artist is antiquated. Nowadays, great literature is a business for sophisticated people, and Gaia's sublime sense of art, her connoisseur's flair, the clarity of her French mind challenge me to peak performance—to which her exotic exterior offers a wonderfully piquant contradiction, for which I dress contrapuntally, choosing the attire of Major Thompson: dark-gray, double-breasted flannel suit with discreet chalk stripes, a tough Horse Guard sit to the necktie, the feather-light hat from Lock Britishly balanced on the eyebrows, the cornflower in the lapel, an umbrella rolled needle-sharp (Rumpelstiltzkin in the dandy: oh, how good that no one can tell I'm carrying a Bibliothèque nationale card in my pocket!). Thus absolved of the profane zeal of a working man, I saunter out into a Paris that fits me as snugly as my dogskin-leather gloves (a Paris teeming with *flâneurs* as perhaps the dog that supplied my glove leather once teemed with fleas).

City of idlers, city of strollers, traversed by packs of tourists, window-shoppers, suburban scouts, provincial boulevard hedonists—while the streets are boiling, boiling away energy, boiling away action, combustion-engine-driven dynamics, every kind of purposeful efficiency: a need for a higher living standard, a desire to shape the future, an economic commitment, a political commitment, an erotic commitment—every kind of greed, drive, compulsion, madness stepping on the gas, throwing the gearshift, clutching the wheel, expelled from the exhaust... The weather is delicious; dove-blue Paris has donned lemon-yellow lights, and I stroll along the avenue Foch as far as the Bois de Boulogne, circle around the pond twinkling with golden scales, study the ducks, the children, the dogs, the loving couples, wander back to the place de l'Étoile and then a bit down the Champs-Élysées (briskly,

briskly! you're getting to the age when you have to watch your form and figure!). At Faguet, on the rue Washington, I select a jar of apple, sour-cherry, or currant jelly for Gaia's breakfast table (should she ever—perhaps on a Sunday—arrange the leisure to relish it). At Fouquet, I order an aperitif and read the newspaper (there's nothing interesting in it). At noon, we meet in a substantial, intimate little restaurant known only to very (but very!) knowledgeable Parisians and not imperiled by touristry (a *blanc de veau chez Anna*, a *sôle aux champignons chez les Fils de Charpentier*). If Madame does not have one of her urgent appointments right after, we indulge in a little treat for the eyes (drop in at the Musée Camondot to look at furniture, an exhibit of illusionist designs at the Orangerie) or we run a few errands (a geode of rose quartz at a mineral dealer's on the rue Guénégaud, curtains for my study at Halard's), and then we separate—*"Allons, mon ours—ferme le pot de confiture—chacun à son boulot!"*—for she's discovered a skiffle group that's more interesting than Ken Coyler's, she wants to cut a few demos and sell them to Odéon, perhaps manage the group. I, for my part, return home to my work. It may not be the ideal hour—I work best at night or very early in the morning—but this mustn't count now, so much depends on this work, Gaia's waiting for my book, she knows it's going to be a big, significant novel, she doesn't however read German, therefore unfortunately can't follow the emergence of the masterpiece step by step, but she believes in me, she loves me for this book, is prepared to sacrifice anything for it, spoils me in order to make writing possible for me, earns the money for my sovereign equanimity, the ironic distance from myself that I must achieve, she won't hear of any other work, I only wasted my time with my scriptwriting, and got nothing in return but debts all around, she cheerfully pays them, laughingly talks me into admitting to those I wanted to keep from her, she is my muse and my Maecenas, I'd be a scoundrel to disappoint her, that would be a blow to her, a blow she could never overcome. So I have to force myself to be disciplined, to try to create (difficult as this may be on a full stomach). I rummage about in the notes, sift carefully through the existing material, work on two pages of a chapter I sketched years ago, shift it around, draw a new structural draft, clarify the situation, purify the dialogue, chew amply on my pen, pour a jigger of whiskey to fire the creative (the Dionysian!) element—it's five o'clock anyway, and what am I supposed to do? I'm no robot, a man's got days when he's in no mood for creative writing, this isn't like baking bread, you know! . . . The whiskey is excellent (Glenmorangie), I pour myself another jigger, realize I'm tired, weary, empty; the incessant enjoyment of every moment wipes me out, saps all my strength; this ought to be depicted—the sweet paralysis of an existence that is lived with all too intense enjoyment (with raised pinky finger, so to speak), unfortunately Huysmans has already done it—and I lie down on the sofa to figure out if and how this can be integrated into the theme of my novel, wake up at seven, thank goodness—I've still got a good hour (she never comes home before eight or eight-thirty) . . . I go through my manuscript from the very beginning, cross out a few pages, rewrite a few others, while the hour passes like the blink of an eye and Gaia is already whirling in (vanilla wind of exotic spice shores), freshly lacquered (she dropped in at the coiffeur), her Moor's cheeks glowing ("*Tu sais, mon ours, il fait assez froid ce soir*"). Glancing over my shoulder at the manuscript ("*Voilà! Toujours à la page treize—comme si je ne le savais pas!*" with scarcely a very fine shadow of bitterness in her voice), she must be in a good mood (thank the Lord!) and when she's in a good mood then it's a festival, it's paradise on earth: the lamb and the tiger catfighting like brother and sister, laughing, joking, nuzzling ("*Je t'ai eu, salaud: tu n'as pas travaillé cet après-midi, tu as bu, tu as dormi et tu as rien foutu—confesse, canaille!*"), I love her, she is my sister, I don't have to lie to her ("*Je te le jure, mon amour: j'ai récrit au moins dix pages et j'en ai gagné au moins trois toutes nouvelles!*"). She asks over her shoulder how many I crossed out, she's already on her way to the bathroom, intending to warm up by jumping into hot water (Lord, preserve this house!), I follow her, perch on the edge of the tub, around the twins of her solid little breasts (the designer's name is Maillol), the hot blue water smokes boreally, an adventurously contradictory geography: an Arctic atoll in the copper light of a desert sunset. In the depths, a sunken continent lies darkly, attempts to rise: Leviathan, from which the waters cascade, telluric birth out of the boiling ocean, growing up into the rain-fecundated Earth Mother, a brown breadfuit tree with honey dripping from its branches, a stream of water runs from her throat, quickly narrowing between her breasts, catching in the pit of the navel, one drop jumps across, races over the smooth curve of her belly and flees into the black bush wedged between her powerful thighs, a rough black chalice. I wrap her in a violet bath towel (from Ernst Jünger's *Paris Diary:* "... She invited me to have a cup of chocolate—I brought her a bouquet of violets"). I rub her dry, powder her armpits with a pistachio-colored puff, kiss her solid purple-brown nipple almost accidentally (*"Ah, non—pas maintenant—arrète! Mais tu es un obsédé!"*). We change into our evening attire—lounge dress, of course; we have absolutely no intention of going out, *au diable* with Lasserre and Tour d'Argent; after all, we're not Americans, *on reste à la maison:* what France has to offer us is (beyond the bell-tolling of her great architecture, the lark jubilation of her painters, the radiantly spiritual gravity of her wines, the full artful piety of her cuisine) *la douceur du foyer*, and we enjoy the sweetness of home solemnly, this is what distinguishes us from the barbarians, from the jetting nomads, the civilized steppe-peoples who are assaulting this venerable continent like a scourge of God—we oppose them with the bulwark of an intimate knowledge, a connoisseurship, known only to the most familiar initiates, a sublime culture of specialty shopping, a trained and picky superiority. Thus culturally and politically tasked, we celebrate our sensory feasts: Madame—in her moss-green wool skirt (with a red underweave, roughly the Menzie hunting tartan), below which shine the silver buckles of her patent-leather pumps (Lobb of Paris); above she wears a lobster-colored silk blouse, a peacock-blue cashmere shawl around the shoulders (why didn't Renoir ever paint a mulatto?)—sets a low table in front of the fireplace in the salon (the staff are not put upon in the evening; they normally prepare the table in the dining room, but tonight we feel like a *petit dîner intime*): heavy English silver (late eighteenth and early nineteenth century, the bowls by Peter Storr), the Baccarat glasses dug up for us by Baalbeck from the collection of the Duc de Mouchy; because of the evening frost, we use the Russian service, a hard, reflecting, ice-colored porcelain with a blue, delicately bled—all but hoar-furred—Cyrillic pattern, and Madame lights the candles in the Empire girandoles; I (in my bottle-green velvet jacket, white spun-silk turtleneck, velvet pumps with embroidered monograms: Camfora of Capri, 1950) break my fingers on the new plastic ice tray. The choice of wines is taken care of, since there's not much more than some smoked salmon and half a cold grouse from yesterday's *déjeuner* (with Putzi Lambrino, Nicky Ravanelli, Marie-Christine de Brouilles, the last almost a bit too *yéyé* for her sixty-eight years), the problem isn't great, and we can down our first cuttingly cold vodka ("*à la tienne, ma grosse cocotte!*"). It's a pleasure to watch her toss back her head as she pours the drink down her throat, her full neck tensing, her chubby brown hand putting down the glass and reaching for the fork, and it makes me weak to see with what pleasure she pounces on the food: she skewers a piece on the fork, lifts it to the sumptuous cup-shaped blossom of her carnivorous mouth (the rich, soft flesh of smoked salmon is an especially tempting prey), the purple bulges of her lips, notched like elephant hide, spring open, peeling from the two lecherously glittering rows of teeth, which open like a trap (with the rosy reptile head of the tongue lurking in the cavern behind), the lip bulges (smooth now when stretched) gape so greedily that the gums become visible (a jagged wreath of sheer, bright flesh over the bone palisades of the teeth: the jousting collar of a cannibal heraldry), the piece of salmon hovers on the fork tines (precarious moment of predator feeding), cautiously approaching the polymorphous beast—the tongue flicks out, glues itself to the crude piece and draws it in, the teeth snap to, the lip bulges close softly and relentlessly upon the fork, which is pulled out empty. What takes place behind the lips now—they hint at it with a kneading, pressing, and stretching—must be blissfully murderous. At this moment I am all salmon: there, in the darkness, I am will-lessly tossed to and fro by the nimble tongue-reptile, minced, slimed, crushed, releasing my juices and shooting down with them into an even deeper, more abysmal darkness. A small cluck, germ of a sob, in the brown column of her throat seals my fate. Thank goodness I can identify with the next and then the following piece; I am entirely flayed, entirely raw flesh (a true-blue masochist would plunge into paroxysms in my place), but only for the duration of the salmon; the cold grouse already has something cadaverous about it—if the Haut-Brion 1923 didn't provide a flamboyant supply of blood for the pale meat, then the notion of necrophagia could spoil my appetite. A pear compote with a delicate touch of clove and a sharp shot of mango chutney restores purity, *à l'indienne*, as it were, then for coffee we move to the sofa, while in the two superimposed glass spheres of the Kona machine (freely adapted from Jakob Böhme) the mocha substance is gradually created from the first, incorporeal primal grounds. I quickly clear the table, Madame meanwhile inserts the afternoon's tape into her portable deck, the newly discovered skiffle group is dynamite, I'll soon hear how good these guys are, she pours the coffee into our cups (recently brought back from Tunisia, turban-shaped, with delightful apple-green and peach-red stripes), I fill two of our beautiful snifters with honey-hued calvados, we snuggle on the sofa. This is right, I participate physically in her professional experience, as she does (by disappointment) in mine. She presses the start button of the tape player, and the room fills with psychedelic emotion, fills with rhythmic washboard scraping and grooved drops of a vibraharp (first indolently, then alternating faster and faster and swallowed up, but then rain-showering down and drawn out by the beat into swinging wave stripes), in almost breathless syncopes the knitting needle of a flute stabs in and joins them in the ghost of an old, familiar tune—I know that, I've heard it some time or other... Under Madame's dark jungle gaze (black moon in white sky) I mull it over, strenuously listening—just what *is* that?...The melody is as ensnarled as an Irish Bible initial—and then the surface splashing brings me the name: Bach, of course, the D-minor fugue from the *Art* of the same, yes indeed, that's it; undulated with vibrations, rippled up and driven down by rhythms, Madame is proud of me, not everyone would hit on it so soon ("*Bravo, mon ours! Mais tu es malin comme un singe! Ah, ce que j'ai froid aux pieds—prends-les dans tes mains, mon petit!*"), her feet really *are* icy, I blow on them, warm them up, rub them between my palms, bed them on my chest (*et tes pieds s'endormaient dans mes mains fraternelles*), she still isn't completely satisfied with the recording, one reason for her (professional as well as personal) success is her relentless perfectionism (mine is the reason for my failure), it is almost impossible to find a sound engineer with an ear, the good people are all under contract elsewhere, the ones left over push the buttons mechanically, they're deaf, they're stupid robots, and every minute costs a fortune... (that's right, darling: chat away, unburden yourself in a heart-to-heart in my arms, it's evening and the fire warms us) if you don't do everything yourself you end up with nothing at all (*nous avons dit souvent d'impérissables choses les soirs illuminés par l'ardeur du charbon*)... incidentally the chieftain of the skiffle group is an attractive young Englishman who looks fabulous with his Viking beard and Bulgarian lambskin jacket... I feel a pang of jealousy: I know the quarter tones in the range of Madame's voice, the syncopes in her speech rhythm: "*Si tu me cocufies, carogne, je vais te tuer!*" Her laughter is defiantly uterine, it drives me crazy, the colored slut, let's reverse the classical model and make it negative, with a white Othello strangling a black Desdemona... she's as strong as a beer-wagon horse, but I've got my tricks, she's already panting under me ("*Attention, ours! Le verre—tu casses le verre, imbécile!*"), I give her enough time to drink up, but then... the great affection makes me indolent, I sit on her lap, she cradles me gently in her powerful arms (*c'est là que j'ai vécu dans les voluptés calmes / au milieu de l'azur, des vagues, des splendeurs / et des esclaves nus, tout imprégnés d'odeurs*), I love her, I kiss her with ardently closed eyes: baby blisses, primordial home of mucous membranes, wonderworld of warm body fragrances (*et je buvais ton souffle, ô douceur, ô poison*... how does it go after that?... *Qui me rafraîchissaient le front avec les palmes*—that's a different part, but it fits: *qui me faisaient languir*—it doesn't rhyme, but it's poetic)... the fire in the hearth burns slowly down, I stare into the glow, which starts to blink at me with black eyes, I'm snugly exhausted, the implacable experience of the singular, the extraordinary, the exquisite, fills me with steady, intense sleepiness,

Madame leafs through the latest fashion magazines, I slowly sip my calvados, even this is a strain: every exquisite move made becomes a cultic gesture, I am too sloppy for such priesthood, I cannot celebrate myself in every moment of life, one really needs the energy of a Rastignac to be a full-fledged citizen of Paris, I don't have it, I'm a lazy barbarian brooding about the ephemerality of things . . . in the fireplace, the black eyes splinter off in the fiery glow and turn ashen-gray, a final log is consumed, a lonesome salamander, I place the fire screen before its flame-darting rump (the reptile hisses softly), I yawn so hard my cheeks crack (good heavens: another day is done, and my book? . . .), she's reading an endless article in *Vogue*, it must be very interesting, I wish I could read, anything, I haven't been able to read for months, at best my weekly horoscope in *Elle*, why bother with anything else? Now, for instance, we could have been in bed for an hour already, sleeping (*D'accord, mon ours—tu penses à ton travail très tôt le matin, n'est-ce pas?*—naturally, what else?), we go to the bedroom, undress—and then comes the big moment (secretly feared): "*Ours! Tu sais ce que tu dois faire—allez hopp!*" and taking an enormous leap, she jumps on my back, it's the nicest thing in the world for her, there's nothing she enjoys more, nothing more intimate (a childhood dream, she's confessed to me: being carried by a lover—no man has ever been prepared to do so)—so I allow one hundred fifty-two pounds of live weight to heave up onto my shoulders, under her impact my ribs crack from the vertebrae, my ears roar, I see red curlicues, but I bravely trot through the entire apartment with her: bedroom, dining room, salon, her study, my study, the vestibule, the guest rooms, three times all around, then I unload her in the bathroom ("*Bravo, ours! Tu as été très fort ce soir—presque aussi fort que le père Bouglion—et Dieu! ce qu'il était fort!*"). I love her, I stand at the bathroom mirror, brushing my disheveled hair, she stands behind me and says, "*Tiens! C'est comme ça que tu te vois . . .*" What? How so? *Qu'est-ce qu'il y a?* "*Rien. Je t'ai seulement vu comme tu te vois toi-même.*" So what? What's so special about how I see myself? "*Tu ne te vois que dans le miroir, n'est-ce pas?*" Of course not, where else could I? "*Et je te vois différemment.*" One hopes. So what? "*Rien de spécial. Pour une fois je t'ai vu comme tu te vois?*" "*Viens, ne dis pas de bêtises—allons au lit!*" And lights out, shuddering with bliss under the fur cover, snuggling together, flesh entangled with flesh, flesh galore, flesh in masses, in mountains, pulsating blood-warm, spice-scented, coffee-brown female flesh . . . I think of the salmon in her mouth and, suicidally, sink the defective teeth of the Caucasian race into her.

Thereafter, my dream . . .

Or another time, a year earlier, the period of my martyrdom. The no less remarkable creature whom I loved during that period was named Dawn. An American. Twenty-one years old. Extremely beautiful. A fashion model by profession. A psychopath. A virgin when I met her (soon no longer, but God alone knows with what terrible effort). Drove me crazy with her unpredictable ways.

At present, she's vanished somewhere in Paris, I'm stuck in Hamburg, Wohlfahrt has promised me a movie, as usual it's taking forever but I can't get away, I'm in hot water, Christa's suing me for her alimony, I've got to scrape up the money for my son's tuition, creditors are beating down my door, my friends here (Rönnekamp, Schwab) are avoiding me like a leper, I've milked all of them for cash, Big-Time Publisher Scherping won't give another penny for the book I've been promising him for years.

Yet daily, nightly, I phone away a fortune. It took me two weeks to find out that Dawn had landed in the Hôtel Épicure again, heaven only knows in what condition. In any case, I can't get her to the phone: morning noon and night I talk to Madame, to the handsome Pole, I leave messages that are never passed on, directions no one gives a damn about, I act like a total lunatic. Strangely enough, I'm working marvelously despite everything, I've written two presentable chapters of my book, it took me only a few hours to hand Wohlfahrt a treatment based on a subject now popular with distributors and he was jubilant ("Damn it, baby, we're gonna knock those guys on their asses!"), and on the side, I've got three subjects of my own that I'm penning, or rather ballpointing: the words are simply scurrying across the paper. And I'm getting fatter and fatter. The broad is fattening me up.

The broad: a chance conquest. Not undeliberate: I've been separated from Dawn for over a month, haven't touched another woman (to put it in cultivated terms); this probably explains a good portion of my hysteria, a symptom of abstinence I'm not used to. Besides, when it comes to monogamous relationships, I have an obnoxious tendency to overcommit myself—and one can see what comes of it, one can tell by the telephone bill. I am at the mercy of the women I love, I become burdensome, like any dependent does sooner or later; love is a child's game—so cruel, so destructive, so ruthless, so stupid, and woe to him who loses, for in the struggle of the sexual organs there is no mercy, and the colder party has the upper hand. In short, I need distance—from Dawn, myself, the *situation* (*hommage à Monsieur Benn!*). Soon I no longer feel like a man; if a woman were to carry on the way I've been doing these past few weeks, she'd disgust you and you'd tell her to go to hell; with a man, this is really demeaning, humiliating. A matter of convention, I know; I can ask myself ten times a day why it's not manly to love a woman, but it just isn't, at least not the way I do it, it's downright ludicrous, and who wants to be a slaveholder? But the broad is, as it were, a fitness exercise. An erotic lightning rod. A spiritual garbage incinerator. A marvelous person.

The broad. I got to know her when registering at the immigration office. As a stateless person, I had to renew my residency permit. As usual, hours were spent waiting in the corridor, wedged in between foreign workers and other ungroomed types, all of them my brethren: circus performers, peddlers, Maghrebinian students, Calabresi, Sicilians, Hungarian refugees, they change their countries but not their shirts, they smell of the shabby clothes they sleep in, hang around government offices, smoke foul-smelling cigarettes, cough up their mucus in the corner spittoon as if they were vomiting. Then who should come walking down the corridor but *her*: a very well groomed petite bourgeoise, bloody fucking middle-class, with the accent on the second adjective, I hope. Her clothes are as flawless as they are tasteless—a bottle-green suit with a nutria collar, a bizarre plant of a hat—the whole creature medium height, a bit plump, which I like (my Viennese formative years), in her late twenties (earlier, they can't screw, too embarrassed or too curious, inhibited; anyway she probably lets go completely), correspondingly sassy—acts as though she didn't see me, yet her nostrils flare like a mare's at the stud station. The strenuous effort to take no notice of me makes her movements jerky; I sit poised on the bench, my legs crossed, I look her over with insolent thoroughness: the hat above all, the breasts (voluptuously snug in Maidenform), the handbag, the ass, the legs (excellent: narrow of ankle, full of calf; see my poor heart it's split in half). My inspection ended, I look away again: neither satisfied nor disappointed, I have merely registered her; I soundlessly whistle a little tune over my lips, peering absently through the window into the pale coastal sky.

I am convinced she's followed every detail of the game; it doesn't matter whether she's seen through it; all the same, it sparks the desired reactions. Now she really becomes aware of herself (and her awkwardness) but switches to the offensive, becomes aggressive in a feminine way, stands ostentatiously (with her back to me) at the window, through which I stare into the anemic heavenly void, but then she turns around, cuts my line of sight again and (certain of not leaving my field of vision) goes to the office door. Very attentively reads the letters of name groups on the door as well as the names of the officials processing the respective group: A–E, Handke; F–K, Löschmann; L–R, Janitzki; S–Z, Kühnle. By all means, study it as carefully as you can, my dear lady. There are situations that, at first blush, seem ineluctable, this can be confirmed by Nadine; they become all the more piquant if you delay them, in your circles especially this is probably considered good form (*à propos:* in art, too, delay is most helpful). But she is more discerning than she appeared to be, and comes back quite emphatically, recrossing my line of vision (hung out, like an Elbe fisherman's line with an earthworm on the hook, in the watery distance beyond the windowpane). Before she can make any further decisions, I shift (to offer her room) half a buttock over on the bench. She promptly sits down; I naturally pay her no heed, absentmindedly light a Rothman taken from the Fabergé case, exude the fragrance of a victorious power. This must collide with early impressions of hers: budding twelve-year-old girl with half a kilo of black-market butter under her skirt goes through the British checkpoint at Aumühle, the last urban transport station on the way to Lauenburg; will the soldiers search her for it? . . . Such experiences make this generation accessible. Early humiliation and anxiety always do a fine job of preparing the erotic soil; smells, for instance cigarette smoke, are an excellent device for stirring up this past in the subconscious; phonograph records come later. Now, the sensoria of the left half of my body register that she has taken the bait, it becomes perceptibly warmer between us, from the corner of her eye she gauges my suit, the quality of my linen, and presumably the quantity of the hair on my chest—well, what do you think of me, dear lady? A distinguished foreigner, no doubt (shit, as if he *needed* to go to the immigration office, he looks like James Bond; even the Persian nut importer *sends* someone to take care of this kind of business for him, doesn't matter if it's his own brother-in-law). Still and all, I am a writer, a film writer, interested in milieu studies; this immigration office is without a doubt a literary gold mine, with all these colorful destinies, wouldn't you agree? Why, these citizens of serf nations could give you the plots for entire novels, nowhere else could you find such a wealth of diverse human situations, at least not in humdrum West Germany; we all know that sociology is invalidated by the society of equality, one need only know the phenotype. Here, however, true life can still be found, although ultimately no one gives a shit. I shoot my hand out from my sleeve, look at my now visible (to her as well as me) Cartier watch, then turn to her with no transition, as though continuing an only just interrupted conversation, and say, "I hope you've brought along enough time." And she very willingly replies, "Oh, this is nothing new for me." She speaks (as expected) a penetrating Hamburg German, in the direction of Harburg. I ask her disingenuously, "You're not German?" She *is* German, but her husband is Lithuanian, only they're divorced (there you are), but her citizenship still isn't cleared up, "all this endless bureaucracy," and last year she wanted to go to Italy. One thing leads to another, and three hours later I'm lying in her bed, a Murphy on the wall of a ten-by-twelve-foot room; she lives in a studio flat with a bathroom and kitchenette in a high-rise development somewhere in the wasteland behind the Hagenbeck Zoo, but she does have "a bit of a yard" (dropping her *r*'s the way people do in Hamburg), fourteen feet wide, thirty-five feet long, the flanks shielded by two strips of canvas against neighborly in-sight (at least from next door); between these strips, the eye rolls as though down a bowling alley (with a leap over the pathetic asters at the far end) into the yawning void of the planned central green space. The housing development is still young, no lawn has been started as yet, but chamomiles, a resistant weed, are stinting out of the mortar-laced soil, a slum-summer breeze that endures year-round seems to have settled in, there is apparently no other season, in any case the playground is as good as finished, it will open next year (the year after at the latest), red and yellow and green and violet paint, the iron pipework of the swings, monkey bars, and slide are already looming from the cement-framed gravel (a Paul Klee execution site: gallows and torture wheel for little stick figures with zeros for heads). Farther along, at a dramatic standstill, the concrete squadron of the high-rises in triad echelons comes thundering toward the playground: instead of gun turrets, the box balconies emerge from the hatches. At sunrise and at sundown, the shadows of the nine (or twelve) giant phalluses (three are always in reserve) shoot east to west, then west to east, across the bare surface whose border is the skyline, there's nothing beyond it, the world ends there in Ptolemaic fashion, we live right on its edge. Here in the foreground, on the wide (first) step of the three composition-stone steps, under a green sunshade with stitched-on toadstools, there are two chaise longues and a small wheeled table with a bottle holder, ringed by six flower pots with hyacinth bulbs, two with brownishly proliferating asparagus, three geraniums, and one mimosa (donated by myself and now without blossoms). Here, I make myself at home when visiting her. It's already quite cool out, there is supposed to be snow in the Alpine foothills, but I'm a fresh-air fiend, I get claustrophobic in the little apartment, she understands. Our relationship has become quite close in a rather loose way. The incredible has happened: In a city where (as my experiences during my married years with

Christa taught me) each and every one of the two and a half million inhabitants (not counting the perioecians) knows everybody else, knows everything about him, has all sorts of connections with him, can check every step he takes (and usually does), she has no idea who I am, our circles never cross, my present Middle Kingdom (like all earlier ones) is on a different planet from hers. She seems to take me for a businessman occasionally passing through (with a touch of the exotic, though: an Austrian? an Argentine German?), she doesn't ask me for details or particulars, not even where I live when I don't spend the night with her (which I seldom do), or if and when I'm coming again. I call her up when I feel like it (at my age, anyway, such needs are irresistible at most three times a week), and simply say, "Are you going to be home this afternoon?" It sounds (and is meant to sound) as prosaic as asking, when you enter a train compartment, "Is this seat taken?" And she's never answered anything but "What time are you coming?" She always speaks in the same monotonous, slightly nasal tone; suburban bleakness then settles into the earpiece, the emptiness of drab, lonesome Sunday afternoons; already spiritually groggy, I show up at her place at the announced time—and then I have to pull off a one-hundred-eighty-degree readjustment act. Adapting to the reality of the 1960s is not easy for me: when, for instance, I reach the building door (I always need at least a panicky half hour to find the right one: one of thirty-six perfectly similar building doors in twelve perfectly identical concrete blocks), I press the button under a certain (her?) name in the aluminum plate (one of sixty-six Bakelite buttons in punched holes under sixty-six perfectly similar cellophane-covered plastic name platelets in twenty-two triple rows like an accordion keyboard—and just what is her name?). At such times, I feel I'm being sucked into a vacuum. I realize these are merely behavioral problems. With a little more practice (perhaps consultation with a psychologist: Professor Hertzog would doubtless make himself available), I could soon easily get the better of them, above all, rid myself of the neurotic associations that still occur. With the venomous buzzing of a wasp squashed under a shoe, the door lock springs open behind my left renal area. The buzzing has something definitive, irrevocable about it: that's how the automatic lock snaps open and shut on the solitary-confinement cell of a prisoner serving a life sentence. Yet I am entering an apartment house in which the community should be burgeoning; why then are these buildings so empty? These termite houses should be teeming with people, whole tribes must be living here, but you don't see them, you barely hear them (and if you do, they're abstracted into a hum of plumbing). Nevertheless, I picture them as anthropomorphic, flattened like the trolls in a Dubuffet painting and yet palpitating (the insane Maupassant foresaw them in the *horlà*, who comes after man). I won't run into them, alas. They have been swallowed up by the residential mechanism, incorporated into it without a trace. I cannot expect any more spiritual utterance than a question from a fetal voice emerging from the sieve holes of the mouthpiece under the buzzer-and-name-platelet mountings before the door lock springs open, a question wrapped in rustling tinfoil and pickled in machine oil: "Hello? Who is it?"

But can I then in good conscience answer "Me?" (Who am I? Who am I in the face of this new world?) And even if I dared to say "Me," I wouldn't be taking a safe position. The signal of technological behavior patterns that would allow me into the honeycomb labyrinths here or there (beyond them the conversation with the metallic voice ghost would not survive), would be irrelevant. The residential mechanism overcomes dehumanization by multi-digited repeatability of the same setup: it basically makes no difference whether I go here or there, I would merely be arriving at an experience that can be repeated at random. Each of these twelve enormous housing machines is threaded with the capillaries of six stairwells (exactly similar to the one I now enter), each of which leads, on each of the twenty-two stories, to three medium-size or studio flats. That, according to Adam Riese (*sic*!), makes 4,752 four-to-six-celled lairs for consumers of the goods of life on an elevated self-service level. Theoretically (with just one studio flat per landing), the same experience with one of 1,464 unattached women, not intrinsically different from the broad, could be granted to me 1,464 times: I enter and find my bearings with somnambulistic sureness in the very same topography; to the left of the tiny vestibule are the bedroom and bathroom, to the right the living room and kitchenette; through the half-open (and intersecting) door, I see a female shoulder busy over kitchen chores (the shoulder covered with the synthetic and wool of a thinnish sweater lightly fragrant with cologne, soup broth, and femaleness; the odors vie for predominance, the female smell wins by a nose over the soup broth, the cologne evanesces in a field of straggling contenders). I sense the erotic appeal of the eel-round flesh of an upper arm naked from shoulder to elbow, the stays of the brassiere under the armpit, the curving of the back adorned with a half ribbon of apron string, the plump roundness of the hip in a plaid skirt jersey skirt corduroy skirt who-knows-what-kind-of skirt, the somewhat crooked seam of the nylon stocking over a full calf. The head is covered for the time being; if it moves and a slice of it becomes visible, then one may assume with a likelihood verging on certainty that the neck hairline, razor-cut too high, would irritate me in all 1,464 cases, that a voice with a monotonously singsong and rather nasally constricted Hamburg tone would say, "Hi there, just make yourself at home till I'm ready, everything's prepared out there—a whole bunch of magazines just came in!"

So I simply go out to the yard; it is not that I am expected, but rather that it is utterly inconceivable that I could stay away. The wheeled table already offers what she calls "a little something to munch on": a small basket of black bread ("Just try it, it's whole-grain bread") rye bread caraway-seed bread graham bread aniseed bread crispbread salt sticks cheese sticks, a little board with ham on it ("Just dive right in, that's homemade cottage-cured ham"), her familiarity is quite neutral, impersonal, noncommittal, the act of taking possession occurs by way of the exceptionally rich offering of first-class consumer goods: smoked goose breast ("It's a home recipe, from refugees from Pomerania"), fat liverwurst ("You'll never get that in a normal store, it comes from Holstein, straight from the farm"), a small crock of butter ("genyuwine country butter"), a stone jug of Steinhäger beer ("Drink some right away, it's nicely chilled"), a bottle of Bommerlunder, half a bottle of kümmel, a remnant of cognac, reams of paper napkins, a small dish of salted almonds, another of sweets, a cup containing cigarettes (Copenhagen brand: gull motif), an ashtray (Rosenthal porcelain decorated by Bele Bachem's artistic hand with a cat-faced debauchee in a corset and laced boots plus a Montgolfier floating high in the air), the weekly magazine pile ("Knowledge Is Power")—all she'd have to do is have my slippers ready ("Why don't you take off your tie, it's a lot comfier"). I promptly stretch out in the chaise longue, hack off thick slices of whole-grain and rye bread, goose breast and home-cured ham, heartily heap up liverwurst on playing-card crispbread, poke the salt sticks in the butter, the cheese sticks in the mayonnaise. I need something to hold on to, something solid in this boneless situation, in this strangely abstract world; the life-giving food has to produce the reality of life I lose when I walk into the hallway here and certainly under the sunshade with stitched-on toadstools in this sunless wasteland. I try to find the reality of life in the illustrated magazines, I peruse *Der Spiegel*, *Stern*, *Good Housekeeping*, *Better Living*, *Modern Woman*, *Radio and TV Guide*; while doing so I slip more and more deeply, more and more hopelessly into abstractness, also losing my (already diluted) identity.

I am most intimately, most personally spoken to (as among gallows birds and pastors' daughters), initiated, involved, drawn into complicity. Editors honor me with letters, fraternally presenting me with their ethical motives (not neglecting to add their passport photos), sibyls whisper their queenly wisdom to me in a uterine tone (with a profound gaze, a Mona Lisa smile around the vulva that appeals directly to my gonads). This is flattering, but it's not meant for *me*; what is meant and addressed is something in me that is no longer my SELF but probably one of the countless sub- and co-selves of my experiencing self. I don't want to be pedantic—that would promote total dissolution. But anyway it's something embarrassingly general into which the substance of my self (perhaps slashed open by the categorical imperative) runs out—whether the ID of the psychologists (according to Sigmund Freud, the pleasure principle rules unrestrictedly there) or the ONE of the existentialists (according to Jean-Paul Sartre, the world of the *salauds*) makes no difference to me, it's not my SELF—yet it is, but not really... There is evidently a collective self in me, into which any other self (together with its idiotic demands) can be projected, a communal multiplicity in which everyone can identify with everyone else, everyone with all the others, all with everyone. Otherwise, I couldn't be expected to let myself be drawn into matters that are not at all my matters, utterly remote from the things that really affect me and certainly remote from the things that I can affect with my *actions*.

Here, the borders of no Middle Kingdom are respected. What in God's name do I care about the Congo? What am I to do, what can I do about the extermination of the giraffes in East Africa or about Konrad Adenauer's stubbornness?... Yet here, these issues are urgently presented to me as though my material and spiritual welfare depended on them, my happiness, my moral integrity, my ethical climate. This surprises me somewhat. I must admit: Until now I haven't expected anything other than a shallow means of passing the time, distraction—at the dentist's, for example, or at the hairdresser's (when I'm waiting for a girlfriend haloed in blue light and hygienically decapitated by the barber's smock fastened under her chin in the thin-walled cubicle, mysteriously deaf and dumb like the Trunk Lady in a carnival stall, giving me the absent smile of Brigitte Helm in *Metropolis* under a massive space helmet of glittering nickel, she likewise holding a magazine in her hands, which are no longer at all connected to her). It can presumably be traced back to this that I had the notion that one reads illustrated weeklies with one's fly undone—

which is to say: with the carefree distraction of a three-year-old playing with his oatmeal. But this is a mistake, people take me for far more grown up than I am, I note this now, here: threatened by five hundred forty balconies that aim down at me from nine residential machines. An astounding development in the consciousness of the global citizen, in the contemporary conscience, in the feeling of responsibility of the individual for the fate of all, must have taken place in Germany during my frequent (often lengthy) absences in the last five, six years, and consequently a simultaneous mobilizing of public opinion, which is yielding quite the audacious results. I am struck by the boldness of the published word. We didn't have this before in this country. It almost makes me feel there is now no danger in making daring statements. Perhaps this was always the case, but intelligent self-censorship always considered the possibility of consequences. However, consequences no longer seem to occur. Anyway, it is flatteringly assumed here that I have taken part in this agreeable development, that I on my end am prepared to emotionally carry out the aggressive new West German journalistic élan. Alas, I am not: I live abroad too much, where events occur much less robustly, with kid gloves on, as it were. I am struck by the combativeness with which, for instance, a government minister is publicly accused of corruption here; since his continued stay in office would lead one to conclude that he can effortlessly refute the charges, why doesn't he do so? There's something out of kilter: Either the accusations are false, which would have to have consequences, or they are correct, which would certainly also have consequences. But nothing happens; the whole thing seems to take place in a vacuum. Perhaps there are two realities: a pedestrian reality, so to speak, in which I move, in which probably most of the Middle Kingdoms lie—that is, in which what I and everyone else directly experiences takes place—and another reality, superordinate, vaster, and more comprehensive, in which the dramatic public events that I see here take place: a superreality, in which the gods struggle as in the *Iliad*...

But then, these latter events go beyond me, concern me only indirectly, as a consumer of destiny, so to speak. I no longer have the *law of action* in my hand. So why should this superreality be brought home to me in such a bewilderingly direct fashion, as if heaven knows what were contingent on my feeling involved in it? The illustrated newsmagazines leap at me, they almost harass me; like a total stranger grabbing my arm in the street and sputtering his conflict-laden experience-broth at me—from his marital problems to his philosophical ideas, his professional, athletic, and erotic perils, possibilities, prospects, his difficulties in raising his children, his traffic delinquencies, his thoughts on urban planning the fight against cancer food for the world ideas on American Russian Chinese Persian Venezuelan domestic and foreign politics Fidel Castro Onassis Anita Ekberg

Karl and Groucho Marx—not because he mistakes me for an old acquaintance with whom he has often discussed such issues and problems (or because he recognizes me as especially open and receptive to them) but simply because he has pulled me out by sheer chance from several tens of thousands, and I could just as easily have been another passerby coming his way—he merely assumes in sovereign schizoid autism that whatever regards concerns occupies excites exasperates him is bound to regard concern occupy excite exasperate someone else, ergo that I must instantly be passionately moved and captivated—

okay, fine: Dostoevsky does the same to me, Henry Miller even employs my libido for this purpose, but with them I at least know that this is fiction, it is meant to pull me out of the reality of the here and now and transpose me into a different one, removed from time and space, a superreality that sovereignly fills its own time and space, so that experiencing it makes me realize all the more keenly what *reality* is, that I may grasp it all the more clearly, comprehend it all the more fully...This is splendid, my eyes ought to brim with tears in sheer gratitude: the poets want what's best for me, they hand me keys that give me access to what lies in (and behind) my Middle Kingdom, beyond the pedestrian reality I can directly experience: its symbolism, its transcendence.

But that is just what the annoying sleeve-tugger on the glossy pages of the illustrateds does not do. On the contrary: he speculates with robust naiveté on the fascination of existence that is transmitted close to the skin, sour on the stomach, and warm as the breath (and granted: such fascination is huge in this modern world, which sails out into the abstract with concept-filled sails!). And it is certainly true of the magazines in this bunch—which I peruse, more and more excited, more and more addicted, more and more obsessed—that they present my pedestrian reality and no other; I cannot doubt it, it's printed here in black and white and color; the camera, as we know, does not lie. To be sure, it has only a wraith-like similarity to what I actually experience (especially here and now: right at the edge of the world, lying on a yellow-and-white-striped chaise longue surrounded by pathetic flowerpots, under a green, toadstool-stitched sunshade, which stands in something that one can describe at best as the negative of a garden, ringed by roaring emptiness, from which 2,336 windowpanes, in front of me, over me, and at either side, gaze down blankly, and 540 concrete terraces are reproachfully held out to me like empty boxes, like beggar's bowls of a humanity cheated of itself), but this reality in the illustrated magazines, parsed in still photos and served up like a well-shuffled pack of cards, is not entirely alien. On the contrary, it is even traumatically familiar, intimate; a déjà vu experience afflicts me several times on every page. I've seen all this before (indeed, many, many times), though most likely just in other magazines; still, I can imagine I experienced these things myself, and could re-experience them at any time at any step along the way—

thus, it is not directly my reality but, so to speak, its pedestrian superreality, meant to be experienced by me in its fullness, as I experience it here and now: from the void of an abstract superreality I have previously overlooked and failed to heed only for lack of sufficient attention and for want of a sense of the factual.

Okay, fine, I'm ready to accept this. My profane experiences hardly suffice to make me fully cognizant of the reality around me. Nor am I surprised that it is so full, brimming with the unexpected, the astonishing, the wonderful—but why are these unexpected astonishing wonderful matters presented to me as the most humdrum everyday matters (indeed, as *my* everyday experience)? I certainly don't doubt that they have reality, are reality, but I am very far removed from it. The struggle of the gods over us mortals may also decide my destiny, but that doesn't mean that I can intervene, that I can interfere and say, "Hey, fellas—calm down! This really won't do!" Then why does the superreality of the magazines simulate this possibility for me? Why does it strike me with every picture (of oil sheikhs lunar-rocket passengers duchesses poisoners), with every report (of earthquakes jungle warfare atomic explosions floods) as the most up-to-date topicality I can encounter at any step of the way? Things become so grandly colorful and dynamic only in literature, in my dreams, at best. There, my hand meets Haroun el Rashid's in the lamb pilaf, I fly to the moon, sleep with duchesses, am poisoned by green-eyed sorceresses, the earth quakes beneath me, machine-gun muzzles emerge from the thicket of fat tropical plants like the eyes of a Douanier Rousseau tiger and aim at me, and ultimately God's wrath blows up the planet... But if I simultaneously experience myself as immobile, trapped in the vacuum of a void from which there is no escape, while a thousand voices whisper to me, shout at me, cry to me, "Do something! Get involved! Intervene! Stop the monstrous thing from happening! Prevent the horrible thing!"—if that happens, then the dream turns into a nightmare, the events pass over me, press down on me, crush me.

And that is exactly what the superreality does in the illustrated magazines on my lap. Their reality is not to be doubted, but it takes place beyond my immediate realm of experience, beyond my Middle Kingdom, it takes place powerfully, sovereignly, beyond any influence of mine; yet its topicality presses under my skin, and no matter how I turn and twist, I can ignore nothing that happens here, it happens to me, happens here and now—though it is a here and now that exists past me, growing beyond its own ephemeral self, of course. The NOW comprises not only the moment, the day, the week, but the entire epoch; the HERE is not limited to the front yard in the high-rise development where I am lounging, to my present Middle Kingdom, to Hamburg, to West Germany—no, it encompasses all realms, all kingdoms, the globe, the cosmos—

and, needless to say, it overpowers me, does not tolerate me outside itself, I merely belong inside it, belong *to* it, in any case: after all, the superreality is the totality of all current events, the magazines draw a weekly interim balance from it, a rough estimate, as it were, with the praiseworthy goal of telling me about everything as far as possible, letting me participate in the whole... On the whole, however, everything (including me) is one and the same, no matter how one thing or the other may behave (however I may behave); everything exists quite simply by dint of its existence, no matter how active or passive—hence I too am in it simply by dint of my existence, whether I intervene "actively" in reality or stay lounging here inactively on my chaise longue, experiencing the events at second hand. I realize I must not confuse the *totality of current events* with so-called *current history*. The latter, of course, requires my active participation. I must not be passive with it. Otherwise I might drop out of reality, be given the go-by, remain forever invisible, eradicated.

To exist at all, then, I must act, I must become a member of the German parliament or detonate a bomb that shreds at least three members of parliament (if not a chancellor), I must fly to the moon or poison someone. The more effectively my action interferes with current history, the more defined is my existence. But superreality is simply not current history, it is the *totality of current events* in its fullness, and in this totality, current history dissolves, whereby all my efforts to intervene actively dissolve as well. There are, as one can clearly see, many different kinds of current history at the same time: that of the United States of America looks different from that of the Congo (hence, Frank Sinatra's looks different from Lumumba's, and mine looks different from Wernher von Braun's). And yet all of us, with our various current histories, are contained in the entirety of current events—all present, whether as oil sheikhs or big bankers, lunar-rocket passengers or record-breaking athletes, movie stars or duchesses, popular singers, politicians, or gangsters, poisoners, bomb-throwers, or other foul-players—or else as amateur gardeners, animal protectors, good Samaritans, quiet book readers, anchorites, blissful navel contemplators, marijuana smokers. Everything exists in the superreality. Thus, it is not *reality in motion*, like history, but rather the unchanging state of Being in and of itself, of which sometimes this and sometimes that becomes visible. And, visible or invisible, everything exists in it; hence I do as well: whether as someone experiencing a collective destiny or someone shaping a collective destiny, whether as a head of state or as a Trappist monk, an anonymous nobody or a wanton seeker of fame and glory. Whatever occurs in the superreality occurs only as something extant, thus entirely without indication of value, the bomb-thrower peacefully next to the navel contemplator, the poisoner fraternally next to the Samaritan...

In this sense, superreality is almost paradisal, its effect is paralyzing, soporific, like an old lullaby that goes "Such is life, my child..." I am challenged to stay on my chaise longue and content myself with what I can experience vicariously (on the weekly balance drawn by the magazines). But on the other hand, what I thus experience is so monstrous and violent, so fills my consciousness to the bursting point with phenomena events occurrences incidents, that it keeps stretching further and further, becomes more and more expansive. Superreality has the explosive character that physicists usually attribute to cosmic events; while I rest here as a silent nucleus of overall events on the chaise longue I simultaneously fly out into the universe at a furious velocity. It is ridiculous to hold fast to the old, out-of-date idea of action, to the obsession with activity or passivity vis-à-vis history—this would mean something only if I had a history in the absolute sense, were allowed to have a history. This history would be the skin, the solidifying envelope, of the person. It would give me contours—and thus form. What once held together my SELF (at least in my imagination), giving it distinguishable, recognizable form, was the notion of a personal history. But this now proves to be a typically subjectivistic error, showing only my infantile limitation of vision; it is schizothymically autistic, correlating with my bourgeois worldview and leptosomic habitus: superreality enlightens me, makes me understand that my conception of self is completely out of proportion. Hertzog ought to prescribe group sex for me, so that I can finally realize that I have no history. The trivial circumstances of my life are stereotypical, and they integrate me pitilessly into the masses. I am (despite the silly trials and tribulations that I regard as circumscribing my personality) ultimately, unavoidably, quite simply, a contemporary. As such, I experience a banal variant of global destiny as a member of Western Civilization—and as such, in turn, am merely a mote of dust in the cloud configurations of the history of mankind, nay, of the earth—in my present situation, I am nothing more than a phenotype of my historical position and destination, by necessity earning money (at least making a living, however tardily), an unwilling taxpayer, renter, consumer, transportation user, and, especially as the last, inevitably a *zoon politikon*.

This is thoroughly impressed upon me here, each article is intent on firmly imprinting this upon my consciousness: The disciplined driving that I expect from others obliges me to maintain the same myself; this can also be understood in an extrapolated sense, in every aspect of life I must respect red and green lights, above all however the rules concerning right-of-way. Should this have escaped me up to now, it is here once more hammered into me. Individualism is suicide and more than that a crime against the collective. What could eventually set me apart from others like me would occur at the mercy of the journalistic organs that I hold in my hand. They alone are capable of thrusting me into the spheres of visibility, of elevating me to the status of being the subject of an interview, a photo essay, a report. But in the absence of such an (incidentally thoroughly untimely) occurrence, I'm not even able to upgrade the unwilling taxpayer in myself to an impressive evader of millions: my image would then appear in equal stature alongside other prominent figures like Aga Khan, Cordin the tailor, Eichmann, the member of parliament Rainer Barzel—so here too, nothing doing. The stroke of luck of extraordinary natural gifts (quiz show intelligence, photogenic beauty, golden vocal chords, etc.) is unfortunately not my lot, nor regretfully any stupendous abnormality (pyromaniac, Siamese twin, heart transplant patient).

But even if I had, could, wanted, and did achieve all of it: it would again only place me within another multitude, a likewise progressively growing collective like that of the anonymous. For of course the other purpose of these pages, no longer strictly informational but rather instructional, seems to be to pin down the extraordinary, to track down all those who in some way, positive or negative, stand out from the masses, who in some way distinguish themselves, to photograph them, interview them, publicize them as representative bearers of experience. Not necessarily in order to rake up the old notion of merit and achievement as a means of character building, but rather solely for reasons of indexing: to set reference points for the inventory of the super-reality. And it's astounding what doesn't receive notice, what doesn't merit attention, the group grows, in line with the zeitgeist, in a process of explosive expansion. Amazing what this right-of-way-obeying humanity still brings forth! This of course in a certain respect cancels out the potential for recognition, even the distinguished criminal heads of government leaders, the banker's faces of politicians and church dignitaries can scarcely be told apart from one another, begin to become interchangeable, not to speak of the mass-produced film beauties, celebrity mannequins, notable athletes, Nobel Prize winners. Even if I were seized with the mad notion of being extraordinary, I would find this extraordinariness multiplied and typified into the multitudinous—for example as one of a few hundred thousand simpletons who delude themselves into thinking they could, with a masterpiece among a few hundred thousand not completely worthless masterpieces, influence the fate of mankind. And were I too actually a writerly talent that united in itself the qualities of Henry Miller with those of Dostoyevsky, and were I actually to bring out a literary masterpiece that propelled me into the sphere of visibility of the illustrated press, I would only be allocated a place among yet another considerably proliferating group: namely, that of the successful literati; and my achievement would in no way raise me above that of the large-scale tax cheat, soccer goal scorer, or opposition politician. For in the super-reality of journalistic organs the concept of achievement is free of value, one's rank is determined solely by *topicality*: what counts is its *contemporaneity*, be it the dynamic contemporaneity of a just done deed or—even better, more stable, more durable—the static contemporaneity of an exceptional condition. Consequently, the relatively speaking rare moral or ethical quality also pales before the more frequent topicality of the criminal or scandalous and of course the consistency of conditional extraordinariness: true, the song of the good man does occasionally get sung (the acknowledgment of beautiful souls is there in small print in the letters from readers), but what can this do next to the *glamour* of Jacqueline Kennedy, the demonic banality of Eichmann, the breasts of Anita Ekberg—these are *existences*, thank you very much, the *Being* ranks above the *Doing*; both can of course in a lucky case combine into peak-topicality as in the muscle-package of Mr. Schwarzenegger, but normally the conditional is the solid basis of contemporaneity in the super-reality: amidst all past achievement in fluttering topicality the extraordinary is more reliably established in radiation-intensities, vital superiorities, existential powers. But I possess none of these things. What I could in the best case bring to bear would be a book, and this would contain from me again only just the historical—thus the untopical; the account of a meandering career isn't worth talking about in the all-American situation of today, especially not in the refugee-story-saturated German social solution. A Sinbad wouldn't have anything special to tell here, world war and travel agencies deliver by the ton the experience of being geographically tossed around; at the level of a weekly magazine report no one would need such a thing. As a physiognomically recognizable, even name-bearing SELF, not even the fleeting topicality of a shooting star would be allotted me, not to mention the constant, if scarcely individualizable, contemporaneity of a fixed star in some galaxy or other. It's more realistic to keep in mind that in reality I don't exist at all: the super-reality of media is denied me, there no notice is taken of me, I don't at all pass over the threshold of public consciousness, don't take up even the slightest place in the superreal order of occurrences and am therefore actually not at all extant, a little particle in the giant collective of the anonymous without reality.

To grasp the notion of the self physically, at least, I must bite heartily into my ham sandwich, chew, swallow, wash it down with a small glass of Bommerlunder or kümmel, smear a blob of liverwurst on crispbread, munch the hard, splintering crumbs well salivated with the soapy mass of liverwurst, push in a cheese stick, rinse my greasy mouth cavity with corn whiskey, counter its sharpness with that of a chocolate-covered peppermint. So I am eating dialectically at least, in boorish theses, antitheses, and syntheses of palatal stimuli. It helps me to feel that I do exist. How? This is given by the situation. Where? This is harder to establish. Hamburg is no longer what surrounds me here; it could just as well be Detroit or Sofia or even Minsk. It is purely and simply suburbia, a geographic superreality with no precise location. That too is an antiquated prejudice, an outmoded experience-cliché of the nineteenth century—Fridtjof Nansen struggling to get to the Pole, Mister Stanley I presume to the sources of the White Nile—but forget that nonsense, one cannot escape suburbia today, it devours the cities exactly the way it does the so-called (here truly) flatland. By tomorrow, I'll be able to take the subway from here all the way to Palermo without leaving the jurisdiction of suburbia, without arriving anywhere but in suburbia, without experiencing anything but the sapping experience of the unreality, suffocating emptiness, abstractness of these death houses larded with a lemur people, the desolation around them, before them, behind them, beyond them... It's to be had everywhere, in Palermo as well as Salonika, in the same consistent quality, the same picture here as there. No matter from what side one views the buildings, they have both a phallic and a sepulchral quality, always looming apocalyptically over the horizon—a horizon without foreland: a bare patch of curving earth. Like arm-amputated grave crosses seen from a frog's-eye view, they bore into the sky, which soon bleeds to death.

But before this happens, I still have a good half hour. I usually come by around five in the afternoon; so on cloudless days, even in late fall (already early winter in the Alpine foothills but still a coolly restrained slum summer here), I've got at least one and a half hours of surrender to the magazines in the sterile light of an eternal Sunday-afternoon emptiness, while the broad, who has been in the kitchenette since four o'clock, prepares something tasty for supper: "No, no, dear, you really can't help me, this is women's work—besides, you've got something to nibble on, anyway. I've got smoked eel too, dear, really fresh, from Kiel."

I could use it, thank you, I need something solid. Otherwise, the superreality will carry me weightlessly out into the void; my collective ego is in a moral clinch, so to speak, with my superego. Like Atlas, I carry the earth on my shoulders—and behold: it is light. Notwithstanding all the problems of determining a fair border for Manchuria, notwithstanding all the difficulties in Nigeria's domestic politics, notwithstanding the mass slaughter of baby seals off the coasts of Newfoundland, even notwithstanding the peril of overpopulation, the globe does not press down on me at all. On the contrary, it is as weightless and iridescent as a soap bubble and carries me, floats with me, into space.

There, incidentally, the day is actually vanishing, rarefying in a way that makes me experience the forlornness of the planet in outer space. The sun is not setting, but has disowned its satellite forever, its light is now a mere echo fleeing after it, the sun steals away, slips behind the diagonally echeloned triple formation of the Western high-rise block, transforming it for brief seconds into the modernistic trinity symbol from the display window of a progressive shop for devotional kitsch, a few final preclusive rays even quickly imitate the monstrance, then the dazzling humbug is snuffed out, three angular, leaden-gray thorns stick bluntly in the flesh of the sky, making it decay, its vital juice decompose, its hemoglobin (horribly filled with pus) congests over the curvature of the earth, running out beyond it, into the universe, only lymph remains, watery so long as a final reflection of solar gold is still trapped in the 396 windows of the southern squadron wing, this final reflection oozes away upward, strangely (as if through a fine-meshed latticework), then comes the moment of tipping over, I have anxiously looked forward to it the whole time.

The instant I press the buzzer into the aluminum plate on one of the seventy-two entrance doors, I know: I have come to experience this dying of the world. The monosyllabic signal exchange by telephone ("Are you going to be home this afternoon?" "What time are you coming?") is already the upbeat for this overture, the leitmotif for a tormenting poetry, a poetry with exchanged light values, as it were, a negative of poetry. It now drenches the essence of the final moments of a day whose borrowed light nevertheless simulated a possibility of life on the lost planet, a *fata morgana* play of definitive refractions. But now it's past, the sky is a flinty polish, with three triple groups of thorn-shaped lead inclusions sticking in it, I feel its dead weight on me, it presses me into the rock where I lounge on a basalt chaise under the dome of a brazen sunshade with toadstool-shaped iron-oxide spots, it pushes me down with my last shriek of anxiety in my throat—I don't want this, let anything happen, let the world petrify, but this *must* not happen, I must not be discovered in this geological era, this will lead to paleontological errors. I do not belong to this epoch of the world, it is not my epoch, it has swallowed me together with my former world and its various Middle Kingdoms, and it is deceptively using their myths. I protest. It was a *human* myth that designed ANTHROPOLIS, the city of mankind; it was the dreams of *human beings*, not of *horlàs*, that this nightmare stole for its own monstrosity. This is corpse robbery. Every cubic meter of concrete from which this Stone Age was formed contains a cynical utilization of rubble. Even its barrenness, its heartrending emptiness, was finagled; it has appropriated the tormenting poetry of the bomb-crater fields of *my* era; everything that might hint at the former presence of human life is stolen from *my* epoch and falsely taken over into this nowness, is abstracted, is doctored into its own negative. I must warn the twentieth millennium's explorers of primordial times: if among my fossils, beneath the stony cigarette butts and petrified ashes, they find the affected figure of a Montgolfier on a porcelain shard, that cannot enlighten them about what a balloon in the sky meant to me in my childhood. The petrified spinning wheel that may be found in one of the honeycomb cells as a decorative old-fashioned domestic item (transformed into a flowerpot holder) does not belong here. The power shovels that dug the foundations of these gigantic death houses bumped into this spinning wheel, unearthed it with other junk, perhaps from houses that once upon a time stood in this place, and pushed the archaic (almost African) ornamentation of their half-timber gables from the blossom balls of the cherry trees into the melting of airy spring cloudlets in the blue sky—in a long-submerged past before the past.

But how am I to prove this? I will be dated not according to the memories under the potsherds of my cranium but according to the contents of my stomach. Remnants of black bread and cottage ham, liverwurst and country butter, kümmel and corn whiskey will corroborate the erroneous assumption that all these things belong together. No one will stand up to testify that this necropolis employed all kinds of anachronisms to feign life. Even the nature of this past before the past, long assassinated, still haunts the detergent-blue sunniness of the ads in the glossy magazines. What can I do to denounce this perfidious abstraction? It is too late, I did not depart from the evolutionary cycle in time, I neglectfully outlived myself and have been taken over as an anachronism into the new geological era. And now I'm paying for it. For three decades of life (misappropriated by the science of prehistory), I (along with untold other museum pieces) have served this stone world as a biological alibi. I will be ruthlessly counted as a part of it in the omnium-gatherum of its archaeological treasures; whether the investigators stumble upon a hand ax or the crank of a funnel gramophone in the stratum a few meters under me, not even a dog will be taken in; I've held both objects in my hands, either one could be my burial offering. Geologically, I belong to the era between the Neanderthal and the *horlà* that comes after man, a tiny span of time in the history of the planet, and whether I would rather be located a minimal fraction of a particle closer to the one than the other in this tiny splinter of infinity is irrelevant; given the spaces of eternity one has to factor into one's calculations these days, half a dozen zeros more or less makes little difference...

Out here, incidentally, it is becoming bitter cold, the flinty polish of the sky is growing dull, the nine lead-gray monoliths, counter to the laws of atomic disintegration, are transmuting into an even heavier metal, moving one step closer together. In the grid pattern of their 2,336 windowpanes, the first lights are beginning to glow in crossword-puzzle fragments, abstract life signs of the *horlàs;* I flee toward them, for whatever posterity may think of me, I now have need of their feigned life. Nourishing kitchen smells already promise it, real, actual—good solid food will be served for supper, juicy roasts and steaks and pork loins, lavish gravies poured over mealy potatoes, sauerkraut and red cabbage, cauliflower and brussels sprouts and turnip greens, slippery puddings in vanilla sauce, strawberry sauce, raspberry sauce, soon it'll come rolling up. ("It's ready, dear! Bring along the Bommerlunder if you want to have another quick drink!") We'll wash it down with venomous Riesling, Krötenbrunn, and Liebfraumilch, perhaps beer, which will keep me burping for hours. Our Lucullanism has a Lutheran breadth, I would never have believed that I could eat so much. Through the chewing noise in my ears, I can barely make out her noncommittal admonishments: "Nice, huh? Bon appetit!" and "Tastes good, doesn't it?" I nod, grunting (one doesn't speak with one's mouth full!); nor, after I swallow, do I object to or contradict her chatter ("Well, at the new self-service store—oh, it's fabulous, dear—they have a contract with a fruit-and-vegetable importer who brings the produce direct so there's no middleman or anything"). What could I say, anyway? When I read an analysis of the Common Market in *Der Spiegel* or an exposé of tax breaks for building contractors in *Stern*, I react at best with a snort. If I put up with the one, then why not the other? Besides, I'm tracking down the poetry of emptiness, I listen for it when the broad talks about her streamlined, well-engineered household appliances ("You've just gotta see it working, dear. A whole new kind of hot-water heater"—the word causes her difficulties, like syncopated gutturals in Arabic: hahht-wawdeh-heeedeh—"it's also a coffee roaster, steam iron, dish dryer, fruit pitter, bottle rinser, garbage disposal, it's brand new, from AEG"). Her knowledge of merchandise, shopping expertise, and awareness of prices are stupendous, I see no difference between them and the specialized learning of a bacteriologist or a Sanskrit scholar. The interpersonal aspect is also included ("Well, you can get the same tie at Münnemann & Möller for only half the price"). She goes no further into personal matters, except in more or less concealed erotic offers ("That blond on the third floor, dear—you've never seen her, she's very chic—well, she's asked me about you twice already, where you come from and so on, I think she likes you, she's got a boyfriend who's with the river police, he's got a small house on the Elbe, which he inherited, they have group sex there on weekends").

Still and all, this is a curtain raiser before getting down to the real point of the visit: the Murphy bed in the bedroom has already been swung down out of the wall ("A real bed takes up more than half the space, to fold it into the wall is a lot more economical"). But it's not so simple, the structuring of sex uses Bele Bachem's corseted debauchee as a model, her claws dig into my hand as it tries to sneak under the sweater ("You little thief, you!"). After some rather intricate fiddling, the brassiere finally snaps open, her eyes deepen, she painfully bites my earlobe, then I'm promptly sucked into the maelstrom of a four-minute French kiss, no sooner can I draw my breath than the struggle with the girdle begins, but no ("I can't just undress like at the swimming pool and spread my legs, dear, there's no excitement in that"), first stocking after stocking must be detached from the complicated garter-belt mechanism, rolled down individually from each thigh, a kiss in the hollow of the knee (which she has artfully slung around my neck: "Trying to drive me crazy again, are you!"), and in order to get to the girdle again, I require some unwinding (Laocoön), pulling it down is then relatively easy (at least no harder than a rabbit skin), it comes rustling off the already damp buttocks, their notch feels marshy, a peat bog burial ground, one heartens oneself with amorous truisms (*une femme qui ne mouille pas—c'est comme un homme qui ne bande pas*). Ramming my right middle finger in all the way up to the proximal knuckle (my hand trapped between iron thighs: "You'd like that, wouldn't you? Want to make me nuts!"), I can finally think about unbuttoning myself (while sucking on one of her nipples: "Oh yes, that feels good, dear!"). For the actual act of love, I then have to carry her like a kill into the Murphy bed ("Just feel those springs under the mattress, dear—chrome steel, it doesn't rust so easily"), a frivolously added-on cliché ("If you don't rest, you don't rust") entangles me once again in the breathtaking thoroughness of one of her kisses: what follows is of the highest technical perfection, with something of the glistening enamel industrial-product luxury of the magazine ads, it aims at one's happiness, which is suspended from a safe interest rate and full-coverage insurance ("Make sure that the excitement curves meet harmoniously in the culmination points!"); all the positions shown in sex manuals are tried out, the accompanying moans have an ad-copy character ("Just see if you can find anyone who's better than me!"), any original features that break through aim to stimulate ("Trying to fuck me to death, are you?"), and the aimed-for fulfillment has psychologically remote-controlled dimensions ("Yeah—now—yeah—baby—give Mama everything!").

But that's it for now. She jumps up, marches into the bathroom, there are alternating gurgles of pipes and faucets while I smoke a cigarette, take a little (cleverly set up) baking soda with a sip of water, slowly begin to dress. She comes back from the bathroom—"Do you have to go so soon?"—the question is asked quite impersonally, a manner of speaking, so to speak, even the finest ear could not detect any implicit protest. While I then lay claim to the bathroom, she telephones for a taxi ("A gentleman would like to be driven downtown"). The leave-taking is (although jestingly intimate) casual ("Well, dear, be good now, but not too good!"). She holds the apartment door open, waiting to say good-bye, and as I pass her going into the hallway, she raises her arm to buzz open the building door, her dressing gown falls open, there is a split second of breast splendor—but before I can even think of returning, she has pulled it out of sight with a quick motion of her left hand. The building door springs open with a hissing squashed humming of wasps, I don't have to turn my head, I know she's still standing there, intersected by the door and door frame in a narrow rectangle of light that is denser and yellower than the neon lymph in the hallway. When I get to the front door, she sends a last "So long!" after me (it topples from a headvoice C down to the A: "So *lo*-ong!"), and I slam the stubborn reluctant door behind me: an air cushion in the cylinder catches the swing, and the door settles with slow dignity and a pejorative hiss into the lock. The final snap is salvation, I hear it as I flee, hunched into the artificial-leather upholstery of the taxi, I give my address to the cloddish male rump in front of me, and a hand (lit by the blue dashboard light) turns a key, the engine, rattling, kicks on, a pull on the gearshift sets the car in motion, in the rearview mirror the outlines of the first, the second, the third high-rise block (covered with radiant square mildew spots) dance darkly in the cobalt blue, and then the entire development is visible: Stonehenge, starting to fluoresce in its decay... It swings to the left and out of the mirror's range while we dip rightward into the bright flurry of an arc lamp.

Thereafter, at home, in the blissful solitude of my rented room, my dream . . .

There is no basis whatsoever for assuming that S. could actually be connected to my dream. It was probably pure coincidence that at the very moment the slip of paper with Schwab's name came into my hand, the fear hit me like a punch in the solar plexus—the fear that my murder was real, was not the projection of some triviality that had slid into my subconscious and been dramatically enlarged there by the residues of old established guilt complexes, was truly what my dream showed me: the gruesome killing of an old crone for no other reason than to prevent some even more shameful ignominy from coming to light. The momentary *recognition* is almost pleasurable: it is a *holy* terror that strikes me . . . but there's no way this sort of thing could be triggered by the thought of S., much less by my projecting him into a fictional character: a ridiculous notion, inspired by an overwrought brain. A hint of burnout, presumably. Nevertheless . . .

I have an astonishing number of notes about S., an almost alarming number. Almost every one refers to him in some way or has a later note connecting to him. But the explanation is simple: I must have reworked most of the other notes during countless revisions of countless versions of my book, with various kinds of structures. Except, of course, for the notes that were done peripherally, so to speak, and not in terms of a specific plan. Granted, this did not come without some specific idea: I cannot deny that I was tempted to depict the character of a certain Johannes Schwab: a generously constructed figure, an editor in a publishing house, intellectual guru, well read to the point of blindness, well informed about anything worth knowing to the point of despair, hence disoriented, painfully aged by abandoning his once passionately nurtured ambition to write a book himself (one of the masterpieces of the century, the classic of the era, needless to say, an opus that would inscribe his name deathlessly in the pantheon of literary titans), a great-minded, great-hearted man, inspired by lovely envy to admire lovingly all those he regards capable of accomplishing such a masterly feat in his stead (Nagel, me), hence (I would almost have said) an alcoholic, based faithfully on my friend S. in all other features and characteristics... I won't deny that I was tempted to capture such a blockbuster of a featured player on the page. Thus the many slips of paper with his name (or the initials J.S.). In the end, the explanation is simple. It can all be like this, or else entirely different.

Still, I likewise cannot deny that I am more and more obsessed with the belief that S. is standing before me, as vivid and physical as in the moment of my *recognition* of my murder. I mean to say, in the same stunning *presentness*, with the same almost blissful terror that hits me like a punch in the solar plexus—no, deeper, below the belt. A *holy* terror, I called it, and I commit myself to this expression, ludicrous as I find it, however much it may evoke the abstruse formulations of my years in Vienna—

Uncle Helmuth's and Aunt Hertha's transfigured secrecy whenever they came home from one of the séances of their spiritist community: initiates who had penetrated beyond the primitive practices of moving tables and conjuring up spirits, penetrated into the occult and thereby into the transcendent; who now virtually had a direct connection to Creation's switchboard, a through line to the Good Lord, who, as chief mechanic, kept a universe of his own invention and personal patent operating eternally by utilizing, as the motor power, energies released by the tension in the polarities of good and evil, light and dark, up and down, positive and negative, and similar pairs of opposites...

no *perpetuum mobile*, alas, if you don't want to place the promised final victory of good at infinity and bury the hope that the light of the Last Judgment and everlasting transfiguration is nigh; still, an illuminating metaphor for electricians and grease monkeys, in which they could read their ranks in the universe on all sorts of do-it-yourself power meters...

a troglodyte theodicy, which I supplemented in those days with my own mental flights into metaphysics—for example, when gazing from the window of our apartment in Vienna's Twelfth District up into the rectangular chunk of starry sky revealed by the air shaft between the front and back wings:

primal situation of man: overwhelming juxtaposition of his nothingness with infinity:

there I sat in the window niche, gazing up into the immense silver-dusted firmament beyond the fire walls, staring bewitched, like a nixie who knows of a different world in the celestial circle above the well shaft, a world about whose alien life she has an inkling as it fills her with strange yearning: exiled, trapped in the narrowness of my self and tempted out of it and beyond it by an enigmatic *something*—

and as far and high as my imagination could carry me out of myself, it never brought me to where *something* beckoned.

For beyond myself, I was stretched over and above myself. My SELF dissolved, was absorbed in cosmic vastnesses. I flew over the city of Vienna and beyond, over all the beautiful cities that mankind has built and destroyed in the eternal conflict between good and evil, up and down, positive and negative, while incessantly dying within itself and rising again from within itself. I flew over continents and over the planet and into the universe, into the icy spaces of Creation, veiled and dimmed by astral whey, where light had not yet been separated from darkness.

And soon the earth was a mere speck of dust scattering with myriads of its kind in a tremendous explosion into infinity. I, my SELF, shrank accordingly, of course: so utterly into the microcosmic that ultimately I was hurled out again into the macrocosmic, as it were: I WAS THE UNIVERSE.

When I, my SELF, burst through my human dimensions, the whole world burst with me in the clattering shattering of categories—and the thing that rose again from it, like the phoenix, was I, my SELF. Though poorer by one universe than before…

My dead friend S. didn't need to feel such anxieties anymore. Now, he *knew*. Now, he was freed from the monkey cage of his self, dissolved in the universe: with the possibility of peering into the plan of the Creator and Head Mechanic of the Universal Mechanism and understanding its wondrous ultimate meaning (or else the even more wondrous lack thereof)… It was regrettable, however, that this knowledge was no longer *his:* he had paid for it with the loss of his self (in accordance with Miss Fern, dispenser of wisdom in my childhood: "You can't eat your cake and have it"), and it was confusing to reflect that a total consciousness is one that is totally released; that is: totally dissolved in everything, hence extinguished. Still and all, such a consciousness promises us a certain state of contentment, and I simply cannot understand why S. is bothering me so much. (So much that, for instance, I am now frightened because I have perceived S. as "*something.*") Schwab's presentness is a challenge, a demand I cannot evade. The holy terror that overcame me when I identified my sense of guilt about a murder with S. is a demand. It comes from where he is now.

Among the notes that his secretary (Fräulein Schmidschelm, called Schelmie) sent me after his death, there is one in which he says that once (during a lunch at Laget: he had seen me home; that is, here, to the Épicure), I inferred that he was planning to write "a book of a religious nature"; i.e., his theodicy. I had to check this: no doubt I made a note of it; after all, our Russian duel as each other's potential biographer was in full swing. Still, I must congratulate myself upon my clairvoyance back then: this intention is now obvious. I feel the need to importune my dead friend with another of the monologues I've made for him. After all, what I have to tell him is in his interest—which he violates whenever he pushes me off into the transcendental. The point, I would like to tell him, is to draw borders: I seek my outline in order to find the outline of my book. Or, if you will, vice versa: I seek the outline of my book in order to outline myself. It comes to the same thing. Micro and macro are interchangeable here too; they are merely symbols of a multidimensional relationship. If, for example, my story is that of a man who carries within himself the picture of a man who carries within himself the picture of an adolescent who carries within himself the picture of a child, and the man and the adolescent and the child are one and the same SELF, then, quite logically, the child carries within himself a child who carries within himself an adolescent who carries within himself a man who is carried within himself by a man who carries within himself a man who carries within himself an adolescent who carries within himself a child and ad infinitum to and fro and on and on... and yet it always remains one and the same SELF...

And now inscribe a book in this SELF (or around this SELF), then you can form a simpler and even more bewitched series: a man who wants to write a book about a man who wants to write a book about a man who wants to write a book... and this diabolical circle is our case, dear friend: we dash around in it in a ring like rats in a trap, without ever reaching each other; and when we ask about the meaning and purpose of the whole business and what impels us to ask about a meaning and purpose, then we really get into a maelstrom. But, whatever, I, my SELF, am nothing but my story. And this story is my book. So I can say: *I am my book*. Regretfully a statement that obviously can't hold a candle to the Sun King's proud words "*L'état c'est moi!*" I haven't even established my kingdom. I have been trying to do so, but in vain, for nineteen years now, two more years than Joyce spent completing *Finnegans Wake*. You may at best expect something equally obscure, albeit far less brilliant. I have been a king without a country ever since you installed me as pretender to the literary throne—with, presumably, the respectful trust that I would find my kingdom and define its borders myself. My deepest, deepest thanks, retrospectively! For even while you were alive, you kept an eye on me, you noted snidely any territory I might have overlooked, you noted my annexations with such flattering envy that I kept going out in quest of virgin territory... It's all too understandable: you didn't want me to disgrace you. You had told everyone so much about my brilliance that any disappointment would have embarrassed you. People were eagerly waiting for my book; it had to be worthy of its initiator... Today, at best only Scherping is waiting for it, because money *is* more important to him than the pleasant spiritual agony of thinking that he'll never earn back the advances he's been giving me all these years. Nevertheless, your demise obliges me to show the world that you were not mistaken and that I am not a loser. I would have to be made of stone not to have sensed the meaning of the gazes focusing on me at your funeral. The book that people are expecting of me demonstrates not only who I am, but also who you were.

And I am still ready to write it, at least, this book. After eight agonizing nights and days, I am ready to write YOU, Schwab. For that's what you are asking of me. How else am I to understand your omnipresence in my mental life? You want me to write you: in your intention to write me as I write you.

Fine: that would be relative child's play. Unfortunately, you won't be satisfied with this. You want to *materialize*, in Uncle Helmuth's terms: from the vaporous or gaseous or ethereal state in which you find yourself as a deceased person (the pure soul, if you please), you wish to transform yourself back into the denser human state of flesh and bone and skin that holds this stuff together. In a word: you want me to bring you back to *life*. This involves great difficulties. You see, the few biographical strokes are enough only for an obituary. Johannes Schwab: the name is a full program equipped with a curriculum vitae, but by no means with blood-throbbing life, especially not a life lived in the melancholy of a Hyperion: heavy with thought and poor in deed. That's what you need me for. Even your full reality has to be achieved in the OTHER ever since our colleague Sartre. You need me as a mirror, Schwab. Just as I need you as a mirror, as the *Other*, whom I must reach in order to be my SELF. Please don't keep pestering me with metaphysical digressions. Don't keep making me dash about in my own brain like a rat in a trap, with the cat pushing its face up close. Do not slit my skin in order to let me ooze off into the transcendental: that's where I truly lose myself—and thereby you. That's trying too hard, man. I can write you by writing myself as you would write me; I can be your mirror, your medium, through which you materialize, in Uncle Helmuth's terms: I can make you come to life, for a writer's quill can create life and certainly wake the dead... but it will be a different, new book that I must write, a book containing me and you... do not try to convince me that this would require a third party: the GOOD LORD. Do not force him into our overloaded, our bursting concept. With you alone as a mirror image and partner in the rat-dash for form, we destroy the wonderful vision that I had of my book during the drive from Reims to Paris: a glass cathedral, shaped according to organic laws, as clear and beautiful as a crystal . . . this, I say, shattered into fragments, extinguished, kaput, even without the Almighty as the third member of the trio. I fear I cannot manage it with him. It would be more honest, for the time being, to again halt my labor on the masterwork of the era, contrite and modest (*ridimensionato*, as the Italians so profoundly put it), take up my work with the movie piglets and my refuge with Nadine.

She'll welcome me. We're of the same stock, she and I. She too lives a literary life. Of course, not in the counterfeit promise of eternally unrealized potentials. She transforms family-magazine literature into the gold of life. As a first-rate second-class film star, she has long since stopped belonging to the cinema; she now belongs to vast audiences of magazine readers—

and thus (mindful of her lofty mission) she now lives the vicarious emotional life of millions, a never-ending series of high-frequency pulp novels:

THE LOVE LIFE OF NADINE C.
Installment #39
The Chips Are Down
The episode is terminated
SUSPENSE!!!
Who will the next man be?

I'm the ideal partner here. The more hopeless the liaison at the outset, the more suspenseful the course of events promises to be. And the more stylized the variation on the everlastingly identical theme of hopelessness (though at the end of course the simple way out, separating, remains open: for after all the game must continue). And the good Lord is kept out of it.

Nor would I have to burden my conscience: Nadine has as little to fear from me as I from her. Whatever we do together takes place in the dimension of hopelessness. We move weightlessly through the space of the zero point. Thus, we'd both get our money's worth, with neither of us having to pay with himself. The alternation of hopeless literary experience and hopelessly lived literature would take on the grace of a *pas de deux.*

And the so to speak chemically pure literature would be set down in the entertainment section of the illustrated weeklies (where it has always been at home):

NEW AND ENDURING HAPPINESS FOR NADINE CARRIER?
Her relationship with Guitarist X came to a painful end. X could not help her get over her disappointment with Bobsled Champion Y. Nor could he help her forget the cataclysm of her love for Fashion Photographer Z. But now, France's most popular screen star has been regularly seen in the company of Screenwriter A (author of such hits as Heart's Blood, The Royal Eagle Project, *and* The Man in the Plastic Helmet*):—leaving nightclub "8" in Rome—*
—skiing in Courcheval—
—shopping on London's Bond Street—
—on location for her latest movie The Prodigal Daughter *(scripted by A) in Cannes—*
—at the beach in Acapulco—
—at the annual pilgrimage of the Gypsies in Camargue—
—on the grounds of the diva's country house on the Oise—

NADINE CARRIER FINALLY IN SEVENTH HEAVEN AGAIN!
Friends confirm the rumor that France's most popular movie queen is planning a May wedding with the very busy screenwriter . . .

A BABY FOR NADINE CARRIER?
Upon leaving the world-famous hospital, the smile on the face of

France's most radiant star (here accompanied by the successful) seems to confirm the rumor...

NO BABY FOR NADINE CARRIER
The disappointment on her face shows all too clearly that...

A DARK CLOUD OVER NADINE'S HAPPINESS?
During location shooting of her movie Take Me! *(scripted by A), the well-known author showed movie starlet B (who debuted in* Fever Curve*) an interest that went beyond professional considerations...*

NADINE DEFENDS HER LOVE!
Her relationship with her steady beau was endangered by a recent crisis. But now the woosome twosome have reconciled and are spending quiet weeks again in...

NADINE DISAPPOINTED BY LOVE AGAIN?
Our photo reporter managed to get a shot of the extremely shy...

A CAREER OVER THE BROKEN HEART OF CARRIER?
Movie starlet B accompanied by Nadine's previous steady beau:—
leaving the Zoum Zoum nightclub in Cannes—
—skiing in Cortina d'Ampezzo—
—shopping on Zurich's Bahnhofstrasse—
—shooting on location for her movie Till the Seventh Member *(scripted by A) in Munich-Geiselgasteig—*
—on the beach at Marbella—
—by the swimming pool of her villa on Lake Schlier (Lake Tegern, Lake Constance, Lake Wörther, Lake Como)—

STARLET'S ESCORT KNOCKS DOWN PHOTO REPORTER!
Upon leaving, on again, off again escort brutally attacked our...

IS THIS THE END?
Her tense face since her separation from her previous and now steady shows all too clearly that . . .

NEW LOVE FOR NADINE CARRIER!
We managed to get this unique snapshot—
—upon leaving the—
—while skiing in—
—when shopping at—
—on location at—
—on the beach at—
—during the annual—
—in the verdant countryside of—

IS NADINE CARRIER ABOUT TO WED
—racing-car stable-owner C?
—coiffure creator D?
—breaststroke champion E?
—sociologist F?
—playboy G?
???
??
?
(Read our next installment, #40)

I, for my part, would merely have shortened the path to contemporary immortality.

For assuming I didn't eat humble pie this time, sparing Nadine and myself a joint pulp romance, remaining here in my hideout, beating down all my weaknesses, difficulties, afflictions, and reservations; feeding on wheat germ and yeast; standing on my head for six minutes every morning to circulate the blood through my brain; and slaving away with Aunt Selma's tenacity in this cell of godforsaken human loneliness until I finished my book (and it would indeed be a book that bore witness, before the conscience of our race, to being a human being in this era—and God would be in it as he is in Nagel's best sellers)—what would be the happy end of this poignant story?

Let Scherping take the floor:

"Damn it, it's not so important what *a man writes. People want to know* how *he brought it about. What does the guy who fabricated this stuff look like? What makes him different from me, what is there about him that he can pull himself out in this* (profitable!) *way from the dismal affair of* TAEDIUM VITAE? *You've got to understand the poor souls who are so bitterly dependent on vicarious experiences. They don't want to hear any more old wives' tales. People aren't interested in stories, people are interested in existence—you understand? Do you seriously believe that anyone today has any interest whatsoever in Ulysses' adventures? As a book for young readers, maybe. But if you can come up with a book that scientifically demonstrates: WHO WAS HOMER?, it'll be on the best-seller list months before it even comes out. Take my word for it—after all, I serve experience to people—values have shifted. Anyone who wants stories goes to a flick or sits in front of the tube or scans the funnies. Today's book reader is a literary scholar—above all, a psychologist. He wants an analysis not only of the book but of the author—personal, flesh and blood: shaving early in the morning, creating, having sex (marital and adulterous), and, if possible, folding his hands for his nightly prayers. The reader wants to know: what induced* this *man to write* this *book in* this *way? The educated reader wants to get to the root of the literary: the dichotomous, the suspicious, the crack in the author's personality. He wants accurate information: what was Shakespeare's real name? how schizoid was Goethe? how queer was Proust? how good was Hemingway with handguns? And so on and so forth... The masses—the masses are adequately served by a hundred thousand publications. But in literature, they now go very personally into everything: color of eyes, shape of nose, cut of hair, and distinguishing characteristics. The literature you create is, so to speak, your own 'wanted' poster. Only then are you recognizable. Only then does the*

public retain your physiognomy. That's how you achieve prominence and get into the newspapers."

So (posthumously or otherwise), it all ended the same way:

OUR PHOTO REPORTER MANAGES TO SHOOT THE WORLD-FAMOUS CELEBRITY
(if possible in exotic company)
—while leaving the—
—while vacationing in—
—while recovering in—
—on location at—
—at his desk—
—at the annual—
—laid out under—

(under floral tributes, today no more luxurious even for Nobel laureates than those under which my friend Schwab finally came to rest).

JACOB G. BRODNY
literary agent

Can you please come & have lunch with me at Calvet's tomorrow?
12:30 OK?

B

Est Deus in nobis, agitante calescimus illo.
—OVID

Whatever we see could be other than it is.
Whatever we can describe at all could be other than it is.
—LUDWIG WITTGENSTEIN, *Tractatus Logico-Philosophicus*

The "I" is not an obstacle in being with people. The "I" is that which they desire.

—WITOLD GOMBROWICZ *Diary*, volume one

All kinds of things drop down the air shaft outside my window:

refuse—

withered linden leaves wafting down off the roof (God knows from where)—

bones of smoked fish—

spit-out peels of the sunflower seeds that the monkey-eyed Algerians chew—

sometimes, in the evening hours: cottony October fog—

and cigarette butts, condoms, sanitary napkins, hairpins—

but no light: not a single unfiltered mote of sunlight.

Only once have I seen the shaft fill with something which in its complete transparency seemed to shine from within, like pure, ethereal gas; namely, yesterday: the morning after the night in which I had been with the girl at the Madeleine.

I had slept for a couple of hours and, in effortless renunciation, eluded the magic image-weaving of some dream (rising smoothly and imperceptibly and bringing with me not a single shredded tangle, like the surfacing merman with watercress on his fish-mouthed skull)—

(Incidentally, I recall dreaming that I had to lead my foster mother Aunt Selma along the narrow ledge of a building wall—I no longer know where to. Anyway, it was high and dangerous, and suddenly a stone crumbled under her foot; she tried to cling to me, but I wrenched loose, she plunged down, and I grabbed hold of the smooth wall, closing my eyes and waiting to hear the dull thud of her body on the sidewalk below. But nothing came, and when I peered down, I saw her: her legs had either dug into the ground or were totally crushed, for she sat in the billowing skirts of a bright summer frock as though in a flower cup, waving happily up to me...)

For the first time in years, I felt myself awakening with no perceptible malaise—and I instantly knew that I was in Paris and under what circumstances and where (in which mangy hotel room) and to what sublime joys and torments with my papers I would have to open my eyes. So I did not open them right away. I lay there, enjoying my precarious peace—

enjoyed ME: yes indeed: me SELF-brimming SELF-towered (the vertical Anglo-Saxon I)

MAN-ANIMAL SELF

and as such, heartrendingly split in two: physical SELF and abstract SELF.

What is a woman like when she awakes? Embedded in herself, twin-hilled: a more intimate body, breathing life, renewing itself from life, physically more uniform: skin-SELF, flesh-SELF, hair-SELF, and yet an inner cavern: SELF *de profundis*, well and source (my foster mother in the flower cup: as if floating on the watery surface: images of flooding)—

WELLSPRING SELF (I'd like to know what kind of a face I make during an orgasm. I once tried to catch it in a mirror: it didn't work, of course. What I saw was an embarrassingly indiscreet face—embarrassingly convicted of its embarrassment. Yet strangely bloated in shock: like when you step on a garden hose. Like Schwab when he was made to see or hear something embarrassing)...

Schwab and the scene with Gaia in the car: we in front (very uncomfortable), he supposedly drunk and unconscious in the back... I must have acted quite predatory: guttural sounds squeezed out through grinding teeth and the like—

was that why Schwab thanked me?... (Gaia by the way came entirely without jungle shrieks, completely interiorized, an inner shudder. Christa sobbed blissfully, albeit only during our engagement. Dawn? I don't remember; I remember almost nothing about Dawn; only her breasts, the way I finally peeled them out of the onion sheathes of her bedtime armature that first time... Few women emit that beautiful cry, like Stella and sometimes Gisela...)

At last (for a long time now) I am sovereignly I MYSELF: undisturbed by remorse that I am as I am. I carry imprinted within myself the image of the girl I slept with last night. Sharply inscribed upon my mind's eye. How does it go in the *Arabian Nights?* "As if someone had sewn it into my eyelids..."

> *the linear curves of a young female body and their punctuation: from the angle of the raised arm propping up the head (the hand drowned in the whirling torrent of hair), drawn in an arc into the seashell of the underarm and then lifted to the apple roundings of the breasts, from whose buds a rhythmic slope runs down to the flat declivities and curvatures of the flanks and belly, where the line, to which the now entirely symbolic flesh is confined, swings out again from the violin-like constriction to the voluptuousness of the hip, from which a thigh rises, exposing its inner surface in a steep, indolent warping.*

She sleeps, very happy and relaxed. So I'm still together as a man (Kisa Gotami at the sight of Buddha: Blessed indeed is the mother, blessed indeed is the father, blessed indeed is the wife whose is a lord so glorious). I am even still young enough to imagine beating someone up—the handsome Pole with his awful arms, for instance. (Schwab always wanted to do that.) He was presumably a lot stronger than I—at least heavier. Cousin Wolfgang also carried a powerful thorax on his somewhat short legs and womanly Germanic hips (from Uncle Helmuth).

In the first of my formative years in Vienna, Wolfgang was tormentingly superior to me (but never took advantage of it), but I soon caught up with him. By fourteen or fifteen (disgusting: the masculine trail of pubic hair running to the navel, on boyish skin), I beat the hell out of him. I wasn't stronger but was tough as a whip and full of evil tricks—*After all, I had the more beautiful mother* (and the evil bewitchment of my foster mother Aunt Selma in my eyes...). By the way, there was nothing nixie-like about Aunt Selma in my dream: she was smiling: *ce si joli sourire de toute jeune fille qui était vraiment elle.*

Both are now dead, mother and foster mother. *Sur le chemin de la mort, ma mère rencontra une grande banquise*... Cousin Wolfgang too is dead; Schwab too is dead; Stella is dead—*elle nous regarda, mon frère et moi, et puis elle pleura*. And in my dream, she had her pretty smile: *un si joli sourire, presque espiègle* (a pretty word: it comes from *Till Eulenspiegel*). *Ensuite elle fut prise dans l'opaque.*

The girl from last night—she too came out of the fog. I recited poetry to her too—songs of life:

Mon enfant, ma soeur,
songe à la douceur
d'aller là-bas vivre ensemble!
Aimer à loisir
aimer et mourir
au pays qui te ressemble—

Ice-dancer language. Gaia on the telephone: swaying cadences—stop (to listen)—start again—then released: the swing of a wide arc—leap—pirouette—she stands still again: the next arc already tensing in her...

I love listening to her: with no one else does French sound so melodious, so artificial... I wait for the glass-bead tricklings of the next few sentences, look at her mouth: scarlet (*gueule*), behind it the predatory teeth of her black father (his lips like stamp pads)...

(Gaia's description: The Moor father of the Moor father arrives to extract his son from the affair; her mother, the Princess Jahovary, relates: "I saw him out the window from above as he was getting out of the car: cute—a short black Moor with his hair gone completely white..." Gaia's granddad: a negative.)

Gaia too is dead. I am surrounded by dead people. Barely forty-nine years old and already in the best society:

silently over Golgotha, God's golden eyes open . . .

I feel it, it's going to be a good day. I could not wish for a better day for my protracted vice, my passion for constructing sentences whose rhythmic tensions and solutions release the Eros of language:

in the mysterious appeal and attraction that the Word achieves in its wizard-like combination with other words: so that not only does it pass itself along to the next word and the one after that, as in the Archimedean whorl, by way of transmitting a specific and intended meaning (so as to make a series of linked signals produce an image with which experience is transmitted, as a sign whose transcendent shadow, shifting like that of a sundial, forces the other signs grouped around it to yield the secrets enclosed within them) but also (beyond language) a kind of whispering begins, an echoing in the spaces around the words, spaces that would have remained closed without the overtones of the multivalence of each word, spaces that now expand like the expiring sound waves of a tolling bell, followed and driven on by further tolling: each stroke of the bell is the assault of a primordial signal on the vessel of our soul . . .

That's how I should have awoken all those days: in calm surrender to bed-warm sensuality. I am thinking about the girl from last night: for a few hours I loved her. I still feel her perfume on my skin. It is taut from dried fluids on the inside of my thighs and under my pubic hair. I gratefully experience the feeling of having done my proper duty as a man—this steels you for future and past defeats. You won't be getting anything out of me today, friend Schwab. My mind is as blank as a Gelderland windowpane. Not a particle of ambition, not a speck of guilt:

nor do I care about the insanity of my existence: locked up in a shabby hotel room, concealed from any kind of creditor, holed up within myself, denying true reality, living crazily in invented realities: a woeful demiurge, cobbling his world together out of paper and ink, paper and printer's ink, an onanist of creation pleasure—yes, a self-satisfier, devoted to the pleasure of words—

I do not care:

I am walking a tightrope. I am ice-skating across the rope: start—sweeping out of the curve—leap—pirouette—into the next curve...

My Doomsday is remote today:

Le ciel est, par-dessus le toit,
si bleu, si calme!
Un arbre, par-dessus le toit,
berce sa palme...

(incidentally, it might really exist somewhere, *cet arbre par-dessus le toit*—otherwise, where would the linden leaves come from?...)

I am in Paris. Are you listening, Schwab? I am in Paris—which you loved so much, "as if it were life itself"

Mon Dieu, mon Dieu, la vie est là,
simple et tranquille.
Cette paisible rumeur là
vient de la ville—

(and you plunge into the *paisible rumeur*—I yank you back—a cabby's head emerges from a taxi and yells: "*Dis donc—le trottoir: c'est seulement pour les putains?*"—do you remember?) It was by the Madeleine, where you picked up that girl—only it wasn't bright out: *la ville lumière* was drowned in fog—the bright, lovely underworld...

and whatever you have to say: my soul will be forgiven

God spoke a gentle flame to his heart: oh, Man!

I know today will be a good day. I am as God originally meant me to be: a breathing creature that does not regard its existence as a curse: I lie here and feel MYSELF in the creaturely bliss of existence. I am still aglow with the images of my dream, images that are signs for other meanings: Aunt Selma's smile means *woman:*

woman's flesh, woman's fullness, woman's warm skin, in which the spherical triangle of pubic hair is sharply inserted in pure contour: powerfully streaming from the base to the vertex, into the closure of the thighs, insular and mystical like the grove around a grotto temple—

here I am SELF-towered:

violently a black horse rears: the hyacinth curls of the maid grab at the ardor of his purple nostrils . . .

I look for the face of a girl and do not find it in me. It is often quite close, but when I think I'm about to recognize it, it dissolves. I am so awash in lazy self-feeling that nothing in me has distinct contours.

I AM

and am content in ME:

I SELF-brimming

The warm mother hen of laziness broods me and makes beautiful thoughts slip from beautiful images.

FOR UNTO EVERY ONE THAT HATH SHALL BE GIVEN, AND HE SHALL HAVE ABUNDANCE, BUT FROM HIM THAT HATH NOT SHALL BE TAKEN EVEN THAT WHICH HE HATH . . .

All my power (and all my fear) is rooted in this verse, and no one is left around me to measure its truth by . . .

Truly, Brother Schwab: your death was a severe stroke of fate for me. You were to the best years of my adulthood what Cousin Wolfgang was to my adolescence: the lovely echo, the magic mirror on the wall. I know every last feature of your face and his. The nervous pride of the brow. The twitching vulnerability of the mouth. The bright lurking and the despair in the half-blind eyes, which could look so sharply from behind the glasses' lenses. —

Your eyes and his were almost ludicrously the same. Never will I forget his gaze when in August 1939—shortly before I went to Romania to be a soldier myself—he came to me in plain military gray: wordless, with the force of an expressionist stage entrance. His globular eyes peered through glasses as thick as bottle bottoms (just like yours: all in all, he could have been your twin), and these eyes expressed, in an ineffably stupid stare, "Well, what do you have to say now? . . ." And they almost burst with fear of finding out what I might say.

Wasn't this often your fear too, friend Schwab? Otherwise, in order to have a brother, I could have made do with Nagel. He was never afraid of what I might say. He did not seek his defeats in me. He evaded me like a man (for that's basically what it's all about, isn't it? Measuring yourself against someone else?)... Let me reveal one of the secrets that made you blush when you were alive, a medium-size depth-psychological secret (but don't tell Hertzog): *I was never afraid of being beaten up by you.* If by anyone, then Nagel (although that's absurd: the poor man has only one arm, after all). Nagel doesn't want to measure himself against me. You always wanted to measure yourself against me. I for my part am sorry: I want to measure myself against the handsome Pole. Remember his arms? Fantastic, man!... I sometimes daydream about smashing him in the kisser—and then... just ask Sherping what happens when a man imagines *he could be helplessly abandoned to his defeat.*

(Schwab's confession: the blush in his face when he told me about how he would come home and run into his wife Carlotta's lovers on the stairs; how he confronted her, and she told him straight to his face, "Yes, somebody comes every day when you're not here."

And John's stony expression when I returned with Stella, both of us still glowing...

or I in front of Dawn in the sleeping car, in the morning: I had lain awake all night in the next compartment, she sitting on the bed, the damp stain half-concealed on the sheet, and I ask, "What about your friend?" "Oh, he left. He got off the train somewhere last night." Our last—no, next-to-last—meeting. She talking in the phone booth, I, outside, hear what she's saying: "But I love you—you can't leave me..." These are male experiences: they lead to measurings.)

Each man seeks his defeat in the other: that's the simple solution to the riddle of brotherhood. (Are you really blushing now? What's it like when a soul blushes? Like when the light in the air shaft outside the window filled up with the redness of dawn?)

However, I am speaking the truth:

Everyone seeks his murderer in the other; that is what makes human beings brothers. It's as simple as a pulp romance novel, ("and so marvelously symbolic," as Fräulein Ute Seelsorge would say). I was always sympathetic to your attraction to Nagel: it is fascinating to watch him fall into despair for sheer courage; but did you really ever take him seriously when it happened? And you don't even know everything about Nagel. What you admired, why you envied him, was relatively easy to endure: his cast-iron character; his boy-scout single-mindedness; the raging ardor with which he wrote book after book; his poignant wrestling with the angel of literature (Hemingway as Gabriel); his touching and unswerving faith in the writer's mission ... What if you found out that he has given up all those things—in favor of political action?

He is a man of honor, our good Nagel ... like you ... isn't that so? May I ask what you died of? Surely not the combination of alcohol, uppers, and downers? I suspect you died because you took it too seriously that you failed to take yourself as seriously as Nagel.

And now I'd like to know what so fascinated you about me, friend Schwab. The evil? ... That's a fabulous notion. Evil. Admit it. Be honest for once (it can't matter to you anymore): What was the measuring between us? What did my irony challenge in you? Or rather: *As what* did it challenge you? as evil? That should have occurred to me for my last draft of the book—what a lummox I am! I have the stuff of seven best sellers in me and stand in front of literature as if it were a barn door—

of course: EVIL was the basis of measurement between Schwab and me. EVIL tempted us in each other ... If that's not a find! ... I'm going to turn it into a movie: *The Tempter* (get the title registered right away!).

BELOVED TEMPTER
An Intercosmic Film
Script: Aristides Subicz. Lead actress: Nadine Carrier (this time playing a man)

If this doesn't put some spring into the curly tails of my piglets! Done very discreetly, you understand, very delicately: a man, by means of sheer irony—okay?—gets another man—his bosom buddy, of course—to—what?—well, obviously: TO COMMIT A MURDER...

(call Wohlfahrt immediately: he'll flip his lid; he'll fly to Hitchcock with the idea tomorrow.)

I knew it: this is going to be a creative day. The idea is brilliant. Eventually, it'll lead to the *theodicy*, which was so important to Schwab. EVIL in its most sublime, most perfidious variations: love, friendship, brotherhood. The brotherhood of Cain and Abel... It would have fascinating dramatic high points: Cousin Wolfgang's appearance, for example: "Well, what do you have to say now?..." Nothing. What should I have said? A man is given the chance to survive at least the first half of a struggle between maddened nations, survive it calmly and well fed in a brown shirt, but his conscience does not permit him; or rather: THE TEMPTER has aroused this conscience in him... So, at the very start, for the Polish campaign, he plants himself before the tempter in a poignantly simple military gray, and his eyes ask with defiant anxiety, "Well, what do you say now?..." Plants himself with clumsy significance before the tempter, like the lead actor in an expressionist play, his very entrance fulfilling a bit of German destiny, the man in military gray symbolizing Langenmarck, Stalingrad... and his eyes, mole blind from reading so much Stefan George, heartbreakingly tragic and defiantly anxious, ask, "Well, what do you have to say now?..."

I have nothing to say. Not to you, either, dear Schwab. I lie here and breathe in the creaturely bliss of existence. I've got eight days and nights of a Descent into Hell behind me and presumably a few more days and nights ahead of me: I KNOW THAT I AM A MURDERER—like anyone who has a brother.

I know my measure of guilt. Even for certain deaths (including yours) for which I am only very indirectly responsible. Cousin Wolfgang, for example, would not have had to pass away so prematurely but for me ("Well, what do you have to say now?..."); likewise Stella; likewise Gaia. But this was, so to speak, the midwife's role I played for death. Everyone plays it occasionally and also finds his own helper when his hour comes. Nor do I want to mention the corpses that still walk about on two feet in broad daylight: Christa in Hamburg or Dawn in her madhouse. And perhaps also my once so deeply beloved son—a growing corpse, a corpse apprentice, so to speak—who will soon mature to manhood, find a trade, woo a wife, make babies: all this as someone who died prematurely, killed by his father... I did it in order *to be close to an Other*. The way Nadine always wants to *be close* to someone. Like Christa, when we first met in the hell of Nuremberg—like Dawn: initially her awakening, her happiness, and then the plunge back into solitary confinement with herself—

Why did you die, Schwab? To reach someone else?... To show me and Nagel and Carlotta and Hertzog and Scherping and God knows who else that your tormented *existence in contemptuous conditions* was no fiction, no literary as-if, but a dreadful reality?... I imagine that your dead eyes must have contained the same defiantly anxious question as Cousin Wolfgang's eyes when he stood before me, dressed in military gray for the sacrifice: "Well, what do you have to say now?..."

Let me tell you what I have to say: Your murder was not properly structured; your sacrifice was in vain; you proved nothing, you only proved yourself to be a biological backfire; you did not kill yourself because your despair at *existence in contemptuous conditions* did not even let you write about it; the truth is: you lived in despair *because you had to kill yourself.*

You taught me a great deal about life, Schwab: you made me realize in what way I am superior to all of you: I ACCEPT THIS EXISTENCE IN CONTEMPTUOUS CONDITIONS HUMBLY AND GRATEFULLY. This is my HAVING for whose sake I AM GIVEN...

I am like that wolf in Bessarabia: I bite at everything around me, slavering, I bite into my flanks, and the bullet that is to release me shoots only my leg off, and I limp away on three legs, grateful THAT I AM ALIVE...

That is my monstrous power: the power with which I murder even when I don't murder with my hands: FEAR IS MY POWER: wolf hunger and wolf tenacity and wolf fear in my sucked-in belly...

The fear, for instance, THAT I WILL NOT WRITE MY BOOK:

this book with no solid ground plan or outline, no foundation-laying idea, no shaping principle. This book, which increases and proliferates like a cancer, nourished by my moods and whims, by my hopes, wishes, dreams, and visions, my ecstasies, illuminations, contritions, despairs, revelations, insights, perceptions, wrong erroneous foregone conclusions, drives, compulsions, likes and dislikes, by my wisdom and by my folly... This book, which grows out of all these things like one of the monstrous houses that fools build out in provincial nooks somewhere, remote from the times, like turned-up giant-dwarf grottoes among the gillyflowers and Aaron's rods of their rustic gardens: with a hundred arches, stairways, galleries, oriels, and balconies; gabled, domed, and betowered; crowned with merlons, steps, ramps, balustrades; adorned with blind niches, vases, rosettes, and lanterns. All the formal elements of our form-proliferating, form-devouring Europe hybridly piled one on top of the other, crusted one on top of the other... thus proliferations of form coming not from a lack of form, but rather from a glut of it. I want to say *everything* in this book: everything I know, presume, believe, recognize, and sense: everything I have gone through and lived through; the way I have gone through it and lived through it; and, if possible, why and to what end I went through it and lived through it...

and I say it with the ardor of credulous simplicity—with blind faith in God—that a specific form must ultimately be ingrown in something that is so immediately and compulsively produced out of necessity (and against all expectations to the contrary)...

... and while I was thinking all these things, a memory flashed through me, terrifyingly, a memory of a conversation with S. (in front of Pollock's canvases at the first Documenta? or later? at some trashy Action Painting show here in Paris?). Anyway, a conversation I outlined rather accurately and didn't come across while going through my papers during the past few days. A conversation then that must be misplaced or lost, like so many other things... and (precisely because it's been lost) seemed to contain something that must finally, as the conceptual essence of my book, contain the key to its form...

A conversation with Schwab about snails and the houses they produce out of themselves as the expression of their species: always quite typical and yet individually distinct in pattern, coloring, and ultimate form... Plus a quotation from Valéry, which Schwab, of course, promptly had at hand, and which I will never find again without my notes and books...

And with that, I was at last fully awake and greeting the dear day.

It was yesterday. I did not get up or open my eyes. I lay motionless and tried to guess what time of day it was: was it early morning? late afternoon? Somewhere within, I was seized with the desire to get up quickly and go to the Madeleine, where the girl I had left last night might still be hanging around. But there was time for that tomorrow. I kept lying there. What absorbed me was the lost note.

It was, of course, nonsense to imagine it could contain any tidings of salvation, a magic word that would be the key to my book. Yet all my thoughts were fixed on it. It seemed to me I should have thought of it when, with the first note about Schwab to come into my hand, the terror of my dream and the *recognition* of my murder pounced on me. And this, I felt, signified that the two were mysteriously connected: the dream about my murder and the lost contents of the note. I ought to recognize this connection so that it might become clear: the *it* that was about to express itself through me.

As far as I could recall (and it was now enormously important for me to recall), I had slipped the note on the conversation back then (when?) into the folder marked *Hamburg—Miscellaneous*: presumably as the model for one of the fireside chats in Rönnekamp's salon: the cultural chitchat—so cultivated as to be stageworthy—of old pederasts in front of disdainfully bored young homosexuals (boys with breathlessly husky voices and skulls clearly marked in their smooth doll heads, exotically beautiful, like Siamese cats) and ordinary seamen dragged over from the docks (stupidly blue-eyed, sweat-fermented, with laborer's fists like hammers, sexual apparatuses bulging out of snug flies, rosebud-like carbuncles where their Sunday shirt collars sawed into freckled necks... all these things in Folder C).

In those days (happy days of innocence!), I took a schoolboy-like pleasure in describing such causeries, and enriching the ghostly self-exposures—the regular Saturday-night stripteases down to the bone of Wilhelmine, Hanseatic humanism, which Carlotta watched with her lazy eyes and sensually puffed cheeks—with small fragments from my occasional exchanges of ideas with Schwab . . . A malicious act against S., of course, a despicably cheap betrayal and, for that, twice as painful to his virginal mind, a treason against our intimate intellectual rapport . . . He would surely have understood immediately what I was driving at when he found his remarks (chastely costumed as questions: "Don't you really think that it might possibly be different, namely . . . ?") placed apodictically into Rönnekamp's tart auntie-mouth—

Rönnekamp's pale, sharp private-eye profile (Arsène Lupin, avenger of the disinherited—the main reading material of my formative years in Vienna) and the fanatically cold vanity in his tropically lashed eyes when he snapped in his hard Baltic accent: "This, gentlemen, is simply the very antithesis of art!"

Happy days of my youthful callowness, when the sketches for my book were still briskly drawn from human life (and who would ever have dreamed back then that it would not be granted me to present it to Schwab in a finished manuscript and relish my first triumph in his beautiful envy)!

At any rate, and be that as it may: now the notes were lost. In the past few days, I had meticulously, yes downright hungrily combed the folder marked *Hamburg—Miscellaneous*, and had not come across the note. Nor had I missed it when going through the folder, even though an obviously related list of idiotic questions about the philosophy of art had come into my hands:

> *Does the supposed distortion of a Romanesque lion have an artistic aim? Or did the Romanesque simply "see things that way"?*
>
> *Is art a by-product? That is: Did Giotto paint his frescoes as an artist or as a pious Christian?*
>
> *To what extent would the literary value of Samuel Pepys's* Diary *be greater had it been fiction?*

(and so on)—

These things could truly have been uttered in Rönnekamp's salon or even in Witte's refined home: as at a round table of *Kultur*-bearers, among whom Christa appeared like a regrettably mute unicorn, quite properly manipulating a knife and fork (what exquisite things she would have yielded had she been granted the power of speech!). Grouped around her: the director of the School of Arts and Crafts with his wife (a former ballet mistress); the publisher of the *Financial Gazette* with his wife (a doctor of philosophy); a cybernetics teacher with his wife (intimidated petite bourgeoise; incidentally, the only one who got Christa to speak, three brief sentences about a pudding recipe). And at the high point of the discussion, somewhere the question "Boots, you feel, are a Freudian symbol?"

Which is patriarchally rebuffed by Witte: "Please, not at the table!"

Again, and yet again: happy days! For just imagine if I could have had that dance of death published back then, that macabre postwar German round: Christa, Rönnekamp, Witte, and Carlotta: the victims of the resistance movement and the sodomy law, the economic-reconstruction miracle, the *Financial Gazette*, arts and crafts and cybernetics, Doktor Oetker's pudding powder and Professor Doktor Jaspers's philosophy hand in hand, and: reach for the violin, Dame Past! *Kultur* starts playing in an Isadora Duncan dress. A bit moth-eaten, of course: the ivy is growing out of *Kultur*'s eye sockets. But these are true values, salvaged from the rubble, dusted off and freshly polished:

but, no doubt about it, that list was part of another (fragmentary) note that I had found floating loosely in the folder labeled *Magma* and transferred to the new folder labeled *Schwab* (although I can no longer recall my intention—certainly not as a model for a conversation with him? Impossible!):

> *—in literature too (militant since Dada) the tendency to emulate artificially the immediacy of involuntary production. Naturally, then, a reliable judgment on the aesthetic value of such products presumes a critic outside the species and genus, as remote from such products (and their authors) as the man is from*

the snail's house whose beauty he recognizes: at the very least, it presupposes a person at a reliable distance in time—as, say, we to the art of Romanticism. Hence the question: How many centuries (or decades—the gap is shrinking visibly) must pass for us to be able to appreciate correctly the style of an era? the thing that adheres without exception to each and every one of its artistic creations, so characteristically that one can fairly recognize it at first sight; namely, the thing that is produced along with it, unconsciously and involuntarily, as if the zeitgeist were guiding the artist's hands (so compellingly that a mediocre contemporary copy is harder to distinguish from the original than a masterful copy done in a subsequent era; and this later copy, in the different penmanship guided by the zeitgeist, reveals itself to be a copy no matter how brilliant the copyist or counterfeiter)?

So far so good: scolding idiots for cultural chatter: Europe transformed into prattle (which is what had made Christa yearn for America: "They at least have their feet on the ground"). The topic for a Round Table Discussion. Participants: the art historian Frau Doktor X, the sociologist Professor Y, the sculptor and Ernst Barlach Prize laureate Professor Z, and the successful writer Nagel as moderator... And now for the bubbling, foaming, and fermenting of the cultural experience:

We are blind to the peculiarity in the expression of our own era (its so-called style). Today, nothing enables us to discern what will subsequently make a painting by Kandinsky attributable to roughly the same time as one by Augustus John—while we can already see that Corot and Seurat were contemporaries, not to mention David and Delacroix. And the further back we look, the more clearly we see the common features in the character of this epoch's handwriting, and the more modestly the individual distinctions in handwriting recede into the background. We also involuntarily retreat from the style of the immediately preceding era (when we have sufficiently detached ourselves from it to discern it). We regard it as unbearably mannered, dusty, trivial. A breaking of images commences, an iconoclasm—until the gradually increasing distance uncovers that era's charms and lets us read between its lines, as it were. This too proceeds in undulations of presumably measurable frequencies and interfrequencies.

So much for the extant note: a pulverized feuilleton, which could be preserved in its dryness, ground into word-gruel, and stuffed into the mouths of characters in novels. Frail Calder mobiles orbit overhead, and the cybernetics man sits in the corner of the sofa with crossed legs and chats about art: "The phenomenon as such, mind you, is highly interesting—may I have a bit more sugar for my coffee, dear madame..."

And though I knew that the lost note could scarcely contain anything more essential, I now missed it with an impatience that drove me to despair. But that meant again that I was thinking of my book, as if I did want to finish writing it after all. It was still alive within me, then. I was alive. In spite of Schwab. In spite of Brodny, whom I had seen, hated, offended, and boorishly left before I encountered the girl at the Madeleine. I was intent on writing my book in spite of him. In spite of my murder. I wanted to live on in my book... And I hadn't yet destroyed everything connected to it, there was still a pile of beginnings, outlines, notes—except for the one.

Let's keep one thing in mind: I had only just awoken. I thought, saw, felt all this in the moment of awakening itself: *it was my awakening*; it coincided with the signals: vanishing dream—hotel room—Paris—now—here—today—I—my—SELF—

my consciousness was still rubbing its eyes at all this; it was still surprised at, and almost caught unawares by, the things it had to register: it was not fully operative; in pajamas, so to speak, and not yet in pants. Its hair was still disheveled, and it was still chewing its emotive breakfast bread: the foster mother in the flower cup, the fear on the building ledge, the plunge and the salvational gesture of waving from far below, the erotic tidings contained within...

behind these things, however, everything else was already seized and stowed, waiting to be processed: a fermenting gruel of images, perceptions, thoughts, associations, emotions, reflexes; the tremendous mass of surging abstractions that a brain must cope with to set a man's day into motion—a writing man, who feeds it with himself.

The accursed nut kernel–shaped beast under my scalp was already roaring to be fed again. It was already raging in its shell again, this disgusting, gluttonous heap of soft, pale, skin-covered, inwardly twisted, layered pudding mass marbled with bloody veins and arteries. It plopped down heavily again upon my existential creature comfort, squeezing the bliss of vegetation, a bliss as warm as cow's milk. It was already eating again into my divine filiality, that fat caterpillar, eating me off the Tree of Life . . .

And I rebelled against it, offered my animalish body against it: my proud morning glory: my SELF-towered SELF: the warmth of my limbs under the blanket, which I had pulled up all the way to the tip of my nose, my dear skin smell, the resilience of my sinews, the solidity of my muscles, the sweetness of my saliva, the vital sustenance of my breath. I mobilized my gonads, which were quite active anyhow: I reviewed the gamut of last night's erotic images and sensations, of other nights of love, untold nights of love, real or dreamed—all this to withdraw my brain's food: *me*. To save myself from myself, carry me into a different greedy center of my life and being, abstracted from myself into the throbbing, swelling, tensing, urging of a stiffening member—

but it now throbbed, tensed, urged into emptiness, into nothingness . . . the images remained images, abstractions; the emotions dissolved in their own echo; the juices produced shot back and operated as poisons: the nourishing juices of abstraction—

what remained was an impatience that snorted, stamped, reared like a stallion: a powerless desire to *realize* myself, to redeem myself in some way from this existence in a vacuum; from this life in abstractness, which my brain mass reflected for me before immediate life.

What the hell had happened anyway? I had once again mislaid, lost, destroyed a note—in any case, done away with it. Who cares? What was it anyhow? Some hot air about art.

Art. When I hear the word, I first see Gaia before me: Gaia in a flowery hat. Whenever a conversation spirals up into cultural heights,

I see Gaia before me with that hat: a giant chocolate doll with a peony cake on its head. Gaia, the powerful, the splendid-bodied: a dark height of six feet, seventy-seven kilograms live weight, one hundred fifty-four pounds of mahogany-brown, vanilla-scented mulatto flesh, shimmering corn-gold at the curve tips and darkening to brownish violet in the shadowy spheres, corseted, ruffled, bowed, and ribboned into a gigantic sofa doll: chubby little hands raised delicately with crooked pinkies, as though wielding a small, invisible baton to accompany her precocious, amazingly knowledgeable, extraordinarily suave and sophisticated sentences . . . The whole thing superdimensional, however; gigantic: Gaia, the chocolate caryatid, bearing upon her head the dusty, disheveled, magnificent patchwork array of blossoms, the blossoms of Refined Culture . . .

And because her skin was earth-brown covered with corn-gold and not anemically colorless; because the mystery of a different race flashed in her enameled eyes, in the glittering rows of her teeth, in the mirroring patent-leather of her hair, denouncing every word of her cultural blabber, giving it a wild, unused naturalness, a red originality of the blood, which still surged under paw strokes and predatory shrieks, close to the earth, which craved to drink it up—because, of all these things, she was barbarously beautiful, cannibalistically ornamental . . .

Yes! She could afford to chitchat about art. It suited her, the misunderstanding that makes the holy effort of banning chaos appear to us as an intellectual competitive sport. It complemented her resplendent exoticism, made it poetic: palm-filled atolls fanning on the blue sea, sugarcane plantations rustling under aromatic breezes, sails billowing: the word "culture" regained its literal meaning: became colonial . . . A Negro in a leopard-skin loincloth is a savage, but a Negro wearing a tuxedo dickey and starched cuffs becomes a poetic picture-book Negro: becomes art—while a lymphatic paleface prattling on about art, a watery-eyed mealworm-skull, who attaches to it reflections on the philosophy of culture—why, these are mere particles in the vomit that this mortally ill white race keeps throwing up—

And I have bathed in this vomit: have taken it for dragon's blood that makes the skin invulnerable—alas, a linden leaf dropped between Siegfried's shoulder blades (from the *arbre par-dessus le toit*, perhaps, who knows?) from somewhere out there in the golden blueness that filled the fog yesterday and is now so brightly illuminating the shadows in the air shaft...

A mood-moment, in any case. This sort of thing should not be underestimated. The weather yesterday was still affecting me. In the weather I recognize myself in my paleontological strata.

Let's keep in mind: for me, weather has always been more of a psychological than a meteorological phenomenon. The days of my childhood, for example (which I count as having lasted until my mother's death), were never marred by even the smallest cloudlet. Sparkling blue sky everywhere (particularly dense, of course, above the Côte d'Azur). The stolidity of my formative years in Vienna was something I allowed to pass over me with my head drawn in: I no longer remember when it rained or when the sun shone. Unusually clear weather (clear as glass and almost painfully cold) prevailed in Vienna in March 1938, at the so-called *Anschluss*, the annexation (or upheaval), and it remained sunny throughout my summer with Stella in the Salzkammergut. Distinct changes in the seasons (childlike delight at the ardor of the snowmelt, for example, at the black crumbly earth thawing free underneath, the starry-eyed primroses sprouting in last year's wet yellow grass, the first bright, tender green on the birch branches and so on, the leaden sky under which the white balls of cherry blossoms explode, weeks of summer heat thick with flowers when the horizons flicker like fire lanes, apocalyptic downpours whipping the silvery, surging cornfields, lightning flashes and thunderclaps, then abrupt silence, a steaming sigh of relief in Nature—the end of the world was only playacted, everything is sparkling again, the red poppy glows again in the yellow of the wheat next to the truehearted blue of the cornflowers, a blinking dripping from the leafy roof of treetops with the clouds rolling apart overhead, the day mistily brooding to a close, a magical mosquito dance as the shadowy webs of evening weave thicker and thicker, then the moon rises big, round, and clarifying, yes, indeed; finally, the blue-and-gold self-immolation of autumn)—these pleasures, long since anachronistic, I could experience after my childhood only upon returning home to Bessarabia. But then, it was almost winter.

And oddly enough, this winter has already skipped across a few years of military events (I spent them under arbitrarily changing climatic conditions, like a mouse zigzagging around inside a cage of predators where the beasts pounce on one another: one had little opportunity to consider the weather). It was the Ice Age anyhow. But true winter—a crisp snowland, in which the kneeling world turns its back on you in the sweeping storm of ice crystals, the angels are frozen to the earth, they cannot raise their eyelids, frozen stiff over their blind eyes—true winter, I say, resumed for me only when the weapons fell silent.

As we know, it wasn't only the weapons that fell silent back then. The cities fell silent too—that is, what was left of them. They were nothing but chains of streets leading through rubble fields, acres of brick debris, mortar, cement fragments under bonnets of snow: white, hilly districts where the frost softened and leveled the harsher contours with its pitiless grasp. Here and there a cracked lighting pole showed its dangling wires, here and there a section of wall loomed, with its back to the horizontal sweep of the ice wind. Basement caves that weren't filled in were tenanted by people. They too were silent (understandably).

I was granted this winter experience in Hamburg-on-the-Elbe (frozen over) in 1945–46, 1946–47, and 1947–48.

Needless to say, various mild months occurred in between. At times, the rubble landscape even donned a camouflage-green-splotched frock. Perhaps, people even sweated there occasionally, healthfully sweated out the excessive water content of cabbage, potatoes, and fodder beets—ultraviolet sun rays might have eased hunger edema—but all in all, the winter withdrew only temporarily and soon returned with an even icier grip on the ruins of the city.

All this is known. Most of my German contemporaries went through it themselves (meanwhile, cinematic artworks have come to us from America envisioning the day after the annihilation of the world by hydrogen bombs: the mood is pretty much the same), so I can spare myself the trouble of describing it in detail. The only interesting thing is that this grim wintertide stayed with me rather traumatically—but only by virtue of its loss.

What people don't know (or at least don't generally remember) is that it was heartrendingly human. It was certainly no radiant humanity (like, for instance, that of the late Herr Doktor Albert Schweitzer, who was being held up to everyone as an example) but, rather, the dismal, gray-faced humanity of slums—and, despite all the anguishing nuances, the story is ultimately of biblical simplicity: the evil are bad, the good good; the lukewarm lukewarm, the fiery fiery; the wise wise, the fools foolish; the smart people smart, the stupid ones stupid.

That's how simple the world was (until the day when the weather changed again as though by magic, marked in my notes as the "day of the currency cut"): almost a picture-book world.

People dealt plainly with one another (almost everyone wore rags). If you had nothing to say, then you held your tongue (although the man who held his tongue was not necessarily the one who had nothing to say); but if someone talked, you listened. If he talked nonsense, you promptly told him so: people weren't shy in those days (they had already learned the meaning of fear). If you asked someone for something and he turned you down, you accepted that as his privilege and didn't hold a grudge. If someone gave you something, you were grateful. If someone stole something from you, you let him go (you would probably have done the same in his place). If you had no bed to sleep in, you pushed a couple of sleeping people closer together and lay down next to them—and if they drove you away, they had bad dreams afterward. Anyone who didn't want to share his piece of bread ate it alone and was ashamed (or else wasn't: that was his privilege). Any man who coveted his neighbor's wife was a wonderboy: just where did he get the calories?!

Most likely, a very few did live in joy, in the lap of luxury, on the gravy train. But they were marked. Marked not to be condemned but to be marveled at: extraordinarily vital (or miserable) existences. To put it tersely and topically: the middle-class categories were canceled. Values were drawn not from ideologies but from living reality—in nouns, not adjectives: my friend the black-marketeer. That asshole of a food official. Unsophisticated, plain, and simple.

All in all, it was a wonderful time.

It was the time when Christa had every reason to be jealous of Nagel. I truly loved him. His makeshift home was a garden house that a couple of nearby bombs had torn askew (our home was the remnants of the adjoining villa on the Elbchaussee: Christa was counted among the relatives of the victims of the Twentieth of July, to whom the assholes at the housing office gave preference). And here, I made up for the boy-scout romanticism I had avoided in wise timidity during my formative years in Vienna (albeit not without secretly envying my cousin Wolfgang, who joined everything). We distilled turnip liquor in an apparatus cobbled together out of two old watering cans. We lay in wait on the Elbe ice to catch starving coots. Once, we even bagged one, and in order to roast it festively, Nagel burned his cello (he couldn't play it now anyway, not with one hand). In the evenings, when we snuggled under an old horse blanket like orphaned brothers, field-flower bouquets of delightful stories blossomed from the fiery mouth of the little iron stove (to which we had fed Christa's portable gramophone—I wanted to contribute my fair share, after all). Christa, meanwhile, lay in bed in the ruined villa and pouted.

No one could tell such marvelous stories as Nagel. He had lived through a lot and was a keen observer. After all, he had made up his mind to write at a very early age—a reader of Jack London and Joseph Conrad, later an enthusiastic adept of Knut Hamsun, and then, of course, Hemingway. He had had all the experiences that I had not had: the hard, deliciously variegated, adventurous reality of life. Everything I still have not managed to experience. When scarcely an adolescent, he had run off with a circus. For one and a half months—still and all. When they caught up with him, his parents put him in the doghouse, but six weeks later, he was off again: signed up as cabin boy on a tiny freighter that plowed the Baltic Sea. Only one round trip, to be sure, but the wind hit Force Nine three times. His father was a beer-brewery engineer in Harburg. At sixteen, Nagel could drink like a fish and was kicked out of the Hitler Youth for insubordination. A resistance fighter, obviously. Shortly before he was supposed to graduate from high school, he punched his teacher, was expelled, and entered the Labor Service. He dug ditches in the hills of the Rhön and learned how to fly a glider; he fell from an altitude of thirteen feet and broke his leg. Wearing a cast, he took a makeup exam; and no sooner could he walk again than he strapped on a rucksack, according to the good old German tradition, and, with the laudable humanistic goal of hiking along the entire route of Goethe's first voyage to Italy, set off. But because he was nearing conscription age, the assholes at the passport office refused to give him a passport; embittered, he went to the coal district of Upper Silesia, where he worked underground for eight weeks with a safety lamp on his forehead (I was familiar with the white-toothed smile in his blackened face from his dealings with the iron stove). Then he had an idea. He went to Munich and, by way of old comrades from the Labor Service, contacted a certain Party agency, which, after a brief training period (he already knew about explosives from the mine), sent him across the Alpine border to infiltrate Austria as a provocateur.

There, however, he didn't spend much time provoking the Schuschnigg regime, which was decaying anyway (his opinion of Austrians was never high; he found fault with me too, certain features that he ascribed to my formative years in Vienna: inadequate solidity of character, for instance, hence also careless squandering of a certain talent for linguistic artistry). He gave up political agitation among the cisleithan assholes and (a forerunner, a pioneer, of hitchhike tourism) thumbed his way across Switzerland to Italy. There (more dynamic than Goethe), he forged ahead through Terracina, all the way to Palermo, crossed over to Libya, traipsed along the North African coast to Ceuta (a florilegium of small adventures—nowhere near as vividly narrated as on those frost-crackling winter evenings under the horse blanket—has just been put out by Scherping). Next, he crossed the Fretum Herculeum, navigating his own sailboat, and, by way of Spain and France (five fantastic days in Paris: brothel visit and so on!), he came back to Germany. While crossing the border, he was intercepted. He had neglected to obey his draft notice, had not promptly answered the call of duty, and was therefore considered a deserter. The outcome could have been unpleasant, but his father (fortunately a World War I veteran, Iron Cross First Class, gold Party pin) ironed the matter out. Of course, his offspring was promptly inducted into the Wehrmacht.

Uniformed, shorn, given hell, thrown in the guardhouse, put on latrine-cleaning detail ("I'm gonna make you slave like Augeas, you fucker!"). Then, as a reward for the work accomplished, he was allowed to belly through the Lüneburg Heath in full battle dress and kit. In revenge, young Nagel (familiarized, incidentally, with the teachings of Sigmund Freud during his travels abroad) drew the necessary conclusions from the twofold Oedipus situation with his father the beer-brewer and with Father State and became a Communist. However, an active cultivation of this anything but popular ideological direction was obstructed by the war.

But in those days, when the ice wind tattered the angels' frozen feathers, something glowed over the crooked garden house of the villa on the Elbchaussee: the star under which our allegedly rationalist yet ardently myth-believing century has ever sought the start of a new Golden Age.

Nagel had ignited the star. He had, of course, enriched it with evangelical rays (he had met God in the war—a story that has been served up to his readers in several versions), but the model was still recognizable.

From among those who had returned and those who had stayed at home, refugees, stragglers, and drifters, a small circle of like-minded and simply conversation-minded people had formed around him, and this circle now drank our home-brewed turnip schnapps, rolled cigarettes out of the tobacco Christa raised on the manure pile (she, meanwhile, lay in bed and pouted), and overcame the unovercomable past (which back then was the present of yesterday). People discussed Karl Marx, Ortega y Gasset, and Hemingway, the Bible, Hermann

Broch, Camus and Sartre, Max Weber, Hegel, Kierkegaard, and, promiscuously and chaotically, just about everything we got wind of. Anyone who came emptied out of his pocket not only crumbs of sugar, ersatz coffee, herring paste, or cigarettes but also the tiny hoarding bag of his knowledge, emaciated by twelve years of Nazi rule. He would bring along a book he had smuggled through the Thousand Year Reich—a volume of Karl Kraus, James Joyce, Musil, Kafka—or simply a foreign newspaper, or a report on a radio program he had recently listened to, probably still with the subliminal fear of being caught. Intellectually too, it was a slum; "but," as Nagel later wrote, "in intellectual matters, hunger is a virtue that yields miracles. Though the loaves be as meager as at the feeding of the five thousand, not only does one eat one's fill, but one also gathers twelve baskets from the crumbs that are left over."

Karl Nagel would not have had to encounter the most fatherly of all fathers in order to add the four rays of the Evangelists to the pentagram of politically applied historical materialism. This too was due mainly to the weather. The weather was so grim that a small iron stove, heated fairly well with now superfluous cultural instruments (we had already tackled the wooden paneling in the villa library and the shattered grand piano in the drawing room), was a wellspring of upswelling gratitude, which, in light of the prevailing circumstances, was bound to overpour into the metaphysical.

The point is, public transportation operated poorly in those days, and for mere mortals (surviving tenaciously despite hunger edema), personal means meant one's own two legs, and some didn't even have that: at least three of our intellectual companions were left with only one—or one and a half, or one and three-quarters. But anyone who came wandering out all the way to the Elbchaussee on foot (or even on crutches!) had to cross the icily whistling wastelands of the Reeperbahn and Altona, thus offering up a sacrifice of almost mystical grandeur—that noble self-renunciation that gives the formations of primal communities a legendary touch. The at first sporadic but then more regular get-togethers, where we talked ourselves into a fever pitch like Dostoevskian students, took on the character of consecrated hours. Even in its spiritual meagerness there was a certain crèche-like intimacy.

All kinds of things were talked about, and if we sometimes reached one of those moments of collective reflection that occur when someone comes out with a newish truth that is not yet shopworn, then something like a simple poignancy in the mind occurred. "Our crèche piety," I called it when telling Schwab about it later: "There it lay before us in the straw, naked and helpless, the new itty-bitty truth; the shepherds can't take their eyes off it; even when three Technicolor kings come out of the bitter-cold, snowy night with an ox and an ass, their eyes remain fixed on it, the itty-bitty little truthlet. May it now grow and become the All-Inspirer. It is already radiating with starry brightness to all eyes that look up to peer at one another..."

This was soon to change, when, in Hertzog, we got our first pope.

Hertzog joined us by chance—but of course Nagel had denied the existence of chance ever since his personal encounter with the Almighty: hence, God sent Hertzog to us. This happened in one of the green-camouflaged months, under the meteorological phenomenon of a violent downpour. We—that is, Nagel and I, the "identical twins," as Christa called us (without anatomical allusion, surely?)—were tinkering around with the roof shingles on the garden house. We were about to take refuge under the overhang when we collided with a figure obscured by the thick slanted hatching of raindrops, who evidently had the same idea. It was an unusually lanky and, of course, given the period, scrawny man—a gentleman, one might say, despite the socially equalizing and also dripping clothes; so that at first I assumed it was one of Christa's countless relatives, who were always dropping in. He promptly and cordially apologized for trespassing on the rubble property, but, as he explained, he had no umbrella. Oh, well, there were worse lacks in those days.

The rain lasted longer than its intensity might have suggested it would. So Nagel, who was bored, suggested that we wait inside until it let up. The unknown gentleman accepted gratefully; we all introduced ourselves, shaking hands and clicking our heels together according to the fine German custom—with the inevitable moment of embarrassment in regard to Nagel when the stranger's hand remained hovering, unseized, until its owner realized that the right hand he had aimed for was missing and the left hand was being offered in its stead. And thus, we were finally in the drawing room, please have a seat, wherever you can, yes, may I over here, wherever you like, there are no reserved seats here, if you like we can hang your jacket on that crate over there to dry out, unfortunately I don't have an umbrella, who has an umbrella nowadays anyhow, there's no such thing anymore, it would really look funny, so you're a psychiatrist? Yes indeed, formerly professor at the University of Greifswald, you know. Paul Hertzog's the name, Hertzog with "tee-zee," if you please, then, of course, I practiced at the various war theaters. Shocks, yes? Traumatic neuroses, and so on—that's right, I couldn't imagine this kind of research could be done in the Third Reich, and at Greifswald, to boot, right? But weren't the mentally ill simply done away with by euthanasia? A few, of course, regrettably, but still fairly late and depending on the war situation; however, research as such did not stop altogether, by any means—Eventually, Herr Professor Hertzog with "tee-zee" got a turnip schnapps and a cigarette made with Christa's home-grown tobacco, many thanks, but I think I have my own somewhere, no, go ahead, it's not Virginia of course, you're much too kind, no, I can't roll them, I'd rather you did it for me, you see, manually I'm awfully clumsy, why you're amazing, with only one hand—here you are, you've got to do your own licking, so research you say? Yes indeed—Herr Professor Hertzog spoke very interestingly about the foundations and objectives of psychiatric research during the Third Reich, Nagel threw in Freud, yes, now, of course the man hasn't been credited highly enough for what he did, but—well, everyone knows that Freud isn't everything, C. G. Jung, now that's a little closer to the bone—

In short, it ended with Professor Hertzog's unshakable assertion that man has an innate and irrepressible need for religion, no doubt about it, one can demonstrate it scientifically, certain mental disturbances can even be diagnosed indisputably as deficiency syndromes in this respect, mental scurvy, as it were, where faith has an effect like lemon juice, I'm speaking to laymen here of course, professionally I would put it differently, oh please don't go out of your way, these are issues we're all very interested in, by the way, if you'd like another, we brew it ourselves, you know, yes, thank you very much, it's damn strong, but the effect is all the more Dionysian . . . you see how even you quite unconsciously keep bringing up supernatural things; as I've said, psychological needs can no more be suppressed with impunity than physical ones, there's a wide-open field here, especially for social psychology. But this is a nice coincidence. You see, we've been discussing this for several weeks now with a couple of friends, more in political terms, why that goes without saying, it is a highly political problem, indeed, just look: your class-stratified state is conceivable only on the basis of the patriarchal principle, without the notion of God as the most fatherly father there can be no bourgeois social structure, naturally not, but that proves precisely what I'm saying: the need for religion is natural and innate in man, just like, say, the sexual drive, and Freud showed us what happens if you suppress it, well, and rationalism is simply the other repression, just tell our friends that, why it's obvious, we saw it in the Russians with our own eyes, despite a quarter century of Communism those people keep swarming into the churches, well, the war machine functioned there for completely different reasons, you can't do without psychology even here, which is what rigid materialism would like you to do, isn't it, incidentally Stalin is also a father, and what a father at that, and you can't say the Russians have a truly classless society, on the contrary, the Kremlin elite has distinctly aristocratic features, granted, not on the outside, no, there's absolutely no way you can claim that, hahaha, but Moscow's betraying Communism in many ways, and the point is: how does a classless society establish its own notion of God, yes, the process must be reversed, first alter the notion of God, then establish the appropriate state, perhaps matriarchal, why not, I tell you, it's the theologians who are at fault here, so listen, just drop by in the evening, then we can thrash this out with our friends, I'd love to, why not, it would interest me no end, you seldom come into contact with open minds, especially in young people, well, we're not all that young, alas, but that makes no difference, you're as young as you feel, so do come by anyway if you have nothing better to do, I couldn't imagine anything better, certainly not nowadays, well really...

He came. Not right away, to be sure. Cunningly, he waited until winter. But then, the green-camouflaged months soon passed. Nevertheless, Nagel was in a bad mood. He evidently expected Professor Hertzog with "tee-zee" to reconstruct his view of the world, which had got considerably out of joint since the encounter with Father GOD.

Until then, it had been solidly founded on Darwin; Marx and Engels were firmly joined on top; and Nagel had even managed to insert the seductive Nietzsche seamlessly and to paste in Freud. But since that encounter with Father GOD, his ideological edifice was stretched thin as though by bomb suction, "puffed through," as the rubble-dwellers put it in their jargon; and his gruffness in discussions bore witness to the awful draftiness in his spiritual home. Whenever I felt like teasing him (no one could so easily and ludicrously be made to fly off the handle as Nagel), I would advise him in case of intellectual inclemency to appeal to the man who had, it was true, no umbrella, but a need for the religious. Where was he anyway? Karl Nagel would instantly get mad as a hornet. However, when winter came, so did Hertzog. A downright epiphany. Since last we'd met, he had joined the resurrected university as a fully tenured professor and senior registrar of its neuropathological hospital, thus appearing among us whippersnappers with a corresponding authority as a complete human being and scientist. Not only that, but he had succeeded in convincing the military government of the occupation forces that he had heroically resisted the euthanasia of five patients—Party members. And true virtue is rewarded even by victorious armies. Thus, he came as a father: bringing along a bottle of real schnapps and two packs of English cigarettes. Santa Claus in person. In his sack of goodies he even had a "paper" down cold (not written, needless to say, though evil tongues maintained later that he had submitted it as a postdoctoral dissertation at the university). He carried this wealth of ideas in his head. He had only to open his mouth and the ideas, marvelously formulated in a gentle baritone, spilled out like treasure. Every sentence demonstrated how conscientiously he had worked through the subject matter. It had become so air- and watertight that there was little we could do but listen. The topic was obvious. Subsequently, it appeared in countless versions, variations, combinations, in many, many domestic and foreign journals and reviews and just plain magazines, thereby acquiring worldwide fame. Naturally, of these publications, only the popular-science ones are accessible to me, those where the expert across several fields, who communicates with colleagues in a kind of Freemason's secret code, speaks to the layman as though to a feeble-minded illiterate. And if I remember correctly, these articles are crowned with titles like "Faith and Psyche," or "Mental Illness and the Bonds of Religion," or "The Psychiatrist as a Christian Minister," or even "Savior vs. Sanatorium." But I may be mistaken. For our little group, at any rate, which he seemed to regard, flatteringly but, alas, wrongly, as the nucleus of the postwar German political elite, the contents of his paper were framed in the title "The Need for God as a Principle for Forming the State."

One must not overestimate the effect of Hertzog's speeches and writings on subsequent German intellectual life. And even less on political life. He merely served as an alibi. Every conjurer knows the term "misdirection": a diversionary tactic that, at the decisive moment, shifts the audience's attention from the fingers about to perform the actual sleight-of-hand. Postwar German development used Professor Hertzog in this way and got along without any actual reference to his ideas. And he was not alone in this respect: the generous occupation-supported interregnum of intellectuals in Germany from 1945 to 1948 (*Kultur, Kultur über Alles*) was a happy but politically disastrous period.

Nevertheless, Hertzog is pretty much the only one of the then princes of the mind whose head (or mental balls) was not sliced off by the currency cut. His academic career remains unflaggingly at its zenith. Likewise he has a steady influx of patients. He is a shining light at all kinds of national and international congresses—that clever fellow who effortlessly manages to reconcile humanism and technology, Plato and Lenin, Freud and Saint Paul (plus Picasso and Michelangelo, Proust, Joyce, the Bauhaus, Apollinaire, Salvador Dalí, Rilke, Alban Berg, Dada, Nijinski, Herbert von Karajan, and, over and over again, Karl Nagel—for, needless to say, he's also keenly interested in the arts). No doubt about it, this is a bravura performance, and indeed one of high symbolic content, if one understands that only a shrink could succeed in pulling it off.

But I digress, and indeed far beyond that wintertide that left so much melancholy yearning in my mind. What I wanted to talk about is the weather: the bitter-cold winter weather during that period, and the hallowed hours in Nagel's garden house. With Hertzog, they openly acquired the character of a church service.

To be sure, we first had to go through a brief and occasionally stormy process of fermentation.

This was due not just to the topic of the "discussion evenings," as our once disorderly, turnip schnapps–fired palavers were now suddenly known. The chief cause was that we now *had* a topic. Earlier, you see, we had jumped erratically from one subject to another—with the rough directness that set the tone in those days. The word "shit," now vivaciously circulating again, was in great favor before the currency reform. But the rough exterior concealed a heart of gold: an almost childlike openness of minds and feelings. We talked about anything "that came up"—and so many things came up, because everything was new as in childhood. From the flat Ptolemaic world, the world had emerged band-box fresh. "The phoenix," said Nagel, who was already tending toward complex metaphors, "naturally knows, like any magician, the most dazzling way to perform his feat: on a *tabula rasa*." If only he had known then how right he would be at the currency cut!

Anyway, we talked about whatever crossed our minds, and, in greatest detail, of course, about the things that were truly new in our lives. Christa, for instance, harped incessantly on the food shortage, Nagel on God, the rest of us on the preparation of turnip schnapps and the American short story, nuclear fission and its possible consequences, existential philosophy, the Anglo-Saxons, Russians, and French and their behavior during and after the war, radio programs ("The Cultural Word"), diverse treatments for the clap, the possibility of attaining higher caloric value by inserting rabbits into the consumption process for cabbage. And over and over again, needless to say, Germany's present and future. With Hertzog, however, this higgledy-piggledy hodgepodge was sieved for so-called *central questions*. And these, in turn, had to be systematically analyzed. The key factor derived from the gap that our unslaked need for religion had sucked out of the world of experience. In terms of a working hypothesis, it was initially most suitable to fill that gap with Jesus Christ.

In the presence of an epistemological stopgap with such lofty moral prestige, we soon stopped laughing (our earlier laughter had been grim, but frequent). Now, I do not mean to claim that our conversations (or rather now: debates) therefore became duller. The chief pleasure had always been the thinking itself—however informal, even innocent (childlike, you see): a kind of intellectual game of tag for letting off steam until you got tired; there was no meaning, much less purpose, to it. But now it became a sport, indeed a club sport under rigid leadership, a competitive sport. Sports too are pleasurable—a competitive sport, however, is a strenuous pleasure, which sometimes comes at the cost of a good mood. And, in contrast to a lively game of tag, a bit abstract.

Hence (and also because the son of God had so dominatingly turned into a gymnastics trainer), a few of our buddies left the group—regrettably, not the worst ones. But those who stayed made it their ambition to show that the missing ones were missing something quite extraordinary.

And indeed: experiencing Hertzog in these discussions *was* something quite extraordinary. He came with better and better schnapps and more and more English cigarettes, and at first he acted very loose, equal among equals, a *primus inter pares* by sheer chance, yet incredibly cheerful, spiritually rubbing his hands together, as it were, at the joyous prospect of a good, juicy conversation, a real roast goose of a debate, nicely stuffed with apples and chestnuts and cloves. He warmed the small community up (which, for its part, was keen on the intellectual skeleton of the goose) with parish priest–like jokes. (Some of them were quite daring. For instance, I remember one about a patient who is in the habit of running around with his forefinger up his ass because he imagines he's got a bee inside that might fly out at some embarrassing moment; he's promised he'll be cured; he's anesthetized; a huge cloth bee from a toy store is placed on his bed, and when he awakes, he's told that the bee has been removed from his body and he doesn't have to worry anymore about its slipping out at the opera or at his father-in-law's funeral; the patient thanks the staff exuberantly, but then he promptly rams his finger back up his ass because he's scared the bee will fly in again, haha-haha!)

at this point, however, Herr Professor Hertzog switched over from humor to popular-scientific seriousness; he explained that the anecdote had at its heart something worthy of study: you see, the little deception of the alleged surgery on the crazy patient (for supposedly removing the bee from his asshole) was an ancient and utterly wise medical custom, a tried-and-tested therapeutic method of shamans: a casting out of the devil, a feigned exorcism; psychosomatic medicine has established the mental and spiritual origin of many organic illnesses; we still have to clarify whether and to what extent such disturbances cannot sometimes be traced to a genuine state of possession—that is to say, whether the actual psychological nidus did not form solely from a self-created malfunction of the mental and spiritual mechanism (which until now has been pictured rather too mechanistically), or whether something from *outside*—let us quite undauntedly use the popular term for it, a *demonic power*—takes control of a man's mind and soul. As far as many neuroses and psychoses were concerned, he, Hertzog with "tee-zee," on the basis of his rich practice and with a likelihood verging on certainty, believed he could maintain that, with a surprising number of cases, which provided ample food for thought, such an assumption could not be brushed aside.

In short: Today we make do with the meager few notions with

which the psychology of the Freudian school operates—you know, "superego" and "ego" and "id" plus "libido" and "death instinct" and so on—but we cannot manage solely with them, in many cases they simply "just don't cut it," as you would probably phrase it, unscientifically but accurately, the concept of "physis," for instance—in the Heideggerian sense, yes? Not of *phyein*, or "let grow," but rather of *phaeinein*: "to bring to light"—that is: *Physis* as the "shiningly open," as the inherent human drive to develop upward (i.e., our innate striving for sublimity, truth, goodness, nobility, beauty, you know) has always been shrouded in mystical twilight, there is some sort of superhuman, if not supernatural, force obtaining here, hence the superego should not be regarded purely as a product of the milieu, it is not merely the cane of the father and similar authority figures that creates and stamps the ethical elements in our souls, no, no, by no means: quite undeniably, there is something else beyond them, a—I shall come out with it plainly—a spirit poured into us (*well, it's Whitsuntide, I ween, when Nature gets so very green*), why shouldn't the id, which gains such a destructive upper hand in cases of a malfunctioning or nonfunctioning ego, which deals with the reality principle, and of the superordinate and controlling superego—why should id consist of more or less repressed drives and not quite objectively—*materially!*—also contain something that opposes that very *physis*, that urge for upward development, for both ethical and aesthetic perfection? Yes indeed, why not truly? If one assumes the one as existing and thus as the acknowledged good, then in and of itself it already presumes its correlative opposite, does it not? However: we are speaking about medical phenomena here, so if I use words like "good" or "evil," then I am applying these concepts much as, say, an electrician employs the terms "positive" and "negative"—I mean, not as value judgments but merely as *termini technici* of a polarity that exists purely and simply, so do not believe, ladies and gentlemen, that we men of science would ever give up our fundamental impartiality, oh no, absolutely not, to a certain degree we even feel compelled to integrate the concept of disease into a universally framed process of life, after all, disturbance, destruction, death, demolition are part of the overall *bios*, one must take into account the constant renewal of Creation, it is, alas, not thinkable without the steady decay of life—however, as far as the above-mentioned neuroses and psychoses are concerned, we can (although the former, the neuroses, have already been recognized as defense mechanisms, febrile conditions of the soul, as it were, issuing in fact from a recovery tendency)—we can thus establish a good number of illnesses that are traceable to conflicts of faith or to an unsatisfied need for faith. All manner of traumatic leftovers, residues of old religious conceptions in the superego, which are now being thwarted by an attempted adjustment to a godless reality, are almost more destructive than a need for religious attachment; like everything else in God's world (inconceivable without the correlative of the devil), faith too has two sides: a positive, health-preserving, healing side, and, under certain circumstances, a negative, health-imperiling, destructive side as well—if, for simplicity's sake, we do not just say a *salvational* side and a side *twisting into the demonic*... After all, the praxis of therapy has shown that even in cases in which religious motives could not be directly established as morbific agents, a cautious guidance to the experience of faith managed to bring excellent results; and whenever one could speak of a true state of possession, the results were magnificent, and nothing else could help but the correlative antidote, like the homeopathic principle *simili curant similes*. The demonic, you see, can be tackled with neither medication nor scalpels, although neurosurgery has made considerable advances thanks to the experiences gathered during the war in an agreeably large number of brain injuries; and modern pharmacology, which originated in alchemy, is now developing specifics that have an amazing and profound effect on the psyche—but here, in particular, extreme caution is advised, we shall have to observe very closely the effects of these on many, many patients... In short, in his discipline—namely, in the task of taking patients who tweet like canaries and leading them back to vital harmony—the most proven remedy has turned out on occasion—naturally, on the basis of a diagnosis founded on a psychological analysis attached to the previous thorough examination of the physical state of health of the patient—(my ears itched: I lost three precious minutes yielding to the temptation of checking the grammatical construction of the clause)—I (Hertzog was saying) have, as I have said, determined that careful and skillful guidance to new religious contents has turned out to be a proven method—but I already said that—as I have said: it has turned out that such guidance to new religious contents and thus to a new religious experience constitutes an effective therapy in regard to mental-spiritual disorders—

Period. Paragraph. A chance to clear one's throat. Could I possibly interest you in another drop of, no, well please, really, many hearty—the schnapps is excellent, by the way (schnapps, come now, this is real scotch!)—anyway, as I have said, let us establish that when I utilize the concept of vital harmony—right?—then I do so from my point of view as a physician, after all, I am no lay preacher, I stick mostly to the relationship between body and soul, the good old saying *mens sana in corpore sano* must be understood as a reciprocal relationship: a sound soul also determines the physical well-being of the patient, as you know, we are now speaking of religion as a need of the healthy soul, but nevertheless its ambivalence still exists as far as I'm concerned—I mean: the immanent double-poled need, which is termed by the working hypothesis as both "positive" and "negative," right? Thus, we know religion can heal, but it can also lead to critical spiritual crises, states of hysteria, and the like; we must reckon with that too, and thus we have to deal with the task of manipulating the bivalent notion with utmost caution, we shall thus find it now speaking for our hypothesis, now against it, and this is fully in keeping with the Marxist (originally, of course, Hegelian) dialectical method: analysis, thesis, antithesis, synthesis—right? Incidentally, this is at heart merely the ancient religious view of the polarity of Being—light and darkness, God and devil, good and evil—simply good old dualism, spirit and matter, faith and knowledge, subject and object, this world and the next world, physical necessity and freedom, and so forth, and so on; nothing but conceptual pairs designating the coexistence of two diverse and ununifiable states, principles, modes of thinking, kinds of worldviews, tendencies of will, epistemological axioms—and in intellectual history also the polarity of life and death, which is something idealism wants to overcome, you know, although it did not quite succeed, of great interest for psychology in this context are, of course, the teachings of Mach; the history of philosophy, alas, grants German positivism merely a subordinate role, but let us not forge too deeply into philosophy, we'll leave that for later, we'll have very different problems to resolve, the present-day intellectual situation simply demands a new theology, volunteers take a step forward! Germans to the front! We have an enormous mission precisely because of our defeat, but back to vital harmony: the equilibrium between opposites, the resolution of contradictions must be achieved, that is the definition of health: yin-yang, the tolling of bells at Easter, purely materialistic health, that is: conception of life, I mean: exclusively rational thinking excludes the world of emotions, which is rooted deep in the spiritual, and without that world man is inconceivable—or rather, conceivable, yes, but merely as an imperfect human being, a cripple, a mental amputee, our friend Nagel will agree with me here especially since he is an artist; the highest, most valuable expression of the equilibrium of mind and soul, as produced felicitously from tensions of opposites, is art, of course—and art, as a predominantly irrational expression of life (which Karl Marx personally foresaw, after all), is irreconcilable with materialistic thinking; it may be achievable in the gaps of the system but is actually an expression of resistance: metaphysical emigration, so to speak—

a short, nervous clearing of the throat because no one has caught the joke (and how can you tell what is meant to be funny? Extreme caution is advisable: you might laugh at the wrong place, it's better to hold back, an attentive smile always looks good on a listener, nothing can happen to you, at worst your facial muscles freeze)...

Hertzog, challenged by failure, now puts his shoulder to the wheel. The notion of health has been clarified, so let's go back to disease, to document what I have said let me give you a few examples—a merry Mardi Gras procession of all kinds of neurosis is drawn up; now it's really hard not to laugh, hilarious, all these kinds of lunacy, things get quite wild, and Hertzog realizes it: he soon calls the neuropathic clowns back and leads us into the real horror chambers of psychiatry, here even the attentive smile is no longer appropriate, so stiffen the corners of your mouth, look at the floor, earnestly but attentively (the ludicrous footwear of the discussion-group members offers diversion), pull yourself together, damn it! Let us concentrate with ethical frowns on the graphically described cases, tut-tut-tut, the things that exist in the world, it's like Hieronymus Bosch, a finger up the ass (Hertzog says "anus," of course) seems like sheer grace in contrast, Botticelli, so to speak—but Hertzog does not wish to be cruel: I feel like Raphael, who, as we know, refused to paint a martyr (even the experts will have a hard time finding the Nietzsche quotation in so much subtlety), so I'll spare you far more dreadful cases (which is too bad: when you read the church fathers of depth psychology, those cases are the most interesting), which cannot be helped by any focus on the experience of faith, alas! Now you will probably say: How can there be such terrible deformations of the human mind? Yes indeed, how? Some most likely have organic roots; schizophrenia, for example, may have something to do with the chemistry of the brain cells, and manic-depressive psychosis may be connected to the glands, this is unfortunately a rather unresearched area, offering science many fascinating problems, psychosurgery, as I have said, is making terrific progress, let me just mention in passing the slicing of certain nerve fibers in the brain, which procedure often turns out to be highly beneficial for some patients who have suffered from incurable states of agitation and depression, for the first time in years they now can leave the hospital and lead a more or less normal life, at times, to be sure, they are a bit irresponsible and carefree and must therefore remain under close surveillance to avoid their doing anything disastrous to themselves or others, in some cases the cure seems worse than the illness to their near and dear, but you don't have to worry about that for the moment, thank you ever so much, that's our problem, I mean for us medicine men—the point here and now, today, in our first discussion evening, which I so heartily welcome, is to establish that neuroses and psychoses are increasing at a terrifying speed; the further our civilization moves away from nature and its compelling givens, the more acute the danger grows for everyone—yes indeed, for practically everyone!—just think of America, where the percentage of mentally disturbed people in official statistics is frightening, just think of the high suicide rate in Scandinavia, the higher the level of civilization, the more dubious the whole business becomes, the question naturally arises whether the unspirituality of this civilization, its absolute rationalism, its narrower and narrower restriction of any possibility of providing a valve for our natural drives—whether, as I have said, this mind-and-soul-strangulating world, in which mankind believes it can erect an earthly paradise in materialism, may not be one of the causes for the obvious loss of vital harmony. He, the philosopher Hertzog, believes that he can decisively affirm this and he would take the liberty of maintaining (and demonstrating!) that faith—yes?—the attachment of human existence to a transcendental object, is an inexplicable factor in this vital harmony, which must constantly be striven for—ladies and gentlemen, just listen to language, that treasure trove of human wisdom: "Savior"—this word comes from "save," Latin *salus*, health, as in "salvation" (a new humoristic swerve, surprising here): As a psychiatrist, I construed "*Heil Hitler*" as a challenge to heal rather than to hail him, unfortunately I was not offered a chance to put this into practice, hahahahaha! This jest finally catches on, and how! After a tour through the hell of psychiatry and the apocalyptic visions of a world tenanted more and more densely by psychopaths, the joke has a wonderfully liberating impact, and Nagel's arm stump evinces a reflexive attempt to bang his missing hand on the missing knee of the man next to him). Joking aside: if we wish to get to the bottom of the causes (and we must), we won't get any further, as I said initially, with psychoanalysis and so forth, Freud is simply too nineteenth century, this has got around even in professional circles, he is stained with the individualism of the era, but even those colleagues who are now finally starting to deal with the relationship of the individual to society, to the collective, and, beyond that, to collective life itself, shrink back from the final simple step: admitting that the soul of humanity cannot be separated from the connection with the notion of the Godly—

an instant of effective silence, voice lowered as we reach the conclusion: "Western Civilization, my friends, is experiencing itself as a moribund culture. Observers can actually pinpoint symptoms of a serious ailment. The question arises whether a transformed, renewed religious experience might lead to a cure even in such a vast general framework—"

(lively once again): "But then that brings us to the actual topic of the evening! . . ."

> *But woe to them that are with child, and to them that give suck in those days! And pray ye that your flight be not in the winter.*
>
> —Mark 13:17–18

Christa meanwhile lay in bed in the villa and pouted. I must unfortunately say: with good reason.

I did creep regularly to her bed to give her the most precise reports on all our adventures (including the intellectual ones) and to seek solace with her when Nagel surrendered all too ardently to Hertzog's ideology and now generally betrayed the tender poetry of buddyship in many ways. Nor did I hold back with all kinds of tenderness, affectionate teasing, and so forth: after all, I loved her very much, if I remember correctly, very physically; it may be that I am now confusing that with the memory of other and similarly ephemeral happiness brought by erotic possession, but in any case it is one of the good deeds of life that have settled as soothing matter in my consciousness, however dearly they may have cost me—

back then, at any rate, her girlish fragrance, her soft, round flesh, and the warmth of her blond skin made up the capital in my emotional household, and I used the interest to make up for my disappointment with Nagel.

Perhaps I should have told her this at some point; she probably didn't know, though she could, of course, have noticed it. Especially when she was expecting a child, I was simply entranced with her, placed my head on her belly, which had already taken on the milky bloated quality of motherhood, asked her to hold her breath, and I listened to see if I couldn't hear my son's heartbeat—the little boy who would trustingly grow up holding my hand and then stride, laughing, towards life, to which I would release him—a sunny life that we upright survivors of the wintertide would have set up for him, perhaps in the city of mankind, ANTHROPOLIS...

Naturally, there was nothing to hear but the growling of her empty stomach, but I loved her all the same, and even though all she had to say to my early paternal ardor was that I had unpleasantly cold ears (she had received the news of her pregnancy not, like me, in a worshipful crèche mood but rather with an annoyed, despairing "That's all I needed!")—she's simply a rather dry person, that Christa, and her poetry too lies ultimately only in her sensitivity.

Incidentally, she didn't spend the entire period in bed, of course, merely the bulk of it, including daytime. The time, namely, that I spent with Nagel & Associates. And just what else could she have done in those days, when even the angels were frozen to the earth and the nearest basement movie theatre was a twenty-minute hike away?... There wasn't much housekeeping to do. I cooked when there was something to cook, cleaned up the two rooms we lived in, pretty much the only livable ones in the villa on the Elbchaussee. It was bitterly cold, after all, and wood and coal were scarce; Christa saved them for the visits by her countless friends and relatives, the scattered blossoms of East Elbe Junker flora that the polar wind blew our way.

During such visits, Christa had every opportunity to demonstrate how proficient she was in bearing her sorrow in a simple, ladylike fashion. If I was introduced to the droppers-in, they communicated with her by means of a glance. Stateless, eh? What was the father? Unknown. I see... They forwent the shrug taking me as a phenomenon of the times. The conversation then continued in a brittle, piss-elegantly booted and spurred class jargon, as though it had not been interrupted; my offer of a sip of our turnip schnapps was declined with thanks. I took the hint and soon left the like-minded alone. For Christa, however, these were pretty much the only events in her sad life. She had probably had different expectations in her heart when marrying me. She had viewed me as John's protégé, the foreigner and almost ally, the PX rations–recipient and travel-order passenger—

no wonder she retreated and preferred seeing the winter through in her bed.

But when I crept to her, there was closeness again, other skin, flesh warmth, intimacy. We still had things to tell about ourselves; we exchanged the tinsel-wrapped life treasures of childhood memories. Christa sometimes chatted very sweetly about her childhood in East Prussia: very clear weather again, a very blue sky, a very anacreontic nature, a huge estate household, golden fields of grain and darkly wooded lakes, at night the mighty copper beeches soughing over the gentle fireworks of the glowworms in the park. A rather eccentric mother, who had broken her neck in 1939 while jumping over a ditch (on horseback, of course); an elegant patriarchal portrait of a father, who had been strung up in 1944 as a hero of the resistance; both parents very much alive in her memory. A flock of brothers and sisters with quaint character traits; neighbors and relatives had saved them from being arrested for guilt by kinship and thrown in a concentration camp: nocturnal cross-country escape on horseback (the roads were watched), two months hidden in the hay of a barn (not without its humorous episodes), soon the all-out chaos began anyway, the refugee trek to Mecklenburg, finally an underground existence in Hamburg, waiting for the end.

A children's book. I soon knew it by heart. Nagel's stories were a lot meatier, more anecdotal, blossomed in tropical brilliance from the *à propos* of conversation. They didn't tiptoe forward step by step on girlish feet; these stories leaped about daringly and surprisingly, sovereignly disconnected, held together purely by a keen eye, toppling over into more and more configurations, like the prismatically reflected picture elements in a kaleidoscope.

What Christa told me was the beginning of a novel, with the glassy brittleness of Fontane's idylls, over which a tempest of Tolstoyan drama suddenly breaks. Very attractive, no doubt, very gripping, but fragmentary, the opus got bogged down in the far too broad beginning, the main character never got beyond the initial stage of development, events rumbled behind the scenes like stage thunder, many things went up in flames, and stormy sheet lightning flashed over graves and execution sites, but the heroine lay in bed and pouted because there were no more county horse shows and no more aristocratic society balls.

Nagel on the other hand—yes! Nagel picked up the splinters and assembled for me a colorful mosaic of a reality whose farthest reaches were charged with the mood of a thunderstorm. No thread was needed to string together the tangle of characters, settings, themes; the drama behind them set forth the situations, put them in order, arranged them. Any humor only made it more sinister. Any sublimity quickly revealed the dreadful bathos of banality—

but from the barbarism, poetry proliferated like bindweed. It's not a civilized plant (whatever one may say); it blooms and thrives best in rubble fields and steppes...

For Nagel was writing now. He had always planned to write and was bursting with accumulated material: the things he had seen, gone through, made up. He was working on several projects at once: various short stories, a play, and even the draft of a novel. There wasn't any further cooling of our friendship, which had suffered because of Hertzog and the exuberant growth of the manger-shepherd circle into a discussion group, but we saw less and less of each other. He worked fiercely day and night, wrote tirelessly, using his left hand with childlike awkwardness. We weren't allowed a glimpse at his literary output. During the discussion evenings with Hertzog he was struck by an aspect of me that seemed to him more suspect than it had before. "You're too Austrian for me, man." I was orphaned.

During this period, the thrifty bitterness began to appear in Christa's mouth, ultimately transforming the artless cupid's bow of her lips into the clasp of a mostly closed purse. I then might have guessed what she was thinking. ("Nagel is at least doing something sensible with your endless talk.") Even Hertzog, whom she had regarded as a slick crook ("He's only using all of you as guinea pigs; he's just observing you and then doing something completely different with it"), she began to see in a new light ("There has to be something to it if it gets Nagel to do some proper work").

Naturally, she didn't put these feelings into words, either. (In general, she was visibly less communicative; even the memories of childhood and adolescence, memories of large cakes on the coffee table under the copper beeches, and buggy rides to neighboring estates, faltered and oozed out into chilly, ladylike silence. Only later, when our little boy could listen, did those memories surge up again, and, much to my sorrow, he absorbed them more ardently than the myths I had to hand down to him.)

But I could tell by other signs that Christa did not view the evening get-togethers in Nagel's garden house merely as an intellectually camouflaged collective waste of time by a handful of bums, alkies, and moochers. She now barely protested when the remnants of the pool table from the half-buried den, then the cue rack and the window frames vanished into Nagel's stove, followed by all the stationery with the engraved patrician address from the table where he wrote (with his left hand). Furthermore, her transient relatives and acquaintances now evinced a certain interest in my doings. ("I understand you've founded a cenacle with friends, for discussion evenings and so on. One of them even writes, I hear? I'd love to meet the man. Who publishes this kind of stuff? I mean: if ever I were to think of writing about my experiences during the escape . . .")

In short, we were becoming respectable.

This was then gloriously confirmed one evening by the appearance of a gentleman whom I stubbornly called Major General Baron von Neunteuffel, which was not his real name—I forget what it was—but in any case, he *had* been a lieutenant general or something like that, and the victorious powers had soon set him free because of his various brilliant qualities. Neunteuffel happened not to be one of Christa's relatives, or one of the many acquaintances who had been closely allied with the family for generations. But before entering the garden house, he naturally did not fail to pay his respects to her, as a man who had almost joined the resistance movement and was an admirer of her unfortunate father—"he's laying a wreath," I said, reaping Hertzog's explanation that according to Freudian teaching my cynical proclivities were a symptom of a prematurely repressed infantile sexuality with subsequent masochistic tendencies.

It was Hertzog who had invited Neunteuffel. But the major general did not come alone. He brought along (presumably as a political alibi) a distinguished-looking character, whom he introduced as a "victim of Fascism." This man was a Baltic German, his name was von Rönnekamp, and as an incorrigible homosexual he had spent the length of the war in a concentration camp. Incidentally, he was later to surprise me and everyone else present by saying he had discerned in me a "truly religious man in the Dostoevskian sense." Major General Baron von Neunteuffel proved to be a versatile, proficient, and—as it turned out—clear-sighted man. With his dependable, alert, and sociable character, he succeeded in loosening the awkward restraint shown toward him by several participants in the group.

Understandably enough, even though we were supposed to be establishing a truly Christian classless society, the (sometimes missing) heels under the dyed coats and battle-dress tunics of most of the men there involuntarily clicked together when confronted by the spruce civilian appearance of the major general, who had by no means lost his military air. But the women, of course, were instantly on his side. In the shattered Wehrmacht, he had been one of the youngest officers of his rank, he had garnered the Iron Cross with Oak Leaf, plus swords, diamonds, WACs, and crab lice, and his blue eyes radiated a zest to share in the reconstruction of Germany with the same spunk and dash that had brought him high military distinction.

So overcoming our resistance, ponderously loaded down with resentment, was only a matter of minutes. "A good troop leader," as Nagel said appreciatively; he did not dislike the major general but actually found him quite agreeable. Even though Nagel had gotten no further than sergeant with the Close Combat Clasp and the German Cross in Gold, he was treated by Baron von Neunteuffel with a certain officers'-club camaraderie; from now on, it was really a dialogue between initiates, which Hertzog as the consulting egghead could gently steer.

So, anyway, Hertzog delivered his paper: a summary of the jointly worked-out ideological principles ("I would especially like to thank—next to our friend Nagel, of course—Fräulein Ute Seelsorge for her tireless..."). The possibilities of practical realization under the given circumstances. Serious doubts, objections, corrections ("I do not wish to fail to express my thanks to a certain friend for his caustically humorous but often for that very reason animating insertions; in our new society, we must also make a place for an Eulenspiegel"). And many thanks for everyone's sincere comradely cooperation, especially the ever-improving distillers of the helpful turnip schnapps (hahahahaha!). Also many thanks to the detergent industrialist Witte, the true host and owner of the rubble property, who has so far been absent from our circle of friends because the all too slow denazification commission has unfortunately not yet enabled him to add the no doubt valuable intellectual contributions of an experienced industrial leader. And in general, many thanks to a kindly providence, which has preserved us from annihilation and allowed us to find one another here in these makeshift quarters, as the primal cell of a new society that far from neglecting tried-and-true human wisdom actually wishes to continue it. *Per aspera ad astra!* Let that be our motto evermore!

Bravo! Be seated! The women have already begun, at their own initiative, to embroider a club banner (unfortunately, silver yarn is still scarce, but sperm threads will do nicely for the moment). We thank Herr Speaker for his warm, lucid words. The newcomer, Herr von Rönnekamp, in particular, can probably not help being moved at the mention of so many warm, gay feelings. With special joy and expectation, we now greet our guest. Major General Baron Waldemar von Neunteuffel (stop scratching your flea bites, Fritz!)—

Major General Baron Waldemar von Neunteuffel took the floor (took it swiftly, virtually vaulting onto it: Münchhausen on the cannonball could not have been a defter equestrian). He said it was hard for him to say how happy he was to be here and see one of his oldest dreams come true: namely, to see the spirit of the future born from the rank and file (that is to say, from the community of all, with no distinction of merit or rank). Especially you, my dear Nagel, must understand how deeply moved I am. Congratulations with all my heart and soul for the excellent work you have done! What particularly impresses me is the unadulterated Hegelian spirit of this enterprise; after all, without this great Prussian philosopher, any future political formation will be built on sand.

So, many thanks to Professor Hertzog (and of course to you, my dear Nagel) for so to speak replanting the cross of the knightly order in the scorched earth and for gathering the liegemen around you in a truly chivalresque democratic way, inspiring them to lay the cornerstone of the new *polis*. Equality, fraternity, and liberty (in obeisance!) are, after all, ideals that have both led to the triumphs of the spirit of Western Civilization and endangered them when distorted; the most daring things are tied to the greatest perils; anyone who truly wishes to dance must dance on volcanoes; we are all forced to do so in the atomic age; anyone who is not a utopian today is not a realist but a defeatist. However, being a utopian does not mean seizing impracticable things from the clouds and designing them into a world of dreams; it means creating the ideal model for shaping and fashioning reality. This reality is at the door; needless to say, it is related to all tried-and-true ideals of Western Civilization. Christianity goes without saying, socialization too, in the widest sense, of course; the new political formation will presumably crystallize on a federal basis; the most important thing now is the economic reconstruction; I can tell you from a reliable source that the Allies have very specific ideas in this respect; in the long run, no one can afford a slum in the heart of Europe; there is still some resistance, but people will soon have to accept that we live in the era of large-scale organisms. Germany cannot be excluded from the European orchestra; we can thus on this point look forward to the future with hope and confidence; it would, to be sure, be dreadfully optimistic to assume that this means the launching of a long era of peace; we must realize, ladies and gentlemen, that the real conflict has not yet been fought to the end; Churchill's far-reaching world-political view was not to allow the Russians to seize half of Europe, but his view was, alas, not shared by all powers; the American now confronts a fait accompli; the ultimate struggle will not keep us waiting for long; we Germans find ourselves in the both embarrassing and yet—for negotiations—advantageous position of being a buffer state with, one may say, the power to tip the scales; it is highly desirable that German politicians of the future remember this; I am, of course, not advocating a new German power politics; that would be lunacy, suicide; Europe must henceforth march together and strike together when it is time to strike again, God damn it. But let us very clearly visualize how this will take place: the first phase, of course, will be an atomic attack on both sides of the Iron Curtain. Here in Germany, it will presumably strike at our newly and better-built-up industrial center, the Rheinland, the Ruhr, and so on. You know, of course, that within twenty-four hours of the eruption of hostilities, by the latest, that area will be a radioactive wasteland. Now add a few more unimportant zones, for instance our beautiful Hamburg here with its hinterland, Hanover, et cetera: within the shortest possible time, the result will be total chaos and of course starvation; a situation that cannot possibly be dealt with by mere organization—different from the famine now, where the supply authorities do guarantee a certain survival minimum by means of food rationing. Well, plundering gangs and hordes will throng into the still-untouched areas, and naturally the local population will defend itself; refugees and survivors from nuclear-struck areas will be clubbed to death like stray dogs because of the feared danger of contagion and contamination: in short, a situation worse than the Thirty Years' War. To prevent this from coming about, dear friends, we desperately require the establishment of an effectively powerful German force for maintaining order. It will naturally require utmost tact to wait for the psychologically proper moment when one can make such an institution palatable to the Germans, who have been disillusioned by any sort of military structure. But bear in mind, ladies and gentlemen, that this step will be necessary and unavoidable—

And here, the unexpected occurred; here came Nagel's crowning glory. Twitching his arm stump in the empty sleeve as though trying to pound on the table with his missing fist, he suddenly blustered and shouted that he had had enough of this shit; if things developed as Herr Neunteuffel prophesied, then he hoped that he, Karl Nagel, would have found a way of emigrating to a place where it wasn't worth the trouble to use nuclear weapons, Korea or Siam or God knows where, and if he hadn't succeeded, then he would prefer plundering hordes of radium-contaminated Rheinlanders or Lower Bavarians defending their forest homeland with clubs to any powerful German force for maintaining order. He was fed up to here with all the stupid talk; he had more important things to do than waste his time with this chitchat, goddammit; after all, this garden house was not the bookstore at the Cologne railroad station, it was a private home, damn makeshift to be sure, but all the same—So get out, all of you! The whole goddamn bunch of you, get out!

It was fabulous. Hertzog was the only one who made an attempt, at the threshold, to remain. All he got for his trouble was the knob of the slammed door in his back. Hurrying to catch up with Major General Baron von Neunteuffel, who was hurrying toward his car, which had just been approved for him by the occupation authorities, he tried to explain that poor Nagel was in the throes of a subliminal religious crisis that made him extremely irritable and also, because of an unresolved father-son attachment, tended towards an unequilibriated functioning of the gall bladder.

The rest of us stood in the starry, frost-smoky night. Herr von Rönnekamp, who seemed uncommonly worked up by the incident, ecstatically shook hands with every last one of us, holding our hands awhile in order properly to relish each friendly gaze. Despite everything, he said, he hoped to see us again soon, talk to us, get to know us better (the hope was to come true in my case). Then, with a bulbously Baltic "One second! I'm coming!" (which spouted from his mouth as a small gray cloudlet in the frosty night), he likewise went to the car. Fräulein Ute Seelsorge quickly joined him to see whether there wasn't room for her too. Some of us laughed. Some felt that Nagel had been quite right. One man said, "Okay, but that won't do all the same!" One girl was weeping silently to herself, and all of us agreed that it was freezing cold. The little group dissolved and trickled apart.

And I was proud! My shirt buttons almost popped off, I was so proud. Nagel, my friend Karl Nagel, had shown what a grand fellow he was. He had driven the money changers out of the temple. He had spurned the tempter. In the teeth of temptation, he had remained steadfast. He had finally, with his own hands (or rather one hand), set sail to steer his life's dream through the winter night.

Yes indeed. That's what he was like. My friend Nagel. A gruff old bastard, but he had balls. I still remember his white-toothed smile in his sooty face (darkened with smoke from the stove) when he told me how he had lost his arm. Somewhere in Russia, he and a group of similar daredevils—wild fellows from a penal column who knew they were done for anyway—were meant to blast through an encircled area. In the middle of the night, they had put on snow coats and crawled all the way to a particularly vicious nest of heavy machine guns and anti-tank guns. Nagel led the way as platoon leader. Now, the morning was coming up (he described its rosebuds on the ice with an ardor that did credit to his later full-bosomed spiritual kinship with the painter Philipp Otto Runge). The moment for attack had come. Nagel raised his arm to signal to his buddies: "Storm the nest! Get going!" But nothing happened. No one got up to storm. Only the Russians began shooting wildly, lashing the terrain with sheaves of machine-gun fire. Nagel looked around furiously for the assholes, who were lying with their mugs in the snow. Why the hell hadn't they started running at his signal? After all, he had raised his arm—

at this point, he glanced at his arm and didn't see it. The arm was gone. There was no arm to give a visible signal. It had been shot clean off when he had raised it.

And so all his buddies were likewise cleanly picked off where they lay, one after another, their faces in the snow. They hadn't seen the arm that was supposed to signal the attack.

At the time, Nagel, grimly laughing, called it "a really stupid story." But I'm not sure. Today, when it comes to mind, it strikes me as dismally symbolic.

How far back, how remote this lay in time, and how present it was in my memory! . . . I could reel it off like Nagel himself:

All I have to do is apply the pen and it races across the paper. Sheer delight. I write even more fluently than when I concoct delicacies for my piglets. Wohlfahrt & Associates, their snouts zealously snuffling, badger me for something they can smack their lips over: some gaudy, juicily snot-oozing subject to lure yet again some distributor threatened with bankruptcy.

("*. . . Well, just listen—listening?—this idea is worth its weight in gold: after all, GLORIA made* Till the Last Man, *didn't they?—Did you see it? No? Well, this is the theme: a political demagogue convinces the masses of his ideas, which are actually criminal; he starts a war, and the very people who were his most enthusiastic followers, who believed that the man only wanted the best, now have to hold out until the bitter end*—Till the Last Man . . . *It's sure to be the box-office sensation of the season. And now VICTORIA's keen on a topic like that, but with a more optimistic ending. The distributors say that the audiences are excited when they arrive but they're down when they leave. Victoria can't afford that—look what happened with* Till the Last Child—*you know: last phase of the war, a crazy old sergeant wants to defend a village even though it's totally useless; since all the men are away at the front, he arms the kids with bazookas, and all of them are wiped out, of course—right? Well, it turned out that audiences were expecting a silver lining of hope on the horizon. So after a good start in the big cities, the flick's been collapsing in the provinces after just a week. Why don't you mull it over a bit? Find the right solution for* Till the Last Woman—*okay? The title itself is sexy; that'll get them to the box office. Besides, with luck even the biggest dummies will notice that it's not meant seriously—but it's supposed to be, you understand, a hard war theme, but not so hopeless; if a couple of broads get bumped off, it doesn't matter, most moviegoers are women anyway; they like it when something* *happens to another woman. So think it over; maybe you'll hit on something bubbly. That's up your alley, isn't it: harsh reality behind the humor—right?—I've already registered the title, you can't expect any payment for the material itself, but you'll get a nice tidy sum for the treatment, money up front is more important for you than a lot of money later on, I'm counting on a script contract for you, but let me just say this much: it's a unique opportunity, you'll be doing business with VICTORIA, so show us that I didn't pick the wrong man when I chose you as the writer...*")

Then I'm in my element. Then I do without the handwritten stuff (what symbolism in Nagel's scribbling left hand!)—

—then I fantasize "the thing" right into the typewriter: attack the keys with nimble, forceful fingers, as if I were sitting at a Bechstein in a concert hall—and what should inhibit me here, anyway? The question of quality?

("... *Our industry can afford an artistic cinema only if it stands on a sound financial foundation—which comes from the box-office receipts of entertainment movies. I, as the producer, am obliged to make sure of this...*")—

I don't even have to ask what sense the whole thing makes. The answer is obvious: my piglets want to tap money, and some of it will be siphoned off to me—

what, then, should hold me back? my self-respect? the lamentable shred of dignity that we of the sad countenances reserve for ourselves in our work?

(to Schwab: "You needn't look up at me all conflicted and embarrassed—I know perfectly well what you're thinking: that it's despicable of me to do this sort of thing—yet you can't ignore the fact *that I can do it*, can bring myself to do it and not give a damn. Isn't that what you're thinking?... Irrefutable proof of the cynic's energy: I can get away with it...")

what in the name of all that's holy would get in my way? my intellectual honesty? the certainty that I am deceiving?

whom?—and about what?...

Just reach into the throes of human life! The teeming of maggots all around. Into Hertzog's Divine World and Neunteuffel's New Reality, into the roaring torrent of commuters and highway rest stop people—what does reality look like in their brains?

A vortex of images, no doubt. A boiling noise-gruel. A flickering chaos of momentary impressions, eardrum sensations:

incident-fragments happening-tatters event-slivers occurrence-splinters—bubbling up and away in the effervescence of ceaseless and ubiquitous occurrence, the total superreality of illustrated magazines—involuntarily captured dissipated perceived interrupted chopped-up ripped-up spliced-up throttled arbitrarily jumbled-up incoherently superimposed like the trailer to a film that is never screened in its correct and meaningful sequence.

A day of the white maggot—how does it pass by? what is it like?—every morning a torturous everyday spawn:

Alarm clock-buzzing-instant-of-terror, everlasting and as explosive as an atomic bomb:

Dream-world demolition, dream-reality annihilation. Collapse of the logic of the multidimensional. Solutionless abruption of all events, identity loss, feelings of guilt for things not taken care of, frustration of non-coping—

Existential panic: tightening dimension-narrowing, powerlessness, primal sense of forlornness, fear, anguish, menace

Irruption of the outer world into the shredded inner world irruption of time into the timelessness of physicality into the world of gravity-defying nonphysicality space-confinement irruption of what is rigidly established into what is arbitrarily alterable exchangeable penetrable irruption of banal design of multiple experience into sovereignly unprecedented unique unheard-of

Reluctant renunciation of the freedom of unreality the uncommittedness of the ungrammatical helpless striving against being moved by the merciless causality of the factual fragile clutching at melting dream-formations a sense of being swindled humiliation of vulnerability degradation through coarsening

Fettering to the physical: mass load inertia bulk: hard things sharp-edged things hostile things—

Resistance to pain as a mediator of reality, defense, arousal of aggressiveness

Rediscovery of the physical sense of self: self-member-stiffness self-urinary-urgency self-hybrid-morning-erection self-bad-taste-in-mouth self-breath self-warmth self-smell

Gathering, finding one's bearings, getting it all together: mosaic-like reconstruction of the human being who dissolves in sleep every night, mosaic-like reconstruction of the world of facts which is demolished nightly, blurry and bleary, partially snuffed—

Arduous pulling-oneself-together to cope with existence

Everyday treadmill of propitiating the trivial physicality pissing, shitting, hawking, coughing, throat-clearing—spitting, swallowing—

Reluctant civilization-ceremony: teeth-brushing, gargling, washing, shaving, combing—

Meanwhile: recapitulation of existential provisos, necessities, duties

Recourse to history: the hardships successes triumphs defeats humiliations satisfactions of yesterday the day before yesterday and the day before that; transmission of expectations hopes disappointments prospects anxieties coercions into today—

And thus: ordering of reality into the effable, the articulable, the verbally expressible, the grammatical, the chronological. Anything that cannot be said can no longer be part of reality, is pushed under the threshold of consciousness, pads existence with congestions of malaise, defense, anxiety, pleasure, pleasure-quests, pleasure-defense-impulses

From now on this reality seems to take place linearly, in the movement of time, steered by more or less conditioned reflexes and in tension and tension-release, kept vibrating by more or less unchecked affects: as a glimmering, glittering chaos crisscrossed by the meteorites of chance, a uniform three-hundred-sixty-five-day reiteration, in constantly changing guise

Irruption of everyday life with the urgency of necessity, of duty, of time: racing with the clock, with the quota, with the demands of the drives, of forced goals. Cowering under the volley of requests, requirements, requisitions from the other—wife child parent sibling friend neighbor colleague superior subaltern contemporary compatriot coreligionist party-comrade fellow-man hated loved feared honored despised—flight into the chaos of teeming masses, anonymity as the ultimate refuge of self-awareness, isolation in protective shells—the suit the car the office the company the union the after-work pub the club the party the creed the nation. Personality shells. Cell existence. Monad in the aggregate of monads. Maggot in the maggot-teeming of a continuous disintegration process—then suddenly unexpectedly: the randomness of event

...this jerk runs across the street and the light's still yellow—crash! he's flopped over a car hood: screeching brakes delayed reaction thud (Jesus! Did I pay my last insurance premium?...) Hey, watch it! Watch it yourself, you're behind me, don't tailgate me, I wasn't, give me your insurance number, it's only a slight dent, yeah but my car's in the garage for the weekend my wife's gone off to visit her brother-in-law, what's wrong up front there anyway? windshield debris on the asphalt, an indolently winding trail of blood—goddamnit, the poor bastard really got it, why that's illegal, crossing when the light's still yellow—and the way the pedestrians mob the scene, like flies around shit...well, we're in for it now, the road'll be backed up for at least a quarter of a mile: cops signals whistles yellow lights siren squad-car ambulance: they're shoving him in like a loaf of dough into an oven—is he dead already? And I'm going to be late to work, that's life...

(And these are the folks I'm writing for.)

And yet how do they feel that they've experienced this life? How does it present itself to them in that other dimension, which, so to speak, races alongside reality in parallel vibrations and against reality in the amplitudes: always one step ahead of reality, a step of hope, of expectation, of preconception? Always one step behind, a step of transfiguration, of dramatization, of twisting things aright?

How do they experience this fleeting, flickering, monotonous chaos in their wishful notions, their daydreams, their deceptions, their obsessions? How do they rationalize it in their figments, lies, solaces, euphemisms, distortions?

Ultimately as a meaningful order? As a dramatic, dynamic course of events that always correspond to some idea, always pursue, or at least bring about, a specific purpose? Thus are always effortlessly identifiable as a series of causes and effects?

—as if the events that charged down upon us chaotically could be broken down into individual components from which we need only select those that can be threaded in a narratable chronicle and strung on the guideline of a learned notion of life—threaded and strung according to a completely arbitrary event-value that we have established—

whereby we would experience our lives as (hi)story: a florilegium of episodes that, containing literary elements, are culled from the wealth of occurrences and carefully cleaned of all the weeds of anything casual, undramatic, or dramatically inconsistent or superfluous:

so that the episodes are ultimately threaded into a novel-like garland of anecdotes, stories, epics, rhapsodies, comedies, tragedies, woven into compellingly thickened peripeteias and rhythmical arses and theses, to be boaed around the person of the SELF and form his myth—

Even the maggots use the literary in order to overcome the chaos. Even they live literarily—

and I'm supposed to make the devising of tales a matter of conscience?!

So, carefree, I attack the keys of my typewriter: my piglets want a story that reads both simply and grippingly, an adventurous, entertaining, and yet meaningful reality, so that even the distributors will be carried away and actually understand what it's all about

(a *story*, then, that can be told in three sentences)

at your service:

Till the Last Woman

Berlin, April 1945:

The roomers in a boardinghouse, which is actually a front for a whorehouse under the experienced direction of the owner (Kitty Schmidt), look forward to the arrival of the Russians and the expected surplus of vodka, cigarettes, money, and food period end of the first sentence

In the basement, however, honest people have also hidden, and the girls, seeking protection from the shelling, witness the rape of a mother-to-be by drunken soldiers, whereby the mother-to-be kicks the bucket period end of the second sentence

This affects them so profoundly that they resolve to give themselves freely wherever a decent woman is threatened semicolon they thus sacrifice themselves each in turn M-dash *till the last woman* colon Kitty Schmidt herself, who at first opposed this sacrificial effort by her girls third and last period end of story

This I can write. With virtuoso life-interpreting fingers, I hammer away at the keyboard of the little Olivetti Lettera. Nothing inhibits me.

This stuff won't get in front of the camera anyway. It is merely spirited out of thin air and laid into thinner air—as a cornerstone for the cloud-cuckoo-home that is known in the piglets' lingo as a "project" or even "our next film project"—

a little fiction, that's all. If it's ever "realized" (i.e., filmed), then in any case it will be as something entirely different.

Then, real money will be involved. Then, fiction and reality will mate. Then, my piglets will become anxious and will therefore work doubly hard. Then, to play it safe ("Damn it, in a movie every image, every line of dialogue, every scene must be foolproof; it can't be left up to *one* person"), we'll start the teamwork.

Then, the startled swarm of producer-boarlets will be joined by the hefty cattle from the distribution side. Then, the reluctant cinematic legal advisers in the moneylending banks will bring along vest-pocket literati, with flat heads barbered à la Bertolt Brecht, as literary advisers

("... Herr Jorguleit was very successful doing this for the radio and he will henceforth be available to Victoria ...").

Then, amid cigarette smoke, cigar stains, and expense-account brandy, the "project" is subjected to a collective process of intellectual predigestion:

every scene, every image, and every line of dialogue is multiply analyzed to shreds, crushed, insalivated with the psychology of the trade, and thoroughly chewed up.

Everybody adds his bit. Everybody draws on his own knowledge of reality and reality-creating fantasy to inject juices that will make the soon boneless subject ferment into a mash for consumers—so that, finally kneaded and streamlined for the public taste, it may slip through the sphincters of the take artists and lens pullers.

Fine! All I'm after is the check (even if they've clipped three-quarters of the amount originally agreed upon).

My name will then stand as the person responsible for a work of cinematic art entitled KITTY'S GIRLS AND THE RUSSIANS—

the story has been changed to the extent that Kitty's girls are no longer employed in a Berlin cathouse, but are now the wards in a boarding school for aristocratic young ladies in Potsdam ("After all, highborn girls interest moviegoers more than hookers, you have to admit that yourself—something like the Empress Augusta School—right? . . .")—

So Kitty (von?) Schmidt is no longer *madame la patronne* but now teaches local history in the aforesaid institute. ("Just think of GIRLS IN UNIFORM—a worldwide success, American remake, et cetera . . .")

"Well, and then when the Russkies come, the whole thing can run along as it did before—but wait a minute, we don't want to remind the audience of unpleasant historical events like the raping spree; my wife, for instance, she doesn't like to think about it. Besides, we don't want to spoil our prospects in the Eastern market right at the outset . . ."

So: the girls merely fear being raped, but a lieutenant of the advancing Russian company, Ivan So-and-so-vitch or what should we call him? Gimme a real Russian name—huh? Karamazov? No, Karamazov sounds too much like a battlefield; that's what it's good for, a battlefield—THE BATTLE OF KARAMAZOV. But not for us. What? Raskolnikov? I like that, Raskolnikov—you too, Herr Müller-Kapetown? You've heard the name already? So what. In the new version, the character's completely positive; you don't have to worry about issues with libel...Well, anyway: Lieutenant Ivan Raskolnikov has expressly told his men not to rape any woman, but the guys ignore his orders, the delirium of victory and the booze unleash their passions—

"Well, and now Fräulein Schmidt—von Schmidt? Uh-uh! What for? We have to emphasize the social contrast. Previously, Kitty wasn't very popular among the girls because she isn't highborn, you understand? That's what makes the story so up to date; otherwise there's no topical message—well, now Fräulein Schmidt throws herself in front—what? Winkelried? That's what you wanna call her? I don't like Winkelried, too pretentious. Besides, Schmidt sounds better for bringing out the social contrast—and she kicks the bucket...

Oh, she suffered
poor Miss Schmidty
'cause the soldiers
sliced her titty...

"Come on now, knock it off with the jokes!...What happens next? The first victim is brought, and then—

"Well, and the girls? The girls are saved by Lieutenant Raskolnikov himself; that makes it a lot more ecumenical, bringing nations together and so on; why should we keep fighting with the Russians after so many umpteen years? Doesn't make any sense in the long run..."

Certainly not. My Supreme Piglet Wohlfahrt (not for nothing is he the business manager and sole owner of Intercosmic Art Films) is once again talking pure gold.

So: in the end, Ivan Raskolnikov marries the girl in Fräulein Schmidty's institute who hated her most because she wasn't highborn—what should we call her? Effie? Effie sounds good, I like it—and now for a real Junker name—what? Von Briest? Von Briest is great. So: in the end, amid the ruins of the garrison chapel of Potsdam—pretty good, right? symbolic and so on—in the end, Lieutenant Ivan Raskolnikov marries Fräulein Effie von Briest

"...And when you see the two of them in the last shot placing a simple bouquet of wildflowers on Fräulein Schmidty's grave—and the Iron Cross First Class—no, wait a moment, why the Iron Cross

First Class? The war's over, damn it! It doesn't exist anymore. A simple bouquet of wildflowers, a lot more poignant—I tell you: with the final shot, there's got to be snot and tears, that's the alpha and omega of cinematic art, as old Erich Pommer used to say..."

Fine! Good luck! And tallyho! I was merely doing my duty as a man: showing my brood of piglets that they can always count on more pearls from me ("the guy is difficult, granted, simply because he gets too many ideas at once—his imagination runs away with him, you just have to rein in his thoughts, then he functions right")—

I wrote the pile of bothersome obligations off my back: the alimony for Christa ("I have nothing but sympathy with your situation, but my lawyer won't hear of it: after all, he's in the film business himself, he knows how much you make"), the tuition for our son in his plutocratic prep school in Holland, the rent, the auto insurance—

I can even think of paying off some of the most embarrassing of my debts—

all this with the labor of a few filthy weeks...

I've finally written myself free for a few more weeks and I can maybe tackle my book again...

which is what happened in these past eight days and nights—with a more stunning debacle than before, to be sure, although the conditions weren't necessarily success-oriented...

But this time the debacle was more thorough, the failure far more spectacular than ever...

What happened?

Something occult, if that's what you want to call it (Uncle Helmuth, his eyes shining, would have called it that):

A Schwab released from the body of cells and floating in air as a pure metaorganism had been annoying me since my return here like a fly stubbornly buzzing around my nose—and I didn't want it to alight. It came from some carrion. My dream had hatched it—not the dream I had only just slipped away from, being absolved by the shy smile of my foster mother from the flower cup and redeemed. It was actually the other dream, the cellar dream, where an old bag of a cleaning woman lay murdered, her face smeared by a shovel into a Rorschach splotch... And whether it was a dream or a repressed reality—whether (and if so, in what way) Schwab was connected—I did not wish to be bothered by it now.

I lay in bed, keeping my eyes shut. For the time being (at last! after all the tortured days and nights), I was not available to ghosts—to any transcendental individual, no matter how interestingly he manifested himself. At least for the brief moment of my setting out into a richly creative day (and all its failure and frustration), I wanted to be untroubled by any sort of basement reminiscences: wartime air-raid basement experiences, Viennese occult basement existence, reality-constructing catacomb societies from the Reichsmark era, basement children of the new Neunteuffelian reality disguised as film producers, the topography and atmosphere of the basement in which I killed that dreadful crone in my dream (and *where* in reality?). My foster mother's smile from the flower cup (*un sourire presque espiègle*) had exonerated me for the moment: I could take a few breaths without lifting the weight of a sin with each. I could afford, then, to think quite soberly about the contents of my notes, and try to restore the one I had lost, which I missed as if it were the key to my book.

It was easy to recall the train of thought. Snails produce their houses at the command of the species; they have no biological choice, as it were; but still, their houses have individual peculiarities. One can tell by the changing styles of art-historical eras that human beings obey such biological orders in the way they express themselves collectively. And one can see that these orders are cyclical in the way they change; that they repeat certain elements of expression in the changing of the expression, reiterate them in terms of time symmetry, as it were (every art-historical phase ends in its baroque)... That was roughly the gist. And oddly enough, it completely calmed me down. I enjoyed the notion of a tide-like now-and-again, of something breathing, pulsing through the world, making mankind lean alternately in one direction, then the other, like a wheat field in the wind (and the winds, as if sparked by Aeolus's divinely musical sentiment, truly blow first from here, then from there into the various cultures). This notion virtually carried me away from the planet, putting me far beyond it, in a demiurgical contemplation:

showed me this mankind *en bloc* in space and time: billions of tiny particles, coagulated into a gray mass that is moved by an invisible power and forced into the strangest ornaments. And this did not frighten me. Quite the opposite: it was an old, familiar thing, like a lullaby. I had hopped into the lap of the world spirit, as it were, and now, relieved (because I was released, for now, from personal responsibility), I curled up in metaphysical relish—

and I watched the grand spectacle purely through indolently squinting eyes:

It proceeded from the primal beginning and encompassed the entire universe. For the force that leads the teeming of mankind to and fro and occasionally pulls it together and drives it apart like iron filings on a piece of paper under which one moves a magnet, this force, operating on an inexhaustible play instinct of forms, was presumably the same one that formed the first cell from the primal slime and then went on to develop Brehm's fauna and Linnaeus's flora, ultimately crowning the astonishing variety of such creation with *man*, the untiring builder of the city ANTHROPOLIS. The planet was infested with mites, which first appeared in dots and specks, then spots and splotches, growing out, soon proliferating hypertrophically, covering the entire surface of the globular shape (slightly flattened at the poles) with mange ... And it must have been the same unnameable power that had hurled this planet out into the universe among myriad others with their moons and satellites, making this powdering of the stars dance chaotically in a tremendous juggler's act ... Nor did it make any difference whether one of them or a million, with or without mites, died or burst like soap bubbles.

This potency toyed with such riches that if galactic systems emerged or perished in the cosmos, they did not need to be given even a fraction of the significance attached here on earth to the hatching or crushing of a louse. In light of this, it would have been childish to speak of free will, decision, the importance of any action or inaction—of ethical purpose and commencement, of moral action, of the causal relationship between guilt and atonement... And it would have been absolutely hilarious to imagine that one could, as an individual, produce something that was not already provided for in the collective expression; for instance: write a book that was not being tackled, indeed had not already been written, by a hundred, a thousand others with an urge to express... It was simply a joke of the world spirit that someone lay there in despair, racking his brain about a lost note—

It didn't help. There was no way out anywhere. Man is free, but his will is not: anything he does takes place in terms of the all-creating, all-destroying divine game—and thus I am, thus you are, not only God's most obedient servant and dearest menial but also HIS partner: we put our noses to the same grindstone... And I for my part lay satisfied in the bosom of the LORD and could hope that sooner or later, as his most obedient servant and dearest menial, I would do my biological duty by throwing Madame on her back in some corner of the Épicure and sticking a nice bun into her oven—a little French bastard who would soon be practicing with a plastic machine gun so as to take part in the game of the great world spirit... and if I writhed like a fly on flypaper because my conscience wouldn't let go, whether because of a murder that I could not entirely forget, because of the lost promise from the catacomb era in Nagel's garden house and Neunteuffel's New Reality, because of my dead friend whom I had cheated, or even because of my book that I would never write—

was it not boundlessly vain and trivial of HIM who fed on worlds like a whale on plankton?...

"This," I said to Schwab, "is the result of my search for God. If HE does exist, then HE has indulged in a bad joke at my expense. I find that HE has gone a bit too far."

I sensed something quite unusual piercing my lids, which I kept shut: some light narrowed to the sharpness of a knife. So I opened my eyes.

The light (like the wan city light in my Viennese relatives' murky apartment) came through a crack in the shutters (I usually keep them closed even in the daytime: I live by lamplight: that is how I elude time).

I could not tell whether it was the ethereal and as yet unthickened light of the first hour of morning or the self-transfigured, renunciatory light of a gloriously waning day of sunshine shortly before evening. It seemed to be neither, and yet it was so fluid and bright, such as even the most glorious day of sunshine never is. Like a sword blade, it sliced through the twilit darkness of the room and cut into my eyes. I had to close them again, and I sniffed and listened (one can hear the quality of time in silence).

It was silent. (It is always almost uncannily silent in this filthy hotel—its sole advantage, by the way. It is so silent that at night I can hear the humming of the telephone on the switchboard in the handsome Pole's desk two floors below me.)

I compared this silence with the memory of other silences into which I had occasionally listened (the dull, heavy ones at night, when everyone was asleep; the brooding, ruminating ones of afternoons when the always freezing Algerians, in coats with turned-up collars and army-surplus scarves to the tips of their noses, crept into their beds in large family groups, and traveling salesmen entered their daily balances in their notebooks or, with intricate knowledge of amorous positions, were inside the women they had picked up; and especially a silence in which I had endured sublime misery three years ago in this very room, when I had waited in vain for Dawn to call me to her) . . .

an unbelievably eloquent silence, which contained Paris like a dissolved pigment

—the essence of the city in its silence, as if it were not merely that certain forms, colors, images, sounds, noises, and smells

worked together to produce its specific, unmistakable impression (the Parisian quality of Paris) but that the myriads of continual, conscious, half-conscious, and unconscious perceptions of a here and now with which the teeming human swarm out there, in the streets and buildings, experiencing themselves as in Paris, *were weaving themselves into something objective, empirically ascertainable, positively material, which entered the people as it did the breathed air, the squares, the trees on the boulevards, and every single stone of this city; and as if this aura of the Paris that is unmistakably to be perceived as Paris first became truly free and perceptible in the silence, so that if one brought a deaf and blind person here without telling him where he was, he would instantly have to sense it as specifically Parisian—*

The silence this morning was exactly the opposite. True, it also contained the city, but not that aura. You could hear Paris in it, but it was an abstract, panoramic, tourist-picture-book Paris. It contained no people experiencing it. Streets, squares, monuments, gardens, gables, and ledges had a Sunday glow to them—and were accordingly empty. Each house was freshly painted, so to speak, with sparkling windowpanes. Each street corner was meticulously swept. Each leaf on the trees in the boulevards was varnished. It was a toy Paris: beautiful, perfect—and, as I have said, abstract. The silence emanating from it was sterilized. It lay there, scoured clean, like a lovely shell on the beach.

Curiosity seized me, and I got out of bed and went to the window, pushed open the shutters, and stuck my head into the air shaft.

It was filled with bright nothingness.

This bright nothingness almost made the air shaft burst. The walls seemed able to stand the tension no longer. They had narrowed, losing their gravity and density. The bright nothingness scattered their molecules.

I looked up. Very high above the rectangular cutout of the peepshow box to which the air shaft had shrunk, the sky was stretching in a deep polar blue. I looked down. Below, on the dirt-encrusted glass roof of the first floor, frost lay along the iron beams. Razor-sharp coldness cut into my skin. I looked up again—and was yanked aloft like a balloon cut free.

For what happened next, the experienced novelist has a few idiot-proof, well-cemented phrases at his disposal, but he cannot use them unless he wishes to be regarded as tasteless:

his heart contracted when he realized—
with a stroke that roiled his innermost being he perceived—
an insight struck him like a fist—
as though an inner turmoil had shaken the scales from my eyes—
thus, I recognized the light and the silence.

They were the silence and the light of the days when the German troops marched into Vienna (in March 1938: it was known then as "Hitler weather": an icy cold blue sky and a Sunday glow over the empty, silent world).

Those days were still sharp in my memory (and kept fresh by repeated and highly detailed reports to Schwab). There was no reason why their recollection (even, so to speak, from an ambush: on the morning after an honestly bought night of lovemaking and looking ahead to a joyfully productive day here in Paris) should rattle me. (After all, it was not unusual to have frost in October. The political situation—according to hearsay; I don't read the newspaper—was as precarious as ever, but not immediately alarming; and sudden clear weather was no excuse for drawing the parallel to historic dates marked by extraordinary climatic conditions.)

March 1938 was altogether different—I mean more unusual, more surprising. I knew it by heart, like certain notes for my book. Dozens of times—if not more often—I had told all kinds of people (not just Schwab) about those days, finding attentive and then soon reflective listeners, whose moved state had lifted my description to artistic heights. During the quarter of a century that had passed since these memorable days, I had turned them into a showpiece whenever the conversation turned to politics and recent history (for I understand nothing of the former and I live past the latter; in order to join in, I tell about the peculiar weather back then):

How overnight (that is, toward morning of the day of the *Upheaval* or *Annexation*), Arctic cold had fallen upon Vienna despite the clear blue sky; and yet I stubbornly maintain that the lilac shrubs were already blooming in the Heldenplatz and in the Volksgarten. They were trampled down a few days later when one or two million enraptured people—the exact figure doesn't matter (I still believe that even today, despite a considerable population boom, one could pack all mankind in a one-cubic-kilometer crate and throw it into the Grand Canyon so that mankind may collectively bite the dust)—as I was saying, the shrubs were trampled down when an entire big-city populace boiled together into a seething gruel of spastically dislocated limbs, twitching arms, hands, and swastika armbands hurled high and thrashing about as if drowning, with undulating banners and roaring mouths. They were welcoming Adolf Hitler, leader, unifier, and expander of the Greater German Reich, to ex-Mayor Lueger's imperial city... But more of this later.

The bizarre thing about the weather was not just the coldness but, above all, the dematerialized light. With such a brilliant blue sky, one naturally expected the sun to come out at some point during the day—even as just a freshly polished brass disk, simply for the sake of the picture-perfect order of the world, which had suddenly gone crazy. But the sun did not show itself. The events took place in a light that did not emanate from the sun's rays. It was the illumination of total emptiness. It was the light of abstraction. The coldness, so razor sharp it cut deep into the marrow of your bones, peeled out the objects, which were more or less logically lumped together, peeled them so very subtly along the contours of their isolation. It penetratingly clarified them as things. It drove connections apart and turned them into adjacencies. All at once, everything was displayed openly and lucidly. Not, of course, in the interflowing tonal values of a brilliant painting. Everything was separated thing by thing, like a pasted silhouette of colored paper. Despite all the particolored variety in the world, an unbelievable simplification had come about... I repeat—and I am ready to swear an oath—the sun did not come out for three days. It had stopped in the heavens, as on the occasion of biblical military actions at Gibeon or Jericho, but it had not stopped over Vienna.

Nevertheless, it was light outside. So light that your eyes hurt—for three days. Until the Führer and Reich Chancellor entered the city.

Naturally, I take the liberty of squeezing historical events together a bit for the sake of poetic truth. It could just as easily have been the fourth or fifth day when the Führer and Reich Chancellor entered the city. But that doesn't matter. For when the sun remained suspended somewhere else in the sky (only not over Vienna; perhaps over Berlin?), time stopped too. I tell you, for three whole days.

That was the bizarre thing about that light: it was not only beyond matter but also beyond time. An everlasting Sunday had commenced and was shining over the world. Had my friend Scherping been present, he would have said, "Now that's a sky! You could fry an egg on it." (He would have been wrong: the sky was more likely to freeze those who were sickened by the times and wanted to survive past the next few centuries, in order to thaw out again when medicine could guarantee eternal life: the SS would subsequently perform the most interesting experiments in this connection at Dachau.) And Vienna was lovelier and more Sunday-like than ever before. It looked as neat as a pin, fresh, with a new coat of paint, as if straight from a toy chest. And empty.

An especially effective vignette in my story was the one about the flower woman. She appears on the first of the three days. All through the night, the soul of the people had boiled. Describing something like this is a choice morsel for a novelist, and I didn't miss my chance. For instance, the encounter with my cousin Wolfgang in a battery of marching columns (they had massed as unexpectedly as the hosts of iron men that King Laurin stamped out of the soil, and they had marched through the streets to the Rathausplatz, crowding more and more ominously), an encounter that was not without the macabre humor that properly highlights something horrible. (For the postwar German cinema, to which I offered the story on many occasions, the mass spectacle was too costly, although they probably could have found a lot of useful newsreel material; at any rate, my manuscript requires only a bit of tightening and revising to be considered masterful; if I remember correctly, it is filed in the folder marked *Prehistory: Vienna IV*, with the description of Wolfgang's funeral.)

The coagulated flood of iron men smashed the groves on the Rathausplatz and soiled the monument to Ritter von Sonnenthal, presumably because King Laurin's warriors smelled a Jew in the name. They did not sing, however (as they usually did on such occasions). The columns mutely set out again, threading their way in murky order toward the Ringstrasse. At their head, in accordance with tradition, marched a division of uniformed employees of the Municipal Streetcar Company (the trolley conductor of my childhood was not among them). They pulled the monstrous thing along behind them: a worm as black as nightshade, crawling along on thousands of legs, aglint with the will-o'-the-wisps of thousands of eyes in which the pale fire of an hour of decision was glowing.

It now crept out of the trampled-flowerbed earth and grew longer and longer and had no end in sight... crept past Parliament and past the Opera and past the City Park and, at Aspern Bridge, into the curve toward the Danube Canal and up the canal to Schottentor and then into its own tail. It thus placed a ring around the inner city.

And thus the Walpurgisnacht celebration began, and lasted until dawn.

At ten thirty on the day that had thus begun, I strode through a completely deserted Vienna.

It unfolded very agreeably before my tearing eyes (tearing from cold, you see, and because I hadn't slept and had seen all kinds of things through the night, things one sees in oppressive dreams; also, the light hurt my eyes).

Vienna flapped open before me in piercingly lucid, brightly colored individual pictures (the colors of Emperor Joseph's time: yellow and copper-green and sky-blue and glacier-white and streetcar-red-white-red). The city flapped open like one of those panoramic folders sold at railroad kiosks to foreigners passing through, so that they know where they have been:

—a townscape in its own notation, so to speak: in which the extreme simplification limits itself to indicating tonal values, and in which, even with the most banal and most arbitrary chaos of heterogeneous and contrasting motifs and styles (cathedral and railroad station, soccer stadium and stock exchange, hero's monument and zoo), a certain rhythm is inscribed, a rhythm that takes up the melodic moods of the individual views, combining with them into a musical theme that is ultimately the same as the one you hear in the complicated orchestration of the city after a lifetime of intimate acquaintance: just as the theme "chicken run" of course has a simpler and more pure sound to it in a children's book than it does in paintings by all the Dutch masters who trained their eye on farm fowl; and especially than all the chicken runs that we have to put up with in real life.

This Vienna was painted by a highly conscientious Sunday painter with a frozen soul (a Danubian Vivin) and patched together into a booklet of picture postcards. And I wended my way through it and took it in one last time in its brilliance and empty glory: *Vienna*: capital of Austria and old Europe, now scoured by passing time and washed up on its strand.

I took it in, bidding it farewell, and filed it away with the things that had become a part of my being and had become abstract along with it:

its tenacious, buckhorn-button Middle Ages and its chamois-leather baroque; its edelweiss-starred rococo and postmasterly Biedermeier; its grand bourgeois Greater German kitsch and its whining petit bourgeois knavery:

—fanfare-loud, panache-sporting self-assurance petrified into state-chancelry emblematics; the ore of imperial sobriety forged into playful latticework; Spanish draconic severity wine-drunkenly dissolved in perioecian placidity... and proliferating from all these the amalgams of engineering and Wilhelminia: ungainly

monumentality and frivolous intimacy, opera and operetta in cast iron and mortar: the Lay of the Nibelungen on apartment houses and the imperial double eagle hanging at trolley stops as a sign of Heuriger wine: in bridge arches, middle-class pride bloated into the swank of paunches bearing watch chains, and, in administration buildings, the grace of courtiers demeaned into the humility of pensioners . . . and, over the Virginia cigar, an insidious wink—

The Sunday glow of the city was piercing. Naturally, I had known since the previous night what it meant: Vienna had surrendered and stood ready as a bride to receive the groom. A noisy stag party had taken place, a boisterous bridal shower, and this was an hour of the most delicate reflection. Vienna took one last look at itself in the mirror.

And yet it was frozen. A completely transparent block of ice encompassed Vienna and its spring air:

the Old German neo-Gothic town hall with the cast-iron knight on its spire, from which a long red flag with a black swastika in a white circle was now licking down like a devil's tongue with a pill marked "poison." The slender octagonal tower of the Minorite Church over the lilac clusters of the Volksgarten. (I am not mistaken: For what's important here isn't the botanical question of whether it's possible that lilacs would be blossoming in Vienna in March; rather it's a question of heraldry. Thus, the papal tiaras of the blossom candles most certainly stood white and yellow in the green balls of the chestnut trees on the Ring: the Vienna of hand kisses and fiacres bade a proper farewell to Straus, Strauss, and Hofmannsthal.) The grille-toothed titanic maw of the Castle Gate, which only yesterday had gargled with rickety taxis, grief-wrinkled fiacre nags, and bicyclists with chamois "shaving brushes" on their hats, was now caught in a gaping yawn, as if it were trying to swallow all the stony lion-clubbing and angel-cloud-billowing drama of the castle and the Michaeler Church into the void of the Heldenplatz behind it. The Graben with the kidney-shashlik skewer of the Plague Column and the tower of St. Stephen's Cathedral looming so spectacularly over prosperous façades . . .

heading down the Spiegelgasse, I turned off to the New Market, and there was the flower woman.

She was the exemplar of the Viennese flower woman, as round as a barrel and (not just because of the cold) wreathed and wrapped in untold layers of petticoats, vests, jackets, coats, shawls, as well as scarves crisscrossing her bosom and back; bluish red like a tulip bulb and with fingers sprouting like fat root ends from her knitted wristlets.

She had left her baskets of primrose, violet, and narcissus posies, and they stood there tempting any dog's leg, while she ran—no, rolled—in a drunken zigzag across the empty square. Only Raphael Donner's smooth fountain nymphs, so beautiful and motionless in their slender grace, were watching her twirl and whirl and swirl, while she flung up her sleeve stumps with the root ends, as though trying futilely to take wing—and she shrieked, croaked, panted, "*Heil! Siegheil! Siegheil!*"... and although Viennese flower women have voices like Anatolian mule-drivers, she sounded very woeful, indeed stifled in the resonance of the huge void, like the lament of a hare drowning in a rain barrel.

Only then did it dawn on me that something extraordinary had occurred: an era had come to an end.

I once saw a city in flames (Emperor Nero would have kissed his perfumed fingertips):

There were so many flames that they looked almost dainty, even loving. Quick as a cat's tongue, they licked out of the blackened window caverns of the houses and up the walls. They flared up wildly in dark smoke and crackling flurries of sparks only when a building collapsed. Then they whooshed and flickered over the glimmering pile of rubble. But overhead, the sky was a dark glow: the incubator of the Apocalypse—

And I stared till my eyes were red, that the image might be seared into me. After all, you don't see that kind of thing every day.

I told myself, "Hey! People are burning in these houses. The basements they've crept into are buried. The heat is boiling the juice out of their bones, they're shrinking into little black monkeys. But if they manage to break out of their cellar holes, then the burning wind will raise them aloft like dry leaves and whirl them into the flames."

But I was only telling myself those things. The wall of fire was impenetrable and was reflected in me just as impenetrably. No shriek pierced it on either side. Then, the young man came toward me.

The young man was gazing straight ahead, imperturbable, striding through the heaps of broken glass, the smoldering ruins of furniture, and the tattered snarls of fire hose. He was walking along the more or less intact right side of Kurfürstendamm (for this took place in the Berlin of 1944, on the morning after a turbulent night: one of the solid bombing nights in which the Wilhelmine splendor of Berlin's Old West Side lost its plaster of paris amid all sorts of illumination effects that flouted the blackout regulations: the loss being so complete that only the sooty walls remained, and even they were mostly joined and entangled like the fingers of a praying pastor—very few of them were still left upright, as a warning)...

He was obviously a young man of good breeding, and he wore civilian clothes. This too was not something one saw every day. For it was precisely the young men of the best families who deemed it an honor to do their accursed duty and carry out their obligation to *Führer, Volk, und Vaterland*, on land, in the air, and at sea, in Minsk and Omsk and Andalsnes and high over the wind-rowed dunes of drifting sand in the Libyan desert and deep down with the fish by Ullapool. His raincoat with a sloppily dangling belt was unbuttoned, and his hands were in his pockets. He was heedless of his good shoes, which trod over upholstery springs and into the twisted spokes of baby-carriage wheels. And when he had to cross one of the side streets, he stepped rather inattentively down from the sidewalk to the road and tripped... However, he caught himself with the inexplicable, clownish skill of a drunk or other deviant and, after briefly reeling, as if drawn on an invisible string, he strode on: without removing his hands from his pockets or his gaze from the nothingness he was staring straight into. What was happening around him wasn't his concern. Nor was it really his concern anymore what had happened to him.

And I realized, something extraordinary had happened to the young man! And only then did it dawn on me:

Something extraordinary had happened.

I almost always append this episode to the tale of the flower woman: as a paraphrase to clarify the theme for the slow-witted and, for the quick-witted who grasp it immediately, as a gratis addendum to be gratefully received. And I quite regularly reap, with a sigh of metaphysical anxiety, the exclamation "Man! You ought to *write* about that!"

Yes indeed, I know I ought to write about it (and a lot of other things too). I ought to write about it for the sole reason that it has something to do with writing itself: it contains a formula that is as simple as it is foolproof. But it's not so urgent as other things I ought to write down. It may be an extremely effective bit of narrative art (at least it's seldom disappointed my listeners). But it concerns me only peripherally (although the end of an era back then—in March 1938—put an end to *my* era: so completely that my previous life seemed to have been lived by a different person than he of the later life: kind of like how my childhood before my mother's death was lived by a different child than the one who then grew up in Vienna, ultimately experiencing that March in the year 1938). But the *extraordinary thing* that had happened in Berlin in 1944—and which the young man in his absent mental state had caused me to grasp as being extraordinary—this wasn't my concern even then—no more than it was his.

I would venture to maintain that the issue is purely an external one. It was (by way of having happened) to have extremely *far-reaching* consequences—certainly not just for myself but, strangely, even enigmatically, for me in particular (although, for the time being, it altered nothing in the externals of my existence).

In any case, it sliced my existence in two again, pushing the earlier portion behind a glass pane, as it were. What now lay behind it was, no doubt, something I had gone through, lived through, at times even suffered through—yet it really had nothing to do with me now. I continued living with it as if I were keeping one portion of me like a tench in an aquarium: more as a hobby than as a necessity.

One portion of myself was entirely abstracted from me, existing in a different element. In a reality that had become unreal. I could observe it with scientific detachment. It no longer aroused my passion, only my occasional interest.

Like Nagel's amputated arm, which lay buried somewhere in Russia while its owner industriously wrote with his left arm in Fuhlsbüttel-on-the-Elbe, that era of my life was separated from me. And even though it sometimes seemed that I could identify with it in some way or other, this was not actually the case. I was prey to the same illusion as Nagel when some sort of nervous reflex in his arm stump led him to believe that he could move the fingers of his right hand.

In a word: I still experienced myself in that portion—but simply as history.

Even later (years and decades after March 1938), I was forced to carry out such amputations of previous sections of my life; for instance, after my divorce from Christa, in a certain way after Schwab's funeral, and certainly after Gaia's death. So that ultimately my story became that of a man who experiences himself in the story of an adolescent who experiences himself in the story of a boy who experiences himself in the story of a child. Or if you prefer a visual metaphor: the surrealistic portrait of a man who carries within himself an aquarium in which he swims like a tench (a tench, it goes without saying, that carries within itself an aquarium, in which it swims like a tench)... And even though he keeps getting progressively smaller and younger and changing his suit so that ultimately, as a dear little golden-curled sailor, he carries nothing more within himself than the nostalgia for the amniotic fluid from which the stork unexpectedly brought him and placed him in a nursery somewhere full of toys and the first terrors of life, he was nevertheless—albeit hazily and mysteriously and tench-like—the very same man! All those cuts separated me from myself like a tapeworm head, from which the same tapeworm keeps growing back (because, in accordance with a biological command, it contains an established design of itself and hence its style, as it were). But none of those cuts supported its effectiveness by using the spectacular circumstances of a historic event. Only the cut in March 1938.

From which one may conclude that my personal history is connected only rather loosely and randomly with World History. *It really does not concern me.*

Hence, now, here in Paris, in 1968, it was not memory that stunned me but simply my small interest in it. My gaze up into the peepshow box of the air shaft, through which nothing was to be seen but a rectangular section of the ice-blue sky, sucked me out of time into a sort of removal from time—into a no-man's-land between the here and now and today and the there and then and yesterday long since and frequently separated from me.

I belonged to neither one now. I saw both as equally remote and abstracted from me: each a wholly different story. I could tell either—but neither expressed me.

I peered simultaneously into my two aquariums, each of which contained the other and me in the amniotic fluid of a tale to be told—as a literary fetus, so to speak. One was a Paris hotel room reeking of bedbug killer and couscous spices; the other, the Vienna of the annexation by the Third and Greater German Reich.

In both, something swam in slow-motion weightlessness: I, my SELF—or at least a human being with an unbearable resemblance to me. In one, standing at the window and gazing up the narrow airshaft to the sky, a man of forty-nine, modeled trait for trait on my wanted poster, and with the same personal data, the same name, the same place and date of birth (and its disreputable circumstances), the same color of hair and eyes, the same nose shape, ear shape, fingerprints, and distribution of liver spots—hence, in terms of all criminological leads, quite unmistakably me. In the other, the same man, thirty years younger—a callow nineteen-year-old, in whom all these traits were just budding, so to speak, not yet settled in creases, leathern and weather-beaten and masculinely marked—yet nevertheless me. Indeed, beyond the shadow of a doubt, ME, my SELF—

and neither concerned me directly. Each was I, my SELF—but simply as history: as my abstraction.

Still, a secret rapport existed between the two of them (the realization they were ME), in which I was not included. They existed through me and beyond me, in a higher form of existence that I had not yet attained. They looked as if they were winking and waving—indeed, even calling to one another, shouting something I could not (or was not supposed to) make out. It sounded like something I knew, indeed knew very well. It sounded like my own echo, but I had forgotten the words of the original call, and the echo had died away no sooner than I thought I had caught it.

They knew the words and had decided to keep them from me. And thus, they (these stories of mine, twice times two times two times two times two stories) aroused my curiosity, forcing me to deal with them and cope with them incessantly, to tell them to myself over and over again, unceasingly—yet without ever managing to become fully a part of their equation, all their numerators and common denominators, their common multiples as well as, ultimately, the solution to their algebra.

My gaze through the tetragonal funnel of the light shaft yanked me up and out into the cold void, in which I floated away from myself like a balloon cut loose. And, like the hazy strips of soft, perforated cloud covers, the rags of other memories, other histories of my many detached and abstracted SELVES, soared past me:

a pond in a now entirely mythical land (known as *Bessarabia*, a name that is speckled like a guinea hen): a small pond in a park, where a delicately old-fashioned boat was decaying

a bridge arching over the Danube Canal in Vienna, under whose slanting shadow, cast transparently into the mealy lit fog, I, my SELF, a boy of eleven, was placing a toy boat in the black water: in it a candle that was to drift to my dead mother

a classroom at the realschule in Vienna's Thirteenth District, in whose mountain sorrel a wheat field of youth was rotting on the stalk, year by year

the nixie eyes of my foster mother, bewitched and strangely hungry for salvation, her gaze with drawn-in flanks, as it were, arousing the same hunger in me

Stella or liberation, sinful lovemaking in the veil the frogs wove with their croaking one moonlit night over Baneasa, furious mating behind a boundary ridge on the highway where the car stands with its motor running, predatory pouncing on each other in hotel rooms rented for hours at a time

and John, whom we—still glowing and breathless and with hands trembling—sit facing, with his perfectly immobile face.

The war:

Cousin Wolfgang, appearing before me in military gray; Berlin in flames, and the gray human faces which the soot of conflagrations has seared so deeply that they shine; the canteen with German attorneys and witnesses at the Fürth law court and the purely physiological gratitude in the otherwise perfectly expressionless face of a young girl who is eating, taking in food with all the senses, all the organs, all the cells of her body

the Yuletide Ice Age in Hamburg: Christa and I holding hands and gazing down at our newborn son

Dawn, undressing an Indian doll here in this hotel room while Schwab and I watch in delight—and her stunned look, her sudden blush, when a giant vermilion penis appears on the undressed doll

Gaia dying and Professor Leblanc chatting away at her bedside

And none of these things really concerns me anymore. They could just as easily be made up and have never actually happened. They have passed away and could, told as several individual stories, become history. Without someone to tell it, it has no reality: as if it had never happened.

The ice-blue bit of sky over the air shaft was, in any case, wholly undimmed by any of this. It had swallowed it all up into its cold blueness: all of Nuremberg with all its spiritual dousing and crawling grave worms as well as the entire month of March 1938 in Vienna and everything I had been through, gone through, lived through, in between or before or after. True, I could wrest some of these things from that bit of sky, I could resurrect them and bring them back to life—with interest, raised to the level of narrative, an object of reflective contemplation, provoking our thoughts. The sky challenged me with a smile to do so, but this was sheer derision ... It had swallowed up so many other things that I had not taken part in: the atomic mushroom of Hiroshima, for instance, and the smoke of the crematory ovens of Treblinka; the kiln glow of the bombing nights of Berlin and Dresden, of Hamburg, Würzburg, Rotterdam, and Coventry and Warsaw, plus the sweetly burgeoning stench of decay from the fields of corpses in the Ardennes and in the Donets Basin, at Monte Cassino and El Alamein and Singapore and Waikiki and goodness knows where else; the defoliated jungles of Vietnam, the Algerians blown up by a hose in their anus—this blue sky has sucked up all of it. Certainly, others were, fortunately, present in those places: they saw, witnessed, experienced, and are capable of wresting these things away from it, resurrecting them as narrative: on the level of an object of reflective contemplation. But this did not concern IT up above, it did not concern IT at all.

The bit of ice-blue sky over the air shaft (sixteen feet square): it had swallowed up all Babylon and was completely undimmed by this, without the slightest frizzle of a bellyache, silky smooth, crystal clear, and as deep as a well. And what if mankind were now preparing to hurl the entire planet after it, including itself? What concern is this of IT, what concern of mine? I have nothing to oppose it with but words.

Up there, in the blue, the man who experienced himself as the story of a man who experiences himself as the story of an adolescent who experiences himself as the story of a boy who experiences himself as the story of a child—I, my SELF, up there in the Arctic blue (still unborn as a story, still not wrested from the blue maws of oblivion, but about to be: always, destined to be so from early on, misborn to mislive my life as a story), with my image I also carried about a piece of human history—

March 1938, for example:

The Arctic-blue emptiness of those days—and Vienna, washed up on their shore like a lovely dead seashell ...

Certainly: as a story, it was smashing. Blissfully, I stuffed it into the light blue of Schwab's eyes, how many times—and these eyes were never fed up, they kept gaping, round as tennis balls, gawking through the thick glasses. And thus I never got fed up with telling stories—that is, wreaking vengeance. For that's what it really was, an act of revenge each time. Revenge for the betrayal of our life's dream, for our wasted youth, our now empty and abstract life, revenge for the loss of reality, for our lost innocence, for the demiurge's shameful game, imposing upon us an existence under scornful conditions: giving us life in order to steal our lives from us . . . Blissful revenge, turning into gall, until even its bitterness was no longer palatable—until I was only chewing ashes: "Yakkety-yak—why am I blabbering to you about the magic and the death of cities—you who saw, who breathed Berlin: a son, a legitimate offspring of the splendid, legendary Berlin of the 1920s, of the first decade after WWI—until 1933, until the oriflamme of the Reichstag fire. That was another radiant star, a sister star of the city of Paris in the diadem of Europe. I mean, before the hopelessly aged, bull-borne girl donned cowboy pants and New Mexico boots, became the hit of the county fair, despite her crone face and multiple unsuccessful face-lifts, the bronco-busting rodeo star Miss Yurop with neon tubes around her Texas hat . . . Back in that faraway morning hour of the world, when we were all boys, you, friend Schwab, and Nagel and Cousin Wolfgang and I—you, as the firstborn, could spend a few blissful holiday weeks there, in that legendary Berlin, presumably in furuncular late adolescence, but blind from too much reading, and mature enough to note the quickening of your pulse when reading Gottfried Benn and ascribing it to increased distrust, and yet happily enjoying the well-crafted wordsmithery of Else Lasker-Schüler, and associating jazz with Otto Dix's paintings of the world war or the brown shirts and red-white-and-black armbands of the SA with the songs of Brecht & Weill, Inc.—devouring all this like a whale gulping down plankton: to drink the world, to be drunk on the zeitgeist—you lucky man! Born to such riches! . . . And where is it now, your precious Berlin? Does it exist in reality and not just on political maps and in *Bild* magazine as the scene of the German

Wailing Wall?... Cross your heart and own up to it: that city never really existed, it was a legend, wasn't it? A dream that a city dreamed about itself?... How can I believe anything else? I was shown a settled spot in Brandenburg and told it was Berlin, and I wandered through it, up and down, in every nook and cranny, before it was destroyed by fire. And I can assure you: nothing there, absolutely nothing evoked even the slightest echo of that legend, of that dream of a city... I am ready to believe in Atlantis and, if you like, in Vineta and, of course, the Baghdad of Haroun ar' Rashid. But the model arch for tinker-toy tinkering (the big Wilhelmine Memorial Church edition in the Kaiser's birthday package for higher social classes, free delivery), this giant bourgeois toy left to the little people in the brown shirts from the back courtyard, this couldn't possibly have been the Berlin that an entire generation dreamed about, even I in the brooding dullness of my formative years in Vienna dreamed about, like a modern Babylon... I had pictured it altogether differently—not architecturally, of course, but in its atmosphere, as they say: in its mood substance. The legendary Berlin of the so-called cursed *Systemzeit* must have been magical, like a jungle painting by the Douanier Rousseau: an adventure dappled in flickering light like the face of a predatory feline suddenly emerging out of the sickle-moon-sliced blue of the tropical night... At least, that was how I had pictured it when I yearningly dreamed about it in the stale air of a puberty-fermenting classroom in Vienna's Thirteenth District. A tropical voluptuousness, especially at night, when the entangled lianas of light were reflected in the black asphalt currents and vice waxed in the moor ponds of darkness, making the overexcited mind fluoresce. So that, from the miasmas of lust-for-life and misery, luxury and crime, the orchids of the intellectual events of art, of strange, bizarre, baroque existences, of anecdotes, blossomed forth... You used to say you envied me for my formative years in Vienna: Klimt and Schiele, Wittgenstein and Berg, Schönberg, and so on... But permit me: In my time, all that was in a different paleontological stratum. It was past and past perfect, not present. It was history, myth, legend: literature, not life. Your Berlin, on the other hand, was, for at least a decade (until 1933), the most vivid present in our existence—granted, not one hundred percent the ANTHROPOLIS of the utopians, not exactly the New Jerusalem of the pilgrim fathers, but a Babylon: cesspool, chaos, yet all the more beautiful for that, all the more seductive...

"But believe me, dearest friend, that was not what I saw burning down in the year of Our Lord 1944, aside from a few remnants not worth mentioning. What I saw was a dried-up, parched-up, silted-up training ground for the populace. A barren metropolis of perioecians, a steppe city that was already, in essence, half Russian and half American long before its division. Hence, the other, legendary Berlin must have died quite a bit earlier, silently. And not in slow, rattling final breaths but from one day to the next, like my Vienna in March 1938... When a city dies, it does so from one moment to the next, while the people keep treading in their tiny ruts of destiny, life in the streets goes on teeming, the traffic keeps moving with no visible break or jam, the buildings still stand with windowpanes glittering in the sun—and all at once, it's happened: an incomprehensible alteration in the feeling of the world, the quality of life, an indefinable but all the more decisive change of the hour, the beginning of a new phase of life for everyone... It is a planetary if not a cosmic event. There is nothing more anguishing than the death of a city before it vanishes from the face of the earth. This perishing of its spiritus loci is a metaphysical process, and not even a Hitler can take credit for initiating it. For all the undeniable merits that this minion of nature acquired in nature's game, I do not truly regard him as directly responsible for the death of Berlin. But rather as an executive organ: the leader of the swarms of maggots that beset a corpse. Supreme functionary of the decomposition, if you will, the most furious enzyme of disintegration, but not *the murderer.* After all, he marched into Vienna only after the city breathed out its soul in the ecstatic "*Siegheil!*" of the flower woman (one of the city's root spirits, no doubt)...

"But let's stay awhile in perished Berlin. Just look: the young man I encountered there in 1944 on a smoldering and sizzling Kurfürstendamm—his stumbling and reeling, the way he kept walking, mechanically drunk, and yet that unswerving gaze into nothingness, that blind seer's gaze that made me realize something extraordinary had happened—that young man was already a citizen of a city of the dead. A walking corpse. He had no living reflexes left. What kept him upright on two legs, and even caught him when he almost fell, was, so to speak, life in a different environment; that was, at best, the reflexes of the teeming maggots inside him—movement, true, but no longer his: a certain sense of balance still, but no longer his. A condition that we perhaps do not sufficiently take into account, we who intend to tell stories about the living. And this, you see, was the extraordinary thing I realized through him. An enormously simple truth: merely marching upright on two legs is not enough to live. You aren't living if you live as if life doesn't concern you. As a biological process, life is eternal, right? It merely changes form. The maggots that will teem in our cadavers after we die are even, biologically speaking, life to a higher degree—though not our life, alas. In order to preserve what we call our life, the mind must, they say, be preserved. But our mind—is this not our life dream?... I know I am telling you very trite things—do forgive me!—the world consists of such trite things, and their phenomenal wealth often confuses us so thoroughly that we lose sight of it—and that is the very point I am trying to express in my awkward fashion. It took a walking corpse to show me that in 1944 I was not witnessing the death of a city, I was attending the cremation of its cadaver: and that the city had died because it no longer dreamed itself... The very genus of city died out because its mind, its dream, its myth died out: because the dream of ANTHROPOLIS, the City of Mankind, had died. We had all died with it, because we no longer dreamed ourselves.

"It doesn't mean very much if a city goes up in flames. Very many cities have gone up in flames—ancient Rome, for example, a good dozen times before Emperor Nero let it go up in flames again. However, its mind, its dream, its myth, have remained alive for one and a half millennia. And especially in regard to the year of our LORD 1944, dozens of cities were going up in flames; there was an epidemic of burning cities. The burning of a city was nothing out of the ordinary; the fiery heavens of the apocalypse threatened to burst open over Germany at any moment so that a powerful angel might appear and blow his trumpet, announcing the end of a city... However, the end had long since come to many cities. In Vienna, the angel had already appeared in 1938 in the guise of a Viennese flower woman, and his trumpet had blared out a brassy '*Siegheil!*'

"Admittedly, in a burning city, it is hard to distinguish between true events and mere spectacles. But in the Berlin of 1944 it took no Brahman's eye to realize that the incineration of this city was merely the completion of an enormous but compelling causality that had begun a great deal earlier. This was being shouted from the rooftops—insofar as any rooftops still existed and anyone was left to shout from them. However, in March 1938, it took an especially fine nose to sense that time had taken a leap—a spinning leap, so that it was now facing away from its normal direction and would henceforth be zooming backward faster and faster to where it had come from. The Twelfth of March 1938 was the cusp in the swing of time's pendulum—or, if this is more up your alley: the instant of turning between two breaths of God. For the LORD breathes while HE dreams HIMSELF in an enormous game of creating and annihilating myriad worlds. And whenever HE inhales in order to exhale again or exhales in order to inhale again, time changes, the dreams of human beings change—and somewhere, I don't know where, the style, the epoch changes—I'm talking nonsense, I know. I know that any newspaper reader can refute me. There are solid causes and reasons for everything and anything; they are delivered to you with the daily paper. Had I read my newspaper carefully, I would not dare make such flimsy claims. One could just as arbitrarily assume that time changed in 1933, illuminated by the oriflamme of the Reichstag fire, which, so to speak, was the match struck for many subsequent conflagrations—an incident, by the way, that I learned about quite by chance and only many months later—please excuse me, but Vienna was so far away in its own past, so distant from all reality, it had so fundamentally betrayed its dream of itself that its people, already back then, five years before it died for good, were living in a kind of limbo—or better yet: were sleepwalking... I, at any rate, arrived one evening at the location of what I had been taught to view as home back then: the apartment of my Viennese relatives, stuffed with horrible furniture: petit bourgeois Biedermeier, plus crocheted doilies, Colonel Subicz's swords of honor—you've probably found analogous things in Potsdam: sword-knot-proletariat; have-nots entitled to starvation pensions and with the most slavishly obedient class arrogance... There they sat in a family grouplet around the radio, my uncle Helmuth as usual, mental substance in his steeple head: *A Manual for Engineers* (a small three-volume edition for domestic use), the Veda and the Upanishads, Sir Arthur Conan Doyle, Madame Helena Blavatsky (née Halm von Rottenstein-Hahn) and Fräulein Fränzel's Prophecies. His spouse, Hertha: a gruel of stupidity and misunderstood femininity. My cousin Wolfgang (whom you often resemble: very intelligent, precociously accomplished even then), having almost furiously outgrown, mentally as well as physically, his boyhood clothes—now staring with his bespectacled eyes and bending slightly, like someone who's got constipation—the better to hear, of course)... And my aunt Selma: the old broken-down cart nag, her bony hands in her barren lap, the bewitched nixie-gaze into emptiness (need I tell you I loved her? She taught me how to live tenaciously with despair)... and from the radio the broadcast of a recording of the Reichstag fire trial welled brassily. A historic event, if you please. When I entered unsuspectingly, hence loud and unabashed, they glared at me indignantly, dressed me down with dirty looks and shushes. You could hear Göring's voice, and then that of the presiding magistrate (do you recall the guy's name?). He was very solemnly saying "*Defendant van der Lubbe—*" And because, at that time, there were no electronic tape recordings, just Stone Age resin disks into which sound waves were scratched in order to be scraped out by a needle, and that record evidently had a crack or a notch, which made the needle keep jumping into the same groove, the presiding magistrate of the historic court of law kept saying "*Defendant van der Lubbe—van der Lubbe—van der Lubbe vander-LubbevanderLubbevander-Lubbe...*" It didn't sound world-historical, God in heaven be my witness. It sounded quite extraordinarily funny, like a fart in the bathtub... And that is the only reason that the event lodged in my memory—if you would be so kind as to forgive me, an exceedingly ridiculous matter even today, your Reichstag fire, an extremely silly oriflamme, and I could never believe that this was the torch that lit ANTHROPOLIS aflame and destroyed it.

"Since then, I have been insisting on my mythology. It is based on my being an eyewitness. In March 1938, I was there. I directly witnessed a historic event—that is, of course, as close as people like us can get. In any case, fully conscious that it was a historic event. That alone was peculiar. Even back then, I did not read newspapers. I was nineteen years old. I had enjoyed a realschule education in the Federal Republic of Austria—that is, historically, not to mention politically, I was about as informed as a carp in a pond. And even though I had grabbed some of the crumbs falling from the richly laden humanist table of my cousin Wolfgang, my horizon of civic knowledge blurred away just behind the Lay of the Nibelungen, Emperor Max in the wall of St. Martin's, and a few operetta stanzas rehashed in terms of current events. It would simply have been going too far to expect me to read the final end of Austria in the flower woman's ecstatically bouncing ass—namely, an end of that amortization fund that had ridiculously posed as a sovereign state, a sinking fund of the Habsburg legacy of petit bourgeois staleness, Alpine folklore, and parliamentary fussbudgeting that was the Federal Republic of Austria at that time, and at the same time also the end of an epoch. And hence also the end, already twenty years prior at that point but lingering in awareness, of a geographic myth, by which the Ortler was still mirrored in the Adriatic, and behind Fischamend the world was still open far beyond the Carpathian forests, all the way to the mule paths of Macedonia and Bohemia and Moravia with their dark forests and sheaf-laden grain fields together with the hazy croaking of frogs over the ponds of Polish Galicia, still fenced in by the same black-and-yellow toll gates—it would, I tell you, have been asking too much of me to see the end of that notion of the Austrian Middle Kingdom as also the end of Europe, that multishaped, tensely dialectic Europe, which bade farewell to the Guermantes in the west while it wreaked bloody vengeance for a stolen sheep in the southeast, with the same

Kalman tunes being fiddled in its ears from Brest to Braila and from Königsberg to Capua; despite the motley of costumes and patchwork of manners and mores, it was nevertheless a formation of the same culture, a world of the same life-dream, the same ideals, the same shalts and shalt-nots, the home landscape of a humanity that, for all the variety of creeds and cults, worshiped the same God, deceived HIM here there and everywhere in pretty much the same way and along with it let the Kalman tunes from the latest Viennese operetta be fiddled in their ears.

"Please try to picture the background that the Vienna of the 1930s provided for this imperial myth: the feeling of imitation belonged in a certain respect to your proof of residence, whereby on top of that the image of the fathers was really everything other than unharmed: You see, the Kalman tunes were not only fiddled into your ears there by café musicians but also, and more often, cranked out of hurdy-gurdies by the medal-showered, stiffly saluting torsos of wounded WWI veterans with the black glasses of blind men under regimental caps, and not with their hands, but with prosthetic hooks... That was more or less what anything looked like if it was left over from the glory that was Old Austria and the old Europe. Vienna may still have been dispatching the Orient Express in three-quarter time, accompanied by the sobbing Gypsy violins and bedbugs of the puszta czardas and the marrow-devouring nostalgia of shepherds' flutes and lice along the Ialomița, all the way to the Golden Horn. But nonetheless Vienna had long since become part of a different myth. It had long since been spiritually incorporated into the longed-for Greater German Reich. Even the Vienna of 1933, when the *vanderLubbevanderLubbevanderLubbe* of the Reichstag fire trial resounded through its philistine homes, had long since been placed as a bride next to your true-blue Prussian Berlin (alas, oh, alas, not the legendary Babylon of the 1920s). On the wall of the classroom, in which I had dozed away my youth, like an unhappy chained dog dozing away a summer afternoon laced with the buzzing of flies—there, amidst the pictures of Old Austrian President Hainisch's prize cow Bella and the protected Alpine flora, hung an oleograph of the German School Association, very active with its political propaganda. Encircled by oak leaves and surrounded by black-red-and-gold flags, the oleograph showed a German-Austrian mountaineer, yodleeolay, in an Alpine jacket and with a blackcock feather on his toadstool hat: with his hobnailed shoe and vigorously bent goalkeeper knee, he was trampling down a border fence-pole and stretching his hand out to Germania, waiting on the other side in an imperial crown, blond hair, coat of mail, shield, and sword... For many, many, countlessly many hours of dull boyhood misery, while some teacher with a chain-smoker voice used the Mocznik-Zahradniczek method to derive the sine and cosine functions of a unit circle, my mind seized on the allegorical union between the Alpine country and the Brandenburgian sandbox under the imperial crown of Charlemagne. And my imagination thrust the border pole into the lederhosen fly of the costume-party mountaineer and wove the protected Alpine flora and oak leaves around it, the way Lady Chatterley plaited anemones in her lover's pubic hair. And my fantasy inserted the pole into Germania, by way of unification, slitting through her exuberant coat of mail, while she forcefully farted out the entire German School Association with its gym squads and black-red-and-gold flags and Mocznik and Zahradniczek as first and second officers of a student corps, riding on Bella the prize cow and alternately singing "Watch on the Rhine" and "Oh thou, my Austria." Sometimes I even did a detailed drawing of the scene on soft-blue graph paper in my mathematics notebook (I was regarded as artistically gifted), thus allowing my neighbors to partake of my lack of nationalistic conviction. And, although they enjoyed my vulgarities with the boyish taste for the trivial, they never left me in doubt that they despised me for this lack of a sense of belonging to the German Nation: I was a man without a father, a man without a country, and I did not share the intense feeling of the era: the collective urge to eliminate violently the particularistic old and strive toward some universalizing new, whatever it may be, so long as it promised the happy absorption of the individual into the community of the many, the most, the very most, everyone. At that time, dear friend, when a brotherly—permit me to say, a Brother Cain–like—Germany lit the torches that blazed over the twelve-year Third Reich of our Austrian compatriot Adolf Hitler and were even supposed to light the way home for us—at that time, in the world-historic, highly significant year 1933, when you were dwelling in that legendary Berlin, which I yearned for because of George Grosz's drawings and Cousin Wolfgang yearned for because the Nietzschean superman was allegedly coming into being there—at that time, I say, the younger generation in Austria was afflicted by the collective urge to unite, to unify, to become one, all for one and one for all, above all with our brethren in the not-yet-achieved Reich; and it was indeed a beautiful, noble urge, based on an ancient dream of humanity: the dream of the New Jerusalem, the dream of building the city of mankind, ANTHROPOLIS ... Nothing could have been further from the minds of the credulous youth than the realization that the cities would die precisely because, with all the striving toward one another, the uniting and the unifying of one and all, they had regrettably lost the individual. While spiritually building the city of mankind, ANTHROPOLIS, they had unfortunately lost *Anthropos* ... and although a few know-it-all individuals had long seen this coming and feared it, their warning cries faded without echo: the roar of the wind of time drowned them out: the spirit of the time was more powerful than the minds of the time. In any case, my memory of those days is transfigured by an unnameable promise that was held in the breathable air: even gray Vienna was filled with it, the way a foggy day is filled with the gold of the sunshine in the blue sky above. You, with all your knowledge of cultural history, surely know what I mean: after all, even the short-lived style of the era contains the optimism of a humanity that is about to shape a new world: the futuristic elements in art deco, right? ... Well, I don't have to tell *you*, do I; you always knew it, and you certainly know it now: at that time, a new era was looming, everyone sensed it in the year of our LORD 1933. And in March of the year 1938, my schooldays were practically yesterday. I owe it to Stella's generous hand that my clothing no longer had the bleak, fermenting stench of breakfast bread and pubescent urine and blackboard erasers from the classroom—a stench I had only just recently escaped with a high school diploma that bore the misleading title of "maturity certificate." And hence, it would be quite wrong to assume that I could have discerned a sign of Satan in the devil's tongue with the swastika poison-pill in the white circle (which, in those March days, would soon be dangling, fiery red, not only from the City Hall but also from the tower of St. Stephen's Cathedral, from the Stick-in-Iron House, from Sickartburg's and van der Nuell's botched-up opera house, from the hotels on the Ring, from the Head of Cabbage Building of the Vienna Secession, from the Diana Bath and Main Post Office, and generally from every flagpole and lightning rod and every broomstick thrust out of a skylight and every window bolt and shutter hook of the city of Vienna... If there was anything devilish about it, then it was some delightfully Viennese diabolatry. The dangling red rag looked like the red tongue lolling out of the raisin-eyed, almond-croissant fig-skull of the prune Krampus, Santa's hellish little helper, whom the Viennese give to one another as pre-Christmas presents on St. Nicholas's day. And this was familiar and festive. Vienna in those ice cold late winter days was as festive as at St. Nicholas's Feast, celebrating anachronistically a pre-Christmas festival going way back to pagan times... For you are not going to try to tell me that what made my flower woman dance across New Market like a whipped top was the thought of incorporating a few goitered peasants of Ötztal and a few Styrian cider-heads into a Germany already free of hoarders and Jews, waving its wheat and building its Autobahn, a Germany that could at last drink Alpine milk. Her engagement with the world and politics was about on my level... No, no. Something far more mystical, more atavistic, had transported this troll in tulip-bulb guise, making it whirl like a fat fly whose wings have been ripped out. Vienna was celebrating the empty festival of a new era... I've already told you: The sun had halted invisibly in the universe during those days. God took a new breath, and *that which was happening happened*.

"It happened on the second of the three days on which the sun did not appear in the sky (although it gave all its light, all its bright radiance—but not itself or its warmth. It came to pass that the emptied city filled up with human beings again—pig swill, I can tell you: a compactness, a suffocating excess of people. Never before had Vienna choked so much humankind out of itself. It rolled out of all the streets, foamed across all the squares, filled every cubic yard of free space from Hütteldorf to Mariahilf to Schwarzenberg Square. It hung in clusters from the cast-iron poles of street candelabra, was baked into druses on the wall cornices, proliferated in umbels out of every window frame, tasseled over the railing of every balcony, and it seethed and simmered. A human gruel so thick that the spoon stood up in it (as in fairy tales about poor people living it up for once)...What had driven them out into the streets? The Reich Chancellor and Führer was coming.

"Okay, Austria had been annexed. Vienna was coming home into the Reich. All well and good. This was—I can only repeat it—not so surprising or overwhelming. People had known that this would happen. It had always been the most ardent desire of the people of the Alpine lands. The cowherd in the picture in my classroom depicted it very graphically. Every second town councilman, to the Aryan core of his being, had always been stuck up to the hilt inside Germania... Of course, the national guard had fired cannon at workers' bastions and policemen had beaten their rubber clubs with equal violence on Communists, Jews, and illegal Nazis. But these had been carnival free-for-alls, in which nothing of importance was carried out that had not been carried out in reality long ago. In its mind, its soul, its Eros, Austria, or rather Ostmark, had long been part of Hitler's Third Reich.

"Well, then, what was happening now? Why had the people of Vienna and the Austrian federal states gone crazy overnight, sizzling in ecstasy, in delirium, foaming over like freshly tapped beer? Certainly not because something long expected had arrived, something long consummated had now finally become evident!... No, no. Something more significant was happening. It had something to do with God's breath, or, if you prefer, with the mysterious whirlwinds that your ancient Greeks talk about in certain speculations on nature... In any case: *it was happening*...

"It was happening in a strangely inhuman way—I want to say, in a way that transcended the human. Over the seething human gruel hung its noise, veiling, weaving, echoing—like the croaking of myriad frogs in the ponds around Băneasa during a moon-rapt July night—surging across the dappled surface of thousands and thousands of heads, pulling up the faces. Every cry that mounted, every voice that rose, every word that emerged from a gaping jaw, was caught up and carried further, like a stone hurled flat across a watery surface, danced off with hundreds of thousands of other cries over the ecstatically raised heads. These were no human sounds; this was a telluric din, whole gravel slopes were ricocheting and being covered by ones that were caroming back—and others were covering these... And then the spring tide roared up from Mariahilf, coming closer in an eardrum-shredding gush—raging, roaring, thundering ahead of a motorcade that zoomed through the chasm in the wild boiling human gruel, a chasm that opened before it like the Red Sea for the Jews. Pharaoh's plumed chariots shattered and perished when the walls of water collapsed upon them, sank with broken wheels in the tumult of helplessly struggling horse legs... But this time the water opened before them, they passed through with dry feet—and speedily: they flew by like ghosts: three, four, five large black open bulletproof Mercedes escorted by rattling motorcyclists, a couple of plainclothesmen clinging like monkeys off the back of each car; inside the cars, wasp-gold on brown Party-bigwig uniforms, blood-red trickle-stripes on generals' uniforms... And in the middle, standing upright, his skull weighed down by an oversize doorman's cap, automatically throwing up an arm like a jumping jack whose other arm has been ripped off—HE: crookedly pasted ponce hair over a doughy face, snuffling morosely on the small black stench of his mini-mustache... It all whooshes by, and the flood closes in on you, you sink with pharaoh's Egyptians, are torn into the depth, struggle, are struck, punched, kicked, and poked, squashed; you gasp for air and your throat is full of your shriek, you choke it up, throw it up with stars before your eyes. The spring tide has rolled over you, and around you everything is swimming, houses, towers, treetops, streetlights, the human gruel in the writhings (afterwrithings) of a collective orgasm. The men have dark circles under their eyes, their mouths quiver slackly, the women have wet spots in their panties, their hair hangs over their faces. Please explain that to me! Something isn't right here. This isn't the way of an explicable world, the kind that's in the news every morning... Even back then, the newspapers were incapable of describing what had happened, words failed them, reason failed them, common sense—at least mine. All I knew was that I had witnessed a natural event—had known it, in the biblical double meaning of the word. Together with Viennese humankind, the Alpine German humankind, I had known Nature: in a tremendous mass coitus—my ears were still buzzing, my knees still buckling, red circles were still dancing in front of my eyes... But what do you want: we had known Mother Nature: BIG, STRONG, HIGH-HANDED Mother Nature...

"She had enjoyed giving us all a brief thrashing so that we finally knew what 'procreation' meant—namely, not a private pleasure, or even a biological duty in the termite's contribution to the universal process of procreation. No indeed. It was a metaphysical event: a cosmic incident, against which even a solar prominence is nothing more than a fart in a bathtub... Certainly, the GREAT MOTHER allows us our little pleasure—I imagine that the myriads of second-long ejaculations in the big beautiful world trickle and prickle agreeably through her sense of life. But occasionally, she lets out a big, full, whole fuck: simply to make us see how serious the matter is: to show us what our real mission is here on earth—just why we were created in the first place...

"Oh, I tell you, she made her presence felt very strongly in those days, this powerful lady: she called the shots, she conducted the orchestra and was also the great theme and leitmotif of the festival performance. She was mirrored in the bright Viennese windowpanes, she leaped at you from the adolescents' red cheeks and powerful leg hair—the young people who suddenly walked with such extraordinary self-confidence—right into your line of vision; she resounded toward you from the whir of voices—in words like "renewal of life," "growth," "people"—and she created the backdrops in a weather that made your pupils pound: ten below zero Celsius and a bright spring splendor in the air . . . And she acted hearty and homey and housewifely: she tied on the blue sky as an apron and rolled up her sleeves for a big spring cleaning. It was as if all the Alpine glaciers had come to Vienna, mountain wind was sweeping out its nooks and crannies, every smashed Jewish skull burst open into an edelweiss . . . Ah, you would feel differently about former followers (more kindly; less scornfully) if you could have witnessed this festive mood of cosmic spring cleaning. You would be more sympathetic, empathetic, you would understand the subliminal homesickness of an upright North German detergent manufacturer like Witte for such an Eastertide whisk of a scouring cloth by Nature (I repeat: Nature!). For everyone was seized by it, by this sudden need for fresh air, order, cleanliness, purity . . . Even Stella, who was Jewish, after all—even she inadvertently said, 'I'm not surprised that the sky doesn't darken and split into flashes of lightning. We're not so childlike in our faith in God that we could believe He would do that for our sake . . . But this freshness, this fragrance of a house that has finally been aired out and put in order—it makes you almost reel . . .'

"Stella: the intellectual, who had spent her girlhood in the fabled city of Berlin; Stella, who as a child had sat on Flechtheim's lap, and Reinhardt's; Stella, who had corresponded with Kandinsky and Else Lasker-Schüler and received a love letter from Archipenko every year: 'My beautiful pageboy . . .' Stella, who kept coming in and out of Berlin with her diplomatic passport (in the piquantly mysterious aura of John's obscure missions) and who ought to have known what a very different play was being performed in the wings. Stella, the standard-bearer of ANTHROPOLIS, spoke these words . . . And you still find it incomprehensible that Nagel (that ship's hobgoblin of the categorical imperative) whipped his arm up for four years as an example to his fellow soldiers in an enthusiastic up-and-at-'em march-march—until one fine morning when his arm was shot off? . . . And you still brood about the fact that Professor Hertzog was a brigadier general in the medical corps (like Gottfried Benn, incidentally, whom Stella knew so well)? . . . Or that Rönnekamp, the Zarathustra Nietzschean, spent the year 1948 with genitally attached comrades, catching up on the officers' banquets that he had, unhappily, been forced to miss in the concentration camp from 1939 to 1945?... Yes indeed, where were you in those intoxicating weeks and months that followed March of the year 1938? Not in Vienna, I know. But presumably in your student garret: German literature and journalism, eh?... At any rate, you were not in Ostmark when it was finally attached to the Reich. Ostmark, which was suddenly much more robustly Alpine, much more costume-happy and indigenous, much more imperial in its cultural mission than Old Austria had ever been since the days of Archduke John of yore... For if you had been there, you would have learned straight from the (mountain-fresh) source what extraordinary resistance it took to keep from giving in to a certain twitching restlessness—how shall I put it? The itch in your skin of a universally powerful mood that included not only the urge for peaks, for pure, thin air and a clear view of distances, but also risk and the pleasurable bewitchment of vertigo—and then into the Alpine hut and into the Alpine dairymaid—goddammit! Into any old black hole, into the big black mother hole of blindly breeding, blindly devouring Nature."

In the summer following March 1938, I found myself in the Salzburg region with Stella. John now had a lot to do in Prague, and he had rented a house for her on the Mondsee, where he occasionally spent the weekend: a wooden house like a cuckoo clock. We lived a rather earthbound Alpine life there from April to September...

One might have thought that we had screwed enough a year earlier (the summer of 1937 in and around Bucharest)—but no: we mated like rutting wildcats, spitting and howling, in the detritus and under the firs and dwarf pines, clawed and clamped into each other, rolling down the forest slopes, panting and climbing up to the peaks to survey the heights and pouncing on each other there like vindictive demons—in mountaineering costumes, if you please: I was the cowherd up there on the slope, wearing lederhosen (very practical because of the fly) and a quaintly green stitched jacket with stag-horn buttons (whose imprint we then found on her breasts—her behind bore the imprint of the pine needles.). I rocked my mountain-lion manliness on bare suntanned knees—and she, she was the sheer Puster Valley with her narrow, dark head (I bit her neck when I discovered the first white threads in her raven hair: *Ô vraiment marâtre Nature, puisqu'une telle fleur ne dure que du matin jusqu'au soir!*). Her almond-eyed Bedouin head rose out of decrepit fringed shawls (great-grandmother's trousseau: we were supplied by every antique dealer on either side of the Inn and over and under the Enns). Tiny wood anemones were embroidered into her silver-buttoned velvet bodice; she laced them in with belts plated with copper and silver like the harnesses of brewery horses. And out of them, the heavy linen skirts (printed on wooden forms) and silk aprons (interwoven with golden threads) billowed into a brood-hen basket. Your highly honored compatriots from Neustrelitz, Brera, and Winsen-on-the-Luhe, who back then were swarming into Salzkammergut, gaped and gawked when they saw us at the tavern garden in the evening... And if we then exchanged a few Romanian words, their spoons fell into the mounds of whipped cream they had dished up (in the Old Reich, you see, whole milk had already become scarce). There was agitated murmuring ("... a certain Latin touch in specific isolated valleys here—that probably explains the aquiline nose..."), and this amused us no end. I couldn't reach fast enough under all that peasant textile wealth; I yanked my almond-eyed, black-haired, milking-stool princess behind the nearest bush, shoved her behind the closest rock protuberance, and with my wild farmhand paws peeled her bare Jewess body out of everything that was homespun, handwoven, embroidered with churchgoing swank, worn out by wedding-night work. I tore her alien-race nakedness free, spread open her cable stitch–stockinged legs... We committed an act of miscegenation that was not provided for in the Nuremberg Laws: we rutted blasphemously with all of Alpine nature... And when I was gasping my last breath and only my chamois-leather suspenders were holding me together, and she was lying in the moss among the crushed fern as though she had toppled from high up on the mountain wall and crashed down here, her arms and legs bent in a swastika, her head dangling to the side, only the not quite closed lids still trembling (she's truly been dead for twenty-five years now, and that trembling of her lids still reaches me—Stella in Alpine moss: overhead, in the star-seething heavens, glittering fist-size fragments: URSA MAJOR, *ursa minor*, Cassiopeia, Betelgeuse, hazy galactic whey—who knows what was already dead while its trembling light still reached us? . . . And cold, white, sawtoothed peaks, towering dark masses shoved right up close to us, megatons of primordial rock squeezing upon our chests . . . and, in the tattered black of the firs, a sublime soughing . . .), when we gradually began to gather our shattered limbs and torn-off antique costume buttons, when we, so weary with wandering, began to drag ourselves back to our cuckoo-clock cottage to sink into the checkered featherbeds (only to be riveted into each other again)—then we knew why we were doing all this: out of fear . . . Not out of fear of Adolf Hitler and his brown squads and gray iron men and knackwurst-shaped civilian officials with huge killer hands (what did we care about them? we were both foreigners: Stella had a British diplomatic passport and I a conscription order to join the Royal Romanian Army as a one-year volunteer). What we feared was: *the big cat.*

We probably didn't realize how correct our feelings were. And we weren't the only ones. Something had come into our minds, something that left everyone around us in a state of panicky rapture, a furious midsummer-light fear . . . And that something, lurking in everything, in all people, all things, all events—like a picture-puzzle face inscribed in them, inhumanly huge yet terrifyingly human—its name was NATURE. We were overwhelmed by it. We served this big, strong Alpine nature, served it with our bodies from dawn to dusk. We never let go of each other. If we occasionally needed to recover a little, we walked hand in hand to the modern boathouse in the reeds along the lake. There, we had discovered gigantic cobwebs in the timberwork under the planks of the pier. We lay down by the webs, caught flies, and tossed them in—and, hand in hand, like Hansel and Gretel, watched them as their struggles in the net of the web signaled to the spider in its funnel-shaped hideout, we watched it stick out its nasty head and then jerk out its thick, furry body . . . watched it shoot out and, with a cruel technical perfection (which raised goose bumps on the backs of our necks), secure the torn rib threads of the web, then scurry toward the trapped fly, paralyze it with a cunning sting, and start to wrap it up in spinning whirls... Our hands stuck together, sweating, while we watched the powerlessness of the fly in this hammock spinning tighter and tighter...

and when the fly was finally spun solid, looking like a caterpillar in its cocoon, we killed the spider and destroyed the web. There were so many, after all; they kept us entertained all summer.

Said Solomon to Sheba
And kissed her Arab eyes
"There's not a man or woman
Born under the skies
Dare match in learning with us two.
And all day long we have found
There's not a thing but love can make
The world a narrow pond."...

"Yes indeed, my friend," I said to Schwab, "that's the sort of thing Stella was doing in those days. Stella: it's not surprising that I was capable of that—I am and always have been an avowed nature lover. But Stella!... However, we must bear in mind that our actions were in keeping with the collective behavior. Something had happened to Stella that happened to pretty much all the people on our old continent: she no longer dreamed about ANTHROPOLIS, the City of Man. The zeitgeist had turned. The cities were dying. Humanity was building its New Jerusalem outdoors. In the middle of nature. People were striving to return to the Great Mother. *She* was the new model in their souls—thought up for the era by our confrère D. H. Lawrence: a magnificent female with fat piglets on all her teats. A perfect specimen of fertility; the goldfish jumped wherever she pissed. A housewife, I tell you, never emitting a fart without instantly transforming it into chlorophyll... THE GREAT MOTHER—it was actually she who was being celebrated in the Alpine land of Ostmark. The purpose of the radiant Yule night of March 12 in Vienna had been to conjure her up. The millions of termites, drunk with light, ecstatic with fresh air, had danced their termite dance for her alone. She had sent out her favorite son, from Braunau-on-the-Inn, so that mankind might celebrate her and so that she might soon show her true face: her dreadful carrion face. That blood-and-lymph-dripping maggot-sack of her body. The sky-high pyramid of skulls on which she sits enthroned... That was she, our dear Mama. The Führer guaranteed that she did not stir only in the wombs of German maidens, in the hopping of little goats on the flowery meadow, in the blissful sour-milk vomiting of babies, in the testicle-shaking rigid marching step of our boys; she also had to show herself in the full majesty of the Omnivore, who needed only to growl briefly like a predator to have a couple of Jews tossed into her mouth—a couple of thousand, a couple of million—and then, if need be, if that wasn't enough, then a couple of million Aryans in the bargain: one's own sons, one's father, one's mother, the grandchild in the cradle...

"Uncle Helmuth had good reason to listen to the voices from the beyond that announced a potentializing of our planet by Adolf Hitler. Austria's greatest son, the former suburban asphalt-walker, whom we had seen as a savior and redeemer, grouchily snuffling into his butcher's mustache under his oversize doorman's cap as he entered Vienna through the divided sea of the people—he truly seemed to be chosen for that mission. Nature had been alienated from mankind, violated by technology and art, and he was restoring her to her full rights—and this took place in the spring wind of the zeitgeist; even someone like Stella, who was born alienated, could not resist.

"No arguments could refute this. Reason—if it was worth its salt—had to admit this was beyond its jurisdiction. The force that pulled and steered was the collective feeling. Everything that occurred in the thin air of an incomprehensible but undeniable, irrefutably powerful enthusiasm came out of the collective feeling. It was so primeval, so earthy, so full of life, and yet so pure! It came virtually from the Alpine glaciers and tasted as clean as mountain air and as fresh as a mountain spring, even over slit bellies. It foamed with the trout streams through the valleys into the lowlands, sweeping souls along with it. Anyone who was not destined *by nature* to be a victim or was totally dull and without functioning sensoria was swept along. His tie was torn from his throat and his shirt collar was torn off and he was offered up—to the GREAT MOTHER. What is man, Czerwenka? Chaff in the wind of time, Herr Professor. And the wind was blowing out again into the open countryside. The Garden of Eden had recently become a nature preserve. Human beings were ensuring its care and protection with rifles. Shielding the Alpine flora and gassing vermin and Jews. The fictions were pine-needle green and rich in vitamins. And the GREAT MOTHER laughed so hard that her sides ached—looking forward to the next big feeding..."

It was like a vicious revenge-taking when I spoke to my dead friend thus: revenge for the sold-out dreams of our youth, for the gone spring wind of the lost halves of our lives, revenge for the guilty part we had played, revenge on myself for his death.

Revenge too on the insatiably alert, bright eyes, clear as water, gaping from his thick glasses—behind them someone busily copying everything down, recording every word in the intellectual's fine-limbed script, inscribing everything with a sharp quill in the greasy gray matter of his brain "as if someone had sewn it into his eyelids."... What's he hanging on to it for? What does he plan to do with it? How is he going to render it?...

"All these things that I'm so recklessly going on about seem to fascinate you no end—or am I mistaken?"

His face is nicely reddened: a blond's thin skin, boy-scout lock combed back over his high, narrow forehead (start of a steeple head: underneath, it's more massive, more Lutheran). A few beads of sweat on it. Restrained excitement. He's controlling himself nicely, but his face is not dominated by his eyes, which, grotesquely magnified, gape out of the round steel frames of his glasses; no, his face is dominated by his mouth: mollusk flesh, quivering with sensitivity.

He nods: "You are not mistaken. I am fascinated!"

Revenge, then, for every sentence extracted from me. For the sanctimonious simplicity in his sharp alertness. For his quick weighing, his swift connection of anything he hears. For the spinning of threads, the lying in wait, the shooting at the prey, for the paralyzing sting, the meticulous wrapping and preserving... Revenge for the smile flying up involuntarily amid light breaths—the cruel smile on his nervous lips. For the occasional light sniff from his nostrils...

"I seem to be giving you a great deal of pleasure with my stories?..." "Indeed you are. Extraordinary pleasure..." The irony he manipulates so much more skillfully than I. His superiority. The gently interspersed questions. The razor-sharp precise comments: the greater suffering, the more cutting experience, the more tested, more knowing patience. And he keeps measuring himself against me. Forces me to measure myself against him. "If you only knew how much you resemble my cousin Wolfgang..."

Rasping fraternal hatred in my voice, the voice of Cain: "Too bad you died, Schwab: you could have seen a new, more thorough era. The last time you were in Paris, I gave you a hint about this. Let's not fool ourselves, dear boy! You've got ants in your pants here, you can't even keep your ass in your chair for three minutes. And the cause? Sheer panic. You're scared of discovering that this lovely Paris, which is nevertheless still beautiful, nevertheless still poignantly Parisian, is no longer itself; you're scared that it died long ago. Just a blank shell: the paling home of a dead creature, still inhabited, but not by those who built it up around themselves out of the compulsion to express their nature. Why, if so many cities have died, if THE CITY, the myth of ANTHROPOLIS, has died—why should Paris still be alive? True, it's teeming before our eyes—or rather hustling and bustling—like I've said: the maggots teeming in a corpse are biologically potentialized life... I mean to say: Without our noticing it, perhaps during one of our absences, a quiet, bright dying may have taken place—like one of those instantaneous life-changes that amputate our past, cut it away from us, so that we undeniably go on living and remain the same persons, and yet no longer live the same lives, even if they are the same on the outside... After all, we know that, normally, a real event occurs discreetly. Dramaturgically, it is not proportionate to what it marks. It may be a stroll during which it occurs to you that you no longer love Miss McDonahue, whom so far you have regarded as the nuclear core of your existence. Or a ride on a bus during which it dawns on you that Karl Marx is not the be-all and end-all of the world. Such things happen entirely without our interference. A relatively nugatory cause for a sudden, thorough revision of previous thoughts and feelings brings about a sudden, thorough alteration of our entire existence. A private turn of the century, so to speak, which transforms the previous future into something outmoded and the past into a conjecture about any number of possibilities. But you believe that this is your personal, private turn of the century. In reality, the change lies in the times, and everyone is affected by it one way or another. For you, however, it was an existential change. And naturally, you go on living, and so does the world, to be sure. The world, as we know, is divided into facts. One thing may be true or not true, and everything else will stay the same. What is truth, what is fact, is the persistence of circumstances. The latter, however, changes all at once, so substantially that we no longer know for sure what was true and what wasn't—and nevertheless, all factuality remains as it was. But no longer—how shall I put it?—no longer in the same innocence... I am expressing myself quite clumsily again. What I want to say is simple, you know. For people like us, the experience of time is a gradual increase of guilt. Perhaps not even personal guilt so much as collective guilt. Original sin. The guilt of belonging to the human race. Especially to a dying civilization. Why else would you have the jitters? Why can't you stay seated? Why do you roam the streets of Paris like a hungry wolf? Like a murderer drawn to the scene of his crime?

"Admit it: You feel that you share the guilt for the death of the city. You too have betrayed ANTHROPOLIS. So you skulk around here to find its corpse—and yet you're too scared to look at it and see your own cadaver. Let me make a suggestion: Let us regard our existential changes as something positive. Simply as new steps. Metamorphosis existence. Butterfly existence. You've got to pass through the maggot stage. Who knows what's coming afterward? Uncle Helmuth spoke of dematerialization. Let's take the chance! It's totally painless. Without the shock of physical death. First, it happens to our environment. A city dies away under our very noses, as it were. You wake up one fine day, stick your head out the window, peer into the air, sniff at the patch of heaven that you can see over the air shaft, and you ascertain that out there the weather is extraordinarily fine, golden-blue—the fine weather that on a foggy day can lie in wait with a sedate and superior smile—time has time, of course. The air is a bit crisp perhaps, but that's good for your smoker's bronchia. So you brush your teeth, shave, put on a particularly attractive necktie, and stroll out into the street—and all at once you notice that the city has died, and you with it, of course. True, everything looks exactly as it did the day before. The houses are standing in their places, the streets are teeming, the cars are rolling shinily along the boulevards, the street of man-in-the-street faces under hats, caps, all varieties of hair, unkempt or combed, meticulously curled or wind-tousled, flows, dances, whirls, halts, dams up, breaks out, ebbs, swells again—and they are all deceased in the LORD, and you are too... Fine and dandy! How interesting! How very literary! You have just sloughed off a form of being that was previously your SELF, and from now on you are a new SELF, forging ahead with new possibilities of experience. The old self sinks back like the dry husk of a larva from which a butterfly has hatched. The burned-out capsule of a rocket. You yourself plunge onto a new path with new bright eruptions of fire out of your behind... Are you disturbed by the abstractness of the new form of existence? It is consistent with our loss of gravity. Do we mourn it? Is it really true that we lost paradise yesterday? Is it true that we were more innocent yesterday? Just what is that anyway—YESTERDAY? A myth. A legend. A fairy tale about ourselves. Dreamed by those who cannot dream a tomorrow for themselves. Is that not the reason for our feeling of guilt? We know that we are a breed without a future. Yesterday, we could still dream ourselves into the future. Today, we dream ourselves back into our dream of yesterday. But keep your spirits up! How does Novalis put it? We are about to wake up when we dream that we're dreaming. Why not as maggots? Without a past, if you please. Without a history. Likewise without a future. Creatures of the present. Highway rest stop people. Limited to a pure here and now. If that doesn't appeal to you—then, dear friend, all you can do is escape by forging ahead: into perfect abstraction. The pure butterfly. Dissolve in absolute abstractness—like you up there in the icy sky-blue. Or like me in my literary existence: as a literary object. Whether my own or yours..."

I stood naked at the window and peered up through the air shaft to the sky. Cold bit into my skin and shriveled my scrotum. I thought of the day when I had looked out of the same window at an angle, down to the opposite window (whose shutters were now closed), and Schwab and I had surprised Madame in her nakedness. I thought of her big, maternal breasts, whose fullness had charged into my gonads. In those days, I was not exactly overfed by the tender virginality of Dawn's breasts (which, moreover, I had not yet relished). At Dawn's age, Madame's tremendous appendages must have been magnificently bursting, with pale, bud-like nipples.

Rarely does one set eyes on such perfection (much less set hands or kisses or bites). I did once, however, when I was frozen stiff in the collapsed air shaft of a bombed-out house in Hamburg, shortly after my arrival from Nuremberg. She was a victim of the widely feared "rubble killer," a deliciously beautiful woman: stark naked and silkily glittering in her frozen matte nymph skin gently strewn with feathery snow crystals; only her face was bluish violet, like an eggplant. You see, the rubble killer strangled his victims with a wire noose on a wooden throttle valve. All he had to do was twist it behind the victim's neck to tighten the wire with a horrible lever effect. The eyes of the corpse very sharply revealed the power of this tightening twist: one eye had rolled up at a leftward slant under the caved-in lid, the other gaped dully at a rightward slant toward the stiff nipple. And her tongue had burst out of the cracked lips as though she wanted to lick it (they say of hanged men that their last moment passes with an ejaculation—what is it like with women?)—

Anyway, it was when I was engaged to Christa that they discovered that woman, yet another victim of the rubble killer, and I believe Christa had a good night after that. I was at my peak, as now.

I stood at the open window and wished to be seen in my morning glory. By Madame, preferably, or even one of the fat-assed Algerian women. Or, for all I cared, by one of the traveling salesmen, or the chambermaid who was probably cleaning a room across the way. Or the handsome Pole, who must have been sleeping with Madame one floor below, after finishing his night shift... I wished for a scandal. A voice furiously shouting "*Tu te fous du monde, salaud?*" A window being slammed shut. The telephone: "*Vous n'avez pas honte, monsieur?*" Someone banging at my door: "*Dites donc: ça vous amuse?*"

I wished for MYSELF AS AN EVENT.

It occurred to me that this too was connected with my constant thoughts about Schwab, with what had appeared to me in our precarious friendship as the *quest for defeat:* Eros, which had let me pleasurably feel the first conscious humiliation of my life, when I had been cruelly laughed at by classmates for an artfully recited English poem. But this was lay psychology. I was hunting for a different prey. For example: the connection between all this and the *something* that drove me to write. Or: what was at play behind the chance occurrence when it produces such a grotesque that it opens up a perspective into the paradoxical—that is, into the negative of logic. Seen thus, wasn't it funny to think that it was really by way of my friend Nagel that I got to meet the piglets and thus came to write at all (not Wohlfahrt & Associates, of course—that rosy little race didn't exist back then—just their biological ancestors, the primeval pigs of the postwar German movie industry, I would almost be tempted to say—but I would then have to beg forgiveness for this locution from Stoffel & Associates, may they rest in peace; it would by no means be meant pejoratively; its function would be purely evolutionary—those species of *Sus scrofa* already domesticated in the Stone Age, in the order of mammals of the setiferous artiodactyla, who are at the origin of the noble families of the European domestic swine).

Decent Nagel, in his aboveboard literary (and human) uprightness, has nothing to do with the nimble little race, of course, although every one of his best-selling novels could have been made into a box-office smash for housewives. But the rise of his star along its celestial course took place in the constellation of Stoffel & Associates, the ubiquitously long-forgotten heroes and forebears of the postwar German cinema.

They too, you see, are part of this legendary wintertide of the years 1945–48, which I (perhaps with a few rare members of my age group) must recall with persistent nostalgia, though they have otherwise slipped away from the memory of the German collective as thoroughly as the glacial periods of the Tertiary.

In those days, in the bronze heavens over Hamburg (rusting soon after midday, toward the evening), near the Bronze Age community around Professor Hertzog in Nagel's (or rather Witte's) garden house on the Elbchaussee, another star arose, a star that would soon outshine Nagel's meteorites until its extinction:

the Astra Film Company—boldly wrested from the hesitant occupation authorities, mainly thanks to the vital energy of a man named Horst-Jürgen Stoffel.

Stoffel had succeeded in saving a wood-processing plant (which had quite profitably supplied carbine shafts to the Wehrmacht) and had seen to it that it survived the war's end with rather large stocks of timber. Seamlessly adjusting to the new historical conditions, he took the enterprise (which had been evacuated to Winsen-on-the-Luhe) in hand and converted it to the production of Christmas toys—

a highly popular item, for instance, was the so-called Eckermann doll: a droll little troll made of branch knots and sporting a flattened back that could be used as a bookend. Scherping was so delighted with it that he planned to throw it in free of charge with his edition of Goethe's *Faust* (copyright 1947, all rights reserved), which had been licensed by the military government.

Because I ought not forget to mention that the publishing industry was already beginning to stir. Just as all manner of life was still teeming in the ruins. The red-light alleys at Gänsemarkt and on the Reeperbahn had also remained intact (like the Davidswache and the City Hall).

Horst-Jürgen Stoffel was not a man whose enterprising spirit could be restricted to the manufacture of cultural goods. After the Eckermann doll, he started producing wooden soles for ersatz shoes (which soles, to be sure, could be purchased only with rationing stamps). However, his lumber supplies were now categorized as "controlled goods" and subject to a quota.

And it came to pass that from one of the allocations, 870 more pairs of soles were carved than could normally be carved by the most efficient utilization of raw material. Horst-Jürgen Stoffel thus found himself in a ticklish dilemma: as an upstanding entrepreneur, he was obliged to register the increased output; but if he reported the overproduction, then inevitably the assholes at the Industry Office would cut the allocations by enough raw material for 870 pairs of soles (or else expect the same overproduction for the same allocation from that day forward), and, moreover, they would demand an accounting for the missing 870 pairs of soles from all previous allocations. Stoffel got out of this predicament by simply "remaindering" the extra 870 soles on the black market.

I don't remember what price was fetched by a pair of black-market wooden soles in 1947—Stoffel, at any rate, got 150 marks a pair from the middleman, a paltry sum when one recalls that fifteen Wild Woodbine cigarettes cost the same at that time. Still and all, Stoffel had 130,500 marks in his hands. To be sure, that was worth no more than 13,050 cigarettes, roughly what an average smoker puffs into the atmosphere, after a brief incorporation into his pleural cavity, over the course of, say, fifteen months—

what could be more obvious than taking the money, which could so easily dissolve into thin air, and investing it in an industry that creates ephemeral shadow plays? Horst-Jürgen Stoffel applied to the military government for a license to produce movies.

Of course, there were other reasons, linked to the times. Hamburg, as we know, is called the Gateway to the World, and during those winter days it was worthy of the name. Never before or since has it been the scene of such animate transience as in the first phases of the mass migrations (not yet arranged by travel agencies but triggered by the advancing Russians), when the natives of Brandenburg (pushed by the Upper and Lower Silesians, who passed through Lausitz and the Magdeburg plains into the Hanover region, and from there northward to Schleswig-Holstein, only to be shoved toward Hesse by the Pomeranians and East Prussians, who were driving the Mecklenburgers before them) advanced into Bavarian territory in order to avoid the Thuringians, who had likewise started moving, while the Rheinlanders, who had been evacuated into the Warthegau, tried to trade positions with the Poles who had been hauled to the mines in the Ruhr; however, the Rheinlanders were severely hindered by the Sudeten Germans, who had been thrown westward and whose flanks were being attacked by Transylvanian Saxons and Bukovinan Germans (Gaia used to say: *What do you need to make a good salad? A spendthrift for the oil, a miser for the vinegar—and a madman to keep tossing it and tossing it*).

Anyway, back then things were extraordinarily animated. Although the means and routes of transportation were demolished and also inhibited by countless checkpoints, incessant swarms of people trickled along the provisionally patched-up nervous system of the Western Zone road network. Trains were so thickly breaded with people that they looked like rainworms after rolling in sand. Railroad stations were military encampments. Basement waiting rooms were like the dormitory of Sainte-Brigitte . . .

And thus, of course, there were all kinds of unexpected meetings. Human destinies interpleated unpredictably, and attachments formed; Christa (whose meager hoard of language was enriched with the lovely images of a farmyard childhood) said, "Cow and donkey harnessed to the plow."

And so where Stoffel's application for a license is concerned, it was assisted by just such an—at first blush—heterogeneous attachment.

You see, the originally involuntary migratory instinct had also seized hold of the moviemakers. But not necessarily every survivor of Ufa Films was incited to move from Berlin-Babelsberg to Munich-Geiselgasteig. A few flocks wound up in Hamburg. There, in the subterranean makeshift waiting room of an eye doctor, Horst-Jürgen Stoffel had his fateful (especially for Nagel and me) encounter with Astrid von Bürger, the emancipated daughter of a professor of metallurgy at the Technical University of Berlin. In blitzkrieg times, by way of the School of Physical Culture, she had become a movie extra at Babelsberg, where a friendly cameraman had got her a tiny part, through which she had caught Reich Minister Goebbels's eye and then quickly risen to Greater German film fame.

Astrid was a smug girl. In later years, long after divorcing Horst-Jürgen, ruefully renouncing the cinematic art, and remarrying, this time a solid electronics industrialist named Häberle, bearing him flocks of children, and moving to an attractive mountain farm in the Alpine lime countryside south of Bad Tölz (and if she hasn't died, then she's still living there today!), she would tell about this meeting in an unadulterated Berlin-Charlottenburg accent:

"Man, if that wasn't love at first dim sight! . . . I'm sitting on that poor sinner's bench in the basement office, waiting to be ushered in to ol' Doc Four Eyes because my specs had dropped and the last Russian in Berlin had tramped on them with his Siberian boots, and without one and a half diopters I can't tell the difference between the 'ladies' sign and the 'gentlemen,' and the guy's dragged down the stairs by two other guys like a plaster war casualty on the Pergamon frieze, and they drop him very carefully in an armchair, and he keeps holding this neatly folded handkerchief over his eye, because while he was inspecting his factory in Dumpsville on Shit's Creek, a splinter from one of his dolls had flown into his eye, and then he takes the handkerchief off his bloodshot li'l piggy eye and gives me such a heartrending look through his veil of tears, like I should feel a little sorry for him on account of his little boo-boo—and all that plus the blond lock over his thinker's brow, ya know, and him taller than a centurion and stuffed to the hilt, his flesh white as boiled cod—well,

I say to myself, Astrid my girl, I say, you're gonna buy that rubber lion, he's one of the blow-up kind, you can let off the overpressure, it's as easy as pie. That's my kind of man—it's not for nothing I'm singing my Häberle's praises still today..."

But I too (in contrast to Christa and, incidentally, Nagel) did not find the combination of Astrid von Bürger and Horst-Jürgen Stoffel to be all that bad. For semantic reasons, to be sure: in my opinion, the two names dovetailed marvelously:

and it was with their names that they first entered my life: through Nagel, who came to me one day and spoke so glowingly of the founding of Astra Films and of the lofty couple.

Apparently, Horst-Jürgen's temporarily and unilaterally dimmed vision had likewise instantly recognized Astrid as his ideal love object.

Because of the above-indicated mutual readiness, it didn't take much courtship; besides, Stoffel had only to give a little free play to his talent for procuring things, and any female would melt. Winsen-on-the-Luhe was surrounded by farms, in which cows, pigs, and all kinds of domestic fowl were still thriving. A wood-processing plant had something to offer, a fair exchange with mutual profit. A good country ham could get a nice number of bottles of whiskey, the whiskey in turn brought willing ears at the traffic office—i.e., a car permit and a gasoline allocation; with the car one could go in for large-scale butter hoarding; the butter could be exchanged for nylon stockings and plenty of toiletries; for a bottle of Chanel No. 5 any farmer's wife in the Lüneburg Heath would give up her resistance and hand over any home-cured ham. In short, a smoothly running *perpetuum mobile*. No sooner were his eyes fixed than Horst-Jürgen read all of his Astrid's wishes in *her* eyes—and behold: her wishes coincided with his.

For what, after all, can be the foremost wish of a movie actress who has only just reached the zenith of her career and suddenly cannot make movies because, as a result of world-historical events, there is no such thing as a movie company? Don't worry about it, darling, we'll start our own. Here's a ham, you can get so and so much scotch for it, for scotch there's Chanel No. 5, for Chanel No. 5 the goodwill of the German secretary (and bedmate) of the military government's cultural officer, he'll give you not only a license but also, of course, film, and several automobile permits with the necessary gasoline allocations, which means butter again (and more of it); for butter, cigarettes again; for cigarettes, ham again; after all, we've got to crank up the economy in this pigsty, and first and foremost the movie business.

And in the movie business, Astrid knew every man who wasn't out of the picture—whether because he'd been killed at the hands of the enemy or on account of holding unorthodox political values or from the postwar lack of food—and every man knew her. After all, the episode with Reich Minister Goebbels had been maliciously inflated by envious and competitive witnesses; everyone in the movie business had been invited there sooner or later, anyone who didn't go was risking his life for nothing—in any case: "Stop carrying on, Karl. When they wanted to stick you in the propaganda company, you opted to take part in *Jud Süss*—right? Just keep quiet, kid; when they strung up your Lisa it didn't have anything to do with the resistance, it was because of the Bulgarian she kept running around with, they couldn't find him then because he'd taken off—right? Don't imagine you can spin something for yourself out of it... So, cheers, friends! To Astra! And to the great future of the reborn German screen!"

We received tidings of the rise of the Astra Art Films Company before this star had ascended in full radiance over the horizon. Horst-Jürgen Stoffel's entrepreneurial dynamics and organizational talent (supported by Astrid's knowledge of the industry) kept him, of course, from overlooking the fact that in order to build up a proper movie-production company (and also to get the license), he needed a so-called project—that is to say, a subject to grind through the lens—and for that, in turn, he required the work of intellectually creative people.

But this too was no problem. Intellectuals too had washed ashore in Hamburg. The occupation-controlled radio had a nest of them. And these people had gotten through the political filters; you didn't have to worry that their intellectual products might be marked with stains of the past—

but unfortunately, they were still intellectuals. The ideas they suggested were miles from what Horst-Jürgen Stoffel's healthy folk sensibility expected to see on the screen, especially at a historic moment when the masses, oppressed by collective feelings of guilt, should be granted messianic promise from that very screen.

("Well, if it were up to me, the movie would simply have to be called *A Silver Lining to the Cloud*—laugh all you want, Astrid, but this much even I understand about movies, I know they're a mass-market article, and so the public alone decides what it does or doesn't want to see—and believe me, darling, I'm not living in an ivory tower, I have contact with people every day, not old Kurfürstendamm coffeehouse hangers-on but farmers, workers, factory managers, railroad employees, businessmen: these people expect us to give them a guidepost for the future, and a future that they understand, that they can tackle with their own hands, that they can see emerging from the labor of their own hands—believe me, gentlemen, and you too, darling: political philosophy is of no interest to people now, they've had it up to here, it'll come automatically anyway, what they really care about is things that are strictly human, that are close to them: Give us this day our daily bread—right? And for now that's it—and then maybe: And forgive us our debts . . .")

Little in this connection could be expected from the intellectuals who were creating "The Cultural Word" at the Northwest German Radio Network.

("Just listen to just one of those programs—why, it's nothing but coffeehouse chitchat—and it doesn't even have the pep the Jews developed way back when at the *Romanisches Café*.")

still, that's where the solution came from. One of the secretaries of the church radio program was friends with Ute Seelsorge, who had told her a great deal about the fascinating discussion evenings at the home of a young writer named Karl Nagel—

in a word: the cinema bigwig Stoffel came and (to put it in the graphic lingo of the executive world, which, thank heaven, has taken over the cultural business) "made a pitch to Nagel."

From the first few discussions with Horst-Jürgen Stoffel and Astrid von Bürger, Nagel returned home with the euphoria of a lover freshly struck by his gracious madness—and thus also duly and ardently communicative. I couldn't help basically agreeing:

"To judge by the name, it seems to be a promising connection: Jürgen as in George the Dragon Slayer with the defiant lofty eagle's eyrie in Horst and the earthbound rootedness in Stoffel—plus the North Star, Astrid, over the delicate sociological synthesis of von and Bürger—the nobility of the mind, no doubt?"

Nagel bared a fang.

"Is she blond?" I asked.

No. *He* was blond: Stoffel. Straw blond. She was dark. An Icelandic queen. I was shown a photo (charming dedication, primitively printed: "To the Nagel in my coffin!—Astrid")—

Aha, so she was the one...

I should have known, of course. It's true I rarely go (and rarely went back then) to the movies, but this face had been hard to get away from in the last years of the war, even outside the movie theater.

Even after carpet bombs had flattened whole city districts, the unshakeable effigy of the beautiful Astrid had kept smiling down from tattered posters at the population (who, according to Reich Minister Goebbels, were not intimidated even by such acts of terrorism) or was wafted along on the singed front page of the *Berliner Illustrierte*, fluttering in the warm-air currents over the glowing remains of conflagrations. The face was beautiful, alert, bold, and base—the human epitome of the invincible baseness of the capital of the German Reich...

But good old Nagel couldn't know anything of this. For all his knowledge of the world ("The Bulgarian is the Prussian of the Balkans"), Berlin remained a blank spot on his intellectual map. Berlin in general, and certainly the Berlin shortly before and shortly after Stalingrad. At that time, he had been in the war, good old Nagel, risking his neck, while I...

For me, in any case, this picture of a sassy female face surrounded by Brunhilde hair immediately brought to mind very specific associations—

I was afflicted by an entire era: three years of draft-dodging in a virtually manless city crashed in on me; the cynicism of these years melded with a cheeky *spiritus loci*, the bad spirit of a city that has given up its spirit... I could hear its (to my Austrian ears) dreadful jargon, the pulp-novel name Astrid von Bürger evoked a whole Berlin ballad, churned out of a hurdy-gurdy like a lyrical toilet-paper roll, collapsing at the end of each stanza in a rooty-toot-toot as if under a cascade of shards, and then unabashedly straightening up again like a bounce-back doll. I was irresistibly tempted to do something malicious: hadn't Nagel betrayed me, his bosom buddy, in the beautiful crèche period, to Hertzog? Hadn't he betrayed our sacred buddyship even further by retreating into his garden house and assiduously writing without letting me in on his plans, his ordeals and triumphs?... Very well! I could write too. It was mainly valuable for myself; an act of overcoming the past—but, of course, it was primarily meant to be funny (in the spirit of my school days in Vienna, naturally): I wanted to make Nagel laugh. And if the verses of the poem that I dedicated to the "poet" Nagel evinced all my hatred of recent historical events, then it was, as Stoffel would have said, "on account of the times." I, for my part, wanted to amuse the good Nagel, not shock, much less offend him. Not even with the title of the poem:

Per Aspera Ad Astra
The Rise of a Movie Star in the Third Reich

Head to Wannsee, my dear child,
Where you'll still find waters mild—
Cool your German maiden's foot
Arm held out in stern salute

Rip that linen off your body
And be a lady!

Throw the ball and catch it quick
Lie down flat upon your back
Then stand up straight as a rod
Bend forward and side to side
Put your hands on both your hips—
That way they can see your tits—
Slip your pubis from your pants
And try your best while in this stance
To smile with chin between your ankles
Careless as a draft evader:
Give the cameraman his fill
And keep still.

For he's one cool customer,
Whom it seems the reigning order
Like a blessing from the sky
Amidst the bombs and flames and cries
Has set right here before your feet—
And for cheap.

And if he's no proper Aryan
Like a Mecklenburg agrarian,
Really you mustn't complain—
What would all the others say
Whose dear beaus have all been done in
Slaughtered round the Donets Basin?
When the Volk *are all off fighting*
Then at home it bears inviting
Serbs and Turks, Indians, Persians
In the end they're all God's children
Just let the man do his best
As ersatz.

Out there on the sunny sand
Give yourself with heart and hand
Joyful sport on his dark hide
(After all you are his bride)
With saliva-softened hand
Coax it out, his merry glans:
For that's where it has to differ
From the Jewish member.

Let him also, without haste,
Feel around below your waist
Germany's youth have a right
To their Aryan delight;
Let the goatherd at it too—
Their kind know a thing or two;
Alas, they know much more besides—
Who knew they came in such a size!
Therefore don't forget, take heed:
Lest the court should judge your deed.

Yielding to a love most hallowed
They won't hang you from the gallows
Wiggle your ass up and down—
You'll almost rip your dressing gown
Whatever else you might exclaim
Just don't reveal the brownshirts' names
Remember as you move your hips:
Loose lips sink ships!

Spare a thought for your old man:
Who in the heat of battle then
Fought bravely, gave it all he had:
Always such a fine comrade.
Had a laugh with Max and Fritz
At our dear Führer's expense—

But while he did so paid attention
That no dirty Jew should join in
If one did—oh man, oh my!
How the shit began to fly!
Out his ears and down his throat—
So long, Jew! That's all she wrote!

For sure, there's not a single bloke
Who doesn't like to laugh and joke—
But none of us would ever shirk—
Duty comes first.

And so every veteran soldier
Puts upon his joy a damper—
If you risk playing the cut up
Next day comes you might get strung up
Better also not inquire
About Göring's Reichstag fire
Or our fellow party brethren
Who were shot in plain reaction—
Good Jew haters, every one,
Hayn and Strasser, Heines, Röhm
Et cetera, et ceteree
On a pretty Alpensee.

And just as the old guys sang,
So we boys can chirp and twang:
To us the Führer is a god!
Though every third shell is a dud
Our belief is strong as ever
In his wise battle maneuvers.

And if in the Donets Basin
Our advance stalled out, lost traction,
Forced us for the nonce to beat

A glorious tactical retreat—
What's it matter?! The Iranian
Who became your war companion
Also pulls back just in time
From that fertile basin thine.

And so no one gets to grouse,
Or make a mess in his own house,
It's filled to bursting anyway—
Crap everywhere, the enemy
Makes for the home front, despite our objection,
No exception.

If Wedding burned and is no more
Just lie down on the Wannsee shore:
There amidst the gentle breezes
You can find a spot that pleases
Racial pigment, in the sun,
Will tan an ideological brown
Moan through love's activities,
Stretch various extremities
Which otherwise would only languish
Idly covered up by fabric
And in this total war would be
Of no utility
For victory.

If the fatherland should yield,
Should find that its fate has been sealed,
You can do your part and more
By waging your own private war:
Black-haired boys with curly locks
With cameras hanging from their necks—
Show them your gymnastics act
They'll photograph you on the mat:

One hundred percent woman
For the film industry's stud farm.

If we've got our skinny flanks—
For which we've got Adolf to thank—
And during this our healthy fast
They roast up crispy, barely last,
It's not just a frivolous game
But rather propaganda's aim.

The whole world must be made to see
That we have no weak tendency!
Babelsberg gives them their start:
Our cinematic works of art
Shall be presented far and wide
And show what Germans can provide:
Willingness to sacrifice
At any price.

When the winds of fate are shifting
Film receives its lofty mission
To instill in every breast
The will to stand up to the test:
Film can drive off with its power
Sorrows from our heavy hours
And move the hand over the heart
Amidst the cinematic dark
The eyes meanwhile look up and see
A fellow Aryan on the screen
Who battles death and devil
While subsisting on nettles—

So that in the end the beauty—
Seeing him carry out his duty
And rise to heroic fame—

Lies with him in the final frame:
He satisfies his mighty will
While making sure she gets her fill.

Don't give in to hesitance—
You mustn't miss out on this chance
To prove in such a prominent place
That you're a credit to your race
And that even in the buff
You're up to snuff.

All the Ku'damm conversation
Touches on your fine proportions
Few there are who'd disagree:
For German ideology
There's quite a force to be deployed
Contained in both your breasts and groin
Soon the moment is upon you
When good fortune shines upon you:
That you might show the boys who fight
And yearn for beauty's sweet delight
Just what those dirty crook-nosed ogres
Would have chosen for their lecher's
Pleasure, had the boys not acted fast
And cranked the gas.

So wiggle your hips left and right
Flaunt your bottom in plain sight
Do a cartwheel, round and round,
Splay your legs and leave the ground
So that between your fleshy hams
You highlight your erogenous zones
While up above, as soft as butter,
Beckons your fantastic udder.
Thus it is you make apparent

What the foe tries to keep silent:
Even the worst terror acts
Cannot suppress the simple facts:
The truth that we call "strength through joy"
Is unaffected by his ploy
And gives us, even 'midst bombardment,
Entertainment.

Don't listen to Mama's protest
When, clad in a high-necked dress,
You appear on the silver screen,
Crying for a Germany
Brought low by base and shameless Jews,
Choked by Versailles's unfair dues,
Sordid and pitifully quaking
Till we received Hitler's waking—
Older ladies' understanding
Cannot grasp film's inner workings.

The path to film celebrity
Begins with your virginity;
But no star can begin to rise
Unless she first should spread her thighs.
The strictest virgin of her day
Has more than once rolled in the hay
Well before the film starts rolling—
This is simply the beginning
Of her rocket-like ascent
Into the starry firmament.

For the road to fame is arduous
On this point there's broad consensus
Certain things you'll find that slit
Upon which German maidens sit;
And as you climb up the ladder

May your stride grow ever wider
Should you find between each rung
A colleague or two (all well hung)
Waiting gamely for to lend
A helping hand.

They're all experts in the trade,
In how Germanic glory's made
To reach the men of every station,
Even 'midst the clash of nations.
If morality is strict,
Still, a luscious pair of tits
Can boost the spirits of the people,
Bringing joy that nearly equals
That which fills a blue-eyed face
On seeing some Jew put in his place.

Besides, the boys in far Donets
Expect the best and nothing less
And sooner rather than later
For our mighty German warriors:
In times of Nibelungen need
It's not just bread that our boys need
Gunther, Giselher, and Arno
Need something to masturbate to
And the Reich's loveliest woman
Makes them hard as iron.

So climb the rungs to filmic glory!
Never tell a soul you're sorry!
See your star higher ascend
While back home mommy tells her friends
Don't mind that climbing to the top
Means climbing on producers' cocks,
Or going with the fellas,

Who are still behind the cameras
Even though their parentage
Requires a little subterfuge
And lots of foreign currency
To smooth away.

A German mother's plain good sense
Is not without permissiveness
If only for the race's sake—
And if the future's what's at stake,
And it happens to be dawning
'Tween the legs of her sweet darling,
Then a mother's sure to foster
Whatever prevents a stricture—
She herself in proud grief might
Regret that fate should deem it right
To curse her with unwanted leisure
When she'd rather have the pleasure
Of herself comporting
With the boys—it's only sporting.

If you manage to get cover
For your plans from your dear mother
You can finally be at ease—
Put your feet up, feel the breeze,
Close your eyes, relax, dear child,
Let the rose-hued fingers mild
Of sunlight play upon your face
How nice, to laze here by the lake
SA commander Roehm
Doesn't have it half as good.

Nor do others have it better
Lying beside other waters
With their noses in the mud

Eels swimming around through their heads
Two-foot holes shot through their guts
Mushrooms sticking out their butts
So the Führer's will to victory
Could be fulfilled economically
If Lebensraum *is our desire*
It'll cost us fertilizer
Where blood mixes in with soil
Germination knows renewal.

Strength through joy: render it service
For it passes through your cervix
In Adolf's plans for living space
The path from forebears of the race
To proudly liberated grandsons
Leads through the thighs of German virgins
Happy then she who can say
I've done my duty.

Bear the hard times then with patience
Cheered by German confidence
Wait in silence, free of scorn,
Necessity will break through iron
If the iron won't break, howe'er,
We know of things that shall endure:
Zille's cast of characters
On the Spree.

Let that fire fill your lungs
And you won't have to hold your tongue
Unless it suits you, then act meek
But sometimes show a little cheek
To let them know, time and again:
You're from Berlin!

Admittedly, the poem wasn't in the best taste. But it depicted the cultural background, the foil against which Astrid von Bürger had to be seen in order to be fully understood and appreciated. And that background could not be depicted in anything but our so-called stave rhyme, following the literary recipes of the greatest German: for a prose description, Goethe would have said, the subject was not important enough.

As for Nagel, it was not only his lack of necessary familiarity with the milieu that kept him from a sociological understanding of the beautiful Astrid. He was in love. Had he known the obvious, he would no longer have believed in the survival of the formal energy of that milieu; he would have regarded the memory evoked thereof as arbitrarily and improperly quoted, and he would have labeled it a rather shabby ad hominem argument. But because he was in love, he took my poem without further ado as sheer perfidy on my part. There was a rupture in our friendship, and it could never again be glued together.

Fine. I had no other choice but to feel ashamed. I had not only hurt a friend's tender feelings but, far worse, transgressed against a tendency of the zeitgeist, against the collective desire to forget.

For such was the situation in that legendary wintertide. People were willing to forget. The world was gray, but it was to be reborn. Yesterday was only a legend now. It had nothing to do with today.

There was, of course, a terrible myth about it. Everyone knew the myth and was burdened with it, as if haunted by the memory of a bad dream. A deeply gnawing malaise, a dull, irrefutable sense of guilt, a constant reminder of an incomprehensible fall of man—this lay at the bottom of reality, padding it darkly and also casting its shadow into the future.

Everyone knew: never again—even if the miraculous should happen, and the houses rose again from the rubble cities, the streets became filled again with the hustle and bustle of people, and there were all kinds of comforts again, some kinds of fullness and all kinds of change and variety, as well as summer skies, warmth, sunshine, instead of just frost and worry and gray wretchedness under hills of debris—never again would the world be the same as it had been an unimaginably long time ago (only yesterday, before its last great decline).

That much was certain. The world had been reborn—but a shade grayer and bleaker. There would be no more carefree atmosphere, no cheery optimism, no happiness that did not taste slightly ashen...

But even though everyone knew that lightheartedness, joy, and optimism were lost for all time, everyone pretended not to know for sure why and how they had been lost.

The dead—it wasn't the dead. We sow our grain in the dust of the dead. It was not the huge murdering. People have murdered since the world began. People will be murdering tomorrow. So, then, what was it?

In those days, snow fell from the iron sky in nastily beautiful crystals, and it bit painfully into the anemic eyelids of the lost, who trudged through the rubble fields with ashen faces and with sharp shoulders pulled up to their ears because of the cold and grief and misery, and the snow pitted and patted the frost-chewed ruin of a city into a glittering white-furred Arctic, over which the charnel-house reality of yesterday hung like the northern lights.

Nothing was forgotten as yet (though everything was withdrawn into the mystical). Death still followed one step behind everyone like an aide-de-camp. Hamburg was stalked by the so-called rubble killer, who strangled his victims with a wire noose. They were found in collapsed rear buildings, stark naked and frozen stiff, with laced-in throats and bluish-red faces, tongues and eyes popping out of them like medieval gargoyles. No one knew the victims, no one knew where they'd come from, where they belonged, or where they'd been going. Hamburg, the Gateway to the World, a world that had become so suffocatingly confined, was a crossroads now for countless uprooted beings, who, with their lost papers, had also forfeited their names, their backgrounds, their reality. Their murderer too lived among us, together with the many others. And now, twenty years later, gazing up at the rectangle of blue sky over the air shaft of a lousy cheap hotel on the place des Ternes in Paris, I felt as if I could have been that murderer—not necessarily the murderer of the nameless victims during the Hamburg rubble period but the murderer of my life-dream, the assassin of the promise into which I was born, into which every human being is born . . .

But what did all that mean now? Around me everything was dead. Stella was dead and Uncle Ferdinand's Middle Kingdom; Cousin Wolfgang was dead, and the Berlin of the gracious beginning of our life-dream. Stella was dead, and Gaia, and the beautiful city of Paris lay dying before me. The old Occidental Europe and with it I myself were a middle shadow kingdom, a myth, a literary invention like my friend Schwab. And it was left to me to take all of this to my grave.

The cremation of my friend Schwab took place three days after his demise on October 18, 1965. In the sympathetic presence of all who were near and dear to him. They turned out to be an amazingly presentable grouplet. It filled out the cremation pavilion at the Ohlsdorf Cemetery down to the last seat; in fact, a few people were even standing in back, craning their necks to catch a glimpse of what was happening. Very little was happening, but all sorts of things were going on. First during a worshipful silence, then during the scrambling clamber of pipe organ sounds in a fugue by Pachelbel (masterfully performed by a radio organist who used to frequent Lücke's Bar and—as it turned out—was Schwab's downtrodden first cousin twice removed. He was now rendering him his loving familial final service as a reward for lifelong scorn).

Honey-golden smoke rose steeply from tall white tapers (Pre-Raphaelitely inspirited by clusters of lilies at their bases) into the vault of the fire temple, which curved through parabolic ribs into a kind of expressionist Oriental Gugelhupf Gothic (an architectural achievement of the 1920s that in the span of our generation's lifetime has already become a historic document).

I don't know who paid for the considerable funeral expenses. Perhaps S. himself had taken care of them with regular payments to a burial society (back then I began to feel he might even have been capable of doing so).

Be that as it may: the wealth of flowers was overpowering. The lily-gilded candles in the apse were foamingly encircled by sprays of white lilac like ostrich feathers on helmet adornments. And in the very midst, where an altar normally looms in a house of God, a blossoming mound of white roses and camellias ascended out of a declivity one step down.

He was presumably resting under the flowers, having finally passed on into the lighthearted self-lavishing that had been so difficult for his prim and prudent character.

A dead man's generosity enabled anyone who might like to worship this prize piece of a flower growers' contest (Dawn's longing for the Mardi Gras in Cannes!) to do so. Needless to say, Scherping was present: as a bearer of culture, employer, and rival. He expressed the first function by means of a silk-lined black hat (which he held in his lap like a soup pot) and the latter two functions with a cunning contentment in his apple cheeks. At times, however, his soft mouth twitched painfully—with the corresponding emphasis of pleasure. The drapery of his face was tied back for the solemn occasion, but with a frivolous touch, like the hem of a Belle Époque cocotte, who sees a puddle on the pavement as an excuse to reveal her calves.

And Schwab's respectable, serially unfaithful former spouse Carlotta at his side was a widow transcending all conventions in so comradely a fashion that no one would have dreamed of asking how many years ago she had left the deceased because there wasn't even the smallest spot left on his head for another horn.

And Witte too, the Nestor of her countless lovers—and patron, laundry detergent king, and culture-fertilizer manufacturer—sat near her; in his lap, the same civic-association-representative black hat that is always sported in Hamburg to show economic prosperity in a dignified way despite a never denied (and certainly never doubted) lower-class background. Whereas Scherping's hat would, when donned, slide down over both ears, Witte usually pushed his own smartly off his forehead: *Stadtluft macht frei.*

Witte sat next to the legendary aunt who, in far-off days of youth, when bearing the name Wiebke, with its sound like the evening song of a plover, had been his betrothed for a time, and for whom he had nurtured tender feelings ever since. He sat sturdily at her side as if ever ready to support her should the need arise—

not only out of devotion but also in the full weatherproof awareness that here—and here more than anywhere else—it befitted him to bear the club banner. His apoplectic skull shone like the cocarde of a champion sharpshooter: blue in the red-framed core, surrounded by the blazing white of his silvery lion's mane.

The aunt had slipped her nicotine-tanned paw into the arm of Schwab's niece Uschi (who so far seemed ready to let any man bed her); and next to Uschi, his thick eyebrows somberly spiraling into the bridge of the nose, sat her new fiancé, Klaus, in stiff, sap-fermenting young manhood, which Herr von Rönnekamp in turn kept jealous watch over, raising his master-detective profile with derisive pride. In short: the more or less immediately affected mourners in this Middle Kingdom were also intertwined by a busily spun sperm thread, which also pulled in more remote people.

In the second row, wedged between the production managers of Scherping Publishers (black hats) and the sales directors (black hats), sat the loyal secretary Elisabeth Schmidschelm (called Schelmchen or Schelmie or even Ellie the Alkie), who had once seen better days, before she had been gently nudged into retirement at Lücke's Bar after Schwab's departure.

And over her shoulder (heightened hump-like by a brand-new Persian lamb coat collar—Scherping with his usual generosity had been forced to pay her off too) peered—oh, graceful folly!—the enchanted eyes of Lovely Heli (it is with such timid curiosity that the unicorn sticks its head out between the oak trunks in the forest to see if its knight is coming). I looked out to see if Gisela was coming. There was no reason why she too should not make an appearance and say farewell to someone who had offered up his soul to her like a youth his manhood on the altar of Astarte. But I couldn't find her. Presumably, she took her profession too seriously. It was a Saturday afternoon, a time when the regular clients (as she had reported) turn up at the brothel (Scherping's bad reputation in respectable Hamburg circles was largely due to his occasional midweek outings there, to devote himself to his dark quest for salvation).

Hertzog too was missing, by the way. True, it's not customary for physicians to come to the bier of patients whose passage to the beyond they have scrupulously made more difficult—and thus all the more desirable (after all, Professor Leblanc did not attend Gaia's funeral either). However, this very special case was more than just a medical relationship, and one might have been justified in expecting that the Great Psychopompous would describe, in his full-weighted presence, the ticklish cases to which he had been summoned to help out not merely qua scientist but also qua philosopher. But as luck would have it (and luck occasionally has a fatality that goes against the rules), a congress of psychologists and psychiatrists had been convened in Münster on that very day. And a dillar-a-dollar scholar of Professor Hertzog's stature could not fail to attend.

However, the ranks of mourners were serried seamlessly even without these two figures (so important in the history of the deceased): from the grieving to the sympathetic; from the mutely moved to the deeply affected; from the long-time supplier (of alcohol) to the relative by marriage; from the dutifully attending representative of the Municipal Agency for Culture (black hat) to the stigmatized newspaper reader who had once felt profoundly touched by a feuilleton by the deceased and had responded with a letter to the editor, presenting his own intricate thoughts, which had eventually degenerated into a correspondence and finally a meeting in person—

(after all, even when moving house, everyone learns how much unexpected property has gathered in the nooks and crannies of his home: because you acquired it sometime or other for a temporary necessity or even quite spontaneously and with no special purpose in mind, and you were too neglectful to get rid of it in time... Now just imagine what has been collected in the spaciousness of a lifetime exposed to so many random events, even if one leaves it in the prime of manhood!...)

Here, a man had passed on who, whether he liked it or not (and whether or not he might have wished for other cities as his adopted home), had been rooted in the solid, land-cultivating citizenry of a Hanseatic Gotham, which, only yesterday, had been planted in the green countryside with gabled gingerbread houses:

—one of the still well-housed comfort lovers whose childhoods were gaily illustrated with anecdotes of the clan, from which a whole chest full of the toy German world comes into being: Grandfather's shop close to the free harbor (which shop proliferated into a supermarket chain) and Mother's farm in the marshlands, which farm his uncle had run into the ground, alas, because he had been rather easygoing and a bit status-hungry during his stint in the cuirassiers (nevertheless, the moor meadows had brought in some twenty million as the building site for a squadron of high-rises); the pharmacist cousin in Ochsenzoll with his jars of poison and his officinal bottles from days of yore (monthly turnover: sixty thousand deutschmarks); and the aunt who had displayed such a great gift for the piano that she had been sent to the conservatory (where she began her rather shady life, which she ended, prosperously, as the owner of a guesthouse on Schwanenteich): all these Buddenbrooks in miniature and mini-miniature had leaped into the new era so successfully that they became its masters; the wind of freedom had swept them out of their respectable nook-and-cranny existences into mass administration, and they now carefully throttled that wind in order to steer it, housefatherly, to their mills—so archetypal in their tough, sly, prudent economics and attachment to objects that any world-beatifying zeal is wasted on them and must ultimately admit defeat in the face of the welfare brilliance of their now-fattened necks—

In front of the flower-laden coffin, their heads were thick and dense as cobblestones. God-fearingly bared or else bonneted with reasonably priced millinery creations, their hair curled mildly, maternally, in permanent waves, or charily parted, thinning, or bald—and from the shoulders down, they were welded into a block. If, overhead, the pipe organ sounds had not been clambering through and over one another like puppies in a basket, I would have expected a thundering hymn, as if from one mouth, from the many mouths of these many heads:

a mighty fortress was their God.

And they acted as if this were true for my friend Schwab as well.

My dead friend's irony allowed the survivors elbow room for their life-lie:

It sovereignly let them falsify his sloughed-off life to bear witness to the upright character of their own, and to declare as humus and topsoil what actually had merely given birth to his hatred and nurtured his questionable majesty:

the ridiculous potentate gesture of the intellectual, who, imperious as Tamberlaine, subjugates the endless terrains of intellect and rules, unrestrained, in the realm of possibility: out of hatred for a reality in which he never succeeds in tearing himself from the tangle of narrow-minded middle-class interests in which his existence is inextricably interwoven with thousands of fibers

Now he had succeeded in doing so (albeit in a different manner). Hence, he could afford to be magnanimous.

He left the field to those whom he had once so deeply despised. He lay there, so well concealed under his hill of flowers that one couldn't even tell whether it was really he whom all the snowy wealth of blossoms had buried there, and whether he wasn't actually viewing the spectacle, mildly amused, from some spherical corner of the crematorium's pavilion vault or even from outside (blissfully enraptured, at any rate): the solemn laying of the cornerstone for the model building of his edifyingly falsified history.

A highly gifted son (and hence afflicted by that to which the extraordinary are susceptible) of the most solid bourgeoisie, rooted in the strongest national soil and shaped by the landscape; and his sense of duty toward the collective had ordered him modestly to exert a broad effect as an editor in a publishing house instead of focusing his uncommon strengths on creating an outstanding work of his own.

Thus he hung on the finally drawn noose of his life story like a home-cured ham from which each of the worshipfully gathered could slice off a piece (washed down with the schnapps of sentimental self-absorption). They were delivering unto the purging fire a lucid, educated intellect that had frequently hinted at genius. A man who had raised his brow over the short-lived squalls of the culture business and held it aloft in the grand wind of the true act of creation. And who, although never personally soaring to creativity, had stalked creativity and recognized it and cleared the way for it, and frequently and happily fecundated it, thus attaining an undisputed rank in the cultural reconstruction of postwar Germany.

And he was flesh of the flesh and bone of the bone of the mourners around him here, and blood of their blood (if not spirit of their spirit).

With all the distance that they, respectful toward his "genuine values," recognized as existing between him and their more modest altitude, he had nonetheless emerged from their midst. They had produced him. And even though he had sometimes made them feel his scorn, he had never repudiated them. On the contrary, he had testified to his fateful attachment to them in many a painful utterance.

And it was to be that way for all eternity. He allowed it. It seemed to amuse him mildly. He was free now, hence without hatred.

And I realized that I had been taken in by his final act of crafty wickedness.

I was attending an ill-timed festival of reconciliation. Not, as I had secretly expected, an apotheotic demonstration of his passionately lived fundamental otherness (some of whose dark majesty I would have shared). He too now made me feel that *I* was what the burghers here considered me to be: chaff in the wind.

Furthermore, I had arrived a moment late, and I sneaked into the devotional temple when the mutely moved hellos and the mutual displays of presence were largely done with and everyone was primed for the actual act of devotion. And once again, I was embarrassed to realize that here too I had joined in more or less randomly, anyway peripherally, and that I had never been properly involved in the social biotope of the man whose intimate confidant, yes, indeed, only friend and spiritual brother I had considered myself to be. So as not to hug the temple door as an obvious straggler, I squeezed forward along the wall, running a gauntlet of gazes, and in so doing my eyes, as they say, were opened.

And quite literally: my eyes encountered another pair of eyes and were entirely lost in them: I henceforth gazed with them—gazed at myself. Saw myself not as in a mirror (Gaia: "*Tiens—c'est comme ça que tu te vois!*"), but with the gaze of the eternally unattained other. And in it I finally recognized myself.

The astonished "*So that's you!*" in those other eyes signified a lightning-like illumination for me: "*So that's me!*" For amidst the lymphatic scattering of Hanseatic heads, in which, between hairline and coat collar, the physiognomic characteristics of Frau Professor Else Schumann (bosom friend of the aunt and culture vulture), chauffeur Jochen Zoelke (African battle cap), housekeeper Frieda Harms, and auditor Horst Herbert Siemers (black hat) had bled out and left only the pale glyphs for *female contemporary* and *male contemporary*, Christa's doll-face stood out sharply: the round Gothic forehead ringed by scattered blond curls and crowned by a small, brimless mourning hat, a so-called toque, its flat, unadorned cake-form giving chic and fashionable expression, if not to a nun's renunciation of the world, then at least to her unconditional submission to the rules of her order.

This most appropriate headgear had often proved to be sensationally well chosen at memorial evenings for the victims of the twentieth of July 1944, and thus it was most likely suitable here too. And under its, as it were, narrow-lipped horizontality, Christa's eternally young sapphire gaze struck me all the harder, saw *me*:

me, sneaking on tiptoe along the wall, without a hat, of course (much less a black one), and in an old raincoat (it hadn't been cold in Paris, whereas here, an early November fog cut icily into your bones), my hair disheveled to boot (due to my "irresponsible speeding" with the windows down):

just barely making it on time to a bizarre, anything but private, yet very intimate ceremony, in which they had, for better or worse, been forced to ask me to participate (since I belonged to the unavoidable flotsam of a life that along with many ups had inevitably gone through many downs, inevitably coming into contact with all manner of undesirables)—just barely making it on time to a ceremony that no sure instinct for proper and suitable behavior would have advised me to stay away from.

Was I mistaken? Did Christa nevertheless give me an encouraging nod anyway? Conciliatory? Encouraging? Had her small, arrogant mouth softened into a smile?

—the mouth that, after each of her spare utterances, retreated and closed as definitively as the purse of a miser who has yielded a penny's worth of alms; the mouth that—softer, purer, and poetic because of a precocious grief—was repeated in the face of our boy, who carried it into the painful ordeal of innate taciturnity:

in the vise of two fine creases as in the grip of tweezers, inserted in the innocence of the round cheeks: a coyly bent Cupid's bow, destined for tenderness, but despicably scrawled by a never-begun love story in the Latin majuscule M, whose right-hand vertical stroke drops in a priori resignation (Gaia: "Sa bouche traîne la patte, pauvre petite"*)—*

yet without the pinched intransigence of the mother who had exasperated me, arousing one of those unjustifiably cruel impulses with which we take revenge for an eternal—because primordial—misunderstanding; letting myself go, I had told her that her mouth expressed the most recent German tragedy: in the pathological drop of its arrogant curve, it resembled, I said, the signature of Adolf Hitler—

(which, the evil words backfiring, naturally led to my never again being able to bring myself to kiss her. Which was why she could not believe that I still—despite this and despite many other things besides—loved her, even though our love had long since become the most efficient instrument in our conjugal torture chamber, because of that primordial lack of understanding, which perpetuated and increased the lack of understanding forever)—

Could it be possible that this mouth had softened into a smile: ready to speak the words: "Come, I've forgiven you!"

No. She did not smile, nor did she nod. It was an illusion—like the illusion that her head was looming wondrously above all other heads and out from among them—

a nixie, suddenly in the still smooth surface of the well:

up to her shoulders in the hasty game of tag played by the rings of water, her hair flowing out and splotched with flashes of green light from the depths she rose out of, her eyes astonished by the alien human world she is gazing at.

It was an illusion, but it made me realize what the lack of understanding was all about that had existed between Christa and me from the start.

Among the papers from 1965, I can't find anything referring directly to Schwab's funeral (the occasion of my final stay in Hamburg, which lasted for just three days).

The date books for 1965 and 1966 are still somewhere with the things Gaia left when she died—I nurse the suspicion that she hid them in order to secretly keep them for herself. They contained our story in playful, foolishly tender code words that only the two of us could understand; and in the end, after her death, I hadn't had the emotional fortitude to rummage through her apartment. Presumably they ended up with other personal effects at the *Marché aux Puces* (from which had come so much of what had often afforded us the bliss of discovery browsers and collectors feel when they make a find).

But I know for sure that while returning from Hamburg to Paris (this time via Saarbrücken), I sketched out a treatise on love. And I think I remember having at least set down an outline of it in the days that followed.

Splendid days, incidentally. The city of Paris was still alive. I was still alive. I had just loved Dawn and I now loved Gaia. Our wanderings through an autumnal Versailles: the brown-blue-golden backdrop to Gaia's exoticism. Her large, brown hand in my coat pocket. The rhythm of our steps in the wet leaves (two of my steps for every one of hers, my caryatid; I, holding Miss Fern's hand as I toddle along the Promenade des Anglais; Dawn at Lake Zurich, toddling along beside me, holding my hand, two doll-like steps on high-heeled shoes for every step I take).

The good silence between Gaia and me. Our even breathing. A word or two exchanged now and then. The calm question whether I'm writing anything else besides my work for the piglets. Yes, a book. (Shamefaced confession.)

"A novel?"

"I'm not quite sure. There's so much chatter about what a novel is and what it isn't that I don't know anymore. In any case, it's a story that begins with the childhood of its main character and ends with his death."

"Is it very important for you to write it?"

"My friend—you know who I mean—"

"I know..."

"Well, he died because he couldn't write it."

"Is it his story?"

"Mine, of course. Who would dare write anything but his own story? Yes—stories. The kind of stuff I write for the movies. Pulp romances—no end of them. I have another friend, a man named Nagel. He churns out three a year. He's a candidate for the Nobel Prize."

"How much of your story do you have so far?"

"Nothing that's finished. I've begun a few chapters. Several hundred pages. Several thousand notes."

"So no outline."

"A sort of notion of the form, all the same. But it's assuming a form all on its own. Or rather, an antiform. An explosion, consistent with the zeitgeist. A hybrid cell growth. After all, cancer too is just an explosion in slow motion."

"And this keeps you from completing it?"

"Sooner or later it'll complete itself—somehow or other."

"Why don't you make it happen right away?"

"Because I love you. Because I can't write and I don't want to write when I'm in love. Because right now I want to live. *Make love, not literature.*"

"But I'll soon stop loving you if you don't do what you have to do."

"I know. But if I do it, my piglets will get very mad at me and not give me any more money. Then I'll have to live on your money, and you definitely won't love me then."

"Don't forget that I'm a professional promoter. I make a good amount of money financing talent."

"Musicians. Do you know what a writer earns on a book?"

"A lot of prestige, with which he can squeeze a lot more money out of his piglets than before. I know. I'm the piglet of my musicians."

And naturally this ended in a paroxysm of amorous blisses and the solemn promise that I would start working first thing in the morning.

Everything that begins with a lie, says Dostoevsky, has to end with a lie. In this case, it was that I soon started putting page numbers on every abortive draft, every commenced and aborted, recommenced and reaborted chapter, every lengthy note, and finally every bit of even slightly bedoodled paper. I could no longer bear the disappointment in Gaia's voice when she looked over my shoulder and said, "*Toujours à la page treize, mon ours!*" I had to make her believe I was forging ahead. After all, I was writing for her and our love. Hence, unassailed by everyday cares thanks to her, I had to write fluently and toward a foreseeable end...

And meanwhile, the hybrid cell growth was running riot not only in my papers, but in her too—in Gaia's chocolate-brown giantess's body.

But this wouldn't come to pass until later. It was still in the future. I wasn't yet carrying it inside me, carrying it always, like all of the past. And added to this now was Schwab's funeral, and it made the burden heavier. The day was already past on which he had lain under his hill of blossoms, waiting to be delivered to the fire in the belly of

Ohlsdorf Crematorium in order so to speak to rise through the chimney in a different, airier state and merge into the clouds of Hamburg, like Stella in her time at Theresienstadt.

Thus I had come from Paris to say good-bye to my friend S. and to be witness to Hanseatic chivalry, according to which you pay last respects even to an enemy, so long as his life can be falsified and re-purposed into an edifying testimony to your own favor in the eyes of God. I squeezed along the wall of the cremation temple and saw myself through Christa's eyes. Still and all, it would have been nice if she really had nodded at me and smiled:

Christa, the relentless woman on whom I had failed so miserably—without ever reaching her, like the sailors in the fairy tale about the magnetic mountain, which pulls the nails from their ships before they can land, so that the ships fall apart in the open sea;

Christa, who always remained standoffish, alien, and who, no matter how hard I tried to get her to forgive me (after our love was lost) had proved so unyielding that my despair made me do all the mortifying things that make any helplessly demanding lover despicable,

the ultima ratio *of the no-longer-beloved, whose lamentable inconsistency draws sympathy to the side of the standoffish,*

the begging tenderness and the feigned coldness that yearns for its own thaw,

the false magnanimity with the schoolmaster's hickory stick held ready,

the mistrustful understanding geared to recognition and the rage with an eye out for reconciliation,

the tears, torment, and torture, and—the worst disgrace of all!—always putting the other in the wrong

(as though a stubborn demonstration that the other is full of failings must ultimately arouse his self-knowledge, which reaches into the depths of his awareness, from which, with all other virtues, mercy too is bound to spring),

in any case, always far too much talking,

the monologues flowing along, as wide as the Volga,

the cascades of chatter, released by the most trivial things and never coming to a standstill until every possibility of bypassing them is washed away by a flood of words, of which—when the verbal torrent has finally ebbed—the vicious words remain, decaying and poisoning the ground;

and all this constant instructing, moral reproving and edifying, preaching of salvation and disaster in the breathless urgency of the indignant man who asks for justice (while sentences bubble out of him like blood, shrieking "Staunch me!"—and all the shamelessly flaunted misery that makes those who are appealed to—and hard of hearing—even more hard of hearing:

because silence is the ultimate haven for dignity).

That's what had become of what had started as love, and I regarded myself in Christa's eyes accordingly, and her smile could have exonerated me. *Mais hélas!*

I saw myself through the eyes of the *others*, saw myself squeezing along the edge of the black block of mourners, along the milk-and-lily-whitewashed wall, on which my wet raincoat was probably leaving an ugly streak. It wasn't hard to guess what those who had known me for years were seeing: hair that had grayed and thinned, a little extra weight, even a certain casualness in the clothes that had once (as Schwab had phrased it) been indecently elegant. They were also, I assume, paradoxically familiar with the alien streak in a man who is a stranger not only here but abroad as well—an alien streak intensified by this alien quality, even though he had returned home. They saw runes of life, which may have given them insight into themselves.

Scherping, seeing me, was cut to the quick, I could tell, at the thought of advances running to tens of thousands of marks for a book that would never be published. But, experienced as he was in many kinds of wile, he most likely could not fail to applaud my frequent success in unbuttoning his pocket. Such relationships, he knew, also lead to a friendship of sorts. So he saw me as embodying something of the obstinacy of money: if you surrender to it on a large scale, then it will always demand some irrational interest from you on a small scale. Perhaps he was even grateful to me. He knew this femininely stubborn pettiness of money, accepting it like a good husband who overlooks minor defects in a wife with a number of merits and pleasant traits. I thus made him feel generous. So he took on the air of a generous man. He looked upon me not without a certain delight. A warm feeling in his chest brought out his better nature, so to speak, and with it, his checkbook.

And Carlotta was at his side, barely aging, the hint of the future matron barely in her face, in the slightly puffy cheeks and tear sacs, under the bovine gaze of a nymphomaniac. She might have been thinking about our first meeting, eighteen years ago, in Witte's office: she was Witte's secretary at that time and his *dame de compagnie*, although still married to Schwab, while I was married to Christa, who had talked me, a young man full of ideas, into taking Witte up on his suggestion and entering the advertising department of the Wittewash Company. Naturally this was not the result of my visit to Witte's office. But it did lead to meeting Carlotta (and, at a certain point in the "conference," to our launching into a fit of laughter that nothing could suppress or arrest). It led to one of those light-as-a-feather relationships never dramatized by either partner, whose basis is for many years the nearest bed or sofa, and which, unmarred by any other demand, prove to be the most durable and most useful friendships (Gisela).

Presumably, then, Carlotta (her real name was of course Hannelore, but she had sloughed off this prosaic name as an adolescent during a three-week sojourn in Florence, where she had assumed the more rigorously formed name)—presumably, Carlotta was not overwhelmed with emotion on seeing me again. She merely sized me up and down with a sober eye to check the extent to which my physical decay, undeniably commencing, could spoil the tastiness of the morsel that she had sporadically inserted into her erotic diet over a long period of time, a quite variegated diet at that. She liked me; that was certain. Besides, she had never put on a show for anybody.

In those days, I had greatly disappointed Witte; furthermore, my separation from Christa, his protégée, had convinced him how fatefully correct he had been to feel qualms about "part-time artists" (he meant, oddly enough, artistically gifted men who were careless with their talents; who lacked the ethical strength to devote themselves totally to art, commit their entire being to it). Witte, of course, had completely excluded me from the precincts of his role as God the Father, promoter, and protector. I figured at the periphery of his Middle Kingdom as a troublemaker; but ever since he had filled his flock almost entirely with full-time artists—ceramicists and interpretive dancers—I did not get all too close to his cock-of-the-walk feelings. He had (like most other people) viewed Schwab's friendship with me as the expression of the non-middle-class leanings that one must accept in a full-time artist (for Schwab's assignment to this category was due to his death, which had proved once again to Witte that a genuine artistic temperament will brook no compromises).

Here too Witte could, quite appropriately, play the generous man. And this, as usual, moved him to feel sentimental about himself. Only the strict obligation of a Hanseatic man to act reserved (and perhaps also the suspicion that a news photographer might be present and could possibly publish the photograph) prevented him from waving me over to shake my hand with deep concern.

In private, he would most likely have been rather glad to own such a photograph. One of his favorite words was "tolerance." Even in his early days as a committed National Socialist (of the Strasser type, to be sure; i.e., an outspoken opponent of Hitler), he had never gone so far as to demand explicitly that the world be cleansed of my sort. In his heart of hearts, he may have counted me among the things and people against which and whom the Wittewash Company was pursuing its campaign of whiter and whiter washing, more and more thorough detergents. Yet his profound feeling was dominated by the generous forbearance of the royal merchant who, when I married Christa, had said to her, "You've danced a bit out of line, dear child.

But still, you've got an interesting partner." He couldn't help letting out a sigh when he saw me.

So much goodwill on all sides began to make me feel ill at ease. It bolstered them against the past the way their padded coats bolstered them against the autumnal fog outside. Old Miss Wiebke, Schwab's wonderful aunt, who had once been engaged to Witte in some lost mythical past, looked at me with loving melancholy, in which nothing recalled that while her adored nephew Johannes was alive she had regarded me as the evil spawn of the lowest cynicism. Had her life's dream come true and she become a theater director, she would have cast me in the role of Mephisto in a modern-dress staging of *Faust*, daringly based on 1920s Berlin Expressionism (and she would then have screwed me out of my salary with the clearest of consciences). Now, she seemed ready to view me as foster brother to her protégé, who, because of me, had sometimes treated her even worse than usual. And oddly enough, her indulgence was now sincere. Not just because of her grief, which was no doubt profound. There was also a sense of salvation in her. It was as if her nephew's death had released her from something that had prevented her from being herself—had released her from a life-lie.

Fräulein Schmidschelm behind her, Schwab's secretary Schelmie, could relish her own triumph. Now *she* would be the leading lady at Lücke's. The field was hers. Earlier, Schwab had dragged his aunt along on his boozing tours (against her will, it turned out), finally landing at Lücke's, where unspeakably ludicrous scenes of rivalry had taken place between Schelmie and the poor aunt. The latter would wear housekeeper blouses buttoned up to her chin, with a brooch and a corseted waist, as though she were still an actress and had gone out right after the performance (of say, *Mrs. Warren's Profession*) without bothering to change, in order to pop into her regular pub and gulp down a jigger of something or other. For all the popularity that the aunt thus attained (and that was far greater than the popularity she had enjoyed in her theatrical days), she must have felt that this role was forced upon her and that Schelmie more authentically played the part the aunt was trying to play in her old-hen love for the nephew, who had left the nest prematurely: the part of a drinking companion and (in the fog of intoxication, in which everything blurred together) occasional bedmate (also dimmed by the subsequent hangover, like the memory of vomiting and similar embarrassments).

Now, the aunt sat between Schwab's niece Uschi and her brand-new fiancé, Klaus (with Herr von Rönnekamp standing at his side as an auntie-father). The old lady had finally become something she may never have wanted to become, but that she had to be and was actually meant to be in accordance with her true essence and true vocation: the upper-class daughter who never married and made herself the pillar of the family. The tavern original of the past twenty years (the former grande dame, known to everyone and always trailing after her boozy nephew) was merely the cross between this actual life-reality and the life-dream of a career on the stage. And even though (or because) it had been a life-lie, it would now give her a certain glory in a life-reality that had finally come true. *She* was the one predestined to become a myth for the family, and not the star-crossed nephew for whose sake she had lived past herself and then in the end to herself.

They would always be victorious in their way—these honorable tavern denizens and sedate brothel regulars, from whose angular shopkeeper-skulls their grandfathers' eyes peered, clear as water (grandfathers who had tilled the marshland between Pöseldorf and Ohlsdorf). The god who was their mighty middle-class fortress never allowed them outside its ramparts. Even their most daring fictions rooted them all the more deeply within its walls. As a result, their major and minor fictions—from world improvement to persecution complex, from artistic intention to manic conformism—all these life-dreams and life-lies, all this constant as-if, were somehow repulsively perverse, a gamble of the imagination with only a seeming risk, an *art pour l'art* of spiritual gesture that turned their lives into the caricature of authentic drama. I now understood the core of John's dislike for what he called the "bloody fucking middle classes," and I understood how fundamentally different they were from the Middle Kingdom of Uncle Ferdinand, Sir Agop Garabetian, and Bully Olivera. "Psychology begins with the bourgeoisie," Stella used to say.

I now also understood what Schwab had meant when he said that the German novel, as *the* bourgeois art form (self-destructively aimed at the bourgeoisie), has to have something of the barbarian splendor of the German renaissance: its country-squire gaiety, through which the still lumpish severity of the middle ages still shone; and at the same time, something of Richard Wagner's kaleidoscope technique, in which leitmotifs, within an extraordinarily complicated structure, produce order, clarity, and recognizability out of heterogeneity. All these people lived in a nonuniformity and noncompatibility of wishes and desires and, consequently, in a steady spiritual volvulus; this twisting of their bowels could not be depicted more lucidly than in an arabesque from which they themselves regularly kept peering out as their own actual leitmotifs.

Here too, by trying to see through me, my trials and possible tribulations, they looked at me through themselves. Herr von Rönnekamp (black hat, but cream-colored gabardine coat with mink collar) let his private-detective gaze, rising darkly from his own private sphere and diving deep into mine, play over me with an ironic smile of sweetly puckered lips, in order to catch me slipping up and thus giving the lie to my claim that I was not occasionally afflicted by homoerotic stirrings. His protégé Klaus, fermenting in more and more densely, more and more darkly hirsute young manhood (which was about to expand to tavern-bouncer dimensions), dreamed of himself in movies through me. And his fiancée, Uschi, Schwab's niece—who could never say no, thus suffering spiritual torments that emanated from her like a sharp body odor, so that any man, from the milkman to her doctoral adviser (her major was German), felt impelled to lay her on her back—Uschi hated me for being one of the many men who had done so. Then, behind these people, I saw a tearstained face—and there she was at last, my nixie, who had announced herself with Christa: Lovely Heli.

Lovely Heli, bravely defying her timidity toward appearing among respectable people, had emerged from the whorehouse to accompany to the grave the man she had loved and would love to the end of her days. Her standing behind Uschi was a subtle irony of chance. For she, Heli, had given herself to any man who wanted her, from the milkman to the professor, because she was trying to make up for the ignominy of normally being paid as a professional joy girl ("A person shouldn't have to pay for joy," she had said to Schwab with professional naiveté; and if it hadn't been for Gisela, who brought her to her senses, Heli would have ruined herself).

She was very beautiful in her powerful, common way, with her fresh complexion and auburn Hamburg hair, which was now demurely upswept rather than loosely tied into a working girl's ponytail. And I envied Schwab for her love, which was pristine, like in a folk song, and which he had squandered with the recklessness of the untrue beloved in a folksong. All sorts of memories whirred through my head—for instance, Schwab and I sitting in Heli's room at Gisela's whorehouse, delighted by our view of the narrow whores' alley, whose serried gabled houses preserved a final bit of pre-Wilhelmine Hamburg; our enjoying the soft, yellow light in the small windows and mellow shadows down in the street and talking about women as being the natural proprietors of reality, each of them able to give birth to a human being, no matter whether a man or another woman; we said that they carried humanity inside themselves and were capable of renewing it out of themselves—while we men bore the curse of unreality because our contribution to this renewal was so abstract and implausible, an ejaculation and nothing more, so that we could not justly believe that we really existed and, in order to have reality, had to realize ourselves in some sort of activity, in a work aimed at re-creating the world, at creating a new reality—in short: some kind of fiction; and therefore, we kept looking for ourselves, always and everywhere, and could not really love anything but what keeps reflecting only us: always only us . . .

It was probably Lovely Heli's loveliest hour, a professionally intimate experience. She could sit at Schwab's feet, her head in his lap, his hand in her hair, and she could listen to him talking to me—

and he had spoken about the nixie, whom he knew from my tales about Aunt Selma, and he had said that the bewitched creature that gazed with listening eyes into an alien world (although something there is calling to it that this was once its world too)—the nixie was to float ahead of the story I wanted to tell in my book, precede it like the figurehead of a ship, her hair flowing in the great headwind and her countenance stretching forward, blindly clairvoyant with listening eyes . . .

and I had to think of how enthusiastically I had gone home, straight from the brothel to Christa and our little boy in Witte's halved villa on the Elbchaussee, in order to renounce all the deceptive promise of the movie piglets Stoffel, Spouse & Associates and to become Nagel's good buddy again, and start on the story right away (for all this had taken place in the mythical past, in the very last days of the Ice Age: Lovely Heli was still practically a child). And Christa and our little boy had been so dreadfully poor that I had gone back to Stoffel, Spouse & Associates after all. And later, I never mustered the ethical strength to emulate our good Nagel and devote myself to pure, literary writing—a part-time artist indeed, in Witte's categorization. And as for the story that Schwab had liked so much, I could never really launch it, I kept bringing it back to the dock and rigging it up again, until it had become its own wild and gigantic construction site and never sailed out on its blue adventure . . .

The nixie, at any rate, was still waiting to be nailed to her bowsprit. I kept encountering her blindly clairvoyant gaze, now wept empty in Lovely Heli's eyes. At last I knew why she had been a symbol for me through the many years, a symbol of the never-fulfillable, of the aiming-beyond-all-reality, everlastingly listening ahead into the nothingness of male love. I realize this shamefacedly. For here, in Lovely Heli's eyes, the female force that maternally says yes to anything, the love that holds reality in its hands—here, it wept itself out.

All this, as I've said, began to wear gently on my nerves. It bewildered me to perceive that the whispering stopped when I slipped into an angle of the visual field of mourners who had not reckoned with my approach from behind:

"*...fall coming so early again—why, I could lie in the sun three hours a day—day in day out...*"

"*...it used to be* the *club in Hamburg, and we're hoping that it'll be* the *club again...*"

"*...well, I'm Protestant, but I've got a certain weak spot for the Virgin Mary...*"

"*...what does it have to offer? It's got a delightful atmosphere, there are chic people, there's a fabulous band—the great advantage is that when you feel like a bit of chic dancing in the evening, then you can...*"

I had thought I knew what it was that made them go quiet upon seeing me. And evidently, nothing had changed in this respect. I was still fundamentally alien to them, hence suspect, even sinister: a member of an altogether different species, whom you couldn't trust any farther than you could throw him. Thus, I was all the more bewildered by the shameless goodwill that now appeared in their gazes. It could not be due to their having grown accustomed to foreign workers in Germany or vacations on the Costa Brava. The more probable cause was that they knew I wasn't going to contest their claim to anything. Not even to a share of his grave.

Truly, I have never been concerned with such possessions, nor do I care about them today. I don't even know the location of my mother's grave. (Presumably, she was fished out of the pond in Bessarabia and then buried somewhere; Uncle Ferdinand had been too tactful to touch on it, and I too cowardly to ask). Nor would I lift a finger to find out whether any sort of paternal legacy has devolved upon me, which apparently is meant to be the origin of humanity (assuming I could determine which of my mother's countless lovers can claim the questionable honor of having sired me). My cousin Wolfgang, as I have said, lies in Vienna's Central Graveyard, to which nothing draws me; and I was not informed whether the corpses were salvaged from the basement air-raid shelter of the building in Vienna's Twelfth

District where, in the summer of 1944, a bomb forever ripped my rather worn tie to my foster parents. And so it has remained.

Thus, facing the hill of flowers into which my brother Schwab had been transformed, I could not understand why his further transformation into the contents of an urn, and eventually into humus under a grave slab, should bind me to the Hamburg soil, which had not succeeded in binding me to itself, even though I had spent years wearing out my shoes upon it—usually during long walks when I brooded about the enigmatic fate that had cast me ashore here in the first place.

True, my dead friend, while alive, had tried everything in his efforts to convince me it had happened so that I could tell stories, to narrate—but what? A glance at the faces of the philistines here informed me that it was bound to lead to a misunderstanding—whatever it was.

For they would again be the victors and somehow turn it into grist for their mills, whether I told them edifying tales as Nagel did or tried to play the little insect nagging at their consciences, even though they kept swarms of them for their own titillation:

—the a capella choir of Jeremiahs, to whom everyday German life assigns the cultural business as a sort of natural preserve so that German Cassandra cries will not be missing from the swan song of the West: in the tenor of the eternal (and, alas, ubiquitously betrayed) values of beauty, goodness, and truth; in the baritone of old, traditional humanitarian principles (that not even a dog observes); in the bass of generally (albeit rhetorically) accepted categorical imperatives—

and yet so very dramatic in the gesture of the decent man who has taken the globe upon his shoulders and now summons the whole world to help bear responsibility when it rolls off; so intimately moved by himself in the role of powerless knight whom no one heeds, so that no eye in the public refrains from widening in fear and pity, and no lips refrain from agreeing: "How true! What a daring and global vision! How terribly ineluctable!"—

while, in the meantime, everyone is making a leisurely effort to get his share of the pie baking in the fire of the Apocalypse, and all people have tranquilly resigned themselves to the fact that everyone's actions are different from what he says and certainly different from what he thinks—

and thus the call of the angel to the Last Judgment is merely one more noise in the tremendous din of universal chatter, a tiny fiber in the overwhelming thread of sound that is caught by a few powerful, opinion-shaping institutions and twisted into the dog leash of the zeitgeist, which irresistibly draws us toward our collective fate—

These people could do just fine without me. They had more than enough cleaning woman fairy tale tellers and culture-pessimistic intellectuals. Their verbal gruel burst through the windows of bookstores and came to them every evening on the more uplifting radio and television programs; it fed the cultural sections in the weekend editions of their family papers (illustrated and unillustrated); it occupied the minds at congresses of their leading scientists and philosophers; it was the major discussion topic in their adult-education courses; it echoed through the utterances of their statesmen and began to break through even in movies (after America had courageously taken the lead, here, too)—

and went as smoothly in one ear as it did out the other. It was part of the sound track of their reality, an "integrating component" of the background noise that the present era used in its drive for self-perfection. And had I joined the concert, then upon my demise they might have treated even me to a hill of flowers, like that man up front there, and during my lifetime they might have paid me all sorts of gratis tributes, but never this eerie goodwill, which seemed to have a smarmy familiarity at its heart. What the hell did they want from me?

In bidding solemn farewell to a man who had nagged at their consciences not in the cultural division but in self-destructive reality, the congregation of mourners had, of course, hired a shepherd of the soul, a pastor (presumably a Protestant of the Augsburg Confession).

In order to greet the grief-stricken and take them into his care, the pastor stood facing his flock, with his back to the hill of flowers (where the deceased, always quite shy and unsociable, had finally found a refuge where no one could get to him); and the pastor, with an ardent assurance, emanated waves of solace as if to say, Do not despair, your beloved relative is really lying here. By way of demonstrating that he truly believed in the faith with which he wanted to fortify the faith of all the others, he had disguised himself as a mountebank at a medieval fair. His robe (raven-black and creased: the domino of a macabre heavenly carnival) flowed all the way down to his fashionable department-store shoes and was tied over the shoulders like a sack; over it, the buzz saw of a gigantic, chalk-white furbelow ruff decapitated him, so that he presented his head as though on a plate—virtually his own executioner. The head was anointed with the grease of the edifying word and was slightly tilted in a posture of humility. The skeleton of a Gioconda smile hovered around his mouth.

He stood there, looking toward me—and I understood: he waited in loving Christian patience for me, the belated straggler. The assurances of solace, which his thriftily smiling mouth had excreted in small, murmuring rations of verbal gruel, had vanished without a trace into the furbelow rills of his ruff. He was now gathering a new little portion for me. His hands were concealed on his stomach, inside the folds of his sleeves, as though doing something indecent (the right hand didn't know what the left hand was doing). Now, they hastily slipped out to seize my hand—

first, slightly arched in the prayer position of Dürer's mother's hands, lurking as a trap to snatch the timidly offered hand like a broken-winged bird: with two simultaneous lunges, one reaching under the prey, the other quickly covering it. At the same time, he closed his eyes—presumably to roll them Jesus-wards behind his lids. And, with his fingers contracting into a meaningful suction grip over mine, his listing shepherd's head tilted back, while his eyes reopened, offering their watery void—sea-blue—to the wafting sighs.

It was as if he had spiritually grabbed me by the balls. I wanted to pull back my hand, but he held tight. And while his mouth over the ruff drawled at me, "You were his best friend—I know!" (how did he know? The church and the funeral parlor were obviously in cahoots, like Interpol), he pulled, or rather pushed, me to a chair standing somewhat away from the first row and directly in front of the heraldic foam of lilac. I compliantly seated myself, thankful that his Lutheranly licensed freebooter grab at my emotional world had not incorporated me, but instead had separated me from his flock—depositing me on the edge of the plate, like a fly that has dropped into the soup.

But I was to be mistaken. While sneaking along the wall, I had pulled the gazes of the congregation along with me like rubber bands; but since little more than my shoulders and the back of my head was offered to their delectation, those gazes had gradually turned from me and were worshipfully fixed straight ahead, until the downtrodden cousin twice removed had surmounted his Pachelbel on the organ. The galvanized pipe clusters, quivering in their steep flanks, were exuding their final, rigorously structured shrieks into the paraboloid vault of the cremation temple. Then, devotional silence, astir with stifled coughs and noses blown into handkerchiefs, fanned out through the space.

As usual, I vividly pictured what had to happen:

To my right, there would be a whispering, like reeds swishing the secret that King Midas had donkey's ears . . . and Witte's giant figure would rise up out of the whispers, hand his black burgher's hat to the aunt, and ponderously stride toward the hill of flowers in order to turn on his heels at the head of the coffin and show us the club cocarde of his countenance: the sea-blue eyes shining in the apoplectic red and surrounded by the flickering white blaze of his silvery lion's mane. He would roll his padded shoulders as though priming himself to lift the flowery slope at his feet—but no: he merely raised his fist to his mouth and cleared his throat resoundingly into his hand, cleared the mucus-lined spaciousness of his cigar-smoker's bronchia into the echoing vault of the cremation temple. Then he dropped his head.

Remained in mute concentration. Jerked his white-blazing skull up again in order to hurl out a gaze and enclose us, all of us, and with us Hamburg—and Germany—and the vast ocean—the globe—the starry cosmos—and in it, GOD—enclose us all with a single gaze hurled out into eternity.

Then Witte would speak. Would inform us that we were standing here at the bier of a friend. And, in accordance with his principle in all situations of life, he would be the exemplary, living proof of this fact: he would stand there, dynamic, at the flowery bier of the vanished friend as though on a conquered peak on which he had just planted the flag.

His word was bronze. It gave eternal value to the personality of the deceased. But it also raised an admonishing finger at the human foibles that the dear departed had sloughed off with his corporeal envelope (and as whose dismal witness I sat here, to the side, on the poor sinner's bench). In this sense, you see, this man (wide sweep of the hand across the flower hill) died vicariously for all of us: filled with the most splendid promise and endowed with all the gifts to make all the expectations about him come true, but foundering on the all-too-human: this gave his premature decease the character of a sacrificial death. Here he lay as a symbol of the fine possibilities inherent in every human being and, alas, not always reaching development because of the all-too-human, a martyr to earthly imperfection (three powerful coughs into the fist, thorax pumped up for the grand finale): here he lies, cleansed of all the slag that marred his earthly travels (involuntary glance at me) and obfuscated his rich talents, so that his road of life was not, alas, a trajectory that hit the bull's-eye of self-realization. But this very failure lends redemptive value to his demise: he died for the average man. His fate is that of most people: much promise and even more expectation sinfully lost to time—Ecce homo! (involuntary scraping of Herr von Rönnekamp's feet).

Witte lapses into silence. His head sinks upon his chest. The club cocarde fades. Now he is no longer the victor on the conquered peak. He stands by the bier of the departed like an elephant hunter, with the sportsmanly hunter's humility before his vanquished noble prey. Then his giant figure detaches itself from the flower hill and, with a sunken head, strides past the pastoral nightshade plant (two nuns humbly bowing to one another as they pass in the cloister), returns to his seat, devoutly lifts the black hat (which the aunt, after holding it in her lap for a while, eventually placed on his chair), and once again covers the now unoccupied surface with the seat of his pants.

And again, a whispering moves through the rows of leave-takers, like evening wind soughing in the foliage of a weeping willow. And (spurred by a poke in his ribs from Carlotta) Scherping rises most ceremoniously and turns and coils in front of his chair like a puppy getting ready to lie down and sleep; and, with a slight bow that tenses the seat of his trousers, he places his black Sunday hat on the chair as gingerly as if he were inserting a brick into a basket of eggs; and he turns toward the flower hill and stares at it with such a painfully pleasurable look, as if extracting a dagger from deep within his heart and feeling as he does so a cunning delight. And then he resolutely heads for the place where Witte was standing; and, while walking, he sends a quick, ironic snort through his nostrils, pulls his head in between his shoulders, like Rumpelstiltskin, and begins to speak. And he says: If it must be so, then he too does not wish to refrain from casting a few words into the grave of the deceased, his dear editor and difficult friend. And now he stands in front of the flower hill like a Baltic beachgoer before his prizewinning sand castle: smirking awkwardly in joyful anticipation of the free beer that the resort provides for the prizewinners.

But of course, I was merely imagining all this. Nothing of the sort happened in reality. Absolutely nothing happened in reality. Except that the silence, astir with clearings of throats and noses blown into handkerchiefs, began to show signs of overextension. Also, a contraction in the skin on the back of my neck indicated that once again many eyes were glued to my nape. Someone in the front row even bent forward to look into my face.

I felt extremely ill at ease. In front of me, rooted near the lilac bushes, stood the pastor, he too a flower: a white disk of petals on a black stalk, with a human head as a syncarp. His eyes too soaked into me. His throat, wreathed by the furbelow ruff, was then cleared—an unmistakable admonition. Finally, a jolt passed through the robe. With flowing folds, the robe began to move and carried the wondrous blossom of the head close to me, lowering the blossom to my nose as though inviting me to take a sniff.

"Would you like to say a few words," it murmured—without a sympathetically vibrating question mark—from the furbelow ruff.

I shook my head, frightened and bewildered, aware of my incapacity.

"It is expected of you."

This was not the time to negotiate *by whom* it was expected and what right *they* had to expect anything of me. So I simply murmured, "I can't!" And feeling that this did not suffice, I stretched my neck and whispered toward the mountebank skull on the furbelow ruff, "I'm too moved."

"Then your words shall be all the more ardent."

It was no use. I had known it from the very start, when sneaking in here and hoping to remain unnoticed. Nothing could be done. I had to go along with it.

So I got to my feet and walked to the flower hill (seeing myself just as I had seen Witte and Scherping in my mind's eye) and stationed myself in Witte's place (hoping that no one would see me there as ridiculously as I saw myself). And I gazed down at the conquered peak of white blossoms—

and there was nothing. Nothing. No Schwab. No dead friend for me to mourn. No corpse with a waxen face. No deceased after whom I could send a few ardent words into the great void. A heap of tightly wired flowers on a socle, which loomed out of a pit in the floor. That was all.

A rat hunt began in my brain. Schwab had snuck away and left me in the shit. Typical. But just who was he anyway—Schwab? Did I even know who was meant when people talked about a man named Johannes Schwab? Wasn't he someone else, and wasn't the one I meant merely a figment, a fiction of mine? When had I last seen him? In

Paris. At Orly Airport. He had wept and stuffed my pockets with money. Then he had vanished faster than that money. Had dissolved more swiftly into nothingness. A memory during his lifetime. And certainly a memory when the news of his death had arrived. My brother Schwab.

When had he become that? During the Ice Age. The lost mythical past. Had that period ever really existed? Wasn't it a pipe dream of mine? Did the people sitting here know anything about it? Had they experienced those years as I had? Had I really experienced them as I imagined? Now, in this reality of 1965, in a world cemented to the sky and inundated with numberless kinds of plastic toys—was it possible to believe in the crèche Christmas of 1947? Could I give a high-rise *horlà* any notion of the neo-Gothic clinker-brick villa looming like a citadel from the surrounding landscape of ruins in 1948—the villa in which the British had installed Horst-Jürgen Stoffel as the first postwar German film producer? A nocturnal script conference there:

with the company scenario editor (former gofer of the last *System-zeit* intellectuals to find refuge at the Nazi Ufa movie studio), the head of production (former chief of lighting at Ufa), the head of distribution (former textile dealer, then war-economy adviser), the cinema consultant of the foolhardy daredevil bank that intended to finance the "project" (a man with a hitherto immaculate past as a teller), the film officer of the occupation authorities (child of Auschwitz victims; he had emigrated in time), a representative of Hamburg's cultural senate, which had risen from the ashes of buildings like a phoenix. All these emaciated executive faces, colorlessly inserted into lamentable civilian clothes and marked with the indelible traces of various winter campaigns, were now notched by something almost more terrible: an urge to overcome the past (by way of the movie business) and to find personal fulfillment in artistic activity ("Creativity, ya know—that's where all these guys in our business get so obsessed!")...

they squat there, half-asleep, as though they had been shit into the titanic club chairs provided by the megalomania of Hanseatic founding fathers: they are exhausted, exasperated after seven hours of grating against one another's narrow minds, ignorance, resentment ("I tell you, gentlemen, if we're to form this brain trust of ours to make our project foolproof, then we've got to make sure that the image of the German woman in wartime is done properly!")—yes indeed! But how can this idea be carried out with the actress slated to play the lead in the "project," Primordial Piglet Stoffel's wife Astrid von Bürger, the darling of the public during the last years of the war and now emerging purged from the final collapse, rape-spree tested, a blend of noblewoman and tease...

poor Nagel! How he loved her!... And how he hated me because of her! And yet he should have known that my betrayal was only a parody... How often had I wanted to explain it to him: "Damn it! Can't you understand that I was trying to make a joke! Granted: it was a bad joke. Blame it on my Viennese upbringing! Your hatred for the Ostmark is justified." It wouldn't have mattered. He was a serious man, our friend Nagel. There was no teaching him that it could be considered funny that a man who has just returned from the war minus an arm, arriving in a shattered Fatherland where everything has to be rebuilt, at last, at last discovers what he was fated for, and writes, damn it, writes, arduously and sedulously with his awkward left hand, penning short stories and the beginning of a play and the outline of a novel and another and another...

and his head whirrs with ideas and images, and his heart leaps blissfully in his body because of the wonderful, wonderful life next to the small stove in Witte's garden house on the grounds of the halved villa on the Elbchaussee—and he's already sold two stories to the radio network, and one is printed in *Die Welt*, which is publishing again, and now the movies have approached him too. ("We have a specific project in mind for you, dear Herr Nagel: would you like to write a screenplay for us? If so, then we'll come to you.")—and he instantly has an idea for a screenplay, a lovely idea, after all it's to be the first postwar German film and it should have something symbolic in it too. So, somewhere in South or Central America—in any case, the guys are wearing sombreros—a man is wandering, a scientist, ethnologist, anthropologist—right?—he's traveling to a remote Indian tribe to study a bizarre custom: you see, the Indians believe that every fifty-three years, corresponding to a cyclical eclipse of the moon (which can be observed from their territory), the world comes to an end, only to be re-created and resurrected the next day. En route, this scholar meets another man with the same destination, and he introduces himself as a government-licensed executioner. He explains that during a famine, a woman of this Indian tribe went to the communal store of grain and stole a handful for her child. According to the natives' law, which is respected by the government, she has to die for her crime, except that the government reserves the right to perform the execution—typical, eh? Hahahahaha! Well, the two men, the scholar and the executioner, reach the Indians at the very moment when they are preparing for the end of the world. Tomorrow night, at one a.m. on the dot, the world will end. Ten after one, it'll be re-created. This is shown very graphically—it's a movie, you know: all fires are put out, everyone strews ashes on his head and lies down to die. Voices howl and teeth chatter when the eclipse begins, and then, when the moon lights up again, the past is past, the world is as neat as a new pin, they rekindle the fires and start baking tortillas with purged souls. Question: does the woman still have to be executed or not? . . .

a nice story, a profound story, as simple as a legend, you can almost tell it in three sentences, and Piglet King Stoffel is crazy about it and even more so his wife, Astrid von Bürger, the Beautiful, the Marvelous, whom Nagel, during the final years at the front, secretly carried in his heart like a schoolboy in love ("Man, if you ever get out of this shit alive—you're gonna marry a girl like her!").

Astrid von Bürger, now making movies with her husband, Stoffel, finds the story fabulous, simply heavenly. But there's that moron of a scenario editor they've picked up, plus a head of production, an absolute prick, who thinks he knows something about moviemaking because he used to push lights around, and then, of course, that phenomenal asshole of a banker who's supposed to finance the project—and those guys check every single scene to make sure it's understandable and probable and psychologically and anthropologically and astronomically correct, and they want the symbolism clear, they want to hit you over the head with it, and Stoffel himself begins messing around with the story because he figures on difficulties in casting and in finding expensive locations...well, to make a long story short:

"Why don't you come along to a meeting, they call it a 'conference,' I'll tell them you're a Young Writer too, then you can see the endless dimensions of human stupidity..."

and I went along and was introduced to Stoffel and his primordial piglets as a Young Writer and was permitted to lean over the hand of Astrid von Bürger and kiss it and peep into her blouse décolletage, and I was forced to watch my friend Nagel being tormented and tortured, to watch a pen-knife vivisection of a fellow Young Writer and to witness a systematic slaughter triggered by an instinctive hatred of one kind of human for another, the murder of the seedling of a work of art—and my eyes bored into the smugly ironical eyes of Astrid von Bürger in order to learn what she was feeling and thinking during this slaughter, she couldn't have overlooked the way poor Nagel loved her, his boyish chivalry and willingness to suffer. And because her eyes endured my gaze so long and amply that they swam, my gaze was lost in them and I suddenly heard her say, "Look, before you kick each other's heads in, let the other Young Writer tell us what he thinks about this whole business. I have the feeling he has some ideas about it."

Was this the right time to say that I found Nagel's story simply fabulous? They kept saying they did—only to pounce on it all the more furiously and tear it to shreds. I figured it was better to point out what they might object to in it; the von Bürger bitch was right, I *had* thought about it while they kept yakking and yakking, and I believed I had found what was wrong. And so I said: I think the difficult thing about all stories with an open ending is that they sound wonderful in three sentences because they contain an insoluble problem in a single situation, but if you tell them in detail for an hour and a half, breaking them down into a series of situations, then you can't intensify the problem or present it any more clearly, much less resolve it. The story always remains a "what if?"—

I wanted to add that they have to get beyond this; that the ending, which they had been arguing about for hours with their narrow, stubborn minds, was quite harshly and plainly obvious: the movie had to end with the young woman's execution. The audience could then argue on the way home about whether it was just or unnecessarily cruel. But they all pounced on me as if I had tried to grab their favorite toy. Even Nagel yelled, "Goddammit, don't you understand that it's us in that what-if situation? Are we supposed to pronounce sentence upon ourselves?"

I was stuck with six men all screaming at the same time, and it was impossible to make them realize, individually or collectively, that they were idiots who had misunderstood me in the stupidest way. So I asked if I could offer them an example of what I meant: "Let's assume that a man shows up at a radio station and claims that God is calling him. His name is Niels Otto Alsen, and he usually introduces himself by his initials: N.O.A. God's voice is calling him, N.O.A., because a new flood is imminent. He says it's high time to warn mankind. The radio station has to broadcast the news that the deluge is about to come and that people have to prepare for it. Needless to say, they think he's a fool and kick him out. But an intellectual who's hanging around the editorial office goes after him and maliciously points out the problem: if God has elected him, N.O.A., to be told of his intentions, it is because he is the only righteous man among millions of doomed sinners. He must not act more humane than God Himself. God won't stand for it. Assuming the radio station really did broadcast a warning, the resulting panic would have consequences more catastrophic than the worst deluge. So: if the LORD intends to destroy humanity but for one righteous man, then he, this one righteous man, should not interfere with HIS workings. It is his duty to build an ark, fill it with two of every living creature, and wait until God has done His destructive work in order to begin the world anew on His behalf. Period. That is the 'what if.' The problem confronting a modern-day Noah becomes dramatic now. Where and how will he start his rescue action? How should he populate his boat? He can grab his neighbor's cat from the windowsill, but things get tougher with the other fauna. There are several hundred species of finch; where's he going to get a pair of each? Where's he going to find lions, rhinoceroses, elephants? What kind of tools should he take for a new mankind? A knife, a cigarette lighter, an encyclopedia? But each of these contains the seed of new sins. Besides, this is 1947, and where and how is he going to get rationing stamps for the wood and nails for his boat? Wouldn't he, the only righteous man in God's eyes, have to commit all sorts of legal offenses in order to carry out God's mission? And so forth..."

but I couldn't get any further. I couldn't demonstrate that this story too could not be told beyond this point because it has no end, it expands like a fan, but without moving, without coming to a dramatic point, without making the conflict clearer than it already is—

I couldn't do it, because they all leaped on me at once and shouted at the top of their lungs: a solution at last, the idea was wonderful, much more plausible, much more symbolic than Nagel's story. Stoffel jumped to his feet and gave one of his conference speeches: "Well, gentlemen, dear Astrid, I believe the solution has come to us from an unexpected source. Here we finally have the film we want, which will liberate the problem of our times from the eternal German guilt complex and raise it beyond the actual German situation to a universal human level..." And with that he opened a bottle of champagne, which back then was a great rarity on the black market.

Nagel, however, had gotten up and left the premises without a word of good-bye. When I tried to dash after him, the idiot, to get it into his thick head that I had wanted to help him with my parody, Astrid von Bürger held me back: "Leave him alone until he's over his anger. He'll realize how childish he's acting." But he never did realize it, my friend Nagel. He never spoke to me again.

Ah, that was the point when pretty much everything in my life began to go wrong. We had our little son, whom I could love above anything else, and he too loved his daddy above anything else, but things just wouldn't work with Christa and me; she kept getting more and more bitter, more and more uncommunicative; I had disappointed her, I had not brought prosperity and conviviality into her life, only want and shame; I, the husband, had lost the war, Hamburg was a flattened city, you could see all the way across town, only the red-light district near Gänsemarkt and the other one behind Davidwache had been spared, symbolically, by the bombs (incidentally, the theater, tax office, and police station too). I was doing my best for the reconstruction of conjugal tenderness, but it was not easy, nor was it successful: Christa's perfidious way, the instant she got to bed, of placing her arm across her face so that her elbow lay on her mouth like a bulwark—the mean little mouth that I liked to kiss so much—frustrated my feeble attempts (until I recognized it as Hitler's signature and didn't want to kiss it anymore). To be sure, she was very frightened, the poor thing, there was a shortage of everything, you really didn't know how you were going to survive from day to day. At night, the rubble killer roamed the streets. I myself often had horrible dreams, I murdered a cleaning woman with a coal shovel in a cellar, ran around during the day in Witte's shattered library and made up cock-and-bull stories for Stoffel, Spouse & Associates—see, I had become the house author at Astra Art Films; every other week, either a new project was tackled or an old script reworked and revised, they were busy for the sake of busyness, and I had to lubricate it with brain grease; but I didn't have the moral grit to toss the whole business aside, there was always that prospect of an incredible amount of money, and it remained a prospect, it soon had something religious about it, this constant promise of pecuniary grace, salvation, and bliss; Christa believed in it with as much ardor and unfulfillment as Witte (a Protestant) believed in the Virgin Mary.

But I also felt a certain defiance toward Nagel. He wouldn't greet me even when we ran into one another in the ever wilder, ever ranker garden of the villa on the Elbchaussee, he wouldn't respond when I called out to him, telling him not to be such an asshole, he turned his back on me and slammed the door of the garden house behind him. The light burned in his little window late into the night; he was nearly done—Witte told Christa—with his first novel and was already working on a second one; his play, said Witte, wasn't going so well, but there were very interesting things in it; as for movies, he (like Witte himself and most likely Christa too) did not consider them real art. In a word, a full-time artist.

Well, I didn't want to be outdone, and so I thought up a number of truly lovely films. For instance, a New Guinea movie: A missionary has spent twenty years trying to get a Dajak tribe to give up head-hunting, and just as the solemn renunciation is being celebrated with a great feast, a government commissioner shows up and offers five pounds sterling for every Japanese head; war has broken out, you see, and the Japanese might invade at any moment...That this too was another story without peripeteia, because it began with a conflict that from the outset was unsolvable, occurred to no one, because it was impossible back then to film in New Guinea anyway; and the other projects likewise came to nought for some reason or other. I kept writing countless and largely unremunerated scripts for Astra Art Films; some of them were even filmed during the next few years, although in completely revised versions. But for Witte, I was and remained a "part-time artist," and, I'm afraid, for Christa too.

I've gotten used to it by now, but back then, script conferences with Stoffel, Spouse & Associates weighed on my soul like millstones. They took place in a Hanseatic villa on Harvestehuderweg, which had been saved by Providence from major bombing damage in order to provide Stoffel's reconstructive will with the appropriate setting. The furniture was old German. The filmmakers, who had been shit out into their Aesir sofas in front of the Valhalla fireplace, turd columns of thick cigars rising from their pursed bud-like mouths, seemed to have been created to fit in with the style. Such scenes aroused the most dreadful notions in my head. This potpourri of a living room—an omnium gatherum of clinker bricks, cast iron, and stained glass—came off as a cabaret parody of a Wagnerian opera, and the gray manager-mugs on the conference-exhausted giants, the fresh-faced heads and uniforms of the rosily well-fed culture-creator occupation officers mixed in among them, fit in nicely in a Götterdämmerung kind of way; and Astrid von Bürger was beautifully typecast in the domestic garment of an Ufa star, a sort of Nibelung dressing gown in royal blue with scarlet lining, which she forgot to button from the mons veneris down, so that each of her calculatedly negligent movements revealed kilograms of German female ham hock. The memory is lodged traumatically in my soul: her arms are flung far apart on the ox-leather bulges of the sofa upholstery; her torso is bent back, her twin howitzer-shell breasts practically bursting through the (here decently buttoned) silk; and over them hovers her—alas—really beautiful Brunhilde head (the head that seduced Nagel at the front, his dream of the "best friend's sister"). A powerful flood of short dark hair, virtually a banner of Berlin freshness, dangles over her eyebrows, and her big-cat eyes are observing the effect of her erotic presence: a drumbeat into the diaphragm of every man in the room. At the center of the room, her husband, Stoffel, is roaring, with a snifter (black-market cognac) in his left hand and a (black-market) Havana in his right. Primordial Piglet Stoffel, his own totem pole, as it were: six feet six inches of bombastic tremendous stupidity whetted by a certain shrewdness; a double hundredweight of crooked cunning combined with the upright joviality of a suburban bon vivant; a gigantic man-child, still emanating the sweet-and-sour odor of mother's milk; blond, fat, rosy, moody, ridiculous, and dangerous: the horrifying epitome of German entrepreneurial vitality bulldozing everything in its path...

There he stands, on solid seafarer legs, inspired by the model of the Hanseatic cog on the windowsill, bucking the weather, towering in the pea soup of cigar smoke and Hennessy vapors, swaying in the waves of emotional logorrhea that have been pouring out of him for hours; with arm stumps and flapping elbows, snifter and cigar in his sausage fingers, he beats time to his rhetoric, and, with hypnotic gazes from his small, light-colored pig eyes and a spooky play of his features, he tries to make his spouse, Astrid (who pretends not to notice), aware that the skirt of her slit Blessed Virgin frock has slipped off her lap so that over the silver-slimy snail paths of her nylon stockings (from the American PX) two succulent, quartz-lamp-browned thighs are visible all the way up to the groin...

It is heartrending to see how greatly this irritates him, even though he wouldn't dare say a word about it or walk over and shift a corner of the old-fashioned dressing gown to cover the splendidly conjugal boundaries that his spouse so hospitably presents. His face twitches like the face of a sleeping man when the legs of a fly stroll across it, his eyes blink, his breathing is audibly heavy, his intonation more and more menacing: "... and so, gentlemen, and dear Astrid, once again, I can sum up the results of this conference as quite positive in the following terms: for me personally, the project seems to have made great strides thanks to the night's discussion and especially thanks to the objections—approved by all of us—the objections raised by our friend from the bank, Herr Jansen. Certain details in the treatment aroused in each of us—and I am expressing myself with some amount of restraint—an impression of superfluous, highfalutin intellectuality. But now, thank goodness, all those aspects have been omitted, and the author will be so kind as to replace them with new and—hopefully!—better things. However, beyond that, we are all—and I believe I am speaking on behalf of everyone here—we are all as convinced as ever about the project—one hundred percent. And if this isn't a film that can bring us back to the peak of the good, old—I mean: the *pre*-Nazi Ufa—yes indeed, dear Astrid, we all know and appreciate your contributions, but you can't possibly claim that the German cinema during your Doktor Goebbels's days could be compared to what it used to be—huh? Well, then! If we can work our way back up to the top with this project—incidentally, I think you've lost a few buttons, darling— What? No, it doesn't bother me, I'm only pointing it out for the sake of order—anyway, as I was saying: if postwar German cinema doesn't show a desire to regain its supreme position, then my name's not Stoffel, and to you, my friend"—meaning me—"I will never speak another word!"

When my experiences ran along those lines, when they made me realize the net I was caught in and that I was getting ever more irredeemably tangled in it because I was chasing the chimera of money, which in the movie business is tossed out left and right—inveigling the needy into leaping at it the way fools leap at confetti during the Mardi Gras in Nice—

when I found myself before the mountain of shit that I had to chomp through in order to be allowed brief sojourns in never-neverland, where I was quickly permitted to play the rich daddy for my little boy and bring Christa some pathetic bit of black-market luxury, which she didn't even want; when I perhaps achieved, temporarily, an even more pathetic bit of respectability, which Christa truly and very sorely missed in her marriage to me: a threshold swept clean of embarrassing creditors and scandalous rumors, a threshold her Junker relatives could cross, willingly and honorably—

when I was walking home from Pöseldorf, the site of the clinker-brick Valhalla that the occupation authorities had requisitioned for Stoffel, Spouse & Associates, and when I headed toward the Elbchaussee, where my darling little boy was waiting for me, as was Christa with her elbow over her mean little mouth in Witte's halved Swiss villa, and when I had brooded enough about what it was that always kept bringing me to strange worlds and alien people and dream-like and traumatic experiences, I would then turn off on the Reeperbahn, right behind Davidswache, make a left on Herbertstrasse, and seek refuge with Gisela in the whorehouse, which had migrated from Gänsemarkt to the more lucrative zone.

The day was usually dawning, even though most of the lights were still burning on the empty Reeperbahn: the stars of the streetlamps piercing the stone sky like needles; and the bulbs in the grottoes of pinball arcades giving off a gaudy, theatrical glimmer; and the garlands of lamps hanging over the war-damaged façades of the dance halls; and, across the street, a wretched kerosene lamp smoldering sootily on the counter of a sausage stand, where a couple of bleary-eyed loafers and gadabouts were hanging around. In the empty vastness beyond this cheaply scrubbed-up poverty, there was something of the forlornness of Bessarabian cities, left all to themselves in the tension between a yearning for the twilight west and the agonizing promise from the east. And I entered the red-light alley as if I were coming home.

I don't know for sure now whether this took place in the midst of the Ice Age or after the grand, world-changing fraud of the currency cut—the criminal conjuring trick in which Stoffel, Spouse & Associates took part as fascinating shamans. It probably occurred on the threshold between the two; the crèche period, at any rate, was past, and one of the few clean places in the world was the brothel.

At some point, I left a few pages there, the draft to a screenplay presumably, it couldn't have been anything else back then. Scherping, who was a regular customer of Gisela's, found these pages, read them, and took them along—ever the publisher. He showed them to Carlotta, who had meanwhile left Witte and had become Scherping's secretary and *dame de compagnie*. And Carlotta showed them to Schwab, with whom she was still living in conjugal union then, and said she thought she knew who the author was—we were seeing each other from time to time.

Thus it was that Schwab, an editor at Scherping Publishers, set out to find me and talk me into writing books. After all, it was reconstruction time, and literature too had to be created *ex nihilo*.

I also don't know whether to interpret it as symbolic that my road to writing began in the whorehouse. But I can see Schwab when we met for the first time. He was taut and lanky, like all of us at that time; the scant wartime and postwar diet suited us. His hair was cropped short, and his thick glasses made him seem as if he were sorry he hadn't died at Langemarck. He did actually appear to interpret the origin of our acquaintanceship as symbolic. He handed me the pages Scherping had found in the whorehouse and said that he, Schwab, had read them with the greatest pleasure. He then made it clear to me with some embarrassment that he knew where Scherping had gotten hold of them, and added with a heart-winning smile, "I envy you your right of domicile there." My brother Schwab.

I knew why the burghers had piled up such a lovely flower hill for him here. They were tied to him in the same way they were tied to me. Their act of taking possession of him as one of their own and the dreadful benevolence that crept into their eyes whenever they looked at me were one and the same. They saw us as failures—and that was why they identified with us. We were all failures from the start.

I could now look up and peer into their eyes and see myself in their eyes as a lotus-eater among lotus-eaters. We had all forgotten where we came from and where we were going. We were all whirling in the whirlwind of our delusion, our epoch's delusion, floating, sailing, reeling, plunging, and soaring up again on the pinions of our fictions and illusions, whirling chaotically in an unreal carnival of realities, while around us the squadrons of *horlà* fortresses grew into the sky and the all-covering cement would soon wipe out our very last traces. And with us, our finest dream visions would come to an end: the gardens and the cities, the Eden of regulated nature and Babylon within it, and the New Jerusalem to be built, the city of mankind, ANTHROPOLIS.

"Peace be with us, Brother Schwab," I said to the flower hill at my feet, "once again you've imparted a valuable lesson to me with your generous reconciliatory gesture under your white flowery splendor: we've got thousands of reasons, but no right and no occasion anymore to despise the burghers here, because all of us have died—you may be a little more dead than we are, here in your blossoming grove; but these are differences of degree; in essence, it's the same: we are all of us dead. We—you and I and our true blood relatives, *our* contemporaries in the highway rest stops—we can now make peace with one another. Granted, they muddled up our lives with their shaman guiles, these burghers, these *bastards of the bloody fucking middle classes,* they screwed up our crèche period in Nagel's garden house with their currency cuts, and in the insanity of their fictions they destroyed beautiful Babylon and all the even more beautiful plans for the New Jerusalem. But in all fairness, we have to admit that we, and those like us, eagerly beat our drums in accompaniment. The drumbeat was mostly confusing, and that only helped them. Yet it was never clear whether we weren't just beating *their* rhythm, and indeed beating it most effectively whenever we thought we were drumming our sheer hatred of them out of ourselves.

"We can hedge all we like, but we are their brethren in this perishing world, and the more violently we rebel against them, the more firmly we follow the logic of our being and our decline. We follow this logic in any case, whether as revolutionaries or as conformists. For just as there is no escape from the cage of our SELF, so too there is no escape from the pens and prisons of our diverse Middle Kingdoms. No matter how isolated we may feel inside them, whether in the defiant pride of the individualist or in the misery of the lonesome man among too many, as a stigmatized reformer or as a cynical exploiter of the system—we merely express the prevailing trends and moods, we are merely witnesses to the state of affairs, symptoms, scale points on the fever curve, points on the life stages of our world within the world. As redeemers or wanton strivers, as geniuses or run-of-the-mill morons, we are tiny particles of some collective whole whose will we carry out—thereby fulfilling its destiny. None of our gestures can be dissociated from these states and currents, which furrow us like a wheat field in the wind—in the wind of the zeitgeist, which, in any Middle Kingdom, sets its own time.

"We should never have forgotten these things—we who sought our salvation in writing. We would have become more tolerant, at least more reticent. We would even have found it, our salvation, if we had realized that this very search for salvation in the art of writing (or any other art) is a symptom of the times of our world within the world and not an individual destiny. It would have opened our eyes to the act of dragging the past into presence that we were committing by deluding ourselves into thinking we were something special—or even: especially alive: Artists, creative people—according to Dr. Sigmund Freud nothing more than neurotics, who are capable of healing their own neuroses—*magari!* Nagel for the Nobel Peace Prize! . . . We are quite simply the children of an artistic zeitgeist and not even its firstborn. We are chaff in the wind of time like everyone else in the world around us.

"We are about to wake up when we dream that we're dreaming—isn't that so? That was the utterance that made us brothers—do you remember? But did we actually awaken? Instead of resorting to anything (even the destruction of our artistic devices) to prolong our ever-frailer, ever-more-transparent trance, to keep dancing the shaman's dance of artists, we late-born senile Young Writers, we sorcerer's apprentices of the anthracite-gray magic of the Word should have realized what we were and what we were doing.

"The way we feel the wind of the zeitgeist when it barely comes up as a breeze, and the arms of our mills move with it instantly, rather than waiting till the storm shakes the trees and makes the fields bow down to the earth—how proud we were of this ability of ours! How we fancied knowing, before others knew, that the time was past when one could speak about the individual and his plights in the collective of others; or that one feels as stir-crazy in the solitary confinement of any Middle Kingdom as in the terrifying capsule of the SELF; and that the knock signals sent from one to the other merely knock them apart all the more thoroughly, these individual worlds within the world; that here too the cells begin to divide and to proliferate, and the entangled circles of the individual worlds, Middle Kingdoms, and Fatherlands fall apart into monads—so that one could no longer speak about man in general, but only of the collective and the completely isolated, unconnected SELF... What bitter dignity haven't we derived for ourselves from this knowledge—but have we grasped the consequences? No! The intellectual in society—or even: The artist and his subject—aren't these ridiculously antiquated topics?... The sorrows of young Werther when he reached for a quill instead of a pistol—for instance, his despair about the things that tried to express themselves out of him and the things that he succeeded in expressing

as if the gods wanted to make us realize that it is not up to us to say what ought to be said, but rather that it was up to their arbitrary will to determine the time for such utterance, as if the gods wanted to force us to realize that this arbitrary will is divine in its enormous wastefulness—

for even the stupidest man, saying something that no one heeds, will sooner or later utter a basic truth, for which a Thales would envy him; something occurs at some point to even the dullest head (and then drops out again), something capable of expanding the spiritual and intellectual horizon of mankind by a good big step; in beer garden conversations, one may hear an insight that, if uttered before attentive listeners, might stamp its utterer as a genius; and in his dreams, every child surpasses Homer and Dante—

while the poor fools who feel destined to speak must earn every word in harrowings of hell until they finally reach the humble awareness that it is a matter of luck whether a crumb falls to them too from the steadily wasted and squandered opulence—

"Sure, we knew all of this. But we kept on living as if we didn't know it. After all, we had a promise to fulfill. HE WHO HATH, TO HIM SHALL BE GIVEN ... A gift means having substance, so they say morality gives expression to this substance; talent means finding this expression in an interesting way, with the insight that the word spoken for communication separates more than it connects, that little else is possible but the flight into absurdity, into humor, satire, parody. Didn't we act as if we didn't know this, even though we gave ourselves to know with meaningful augur's gazes that we knew all too well? ... above all: that we aren't ironicists and parodists by nature but rather stolid souls—but called by the zeitgeist to transform our sadness into mockery—of that which we secretly held to be our true calling: to become great writers: to speak beautifully of the world in which we live. Let's leave that up to Nagel. He does it with so much devotion that he's forgotten to say how this world truly is. Let's be of good cheer, brother! The truth of this world in which we live now emerges only in caricature. We can hold our heads high. We are the Eulenspiegels of our time. We finally admit to being what we had always been before, unconsciously and with the ludicrous arrogance of various kinds of grandeur: the clowns and court jesters of the middle classes. Albeit with the fool's privilege to say what's on our minds. Now, we believe we're finally doing for fun the things we had once done in holy beery earnestness: celebrating funerals. We anti-burghers thus carry ourselves to the grave in the universal carnival of 'realities.'

As the clowns of the burghers, we are burghers in the final phase of a logical development. Just as parody is the final phase of an art, so too the burgher has to become his own parody as an artist and bohemian. Indeed, if possible, as a celebrated artist and bohemian. To recognize the burgher in his apotheosis, one must see the procession of the BIG ELEPHANT BALLYHOO as *pompes funèbres*. Only then do the values reveal themselves. This is the only way to show how awfully futile it was, the only thing we really wanted to do: take revenge.

"He who writes takes revenge—wasn't this too a discovery that mellowed our suffering, that gave us a feeling of majestic superiority? Now, we have the choice: either nobly to forgo revenge and hence final salvation and enter the icy void without further ado—like you, my dead friend—or else clamp our teeth into our neighbor and proliferate with him in the slow-motion explosion of metastases, and, as everyone knows, one's neighbor is really oneself, right?

"This is the final, macabre joke of the middle-class jokesters: the hara-kiri of the brains. The voiding of the contents of brains for a trichinosis inspection before blue philistine eyes. The presentation of the no longer expressible SELF in its timeless presence, in which the past and the future are shuffled together, memories and wishes, traumas, anxieties, and fears, like a well-shuffled pack of cards, and formless, proliferating with millions of its kind in a fermenting dough—SELF split up into millions and proliferating into a monstrous cancerous tumor with rapid hybrid growth—an explosion in slow motion—

"and we have tried to keep living individually, have stubbornly and contrarily kept believing in ourselves and our mission, have tried to fulfill our promise, as if we didn't know any of this—

"and yet we knew it ever since the days that cut us off from the first half of our lives. I, at any rate, knew it since 1938.

"It was on a day in Vienna—the last of the three days on which, as I stubbornly maintain, the sun stood still in the heavens. The Führer and Reich Chancellor of the now truly greater Greater German Reich was staying at the Hotel Imperial—the world comes to an end nobly and symbolically!—and now he wanted to show himself to the ecstatic people of the Ostmark. Not just whooshing by, as on the second day—through the dividing sea of the people, hurrying as though fleeing—but static at last, lapidary, and entire: that is, as a bust. For unless, in accordance with nature, we place a great personality on four legs by inserting a horse underneath him, then he is most effective as a bust—there must be something wrong with our extremities, they seem humanly convincing only on crucified bodies.

"The Führer and Reich Chancellor knew this, of course. He wanted to show himself to his Ostmark people as monumental, as rut-breasted, so to speak: I embrace you, all you millions. Let me kiss the whole wide world! (In the enveloping battles later on, the text was varied: Let me kill the whole wide world!) And the ecstatic people of Vienna came swarming out in oppressively full attendance to throw themselves at this bust. The Heldenplatz was packed full. Vienna was empty again. As shiny as a shell washed ashore. It became clear what a city really is: this enormous hive, this once so beautifully formed and now stone honeycomb, proliferating hybridly and pumping millions of human beings through itself in a pulsating osmosis—but only so long as it's alive, of course: and once it dies, it's nothing but a many-pored crustacean shell grown into and carved out of the earth, produced by the unconsciously guided will to form of the particular species of life-form that lived within: witness of this strange collective urge toward form (which WHAT directs? WHO? With what intention? According to what plan? To what end?...

"You see, friend S.: the difference between our current states of being—mine here at your flower mound, and yours underneath it or perhaps dissolved in the air we breathe, in the heavenly blue with which even this rainy-gray day may be lined—this difference only in degree between two varieties of dead man boils down to the fact that I have to keep asking the same old questions, while you—unlike the pastor, who believes he has an answer to these questions—no longer have to ask them. Witness to your satisfaction that this time it is I who envy you).

"Back then, in Vienna (and we must not forget: it was always the same weather, beribboned with springtime blue but arctically cold, and the sun stood still in the heavens), back then this honeycomb was pumped empty, down to the last rat hole. Anyone with legs or even without, anyone who could at least manage to creep or crawl or drag himself along on crutches or on the leather seat of his pants, or roll himself along on a rolling board, or be supported, carried, or pulled along by a nurse, a son-in-law, a daughter, a grandchild, on litters or in a mackintosh sack; everyone, down to the last man, the last woman, the last child, the last old man, the last old hag not yet dead in some cellar was sucked out of his home and had flooded to Heldenplatz, Heroes' Square, and was damming up into an enormous gruel of human flesh, thickening into a human dough strewn with particolored sugar and proliferating and fermenting and rising higher and higher: the horses of the rescuer from the Turks and of the victor of Aspern reared in vain to escape this human dough, which welled and swelled up to them and eventually covered them, a dreadful cake of millions of individual creatures—and it roared.

"The human dough palpitated and roared in short, gasping breaths at the icy blue sky stretching overhead: *Hee-ha, hee-ha, hee-ha, hee-ha, hee-ha*...

"The individual voice might have been articulating the flower woman's hysterical *Siegheil!* on the first day; but in millionfold accumulation, it was a fluttering, shallow-breathed roar. And it rose all the way to the celestial vault, which sent back a ruthlessly icy smile, and the roar reverberated back, echoed hauntingly through the empty city, which had now become its own charnel house: *Hee-ha, hee-ha, hee-ha, hee-ha*...

"And then it choked, whirling and retching, bellowing in a vomitatio that turned the innards inside out and burst into the cosmos...

"for far, far beyond the vast square, over there on the sandstone-colored façade of the imperial castle, where the thick black-and-white swastika spiders of the national insignia billowed restlessly in a tangle amid the bloody surge of flags, a microscopically tiny, mustard-brown manikin had stepped out on a tiny balcony and shoved his chest against the balustrade and raised a tiny arm for the Nazi salute and turned his minimal tiny head (now without the oversize doorman's cap but merely smeared by the skewed ink-wiper of a strand of hair), turned it to and fro, slowly—a tiny mustard-brown particle, a single part in the proliferating human dough (think how infinitely tiny his snuffling pleasure-seeking mustache must have been!)...

"You must forgive me, but I was really standing very far away—or rather, hanging very far away from the manikin, hanging in a cluster of people, with Uncle Helmuth and Aunt Hertha and Aunt Selma, on the shaft of a candelabrum beyond the vast square at the gates of the Volksgarten. We had not been able, alas, to conquer any better places in the human dough; Cousin Wolfgang, however, had been rewarded for hush-hush underground loyalty and, freezing in the white shirt and black-booted trousers of the national warrior, he was permitted to stand in the middle of his marching column barely a hundred and fifty yards away from the Führer and palpitate in the rhythmic *Siegheil!* of the mass beast—again in rhythm, I say. For after the mustard-brown manikin on the far, far balcony let the booming incense of the shouts rise to the heavens for a while, he lifted his hand, and the roar was now chanted as a stomping *hee-ha, hee-ha, hee-ha*...

"And the manikin (he was now surrounded by a bronze-brown and blood-rippled general-gray retinue—and Cousin Wolfgang told us afterward he had even seen the blue eyes of the Führer surrounded by his henchmen), the manikin let the *hee-ha* boom into the heavens for a while and reverberate from the emptied Nibelung city (and Uncle Helmuth bellowed into my ear that such a concentrated, rhythmically organized discharge of sound from such a tremendous human aggregate had to transform itself into energy waves, which charged the willpower accumulator of the manikin up there on the balcony with unbelievable tension). And then the manikin lifted his hand again, and silence reigned—what am I saying: a column of silence descended from the heavens and pressed down upon the human cake and choked every sound...

"and the manikin began to speak (and his voice thundered through the aggregate of the many hundreds of loudspeakers suspended among the chestnut candles, and his voice was almost as tremendous as the roar of the mass monster),

"the manikin began to speak and he said, 'I...'

"and whether it was the fault of the metallic tone of the loudspeakers or the rapscallion baritone of the manikin or his understandably profound emotion (for, after long years of struggle, he was back in his homeland for the first time, returning triumphally as her greatest son—recognized at last in his greatness and at last victorious)—

"in any event, this 'I,' this *'Ich,'* came out as a shaky umlauted *'Üch'*—and was instantly reattacked by the driving *hee-ha, hee-ha, hee-ha* of the beast, a human tumor—

"and it was repeated lamentably: '*Üch...*' And once again, the roaring predator's breath of the monster, a human metastasis, pounced upon this yearning umlaut and yanked it down and into its panting *hee-ha, hee-ha, hee-ha...*

"and the manikin courageously reiterated his lamentable *'Üch...'*

"the tension of the willpower accumulator did not yield, but the record evidently was scratched or cracked: the needle kept hopping in the same groove: *'Üch...' Hee-ha, hee-ha, hee-ha... 'Üch...' Hee-ha, hee-ha, hee-ha. 'Üch...' Hee-ha, hee-ha, hee-ha... 'Üch...' Hee-ha, hee-ha, hee-ha...*

"and finally the manikin managed to blurt out, 'Oy am sooo happppy...'

"But this was just so much blubbering: it sounded squashed and washed out and dull, like a fart in the bathtub: *vanderLubbevanderLubbevanderLubbe...*

"Yet the thing that rose grandly to the heavens, where it was eerily registered for the rest of my life, was that apocalyptic cry, rising heartburstingly above everything else, that toad's croak: *'Üch...'*—oh no, no majestic manifestation of sovereign self-assurance, but a fluttery call for help, which rose, forsaken, from the fermenting human dough: a cry for help from this very mass of people.

"The manikin had vanished from the balcony. And the human dough kept palpitating in its resonant, million-throated *hee-ha, hee-ha, hee-ha*...

"and flattened it again into a shallowly surging roar, for now the manikin was suddenly in the midst of the human dough and cutting through it.

"This time, he sliced through it like a shark's fin, slowly and calmly—after all, he was entirely in his element. He stood upright and exposed in his bulletproof but open Mercedes, but neither the car nor the cops encrusting it were visible, they were kneaded into the fermenting dough. Only the manikin loomed above it and sliced closer, ringed by the roaring madness of ecstasy all around him. And he kept slicing closer through the human dough, closer and closer, toward me, until I could look into his eyes.

"He had put his oversize doorman's cap on again and was snuffling morosely on his minimal mustache. Very slowly, like one of the automatons in the Prater that begin to move when you hit the bull's eye on their bellies, he lifted and lowered his right arm, displaying his slightly curved palm. His left hand held tight to his belt buckle, as though he were afraid that his pants might fall down. He seemed withdrawn, pensive, and very solitary. And his eyes radiated, sky-blue and foolish.

"Eight years later I managed to witness another historic event, which, after this and several subsequent ones, more or less summed things up.

"At the defendants' bench in the Nuremberg court, one defendant gets to his feet, eerily lizard-like, a saurian emerging from the primal ooze: Rudolf Hess, the Führer's deputy. He lets his arm move up in order to be sworn in as a witness with a lamentably raised forefinger.

It is impossible to say whether he is merely pretending to be crazy or really is crazy. If he's just pretending, his act is brilliant, with a highly effective dramatic climax at just the right moment.

"It is the tormenting hour when the defendants make concluding statements before judgment. For nine months, this hour has been marked in all minds as a coming event. For nine months, they have looked forward to it impatiently. More and more hope has adhered to this hour. The hope that these final words of the defendants would make it clear what monsters and monstrosities have been on trial here. The hope that this leadership elite of the Third Reich would finally own up to being the true perpetrators of the crimes they are being tried for here: the destruction and conflagration of a continent; the rape of a civilization professing Christian principles; the bloody besmirching of the name of a once great nation until the end of history; the final annihilation of faith in the moral reliability of mankind.

"For nine months in Nuremberg, people have been waiting, in greater and greater despair, for one of the twenty-two prisoners at the bar to step forth from behind the mask of a banal average man, a mask that has made it impossible to comprehend that he—an irreproachable officer, an excellent office manager, a solicitous paterfamilias—had allowed what happened to happen, a mask that made it hard to believe it really had happened and had not just been dreamed or invented by sick minds. Nine months, prolonged more and more unbearably, with weeks of tedious readings of documents and interrogations of witnesses, days in which horror has become an everyday routine and finally a matter of the bleakest boredom. And throughout these nine months, one has looked forward to the moment when some dark confession, some satanic word, some perverse thought—expressed defiantly or involuntarily—might reveal that a drive, a desire for evil had been operating, and that the dreadful things exposed and testified to every day had not taken place only *because they had not been prevented.*

"Such a revelation would give the prosecutors and judges the security that righteous men feel toward insane criminals and monstrous evildoers. This trial has been put on too hastily, with too much governessy indignation and idealism and on a very flimsy legal basis, and the hoped-for revelations will make it look more like an act of justice and not just a superfluous humiliation, a process of revenge wreathed in embarrassing cant and carried out against inferior losers by men who just barely won, and who might be accused of the same crime tomorrow, since they too had failed to prevent what had happened from happening.

"However, the expectations are not realized. The evil won't be grasped. The defendants of Nuremberg cannot be made to fit the proper dimension and proportion in regard to the crimes they are being tried for. No dolus can be demonstrated. Their crime is that of mediocrity.

"They are a representative average. The incarnation of everything that John and Stella hated about the *bloody fucking middle classes*; everything that today is hated, despised, and blamed by itself for the betrayal of the dream of man in the name of bourgeoisie. Their demonic quality is that of utter lack of imagination. Their perversity is the fundamentalist attitude toward rules and regulations. They merely did their duty. They remained true and loyal to their Führer through thick and thin and night and fog, that's all. It never occurred to them that they were dangerously behind the times, and that in the world of relativity, they were practicing the unconditionality of the virtues of medieval vassals. As average Europeans, they drew their models from the dumping grounds of history. They learned how to obey in silence. They signed thousands of death warrants in their bureaucracy and were responsible for running it smoothly. That was their job, and that was what they got paid for. They can cite this fact. This too is law. It was valid for their accusers and judges too. They have nothing to reproach themselves for.

"They have insisted on this for nine months. Was it not naive to expect that now, at the last moment, they might admit to being artful scoundrels, and that, in their last words to the public, before a noose around their necks cuts off any possibility of further utterance, they might reveal something of the secret of how the evil nesting in souls erupts suddenly and leads to the annihilation of the world?

"One of the concluding speeches has already been given. Amid an embarrassed silence in the courtroom, Göring, the first to speak, has cast down a bit of nasty, bumptious cant. He was plainly nervous, annoyed and muddled. Even he, who, with his occasional vestiges of personality and authority, had maintained something like the dignity of a gang boss and something like gallows humor, now seems pathetically second-rate and humanly shabby. His words are cheap rhetoric. Whatever the court decides, he sullenly barks, he leaves the actual and final judgment to history: the future youth of Germany will pass the just verdict on him and his comrades. Period. He sits down again, fat, pale, disreputable.

"If everything else had not been in this style, then his words would sound horrifying. The future youth of Germany is growing up out there, in the rubble fields beyond the walls of this courthouse, guarded like a fortress, beyond its barriers, beyond the heated rooms, all the food in the cafeteria, the fragrant cigarettes and manicured fingernails of the secretaries and all the grandiose fictions and abstract rules of the court proceedings. There, beyond this Middle Kingdom here, an entirely different reality prevails. The youth growing up out there was conceived in Quonset huts by more or less maimed fathers and dropsical mothers; no sooner could this youth crawl than it learned how to pilfer potatoes and risk its life gleaning coal chips on railroad embankments and filching cigarette butts from the fingers of Allied soldiers. In all likelihood, this new generation will create its myths independently of moralistic reflections on history. Yet here, in here, those words sound like dreadful cant. Embarrassing cant: they remind everyone that here, everything is cant and must remain cant. That the more and more threadbare, more and more brittle as-if—which was meant to apply the legal conception of the civil code in punishing the deliberate and generally perpetrated annihilation of entire human races—cannot end in anything other than cant.

"The dreadful thing, the ridiculous thing, the poignant thing about the Nuremberg Trial is that it is built upon cant and thus has nothing else to put forward but simply cant. It is the desperate attempt at inflating the cant on which our civilization rests, the noble, sad, quixotic tilting of Western fictions at the windmills of the reality of human nature. Of course, the magic of these fictions is still powerful enough to keep the trial going. Their magic has sufficed not only to make the prosecutors act shocked, indignant, and full of holy zeal, and the judges dignified and aware of their high office (albeit with an occasional skeptical shake of their heads), but (more astonishingly) to make the accused perform their parts as lawful defendants. Yet that is precisely what makes the events here so spectral. It turns them into a ghostly spectacle. Nothing has any reality.

"The worldview of these men allowed them to, actually demanded that they, kill millions of people in order to guarantee the purity of their people's blood. And it is not possible to accept that the defendants will now try to wriggle out of these charges like cheap crooks in a provincial court. It is a ghostly experience to see with what servile eagerness these cynics of the will to power, these fumigator executives of racism outdid themselves in lending a helping hand to the judicial process when they had to assign responsibility to a former brother-in-arms and present themselves as victims of misunderstandings. It was absurd and repulsive to watch these ever faithful, upright citizens with their miens of injured innocence and gestures of insidious hostility, with their attempts at self-justification by citing orders they had received and official duties they had had to perform as a matter of course. So that Jewish prosecutors, beside themselves with fury, despair, and mortification, were suddenly playing devil's advocate, using arguments taken from Nazi ideology merely to attach to their defendants some small degree of freedom in having chosen to commit their crimes—and thus give them a final shred of human dignity, thereby rescuing the dignity of the court, which dignity threatened to dissolve in the miasmas of cadavers and the stale, stuffy smell of petit bourgeois order recipients and program executors.

"True, when Ribbentrop, as third speaker of the concluding statement, was talking, he said something about the incompetence of the court, arrogantly grumbling that if he were to be hanged, he would not formally recognize it. But it's a bit too late for such protests, and his words go unheeded. They too remain cant. Besides, they sound like everything else coming from him: insolent, presumptuous, and stupid. And anyway, the real sensation has fizzled out: Rudolf Hess's concluding statement.

"Now it's his turn. He was Adolf Hitler's deputy. His most loyal vassal. The John among his disciples. Here, he no longer seems to be of this world. He sits there, mentally departed, with a blanket over his legs, like a resident of an old-age home. A military policeman—his face contracted like a bulldog's by the polished chrome-steel helmet with its tight chin strap—sticks out his junior-officer paws in their full-dress white-cotton gloves and shoves the microphone under Hess's nose. But, with a motion like he's brushing away a cobweb, Hess pushes it aside and raises his forefinger like a schoolboy who wants to leave the room.

"It is a pathetic little white worm of a forefinger. It rises, timorous and crooked, as if crawling out of a hole in the ground and peering into the hazardous world with a nauplius eye on the fingertip—a dwarf-like harbinger sent out for reconnoitering by its lord and master.

"His head also seems to be emerging from the primal ooze, it too squints perplexed into unknown creation. A saurian head: the weight of the upper skull has squashed the mouth into the flat lower jaw and distorted it into its breadth, hopelessly unsated. Yet this is a tame, a humble saurian. Its eyes are so gloomy with despair as they ogle out of the shadow of its Nietzsche brows, which hang bushily from the socket arches and grow together at the top of the nose as in a criminal's face; indeed, the eyes exert an almost suction-like effect. One looks into them as into the apertures of two periscopes that are camouflaged for maneuver purposes and that are slowly screwed upward as they turn to and fro, scanning around.

"They turn on the pale stalk of a withered neck, which grows out of the now oversized shirt collar; with a male choir singer's Adam's apple whipping up and down between baggy skin and sinews, the throat emits a sullenly lamenting little voice. Extremely submissive, this little voice asks the High Court for permission to remain seated during the reading of the concluding statement.

"The black-smocked Punch-and-Judy torso of LORD JUSTICE Lawrence at the judges' table opposite the defendants' bar nods paternally as in a puppet theater, his iron-framed spectacles sliding down his nose; with the old-man tremolo of dignified Anglo-Saxon bombast in his voice, he proclaims that the request is granted in light of the defendant's poor state of health.

"The defendant utters his thanks, audibly touched by such patriarchally strained humanity and, while his periscopes scan an imaginary horizon, he pulls a few sheets of paper from the folds of the blanket slung around his knees, the blanket of a Baltic Sea vacationer. The room is deathly still, the defendant's fumbling very ponderous. Finally, he's ready. In a droning voice, Hess begins to read off a text that was obviously prepared by his attorney.

"This too is merely cant. The protestations of a completely honest man who must deal with charges that are not quite groundless yet unjustly harsh, and who must now make a manly upright effort to kiss a few asses rhetorically, to creep into any available hole inside or outside the court, and to do so quickly, making the best possible impression before a general closing of sphincters.

"There's a hollow feeling in the pit of everyone's stomach, even, apparently, the defendant's. He lowers the sheets of paper and shakes his head indignantly. No, he says resolutely, he won't go on. They have forced him to read his text in order to hinder him from communicating something of extreme importance. He is visibly agitated and gets to his feet after all, but so shakily that the papers and the blanket slide from his lap. Göring, who sits next to him, tries to pull him back on the bench by the tail of his jacket. But Hess shoves Göring's hand aside and hisses to him that he has to let him do his duty. He stands there, large. Stands there and moves the periscopes of his eyes about as though seeking something.

"He seeks it far, far beyond the table with the Last Supper figures of the eight judges facing him on the long wall, far behind the now empty witness stand on the short wall to his left and the glass lock-up booth next to it; behind it, the simultaneous translators are waiting for his next words in order to instantly recolor them into French and English and Russian and let them whir up like a bright flock of birds.

"As a rule, one scarcely hears it, this bright flock of words. It whirs up and scatters, slipping into the rusty and encrusted headphones made of former Wehrmacht supplies and hanging from every seat in the courtroom, albeit seldom used. And even though the words trickle out as dwarves from the uselessly dangling earphones, it is so still in this room that you can hear every one of them. The periscopes of the defendant Rudolf Hess sweep through the space.

"They scan an imaginary horizon. He turns them to the right, they sweep across the stunned heads of the attorneys, who are looking at him, and across the tables of the prosecutors and their astonished miens to his right, across the barrier separating the public, from which hundreds of pairs of eyes are staring at him—but what they seek lies far beyond, outside this room, far outside this building, guarded like a military camp, and beyond Nuremberg, shamefully bombed and flattened, and beyond Germany, covered with silent lunar craters, and beyond Europe, smashed and shattered, and perhaps even beyond this planet, which the mange of mankind has so dreadfully attacked and violated. And while they search, his saurian head speaks, and his sullen and exhausted little voice says that the important information which he has to communicate and which they have been trying to hinder him from communicating concerns matters that the initiated have long been aware of, but that have not been made sufficiently accessible to the general public. During the great show trials in Russia, the press pointed out the incomprehensible self-accusations of the defendants and expressed the suspicion that these self-accusations could have been obtained only with the aid of drugs. Nevertheless, it still has not gotten around *urbi et orbi* that certain pharmaceutical preparations, in the form of injections or tablets, are able to transform the most solid character into a toy with no will of its own, a malleable tool for any intention whatsoever.

"Now, all at once, the suspense of sensation crackles in the room. All past events suddenly become more present. The light of the neon tubes becomes harsher. The nightmare mood becomes more intense in the small courtroom, which is almost boudoir-like, intimate, after nine months of horror-filled proceedings. Reality becomes real.

"This is now transmitted telepathically throughout the gigantic honeycomb of the Fürth Palace of Justice. Outside, the corridors and the other cells are alive. All at once, the termite hill teems. Even the most out-of-the-way nooks and crannies have been alerted that something is happening in the magically charged core cell, where, throughout these months of tenacious exposure of atrocities, horror has gradually become boring and indignant gestures have become bleak. At the same time, a sense of frustration has developed, arousing a universal wish for something extraordinary to happen, no matter what, no matter how, no matter to whom—merely to end the awful stagnation of horror, to stir it up, to bring the salvation of movement. No matter what might happen—the personal appearance of Hitler, still alive and remorsefully declaring his readiness to turn himself over to the Nuremberg judges; or the entrance of a host of angels, opening the prison cells with flaming swords, because the prisoners are innocent—even the most fantastical thing could happen so long as it *occurred as an occurrence* and released the events here from their *state of static being.*

"For this is the torment that everyone here feels, even a rubberneck sticking his nose into the Nuremberg Trial: the ineluctability of a state that cannot be changed. The static, immobile presence of horror (so oppressively depicted in the best present-day writing from Kafka to Beckett—isn't it?). The omnipresence of hopelessness. The anonymity and ubiquity of evil. The continuous existence of murderousness in the *condition humaine.* The impossibility of eliminating that existence...

"The habituation to horror has paralyzed every person in the Nuremberg court. Its omnipresence has allowed no movement. One murder is dreadful and reprehensible. The murder of ten people is an abomination. The murder of one hundred people goes to the limits of the imagination. The murder of several million people is an abstraction, to be grasped only with statistics. Crime becomes a matter of quanta. The murderer cannot be placed in any conceivable relationship to his deed. One cannot imagine a just punishment for him. He is no longer a murderer by means of a direct deed. He is an executive particle of an overall executive action. He no longer acts. He performs his part in organic events. The causality of guilt and atonement is canceled. Indeed, all causality is thereby canceled. Time stands still... I don't know who said that limbo must be worse than hell. So it doesn't matter what the event may bring, it will bring temporary salvation. Even if it spelled an end to any further attempts at distinguishing good and evil, it would still be the final fulfillment of an increasingly vital wish.

"And this great moment seems to have come. The room fills up with people. No one hears them or sees them coming. They jam in. The room fills up like a pond with an underground source. Where one person was standing there are now three. Three heads stick together to hear the translations out of earpieces of antediluvian headphones from shot-up tanks or crashed airplanes or sunken U-boats, tangible testaments to the reality of the horrible. What will he say now, the defendant Rudolf Hess, the deputy of that "*Üch*" of March 1938 in Vienna? Will he reveal that the accused of Nuremberg are drugged? Or that they were drugged in the days of the Third Reich? Or the judges? The prosecutors? People wait in utter suspense.

"The defendant Rudolf Hess once again raises his small, white worm of a forefinger. This time for the oath. He pronounces the formula. He swears to tell the truth, the whole truth, and nothing but the truth, so help him God.

"And even though the black-robed torso of LORD JUSTICE Lawrence at the judges' table opposite him clears its throat, reminding him paternally that the defendant need not say the oath again, since all his statements here in the courtroom are under oath anyway, the defendant declares that he nevertheless wants to tell the truth this time and nothing but the truth.

"Then, he starts talking. He tells about his flight to England and the way he was received there after landing; his reception was at first formal and reserved, and then he was interrogated and taken to a camp, where he was treated with utmost courtesy and solicitude. In particular, his physician, a man named Dr. Johnson, soon grew so close to him and was so unreservedly friendly that he, the not yet accused, the as yet still interned Rudolf Hess, finally told him, Dr. Johnson, something that had been on his mind for some time: all the people he had come into contact with, all the officers and functionaries who had interrogated him, as well as all the guards in the camp, had strangely radiant blue eyes, as clear as water...

"Now, they all feel shudders up and down their spines: Everyone knows who had such strangely radiant blue eyes, as clear as water. Aryan eyes, the eyes of pretty much everyone in the Greater German Reich, and they know that those eyes supposedly exerted an irresistible fascination on everyone who encountered their gaze. Is this what the defendant Rudolf Hess is aiming at?

"Even though it's not altogether clear, is he ultimately trying to say that when he was in England, he realized that Adolf Hitler, the man who led Germany to destruction, had been under the influence of drugs? Or was he the involuntary tool of the secret service or some far more obscure and anonymous power in the background? The Freemasons perhaps? Or the Elders of Zion? Or some mysterious Mr. X? Or the Jews themselves?...

"But this is too literary to be probable. Too parodic. Too artistically dramatic for the pulp fiction of life's reality. Such spectacular devices are used only by the guild of adventure novelists and comic-strip authors. For the most intricate plots, reality has far less demanding dramaturgical devices. Usually, the crudest motivations and stupidest solutions. The suspense gets unbearable.

"Yet the defendant Rudolf Hess won't let the cat out of the bag right away. He stretches the suspense to the limits of patience. He goes into detail about which people at the camp in England had these strangely radiant blue eyes, as clear as water. And he tells of how Dr. Johnson now observed the very same thing, coming to him every day with a newly discovered pair of blue eyes as clear as water. Until—yes, until he, the defendant Rudolf Hess, was forced to perceive that he too, Dr. Johnson himself, had these strangely blue eyes as clear as water...

"It was still deathly silent in the Nuremberg courtroom. No sound, no motion. Nothing stirred. The dammed-up human pond stood still. But all at once, the suspense was gone. It was gone in a bizarre way. It had not let up. It had not eased up little by little to tear off like a hanging thread. It had, so to speak, run out of this world. It had crossed some mysterious threshold and had run out into a different dimension. The pond was dead. It was no longer dammed up and it did not flow out. It stagnated, it began to decompose.

"And it remained so as LORD JUSTICE Lawrence, after clearing his throat with literary thoroughness, so to speak Dickensianly rapped his pencil on the tabletop and spoke in a paternally strict voice to tell the defendant Rudolf Hess that he should finally get to the point, he had already been speaking for twenty minutes, and he must bear in mind that twenty more defendants were waiting to make their concluding statements. And when the defendant Rudolf Hess responded by shrugging his shoulders and sullenly saying that if they didn't want to hear what he had to say, he would simply stop; and he very ponderously rolled back into his wheelchair-invalid blanket and sat down to stare with empty periscope shafts into the void.

"Nothing had happened, and what had happened was meaningless, both for the defendant Rudolf Hess and the Nuremberg Court of Law, and for us who were permitted to witness this historic moment. And it was meaningless for the world outside, beyond the guarded walls. And certainly for the new youth of Germany who were growing up out there in the rubble dumps. All of us had long since passed into a different state, into a dimension that had not been human for a long time.

"Nothing more was happening to us. There were no murderers anymore and no victims, because there was no more human reason able to distinguish between good and evil. Madness was growing hybridly, welling and swelling and forming metastases like everything else around us. There was no more guilt and hence certainly no more atonement, hence no destiny and thus nothing more to narrate. We should have known this, my brother Schwab. We shouldn't have pushed one another to write. Why? For whom? To what end? Peace could have been with us long ago, my brother Cain."

Naturally, I said none of these things at Schwab's flower hill. They merely passed through my mind while I said something totally different. What? I don't even know anymore. And it made no difference at all, whatever it was. For I hadn't noticed that a microphone was hidden by Schwab's presumable head in his new condition as a flowery hedge. Without realizing it, I spoke right into the microphone, and even though I spoke softly, my voice boomed a hundred, a thousand times louder through the cremation temple, bellowing into the paraboloid vaults and thundering and crashing back upon itself—an acoustic pandemonium, deafening every eardrum in the place. Afterward, Carlotta told me that her ears kept ringing for hours.

I kept my concluding statement as short as possible and then, quickly as I could, returned to my penitent's stool.

Meanwhile, however, the black-and-white pastor-blossom had ambulated over to Schwab in his new condition; perceptively, he stationed himself at the putative feet, far away from the microphone, and now he chewed a small portion of consecrating verbal gruel. At almost the same time, the downtrodden cousin twice removed began to play the organ; and while he made a steep fugue of pipe tones rise into the vault, I saw—first with terror, then with mounting delight—that Schwab was sinking into the pit from which he had been looming, and I saw two curving walls at his flanks, and they closed over him, forming a small barrel.

He had passed into his element.

CAIN

The Last Manuscript

Translated by David Dollenmayer

EDITOR'S FOREWORD

THERE IS no basis for the claim that the finder of the manuscript presented here knew what it was the minute he laid eyes on it. Although the attorney Dr. Fritz Engelhardt appears to be an astute reader of my books, his knowledge of them presumably doesn't go beyond the *Tales of Maghrebinia*, and it is doubtful that the names occurring in the pages he discovered—Schwab, Scherping, Nagel, Witte, etc.—would have led him to guess their connection to *The Death of My Brother Abel.* Only the preface by the producer Wohlfahrt—which was meant to be an introduction but by accident was stuck in at the end of the folder instead of the beginning—must have suggested that a happy chance had put into his hand Folder C of the manuscripts of Aristides Subicz (or rather, Schwab), which had been missing and thought lost for almost thirty years. (Folders A and B were published in *The Death of My Brother Abel.*)

Upon closer inspection, however, various inconsistencies and even contradictions began to emerge. According to Aristides, Schwab's secretary Fräulein Schmidschelm turned the folder over to him after Schwab's death, yet it contains passages in Schwab's hand that were obviously written after his body had been cremated at the Ohlsdorf Cemetery in Hamburg in 1964, as described in *The Death of My Brother Abel.* Fräulein Schmidschelm—a secretary in the editorial offices of Scherping Publishers and known to everyone affectionately as "Schelmie"—had unfortunately also passed away in the meantime, so that she could not be asked to clear up the discrepancy. To increase the confusion even further, moreover, Wohlfahrt, formerly a movie producer and subsequently a publisher, declares in his presumptuous preface that he regards himself as the legitimate owner of the folder from Aristides's literary remains, namely, as compensation for a prepayment he claims to have made for a film script entitled "The Lost Daughter," which was still undelivered when Aristides lost his life in an automobile accident in late 1969. I do not intend to get into how grotesque it is that Wohlfahrt exploited this supposedly "legitimate literary possession" to switch from movie producer to publisher. It is highly implausible in any case that he could ever have expected to find a script for the movie "The Lost Daughter" in Folder C. A review of the evidence has revealed that that was an intentional misdirection—unsurprisingly, given the bankrupt Wohlfahrt's customary business practices. Fragments of a treatment for the script in question have turned up among the papers of his French coproducer, but that does nothing to explain the contradictions in Aristides's manuscript, to say nothing of the fact that all the names in Aristides's writings—presumably including his own—have been replaced by made-up ones. Not all the personages who appear there are identical to actual people living today or alive at the time of writing; the same goes for the events depicted vis-à-vis historically documented occurrences. Incidentally, to insist they be identical would mean forbidding the novelist an imagination.

In this case, however, investigations were able to be conducted on the basis of reliable information. Dr. Engelhardt purchased the house on the Tegernsee where the folder was discovered from the producer Wohlfahrt (or rather, from the actual person who bears that name)—fully furnished and containing surprisingly complete files of commercial documents dating back to 1959—shortly before the producer (undoubtedly identical to the "supreme movie piglet" in Aristides's *Death of My Brother Abel*) fled the country under multiple indictments for fraud and tax evasion. (Dr. Engelhardt surmises his current domicile to be somewhere in the Caribbean.) Full as they are of crackpot (if not intentionally fraudulent from the get-go) movie projects, the files clearly include not a single film with the faintest similarity to the one in Wohlfahrt's preface, also described by Aristides in *Abel*, namely, the one entitled "The Lost Daughter." In fact, both

Wohlfahrt and Aristides make many implausible assertions about production details, especially that Nadine Carrier would play the lead role. But perhaps we can attribute that to an attempt at obfuscation by Aristides, which Wohlfahrt was all too happy to seize upon in order to substantiate his grotesque claim to the manuscript. In any event, as was to be expected, attempts to make inquiries of Madame Carrier were fruitless. The very number of individuals who had intimate relations with her over the years made a precise sifting of the evidence out of the question. The diva could not be cajoled into reading and commenting on the relevant passages in *Abel* ("There's been so much written about me..."). So how did Wohlfahrt get his hands on Folder C? One thing the files from Wohlfahrt's house on the Tegernsee prove beyond a doubt is his connection to the long-serving editor at Scherping Publishers, Johannes S.

Who he might be—or perhaps, who the publisher Scherping stands for in reality—doesn't need to be disclosed: it's all too obvious. By the same token, however, it's evident how Aristides (or the author concealed behind that pseudonym) understands the concept of "reality." His skepticism toward this "most protean of all abstractions" is a leitmotif running through all his works and he leaves not a shred of doubt that for him, however fictive it may be, "literary reality" seems to come closer to the actual truth of what's happening than the multiple interpretations of the factuality of events. This makes it a priori impossible to read *The Death of My Brother Abel* as a roman à clef; to be sure, its supposed transparency would allow us to recognize the flesh-and-blood models for the figures and occurrences contained therein, but we would lose sight of the meaning of the book. And of course, the same goes for Folder C. In my capacity as editor of the writings in Folder C, its distinct "literary reality" seemed to me more important than finding a key to the factuality concealed in the fiction, a key which—as Dr. Engelhardt assumes with forensic persistence—could possibly correct if not totally eliminate the discrepancies between the accounts in Folder C and those in *The Death of My Brother Abel*. All it takes is a few pages from Folder C and one soon falls under the narrative's spell and has to admit that the apparently accidental and heterogeneous arrangement of its accounts actually represents a carefully structured and coherent literary product with a thoroughly justified claim to unmediated authenticity. Even such a puny intellect as Wohlfahrt's, whose own sense of business ethics often tends to manipulate and relativize the substance of reality, recognized that what we have here is not a supplement to or, if you will, a completion of the book *The Death of My Brother Abel*, but an independent piece of literature in its own right. Let the grotesque nature of his preface bear witness to that fact.

Surely the motive behind the notes in Folder C that seem fragmentary and, at first glance, unrelated to one another is the same as in *Abel*, namely, an attempt to get to the bottom of the act of writing—that is, novel writing, the authentic invention of reality. Aristides's various approaches to this problem, his "wrestling with the angel of truth in the 'as-if'" and continual failure in the attempt, as agonizingly and tortuously reported to the literary agent Brodny and to Schwab in *Abel*, seem to be continued here, although they stay closer to the topic, deteriorate less into blather, and thus seem more disciplined and orderly—small wonder: they are pieces of work that Schwab collected and sequenced with a view to completion and eventual publication which he, Schwab, would have overseen as an editor at Scherping Publishers. Aristides could at this point interject: it's a job Schwab would have had, had he not died. But that was not the case: Schwab was still alive when the cover of Folder C was closed.

I leave it to the reader to solve the mystery hidden therein.

—G.v.R.

INTENDED AS A PREFACE

by the producer Heinz Wohlfahrt

When I hereby release the manuscript of "The Lost Daughter" in printed form, I do so in unimpeachable legality on the basis of the authority vested in me as sole proprietor and CEO of INTERCOSMIC ART FILMS, Vaduz, Principality of Liechtenstein, P.O. Box BX 391, whose executive and sole proprietor I have always been and remain to this day. Thus it is not some shady deal, as has been claimed in certain quarters. It has always been—and up to the present moment still is—my principle to invariably honor obligations my firm has undertaken, even such as are against my better judgment, but also vice versa. I've stuck to that in good years and will keep it up in times of crisis too; some may call me crazy, but I was fanatically devoted to the beautiful profession of filmmaking—however, even the gods strive in vain against a wall of opposition.

There have been some hostile comments made about me recently which I here wish to publicly repudiate. I would like to again lay out the facts, one after the other, in chronological order, especially for the gentlemen from a certain newspaper for egghead superstars, a.k.a. intellectuals, who've suddenly discovered a supposed genius in Herr Aristides, even though they knew him before without noticing anything of the kind.

Herr Aristides (with a person in his line of work you can never tell if that was his first or his last name or if he really was called something else entirely) was a victim of driving at a speed that even I have to call irresponsible, and I like to drive fast myself. He lost his life in a crash in which no one else was injured, thank God. It was in France, thirty kilometers or so beyond Avignon, on January 13, 1968, between 5:30 and 6:00 p.m. precisely. That exact date—probably the only certain one in the life of a man like him—has stuck in my memory so well because it was when the disagreeable arguments began with my French coproducer at the time, arguments that led to a falling-out (which, as far as I personally am concerned, has been flawlessly resolved) and so to the collapse of the *Lost Daughter* project and thus to the provisional liquidation of INTERCOSMIC ART FILMS, all because of a certain Herr Aristides, today celebrated as a poet by those of his ilk.

In point of fact, at the time of his accident my screenwriter Aristides found himself, under my contractually stipulated directive, en route from Paris to Cannes. Waiting there for him and the completed script for the film *The Lost Daughter* was a camera-ready crew—everyone from the cameraman to the best boy and the actors under a renown, first-class director—which it was my job as producer to have up and running. I was staying at the Hotel Martinez and punctually at 11:00 p.m., I received a call from the highway patrol advising me of the accident and cause of death. On the spot and still in my tuxedo, I personally set off directly from the bar to the scene of the accident, which—on account of extremely adverse road conditions in what will be remembered as that unusual winter of 1968—I did not reach until 2:00 a.m.

I herewith declare under oath that, despite personally conducting a thorough search, I did not turn up among the papers found at the accident scene a script entitled "The Lost Daughter." Nor did such a script emerge during later searches of Aristides's paltry literary remains in various third-rate hotels in Hamburg and Paris. The one and only thing contained in the folder marked "The Lost Daughter" was the manuscript being published here.

Claims to this manuscript have been asserted by a lawyer representing the mother of Aristides's underage son (they divorced in 1952) as well as by Herr Klaus Scherping of Scherping Publishers, Hamburg, and the stockbroker von Rönnekamp, also Hamburg, all under the pretext that it is not simply a movie script but a literary masterpiece and that it belongs to them.

Be that as it may, it only shines a harsher light on the dark ignorance of those ladies and gentlemen, who are not even aware of the fact that in this manuscript their friend Aristides depicted with microscopic precision the roles they play in it, such that from the very first page, anyone with half a brain knows with one hundred percent certainty what I suspected from the very first, and which Aristides even has the gall to admit himself—namely, that with their total support it was his intention from the beginning to double-cross INTERCOSMIC ART FILMS—a.k.a. in this case me, Heinz Wohlfahrt—in the most cynical way, by never intending to write a script but a work of literature instead.

That is confirmed by the statements of other equally experienced, top-notch experts in film production whom I have consulted. Their unassailable conclusion is that not even one of the madmen who were yesterday dubbed the "New Wave" and today find themselves on top—not even one of them could make the manuscript in question into a movie, much less a box-office hit of the kind our financially high-risk industry is dependent on, for better or for worse.

And now they expect me to sacrifice my interests to their opinion? Even though it was against my express warning and opposition that the fellow was contracted to write the script on the basis of—if you can believe it—nothing more than a treatment of three (3!) typewritten pages. My French coproducer insisted on it in consultation with the distributor against my vote as executive producer, because Aristides's oral presentation of his idea was supposedly so brilliant that he was to set to work immediately on the shooting script, skipping the treatment that is standard in the industry. I have a memo of September 4, 1967, as proof that the distributor agreed with the French coproducer and therefore put pressure on me at this time of crisis to pay an advance out of my own personal pocket (certainly not the usual practice for unknown authors in my country) and promise to take over half the costs once the script was ready. These partners were then content to get an occasional look at only a few pages of the script that was purportedly in progress. The contracts for the actors were drawn up from a cast list handwritten by Aristides. Here I want to stress that this unthinking lack of caution was encouraged by the influence of the female lead, Nadine Carrier, whose relationship to Aristides he himself depicted in a way that leaves little to the imagination.

If I am now going to be accused of possibly being at fault in the early death of a writer who would have restored the global role of German postwar literature à la Böll and Grass, despite the fact that no one else but INTERCOSMIC ART FILMS—i.e., in this case me, Heinz Wohlfahrt—ever had need of his artistic talents, I can only respond coolly that it's quite possible that Aristides—at the time utterly unknown and financially dependent on my advance, having pumped all other wells dry so that even his friends Scherping and von Rönnekamp (as he regretfully admits himself) wouldn't advance him another red cent—caused the accident intentionally to cover up the fact that he had not met his obligations to me. From my personal examination of skid marks at the accident site, I can affirm that the facts are otherwise. The results of the police investigation at the scene, where I was personally present a few hours later, as well as the unimpeachable statements of credible eyewitnesses unambiguously show that the trailer of a truck had begun to skid on the icy curve, forcing Aristides's car, approaching from the opposite direction and, as usual, traveling much too fast, into a dangerous maneuver, and Aristides himself at the wheel tried everything he could to regain control of his vehicle before it crashed into the concrete mast of an overhead power line that crosses the road at that point.

Which leads me to this conclusion: not only did I have absolutely nothing to do with the accidental death of Aristides in a traffic accident; instead, he violated my trust, which gives me the right to regard myself as the sole legal owner of the only known copy of the recovered manuscript of "The Lost Daughter"—as has also been determined in an injunction of the state court in Hamburg—with all the customary rights to translation and publication in other languages, distribution in film versions, radio and television broadcasts, as well as in all future media of the same or similar kind. Fees resulting from any of the above will serve solely to compensate me for damages suffered through Aristides's breach of trust.

No one can accuse me of the slightest misuse of my authority as the legal owner and publisher of the written—not the filmed—work entitled *The Lost Daughter.* I have not altered, deleted, or added a single syllable to the manuscript, despite the fact that the manner in which Aristides writes about the movie business—and especially about my person or the person of Horst-Jürgen Stoffel, doyen of the reconstruction of postwar German film, or for example the way he presents certain men like his Gerdjochen Witte, doyen of Witte Laundromats, when we know exactly who is concealed behind that pseudonym, namely, one of the most respected figures of Hamburg's business community—would have caused anyone else to truthfully gloss over the bald facts. Unfortunately, the facts speak for themselves and against him. After all, it's well known that in their politics our so-called intellectuals are more on the rosy-red left wing and therefore have no real contact with leaders of the business community. I hope I will be forgiven for this publication because Aristides's manuscript is, after all, more poetry than truth. That is attested to by the testimony of a highly intelligent young man who unfortunately has not yet made a name for himself but surely will going forward, a certain Dr. Wieland Haslitzsch, PhD, professor of German, whom I have hired as an expert consultant on literary matters for INTERCOSMIC LITERARIA. He writes, for example:

> There is no doubt whatsoever that in this manuscript, extremely personal experience strives to achieve poetical form. It is, however, by no means a conventional autobiography. What seems to be the author's account of how he was moved to write the book is in fact the architectonic floor plan of the book itself. Very deliberately, events and the experiential impressions they leave on the experiencing subject are selected and arranged to create the illusion that this is only a first sifting of drafts, beginnings, and experiments that have been assembled in order to review their suitability as material for a book to be written in the future. In reality, the result is this very book in its inventive form, a form however, that in the final analysis is a dead end.

> As if in a mannerist painting, more or less finished sections of the work as well as the artist's tools of the trade are arranged in an atelier still life and reflected in the mood of the artist—in his own personal problematics—constantly revealing new and surprising aspects that proceed from the artist himself, who also looks out at us from these reflections. The result is an insight into the structure of the work *in statu nascendi*, i.e., in its origin in the creative artist, and thus also his self-portrait. Everything written in this book is the experience of a writer, i.e., a person for whom writing is not just a calling and a profession, but existence itself, in a word: destiny. Accordingly, what we have is a way of experiencing that is fundamentally different from that of a nonwriter. The author's claim—based on a quotation from Nietzsche (the prediction of an "artistic era"?)—that thanks to a predominantly literary education, modern man is already a potential writer and thus experiences reality in the same way as the writer, assumes a general awareness of the process that is being described: the continual transformation of factual events into literary material. The dissection of this process also reveals the falsification necessarily inherent in all novelistic literature.

Personally, I have nothing to add to this impeccable evidence of the poet Aristides's respect for the truth.

One reason I am publishing the manuscript of *The Lost Daughter* is to document the lamentable fact of alienation from reality and the unfortunate neglect of box-office receipts that has rightly been levelled against the movies and is solely and exclusively due to the collaboration of madmen of the ilk of Aristides.

Munich, September 21, 1984

Heinz Wohlfahrt
INTERCOSMIC LITERARIA
(formerly INTERCOSMIC ART FILMS, Munich)

Handwritten enclosure, presumably not for publication:

As a former journalist and the current wife of the producer Heinz Wohlfahrt before I came to the movie business via television, I would like to add a few personal words to my husband's preface. I am of course not sufficiently familiar with the technical details of the rights to the Aristides manuscript to form a conclusive opinion. I know my current husband well enough to be able to say that he is incapable of any dishonest behavior whatsoever. At least for my own person, I applaud his decision to have Aristides's manuscript printed in book form, thereby applying the organizational skills of an entrepreneur more to literature in these times of crisis, which in the end must also benefit film.

Of course, the Aristides manuscript interested me from a literary standpoint. Like Wieland Haslitzsch, I see it as coming to grips with the problem of reality. The writer creates his own world, which for him is often more real than genuine reality, with which he then naturally loses contact. I therefore would like to suggest as an epigraph the following pretty quote which I found while leafing through a Chinese book:

> *I dreamed I was a butterfly that dreamed it was a man. Now I don't know if I'm a man who dreams he is a butterfly or the man the butterfly dreamed.*

Wiebke Keller-Wohlfahrt
Current address: Tutzing on the Starnberger See

Folder C

We are about
to wake up
when we dream
that we're dreaming.

—Novalis

THE ICE AGE, 1947

If I would seek my ending
as well as my beginning
then I must sound out God
and fathom Him within me.
I must be what He is:
a gleam within His gleaming,
a word within His word,
a god within my God.
—ANGELUS SILESIUS

—.where'd you get that idea? you tell me, what should I tell you? please don't start in again, please! I can't stand it! well a person can say what he thinks, can't he? you should be ashamed of yourself! stop it, you two! Just a sec—fine—well?—well if I understand you correctly—yes, go ahead, I'm dying to know what you think, that's exactly what I wanted to do, to summarize briefly: if I understand you correctly, you wanted to say—I'll express it very simply...yes?...that the precondition for a constructive conversation here this evening, but also in general with respect to our topic—eh, the precondition for such a constructive discussion of a new and yet-to-be-determined form of government here in postwar Germany, following the collapse of all values formerly considered worthwhile...yes?...eh, so the prerequisite for a form of society that conforms completely to all previously encountered psychic conditions—if not requirements—of man *in genere* is our agreement on the existence (whether objective or subjective plays no role at this point), anyway, on the existence of an object which, while not rationally comprehensible, can be psychically experienced—right? *transcendental* object, if I may, and it's psychologically necessary to enter into religious association with it, which, in the event that such association is suspended or never existed in the first place, or only temporarily—in childhood, for instance, but not later—expresses itself in a need that can often increase to the point of emotional disequilibrium and neurosis, and as a consequence must absolutely be taken into account when creating a new state structure as an integral part of the—if I may—psychic environment in which we live, for better or for worse—agreed? That is the precondition, is it not? Did that sum up what you wanted to say?

Man, pull yourself together! All eyes are on you (on me is good! They're on me like leeches). Show these intellectuals and viragos what you're made of! Show 'em you've got a brain in your head too! Now's the time to show your mettle, the moment of truth (Heil Hemingway! *For Whom the Balls Tell*). The existentialist has to realize himself every minute of his life, even in the outhouse. So roll up your intellectual sleeves and get down to business: the prerequisite for a constructive etc. etc.—so far so good—is our agreement... Here! There's the catch: why "agreement"?—but that probably emerges later in the sentence; it has to or I wouldn't have started it out that way—so go on: is our agreement on the existence of an object which, while not rationally comprehensible—absolutely right, I agree one hundred percent (this guy really knows his text, damn it all!)—so: while not rationally comprehensible, can be psychically experienced—well how the hell else than with the psyche? With the large intestine maybe? (Careful! If I say that out loud he'll say I'm anal)—so "experienced" in any case, can't argue with that, all the psychic conditions man has experienced up to now confirm it, a few dozen millennia of not just Catholic religious ecstasy look down upon you, Christian Soldiers! It's just the old duality: light and darkness, Ormus and Ariman, Baldur and Schirach, all nicely transcendental, so that's okay, and it's psychologically necessary to enter into religious association with it ("religious association" is actually a pleonasm, but what the heck), a psychological necessity—just like when you did something bad as a kid: first you get down on your knees and pray they won't find out, they usually do, but that's just the way humans are put together—the bastard is right, damn it, he's a scientist after all, PhD in head-shrinking, an inspector of underpants trained by Papa Freud, and they don't hire just any clown at the university, he's not a Nazi either or he wouldn't be thick as thieves with Freud and the Tommies, an intellectual reconstructionist appointed by the military government—appointed for what? to drink their whiskey... but stay on track here, it's so aggravating to have your thoughts drift off, it's probably due to the damn schnapps—or rather whiskey (I can't even be precise about a thing like that and I'm crossing swords with a scholar?!)—you shouldn't drink on an empty stomach, the Golden Rule, but what're you gonna do when you've got nothing to stuff your face with? let's get back to his (or rather, my) sentence or they're gonna think I'm completely soused or just nuts, or possibly they'll blame it on my leg (who was it who brought that up anyway? They're gonna be sorry they did!) what's that supposed to prove anyway? a cripple's psychology, trauma, amputee and only half a man ... just because you were hit (to the right of the scrotum, thank God: a gentleman carries his on the left side) and not in a vital organ, doesn't mean you're obliged to choke down all this religious content to understand the meagre ideas of this bastard Hertzog (with tee-zee), what a joke, a bit of dialectics (all Teresas and Annalisas, Freudian prick prosthesis)...what were we talking about? the formation of a future state—what a joke! By then we'll all be dead and gone (not him, of course; he's thick as thieves with the Tommies); but me for example, all I need to do is catch my fucking crutch in a hole under the snow on my way home and I'll be lying there like a bug on its back, Kafka my contemporary, and I can wiggle my legs until I'm frozen to the ground, *requiescat in pace* on Brahms Blvd., and I could give a shit about a future state, whatever it turns out to look like won't matter to me, so if there's a psychological necessity that can increase to the point of psychosis, then he's absolutely right—after all, the man's a psychiatrist, a professional—

then he can serve up a state to his crazies that corresponds to their neuroses, a perfect metaphysical comfort station in harmonious accord with everybody who wants to participate, it's just a shame that my buddies over there are all in on it, I thought they were my friends—but the way they all started attacking me! the dames were the nastiest, of course: "you know what we're talking about"—what do I know? what the hell do they think? that I'm a spy for the East or something? some of 'em are Marxists themselves—but it's not worth getting all riled up about, they're just crazy, the whole lot of them, Hertzog's patients from the word go, they're right to get themselves a house psychiatrist, but they used to be so nice, they were once true friends, real buddies, hungry, no future state, just nice people, I liked hoofing it out here, even though it was hard with one leg gone, it sure wasn't for their crappy turnip schnapps and their shitty hand-rolled smokes, what a pile of shit it all is, and now they're gonna invite the savior too: Come Lord Jesus, be our guest, may the shit you've dished us now be blessed! and in the same breath they swear by Karl Marx, comrades hear the happy news: the baby Jesus is the real founder of the classless society, the model of a metaphysical need fulfilled: in constant, active contact with the transcendent Big Daddy while completely free of any Oedipus complex thanks to his virginal Mommy, what do I need them for anyway? best thing would be to just beat it—this guy here, the Germanic Führer with tee-zee—etymologically without tee: the "herzog," the duke to these blond-bearded assholes, the arch-asshole—he just puts me in the shade, he's made to order for them, hand-tailored by the providence of the immortal Führer, the stiffs got scared by their own daring, reorganizing the globe in accordance with their weltanschauung blew up in their faces, let's stick with time-tested Western values, with all of them if possible, without regard to what we're losing: when in doubt, the good, the beautiful, the noble, and the true are innate human needs, no question about it, if we lost sight of them it was collective guilt, just ask the military government, turn yourself over to a trained therapist, Hansel and Gretel get lost in the forest so easily—that's how it is:

they're scared shitless, that's all, just look at 'em, the way they look at me, like I was going to steal their mental crutches (accompanied by the chrome-steel baritone of that asshole there)

...did I more or less summarize what you were trying to say? (Okay, pipe up now, Willem!)...

...well sure, partly—I mean: some of it was exactly right...

and the other parts? (I wish they wouldn't look so gleeful, waiting for him to crush me, nice friends I've got...)

...well now, on the other hand—you know, I've got nothing against God—I mean no fundamental objection (or: in principle—or what's the best way to put it?)—I mean, I'm not particularly unbelieving...

but what?...

but nothing (why'd he say "but what"?), Jesus Christ too, right? it's all okay with me—I just mean about the "agreement" part...

Yes?...

I mean, I admit that in a certain sense, Christian teachings—in their original form, of course—yes?—naturally those teachings represent in a certain sense an end point of social thought (why're they squirming like I'd kicked them in the stomach? did I say anything against Karl Marx? or even Karl Nagel? just 'cause I'm drinking his turnip whiskey?)

...yes, I'm listening...

(the way that sounds: "I'm listening"! it's like being interrogated by Roland Freisler)

... I just meant to say we all know what the church did was a load of bullshit (shit! that was a mistake! it just slipped out—talking like a grunt is definitely not in the right key for a serious discussion of central questions of political philosophy—and here comes his unrelenting baritone again: "Well, for the time being that's not what's at issue"—all that's missing would have been for him to let it pass without comment! such a compelling thinker) ... I only said that to formulate—I mean, just simply to express—yes?—that the idea that a new state in future should naturally be founded on original Christian principles—yes?—well, that in that case, of course I'm in agreement ... (however—but then the whole shitty discussion will start all over again; let's leave it at that)

... so, as I said, I agree (I'm about to beat it anyway)—

Once articulated, inventions, insights, and discoveries gain a reality that makes their obviousness unassailable and omnipresent, independent of their communication by the spoken or written word. Everywhere and simultaneously they are invented, comprehended, and discovered—

as if it wasn't just a single person they would have occurred to but instead, from a particular moment on, were ripe for discovery, floating in the air we breathe, and could have occurred to anyone—would soon have occurred to everyone:

as if no one could avoid them reaching him as well—

... couldn't even broach the subject with him. He always cleverly changed the subject to the immediate postwar years, which he called the "Ice Age." He stubbornly kept returning to his pet topic: the "rubble killer" who was never found or punished for his crimes. Corpses of women had been found in the rubble of the ruined city, all stripped naked and killed in the same manner. They could not be identified; it was a time when all sorts of people were moving through the city, God knows from where, nobody had papers, countless numbers were missing, disappeared. Unless there had been a notice of a missing person with precise information that matched one of the murdered women, there was almost no chance the victims would ever be identified; and none of the existing notices matched them. It wasn't just the anonymity of murderer and murdered that fascinated him. It was primarily the instrument with which they had been killed: a wire loop with a toggle that could throttle them in the blink of an eye. He never tired of praising the "admirably ingenious" simplicity of this murderous tool ("loop it around her neck and twist the toggle—couldn't be quicker, cleaner, quieter . . ."). And he carried it to absurd lengths, claimed this lethal loop had already been in use in the Egypt of the pharaohs, he'd seen with his own eyes a wall painting in which a dignitary was holding one in his hand like a hieroglyph—"no, I'm sure I didn't dream it, I do sometimes dream about a murder—quite often in fact—but never with the garrote, I wish I could kill so elegantly, my murders are gruesome, base acts of violence, that's what makes them so distressing . . ." If his listeners showed signs of getting bored, he served up the story of the girl from Buxtehude who'd been given a ticket to the Holstentor Theater and had come to Hamburg for the performance. The sight of the rubble around the train station was enough to give her the creeps already. She didn't have a return ticket to Buxtehude. After the play, she would have to walk in the dark to Rothenbaum Avenue where a relative of hers lived. She hadn't even had time to let this relative know she was coming and of course, she'd heard about the rubble killer lurking in the ruins—in a word, she was very restless during the first act and was thinking she should maybe forgo the second act and set off right after the curtain came down on the first. She got so fidgety that the man sitting next to her asked if there was anything wrong: did she have fleas or need to go to the ladies'? He was a nice middle-aged gentleman and seemed trustworthy enough to tell him what was worrying her. "You can stay here and relax," he said. "I live near Rothenbaum Avenue. When the play's over, I'll walk you there." So she sat back happily and enjoyed Shakespeare's *Taming of the Shrew*. Helmut Käutner was directing and was riding his hobbyhorse: there was a tango interlude in which a Spaniard in a bolero jacket whipped his partner into obedient lockstep. And sure enough, when that magnificent spectacle was over, the helpful gentleman was prepared to accompany the girl to her relative's place through a landscape pocked with craters and piled with rubble.

They didn't talk much on the way. It really was quite oppressive and totally dark in some stretches. Here and there, a lonely stoplight glowed. Any houses still standing had boarded-up doors and windows and looked quite forlorn. Instinctively they pressed against each other and at some point in the gloom between two pale islands of light the good Samaritan gave in to his desire for more intimate human contact and tried to kiss the girl. As I've said, he was a sympathetic man in his mid-thirties, as well dressed as it was possible to be in those days, and he'd shown himself to be friendly and helpful. Under other circumstances the girl would have been quite willing to let it happen. But for some unfathomable reason, she instantly panicked, the suppressed tension of the preceding hours broke through and tore a scream from her throat, a scream so wild and terrible that her escort took fright himself and ran head over heels in one direction while the girl fled in the other, screaming all the while. She ran and screamed to the point of utter exhaustion when she spied the lighted sign of a police station in the distance. The officers on duty were already pouring out in response to her screaming. One took her firmly by the arm. "Where is he? Which way did he run?" She struggled for breath. "It was nothing—I'm so frightened—He just wanted to—" "Which way did he go?" the policeman yelled at her. "Somewhere in the other direction."—She heard the sudden roar of the motorcycles, a swarm of police raced off in the direction she was pointing. "But he just wanted to..." "Come with me!" said the officer still holding her by the arm. He led her into the station and in front of a mirror. Around her neck was a wire loop with a toggle...

He told it with great dramatic effect and the reaction was usually what he'd hoped. But he had to be reminded that the story had been making the rounds for a decade or more. "That's exactly why I keep telling it," he said. "At least people from those days will recall it. Everything else has been erased, suppressed, never happened. And there's hardly a more vivid way to bring that time back to life, the Ice Age that sucked the marrow from your bones: a mixture of anxiety, fear, and lust..." "Lust?" his listeners would ask. "Yes, lust. Freedom that might even become blood lust. There was nothing left to keep people in check. No commandments, no restraints, nothing. Sheer, naked survival was the only thing that mattered. People could do whatever they wanted. Everything was permitted. No wonder they never caught the rubble murderer. Even if all his victims were killed in the same way, it doesn't necessarily follow that there had been only one. What if the girl's escort had just decided to try out the role? Put a wire loop in his pocket to see what would happen IF... Can't you imagine the delicious curiosity to see just once what would happen if you cast off all inhibitions..."

THE BACKGROUND (BESSARABIA, 1940)

Uncle Ferdinand chats about the phenomenon of time:

"...people these days are all excited about relativity, especially the relativity of time discovered by that Jew, that Einstein fellow—well, it's something all of us have experienced—for example, you're at some event and bored to tears, so you disappear with the wife of another guest and spend a little while with her in an adjoining room—well, for you it was a nice quarter of an hour—right?—but for her husband—right?—who can feel his horns growing the whole time, it was an eternity..."

But that's a piece of shop-boy wisdom. I'm sure it's not what what's-his-name—Einstein—had in mind. If that was his discovery, he wouldn't be so famous. He must have been interested in something else, something to do with mathematics, which I know nothing about. But someone just as smart could have come along sometime and realized something else, namely, the way time suddenly shifts. What I mean is the way the quality of time, an era's sense of life shifts. All of a sudden everybody experiences time differently than they did yesterday or the day before. You can't tell exactly why it is: historical events, like maybe wars, revolutions? They didn't touch it off, didn't cause it. Not at all: they're just the products of the shift. They never could have happened without that abrupt, mysterious change. Today's experts are utterly nonplussed by it. Even the theologians can't think of anything to say about it, for instance, that God must be in a bad mood or that He just inhaled and then exhaled. It's something worth studying: what makes two eras different from each other? Do they return in some guise or other? Are their fundamental principles transformed into their opposites? At any rate, you can't ignore it. Everyone's felt how the world can change from one day to the next. The difficulty is that you don't notice it right away. It takes a while to realize that since such-and-such a day, everything is different..."

I was born in the forest. My mother washed me in a spring, laid me in the moss, and covered me with her hair. Her face hung over mine as I blindly slept through the night. In the morning she took her hair from my face. The sun warmed my little body. The fragrance of strawberries penetrated my skin. I was a child. I played with the doves that came to drink from the spring. When I was a boy, the kingfisher was my playmate. My limbs grew like willow boughs. Sometimes when I was tired, my mother took my head in her lap and let her hair fall over me. Then I dreamed I found my father who was missing in action. "Hey," he would say, "who's this then?" And he would grab my locks with his hard hand and lift me up like a puppy to take a good look at me. But I would scratch and bite until he let me go. "So that's the kind you are," he would laugh and try to catch me again. I would run away. I was quick and knew the forest. I would lure him away from the spring where my mother lived in a hut of ferns. Then I would go to her and say, "I found my father and now I'm going off to war with him. Let your hair hang down over me once more and let your tears fall on me."

I left my mother and the forest with its shy animals to follow my father to war. Soon the war laid waste the land. People told me my father was a bad man and they had hanged him. So I became a bad man like him. I burned down many houses. I watched many roofs collapse into the honeyed light of the flames that fell from the rafters like a woman's loosened hair. Once I came to a house where there was a beautiful daughter. I took her with me and loved her. She bore me a son, I don't know where. There is no more forest. They felled it in the war. I want my son to seek me. I want to find him and grab his dark locks to lift him up for a better look at him.

Preface (Draft)

> The best part of this book are the drafts I told to someone or other and immediately forgot; they are the chapters of happy invention I neglected to write, the important themes I pursued for a while and then lost the sense of, ideas and accidents I was too lazy and neglectful to note down—in short, everything not to be found in these pages.

The man who left us these notes (without a doubt, they are for the most part autobiographical) was born in Bessarabia, which had just become part of Romania, in 1919, shortly after the First World War. Although it would perhaps be wise to take this symbolically, he spent a princely childhood in extremely feudal environments on country estates there and in the villas of his various "uncles"—a.k.a. the lovers of his happy-go-lucky mother—on the Côte d'Azur. After the untimely death of that beautiful woman, orphaned and forgotten by his mother's benefactors (his father can only be conjectured as one of their number), he ended up with relatives in Vienna and "wilted," as he put it with bitter sarcasm, through a dozen nightmarish years, studying in the sweltering stupor of various third-rate schools in the outlying suburbs and living in the narrow (in every sense of the word) confines of a "starched-collar bourgeoisie" degraded by war, inflation, and what might be called a smoldering Socialism, until in 1937, only a few months before the Anschluss, the Jewish wife (the "Stella" of his manuscripts) of one of the legendary patrons of his childhood, the shadowy British diplomat John, discovered him and, by taking a more than maternal interest in him brought his "existence back into bloom," a good deed for which she would later pay with her life.

What he calls the "blossoming of his existence" will suggest to anyone more or less familiar with the psyche of writers what his destiny would be. The passages of his manuscript that refer to it sound like a catalogue of the wishful thinking of those who, according to Flaubert, "*sont faits pour le dire, et non pour l'avoir.*"

The times did not favor the fulfillment of those wishes. When German troops invade on March 12, 1938, and Adolf Hitler makes an appearance in Austria, it "mows down the naive conscience of those happy beings who were able to take part in the beauty of the world." Although the author of the story spends that summer on a lake in the Salzkammergut with his beloved, "confidently wrapped in a cocoon of togetherness that recognizes nothing but itself," the winter of 1938–39 separates the pair. Stella manages to arrange her protégé's return to Romania and his reunion with another patron of his childhood, "Uncle" Ferdinand. By the winter of 1940, he is a Romanian soldier stationed in Bessarabia. The "world of iron men" has begun and with it the "Ice Age" that will last until 1948.

How he passed the war years is still an open question. He hints that he was in wartime Germany with dodgy papers that kept him out of the conflict. Stella makes an insane attempt to see him in Berlin and gets caught in the bone-crushing machinery of the Nazis. He is unable to save her and will feel guilty forever after. In the war's final days, he witnesses the destruction of German cities and the "death of Europe." The war ends in 1945 and in the world of rubble and the "unfortunate reconstruction" that follows, he is in Hamburg, where his story really begins.

He never tires of telling it from all possible angles. Stella's husband John, who always played a not completely transparent role in the thicket of British foreign policy, has the grotesque idea of calling on him to testify about Stella's death at the Nuremburg Trials. While there, Aristides meets his future wife Christa in the cafeteria of the courthouse in Fürth. His son is born and Aristides, who is not trained in any profession and is in many respects as unworldly "as Kaspar Hauser," "sleepwalks" into a chance to earn his living: thanks to a concatenation of circumstances, he finds work as a screenwriter for the reviving postwar German film industry. Just as in his marriage and most other personal relationships, however, the passionate need to write his book gets in the way.

That book can contain nothing but his personal story. What that means to him is not just a record of ongoing events and experiences, but also "the exasperating telescoping of present and past, the enduring presence of all one's experience," in a word, "the torment of not being able to exist without history." The result is his compulsion to recount his entire life with each new experience—and thus the obsessive idea that his life is designed to be narrated, could have no other purpose than "*to be a book*." "From the days of my childhood," he writes, "with awakening consciousness and then forever after through all the years of my life, I was engaged in producing this book *by living its story*."

Note:
Got into an endless debate over that sentence with Scherping yesterday. He thinks it's so obviously true for an autobiography that saying it sounds like a "gimmicky commonplace." Since I didn't want to get into another argument, I just laid a typescript on his desk (following Schelmie's good advice). Scherping can pass it on to his gofers.

In the first place, it's not the author's autobiography, it's the biography of his book. Of course it's Aristides's story, but "story" and "history" are terms that recur in many guises and in the fullness of their semantic possibilities in A's writing. He understands history as both a cultural fact and a chronicle, a written record or oral tradition of events that concern human beings, whether those events be collective or individual—thus as both *res gestae* and simple stories or anecdotes, but in addition—and this definition underlies (so to speak) all the others—truly transcendentally as "actual existence" ("I have no other reality than my history"). Not by way of deduction from ontological contemplation, but through examination of the essence of his work—writing and especially the writing of novels—he reaches the same conclusion as for example (to choose a contemporary metaphysician) Ortega y Gasset: "Man is the novelist of himself, whether it's original or plagiarized." And according to the rule that "for the writer, any basic insight into human existence immediately becomes part of his literary program," he draws a practical literary conclusion.

(It's a waste of time trying to explain this to Scherping. What he wants is a juicy narrative that includes the liveliest possible scenes from a picaresque career. And make it as sexy as possible, please.)

Apropos "gimmicky commonplace": as he says that, Scherping leans his head to the side as if it was a nervous tick. He narrows his eyes behind his glasses. The plosives burst from his lips. "He's foaming at the mouth again," as Christa Reiterlich says. What's his problem? Is it the publisher's mistrust (remorsefully foaming at the mouth as though in self-incrimination, he refers to himself as a "bookseller")? Is it the unease of a middleman toward the authors who earn him a living? The hatred of the half-educated for "intellectuals" (especially me!)? Or simply his helpless wrath that Aristides is costing him money? Whichever it is, it gives him pleasure. After our irritating argument, I unfortunately found myself adrift and stumbling into a low dive, return home veiled by benevolent amnesia.

Postscript: a preface is probably not necessary.

Postscript to Uncle Ferdinand's chat about time. The way time "slips from your grasp": experience accumulates and always remains present while "pure" time flows away unnoticed. "We pour our lifetime through a sieve. It catches not just the facts but also what moved us inwardly; and the finer the mesh of our sieve or net, the more intensely we experience 'time.' But we don't feel time itself; it flows away while everything else stands still and is always there..." (include in the preface?)

HAMBURG, 1949 (?)

"As if he had been cast away among the lotus-eaters, he seemed to have forgotten his fatherland. He knew he was a stranger. The tired ocean-wind told him so, tossed it into his face—the wind that blew, day in, day out, sweeping across bleak marshland and weed-choked rubble fields and straying into the gaps and ruins of meandering streets."

That's how he had wanted it to begin.

How long have I lived here? he asked himself. He couldn't remember. The bloom of reconstruction after the Ice Age had erased his memory. As it thawed, fog drifted in. He saw the world through a veil. The constant trickle of tinny vehicles through streets that shortly before had still afforded distant panoramas of the rubble fields flickered before the image of the resurrected city and distracted him. Sinister things were in progress here, high-rises sprouting from the bomb craters like mushrooms. Over the fire-blackened ground, a herd of construction cranes stretched out skinny necks like skeletal dinosaurs, nest-building monsters designed by Paul Klee. Cement covered yesterday's rubble. Mortar dust obscured the daylight and made him thirsty.

The room he entered, down a few steps from street level, was dark and narrow, a tunnel dug into the subsiding walls of an old half-timbered building that encased the bleak new space: the rudiments of superannuated good old days, folkloristically preserved and dedicated to the dullest of all vices: sitting on a barstool to soothe the soul. Like the careworn face of a war widow, the light of an autumn day pressed against two narrow windows at sidewalk level fashioned from bottle bottoms cased in lead. Twilight reigned in the depths.

Dark paneled walls and carved wooden dividers between the booths: thick clusters of grapes and putti wearing grape-leaf wreaths—bacchanalian German baroque. Pools of shadow swallowed the light his eyes had carried in from the street. He couldn't see a thing and only sensed the presence of people in the booths, caught the scent of their rain-wet clothes below the sour smell of beer. Above the bar at the far end of the tunnel, neon tubes flickered. Red and violet stars were reflected in the zinc sink where the glasses were washed. Like an aurora borealis cased in metal, a resplendent jukebox pushed back the darkness, shimmering in all the colors of the spectrum. Its lantern-jawed visage bared the teeth of selection buttons and farther back, the baleen-like rows of 45s.

He pushed his way through the silence that had instantly descended at his entrance. The back of his neck prickled from imagined stares that were probably not following him at all but made him feel like an outsider, importing foreign weirdness: a samurai perhaps, in a dragon helmet and lizard armor and studded with swords; or a camel with a cage on its hump, a Turkish crescent jingling exotically; or Caesar and Cleopatra driving a yoke of leopards. He felt their glances, believed the sea-blue, blinking eyes of the coastal populace directed toward him, as if sizing up his value as driftwood. He saw it at work behind their high foreheads, beneath their unruly corn-yellow thatches, saw how the worldly wisdom of these port-city inhabitants was piecing together what to make of his strange appearance, saw himself dissected into various exotic elements and then slapped back together at clumsy angles, saw how their sensory equipment palpated those angles, seeing if they hadn't injured or rubbed themselves raw on something like this before, if open hostility was called for, or at the very least caution, suspicion, basic disapproval... He saw reddish-blond wives embarrassed by their gender becoming restless, shifting in their seats, putting themselves on display... but no, it was just his imagination, he knew they were paying hardly any attention to him, not even as an interruption of their dribble of conversation. Their silence didn't mean anything, it was an involuntary reflex of seaport inhabitants who were used to foreigners but had never entirely accepted them. Everyone who came in snapped their brittle sentences in two, and they only grew back together once he had passed. They didn't need to look up to have him sense that he wasn't one of them. They weren't hostile, he felt, or even curious, only forewarned against foreignness. Nevertheless, the few steps to the bar were as far as in a dream, when gravity seems both suspended and multiplied a hundred times, so that lead weights on our feet hurry us toward a goal we will never reach.

Don't look back, he told himself. It's like a fairy tale: whoever looks back turns into a stone beside the path. A group of teenage boys blocked his way to the bar, would-be hipsters in what passed for fashion in Germany: blue jeans and cowboy boots, their greasy blond hair combed into Elvis ducktails. One broad back in a leather vest blocked his way. To avoid bumping into it, he loudly cleared his throat. No luck. With more irritation in his voice than intended, he said, "Pardon me!"

That was a mistake. He realized it from the faces that turned toward him, suddenly alert as hunters. "Pardon me" was a foreign affectation no true foreigner would ever use. It placed him pretentiously outside their communality, was intended to create class distance. It wasn't a foreigner who said something like that, it was a prodigal brother and therefore an enemy. He stood there, waiting, his heart beating. The back in the leather vest turned so minimally to let him pass that he brushed against it. He suppressed the impulse to shove it brutally out of the way. Such temptations befell him all too often. The anger that surged up and then sank back helplessly was his soul's daily fare. It nourished his hatred.

He stepped up to the bar. "A Coke," he said to the bartender. He felt the need for a schnapps but it would have sounded like he was trying to be chummy. Drinking as a male bonding ritual.

The teenagers were also waiting expectantly. They had grouped together right behind him, including the back in the leather vest, now returned to its original position. He was trapped.

A man dressed in suspiciously elegant clothes who says "Pardon me" and sips Coca-Cola—they'll think I'm a fag for sure.

(Of course, they themselves are potential prey for fags. I ought to tell Rönnekamp about this place. They're all set up for it with their Elvis coifs and tight jeans. Their being, their *Dasein* and *So-sein*, as their philosophers call it, is bursting out of their tight jeans. My *So-sein* hangs on the clothesline—a counting-out rhyme for adolescents.)

"Eighty," said the bartender, took a bottle of Coca-Cola from the refrigerator, pried off the cap, stuck a straw in the bottle, and pushed it toward him.

—The world-famous trademark, top-of-the line product of the synthetic beverage industry, spouting hundreds of geysers from Karachi to Caracas, conjured up from the crust of our spinning planet by a wave of the hand of powerful business interests, from Dallas, Texas, to Paris, France; from Heidelberg, Iowa, to Heidelberg, Germany: Take a Break! Shove your hard hat, bus driver's hat, or filling station cap off your forehead, lift the bottle in a toast to the milk-and-roses face of the blossoming girl at your side (warmhearted foreman's smile exuding solidity), her spring-fresh, Pond's-Almond-Cream face—lift the plump bottle—conveniently ridged like a hand grenade—and its starry tingles in salute to the glistening Colgate teeth of that fragrantly clean daydream of a creature in her summer blouse, straining two full, bulging handfuls of proffered pleasure toward you: eros of consumer excess—holding up for your inspection the giant economy-size, small-change, fractional economy, it's the turnover that counts, billions from Greenland to Palm Beach, from Sauerland to Tierra del Fuego, from Flanders fields where poppies grow to Maya-Land, Watusi-Land, Singhalese-Land, and old Atlantis, webbed and crisscrossed by superhighways and airline routes, bald eagles and ibises, land of tourist brochures, a Hindu lad waves to the stewardess from his zebu's hump, igloos, silent ivy-covered castles reflected in water-lily ponds, Rob Roy, hero of the whiskey tartans, Cesare Borgia of the Dukes of Supercortemaggiore, oil rigs boring through the megalithic tombs of the Lüneburg Heath, stockyards in the

Zane Grey prairie, like swarms of ants the buffalo herds trickle away over the distant horizon into a gigantic jar of Bovril meat extract, Quaker-Oats-Land, Singer-Sewing-Machine-Land from the calving polar ice caps to the coral coasts, from the foam-flecked strands of the Spice Islands to the rocky islands where seagulls flutter and the atolls are alive with crimson fish—

the cherry-slim, invigorating beauty arches toward you, soap-fragrant, firm to the touch, the coolly fogged consumer grenade, the geyser of synthetic sensual satisfaction, extracted from the wilderness and sterilized on a distant star, the juice of meteors...

He placed a coin on the zinc bar, heard the cash register whirr, and waved away the change.

The bartender took hold of his hand. "You gave me two marks."

"Did I?" he said distractedly. Now he was probably just making a ridiculous impression: the absentminded bourgeois, the mama's boy. "I thought it was just one." He tried to extricate his hand.

The bartender still held it fast. "You got one twenty coming."

"Yes," he said, "I made a mistake. I intended to give you a twenty-pfennig tip."

"But you gave me a two-mark piece. I can show it to you."

"No need to. I believe you. If you'd just let go of my hand, I'll take a mark back."

The bartender let go of his hand. "A mark twenty. Gotta keep things straight," he said.

"I'm not trying to cheat you." He was indignant about his captured hand.

"Not the point," said the bartender. "Gotta keep things straight."

He could feel the young men breathing down his neck. "Well now they're straight again, your things," he said, irritated against his will. "Now can I drink this stuff in peace?"

"Yes you may," said the bartender. "You're allowed to drink as much as you like here. Not just this stuff, as you call it. Here you're allowed to drink till you fall down. As long as you pay, that is."

"I did pay," uncontrollable anger sharpened his voice, "didn't I?"

"Yes, with a two-mark piece. Didn't I give you correct change?"

"You did indeed. Now I'd like to be left in peace."

"And you will be, mister," said the bartender. "But that doesn't mean that anybody can tell me to keep quiet. Not in my own bar. When I say you were mistaken, it's to your advantage."

"To my advantage?" This was starting to be amusing.

"Yes, of course to your advantage!" said the bartender. "You'd've been throwing a mark twenty away. And when I point out your mistake, you should be grateful, mister, and not tell me to shut up in my own bar. And if you don't like it, mister, then you know where the door is."

"Now kindly allow me to drink the cola I paid for in peace."

"I'll allow you," said the bartender. "But nobody's ever told me to shush up in my own bar before, not in thirty-five years in the business." He raised his voice to a threatening lament. "There's been a bar right here on this spot for more than a hundred years, mister. These young folks can tell you if you don't believe me. They're Hamburgers born and bred, mister. This bar survived the terror and it'll survive whatever else comes along. It was here when seafaring was still a Christian occupation."

He thought he detected in the bartender's voice the compulsion to spin a yarn. In a chatty tone, he said, "Must have been nice back then. Too bad the old interior didn't survive. Mermaids and ships in a bottle, right? Were they destroyed in the air raids?"

"Plenty more than that was destroyed," said the bartender. He was washing glasses. "You can still see the mermaids—right around that corner. But my wife and four little children died in your air raids."

"I wasn't in any bombers," he said, tormented by guilt.

The bartender started drying the glasses. He did it in a peculiarly clumsy way, more like an inexperienced servant girl than an old barkeep. He screwed a corner of the dishtowel into the glass till it reached the bottom, stuffed the entire glass with the balled-up towel, held the protruding end with one hand and turned the glass with the other, and then pulled out the towel and held the glass up to the light to see if it was clean, closing one eye as though taking aim.

"I wasn't in any bombers. I did play at soldiering once, but thank God not in the war."

"Well weren't you lucky," said the bartender. "People like us didn't have it so good."

Now the silence of all those around him was thick enough to cut with a knife. He thought he could sense their contempt. "You didn't have to start in about it," he heard himself say, "about the war, I mean." He listened intently for the silence to become malevolent. Ready to fight. It would have been a relief to throw a few punches. But that was just what they were waiting for.

Should I go over and put a few coins in the jukebox? he thought. Play just any old record—probably nothing but wild rock 'n' roll in there. Set off a racket to accompany this unreal reality; unleash the hullabaloo they use nowadays to smother thoughts of the past; transport the senses into blazing intoxication to match the psychedelic, spectral light of this new world . . .

> Strike up the jukebox and the magic begins! Shove a coin in the stamped-tin slot, give it a push with the ball of your thumb, rough and brutal, and the spirit of the times begins to twang: droning, clanking, blaring, eardrum-bursting, the hand of the times unleashes the din, the hand of a young wildcatter, gas station attendant, or trucker, a boy's hand but already a workman's paw, a few grips learned by repetition is all it knows: the grab, the yank, the shove, the twist, the push, ignorant of relaxed, idle fingers, eloquent gestures that remodel a word, make a thought spatial, suggest a caress. The hand of the times, no longer an instrument to initiate sublime events, no longer a hand that paints like Piero della Francesca, not a hand that sets tones singing like the hands of the boy Mozart, not a hand that writes like the poet Eichendorff. A mercenary's hand, the thumb horny from counting its wages, sliding the bills again and again

across an index finger bent from pulling a trigger, smooth from familiarity with the utensils of murder: money-grubbing hand—let the coins begin to jingle, shove them into the stamped-tin slot; no swindle possible: the machine is finely adjusted to the size and weight of each coin, it registers the slightest deviation, the smallest irregularity, the most trivial-seeming difference and immediately jams, your hand has to push it in with horny fingers, roughly, so the whole cabinet shakes, the heavy, bulky cabinet of iron, tin, and plastic, all sorts of serrated, fluted, stamped, shopworn, dented tin, all sorts of plastic bulges and groins, plastic with tin inlays, tin with plastic inlays, a mongrel of cowboy saddle and squeezebox, oil sheik's Rolls and vaquero's guitar, soda fountain and Mexican revolver, the tropical night lurking within, full of jungle screams, gives it a good whack, it's a bit sleepy, the old gorilla, doesn't react in a split second like it used to, Tarzan has it easy, his thumb gives a shove, the coin clatters into the metallic entrails, a soft, elastic click indicates it has come to rest in a kind of trigger guard, the final instructions have yet to be given before the spinning soup pot rises into the ionosphere, the triple rows of plastic-button teeth in its shark's mouth transmit them telegraphically, the selection-button molars pass them on to the sharp incisors of tin-rimmed cards in the title catalogue, which convey them to the vertical stacks of baleen discs—the three stages of ignition—then the horny thumb gives another push, pushes from the shoulder with a brief twist of the upper body taken up by the hips, a dry shove of the bent arm, a thrust into King Kong's heart, the bulletproof armor plates of the prehistoric monster clank in alarm, the iron entrails of the enemy-occupied space station are jostled together until at last the release is accomplished amid flickering electric discharges: apotheoses of flaming light, blazing spectra coil in slowly rising and falling spirals, aureoles fan out and disperse, geysers of synthetic visual stimuli join the billowing wreathes of light which curl up like incense smoke and undulate down like a desert god's pillars of fire into arcaded arches, erecting cupolas, oil-sheik Alhambras melted down into Sabena-borealis, grand vomitatio of ice-cream colors, tapping a super-rolling mill of sound: like a burst of fire the aural fare shoots out of the triple-toothed baleen whale's gorge, Jonah the American, pours out in the primitive form of a musical motif, gets caught under the pile-driving beat and is squashed, hacked, steamrolled flatter and flatter into cheaper and cheaper clattering tin, grooved, serrated, stamped, processed to be consumed by trash dumps from which the lime slurry of neon tubes flows into the starry sky on high, the lymph of suburban mange: the mournful wailing of suburbia that has devoured the city and all cities.

He turned to face the teens standing silently with beer glasses in their hands. They didn't seem to be waiting for anything, were without thought or action, completely given over to the trickle of time, and he wondered in what sense they belonged to reality, the reality of reconstruction, of the unleashed restoration of misunderstood facts, the abstract reality of resurrected cities and the ruthless rhythm with which they sprouted from the mounds of rubble.

Nothing is resurrected. Nothing but the chinking of the cash registers, the banging on the bars of the cage you inhabit, the prisoner of money. You can't take a single step without money running through your hand, every move you make is immediately confirmed by the clatter of the register that lends it a definitive air, checks it off, establishes the causal short circuit that every action must be immediately followed by a payment: you pay and get paid—even for murder—that's how every act is transacted, even the most inhuman acts, with every activity thus completed, the compelling certainty grows and finally incorporates even the initial impulse to act, the motivating need or desire, into the causal circle of being paid and having to pay—the desire inspired by the cherry-cheeked daydream of a creature with the twin faucets and their sterile promise of pleasure: that great household teat is only there to fool you, lure you into the fallacy that the more you consume, the cheaper it is—the certainty that you must pay is not thereby cancelled: on the contrary, its rhythm is accelerated, more and more harrying and harried. Your scream into the starry sky merges with organs, bells, vaquero-guitars, revolver shots, factory whistles, lonely locomotive shrieks, packs of moonstruck saxophones, kettledrums and trumpets, Jericho trumpets that bring the walls of cities tumbling down, you gasp and sob, your voice quavers and shakes, gurgles and cracks, buffeted back and forth in ecstatic convulsions, you're a world-war trembler swatting at invisible flies, foaming at the mouth, sweat dripping from your Mexican tresses in the merciless beat, your mangy homesickness for some unseen land of suckle and reassurance, for cities as many-towered as Monsalvat, for all the cities you've known and lost, all you've not known and lost, the blues of my life, my lost, squandered, misplaced fatherlands on the mangy crust of this planet hurtling through space: no confluence or interweaving of events is permitted unless it's been chopped up and riveted back together by the bang of a rubber stamp—payment received!—no longer do actions blossom from mysterious sources and sow their seeds in the wind that carries them where it will, no longer can an idle whim connect events in a round dance, the staccato of the rattling cash registers grinds them into chaff, a sum of separate processes, each of which demands to be dealt with at once, and *woe betide you* should you evade paying immediate attention, *woe betide you* should you break free, delay or even prevent the short circuit of performance and payment, *woe betide you* should you withdraw your deeds and wishes from this universal law, do something without money, wish for something without money: you'll be as culpable as if you'd interfered in the harmony of Creation: they'll pursue you like a blasphemer against almighty God, someone whose example—God forbid—could be imitated by others, by several others, possibly by many, even by all, could lead to the planet being thrown off course, the planet that's harried, clanking and rattling, through space by the pulse of thudding cash registers, in cosmic rock 'n' roll, while on its crust the rabble of humanity slaughters and strangles one another, one tribe wipes out the other, one people lets another bleed to death *ad maiorem dei gloriam*: slaves to the great mammon—thou shalt not sin against it! Otherwise, continents would escape from the nets spun by airlines, the coral coasts would drift away from the iceberg-calving polar glaciers, Karachi and Caracas would separate from their embrace of fervent agreement that consumption must rise whatever the cost, because cheaper consumption means increased consumption, Dallas (Texas) and Paris (France) would fly apart with explosive speed . . .

In my far-off fatherland they came once a year, on New Year's Day, in the entourage of the children dressed as the Wise Men who came singing door-to-door, collecting charitable donations. First came the tenants in new white stockings; they left their shoes on the doorstep. They brought venison and poultry and lovely fish, jugs of wine and honey and stacks of golden winnowing baskets. Then they went to the overseer's to pay their rent. In the afternoon the vendors came crunching down the frosty road from town in jingling horse-drawn sleighs. They presented the overseer with bills, which he went over carefully, and it lasted into the evening. Uncle Ferdinand stood by the window and watched in frowning contempt as they departed one by one or in groups after repeatedly bowing in thanks to the overseer. When the last one had left the yard, Uncle Ferdinand washed his hands—

I was never allowed outside with bare hands. They always made me put on chamois gloves. I was never allowed to touch money. I knew the old pennies with snipes on them in Uncle Ferdinand's numismatic cabinet long before I could make change with the coins of the currency then in circulation—

> and all that was less than a quarter century ago and maybe it's not even real, maybe it never happened in flesh-and-blood reality. Maybe it was only invented by some dreamer who told it to me or about me, or maybe I invented it myself. Who'd be able to confirm it, or even want to? I lost my fatherland. It's extremely odd and quite extraordinary. And I don't even know who my father is. I carry my mother's name (assuming it was her real name)—

"I'm not going to drink this stuff," he said, pushing the Coke bottle away. "Take it back and bring me a schnapps."

The bartender widened his pale blue eyes. "You want to exchange your drink?"

"No. How much is a double kümmel?"

"Two forty," said the bartender, giving him a very suspicious look.

"Here's three marks. Keep the change, give me a double kümmel, and keep your mouth shut till I finish it and leave."

From the handful of change in his pocket he sorted out three one-mark coins, shoved them one by one with his thumb over his crooked index finger, and with three sharp snaps placed them in a row on the zinc bar. The gesture gave him spiteful pleasure. The horse trader's ostentatious display was surely a provocation for the bartender and the teenagers and also a sneer at the miracle of reconstruction, a miracle produced entirely by money, worthless paper become hard currency overnight, hastily hardening hearts and heads—

> it was exactly how Mommy snapped down her solitaire cards on the green baize of the little card table—the contempt of the rich for small change...

> He sees himself sitting with John and Uncle Ferdinand, watching his mother play solitaire: three lovers, and him at seven years old by far the most ardent. It must have been at Uncle Ferdinand's estate in Bessarabia; the lighting is as it was in those days. Nowhere did I ever see such light again. In it, the

world was infinitely wide. When the sun shone, it lit the wetlands along the Pruth River with all the bright distance from the Don to the Côte d'Azur: our hunting grounds: Balkan castles and casino palaces. Courtesan country. Mommy the high-class courtesan, the marionette of a paying gentleman on each of her slender fingers . . .

The cards bloom in neat beds on the dark green baize. Mommy took them out of a little tortoiseshell case, tiny cards with pink and powder-blue backs on which a pair of doves bill and coo in a black frame of filigree rose tendrils. On the case is an enamel showing the aces fanned out: the ace of hearts, spades, diamonds, and clubs, held in place with a brilliant. Everything Mommy owns is tasteful and luxurious, earned on her back with nonchalant grace. And I, her darling, was also earned on her back: Uncle Ferdinand could just as well be my father as John or one of our other benefactors from the Côte d'Azur, Bully Olivera or Sir Agop Garabetian. They will all repudiate me when Mommy dies—

Unwillingly, he sees himself in Vienna, an orphan, living with relatives made shabby by inflation. Not now, not here, where hatred of these philistines is already choking him. What he needs now is propping up: he's on the verge of losing himself here in Hamburg, in this patched-up world of rubble, busy rebuilding everything that only yesterday led to its utter ruin—

I don't want to think about the way I was when I wasn't allowed to be *myself.* I'm not allowed to here and I wasn't allowed to back in Vienna. I need my myth: the pipe dream of my true self: *me*, not the stranger, the odd one, the cause of offense, but as I was back then: snugly nestled in everyone's goodwill, the Little Prince, luxurious little son of a whore. I worship Mommy but I don't like the way she snaps down the cards. It doesn't go with her elegance. It's vulgar. It's nothing but . . .

she cheats: instead of drawing three cards from the pack each time, she draws them one by one. The rings on her fingers glitter, her polished nails are hard and pointy. When she casts a strategic eye over the colorful field to see where she can play a card, or if it will be discarded, she purses her red lips as if to whistle a silent song. Kissy-mouth. I read rapture in Uncle Ferdinand's eyes. John's face is cool. Both know Mommy's passion for cards. She has cost them both a fortune . . .

now Mommy has spotted a place where she can play her card. Her lips part in an incipient smile that would be cruelly triumphant if she allowed it to ripen. Her eyes flash. She presses the card onto the green baize with such enthusiasm that it bends double. Then with her thumb she snaps the lower edge over the last joint of her index finger. I can't help thinking it's like when someone squashes a flea with their thumbnail, a nasty sound. Where did I learn to think so? Was it when one of Uncle Ferdinand's foresters was de-fleaing his dog? A mundane idea. Better: in his dressing room Uncle Ferdinand has a Sèvres porcelain, "*Le puce.*" A shepherd kneels behind a lady who looks invitingly at him over her shoulder. She's pulled up half her crinolines to expose her naked bum, plump and rosy, on which sits a flea. A pastoral: just a game, like Mommy's solitaire, a game that can turn dangerous at the chemin-de-fer tables in the casino, where fortunes are lost. A man can be squashed under her thumbnail. (Pulp fiction!) MONEY IS HARD. Gisela told me that, and Christa says the same thing every day—

He snapped the third coin onto the bar and looked up. The bartender just stood there. His lips pursed as if to whistle a silent song, he added a fourth mark and said, "Eighty cents for the Coke and two marks forty for the schnapps, comes to three twenty."

"Exactly!" snorted the bartender. "I thought you were trying to get away with three marks."

"Nothing's too much to get out of here, not even if you made me pay twice for the Coke."

Bewildered, the bartender started to object. "Forget it," he said. "We can't all do sums in our head. Keep eighty cents of this filthy money for yourself and throw out the Coke, or..." with the beginnings of a malicious smile he turned to the boys behind him, "...give it to these gentlemen here. A refreshing soft drink for youngsters."

None of the boys moved. He waited three breaths, then turned back to the bartender. "I'll have a kümmel or a vodka. Or a Steinhäger, please. Or whatever you have on hand."

Without a word, the bartender took the brown stoneware bottle from the cabinet and poured a glass. He picked it up and tossed it back with studied nonchalance. The schnapps burned his throat.

"Keep the eighty cents yourself," said the bartender belligerently. "I'm not taking no tip from you."

But he'd already turned on his heel and waved off the threat, twiddling his fingers at his temple like he'd seen Gary Cooper do in *Morocco*. Where had that been? In Vienna, a fallen world ago. As an orphan, a boy not yet fully grown: a dreamy experience in the world of the philistines. Long before he'd met Stella. Long before the advent of the Ice Age in which the world of the philistines would disappear along with the world of the fortunate—only to rise again with doubly hardened hard currency.

The unresisting hipsters manqué opened a path for him. Halfway down the tunnel he heard a voice calling a bitingly sarcastic "Bye-bye"...

...was already writing back then, laboriously, with his left hand, the damned right hand together with forearm and a good half of the upper arm having been left behind in Russia—he wrote in simmering fury at how clumsy the pen was and at the scrawly letters it scratched onto paper, the stack of writing paper I discovered in the villa under the ruins of a desk and brought out to him in his garden house. The letterhead bore the august address *Hamburg, Elbchaussee* in elegant cursive. It looked very cultured, genteel as a frock coat, and Nagel's scribblings on the page below were quite touching. At first glance you would think they were the clumsy attempts of a well-brought-up grandchild to write a birthday letter to Grandpa, a prince of international finance. He wrote on that paper with grim and stubborn determination.

Nevertheless, he still never missed one of our gatherings. Poured turnip schnapps with a generous hand and shared our homegrown tobacco. When Hertzog and the others left, we'd have a little hour of quality time, just the two of us. The joys of friendship—and only yesterday, but it wasn't just our friendship that had vanished. In the meantime the whole world had changed.

Of course he wouldn't show me what he was writing, not after the offensive remarks I was guilty of, evidence of my cynical, godless attitude ("which I really wouldn't have expected of you, dear friend!"). He kept it from me like a secret lover (I was able to buy it in a bookstore a year later). But once he had gotten his fury off his chest by talking, he found his way back to our old intimate tone, his teeth shining white in a face smeared with soot from the stove. He worked with his brain instead of his hands now, and in place of his miner's lamp, his forehead glowed with the sublimity of the successful creative process. We talked to each other again, had conversations instead of discussions, exchanges of ideas instead of debates. We forgot our utopias and turned to daily life, the adventure-filled daily life of those Ice Age years. In brotherly cooperation we pursued the day's business (usually black-market business). Sometimes Nagel even made a little joke at Hertzog's expense, but then he had a relapse, became deadly earnest about the nights of discussion—or rather, about their noble goal: "thinking through" a new society—

or did I deny that this was a matter pregnant with significance and consequence?

No, no, not at all. I only admitted that in this regard, I was totally without ideas. I was abashed in the presence of such passionately engaged people as our one-legged friend Wilhelm; I wasn't suffering under the current conditions, after all. Given the current state of affairs, I was remarkably contented—

and Nagel got excited again: Do you realize what you're saying, man? The country's bombed to smithereens, a horde of starving people are controlled by a foreign military power and barely able to keep from giving up the ghost—and you're content?...

I had to declare myself shamefully devoid of any sense of national pride. I wasn't a German, after all, hadn't anything invested in the lost cause, hadn't risked my neck—an arm off here, a leg off there—no, no, the times owed me nothing... but that's not what I'm talking about; it's the future of Europe as a whole I'm worried about... exactly, and that's why I was so contented: that future could only come from the total destruction of the existing order, right? In that regard, Germany was an exemplary country... But that's pure nihilism!... Could be, I said, sure. I'm quite aware of that, but I'm simply a very radical thinker who happens to have no allegiances whatsoever, always an outsider, alas, I've always been a lone wolf—in short, the hunter-gatherer existence in this arctic, archetypical landscape suited me. It corresponded completely to the world of inner experience (as Hertzog would call it) that was formed by my experience of the war, and from that, from the acceptance of that, something new might emerge...

(Honestly, back then I seriously thought it could be possible. I was dazzled by freedom, didn't see what was coming. That is, I saw it but refused to see it. But even then, Nagel didn't buy it.)

He was pissed off: So why the hell are you even here!?

In fact, that's a very touchy subject, I said. I couldn't really tell you without hurting your feelings... Come on, don't beat around the bush and play Mr. Sensitive, just spit it out if you can... all right then: I'm looking for a spiritual experience *de profundis* as well—in fact, I feel like a pig in shit at our evening discussions—but I don't find it in what Hertzog has to offer (I have no intention of becoming a cabaret comedian). But I think it's enormously worthwhile to observe the impression he makes on our friends and where it presumably will lead—that was a significant spiritual experience, wasn't it?...

Nagel pricked up his ears: What do you mean, exactly?

Well, what it takes to make a new society... For instance, the development of a catacomb congregation into a church—

Come again?

The metamorphosis of spiritually impoverished people, touched by God's finger, into staunch spiritual bookkeepers—

Nagel made a superhuman effort to control himself, but below the surface he seethed and rumbled alarmingly. The stump of his arm thrashed about involuntarily, making the empty sleeve of his dyed field shirt flutter, but he was listening—

And that was wonderful and amazing: persuading Nagel to listen seemed like a gift, a gift from the god of friendship. It made me serious; I dispensed with the cheap thrill of teasing him and taking it out on him instead of Hertzog. I even made an honest attempt to suppress my bile against Hertzog, my bitter rejection of him for intellectual—no, for physical, for physiochemical reasons with an admixture of straightforward schoolboy envy. I loved my friend Nagel but there was something about the man who called himself so pretentiously Hertzog with tee-zee that concentrated all my hatred, my hatred of the curse inflicted on this country, this people, and of what would soon return—relentlessly step by step—and one day change the world instantly and forever.

Sometimes I was so overcome by despair that everything within me was destroyed—literally: my will to live, my ravenous, wolf-like will to survive, the hungry, emaciated beast from the steppes that had kept me safe through the infernal madness of the Third Reich and its destruction and was determined to hang on by the skin of its teeth through the Ice Age that followed. Resigned to its fate, it sank impotently to the bottom of my being and lay there in feigned peace—

it was a remarkably happy feeling of dissolution, of being adrift in the current of time...

Why the hell was I here? No reason. I was washed up here. Uncle Helmuth would call it my karma—and he, Nagel, angrily returned to his garden house and wrote—wrote page after page of his first book with his left hand—how envious I was behind all my irony! How impatient I was to be seized too, seized somehow or other by such devotion to something, to be redeemed by a passion . . .

(In memory, it's all connected to the sight of the bleak, icy landscape across the frozen Elbe: a streak of crepuscular red haze in the glacial blue limns a desolate horizon. In the foreground, the dense filigree of bare lilac branches on the slope facing Övelgönne cuts a black border between the ruinous premises and a world gripped by frost. Above them the villa's silhouette rises into a sky of iron—a neoclassical structure, half Schinkel and half Palladio—in massive Wilhelmine pretension, but the mangled left wing lends it the romantic enchantment of a ruin—a foreign world: wildly foreign and bedecked with icicles like wintry Bessarabia long ago—and in it, me, the foreigner, turned into a foreigner . . . Isn't it weird that I should yearn to go back, that I feel homesickness when I think about it? . . .)

Teutonically gigantic in a dyed soldier's greatcoat that reaches down to his feet; his hands buried in its pockets and a head like Luther's, topped by a grizzled shock of blond hair and thrown back haughtily in the turned-up coat collar; his sensitive mouth clamped bitterly shut, he gazes dully forward at nothing through thick glasses, striding through the seagull ruckus of the girls' jeering welcome. He carries a whiff of contempt, the good citizen with his ambiguous morality, cast iron, corrupt and rotten: the right hand should not know what the left hand is doing. Has he come to snatch the prey from one of them again? Last time, he led away a patron who'd been under treatment by Gisela for three days and nights, led him like a prisoner. In this same gnomish rigidity, hounded by curses and threats, he'd walked along beside the john who was still racked by sobs of happiness. And everybody had known their cries of protest were hypocritical. Nobody wanted anything more to do with that fucked-up guy he was leading away. He'd been fleeced to the last penny; his watch and even his gold eyeglass frames were gone; shreds of shirt hung out of his jacket sleeves because someone—probably the supposed pimp who had been hired to beat him up—had ripped out his cuff links. But who asked him to come get the guy out of here as if he needed to be rescued from something? He had come and stayed of his own free will to the end of the treatment. Gisela wouldn't have released him any sooner even if she'd been threatened with violence; she's a reliable girl who takes customer service seriously.

It's especially not the job of this former POW in professorial spectacles to meddle in this business. What's he really want? Gisela has no customer at the moment. It's high noon and business is slow. Out of rank boredom, the girls make catcalls as he passes. Some tap their keys angrily against the glass of the windows behind which they loll on display—not to lure him but to draw his attention: look here, we're whores and we despise you! Why aren't you at the office or home eating Mommy's hash? Or are you up for a quickie?...

Maybe he came for a session of his own with Gisela? He looks like he needs it. His miserable existence is written all over his face. You can tell he drinks so he must have a reason to. This is where the girls can give you solace, a shelter for the lost. But you have to be profoundly desperate to come here in the middle of the day, driven beyond the limits of the bleak, blessedly dull escape from yourself to be found in the bottom of a bottle.

It's different when the lights go on in the evening all around the little gingerbread houses spared by the bombs hailing down in the fire-breathing nights of the Ice Age, as if a magic spell had protected Whores' Alley from the fate of the respectable town that was collapsing in a fiery mass into its burst-open cellars; when those squat houses with their old-fashioned gables—still intact among the ruins that are sprouting more and more concrete cubes—stand jagged against the smoke-blue sky that soon turns inky and would swallow them up if not for the windows of the girls' rooms, shining yellow as buttercups; when the glass boxes light up to display the half-naked girls sitting on plush sofas in tiny carpeted parlors, teasingly tricked out in black silk bodices and fire-red feather boas, thighs showing white through their net stockings; when their harem pants and plump tits in open-necked sailors' blouses and Spanish boleros advertise the motley, wonderful, erotic as-if in the golden light that fills the narrow alley, then the hour has arrived for those who hope to press a few moments of oblivion from the last dregs of illusion, the wine of self-deception. Anyone who comes in the middle of the day has realized what constitutes redemption; he's heading straight toward his own destruction.

The girls are mistaken. They don't know him yet. He has only recently been released from a POW camp. Though he was born here and was a longtime resident, the business of committing genocide has estranged him. In a city where in good times everyone knows everyone else and everything about them (a truly democratic city: the mayor is the cousin of the waiter serving the soup at the banquet for the town council), now he's just another of the countless people who've washed up here: refugees, forced laborers, the stateless...

The girls have no way of knowing that someone will write of him:

> Because he exudes an aura of weighty destiny—or at least, an extraordinary sensitivity, a bitter consciousness of being helpless in the face of the termite-like power of all the vulgar, malicious, stupid people in this world, a consciousness that cripples him and lends him the pathetic unwieldiness of a fallen giant, a Titan with severed tendons—one can't help but perceive all his impulses as much too forceful, much too sweeping and tragic, all his utterances as grandiose and brittle, his person as an ivy-clad ruin, thereby overlooking the alertness of a sensitive and vulnerable person as well as the quite concrete stratagems by which he copes with daily existence: his healthy sense of the practical and merciless eye for the ridiculous, his shrewd and often hard-nosed tactics for handling others—in short, all the routines that make possible the paradox of an emotional economy that keeps the hatefulness of his environment at arm's length and at the same time allows him to wallow all the more extravagantly in his melancholy—
>
> majestically, of course, behind a decisive "No!" to everything mediocre, banal, and sentimental (under present circumstance

> a suicidal line to draw)—and majestically unconcerned with the damage he does to himself thereby (as well as via hard liquor and pills)—

What he's looking for in Whores' Alley is a manuscript. Another of Gisela's customers left it with her by accident. He doesn't know him, hasn't seen the manuscript either, but only knows about it from the account of the man he fetched out of here after having seen to it that the latter's three-day absence from home and workplace did not result in a missing-person bulletin. The manuscript is supposedly a film script and apparently extraordinarily brilliant and inventive. As an editor in a publishing house, he works with manuscripts professionally, and the man he led away from here, the discoverer of the manuscript, is a publisher. How the latter was able to get a look at it in the midst of a seventy-five-hour frenzy of torment and lust, an organ symphony of alcohol and drugs, can only be understood as an unbounded *déformation professionelle.*

> Gisela's "treatment" is symbolically organized. She begins by undressing the john and putting him naked into a crib as if recently weaned. Gisela kisses and hugs him like a good mommy, fondles his member, but punishes him—still laughing and joking—when it gets stiff. That's cute and all, but not allowed yet. And then things get stricter: he's gone pee-pee in bed, bad boy! He gets it—whack, whack—on his bare bottom. Then more tenderness and a treat—don't ask about its pharmacological ingredients. Now the little guy is wide awake. He's reached school age, wears short pants, little socks, a school shirt, and a big polka-dot bow under his chin. She sits him down at a little desk and gives him assignments. But the bad boy has blotted his paper. That's going to cost him a caning. At his age, there's plenty of lesser and greater offenses he's guilty of. The day passes, full of praise and punishment. Mommy Gisela is strict. Fair, but strict. The punishments are more elaborate than

the rewards, but the latter are also excitingly painful. Now he's in puberty. Gisela temporarily plays a new role. As his fellow pupil, she introduces him to the anatomical differences between boys and girls. But alas! He goes too far during the inspection. His playmate is insulted, angry, and uncommonly inventive in the half-kidding, half-malicious infliction of pain; she pinches and jabs and scratches and bites. Then Gisela, once more in the role of governess, catches him at the vice of self-abuse and exposes him publically as a masturbator. She invites in a group of her girlfriends and puts him on display. The girls mock and scold him appropriately and make cruel jokes about the size of his member. They try pulling it to make it longer. More blows rain down since no erection is forthcoming; then even more when it finally begins. His back is striped with bloody welts. That night, he's permitted to chat with Gisela and sleep a bit.

Day two: now comes the manhood phase. His virility must be tested. Gisela finds occasion to punish him cruelly for his failures. They copulate continuously. Her ability to spur him on to climax after climax is stupendous. As is her ability to invent more and more reasons to mistreat him. Nor is the element of surprise lacking: a supposed pimp invades the room while the two are lying in bed, takes him unawares, thrashes him good and proper, and robs him of his last penny. Gisela watches with a wicked smile, calling words of encouragement to the pimp. The line between pretending and real life blurs. Gisela forgoes her roles and presents herself frankly as what she is: a heartless whore. "As-if" becomes nightmarish reality. She makes continuous demands, expresses expensive wishes. He is in a condition of utter lack of will, completely exhausted mentally and physically. His head is seething with drugs and alcohol. He writes checks for sums that really frighten him. He wants to flee but finds himself at her mercy, powerless and even enjoying it.

> Day three: now he gets chained up. It's done with such skill that he can't move a finger without excruciating pain. He hangs in his chains, his arms extended, crucified. Gisela ridicules him, belabors him with a whip, and leaves him alone. Hours go by. He starts to cry for help, but no one comes to release him. At last the cleaning lady shows up but pretends he isn't there. She starts to straighten up, all the while uttering complaints about what a mess the room is in. She tosses his clothes into the trash can and pays no attention to his cries. After scrubbing the floor, she leaves. After another eternity, they finally set him free. They say one of his employees is waiting for him downstairs. He's there to gain his release with a hefty ransom of several thousand marks. (Later, the police would suggest that Gisela not overdo things; the Hanseatic town's reputation was at stake.)

And yet the object of such treatment was so eager to find as yet unpublished material that in one of the pauses to catch his breath, he was able to take a look at a pile of typewritten pages one of his predecessors had forgotten among the illustrated magazines on Gisela's bedside table.

—and I wear his clothes: his shirts, his pants, vests, and sport coats, his tweeds and flannels, he has to hang onto his dark suits for official occasions. He dresses me just as his wife once dressed me a dozen Ice Age years ago, me, a youthful pavement pounder who became a dandy at the hands of a woman of the world—no, not by any means a gigolo, no cold-blooded lounge lizard or gold digger. I was too sentimental for that. I loved Stella and wouldn't have traded her for Garbo, to say nothing of Dietrich. I didn't know any other worldly-wise women, my memories of the Côte d'Azur having been buried under twelve years of schooling in the lap of my relatives' family: Uncle Helmuth, Aunt Hertha, Aunt Selma, and Cousin Wolfgang. Even the fashion magazines Aunt Selma bought on the sly didn't excite my daydreams as much as the movies. The "wide world" was the one on the screen: Adolphe Menjou in a silk suit and Panama hat brings Marlene Dietrich a fresh, dewy bouquet of roses at the edge of the Moroccan desert, but she won't stay with him. She'll follow me, the French Foreign Legionnaire Gary Cooper, into an uncertain future. Stella doesn't give a fig what John, his fellow diplomats, or Viennese or Bucharest high society think or say about her either. Nor does she have to throw away her high heels like Dietrich to walk more easily through the sand (how her tender soles will soon be burning!); she doesn't have to grab a goat by its horns and drag it along in my wake either. She, Stella, takes me by the hand and leads me to Prix and Knize and has me measured for half a dozen suits. A woman of the world likes to dress up her baby doll—and John grins and bears our game. He grins and bears all the games here in Nuremberg too and assumes—no, uses his grin to force the others to grin and bear his game, for example, the absurdity that he's brought me here to testify about Stella's murder. Just imagine testifying about the murder of a single, solitary person when what's at issue is the murder of millions. Why does he do it? It can't be for my sake; I'm not important to him. It was purely by accident that our paths crossed again in Hamburg, in front of the Hotel Atlantic. The thing that led me to be walking past was my aimless wandering through Hamburg's construction sites and the fields of rubble where some testimonies to the city's proud past were still standing: the town hall and the stock exchange, some luxury hotels, the villas of the moneybags on the banks of the Alster, the dance halls on the Reeperbahn, a few churches, and the gingerbread cottages of Whores' Alley, all surrounded by ruins, rubble dumps being shoveled out for new foundations. I wandered through this Baalbek with my ribs showing and happened to pass the Atlantic just as he, John, was coming out with a group of resplendent top brass from the occupying army. He spotted me and couldn't believe his eyes at how sharp-featured and run-down his wife's youthful lover had become, but it couldn't have moved him a bit. John was anything but softhearted. So why did he unceremoniously pluck me off the street with the same cold-bloodedness with which Uncle Ferdinand had welcomed me back to Bessarabia in 1940 after fourteen years (*"Ah, te voilà, finalement, il était grand temps qu'on te voie...*"). It'd been seven years since John last saw me in Bucharest. Back then I too was in uniform, but with much less brass on my lapels than his friends in front of the Hotel Atlantic had. Then as now, he was wearing one of his Saville Row suits that now fit me like a glove. I'm again part of the civilized world of the victors, but in front of the Atlantic in the condition of a raggedy refugee driven from his homeland, it required the exorbitant self-confidence of a John to introduce me to his entourage of brigadiers and wing-commanders as if it was only yesterday that the two of us were together for a weekend at the Duke of Westminster's. Why did he do it? What moved him to quarter me forthwith in the Atlantic, feed and clothe me, once again provide me with dubious papers which, however, commanded respect from dutiful officials (a travel document from the military government for an "individual of doubtful nationality"), and finally to order me to Nuremberg? Was it the memory of my mother, the high-class courtesan he had had a stormy relationship with—so stormy that he almost couldn't grin and bear her cruel game before she found eternal rest in a pond in Bessarabia?... Stella had been much more passionate about memorializing her. She took a literary interest in the career of Ilse Subicz, who gave herself the stage name Maud (the bed as stage?). Stella found her exceptionally audacious. An officer's daughter from the world of Austro-Hungarian garrisons that stretched from Udine to Kecskemét to Zhytomyr and a beacon of emancipation, she turned the heads of the richest, most pampered and hard-nosed men of the era until they jigged before her like organ-grinders' monkeys. Stella collected everything that could document that career. Some things—photos, clippings—I still have, preserved in my magic box—that was all that I could call my own except my rags, a comb, a toothbrush, and a fingernail brush when I washed up in Hamburg-on-the-Elbe, of all places! It all served to confirm my mother's legend, the legend of the beautiful Maud; and so it also served to confirm the legend of me, her love child. But what's all that to John? It's a million miles removed from even the remotest likelihood that John could regard the earthly existence of his onetime mistress, my mother, with the same literary interest as Stella, to say nothing of being so fascinated by the legend's factual aspect, congealed into the concrete existence of a bastard child, that he would feel compelled to take this living evidence—me—under his wing... so what did he want from me? In some complicated way, am I supposed to help him take out his anger on the Americans? It's so obvious he hates them that I'm often embarrassed to be seen with him. They're in charge here in Nuremberg, and I get the jitters when he starts in in my presence about how one nation founded on genocide—the extermination of the redskins who owned the land where the stars and stripes now wave—shouldn't presume to sit in judgment on another, much older, incomparably more civilized, nation that did nothing but undertake the elimination of a foreign body from its own organism. The people he says this to can't believe their ears: their shocked gazes slide involuntarily in my direction. What's my connection to such a madman? In intimate contact with the most prominent figures of this "show trial," as he calls it, he can afford to act like that. Although nobody knows exactly what role he's playing here, the more obscure it is, the more important it seems to be. I, on the other hand, the stray nobody at his side, an "individual of doubtful nationality," still half-starving but accoutered (if only in hand-me-downs) by Turnbull & Asser and Huntsman, supposedly a witness in the trial—called by whom? testifying for or against what?—I am an extremely suspicious figure. They let me know it wherever I appear. They give me the cold shoulder. So I stay in the background as much as possible and wander the labyrinthian corridors of the gigantic courthouse in Fürth. I don't eat in the Allies' canteen, but with the untouchables: the Germans and stateless, displaced persons like myself. The food is the same as in the Allies' canteen, but for the likes of us, it's dumped out like slop for pigs. Whether they're a certified defense attorney for the accused, a worn-out general who avoided indictment and hanging by a hair's breadth thanks to the Twentieth of July, or a newly appointed party chairman and future chancellor, they're all under the thumb of an officer of the court whose job is to keep order in this swarming nest of termites and who, as a praetorian guard, has nothing but contempt for them. The other thumb they're under belongs to a highly suspicious individual by the name of Gaston Oulman, his ancestry as indefinable as mine, who styles himself the beadle of the German press corps, runs around in a homemade uniform of highly martial cut, and is treated with corresponding respect. Everyone fears him. Everyone dances to his tune except me, and he knows exactly whose protection I'm under and avoids crossing paths with me but doesn't exactly contribute to my feeling at home here—"at home," yes, that's exactly the term for it. The historic significance of this trial, the polarity of good and evil, of glorious victors and bloodstained vanquished, the back and forth and up and down, the tension between right and wrong, moral outrage and hypocrisy, heart-stopping horror at inconceivable crimes and forensic hairsplitting, shock and indifference, the daily emotional roller coaster under the downpour of newly discovered, monstrous evil and the excruciating doggedness and bureaucratic pigheadedness of procedural process, the banality of evil and habituation to dealing with monsters—all that squeezed into the beehive of Fürth and its queen-bee cell, the smallish courtroom at its center, all heavily guarded, sealed off, a fortress bristling with checkpoints, encircled by tanks and ordnance in a landscape pockmarked by bombs—all that, I say, constitutes a biotope, a cramped little world whose spell no one can escape. Everyone is marked by it like the participants in a battle—Verdun or Stalingrad—there's even a certain camaraderie. I sense that one can be incorporated and begin to feel at home in it. I can see it in those who work here writing press reports, wading through files, writing out affidavits, working for the prosecution or the defense. But here too I'm just a flaneur, suspiciously idle, an outsider with no real connections, no obligations, but sharp-eyed, a silent observer, so probably a spy. People can't see my uneasiness. Not a syllable, not an expression, not a look betrays how the conflicts, the contradictions, and the absurdities here are eating at me. John doesn't hold his tongue when the talk turns to the world-historical significance of this trial: "World-historical significance!" he sneers. "It's a scandal, a farce that will permit us to play the Last Judgment through the next century and always be the judges, never the accused . . . Who set up this Punch and Judy show? What does the Nuremberg Tribunal represent? Surely it's not a show trial for the victors to humiliate the vanquished? No no, we're much too pure and noble for that. We believe in the rule of law; didn't the Hague Convention of 1926 brand war a crime? All well and good, but it didn't provide us with the legal tools to try to punish those responsible. That's what we're out to accomplish here. To condemn the intention to go to war when you have to go to war? A moral analysis of the reasons to do so, after the fact? How are you going to accomplish that? With the flimsy charge of conspiracy? When the next conflict breaks out, would anyone have the nerve to indict the presidents and prime ministers of the nations involved for conspiracy—I mean, without making himself a laughing stock? And how would he proceed? According to what legal principles? Germany and most other European countries follow the ancient Roman principle of *nulla poena sine lege*. On the other hand, there's the Anglo-Saxon conception that the judgment arrived at and carried out in a proper trial sets a legal precedent, i.e., has the power of a law that can be invoked in future cases. So here in Nuremberg we have an Anglo-Saxon court judging Germans, i.e., a court imposed from without, a court of victors. But no, that would have been immoral; that would not have been in line with our lofty ethical principles. The Nuremberg Court, so they say, was installed by the Germans themselves. To be sure, there was no German sovereignty to install it, so the Allies had to jump in. On the basis of Germany's unconditional surrender, the four victorious powers comprise the present German government. And this government installed the Nuremberg court. And that's why it's judging not according to German law but to Anglo-Saxon law. What may have been overlooked in the process was this: Which German signed the unconditional surrender and may perhaps be strung up—General Jodl, for example, or Admiral Reeder—and has thus signed his own death warrant . . ." John is immune to the babble the follows his words. He cold-bloodedly plays the bull in the china shop and doesn't care if they openly accuse him of being a German sympathizer. He knows only too well that most people here agree with his most cynical statements, especially the anti-Semites among them. Besides, he's invulnerable because all his encounters and contacts are open to view. He's never alone with anyone but is always accompanied by officials of the relevant authorities. As his protégé, however, I hang around with the reptiles in the undergrowth of this jungle. What reports about them do I deliver to him? What messages do I carry back to them?... and yet I know that my activities don't interest him in the slightest. They float above—or rather, slip below—the horizon of his concerns, are too far removed from the world of his thoughts for him to pay them any heed. Should he really need me for anything, he'll make use of me (and devote about as much thought to me as he does to the bootjack in his dressing room), and if he should lose track of me as he did when Maud drowned in the pond in Bessarabia, he'll make as little effort to find me as he did in the fourteen years after Maud's death and the last seven years since we parted in Bucharest. Our encounters are planetary; each of us follows his own orbit and eons pass without them intersecting. And if they do, neither one is diverted. Uncle Helmuth would surely be able to explain that using Hindu cosmology...

A thought in the middle of the night (I'm having a miserable time falling asleep; I lie awake for hours and watch the sky turn gray):

Rub Scherping's nose in Gertrude Stein's "people are not interested in stories, people are interested in existence." *No more artfully dramatized sequences of events in which characters appear as "actors," determining the flow of the story by acting and suffering. Instead, the weaving together of existences in the motionless time-space of the narrative—existence is pure present, has no chronologic development, is in the simultaneity of past, present, and future—*

no thread is spun, but a static piece of fictive reality is woven; events that occur within it are subjectivized and no longer exist as something that can be generally experienced. Instead, they stand by themselves as a pattern, the pattern of the weave in each separate existence.

(The difference between Tolstoy and Joyce—with luck, Scherping may be familiar with their tables of contents.)

Centrifugal and centripetal narration—

To obtain nuances, highlights, etc., take up some things not germane to the action—

(Scherping's almost unimaginable astonishment that I'm plagued by such thoughts even at night [and thus definitely outside office hours], as if I had a personal interest in them, and not just as a wage earner. In fact, they're a blessed distraction from the swarming nightmares in the Brueghel landscape of insomnia [my murder!]—

thus: literature as escape even in this sense—)

SCHWAB

Biographical note:
He can barely recall his boyhood years (and his childhood, not at all). He dreamed his way through them. He gets self-conscious when asked about them, pussyfoots around the facts as if they embarrass him. The truth is, he has trouble reconstructing them. They lie befogged in the diffuse light of the daydreams woven through them. The "way it could have been" always superseded what was actually happening.

So he's almost incapable of telling the story of his life as it played out in the eyes of his family. They try to remind him of this or that event and he accepts it as a possibility. He can only conjure up something approximating it if it's interlaced with a simultaneous dream motif whose emotional color allows him to recall that epoch. The tone, the nuances in the span between major and minor allow inferences about the character of actual occurrences. For instance, the anxiety at moving from a spacious, sunny, and comfortable house to a meager, narrow apartment after his father's death; or the grueling, eye-straining hours of study so that he could escape that cramped place as soon as possible. His dream adventures rob those days of their reality. Replayed against the pale screen of life's trivial happenings, his dreams are incomparably more intense and he is unable to discern their motifs and elements in the actual occurrences. Reality took place (a curious way to express it, but it captures the working-out of reality) without giving the experience of the past a sturdy framework, some sort of bone structure. And so in retrospect he himself is composed of feelings without a skeleton, a sort of mollusk. It's up to him now to give what he dreamed then a framework and thus plausibility. He has countless possible biographies within himself. (Compare that to Aristides, whose memories are a series of concrete events only retrospectively illuminated by emotion.)

The loss of reality in the realm of the factual also determines Schwab's relationship to the persons allotted him as family. To manufacture them he has to slot them into social categories. His mother: typically déclassé, a lady who had "seen better days," suppressed indignation in every bone of her angular body, the "daughter of a good family" fated to become a domestic slave (in contrast to Aristides's Aunt Selma, who was just as "worn out by housework" but without reproach and without dreams either, according to the testimony of Uncle Helmuth and Aunt Hertha). Her love for her son was strict and ambitious; she was not about to let him think that lack of means led to social decline. Poor but proud. Emphasis on intellectual, culturally elevated pursuits. Idolized father: a frock-coated professor of the Wilhelmine era, incurably behind the times, his horizon blocked by the spines of his books. Highly respectable in his role as the noble philologist. Too sure of his own knowledge to become didactic. His son perceives it painfully as open contempt (in contrast to Aristides's Uncle Helmuth: the flat-footed engineer who sometimes indulges in an excessively good mood, tells jokes, feels an affinity with the poltergeists that serve to lubricate the sticky spiritualism of séances. Not to mention his taproom politicizing).

Schwab, never ever called by a nickname but always by the sternly biblical "Johannes," was haunted by the joyless atmosphere at home, which in a way was a monument to his deceased father, a monument erected against the shame of impoverishment and meant to put both paternal and maternal relatives in their place. Although much better off, with deep roots in the culture of suburbanized citizen-farmers, all those merchants and bureaucrats descended from the marsh-dwellers who farmed the heath gave way deferentially to the academic but had no intention of being bullied by his poverty-stricken widow. However, they pay their respects to the deceased whose glory reflects on the entire clan. His scholarly publications are mentioned reverentially, the books he edited shelved alongside Schiller, Gustav Freytag, and Treitschke in glass-fronted bookcases. His funeral (his son is sixteen, his lineage betrayed by glasses with a hair-raising diopter number) is not without political embarrassment. One of the speakers, with a Party pin in his lapel and obviously drunk, ventures to say that the best proof of this outstanding intellectual's National Socialist sentiments was his grasp of the fact that the Röhm purge was not a liquidation of pederastic traitors but the overthrow of good old naive brown-shirted yokels. (They arrest him right there in the cemetery.) The deceased's son, an ogreish giant a-tremble with neuroses and risible in his faded Hitler Jugend duds, listens with loathing but is preoccupied with dreaming himself out of what is going on, out of his effective reality: his massive body, weak chest and shortness of breath, rachitic knees of a wartime infant, oxycephalic forehead (cf. Cousin Wolfgang)—a few years later all that would be packed into a field-gray uniform. His experiences in the war are terrible. Even today he still wakes up screaming. That is a reality he can't dream his way out of. His ability to escape the here and now into a field of fantasy has been obliterated. Hence his melancholy.

P.S. His two closest relatives: an "aunt" who by hanging out with bohemian barflies completes the image of a middle-class person with petit bourgeois lifestyle but pretentions to the prestige of the upper classes. And in addition a nymphomaniac niece. Both of them embodiments of his bad conscience. Unavoidably, he's slept with both and would give his life not to have done so.

Depict as anecdotes:
The currency reform of 1948. Parallels to March 12, 1938, in Vienna (Nazi invasion). Beginning of a new era. (Cf. Uncle Ferdinand's theories: a new epoch begins every time God inhales and exhales.)

The effect on Christa: the definitive de-heroizing of her erstwhile (run-down) table ally from the Nuremberg canteen; the deterioration of the oddball in Nagel's primal community into a complete loser who won't line up for the opportunities offered by reconstruction.

Schwab meets Nagel.

My relationship with Nagel (friendship? blood brotherhood? Brothers—yes, the Cains and Abels) is getting more and more difficult. Since chasing the thieves (Hertzog and his cohorts) out of the temple of our little community and thereby destroying the temple as well, he's recapitulating in the new era the developmental stages of the post–Ice Age. At first the furious chronicler of events in the recent past (his first novel, *Craterland*, is in its third printing), he was soon carried away by the pull of market forces: radio dramas, a play (which hasn't yet been produced), and recently film scripts for Stoffel—or rather, for Astrid von Bürger with whom he's head-over-heels in love. He was careless enough to introduce me to them, so now I've met Horst-Jürgen Stoffel, founding father of postwar German cinema, first licensed producer of a movie in the British Zone, and his wife, Astrid von Bürger (Nagel's not the only one to rave about her), joint proprietors of STELLA FILMS.

It isn't immediately apparent what qualifies Herr Stoffel to be a producer, although his exterior doesn't rule it out: typical entrepreneur of the German reconstruction from the cadre of those exempted from military service for the sake of the wartime economy (son and successor of a manufacturer of wooden articles in the town of Winsen-on-the-Luhe; main product: gun stocks). In his early thirties and obviously well fed even in times of scarcity, viz: plenty of lard on a six-foot-one frame, flaxen haired, theatrical, booming voice. Educational level: left high school before graduation. But sly: a shrewd eye, quick grasp of a situation, without doubt ruthless. Clearly knows next to nothing about film but can bluff with the opinions of an observant moviegoer. ("What drives me crazy is that in movies, nobody ever gets change from a cabbie" or, "Have you ever seen a man get dressed and tuck his shirt in *after* he's buckled his belt?") He owed his license to his wife Astrid von Bürger's relationship with a film critic, an émigré who returned to Germany as cultural officer in the military government. (That good fellow, one Mr. Fletcher—formerly Fleischer—is a fan of Astrid's "Niffelheim beauty" and stoutly defends her against the accusation that during the war, she used her fame as a movie star to at the very least aid the Nazis in their push toward a final victory.) Meanwhile, in addition to her, Stoffel had the trump card of a million reichsmarks in hand (God only knows how he got them), not to mention his excellent connections to self-supporting Holstein farmers eager to trade their surplus ham and butter for Scotch whiskey. Thus he was able to found STELLA FILMS even before the currency reform, after which banks with large D-mark reserves swarmed onto the risky investment like flies onto dog shit.

Nagel is well aware of all that and appropriately repelled intellectually and morally, but not strongly enough to forgo his chance to write for the movies—to say nothing of spending a few hours each day in the presence of Astrid von Bürger. He'll have to do penance for it, however. She takes a lively part in all script conferences and voices very strong opinions. But even if they aren't always in artistic agreement, good old Nagel at least has the good fortune to sit down together in a cordial, collegial atmosphere with one of the masturbatory pinups of his infantryman's days in flesh and blood and skin and hair and come-hither looks, with a good view of her cleavage and sometimes, when she casually crosses her legs, even up her skirt.

She greets me graciously. She's undeniably beautiful, with a magnificent body, dark haired (Brünhilde's mane), her voice a bit metallic, but ringing. She knows how to modulate it and is one of those German women who seek to establish with each person they meet a secret affinity between allied souls, a sort of elective affinity at first acquaintance that doesn't exclude others but gives the person toward whom it's directed the illusion of being singled out. Stoffel does something similar. He obviously doesn't know what to do with me at first and is on his guard, but nevertheless turns to me with an occasional remark about the others present (including Nagel), as if there already existed a more intense relationship between him and me. It is just the feeling I'm receiving inappropriate attention that makes the exchange uncomfortable. (I don't know how Nagel couched the suggestion that I be invited; what's more, I'm embarrassed by the whiff of homoeroticism lurking in every meeting between two German men.) What unsettles me even more is that his spinning abstract threads of a relationship between him and me is a continual, potential betrayal of all the others (and likewise, between him and them, of me). The atmosphere is thick with treachery, the relationships slippery.

In his desperation, Nagel had brought me along to a script conference to help him defend his artistic ideas. The discussion takes place in the Stoffels' new house on the bank of the Alster. Interior decoration: dark wood paneling with miniature Hanseatic merchantmen as chandeliers. Besides Astrid, Stoffel, Nagel, and me, in attendance were the STELLA FILMS dramaturge, a pimply young man who would have fit right into Nagel's primal community if he hadn't immigrated too late from the Eastern Zone; the investment bank's film consultant and attorney; and two stereotypical gray-faced employees waiting like cats at a mouse hole to pounce on the bizarre notions of artistic types. Nagel had presented a marvelous idea. The treatment read like the ideal metaphor for Germans' coming to terms with the past, poetically shifted far enough into the realm of symbolism and humanity in general so as not to seem uncomfortably allegorical. But with plenty of dramatic tension:

> A native tribe in Central America (it was a saga Nagel brought home from his globe-trotting years) believes that every thirty-five years, the world is destroyed and renewed overnight. The fateful day is preceded by a time of scarcity. The tribe is threatened with starvation, and whoever steals from their meager food supplies is condemned to death. A woman steals a few ears of corn from the village storehouse to feed her starving children. The tribe has its own court that can issue death sentences, but may not carry them out itself. Now they are waiting for the executioner to arrive from the capital city. He arrives

> the night of the expected end of the world. The tribe is preparing for the end of the old and the birth of the new. They extinguish all their fires and destroy their old possessions. They await the morning on which a new world era will begin. The executioner must decide whether it is his duty to execute a prisoner condemned in the old world on the first morning of the new one.

In his treatment, Nagel has already described some scenes (extinguishing the fires, the tribe's mood in the face of the destruction of the world) vividly enough to provide the men from the bank a picture even they can imagine. However, the first thing they do is start picking apart the content in minute detail—apparently feeling it their duty to the employers who put food on their table to make the movie so foolproof that even a department head couldn't have anything against financing it. The arguments are correspondingly predictable: Will it be possible to convince moviegoers there are people who really believe that every few decades or so the world is destroyed and then raised from the dead the next morning? (I venture to interject that the miracle of the currency reform must have convinced most Germans of such a possibility, but I'm met partly with blank incomprehension—"Whaddaya mean?"—and partly with barely contained indignation, as if I'd called into question the inviolability of the monetary system and thus of the banks.)

Another objection: Why does the executioner have to come from so far away? ("Can't these people string up their own criminals?") Nagel patiently explains that after all, the tribe is subject to the laws of the country even if the government makes allowances for ethnic traditions and permits them to try their own cases. Carrying out the sentences, however, is reserved for the organs of the central government. Although she's only Stoffel's representative, Astrid von Bürger has taken charge of the discussion with a good deal of personal authority and asks somewhat mockingly (glancing at me for complicity) how they are going to inform the moviegoer of this complicated judicial situation—with a screen of written explanation, perhaps, listing the applicable precedents? (She's already secured the complicity of the bankers; as chair of the meeting she has to support everyone equally.) Nagel squirms like he's suffered a psychological shot in the belly. No, he says in a somewhat hoarse voice, the executioner himself could explain it in a few brief words—the treatment already has the movie beginning with an encounter between two strangers, the executioner and a world traveler who narrates the events. They meet at a campsite, both on their way to the natives. "Narrates?" Stoffel interjects in a booming voice. "I hate films that need voice-over narration. Film is a visual art, as proven by the decline in quality when the talkies were introduced..." Nagel interrupts him peevishly. "First of all that's nonsense, and secondly, there's no voice-over to what's happening on-screen. Nobody explains what's going on. The foreign traveler witnesses it all and we see what happens through his eyes."

Stoffel is disgruntled. He doesn't like being corrected. "What I said about the decline in quality isn't nonsense because..." Again, Nagel interrupts him rudely. "Are you planning to make silent films?" Stoffel replies superciliously, "No, but I'm going to make films where the action is so obvious that at most, the dialogue serves to express the emotional reaction of the actors without needing the exaggerated miming of silent films—as straightforward, clear, and economical as possible, of course. Let the stage—the theater—celebrate the spoken word. Film is film!" That comes so close to voicing every possible platitude that even Nagel is struck momentarily speechless. Stoffel's P.S. crushes him completely: "And by the way, I can't see any role for Astrid in your story. As a native condemned to death, all she could do is get tied up and sit in her hut, waiting for the hangman." Astrid says she doesn't have to be in every STELLA FILMS production, and besides, exotic roles don't suit her—except for Carmen. She worshiped Carmen when she was a little girl, but she's no opera diva—and besides (she glances at me, looking for confirmation—I can't help thinking of Christa), it's Nagel's job to introduce another, more attractive female character besides the candidate for execution. However—and this concentrates the smoldering skepticism of all those present on a common denominator—how does the story end? Does the woman get hanged or not?

At this point, the pimply dramaturge pipes up to say that a story like this contains the elements of Greek tragedy—namely, an ethically and morally unresolvable conflict in which all involved must perish, engendering pity and terror. Clamorous protest from the bankers, who can't agree to such a pessimistic outcome. Stoffel sides with them. ("The moviegoers will stay away in droves after the premiere.") Astrid objects that, however the conflict is resolved, she still doesn't know how to "visually conceive" the end of the film. Nagel growls that it's very simple: you'll see the woman either being untied or dangling from a branch. He's become quite grouchy. Trying to help my friend out, I say you have to leave it up to the viewers to sort out the clash of two ethical principles. Let them talk it through in the pub after the movie's over. You can't ask more of a film than that. Again, I'm met with blank stares. "Whaddaya mean? What kinda clash?"

I say, "Imagine yourself in the following situation. All of you have a highly developed sense of the need for moral improvement and at the same time a lively feeling of responsibility for correct rules of engagement in war. So let's assume you're a missionary—in Borneo, say—and have spent long, weary years laboring to persuade a tribe of Dayaks to solemnly forgo head-hunting. A great ceremony has been planned to mark the historical importance of their pledge. Just at the culminating moment, a commissioner of the colonial government appears and promises the Dayaks five pounds per severed Japanese head. They're at war with Japan and fear an invasion. How would you react?"

That remark unleashes a paroxysm of enthusiasm. None of them is willing to see that my story was nothing but a sort of inversion of Nagel's, with the same dramaturgically insoluble outcome: no ending is able to be completely satisfactory to those involved. Stoffel loudly and illogically announces, "That's exactly the solution!" And even the bank stiffs nod in agreement. "Solution to what?" I ask in confusion. Stoffel's meaty hand wallops me on the shoulder. "For the movie, man! We've got you to thank for how to get this done. Aside from making the awkward parallel to Germany's fate much harder to see (do we have to be condemned for our past even now, when the world has moved on in a totally different direction, toward freedom and democracy?)—I say aside from that, your version makes a tangible product so real I can taste it." He waxes visionary, starts to show off for the bank guys. "Borneo sounds like a long way off, but it's under British administration. Our occupiers will certainly have a more lively interest in it than in Mato Grosso or anywhere else in South America. I could imagine involving an English company in a coproduction. Astrid has good connections to Rank Films through her old friend Billy Fletcher. I've got an exchange between occupation zones in mind too: I think we could shoot in the studios in Munich-Geiselgasteig. The Yanks won't find anything to object to in a film like this. Hamburg doesn't have big enough studios and besides, in Munich we can interest American distributors. And Borneo is just a spectacular location: jungles, the safari experience, and so on..."—I can already picture him running off to the tailor to get measured for bush jackets—"Although, the weather in Borneo is unpredictable. We'd be in trouble if the rainy season started too soon. I see that I'll need to go out there myself..." To do what? Teach German punctuality to the clouds in the sky?

He forges ahead with visionary plans. I've given up trying to straighten out the misunderstanding that has stretched its tentacles like an octopus into every aspect of the topic. I shrug and nod in agreement when he asks me, "Are you prepared to write me a treatment of your story? I assume the content isn't copyrighted; it really happened, no? So we won't have to purchase the rights?"

Just to Astrid, I say, "Sorry my location is exotic too. But for sure there'll be a lovely role for you to appear wearing a flower behind your ear and topless," and get a look in return, a look that a woman at the turn of the century would have coupled with a sharp rap from her closed fan—

and with all that going on, I have failed to notice that Nagel has left the room, fuming mad, presumably. It's too late to run after him. I don't find him in his garden house either, and he remains invisible for the next few days. I respect his anger and wait for it to cool down. It's pointless to explain that it truly was not my intention to poach on his territory. He won't believe me anyway: what strengthened our friendship from the beginning was his frank distrust of me. Christa is equally skeptical of me as a screenwriter. "Not a very respectable job." What else should I do? What could I do? Write ad copy for Witte's laundromats? He's hinted there might be a job there for me.

Handwritten note:

For later:
The history of film projects during reconstruction:

Either: The producer has an "idea" for the subject matter—a title—doesn't matter where it comes from. The first thing he does is secure all the rights. So he also owns what the screenwriter thinks up and writes under that title. At best, the producer pays for the treatment written on the basis of a short synopsis, which is never paid for.

Or: The screenwriter suggests his own subject matter. Again, the first step is a synopsis. With luck, it gets expanded into a treatment. Since other writers, the producer himself, usually also a dramaturge working for the financing bank, the actor chosen for the lead, to say nothing of the presumptive director and in Stoffel's case, the producer's wife, all also get involved, the treatment gets so worked over and discussed to death that the screenwriter who initiated it can't claim any rights to it.

At this stage, the final product, the movie, is completely secondary. What's important is the "project." At the latest with the treatment, it begins to have substance, i.e., negotiations with the financing bank have begun. According to whether they take a positive or a negative turn, the treatment gets changed, that is, gets made more palatable for the money people—the banks and distributors. And even if a screenplay finally gets written, it only serves as a basis for negotiations to extract more money. The screenwriter doesn't get paid until final acceptance, i.e., hardly ever, since in most cases the "project" is not completed—nor does it need to be, for the producer has in the meantime gotten together enough money to keep himself and his company afloat. To cover the monies obtained for this project but not spent, he starts a new one.

If it happens that a movie actually gets made, the backers are steamrolled by the avalanche of cost overruns. The screenwriter has long since been tossed overboard, but the production company is flourishing. If the project fails before a film is made, the intellectual property rights can be sold to some other production company.

Wohlfahrt: "Keep the rubles rolling, man, that's the main thing!"

Because whoever resurrects an event in order to place it in relation to the past and the future—and in the end to eternity as well!—is performing a moral act. I would even say *the* moral act per se. Doesn't our conscience operate in the same way, by measuring what we do or fail to do against previous good or bad deeds, with regard to future deeds, and all in relation to the timeless absolute, eternity? Thus a story is the mother of morality, and the telling of stories is morality in practice. And so we will end up on the cross with our practice of morality—all of us who take the stories we tell seriously.

Dream:
Christa, S., and I are standing on a bridge suspended on steel cables high above a river. I know they are about to snap. I want to test the tension in the midsection of one of these cables. I pluck it and listen to it vibrating at a high pitch, like a violin string. I've never played an instrument in my life and I'm enchanted. I discover I can play like a virtuoso; it sounds like a harpsichord concerto. S. is also ecstatic. Even Christa marvels at me. I become aware that under my fingers, the cable is fraying. With every pluck it gets thinner and the tension increases. I know it's about to snap and the bridge will collapse, but still I keep on playing without warning S. and Christa. Below, Nagel is waiting. He won't catch any of us.

Handwritten note:
Select and tailor one's figures so they become stereotypes—or rather, phenotypes.

But is there any other way?

Caught myself trying to move as I imagine he moves: lightly, elegantly, gracefully, without affectation. Fell deep into alcohol at the shame of it (and also haunted by dreams: my murder!). Ran into Schelmie and my aunt in the pub. Their intimacy (at my expense) is very suspicious. Was unintentionally quite rude; embarrassed to think how I played the big boss toward Schelmie, the lowly employee. Even more shame. Back home, an auto-da-fé: destroyed everything I'd written in the last week. Lost all idea of what it could be good for.

GISELA

She is a living testament to the truism that a woman is never humiliated by what she does, but only by what happens to her. She never talks about where she comes from but she doesn't keep it a secret either. She thinks it's insignificant and not worth mentioning whether she comes from a middle-class, lower-middle-class, or completely unclassifiable family. Her existence begins with the decision to become a whore. She didn't fall into this profession by accident. She chose it as her best chance to survive—and not just survive, but do so without being exposed to what could have happened to her (at the very least, to be seized, forced to submit to a man or several men: the inescapable fate of a poor, solitary, and very beautiful girl). The times were hard. We are already beginning to forget that back then it was possible to starve to death unnoticed. Only two years: the day that separated the two worlds was only one of them ago.

She describes the dumbfounded expressions on the faces of the vice squad when she went there to register as the occupant of one of the whorehouses on the Reeperbahn, tells how one of them jumped up to offer her a chair, tells of the respect with which they took down her particulars, the dignity with which they repeated her name, birthdate, and previous addresses. And then the glances: each one a potential customer. She describes the spontaneous camaraderie of the girls who resolutely embrace the calling of whore and the envy and resentment of the others who have arrived at this point from desperation or carelessness. And she chooses her customers too, but seldom turns one down because she doesn't like him: professional ethics. She has no right to be picky, makes her choice based only on the desired specialties. And so she became Grand Mistress of the Order of Sadomasochists. Hardly ever sits in the window to lure customers anymore. Works mostly to order. By arrangement. She took me on because none of the other girls were free. We got into conversation thanks to her lightning-fast recognition of my intentions. First reluctant reaction: Let's get down to business! Don't waste my time. But then immediately relented once the financial arrangements were taken care of. "It's not just my physique that's for sale. I'm well paid for fantasies and sensitive to the psychological needs of my customers." Maybe it was my understanding of her motives that won her over: the principle of fun. That's how our cold friendship became close. I don't need to pump her. She knows my curiosity is germ-free. We both enjoy ourselves.

And she is wonderfully discreet. Never a personal question. What I tell her—or could tell her—about myself wouldn't be compensation or an exchange of confessions. Our subject is *the world of her experience*. She examines it with me and through me with the same detachment and observational interest. We are most amused when one of her regular customers is at the next table in the swank restaurant I've taken her to—ideally with his wife and children—and is on pins and needles fearing she will expose him.

Her bearing is similar to Christa's: slim and straight as a reed. In Christa's case, to appreciate it fully you have to see her in dressage. Gisela has a freer stride. For the rest, it's still an ironclad rule that I have to pay every time I want to sleep with her. I think it would be easier to borrow money from her than to talk her into a free fuck.

The stars have turned senile . . .

Hamburg, 1950: Ran into Herr von Rönnekamp on the Jungfernstieg. Cordial reunion: his detective's face (Arsène Lupin, avenger of the dispossessed) steamrollers you with amiability. In his rich Baltic accent with the swallowed umlauts that earned him the nickname "the

Bütch" he declares, "Hoven't zeen you in a dock's edge!" Invites me to a "little chat" in the pastry café of the Hotel Vier Jahreszeiten. On the way he tells me about the tragic fate of another member of his brotherhood: Unhappily in love with a young man he picked up on the street and hired as his servant only to be swindled and robbed in every possible way, his despairing friend had decided to kill himself. At the moment he's raising the pistol to his temple, his servant-lover enters the room. Caught in the act, the startled suicide shoves the pistol into his pants pocket. It goes off and shoots off "bows nuts, chust sink off it, shoots off bows testikels." *Tableau.* (From his narrow mouth "testicle" sounds like the name of a Baltic landed estate: "For seven hundred years, the Rönnekamps have been the lords of Testikel.") What moves me is not the tragedy of the man who shot off "bows nuts" or rather "bows testikels," but the love story behind it. So that sort of thing still exists—although probably only among queers. Rönnekamp too won me over with his capacity for love. Unforgettable times in his gingerbread cottage in Pöseldorf: him in the midst of his lover-boys—of the teenager or ordinary seaman variety—muscular young lads with fist-sized boils on the backs of their necks beneath their yellow Lorelei-manes; him boasting in his Baltic aristocrat's manner that tenderness is unmanly and laughable, and an immediate, rising chorus of young male voices: "You? How can you say that? You! Just a little kiss and you're right down on your knees!"

(Handwritten note: Attention! cf. Abel*)*

I see him standing at the window, in his hand a book he's going to recommend to his favorite, Dieterkins (a mechanic's apprentice). (What heterosexual still falls in love with a girl from the "people"? Romanticism flourishes only in tennis clubs these days. With predictable consequences.) Rönne's anguished attempt to explain the beauties of Joseph Conrad to the dull-witted boy. Loving instruction. Wanting to give the best one has. His knife-edge profile bent in Pre-Raphaelite humility.

In the pastry café (coffee and cake for him; cognac for me in the absence of whiskey), talk turns to the days of the primal community in Nagel's garden house, where we met. (General Freiherr von Neunteuffel, in whose company he had turned up, is in Bonn by now, busily engaged in the project of rearmament.) What Rönne articulates with fetching impersonality is an excellent analysis of events since 1945: at first, paralysis after the shock of total defeat (Nagel's "Craterland"), then the primal communities born out of it, gatherings of fanaticized starvelings too inept for black market business. Escape into the intellectual sphere, the cultural and political spheres. The latter especially—a playground for the utopians; equally fertile ground for sharp-eyed strivers. Everyone who barely managed to survive—scruffy, tattered idealists with their heads in the clouds, disabled sleepwalkers, eternal students missing a limb or two, dyspeptic intellectuals, exploiters of ruined ideologies—they all devote themselves to intellectual reconstruction. Including the cobweb-shrouded Weimar Republicans rounded up by the western Allies from liberated concentration camps, state prisons, agricultural forced-labor camps, and other hiding places as pitiful proof of originally humanitarian war aims, in order to give them a quick dusting off and introduce them into the mother liquor of apathetic turnip eaters as catalysts for the hoped-for crystallization of a new German democracy. Although officially appointed, they too operated at first in an airless environment outside the bounds of general awareness—until, in fact, a sort of crystalline precipitate formed (similar to the famous Karlsbad salt) with a crust of professional politicians surrounding it. This new race is now determining the new German reality. Its first coup was the currency reform of 1948.

However, Rönne says, this process would not have been possible without the distracting maneuver that every magician uses to divert attention from his actual manipulations. It was produced by the interregnum of the intellectuals. The radio dominates reality. An enormous backdrop of chatter is erected. The most obvious evidence: Professor Hertzog and his intervention in the intellectual magma of the primal community, his distracting game of supposedly bringing order to the chaos. The radio broadcasts journalistic imitations of it in the evening while actual politics (e.g., Bonn's appointment of General Neunteuffel) takes place behind a curtain of threadbare news reports.

When Rönnekamp talks, his incisors drop down from behind his upper lip and appear very large. Does he have not very well seated false teeth? Very disconcerting. I have to force myself to pay attention to what he's saying and not to the epiphany of his front teeth.

Herr von Rönnekamp thinks that given the currency reform, the intellectuals can be dispensed with. Protesting loudly, they'll recede into the background of what's happening. The new German world time—shelled so wonderfully out of the preceding time by the devaluation that there is absolutely no remaining connection between yesterday and today—is now in step with universal world time. Gathered home into the American Reich. Hertzog a prime example of that as well: his remorseful (Rönne says "raymorzfoll") return to the Freudianism he had opportunistically sworn off during twelve Nazi years. Among the survivors of the primal community, its founder (actually only its host) Nagel is also an example of developments: from fiction to film. Rönne prophesies an age of media.

All that, however, stands in the spotlight of what is happening in the Russian Zone. There, politics is not a morally fraught concept whose retroactively disastrous effects get registered in questionnaires. On the contrary, it's the central word of a new ethos. While on our side, the God who (based loosely on Nietzsche) no longer exists still casts a terrible shadow from his cave, in the Eastern Zone he's dressed in new clothes and shines in his old glory. His radiance does not admit of any guilt feelings. His yoke rests lightly on shoulders used to carrying it under his old name.

Exhilarated, we bid each other farewell. Rönne's handshake is like a suction cup, as is his parting glance. It seems to be saying, "Haven't you recognized who you are yet?" Like all queers, he surmises one of the brotherhood in every man, just like a masochist suspects everyone else of masochism (while hoping for a sadist). His long front teeth flash in his good-bye smile as though firmly rooted.

On Christa and Aristides:
In order to remind him that as his wife, she has a claim to part of the money he supposedly rakes in bushels of working for Stoffel & Co. (in reality, he works without pay as an idea man and besides, he has pulled back almost completely to leave the field free for Nagel, its lawful occupant), she decides to buy some new clothes. She's surprised to discover how familiar he is with questions of feminine couture, but of course has no idea that his knowledge comes from the shopping sprees on which he accompanies Gisela as an advisor. With his bad conscience, A. can only half appreciate the humor of the situation.

Even his bad conscience is ambivalent. On the one hand, he welcomes his relationship with Gisela as a liberation from the erotic obligation that binds him to the standoffish Christa, leaving him unhappy; on the other hand, he is sorry to see what he's destroying. He's also stung by the fact that he has to pay Gisela for every copulation. He tells himself he's encroaching on Christa, taking it from her already meager housekeeping account, so to speak. But then again, the idea of taking some sort of revenge is a satisfying feeling. His relationship with Gisela punishes Christa for the coldness with which she responded to his passionate courtship. With pure schadenfreude, he now sees that Christa has gotten wind of his infidelity; the fact that it's with a girl from Whores' Alley on the Reeperbahn is beyond anything she could imagine, not to mention that his relationship to that kind of rival could have become so intimate that he goes clothes shopping with her. All that flatters his sense of irony, but smacks unpleasantly of bourgeois complications: he cannot help calling it—with Stella and John—"*the fucking problems of the bloody middle class.*" In his heart of hearts he tells himself that the Hamburg milieu is beginning to rub off on him. From a nonbourgeois perspective, his marriage to Christa is a banal misunderstanding on which any emotion is wasted, while his deep-frozen but intellectually fiery relationship with Gisela is a pleasurable adventure. (Two different aesthetics. Muddied when morality puts in a word).

Perhaps superfluous. Hard to connect it with more important questions. Interesting, of course, from a psychological point of view. Gives A's figure more profile. But—you need to know things like that, but you don't need to say them.

"The activities of the mind arise solely from adequate ideas; the passive states of the mind depend solely on inadequate ideas."

—SPINOZA

NOVEMBER 1949

Cultural event: Debut of the film star Astrid von Bürger (gloriously denazified but still deeply controversial) in *A Woman Plays Foul*, her first postwar role (screenplay by Nagel). Producer: Horst-Jürgen Stoffel, her spouse (production company: STELLA FILMS). Location: the Anglo-German Club on the Alster (following the screening in the Holsten Theater).

Went there to forestall arguments about it with Scherping. Accuses me of intellectual arrogance when I stay away from such things. Nothing much different in the club since the forlorn gatherings of creative artists in pre-currency-reform days. Nevertheless, more relaxed interaction with the British occupiers. (Recent exchange between two club friends: "Hello, Heinz-Günther!"—"Hallo, Percy!" pronounced "Pörsü." Percy was clearly a frequent name in Hamburg as well, testimony to Hanseatic relations with the Anglo-Saxons: my cousin Percy Fettkötter.) Duly noted, the rearmament of fashion: the triumphal procession of German textiles begins. Silvery bowties everywhere (symbols of "nothing to hide"). Axel Springer's natty pseudo-English downtown Hamburg elegance in contrast to Witte's almost Russian boorishness (his apoplectically red, Falstaffian face with the sea-blue gaze of a "gatekeeper to the world," haloed by a lion's mane of white hair—a bourgeois cockade). Equally eager to make visible his reclaimed urbanity (with a tinge of Winsen-on-the-Luhe, however): producer Stoffel, stuffed into a double-breasted pinstriped suit like a gangster in a hit from the Roaring Twenties. Scherping too, Hamburgishly Anglo-Saxonized (somebody's persuaded him that you don't have to wear gray flannel pants with a checked jacket; it's more fashionable to wear pants of the same pattern). Once again, it's painfully funny to see how hard he tries to downplay his status as the representative of high culture, joking about the book trade, playing the clown—you expect he'll begin turning somersaults any minute—kidding me, "Well, what should I call you, editor-in-chief? Or maybe just chief? Chief sounds like a dog's name: Heel, Chief! ... That is, if you're not already planning to become my boss! Go ahead! You think I'm illiterate anyway!" He's looking for his daily dose of abuse and humiliation. I have to control myself to keep from throwing up.

Surveying the physiognomies present I can't get out of my head the image of the hostages being shot in Crete: Father and son standing together in front of the firing squad. Two gaunt, noble peasant faces, the son with eyes closed, the father looking almost peevishly straight ahead, a second before the crackle of the salvo: the complete, inward collectedness of their composure, nothing demonstrative, no heroics; just a proud coming to terms with an absurd fate—including a cosmically boundless contempt for fate's violent henchmen ...

these bloated pusses by comparison: Herr Senator Meier-Müller or whatever his name is: I can't stand his face, prefer his ass. I can recall it packed in field-gray trousers, general-staff tucks along the side seams. He staggers around, drunk. The staff is quartered in the remains of a villa. On a tattered sofa lies a little dog the grunts have picked up as a mascot, still a pup, wagging its tail in excitement and greeting everyone who comes near—and the ass approaches and plops down on top of it. The major is too drunk to notice what's there under his bottom, whimpering, its chest crushed and legs broken ...

With every glass of the generously available (gastritis-inducing) expense-account champagne, increasingly severe palpitations. Professor Hertzog's pills obviously have conflicting effects. Keeps me on a short leash in any case; if I ask for more, he blabbers about Thanatos. (As if the wish to be no longer a part of this world belonged merely to the subconscious ur-elements of the psyche and were not urged upon us by every step we take through our environment.) Didn't even confess to him that I now and then swallow whatever I can get hold of even without his prescriptions. But perhaps not so harmless after all, in combination with his pharmaceuticals.

By the way, on the subject of new German fashions: my kind, artists and intellectuals, still cling loyally to our old duds: baggy corduroys, anoraks, and berets. (In the days of Rinaldo Rinaldini, highwaymen too wore distinctive and easily recognized clothing.) But even the lads from the radio already betray a tendency to rebourgeoisify into manager types. Gone is their buccaneering candor. The currency miracle's caused shockwaves. The stroke that separated today from a swashbuckling yesterday in the bombed-out landscape cuts through one's character. The innocuousness of those who had nothing left to lose in the poorhouse generosity of the hunger years spent in cellar holes and Quonset huts belongs to another race of men. I wonder if the trip through purgatory was a process of purification? It's a long road to travel from former Party member to nihilistic existentialist to arch-democrat and citizen. Can't get rid of the impression that it happened almost without any—or at least with mostly unconscious—involvement on our part, over our heads, so to speak. Collective fate. The times are pregnant with it. (I'm afraid to encounter myself in the mirror: yesterday, gaunt as a Belgrade hackney nag, but with bright eyes [bright with horror!]; today, drunkard's eyes like old oysters behind thick lenses, pillowed in the fat of the all too abrupt dietary shift of the miraculous reconstruction. Specifically German in bearing and gesture: a routinized display of droning uprightness: "True blue and always honest!" as a program for worldwide profit. By the way: the post-currency-reform spirit is dropsical: the edema of yesterday's famine shines through; the pressure mark of a finger takes several minutes to fade.)

In response to all that, the occupying Brits in their dysentery-yellow field blouses maintain a stiff upper lip. No longer the masters in their former officers' club, they mingle in uneasy nonchalance with the horde of German cultural managers busy devouring rolls while balancing champagne glasses as if they had no memory of the raggedy cigarette-butt collectors of yesterday ("Exskyooze me Zurr, I vant to ax you for a purrmeet to go to Buxtehude to fetch my zister. She iss a ferry pritti gorl"). Done and gone their colonial grandeur, when the Ice Age Germans were the coolies of the British Labor-Sahibs. A people's prestige is measured by the hardness of their currency.

For a while I stand by a group talking about the recent past and what a disgrace it was that many of our countrymen acted after the defeat and under the Allied occupation: denunciations, self-abasement before the victors, begging for cigarettes and chocolate, turning tricks for nylons, and so on. An occupying officer turned cultural advisor stands there listening. He is young and the very model of an Englishman: clay-colored field blouse; tangerine-colored hair; banana-colored mustache; innocent, steel-blue eyes framed by egg-yolk-yellow lashes; rabbit teeth; and a long, pointed chin like King Thrushbeard. Someone turns to him.

"Tell me, John, don't you think it was a disgrace? If we'd invaded England, for example—you've got to admit, we almost did, with that mess in Dunkirk—so, if we'd occupied your island, could you imagine anything like what happened with us here in Germany?"

King Thrushbeard blushes and bats his yolk-yellow lashes. His chin gets even longer and sharper. After overcoming his obviously genetic Anglo-Saxon bashfulness, he comes out with, "I can imagine that in that case, just about everything you've mentioned could happen to us just as it did to you—except for one thing: this conversation."

No one seems visibly affected by the screening of the embarrassingly bad cinematic work of art. Except for Nagel, of course, who's seething about how the brain trust of director, star, and her producer husband as well as the distributor and the investment bank's film consultant made a hash of his original screenplay. He claims he can't even recognize his own work. But even Nagel has no ear for the disgrace of this concoction's warped attempt to overcome the past, especially since the only thing it's meant to overcome is the exceedingly banal past career of the former Nazi film star and present leading lady, Astrid von Bürger. Good old Nagel is too much in love to see how her biography is glossed over in the cinematic legend he's been force-fed: her rise—amid the death throes of Universum Film Inc.—from an athletic starlet to the popular image of young German womanhood, thanks to the patronage of the Reich Propaganda Minister Dr. Josef Goebbels, while shielded from that mighty man's more intimate attentions by a feigned friendship—at first only a hypocritical simulation but soon becoming a real bond—with his wife, Frau Goebbels, whom she, Astrid (in the film she's called Helge), does not betray even in the critical hours before the suicide of the entire family, and for that is retrospectively accused of collaboration in the crimes of the Third Reich.

(If only it had been like that! But what irony in the double entendre of the title "A Woman Plays Foul"! Irony masking as profundity. Nagel is genuinely proud of it. I'm having trouble persuading him not to make a novel out of the story. Moreover, some very unpleasant arguments about it with Scherping, who's all fired up about the project and willing to underwrite it if only to contradict me.)

Insufferable remarks by Stoffel, producer and husband of the leading lady (". . . I'm especially proud of you, my dear Astrid, making such an important contribution to correcting the image of collective guilt . . ."). Abashed faces on all sides.

By the way, Nagel brought a friend along who supposedly lives with him in Witte's bomb-damaged villa on the Elbchaussee. An exotic apparition (here?). Pleasant, but with something faintly disreputable about him. Elegant clothes that don't seem to belong to him. Fashionably well worn and out of date. Out of the ordinary, at any rate. He's one of those people whose features you forget sooner than how they affected you. In retrospect, he escapes precise description although leaving a strong impression. Only a sketchy physical description is possible: strongly built, pleasant outward appearance without distinguishing features—perhaps except for very bright, intense eyes; melodious voice; cultivated manner of speaking with unmistakable Austrian overtones, but speaks a vaguely alien German, as if it's a perfectly learned language but not his mother tongue. Said to be from Romania. I noticed him as I was standing at the window gazing out at the foggy Outer Alster. The clubhouse, originally requisitioned for the exclusive use of officers of the British occupation and now serving the cause of German-English rapprochement, stands almost exactly opposite Witte's house on the opposite shore. (Witte's residence in town; his bomb-damaged villa on the Elbchaussee was left standing for the time being as the half-ruined and barely habitable domicile for Nagel and his friend.) Interpolated correction: Nagel lives in the garden house. Only the friend and his wife are in the villa.

At any rate, you couldn't see the far shore of the Alster at all. It had been swallowed by a thick, yellow fog. The world lay under that misty blanket and even the surface of the water could only be guessed at. Soundless and weightless, two ducks glided by through the gray pea soup: a Zen image. Abruptly walking over to me without having exchanged a word or even being introduced, the stranger said, "Beautiful, isn't it? A Japanese screen, the gold a bit impasto. German roux. What might lie behind it? In the war they're said to have built dummy buildings out into the water as camouflage to fool the approaching bombers. I always imagined they could have been pagodas or Attic temples. Or maybe Indian teepees or Eskimo igloos. Why not? If you're going to do it, do it right. Nothing gets in the way of art, after all. Don't you agree?" For a moment I was captivated by the vision: an artificial city installed in the real one, starkly picked out of the darkness by the light of slowly falling rocket flares. As if he sees the same thing, he continues. "Hamburg is still back there, isn't it? The Gateway to the World?" A surprise question I prove not equal to answering, and remain silent. Must have seemed fairly dull (and drunk). While he continues to look out into the fog, I awkwardly declare myself allergic to anything that reminds me of the war. I can't escape the awareness that there was no point to that global conflagration. The constant thought that we were standing on fields of corpses and reconstructing exactly what led to them in the first place...

He gives me an ironic look out of the corner of his eye, nods briefly and, it seems to me, with astonishing cordiality, turns away, and leaves.

Almost at once, Scherping accosts me. "Did you talk to him?" Excitedly: "I think he's the author of the script I found at our friend

Gisela's place" (convulsive bleat of laughter) "and left there by accident. He seems to be for Nagel what Merck was for Goethe." (Interrupts himself and gazes up at me like a jackal)—"Okay okay, I know what you're going to say. I shouldn't go around parading my solid partial education, but if you would please drink a little less and look out a little more for the interests of the publisher, you'd go after that man. An interesting apparition. How else would his manuscript have ended up with Gisela? Fellow brothel patron." Another bleat of laughter.

I turn around and walk out into the fog.

Sentimental idea: Le grand Meaulnes. *Powerful urge to throw up.*

> For by thy words thou shalt be justified, and by thy words thou shalt be condemned.

Since S. has been coming to the house, a certain interest in me seems to have reawakened in Christa. "As if you had discovered," I say to her, "that an old hand-painted chamber pot can also serve as a vase for flowers." She doesn't answer. Her haughty little mouth remains disdainfully shut. She finds my comment tasteless. Correctly, I have to admit. A vulgarity from my school years in Vienna that I haven't been able to shake off. A cynicism born of opposition to the milieu of Uncle Helmuth, Aunt Hertha, Cousin Wolfgang, and Aunt Selma. An occasional fart to clear the air.

I'll leave aside the question of whether such means are effective in a marital situation. In any event, they're part of the chemical composition of the prevailing miasmic moods. You grasp at anything that could enrich the air you breathe, even the pinch of resentment that prevents a tepid resignation from precipitating out of sheer habit. Give us this day our daily drop of gall! It gives us a taste of how deeply the slightest error in the choice of spouse cuts into one's life. Especially ours!

Poor Christa! That I succumbed to the enchantment of the young equestrienne (the female edition of the standard bearer in *The Lay of the Love and Death of Cornet Christoph Rilke*? What an illusion!) in the canteen of the Fürth courthouse is all too understandable. How could I resist? What primal privation had led this pretty young woman to wolf down the canteen slop? It was terrifying to watch her stuffing it in, utterly preoccupied in chewing and swallowing, so completely absorbed in ingestion that her entire being had trickled into this process and only her sapphire gaze, glazedly turned inward, bore witness to a bewitched higher form of existence... It was enough to melt a heart of stone. But her? What delusion took her in? She was the victim of a much more banal misapprehension: if it wasn't going to be a prince from the fairyland of the Allied press corps come to rescue her from the humiliation of German defeat and a starveling existence, it might as well be her stateless mess companion under British protection. In any event, somebody with access to the heavenly delights of the PX (nylons, Hershey's chocolates!) and the cocktails and floor shows in the Grand Palace Hotel Excelsior (or whatever it was called). At any rate: "Something else for a change," as they used to say in her circles. Big mistake!

I could read this lapse in the eyes of the constant, ant-like trickle of her innumerable close and more distant relatives and friends—friends of her parents, friends of her youth, bosom buddies, friends of her friends—who came to see us in Witte's half-destroyed villa on the Elbchaussee. Hamburg is still a refugee center and transit camp for nobility from east of the Elbe who've once again managed to more or less survive or make a precautionary getaway; even today I still have occasion to read in the eyes of the Junkers my existential error. Most of the young gentlemen are somewhat injured—but I'm used to that from Nagel. He left an arm of his own in Russia, and I don't have to feel guilty for every amputee. Of course, the whole lot of them (like Nagel) are dripping with medals; all sorts of Knights' Crosses with and without oak-leaf clusters, all sorts of Iron Crosses and German Crosses in Gold, Close Combat Clasps, and Lord knows what else—but that's not all they have over me: I'm a *Homo novus* among them. Not just a nonparticipant in the war, but of dubious type and background. They quiz me accordingly. Christa doesn't come to my defense, quite the opposite in fact. She listens in malicious expectation. Regularly, a meaningful exchange of glances occurs between her and my interrogators, and from it I can deduce why most of her kind, including her, see me as "out of line." Whatever it is about my exotic appearance that they consider deceitful, or about what I say that sounds suspicious, is a downright provocation for Christa's social equals. They are tempted to dismiss it as a bald-faced lie probably in the service of some sort of swindle, a clumsy attempt to associate myself with an even higher caste, and moreover at precisely the historic moment when their caste is about to drown in current events—typical for some nameless, rootless sort without traditions, the opposite of fair play and never kicking a person when they're down. But who would expect fair play from someone like me? That was only to be found among their social equals. At any rate, no one knows me or anything about me, but they discover that one of their kind has married me in an unguarded moment and thus I've invaded the citadel of what used to be the Junker class, settled in without being able to show any document that would give me that right. Accordingly, suspected from the get-go of being a fortune hunter if not worse.

"As a Romanian you must have been in Stalingrad. You were our comrades-in-arms, right?"

"At the time of Stalingrad I wasn't a Romanian anymore."

"No? What were you?"

"You could call me a Russian, if you like." (Quick exchange of glances between the questioner and Christa.)

"A Russian? How so?"

"I come from Bessarabia and it became part of Russia in 1940." (Pact between your friends Ribbentrop and Molotov.)

"But you were living in Bucharest, right?"

"Yes, at the time. Shortly afterward, in Germany." (Exchange of glances.)

"Why weren't you interned?"

"We were comrades-in-arms!"

(Distraught look at Christa. Irony is malice.)

"And your compatriots, the Romanians—you just ditched them?"

"My mother's Austrian. So I was one of the so-called ethnic Germans."

"But nevertheless, you didn't get drafted?"

"No. I didn't get returned home to the Reich with other ethnic Germans, so I had a pass declaring me a stateless person." (And all sorts of other equally dubious papers.)

Christa locks eyes with the questioner. "You could have exchanged it for a German passport."

"Nope. In wartime you couldn't become a German citizen without being a German soldier. And vice versa: you couldn't be a German soldier without having German citizenship." (I could have added that, bastard that I was, I had no father to show either. I might not have been—God forbid!—pure Aryan, might even have been half Jewish or at least half Gypsy. After all, my mother's family was from Bosnia. But out of consideration for Christa I didn't say so.)

"And so?"

"And so I was a stateless person in a Germany at war and that's why I couldn't get out of Germany." (I could have added that thanks to Uncle Ferdinand, I was working as a multilingual interpreter in the Romanian embassy, armed with more than transparent documents that were, however, plastered with enough seals and stamps to awe the German officials. Nor did I mention that at the critical moment when my cover—my whole beautiful camouflage system—was about to be blown, I had, as it were, volunteered for the German Army—cynically, knowing full well that I could never be inducted. The Gestapo was getting ready to take a deeper look into my situation. But volunteering made me a hero on the home front.)

"And you just watched while others were putting their lives on the line?"

"For what?"

"Well really! For Germany, naturally. I mean, everyone for his ideals, of course. For Volk und Vaterland. For his traditions."

"I have neither the one nor the other."

"Right. Exactly. Remarkable in any event." (Drawn-out exchange of sympathetic looks with Christa.)

"And how did you end up in Nuremberg?"

"As a witness."

"Witness to what?"

"Murder."

"Murder *tout court*?"

"Murder *tout court*." (Somewhat paltry for Nuremberg, I admit, where if you couldn't testify to the murder of at least a couple thousand, you didn't even rate a spoon in the canteen.)

The questioner now turned to face Christa directly and look her in the eye. "What about you, Christa? How did you get to Nuremberg?"

"I was with Grandma." Blinking her round eyes. "She had to testify about Grandpa being executed for the Twentieth of July plot."

Head nodding sympathetically: "Did your grandmother know anything about your grandfather's heroic resistance?"

"Not much. She was too busy keeping house and running the estate. Canning and such. We were self-sufficient." (A paradise from which they were driven by the Russians, as everyone knew. A bitter fate. I could have added, moreover, that this was after the German comrades-in-arms had killed Christa's parents.)

The questioner, facing me again: "An interesting life you've led. And now you're going to write a book about it?"

"I don't think they're expecting a book about my life. Probably something else, I'm not quite sure myself."

(To be precise, Stoffel's expecting a story for a movie. What S. expects only he can know. In any case, his interest is what reawakened Christa's interest in me. Should I too perhaps abandon the mundane writing of film scripts and become a serious writer like Nagel?)

"Well, our sort could tell a story or two as well. How things used to be, and then the war, fleeing our old homeland, etc. . . ."

For the sharing of stories that follows I don't count. All I can do is listen and learn which of their close or distant relatives, acquaintances, friends of their parents, of their youth, bosom buddies, friends of friends from their good old lost homeland a few miles across the Elbe is still alive and who fled to where and found refuge or is still a vagabond looking for a place to stay. It's been just four and a half years since the end of the war and the refugee crisis is not over yet. ("You'd think that people of the same class would *eo ipso* show some solidarity. But surprisingly, experience proves otherwise...")

Christa says it was a piece of luck that we found shelter in Witte's bomb-damaged villa. Not of the same class of course, Witte, and not a Hamburg patrician either. Comes from a humble background, mother ran a little steam laundry, but by his own initiative he's joined the business elite. "It's a well-known fact that the old families of Hamburg councilmen were too proud to accept patents of nobility..."

> ...but I really did love her. It wasn't just being moved by her appearance in the canteen in Nuremberg or my deep sympathy with this fellow creature whose conscious sense of self consisted of nothing else than the almost forgotten pleasure ingestion and digestion produce in the alimentary canal—
>
>> as though the World Spirit could be fulfilled on its way through her maw—
>
> It wasn't just the German tragedy in her childlike face that tugged at my heart, not just the fairy-tale eyes and beneath them the small, tight mouth whose one end the conflicted tension between self-pity and arrogance forced to droop as steeply as Hitler's signature—
>
>> it was also quite concretely the beautiful, lissome young equestrienne with smooth skin and hair bleached bright by the sun of morning rides—
>
> and how does Schiller put it? "When I encounter a body I also see a mind."
>
> Well then! My mind has rubbed itself sore on hers, but that doesn't alter the fact that I loved her body with a love that is too large to end and so continues as hate—

> a gnome's love: *With hungered flesh, obscurely, he mutely craved to adore*

and I can't blame her for having higher expectations of me and being bitterly disappointed—

because except for my gnome's urge to clamber all over her at night whether she wanted me to or not, I'm an underachiever. The heavenly delights of the PX (nylons! Hershey's chocolates!) were abruptly at an end after I confessed to John that I intended to marry her ("Oh, well—my congratulations!" and not another word), and then in the following years of the harsh fade-out of the Ice Age in Hamburg, I let her starve as if I was the one who'd lost the war and personally responsible for the ice-covered condition of the world—

> the world around us, which lay in silence. But we blatherers in Nagel's garden house talked ourselves dry with cracked lips about our dream of the future, of at last reshaping this world to be good and beautiful and true

and the bitterest disappointment is that I am not reviving that dream, now that everyone around us is revivifying a dreamland of unfettered consumption.

> and yet I had so many interesting things to offer from the world of film (a friendship with Astrid von Bürger, for instance. *A Woman Plays Foul*). If I wasn't going to blossom out into a serious novelist, at least there was a lot of money to be made in film—

And how can I explain to Christa that the movie money, which (provisionally promised) I first have to earn before I get it (and thanks to the arithmetic of my swinish bosses will probably get only a fraction of, if any at all)—that this money is a much more dubious currency than the old reichsmark was; although it's sometimes paid out in hard deutschmarks, it slips through my fingers before I can hang on to a fistful—

and now S. is the sole bearer of all her hopes—S. and the book I'm supposed to write (Nagel's already gotten an advance on his third book; they say by now he has some gold bars stashed under his bed in Witte's garden house)—

I notice Schwab exchanging looks with Christa too. He comes to see us often now—that is, he "drops by" after visiting Nagel in his garden house. Nagel doesn't come with him. The gatherings of the primal community under the direction of Professor Hertzog (Hertzog with tee-zee, if you please) are almost legendary today. Now Nagel lives for nothing but literature: short stories, novellas, books, and plays for stage, screen, and radio. He's not on speaking terms with me since I stabbed him in the back with Stoffel in front of Astrid von Bürger. In his fury at that, he has left the Stoffel field to me. Even his passion for A. v. B. is snuffed out. Nagel, the super-grouch. If he still had his right arm he'd try to "bash my face in."

So S. and Christa glance at each other when talk turns to my past. But that has less to do with the fishiness of a "stateless individual of obscure origins" than with my fantastic stories and the tissue of lies that makes me doubly fishy. And yet that is exactly what I'm supposed to do from now on: tell fictitious stories about myself. In book form. S. is waiting for them. He spurs me on to tell stories, any stories, like a new Baron Munchausen. Even if it leads Christa to secretly take me for a confidence man.

S., on the other hand, admires my stories, my endowment of poetic inspiration. (Is he perhaps a bit envious?)

"Show us something from your magic box," he says and bores his Germanist's eyes, half-blind from reading, through inch-thick lenses into Christa's sapphire ones. They are always wide open, those round, bright blue eyes. When Christa blinks, her shining azure winks on and off like the blues on a police cruiser, but whenever her gaze plunges into another pair of eyes to seek and find agreement, no blinking eyelid extinguishes it for even a fraction of a second. It stays open and beaming, offering itself in crystal clarity, penetrating its object with superior knowledge of the truth. It's not the gaze of an augur, no, it's druid fire from the depths of the sea . . .

(And in its presence, me: a ragged Scheherazade, a fibbing Punch. How well I understand why S. has also fallen under her spell!)

The "magic box" is my only possession. The dowry I brought to the marriage with Christa; accepting it is the last thing she'd do. I've hung onto this box through all the perils of the last few decades: the prewar, wartime, and postwar years, through all my wanderings and escapes from inopportune surroundings and historic events drawing uncomfortably near . . . More by accident than on purpose, it's stuck by me. Whatever else I may have lost, thrown away, or squandered in deserts and depravities, Ice Ages and Ages of Gold, it has survived. No wonder Aunt Selma watched over it like a treasure; it was the travel case for the jewelry of her beloved sister Ilse who had gone (enviably) astray. The legendary "Maud." The high-class courtesan. Loved and spoiled by the most frivolously wealthy and powerful men of her day. A source of shame for the Subicz family (and of daydreamy reliving for Aunt Selma).

> Aunt Selma, the cart horse who knocks herself out to schlep the poverty-stricken Viennese household of Subicz descendants—herself, Aunt Hertha, Uncle Helmuth, Cousin Wolfgang, and me, the son of a whore—through our mundane existence. For an—alas!—all too brief interlude she has laid her hands in her lap. Uncle Helmuth and Aunt Hertha are "at work," he at some factory with gigantic machines, she in her moth-eaten music publishing company. (A university graduate despite being an underpaid employee, he has some claim to professional respect; she has double pretensions: by birth a Subicz and a von Jaentsch on her mother's side. "I kiss your hand, dear lady!" The bankruptcy assets of the Imperial and Royal Habsburg Monarchy readily absorbed into the lower

middle class.) Cousin Wolfgang, that model son, is at school like a good boy. I'm playing hooky (or have a cold, an upset stomach, or something else that releases me from the drudgery of that institution of public education). Between Aunt Selma's hands on her lap, on the coarse linen of her apron, lies the magic box. Crocodile leather, even then fairly well worn. It no longer contains any jewelry. Gone are Mommy's thick strands of pearls, her diamond necklaces, headbands, bracelets, jeweled clasps, her rings with solitaires—emeralds and rubies. Now the box is full of photos gradually going yellow. Aunt Selma and I have looked through them for the gazillionth time: the glory days of the deceased Ilse Subicz, my mother, who had given herself the showbiz name (*nom de plumeau*?) Maud. We spread the photos out before us as if they were solitaire cards: pictures of society events, gala dinners, balls, parties, and receptions, portraits of my mother, portraits of her beaus, snapshots from the daily lives of hedonistic idlers (beach scenes, tennis and polo matches, snowshoeing, casinos, masked balls). They are the visual catchwords of a legend that reads like a dime novel: A beautiful girl goes astray, lives life high on the hog, and dies young, leaving behind a bastard child destined for great things. As an artist he will come into her intellectual inheritance. Every artist had a whore for a mother. Aunt Selma weaves the backdrop for this saga. There's always something else to fill in, explain, place in the right context.

"Even as a child she was something special..." Massively spoiled by their father, my grandfather Colonel Subicz (he too was a legend, fallen in the very first days of the First World War), also spoiled by their mother, born a von Jaentsch ("I kiss your hand, Frau Baronin!"). An army brat whose reputation as a pleasure-loving beauty preceded her in every garrison to which the patiently starving Subicz was posted between Przemyśl and Ljubljana, rising through the ranks from cavalry captain to major, from major to lieutenant-colonel, and finally, decades later, from lieutenant-colonel to colonel while his three daughters grew more and more beautiful and the youngest most beautiful of all. "... and our father told her repeatedly, you're something special, not made to be submissive. You'll always dominate, give orders, have your way..."

And then plunged into penury: their father's heroic death, the hardship of the war years, defeat, destruction of the world of the Subiczes and von Jaentsches, years of hunger, inflation, and inexorably miserable existence. "She couldn't stand it, so she escaped..." (So goes the legend. In fact, the wicked girl gave in to her urge for freedom even earlier. I was born in 1919 so she must have already run off in 1918. John was serving in an international commission at the time. In any case, she ran off...)

Ran off into the "great life." Not, however, as a grande dame. Maud, the high-class courtesan, was presumably snubbed by the grandes dames of the epoch. But not humiliated. (Aunt Selma says that when Ilse-Maud was still a girl her mother, born a von Jaentsch and always careful to maintain social rank by speaking French to her daughters, had told her, "*Si tu continueras comme ça, tu finiras dans un bordel.*" To which Ilse-Maud replied, "*Peut-être. Mais cela sera toujours un bordel de premier ordre.*" (Notation in the margin: Caution! Cf. *Abel.*)

We weave the myth of the beautiful Ilse-Maud just as later, in the winter of 1940, Uncle Ferdinand would weave the myth of the "Middle Kingdom"...

... and so I too am resurrected from the pictures in the magic box, the princely son of a whore, soon to be the orphan boy in the misery of the Viennese starched-collar bourgeoisie, Stella's gigolo, and finally a castaway in the land of the lotus-eaters,

> who never had a real fatherland but was a prince in a childhood realm, a gift from god, cuddled and kissed by everyone—and one day forgotten, abandoned to the world of the lowly and disinherited

S. points to a Kodak photograph. "Who's this?"

"My mother on the Côte d'Azur."

"And the huge old coxcomb next to her?"

"Uncle Ferdinand. A Romanian prince." (Possibly my father. I don't say it, Christa does, with a steely blue gaze into Schwab's thick lenses.)

Undaunted, for decades I've been documenting myself with this box! It's a well-known fact that the camera lens doesn't lie. People expect me to perform my myth—and they get what they ask for:

"Here, this is a good portrait of my mother—beautiful, wasn't she? Yes indeed, ravishingly beautiful, especially the shape of her eyes, so pleasantly un-Germanic, not at all aggressive and round as a bull's-eye. The upper lid an arc soft as moonlight above the straight lashes below—as if the radiance shone anew each time she blinked. Max Factor turned out a whole generation of starry-eyed beauties in Hollywood with that trick. But in little Ilse Subicz, it was a natural gift, inherited from Bosnian mountain-farm women from the days when the Orient still ended at Europe's threshold. Thence also the sly wit in her glance, her irony... Ah well... and the curly head in her lap is me, of course. I must not have been much older than a year when—cute baby, no?"

(Exchange of glances between S. and Christa: it could be any old baby; they all look the same at that age...)

"The farm woman holding me on her arm? Probably a Romanian nursemaid. It must have been at Uncle Ferdinand's in Bessarabia in what's now Russia—or rather, in what was then Romania... To tell you the truth, it gets boring to give your birthplace when you have to supply an entire outline of Eastern European geography and history along with it—at any rate, it was geographically somewhere between the Carpathians and the Kyrgyzstan steppes, temporally between two orgies of cataclysmic hate, World War I and World War II. Between different worlds and times, as they say. But as you can see, when I was a little boy, none of that left any traces on me. For the first seven years of my life I was very happy, well bred, and well fed, very spoiled, very cheerful, and unselfconscious..."

—my earliest memories? Light falling obliquely through a large window, slanting across a bright room, even brighter than the sunlight outside, all bundled together in the words "summer happiness": it paints the four quadrants of the rectangular window onto the mirroring parquet, fragrant with floor wax, and sparkles in a hundred lights on the silver tea set—

On a console table, a big bouquet in a porcelain vase—

and outside, billows of lilac along the wall of the park—

the fragrance of freshly mown meadows—

and Mommy laughs and picks me up and kisses me—

the smell of Pears soap on me, dark as old beeswax; my skin is red from Miss Fern's unforgiving scrub brush—

Excursion: the bobbing rumps of the coach horses, notched like a peach. The parabolas of their coarse tails lift and from the rosettes of their anuses, opening iris-like, emerge apple-round yellow tubers that plop between their sweat-flecked haunches while the mallow-colored rosettes close up again with beautiful efficiency—

—my mother doubled over with laughter and imitating Uncle Ferdinand. He gives a lordly wave to the tenants stepping back respectfully into the ditch as we drive past. "*Bonjour, popor!*" (*popor* means people...)

—in my memory, the bearskin caps of the boyars in the portraits of Uncle Ferdinand's ancestors: I have declared them mine as well; I come from a princely house—

Miss Fern's hateful index finger snapping the hat brim I've turned down at a jaunty angle back into the circular brim of a child's hat—

—the viscous, dark blue sea beyond our garden gate on the Côte d'Azur, continued in the purple waves of the lavender beds; higher up, the clear contour of the coast, the hillsides crosshatched sepia and silvery olive-green, the cloud-blue mountains—

the swaying masts of the boats rocking gently along the pier, crossing one another in a symbolic fencing match: Japanese theater. Sky, sea, and coast all brutal spots of color: land of the Impressionists—

the coastal breeze rattles the palm fronds along the esplanade—

—white parasols, Panama hats, and blazers with gold buttons. We're on the deck of Uncle Agop's yacht. Uncle Agop lets me look through his telescope at a distant fishing cutter. I can see the red pompom on the fisherman's cap...

"But look at those trees in the background—no, not those. Those are cypresses and they don't grow in northern Bessarabia. There was a dense forest of them in Saint-Jean-Cap-Ferrat, where we spent the winter with Uncle Agop the oil tycoon, *we* being my mother, Uncle Ferdinand, my nanny Miss Fern, and me. At home in Bessarabia we were very near the Russian border. Only the Dniester separated us from the evil Bolsheviks. At night shots often rang out from across the river. We didn't think much of it. But we spent the winter on the Côte, and what I wanted to show you weren't the trees there, but the ones in our park at home, as I called Uncle Ferdinand's estate in Bessarabia. Here, take a look at these gigantic beeches—not those, those are plane trees. There were some of them in Saint-Jean too—or rather, in Antibes, in the garden of Uncle Bully Olivera's villa; Bully made his fortune in Bolivian tin and was another of my mother's devotees. She would easily confuse them, especially if you could see lions at the garden gates, because there were lions both here and there—I mean, in Antibes and also in Saint-Jean and at home in Bessarabia... I'm sorry I'm showing you all this in such disorder, but that's also how memory functions—if it functions at all. The selection of images out of the thousands of impressions we've experienced is as random—or inexplicable—as whatever it is that guides my hand to take a particular photo out of the box. All of a sudden, one of the countless snapshots our five senses have stored up, called forth God only knows how and by what, assumes profound significance—for example, the lions at the gates of all the houses my mother and I lived in. Mommy had a real passion for those slightly bourgeois doorkeepers. Uncle Ferdinand called it one of her "quirks." She had copies of Uncle Ferdinand's park lions made and gave them to Uncle Agop and Uncle Bully for their villas on the Corniche, marvelous examples of kitschy outdoor accessories if I do say so, although not the banal kind with plaster ringlets you see at the garden gates of small-town mansions. No, these were medieval and fierce, dreamed up by a local stonecutter who'd never seen a real lion. They were a cross between a dog and a giant tomcat in a powdered wig and fetchingly curled up mustachios above snarling mouths. It's a shame I don't have a photo of them, but we were so used to their being wherever we stayed that no one ever thought they were anything special except Mommy, who named and constantly renamed them after her lovers. If you could see through these trees here, you would see where they stood: in Bessarabia on top of the pillars of the wrought-iron gate beyond the bridge over the deep, transparent, darkly flowing stream, sparkling gold in sunlight and shaded by wondrously large coltsfoot leaves, water whose constant, strong current combed the yellowed swamp grass in its depths. It was as if they too were lined with gold, the bedroom of the beautiful Melusine. I would often watch the riverbank crabs crawling over it. In their armor they seemed like heraldic relatives of the lions, somehow connected to their passionate anger, the petrified fury with which those big cats sank their griffin claws into the blank shields they held before their wasp-waisted bodies . . . Yes, and then the stream emptied into the pond where my mother—but that's another story. Here's a picture of Uncle Agop's yacht off Monte Carlo—"

(By the way, these are photos Stella collected for me, amused by the acquaintances and friends she and my mother had in common without knowing each other . . . Would mentioning that increase my credibility? It would for S., but what about Christa?)

Schwab's rapt attention and Christa's long-suffering skepticism: if she wanted to, she could counter my myth with one of her own, a less exotic one, of course, but all the more tangible. Its guarantors come to tea on a regular basis and it didn't need to be documented picture by picture. Photographically it was already a new generation that shot its pictures from the hip, so to speak, in a habitual routine. That created a somewhat less emotional, less intoxicated background, which in Christa's case was no less grand, not at all: East Prussian lake district, the light and air harsher but clearer above golden waves of grain, the views more expansive, setting out fresh for bright mornings on horseback. And the view down the long suites of rooms in the castle, their walls also lined with ancestral portraits (ancestors documented and not merely imagined!). There were uncles as well, genuine ones, and aunts, all from the same family and not plucked from hedges and fences like mine. Legitimate genealogies, no gaps even in the prewar period. Aristocratic grandparents and progenitors, white haired and bent under the weight of their dignities and duties . . . Here too a park with giant centuries-old oaks—"and they strung up Grandpapa from the thickest branch . . ."

"Our kind doesn't make a big deal about it," Christa would say, if she ever mentioned it. After all, it's history and not some mythic land. Their flight before the Russian advance was interesting. They tried to get carried along in the retreating stream of Wehrmacht soldiers but couldn't keep up. The German retreat was flowing faster than the refugees could flee and the Russian tide advancing even faster... "Naturally there were marauders among the half-Polack populace and you had to hide from the Gestapo too; they stayed behind on the lookout for traitors' relatives—guilt by association, you know. So we traveled only at night in a wagon abandoned by the reserves, pulled by half-dead horses, and during the day we hid in the hayloft of any barn we could find. Uncle Heribert was terrified—he was well over eighty—and we made a joke out of frightening him: 'Uncle Heribert, the Russians are here!' And he peed in his pants every time! Lord, how we laughed..."

I concede that's more believable and true to life. I run out of steam: "No, the man next to the baby carriage isn't my father—why, do I look like him? because that's what many people say... it's probably just mimesis, a little boy's simian imitation. No, it's my uncle—all right, *so-called* uncle, on my mother's side, so to speak—Uncle Bully Olivera, the tin magnate from Bolivia, as I said—or hang on for a second—no, my mistake, it's Uncle Jean Fégonsac—sometimes I confuse the two of them; they look like twins in their polo togs..."

(S. and Christa exchange a look, S. visibly with a guilty conscience.)

And suddenly Christa makes a comment, which is rare. And even rarer, an ironic one. "There were a lot of them—the uncles, I mean—a disconcerting number." (S. stares at the floor.)

"You can say that again." I smile at Schwab. Little beads of sweat are shining on his upper lip, which trembles almost imperceptibly. "I have at least a dozen hypothetical fathers. For example, here's Uncle John—I told you about him already. Christa met him, briefly, in Nuremberg. He at any rate was my protector there, and was also one of my mother's friends, if you will. It was with his wife that I later—here she is: Stella—what a magnificent Semitic profile, eh?... in a dirndl, no less. For a while we were in fact living—adulterously—in the lake district near Salzburg—but that was already 1938... what I'm really looking for... here it is: me in my pony cart, at home, I mean in Bessarabia. Hard to recognize me, however"—

(Christa bores her eyes into Schwab's. He looks down like he's been spanked.)

—and I revel in his embarrassment. What's triggering it? Is it Christa's severity, her unassailably unpoetical standpoint? Or is it envy of my audacious self-invention?...

"The stern person next to me is my nanny Miss Fern... Gloves, yes, one wore them back then, even as a child, and of course, especially when driving a carriage—it sounds funny to you, but Christa can confirm that, at least... You wear gloves to set yourself apart and at the same time, as in handling the reins of a carriage, to have a finer feel of control.—But can you make out the background in this photo? There on the left, beyond the birches, must have been the pond—we'll find a photo of the entire thing soon. It plays an important role in the story of my childhood..."

"... and you don't know if she did it herself...?" Cousin Wolfgang's whisper is oily with curiosity—childish curiosity, the kind of primal curiosity about creepy, spooky, gruesome things that trickles down your spine and raises the hairs on the back of your neck... and what does he know of my distress at not knowing what happened, not having any picture of her death, only the nothingness her disappearance left behind, the hole in the world into which I've fallen...

It's black as pitch in our room—a servant's room in earlier times when this floor of the run-down apartment building hadn't yet been divided into flats for the lower middle class and they didn't have to live like proles—Aunt Hertha and Aunt Selma's constant lament. Uncle Helmuth grimly accepts it. He himself was one of nine siblings, the children of a pastor in Thuringia, so he has no sense of the bitterness of being déclassé. As a university graduate, his prestige is assured. His engineering diploma ennobles his jacket's threadbare elbows. Cousin Wolfgang has never known anything but this petit bourgeois fustiness. He was born in the General Hospital and was brought here almost as soon as the umbilical cord was cut. At least he had this room to himself for the first few years, the proud occupant of his own room until he was assigned me as a roommate, me, the bastard, the foundling in silk suits and high-button spats, an object of ridicule and contempt for the children of the back courtyards. I am the aura of pony rides through the estate park, of *thés dansants* aboard the yachts off the Côte d'Azur in which my mother, the beautiful and infamous Maud, was one of the brilliant queens... Me, bursting with fairy-tale stories I whisper in the dark to my fearful, philistine cousin...

It's black as pitch in our cramped room. Only a single thread of dim light penetrates through a narrow slit in the shutters and cuts a straight line across the blackness into the blackened blood red of the linoleum floor before climbing up the shit-brown dresser and breaking off on its white marble top... It's stuffy in our crypt-like bedroom, moldy as a grave: since it gives onto a light shaft it never gets properly aired out. We've inhaled the last bit of night air and lie in our beds under rumpled quilts, our eyes staring into black nothingness, all our senses focused on what we hear—

and so I can conjure with my whisper and banish Cousin Wolfgang and everything around him—Uncle Helmuth, Aunt Hertha, and Aunt Selma—into unreality, as if they were only a bad dream, and free myself from distress, the incomprehensible transformation of the world that snatched me from my bright, expansive, fresh, jovial, blissful former life and stuck me in this dull, narrow place—

can lend fate's cruel triviality a note of something intended by a supernatural force—wasn't my mother driven into the pond by a curse pronounced on her by higher powers that provoked horror in everyone. Even Miss Fern, who until then had cared for me like the apple of her eye, shrank back from it, brought me here, and departed as though she had to flee from me...

"This picture here is from much later." (The box isn't empty yet.) "An adolescent already, in my school years in Vienna. That frumpy woman between us—that is, between me the orphan boy and this ur-German youth here, my cousin Wolfgang, who looks so much like you—is my Aunt Hertha, Wolfgang's mother. What an impossible hat, don't you think? If there's such a thing as an unmistakable symbol of social status, then it's the hats of middle-class ladies . . . No, of course it's not India—very funny—it's the Palm House in Schönbrunn. I often went walking there alone, even when I was young . . ."

—And here I can ride my hobbyhorse and conjure life from the banal snapshot of an adolescent who's skipping school and wandering around gray Vienna, fleeing into the once feudal domain Uncle Helmuth calls "the Schönbrunn greenery." It represents the topography of his mythical land: a park! An extensive park! The home of his yearning . . .

genuine life experience—not pieced together from clippings out of long-since-lapsed newspapers, not a dime-novel land no one else would think to call home—

—Truth, tangible reality: a pavilion in the formerly imperial and now nationalized park open to the public (documented history, adapted to the spirit of the times) and in front of it, the adolescent in question, gray of face and too quickly grown, skinny, a poorly dressed child of the present—

(S. might be able to recognize himself in that image if his similarity to Cousin Wolfgang was not more blatant—)

—and the lad in front of the Palm House has something wolfish in his gaze, a hunger for life that's out of the ordinary, not to be fobbed off with bourgeois adventures in emancipation—

"And forget about the laughable *Steppenwolf* of your much admired colleague Hermann Hesse—have you ever read anything as ridiculous as his characterization of metaphysical starvation in the lines

> I'm Steppenwolf, trotting and trotting,
> the world is white as snow,
> a raven wings from the birch tree,
> and nowhere a hare, nowhere a doe—

Isn't that laughable? No, dear friend, even if such distress makes the tears roll down your cheeks—nowhere a hare, just imagine, nowhere a doe. What's left but to traipse through the world of philistines and find comfort in a group fuck? Self-discovery! Liberation! From what, I ask you? From starched collars and sleeve protectors? Ask Uncle Ferdinand or John if they ever felt such an itch. No and again no, honored friend, that was not my kind of wolfishness. The tropical world of a tamed jungle in Schönbrunn's enchantingly beautiful iron and glass palm pavilion is not a symbol for some world of adventure that I was missing out on and searching for back then like our friend Nagel, the round-the-world yachtsman. No iridescent parrot "wings" from the agaves, suggesting there's no aardvark and no gazelle for poor hungry Bingo, and for the time being no group fuck in the apartment blocks of Vienna's Twelfth District that could redeem his suffering soul. No, no, that was not the impetus behind my trotting and trotting (a Rilkean cornet hoofing it) through the lovely town of Vienna. My hunger was not for the usual needs. I was not hunting for my Tom-Dick-and-Harry-, my Jean-et-Jacques-, or my Ivan-Ivanovich-identity like your Hesse's Steppenwolf; nor was I after some lost paradise: Bessarabia and the Côte d'Azur were my inalienable possessions. What I was searching for was the *meaning*, you understand?—Back then, same as today, I was looking for the *meaning*."

(Consternation. Sweet revenge for their exchanging glances. I take my anger out by making them uncomfortable. If S. now looks at Christa, he's not seeking her agreement but trying to convince himself that she doesn't notice his confusion. She notices, of course. And what a joy it is to make her lose her stirrup too, as the equestrienne in her would have put it. The eager young man I'm presenting can't be observed from an ironically skeptical distance like the mythic little prince of my childhood years. The distress he suffers is a phase everyone is condemned to live through. Involuntarily, one goes through it with him in the recapitulation and S. and Christa wait fearfully to see how I'm going to chop this psychological state into pieces.)

First, a meticulous depiction of the milieu. S. doesn't know Vienna and probably imagines some Alpine version of Dresden, "Old gold like a stem of Kaiser's crown lost in a green meadow," he says. (Christa's sapphire eyes betray no inner image whatsoever, to say nothing of her parsimonious mouth. She'll agree with any cliché.) I drape their beautiful vision with tattered, grayish-yellow Habsburgian baize, moth-eaten to a filigree by the inflation, and against that background paint an autumnal late nineteenth-century Bruges. But in place of Beguine Sisters silently scurrying down deserted canyons still as canals between neo-Gothic palaces of finance, we have potbellied, goateed old Socialists in frock coats worthy of privy councilors marching in silent protest against the rise in the subscription price for public soup kitchens. From the darkly reflective windows of coffeehouses lined with plush smoke-stained as a meerschaum pipe, they are followed by eyes that clamber over the top of yellowed newspaper pages with the sluggishness of clock hands and after a wintery, flat trajectory sink back, unsatisfied, into their nests of printed letters.

I say, "Please don't believe what you hear: there, no 'quiet songs implore you.' It's dead silent in Vienna. Music needs sky to rise into, and there's no sky there. Above Vienna is a vault of iron and glass, a train-station ceiling over the Danube city that isn't even on the Danube but on a sewer-like side channel of that river of waltzing waves. The city's character is the inevitable consequence of this geopolitical situation. Vienna is the last exit on the Nibelung line, its rails petering out soon after Fischamend. To be sure, Germany's number two river of destiny was and is imbued with a tenacious attraction. Before and during my time, it pulled one Balkan-wards, and a correspondingly high number of expressive, artistic values had already drifted in the same direction. Schubert had long since transferred his activities to the Gellert Spa in Budapest; Haydn fiddled for the Telekis in Transylvania; Mozart—today en route to a long-term guest appearance in the Palestinian protectorate as a public-relations agent for the Bösendorfer piano factory—was at that time sojourning in the valleys of Kirtschaly where Richard Strauss cultivated roses. In the meantime, the eastward undertow of the cultural province had drawn Richard Wagner to the racially impeccable Linz, from where he directed operations. The Rhine Maidens, born in the Bohemian forest, built the Café Vindobona under the cast-iron ceiling of the Hauptbahnhof, much to the comfort of travelers to be sure, but unfortunately not to the promotion of the arts, as originally expected. Music, which rises, soon condenses on the volkishly antiseptic tiles and trickles down to coalesce on the folkloristic station mosaics to the tune of the Fiakerlied or the Radetzky March, or drains off into the Danube Canal in accordion chords of Schrammel music. The river swallows them in accord with its official duty as effluent drain, from time to time unofficially, at the end of the work day, and in pond-like aplomb, merely belching up a few bubbles of primal Viennese sound, the uatch-ewop-guop-shmoatz of a Heuriger song which, in strict adherence to the bylaws of the Schrammel guild, may only be performed by cleft palates."

I banish the last crepuscular sun beam from the imperial town, sweep its corners free of chestnut blossoms and countesses and expand the night, give it echoing room above its well-still waters whose stony banks I clamp together with the heavy clasps of the bridges. I weave mist over their dark depths in which the five pale stars of each embankment lantern float like milky, suddenly luminescent colonies of water lilies.

And for good old Schwab who listens with bated breath, right there in the middle of the mind thus prepared to accept it, I place an enhanced copy of myself (or himself?)—like the egg of an ichneumon wasp that will hatch a murderous larva—projected in perspectival regression back into the purer element of boyhood, of the pale water-lily moons of Endymion to whom was given eternal youth but not immortality... and yet we have passed the threshold to the next, less pure phase of life, afflicted by wild dreams. No longer is it the beautiful boy; it's me—me as I sit here like a Norn hunched over my magic box—but less impure of course, absolved of fourteen botched years of my life, not the twenty-nine-year-old of the here and now, Hamburg on the Elbe, in the half-standing villa of a merchant king—but rather *me* transported into the magic illumination of times gone by, purified in the mythic fountain of youth: orphaned prince of the blood, torn from the royal fatherland he has forgotten like a castaway in lotusland—a fifteen-year-old with my features, but ennobled and refined, a skinny adolescent with my character, but without the wolfishness, dreamy and bewildered, knowing and innocent, pious and disappointed and grieving from the beginning of time, wearing a wreath of Maytime confidence yet with dismay at the suffering world already in his eyes: a desperate lad in his thin schoolboy coat, driven out into the night by the bestial rectitude of his dutiful relatives.

Suicide? How could it be otherwise, I ask you! Of course it was a temptation, luring me into the canal's black mirror. With relish I tell how I clambered down the steeply paved embankment with the desperate intention of drowning myself, but comically afraid I might slip on the cold wet stone and fall into the cold water, afraid of the policeman up on the bridge whose dumpy silhouette (together with that of the man he was inaudibly talking to), surrounded by a bloodless aureole, dug a dark hole in the thick fog glowing in the light of a streetlamp—a double hole, since the plump, lightless volume of the cop cast a large reflection into the foggy light. The silhouette was thus transformed into negative space: negative space of negative light and its pale echo; lightless, hollow pattern and its material reverberation as light. Yet both are weighty: weighty the dematerialized core of negative light and the husk of etiolating material light, weighty-unweighty in padded, cylindrical volumosity; the thick winter coats of the two men bulging rollers of negative light with handles of bulging roller-sleeves, raised up on bulging pant-leg pads; the dachshund on a leash frozen hard as iron, a sausage-roller; the policeman's cap a sausage slice on top of a sausage wheel; the man's Tyrolean hat a sausage-end; the breaths of man and cop a sausage bubble finely integrated into the crackling light, blown delicately as glass into the Christmas Eve glimmer of frost-heavy fog, breaths united in a cloud of rime. (Of course, I hadn't eaten anything all day, just roamed around against my Christmas Eve yearning in the mirrored lights of the canal; of course, I was sick with hunger; of course I was cold in my thin little coat...)

And then, the other thing, compacted of deeper, more formless and sinister darknesses: a blackened double creature at the base of the bridge arch, something indeterminable lying heavy and motionless on the footing, and indeterminably joined with it something uncertain bending over it and preparing to—what? Murder it? Shake it awake? Throttle it? Rape it? Copulate with it?—And no way for me to escape: impossible to scramble up the slick blocks of the embankment, impossible every step backward on the narrow ledge... (rising from the water the crypt-like breath of cold putrefaction)—

—and the roller-policeman on the bridge turns—swinging his overcoat-roller around its axis, taking leave of the roller-man on the bridge who raises his sausage-end and is dragged off by the dachshund-sausage at the end of his iron rod—he turns and strides off weightily, growing smaller as he disappears into his endlessly increasing light echo—

(—and I feast my eyes on the entranced, despairing childlike eyes of S., his empathy for my—his—suffering, the boy in distress; his pained poet's eyes that envy me, the liar in his glory—)

—and me at the bridge arch, chilled and feverish in my thin schoolboy's coat, my pale young face taut with cold, the pounding of my heart in my temples, my breath hammering on the anvil of my larynx, planted in my tracks, driven like a thunderbolt onto the narrow footing of the embankment with stringy mandrake roots of fear, trembling with every soundless step of the retreating policeman on the bridge—

—I stood and, with the bird of my fear violently fluttering against my chest and eyes, held *my guilt* captive—my guilt for everything happening to and around me, for what was going on there in the darkness at the base of the arch, for the cry I never uttered that did not bring back the policeman, for my intention to drown myself, and for the fact that I never would drown myself, the guilt in me for everything the monstrous body of night was pregnant with—indecipherable, uninterpretable, unspeakable.

Driven onto the embankment's footing by the trip hammer of my heart, trembling at its every beat, I glued my eyes to the pregnant belly of night, riveted my gaze on its dark fruit, hoping to eviscerate it, to decipher the indecipherable, interpret the uninterpretable, suck speech from the unspeakable . . . the meaning, the MEANING . . .

And in S.'s hand, the involuntary gesture of resistance, of overtaxed patience . . .

Since he doesn't know what else to do, he says in a mockingly forced falsetto, "It really happened that way?—Or did you just this minute make that all up?"

I'm exultant: "You're trying to persuade me to write a book, no? So what'll it be? Ideally something after the heart of your boss-man Scherping, right? Something for the series *Truth Is Better Than Fiction*? Maybe the refugee tale of one of Christa's relatives and friends—the good old days and what happened to them. At your service: I can do that. Get it off my chest. As we all know, the poet sings just like a bird: today—splish!—deign to lend your noble ear to my humble song; tomorrow—splash!—onto the great guano pile of world literature. Why not give it a try yourself? You're hatching a book plan in your head. I can tell by looking at you: you're not making notes every second for nothing. Well then, what's holding you back? Juvenile literary retention out of respect for the false idol Art? Because creating is valued more than plain reporting? But then where does that leave friend Jean-Jacques Rousseau, whom we both so admire? Still on his pedestal? Because it doesn't depend on what you have to say, but on how you say it, namely, as self-sacrifice. As a butcher's counter of author's ego-entrails, and the reader as haruspex . . . You see? So you've got to leave me a little room for embroidery too. Content's easy to come by. If you're coming up a little short, feel free to borrow some. What's mine is yours. The main thing is that the report retains its confessional character—just like in Master Jean-Jacques. This is just for your ears, dear Diary—and leave the print run to Scherping. Whether it's authentic or not concerns at best only the arch-idiots of literary history. What does 'authentic' mean, anyway? Don't try to tell me you didn't see yourself in the boy who wants to drown himself in the Danube Canal! You, the Endymion of pale water-lily moons in the black-mirrored water that terrifies and attracts him... 'From the starry pond the angler pulls a big, black fish, face full of cruelty and madness'—right? You, the congenital orphan yearning to go home to the womb of Death until a good citizen holds you back with the words 'Life is beautiful!'... You're asking me if I really experienced what I was telling you? But of course I did: I experienced it—in your eyes. You experienced it for me while I told it. Isn't that authentic? Take something authentic from my magic box: that picture we looked at and you thought was me—and the camera lens doesn't lie, as we know—here it is. Actually, it's a picture of my cousin Wolfgang who looks so much like you he could have been your twin. Does it matter at all that he was in Vienna and you were in Hamburg at the time? This picture—if I may—is *you*: the strapping adolescent with the blond thatch and fabulous grades and glasses so thick your eyes look perpetually astonished, with young man's fuzz on your upper lip, a pimply chin, calves with more than fuzz, and a cowhide briefcase which—thanks to misplaced sandwiches and damp swimming trunks—has taken on a disagreeably cheesy smell that announces the model student's return home from school, soccer field, or organ practice in the chapel when he's still coming up the stairs, a little out of breath under the load of pounds of books, every one of them a thick, crabbed tome containing pure intellect—is that a portrait of me, of you, of Cousin Wolfgang, or simply the image of a prototype, the stereotype of a social situation? Unfortunately, I never had the honor of knowing your honored Papa—he was a German professor, wasn't he? Beg your pardon, a classicist—but I seriously wonder if he wasn't in the depths of his being any different from Uncle Helmuth. In him, in Uncle Helmuth, you have the stereotypical father of the stereotypical son—

"Take a look at this engineer's face marinated in active spiritualism. It could be included in the natural history collection of every middle school, but it wasn't among the visual aids in mine in the Thirteenth District of Vienna—included as a deterrent, I mean, a catastrophe of the West: the millenarian engineer, slide rule in his vest pocket, *The Foundry: Handbook for Engineers* in his bookcase, a disciple of Madame Blavatsky, Teutonic knight under the command of Jörg Lanz von Liebenfels, who believed in the renewal of the world by Adolf Hitler... Your honored papa the classical scholar probably didn't. On the contrary: he probably detested that popinjay with the artistic lock of hair falling across his forehead, but the category is the same: bourgeois fathers—John had a nasty name for them: '*bloody fucking middle class*'... and here, by way of comparison, another of my so-called uncles, Sir Agop Garabetian, the oil billionaire in a thousand-and-one-nights getup aboard his yacht off Cannes. It perhaps gives you an idea of the simultaneity of various worlds and of the reversal of environments I was exposed to at such a tender age! It bewilders the mind, my dear fellow. One struggles to unite such basically dissimilar realities, but it only works with the assistance of the imagination, and in the process, the authenticity of events becomes of secondary importance.—Here, take a look. Yes, that's me as well. I admit, it's an almost unbelievable transformation. The metamorphosis of an unkempt schoolboy into a Bond Street dandy—Stella's doing—here we are in Stella's car. In the summer of 1938—so already after the so-called Anschluss of Austria—we were still cruising around the Salzkammergut and surroundings in her open Hispano-Suiza—that's right, she always wore a dirndl to go with that Old Testament profile: Sarah, Esther, Rachel... as for the Nazi stiffs, the car just took their breath away; a miracle of elegance, already almost ten years old at the time, from the absolutely best era of automobile manufacture—what lines, eh? And the thing ran like a gazelle. Too bad we didn't know each other back then. It would have been such a treat for me to go speeding over the Grossglockner Pass with you—whereas you once told me your Volkswagen had to sweat even to make it over the Geislingen Pass in Swabia... of course Cousin Wolfgang, the son of his father, turned down an excursion in that vehicle of the Jewish plutocracy... And now let's look a little further. Look how what you call authentic reality develops by leaps and bounds: this is a miserable photo of me with my "Teterist" buddies—comes from T.T.R., *Tânar cu termin redus*, the official designation for the one-year volunteers in the Romanian army—so me doing my military service. No, not in the war. God forbid!—I have to confess I misunderstood the zeitgeist's charge to my generation. While my buddies marched straight off, heads held high, into a wonderful vision of the future and the open graves it contained, I turned on my heel to look back and understand what had happened, what was actually happening... to grasp its *meaning*, you see?—the sense that all those things were happening in order to be *said*—you understand what I'm saying, don't you? The sense that it would never have happened if I didn't say it—can you already see it in the way I look in this photo? Move your finger a second—yes, that's me: third from the right in the standing row. The one with the wolfish gaze, in honor of our colleague Hesse! Nevertheless... I told you about the wolf in Bessarabia, didn't I?... What became of my Viennese relatives? They were all buried in the rubble of a bombing raid in 1944: Aunt Hertha, Aunt Selma, and Uncle Helmuth all together. Cousin Wolfgang had already died a hero's death for Volk und Vaterland three years earlier."

Embarrassed silence and uncontrollable agitated movements as after an unpleasant coup de théâtre. S. huffs uneasily. Christa's blue lights tinkle solo. Her little mouth is disdainfully shut. Once and for all.

At night, took out Nagel's *Craterland* again and read it into the gray dawn. Some depictions (returning home) excellent. Very vivid scenes of combat. Fundamentally different from what I experienced under the hail of aerial bombardment: the illusion of being able to influence fate. ("The wise man smiles.") His depiction of people, formulaic; of human relations, disarmingly naive. I found myself getting angry about it. I had expected him to produce something better than what I could have done better, even with my left hand. In one of my ugly moods I wrote a poem about Astrid von Bürger. The tombstone of our friendship. All the more shameful because it's a shame it's over.

Draft:
He's been invited to dinner at Witte's. The reason why is undoubtedly Christa: she and her East Elbian entourage are an extremely convenient avenue for Witte to procure an entrée into the Holstein aristocracy, possibly even to Bismarck's descendants in Friedrichsruh ("civil pride before the thrones of power!"). And in fact, among the guests is—along with Rönnekamp and just as queer—a Count Lentzau-Wilmersbüttel, doubly interesting because on his mother's side, he comes from a patrician Hamburg family (the Timermanns, with two *m*'s, as opposed to the proletarian Tim*m*ermanns with three). Everyone else present is only family. A niece among them deserves special mention, a widow (husband fell early, in Poland) with a pair of fourteen-year-old twin daughters. Witte, magnanimously presiding at table, drones out praise for the "valiant commitment" with which the mother got herself and her children through the difficulties of the war and the still greater difficulties of the postwar years without masculine protection and support, all the while seeing to it that her daughters received a perfect upbringing. "To have achieved what you did, my dear Helga, you owe wholly and completely to the ironclad rigor with which my beloved sister, Wilma here" (she sits facing him at the other end of the dining table as ersatz lady of the house, bolt upright, ice-gray bob, a schoolmarm's steel-rimmed spectacles) "raised you, according to family tradition, in the spirit of our unforgettable mother, your grandmamma" (that presser of gentlemen's fine undergarments), "who never let us get away with anything either. If even the smallest thing was not as it should be, she said: Children OUT!—" The word isn't yet fully articulated, its final, explosive *t* yet to sound, when the twins leap up and start to leave the room in lockstep. Everyone calls them back amid general hilarity. No, no, Uncle Witte didn't mean you (this time). He was only showing how things were when he was a kid. Obediently the twins sit back down.

There are other children at the table, the youngest among them showing signs that the traditional rigor of a Witte upbringing was not as ironclad as it had been two generations ago. A particularly cheeky little miss insists on telling them a riddle. Witte—obviously it's a favorite niece of his—gives his permission. The child blares, "What's the difference between a squirrel and our head teacher, Herr Müller?" Everyone pretends to ponder this question seriously; at last they ask for the answer. The girl merrily crows, "The squirrel has a long, red appendage and Herr Müller doesn't." A second of shock, embarrassed silence, nervous clearing of throats; then someone (probably Rönnekamp, glancing imploringly at Count Lentzau-Wilmersbüttel): "Can anyone fouch for zat?" The girl's mother feels called upon to reply with dignity, "The child means on the backside, of course."

For dinner there's eel soup, a Hamburg specialty. Piping hot and fatty, it's prepared only in the summer, unfortunately. Served with Rhine wine. Conversation wanders from one topic to another—that is, everything that comes up here or there is taken up by Witte and dispensed with apodictically. The Economic Miracle, for example: Rönnekamp (cynically) voices the opinion that it could be attributed to the Allies' stupidity. "What did you expect? If you bomb a country flat and then equip" (he says "eekvip") "its rebuilt industries with the most modern machinery, it'll outstrip other countries with their out-of-date paraphernalia." Witte sends a shot across his bow, "But without our German work ethic it wouldn't be possible. Machinery isn't everything. What counts is human material. I'd like to see if others could do what we've done if we'd ironed them flat." Once, Witte's sister Wilma joins the conversation. They're talking about the revival of horse shows. Count Lentzau-Wilmersbüttel describes with indignant giggles the outfits of the farmers' sons who jump the course these days (and admittedly, perform equestrian miracles) instead of the gentlemen jockeys of bygone days. All the more shocking are their violations of etiquette, especially when one is trying to rebuild social life. "Instead of a riding stock, these people wear white bow ties as if they were going to a farmer's wedding. And then, you don't see any properly made boots anymore. These people wear rubber boots with their red coats!" Lying in wait, his giggle breaks forth with a highly indignant snort. One of Witte's younger nieces, obviously emancipated, declares that boots are a Freudian symbol. "Boots? A Freudian zymbol? How zo?" asks Rönnekamp incredulously. Aunt Wilma's stern warning can be heard from the lower end: "Not at the table, if you please!"

(Attention! *Abel!*)

Vergangenheitsbewältigung—coming to terms with the past—is also brought up. Now Rönnekamp gets on his soapbox, frequently seconded and supported by Witte. For all his affected Sherlock-Holmesian coldness, even Rönne can't completely conceal his indignation. It is directed at the falsification of history now under way with the apparently universal assent "of every Tom, Dick, and Harry." It's not a question of the fact that every single German claims never to have been a Nazi, although the number of former Party members stands in "appzolutely ap*pal*ing contradiction" to that claim; that, says Rönne, is all too transparently an act of cowardice and lack of character, in a word, of opportunism, and nobody believes it anyway. It is indeed a historically misleading falsification. What caused it—and, if one will, what even excuses it—was the depiction of National Socialism as being from the beginning the embodiment of everything evil and inhuman. At first, National Socialism did not appear to be a criminal movement at all. On the contrary, it was full of promise. (Witte: "Absolutely right!") The violent acts of the early years were just part of the times. The whole epoch was a priori inclined to violence. So bands of marauding SA men beating up opponents were the excesses of a rowdiness potentially lurking in any human community and especially virulent at that time. If their violence took place with the overtly malicious assent of many people, that was attributable to a population generally coarsened and embittered by the aftereffects of the First World War; the collapse after 1918 was much more harrowing than after 1945. "Back then, after the shock of the first genocide, the old order was destroyed from the ground up." (Interjection by Witte: "Very true! The citizenry was completely disoriented!") "In the meantime, from 1919 to 1939" (Note: John says those years were just a ceasefire in the same conflict), "no stability was created. On the contrary: every damaged institution that continued to exist was robbed of its last shred of"—shrett off—"credibility." Again, Witte agrees: "Totally congruent with what I've always said." "It's patently obvious," Rönne continues, "that in such an epoch of uncertainty and the re- and devaluation of all values, the promise of order had to strike a spark, no matter who claimed to produce that order. Of course, the Reds didn't do that. On the contrary: their program was to continue the destruction of the old capitalistic system. So only the conservative forces remained." (Witte: "Just like today!") With the diabolical element at the heart of every political manipulation, Rönne says, the National Socialists understood just how to present even the excesses of their goon squads as a service to the restoration of order.

With cutting irony, Rönne defends himself against the suspicion of being a fellow-traveler: "Now you can probably guess that I had no reason to love the Nazis—although" (a coquettish sidelong glance at Count Lentzau-Wilmersbüttel, mother a Timermann with two *m*'s) "there were some pretty gorgeous boys in those chic uniforms, especially in the SS . . ." (General chuckles of understanding, tactfully suppressed: when the lock of hair makes the man, you have to speak the truth in dulcet tones.) But with a sudden return to intellectual seriousness, Rönne continues in an almost passionate voice, "What people today suppress" ("Vat beeble today subbress"—as Rönne gets more involved, you forget his knotty Baltic accent) "is Nazism's irresistible seductiveness in its early stages. Its timeliness." Now Rönne is speaking with the razor-sharp clarity of a master sleuth analyzing a case. His audience is enthralled by how his incisors drop shut and get readjusted. "Besides their idiotic party platform consisting of nothing but half a dozen barely comprehensible slogans like 'smashing the feudal system' and similar nonsense, the Nazis were ready to catch every current of the times. Meanwhile and quite independent of them, the promise of a new world order was in the air in any case. The Bolsheviks were promising one too. In this general proliferation of ideologies and utopias, the Nazis had all sails hoisted for every wind, especially the wish for a reform of every aspect of life, from health sandals to Teutonism, from tarot card reading to phrenology, from Coué's autosuggestion to Sylvio Gesell's 'shrinking money.' Everything and everybody needed to be—and wanted to be—reformed, rethought, renewed—it's not as though that was dictated to the people from above." (Witte: "Ex*act*ly. Nobody forced us into anything!!!") "It took root and thrived in everyone's mind." The epoch's expectations of life and hope for the future were virulent in every individual. And despite the obvious trend toward mysticism and arcana in this evocation of the future, the belief in the rational progress of technology remained unshaken. It was technology above all that would liberate humanity from the drudgery of their former blind enslavement to work." Rönne waxes lyrical. "It's almost impossible today to imagine the strength of that trust in the coming of a new world era. Today, we no longer harbor any hope. Quite the contrary: we look bleakly into the future. Especially threatening is the promise technology holds. Even optimists live from one day to the next as if traveling through a tunnel: it's possible we'll emerge, but no telling when. In the years after 1918, it was utterly different, and you've got to grant that fact to the poor stiffs who followed the pied piper Adolf Hitler. The so-called weltanschauung of the Nazis, their philosophy and ideology, was larded with promises that played to the needs of those poor saps. Because they suffered privation during the inflation—déclassé, plundered, unemployed, starving—and intellectually starving because the traditional ideas meant nothing to them anymore—they wanted to take part in the creation of a new reality from which everlasting injustice and everlasting suffering were excluded."

Rönne now turned to me. "In your gatherings in our host's garden house, dear chap, you and your young friends—especially your fraternal buddy Nagel—used to knock together all sorts of utopian models. And if all that was—if you'll pardon the expression!—almost touchingly irrelevant, it wasn't just on account of the hopelessness that followed the terrible disappointment every German—Nazi sympathizer or not—had to feel after 1945 at the collapse of the general expectation of salvation. It emerged from the spirit of the times as well. It wasn't just the Germans who had been bled dry, it was the entire world, the times. You and everyone around you were too anemic to produce anything new from the German world lying in ruins. You didn't lack for noble intentions or spirit, just for an impulse from the zeitgeist. It had been the zeitgeist of the still-young century that like a bowstring had launched the arrow of National Socialism, and although its tip was poisoned and flew into the eye of the bowman, the audacity at the heart of the ideology had something infectious. You're going to say it was a cynically misunderstood Nietzscheism, exaggerated to the tipping point. Agreed. A mortally dangerous field of thought to enter, but watered by arch-Occidental springs, out of a need for order and purity on the highest intellectual level. Already expressed, if you will, by the wishful thinking—widespread at the time—about reviving knightly orders—what Ernst Jünger and Hermann Hesse have in common: the dream of selecting the most highly developed intellects to brew up an alchemical concoction, the essence of all Western thought, out of which would precipitate the philosophers' stone, a monastic elite of unheard-of intellectual freedom" (Witte's interjection: "Right! I'm with you one hundred percent!"), "which elite, however," (with subtle sarcasm, Rönnekamp purses his razor-sharp detective lips while his teeth remain obediently in place) "—and this reveals the cloven hoof of Nazi thought—would forgo any pretention to power. Obviously not the case with the Nazis." (Witte, subdued: "That's for sure!") "But even the blatant thirst for power—i.e., in a conception of power as a necessity in the service of an ethos—was a temptation that was hard to resist. The individual in the onslaught of the masses: that was the idea, to be defended against the dissolution of individuality in the distorting mirror of Leninism. The Nazis wanted to do something audacious: salvage the individual in Socialism."

Witte's sister clears her throat as if to suggest that the monologue was depressing the mood of this social gathering.

"And the decisive thing," Rönne continues in Baltic indifference, "the thing that distinguished the forerunners of the National Socialist ideologues from the crude revivalists of early Christian ideas in the era of mass culture, was their aestheticism. Even the promise of order—from the highest intellectual level of the last of the knightly orders right down to the trivial obsession with the political and moral housecleaning of corruption and perversion and every variety of dissident and minority—all that had more of an aesthetic than a moral character. Aestheticism was a basic characteristic of the epoch's sense of the world. 'Strength through Joy,' 'Joy through Beauty,' etc., slogans everyone endorsed; just think of the choreographed masses in Moscow as well as Nuremberg: pretty, club-swinging lads and maidens—the new humanity was blond, strong, and beautiful. The unbeautiful was denied the right to exist. Hence the silent agreement of just about everyone on the extermination of the Jews." (Witte again, robustly: "*Jawohl!* That's how it was!") Rönne smiles and continues. "But these are subtleties that the flat-footed, polemical ignorance of present-day historians doesn't get into. Both sides work to falsify what happened, both the prosecutorial standpoint of former pacifists and the guilt-denying standpoint of the Germans themselves. Both pillory the evil of National Socialism as an ideological project and not, as would be more appropriate, its execution by the filthiest of the minds it swept up. Hitler, Göring, Goebbels at the tip of a pyramid of criminals and ghouls, based on the worst petit bourgeois resentments—that's not the only thing that's meant by National Socialism. And that's why I wish someone would correct the conception widespread here and everywhere: it wasn't the Nazis who were responsible, but the greatest enemy of all humanity: stupidity. The Germans weren't led astray by a group of conspiratorial villains like children by the Pied Piper of Hamelin; instead, the German philistine with his well-known musicality composed the most sublime, poisonous, and seductive flutings of the zeitgeist into a march, and marched off to his own perdition in stalwart lockstep. A perdition, by the way" (with an eloquent gesture that comprehends the sumptuously set table), "that ironically enough seems to be turning into salvation."

Awkward silence around the table, broken after a while by Witte's sister Wilma with the brittle sentence, "I don't think you can call Hermann Göring a filthy mind." (His peccadillo: art theft. Speaks for his good taste, doesn't it?)

Report from Nuremberg:

Sentencing. Although everyone knows what the verdict will be (and the rationale for it will be much more important for the significance of the proceedings), tension is at a peak. All security precautions have been doubled. Every entrance and exit to the Fürth courthouse is being guarded by heavily armed units. Fürth's Palace of Justice is bristling with weapons as a bulwark against an attack by unarmed, edematous Germans. The nucleus of the place, the small hearing room in the center of the gigantic hive, is full to capacity with VIPs from every faction. The accused are fetched from their cells individually and led in through a barred walkway like big cats into the caged ring of a big top. First comes Göring. He's wearing the togs of demobbed camp kapos and Gestapos: a civilian jacket, jodhpurs, and high boots—but the jacket's a festive silver-gray. The general field marshal's trouser stripe on his jodhpurs is a bloody red. If it were not so full to bursting, his double-breasted jacket would look as elegant as a gigolo's. His boots are as soft as a Krakowiak dancer's. (Eerily enough, it'll become the standard getup of the black marketeers who survived the death camps.) Göring enters the room as self-confidently as ever, emanating unmistakable irony. Relaxed and in mocking expectation, he looks toward the judicial bench across the room where Englishmen and Americans in carelessly donned robes, Frenchmen in the bat-wing sleeves of Daumier's lawyers, and Russians in field jackets with epaulets stiff as ironingboards are staring at him as if he were a poisonous insect. Lord Justice Lawrence rises to read the sentence. Göring puts on the headphones that connect him to the glass-enclosed chatterbox of simultaneous interpreters. Lord Justice Lawrence reads a long, formulaic sentence that ends with the words "... condemned to death by hanging." The last word "hanging" rings out in the deathly stillness like the crack of a whip. Göring shrugs his shoulders and points to the headphones. Some disturbance in the line: the sentence has not gotten through to him. One of the guards standing next to the defendants' benches in a mirror-bright helmet and parade uniform hurries to fix the defect with his praetorian mitts sheathed in white cotton gloves. After some fumbling around he roughly prompts Göring to listen better through the headphones. Lord Justice Lawrence repeats the sentence. Again, the words "death by hanging" snap through the packed room where everyone is holding their breath, and Göring—by now obviously amused—again shrugs his shoulders: he still can't hear anything. With a grin, he hands the headphones to the praetorian guard. The hulking fellow kneels down, red in the face, and fiddles with the cords under the bench, then gives the headphones back to the recalcitrant Göring, still deaf to his death sentence. For the third time, Justice Lawrence repeats the sentence, "... condemned to death by hanging." Now Göring dispenses with his irony. The equipment is still not working and as a former pilot, he's interested in finding the problem; he kneels down next to the perturbed guard and fiddles with the connections himself. As the nerves of all those present are just about to snap, with the patience of Job Lord Justice Lawrence reads once more, "... condemned to death by hanging!"—and behold, Göring's intervention has worked. The connection is restored. The news has reached him, the headphones have functioned. And Göring beams. The news has reached him: "condemned to death by hanging!" He pulls off the headphones, slams them onto the bench, turns on his heel, and disappears down the walkway. Next, please.

I declare that I have a name: Aristides Subicz. Subicz from my unwed mother; Aristides from one of my many potential fathers. (Aristides Blanc, the operator of the casino in Monte Carlo? Also one of Mother's lovers? Possibly. At any rate, a close friend of John's.)

By the way: Johannes Schwab. Also fits very well. Remains to be seen if I can conceal myself behind it.

At Home

From the 1821 travelogue of Count Karaczay: This region, bounded by the main branch of the Moldova, the Dniester, the Black Sea, and the Danube, consists partly of gently rolling hills, but is mostly level and extremely fertile. It constituted the province called Bessarabia. The principal town was Kishinev, the seat of a princely clan ruled by Benderli Ali Pasha. Before the Russian invasion of 1807 under General Mayendorf, Bessarabia was inhabited by Volga Tartars who migrated here in 1568. They cultivated the soil, raised livestock with especially great success, and were known for their honesty, kindheartedness, and bravery.

In the warm seasons of the year, the land suffers from drought. The valleys are marshy and full of reeds. There is no woodland, not even scrub growth, and a bushy grass called burian as well as reeds are harvested, dried, and used as fuel. Winters are very harsh.

Under the general name Government of Bessarabia, Russia has incorporated this country into its empire and the little town of Kishinev, not far from Dubasari and almost exactly in the middle of the country, is the seat of government. Bessarabia is bordered by the Wallachian Moldova and thus constitutes a Romanian region despite its separation by the Pruth River. It is administered by Greek princes, the so-called Phanariotes installed by the Turks. The Moldavian peasants are of sturdy stock. The men wear linen shirts, long trousers, and wide leather belts; in summer a white or blackish-brown jacket made from a material prepared by their womenfolk, and in winter sheepskin coats. Their hair is cut short and their usual head covering is a sack-like cap of lamb's wool. In rainy weather they take their caps and stuff them between their shirt and belly, where they also often keep their lunch, which always consists of a sort of polenta of cornmeal (called *mamaliga*), and then pull the hood of their jackets over their heads. In summer, the apparel of the women often consists of a simple smock with a light belt, and a white kerchief on their heads. Sometimes their underskirt is replaced by a striped apron, usually of black wool, tied around the waist. This apron is sometimes tied with a narrow wool belt, usually of a bright red color. Their chemise is long, reaching almost to the ankles, very close fitting, and of a fairly fine, well-bleached linen, made at home of fine-spun yarn and often interwoven with stripes of cotton or silk threads as decoration, and always embroidered, often very richly. There are no unembroidered women's chemises among the peasantry. The embroidery is of silk, and sometimes spun gold and silver or even glass beads are worked in. The primary embroidery is on both shoulders and always at least a hands-breadth wide. In addition, two stripes run left and right down the entire chemise and on the sleeves one often finds many straight and slanting embroideries, and frequently red and blue flowers as well. The white kerchiefs on their heads are even finer than the chemises. They are the masterpieces of the women's handiwork. They are usually white and often embroidered with colors, with very tasteful decorations worked in along the edges. The way they arrange this kerchief on their head without a mirror and even without pins is a tribute to their good taste. It covers the head more or less like a nun's wimple, but without stiffening or constraint. Its ends hang down somewhat and are secured at the throat and halfway down the breast by a number of clever folds. The free ends are usually thrown over the left shoulder. One sees women and girls thus attired coming to church or into town, but also working in the fields. Especially when the weather is cold, some wear a sort of sleeveless vest of silk material usually trimmed with a narrow band of fur. Their bare feet are a striking contrast to this quite fetching costume, especially when it's muddy. Only on holidays and in the winter do the women put on boots of strong yellow morocco.

The apparel of men of elevated rank is extremely costly and very Oriental.

The Moldovian and the Greek shaves his head and wears the red

Turkish fez pushed forward. His undergarment is of costly silk, and the wide gown with open sleeves reaching only to the elbow is of the finest English cloth or costly Persian wool or silk.

His undergarment is belted with a genuine shawl, of which he has dozens to choose from, worth 100 to 200 ducats each.

His head is covered by a light, padded cap of gray lamb's wool representing a Turkish turban, or frequently by a shawl wrapped very much like a turban, so that at least from a distance, one could take him for a Turk. Scarlet red Turkish pants and yellow slippers of morocco with soles of the same leather complete his attire. The love of fancy clothes appears to be widespread, and an aristocratic boyar may well show himself in the course of a day in two or three different outer and undergarments, one more elaborate than the next. The rich wear costly furs, usually sable, but only in the winter; by contrast, a man of the next lowest class will wear a very wide, short-sleeved Oriental outer garment, usually of silk lined with ermine, all year long.

The fairer sex has a lively, fiery temperament, very susceptible to feelings of love, and clinging to the beloved with burning passion, no sacrifice too dear to preserve his affection. However, one would be making a great mistake to think that this high emotional energy was a source of sensual error or excess. On the contrary, these tender and passionate creatures possess an extraordinary degree of restraint. No matter how powerfully their spirit is convulsed, their exterior always maintains a calm and dignified appearance and anxious modesty accompanies all their actions. But alone with their lover, they surrender themselves all the more completely to the storm of their long-suppressed passion.

In the highest echelons, one finds individuals of the most refined customs. Both men and women are fluent in the French language; many even speak German, and some boyars possess not inconsiderable libraries.

BESSARABIA, WINTER 1939

Uncle Ferdinand speaks of last things:

"From physics, we're all familiar with the law of conservation of matter. Now, this raises the question: What is included—or not—in the concept of 'matter'? Water is matter even if it's converted to steam. Every gas is still matter, quantitatively measureable, even if it's very volatile. So that must allow us to assume that completely dematerialized materials—so to speak—also exist in limited amounts, even if they're so dematerialized they can't be measured by the means available. What I'm talking about is the soul. In our Christian faith, it too is a substance inhabiting the living body, which it leaves when the body dies. You can see that in the frescoes of monastery chapels, but not just there; it's also expressed in the fact that at the head of graves in burial grounds of very early times, they erected poles, not crosses: tall wooden poles and later stone stelae, as the first thing the soul just escaped its body could shinny up, so to speak. And what's more, they planted trees nearby, as though souls were birds that could perch in them. You get the impression that the soul of a recently deceased person first had to become accustomed to the new element of freedom after departing the cage of the body. I mean, it can't just take off at the drop of a hat. Many can't do it at first. Instead, they flutter around nearby for years or decades—some even for centuries, if you believe the ghost stories you've heard—but time doesn't make any difference to them. They can haunt the place until we've become spooks ourselves. Personally, I myself have never encountered a ghost (leaving aside my first wife, but at least she was still alive, even if really terrifying). However, they say that Putzi Cottolenghi actually moped around for years after he died. They had to sell the house, one of the most beautiful palazzi in Ferrara. He's said to have behaved obnoxiously and already fallen out with his entire family while he was still alive; they were furious with him because of the inheritance—or rather, because there wasn't any—he'd spent it all. But despite that, I don't believe in spiritualism and the kind of humbug you told me about in your Viennese relatives, or what that Nostitz woman was up to in Vienna and God knows who else from society in other places. They all fell for Blavatsky and she was an out-and-out fraud—that's been proven in the meantime. But what I wanted to say was this: it can't be that easy to sum up all the souls of the dead. Just think about it: since the beginning of mankind—and that means for millions of years, as science has now shown—souls are supposed to have left their bodies and floated around freely in space, billions and billions of souls. Now I ask you: even if they're dematerialized and not a measurable substance, there must be something there that's released and then accumulates somehow. Our churches teach that the soul first goes through purgatory and then to heaven or hell, and you can see that too, very vividly depicted, in the frescoes of monastery chapels and in primitive art in general; but even if you think of the Kingdom of God—I mean the one in the hereafter, right?—as being infinite, it seems to me there's a hardly believable quantitative discrepancy. And the stuff's got to come from somewhere. It can't just renew itself on its own from age to age. Don't misunderstand me: it's conceivable, and even quite amusing. It would be a genuine *perpetuum mobile*, an energy constantly giving birth to itself, breathed into all living things and then liberating itself from them. But not only does that conjure up the idea of something present from the very beginning—an insubstantial ur-substance, so to speak—I don't mean to call it GOD; that would be sacrilegious; the Creator stands on the side, so to speak, observing himself. But I mean, that's exactly what argues against that substance arising from the void and becoming more and more and more and returning back out into the void... That would be nothing more or less than a blasphemous image of the Creator as a creative void. I don't mean to say that. On the contrary, I consider God to be an extraordinarily efficient engineer, at least as far as his creation Nature is concerned. There, everything is most minutely interconnected and proceeds in constant circulation—yes, of course, help yourself to more cognac. Don't wait for me to offer or even pour it out for you. That's what it's there for. Or would you rather have some calvados? It's very good. I got it from Fégonsac.—No, thanks, no more for me... Where were we? So the observation—right?—that everything runs along in an eternal cycle, nothing gets lost, everything fulfills its purpose—all that led me to the idea that that's also the case with the substance—if we can call it that—of our so-called soul. I mean, the Indians think of it that way in metempsychosis—the transmigration of souls—or rebirth, or whatever. For them it's simple: the soul that becomes free at death remains homeless for a while (but as I said before, time plays no role at the level we're talking about) until it slips into some other body, and I'm of the opinion that that's what happens. Mind you, the new form it takes is not verifiable. Take Putzi Cottolenghi for example: once he'd croaked to annoy his family, he wouldn't be reborn as his niece's dachshund or anything like that. Or take my first wife, bless her soul! She wouldn't come back as the operetta soubrette she always wanted to be. But instead, as substance, as a part of the universal inspiriting substance, whose amount would thus remain constant and plugged in to the eternal cycle. That explains a lot, for example, the fact that today, when there are millions more people on earth than in times past, much less of the substance seems to be in the individual than before. You need only compare some desert prophet with—let's say—my overseer, who's a very competent fellow. Of course he steals, they all do, but as a person he's simply an oaf. And just in general, wherever you look, they're a miserable lot nowadays. But naturally, that can lead to the incorrect hypothesis that because there were only a few people on earth back then, each individual automatically had received more human substance than the likes of us, so a Neanderthal, for example, must have been a much more valuable person. Of course, there are differences. It isn't all equally distributed—but if you're tired, go ahead to bed. It's only—what time is it anyway? Three thirty?—So if you need to get to bed, go right ahead..."

Note:
Nothing can be learned about Uncle Ferdinand's whereabouts. All that's definite is that in 1940, when Bessarabia had to be ceded to Russia as part of the Hitler-Stalin Pact—Aristides was a Romanian soldier at the time and had retreated across the Dniester with his

regiment—the prince refused to leave his house and estate. It's assumed that the Russians transported him to a camp as far away as possible, probably in Siberia. Not even John managed to find out anything definite about his fate. For his part, once back in Bucharest and provisionally demobilized, Aristides takes advantage of the lack of clarity about his background and, with the help of Stella and John's connections, remains there for a while until they succeed in shunting him off to Berlin to keep him out of combat. (Stella's role in Bucharest: a Romanian Jew but married to the English diplomat John; once Romania enters the war on Germany's side, she has to leave Bucharest. Soon thereafter, her crazy attempt to meet A. in Berlin.)

Trivia:
A.'s attitude toward money: After the bitter penury of his school years in Vienna in the care of his relatives, Stella teaches him to spend money without a thought; docilely he falls back into the frivolous extravagance of his childhood milieu, cares as little about the relative value of money as about where it comes from. He loses it too, casually, just like his mother misplaced or lost pieces of jewelry. (A childhood memory: John tosses a string of pearls into the lap of the beautiful Maud. "Here's something for you to lose.") Perhaps in closing, a reflection on money as the deity of today, the only true religion of the West. It determines contemporary life to the same extent as, for example, religious faith did in the fourteenth century. Every offense against money is a sacrilege and gets punished more severely than anything else.

Sylvio Gesell's "shrinking money": could that have been a topic of conversation in Nagel's garden house?

Handwritten:
. . . what exasperates Scherping is a common misunderstanding caused

by my unfortunately large and ungainly appearance. (Is it so completely separate from what's "essential," however? And what would the latter be?) Carlotta calls me "the *starosta*," but that doesn't fit; I lack the necessary charisma. My "aunt" sees it more accurately, if all too poetically: I'm like the surface of a bog pond that doesn't disclose how deep or shallow it is. Indeed, I know what I owe to that fact: without lifting a finger I'm able to dramatize myself. And after all, I've got anguish to spare. All I have to do is open the sluice gates and it surges over me. To more or less save my skin, I need to mobilize the beast in me, the "wolfish nature" I ascribe to A.: the sheer bestial will to survive. In the end, it drags me out of seething despair and saves me—all too reliably, however. And so I practice a deception to fool myself: a cold, pacified despair that gets staged to give the hysteric in me a playing field where he won't be in immediate danger of collapsing into himself. (A.'s ironic smile and shrug as wishful thinking that may not be so unattainable.) At any rate, my insight into this ploy is irritating enough to drive me to the nearest bar. (Most drastic experience at the front: a bottle of cognac while under fire from Stalin's organ pipes.) Paradoxically, I can only get free of myself when I—as here—project myself onto a piece of paper.

Nagel encounters God (from the novel *Craterland*):

. . .

She strokes my empty sleeve. "But you can still feel in your stump that you had a hand with fingers?" The precision with which she expresses herself fit with her Slavic accent.

"Yes," I said. "I feel as though I could move them if they were still attached."

"And when you think about the Virgin, can't you also feel something of what you felt for her as a child?"

"I'm a protestant, Ljubenka. A Lutheran. Or at least, I was. Today I'm not that either anymore."

A shadow passed over her face. Quietly she asked, "What about

God? You did believe in God before He—as you put it—got shot down, didn't you?"

"Unfortunately, He was shot down. In bursts of fire that took off my arm and a couple hundred of HIS chosen people too."

"And Jesus Christ? Do you believe in his gospel of love?" Her hair was touchingly blond.

"I believe in Jesus Christ as a revolutionary. The leader of a revolt of the poor. Like Gandhi."

"And his suffering for us all? His death on the cross?"

"Gandhi was murdered too."

"You don't believe the Savior freed us from guilt through His death?"

"Did He? Is that what your monsignors tell you? Why don't they teach you to see in his crucifixion the incurable bestiality inherent in all humanity—"

"Unless you believe in God's mercy," she gently interjected.

"God's mercy? Where've you been living, girl? Did you forget the mass grave your parents and siblings are lying in? The backhoe they used to fill it in when you weren't sure they were really dead?"

I was pitiless. I wanted to hurt her because it was tearing me up. I didn't care about the tears streaming down her cheeks. The paler her lips got, the more painfully I wanted to wound her. "God's mercy that allows a madman to drive millions into unimaginable misery and a wretched death. Just look around you! It's already been two years since the war ended and God stands by and watches the bellies of newborns swelling with edema. Was that the point of the sacrificial death of his only son? The crucifix as a symbol for the cynicism of the Allfather Creator..."

She put her finger on my lips so slowly and gently I couldn't push it away.

"Don't talk anymore. Come with me!"

She led me to her bed. On a stool she used as a nightstand were some books; a half-burned candle was stuck into a drinking glass.

My senseless anger melted away in the sweetness of her embrace... at some point it seemed like she whispered into my ear, "Believe me, God is merciful!"

Trivia:
His eyebrows knitted in extreme concentration, holding his breath, and delicately probing his incisors with his tongue—he files his toenails.

Sketch:
An official banquet at Witte's—not in the family circle, no nieces and grandnieces, but only his sister as ersatz lady of the house; instead, a senator for culture with his wife and a university professor (also wifed up), whom Rönnekamp—acting even more queeny than usual (one has the impression he would sizzle if you touched him)—identifies as an important art historian. A. has the audacity to remark that unless you're a Worringer, art history as a field combines exceptional learning with the convenience of never needing to have an idea of your own. He hasn't reckoned with the man in question being able to hear him—which he does—and A. gets a correspondingly poisonous look. For the rest of the evening he remains monosyllabic as usual—and here, it's obviously advisable—until Christa, who always gets unexpectedly lively when she's had some wine (Witte, encouragingly: "Drink up, my child, it's an extraordinarily good vintage"), during a conversation about the problem of form which almost everyone is taking part in, prompts him—A.—to describe an idea he'd monologued into her patient ear at home. A., whose thoughts have in the meantime strayed far afield, at first has a hard time getting oriented. At once, the art historian stridently challenges him to come out with whatever it is he has to say on the topic of "form." A. protests that Christa seems to be referring to something else. He's never talked about the problem of form in art, which he knows nothing about (interjection of the professor: "Oh really? But I thought..."), Christa was probably thinking of what he once said in reference to the condition of German society after 1945. "And that would be?" That would be a few things about the astonishing persistence of traditional social forms, levels, and groupings even after their supposedly complete destruction.

He's asked to elaborate. Wasn't it remarkable, he said, that in the

Germany of today, 1950, despite all the social leveling already brought about by the First World War—to say nothing of the Second and the lean years until 1948—one finds the same stratification of classes and social prestige as around 1914, namely, an upper nobility still deeply revered despite its stratospheric distance from everyday life, an also admired but less lofty aristocracy, a compromised and disoriented middle class guiltily conscious of its status, and then the mass of all the more self-confident petits bourgeoises. (Here Christa, already fairly sloshed, interjects a mocking "My husband is especially familiar with the highest circles; that's where he grew up," which Witte gallantly seconds "... and also married into. Prost, dear lady. *In vino veritas!*")

Rönnekamp remarks suavely that however anachronistic they may be, the miraculous reconstruction of German social classes is explained by the national talent for competition—especially in exaggerated imitation.

Lacking an ear for Rönne's irony, the art historian demands an explanation of that too and Rönnekamp points out how rapidly the Americanization of the country is progressing, while at the same time there's a tendency to manufacture traditions at any cost. "Nowadays when you enter a house of the nouveau riche, you'll find a lot of family portraits on the walls, supposedly great-grandparents from the nineteenth century if possible. Regrettably, however, the Anschluss is missing: no grandparents or parents. They remain obscure." (Witte's sister clears her throat.)

A. watches Christa and feels an urge to pay her back for her snide comment. "If my esteemed spouse had the occasional goodness to listen closely, what I was trying to say in my monologue about the restoration of social structures might not have sounded so new to her. Its very specific character, I mean—"

He's interrupted by the combative art historian. "You aren't seriously claiming we have a class system in the present Federal Republic?"

No, says A., he wouldn't want to claim that even as a joke, although paradoxically—as with everything nowadays—it would come dangerously close to being the truth. In any case, more interesting than the appearance itself is what it produces—(again interrupted by a sharp "Namely?"). "Namely," he says, "the peculiarity that informs the national character like a specific crystallization informs a mineral. Whatever structures the Germans develop (and this is a truism, by the way) have a telltale signature—"

"And what would that be?"

"Philistinism," says A.

"Philistinism? What about our cathedrals? What about Dürer and Riemenschneider?" exults the art historian contemptuously, looking around for applause, especially from the senator for culture—

"I'm talking about social structures," says A. ("Isn't art a social structure?") "Philistinism doesn't preclude grandiosity," A. declares. "It's quite capable of rising to that level, as it does in Riemenschneider's case." (Witte's sister, outraged: "Well, I never!"... She too looks toward the senator in charge of the cultural desk.) "Moreover," continues A., "we were talking about rebirth—or rather, the reinstitution of anachronistic societal values, which even if they are similarly preserved in other places, seem especially absurd in post-1945 Germany. And not solely because they're the most idiotic, shortsighted, destructive way of processing the rubble." (Witte's sister: "That's out-and-out Communism!") "No," says A., "but you've got to try to imagine what's going on across the Elbe in the head of a citizen of the other, communistically organized half of Germany when he picks up one of our illustrated weeklies and skims the three pages devoted to an article about the wedding of Princess Ilsebill von Hüblingen-Kreutznach-Hinterstetten with Count Wurmfried Wölflingen-Hassenroth. He really can't take it seriously—I mean, if he's someone living so close to present-day reality that willy-nilly, he has to see it—and isn't blinded, like us, by the eyewash in the Americanized media."

"But blinded by other eyewashers," Rönnekamp corrects him. "By the way, we mustn't overlook the fact that the ladies and gentlemen in the *Almanach de Gotha* have to shill for a brand of sparkling wine."

"That would make it even more amusing," A. concedes, "if it didn't plunge me into despair."

"Oh well," says Witte, "it's the same old figures of fun: the petty prince and the grenadier of the guard. They were already degenerates in the old days."

"No, no!" A. protests more vehemently than he meant to. "That's not what makes—or made—them comic models of remoteness from real life. If being a fool and even sheer stupidity were funny, we'd never be able to stop laughing and we wouldn't need any help from them. It was always the specifically German thing about these lower ranks that made them more ridiculous than amusing—their philistinism. It infects even the highest circles in this country: their inveterate pomposity, bigotry, unworldliness, and absurd self-regard. And all that's been carried over from the frozen, foggy hell of the Quonset huts into reconstruction and the Economic Miracle as a sort of structural legacy." He turns to address his adversary directly. "We're missing an art-historical epoch, my dear Herr Professor. We got tripped up in the rigid forms of the baroque. What we lack is rococo: the graceful form of being able to laugh about things..."

What am I saying? What nonsense am I banging on about? I wanted to score one against Christa and her clique and once more got carried away, masturbation with my spouse, again and again! Why do I let myself get sucked into jabbering about culture? Please don't listen, Herr Senator, just follow the course of the contest and my probable defeat. I presume you also regard the situation as a kind of sport: conversation (one of the delights of life, says Goethe) as a duel—Bang! That'll show the guy who's boss! Not a game in which one person catches the ball of another and throws it back, with every catch a reward for all the players—probably the only person here one can talk with is that boozer Schwab...Why the devil am I letting myself be interrogated like a naughty schoolboy—it's the teachers who produce the philistines in this country, the inbred dyed-in-the-wool schoolmasters—

A memory from the war: An air raid in Berlin, 1944. One side of the street is on fire. At the first building, air raid wardens have ordered people into a bucket brigade. Full buckets are being passed hand to hand from a hydrant on the corner up to the edge of the conflagration and the empty ones are passed back to be filled again, a pathetic undertaking. The water steams away before it ever hits the fire, but the dazed citizens, ragged figures with raw hands and eyes white in their soot-smeared faces, mustered from their cellars in the neighborhood, continue their irrelevant firefighting efforts undeterred while the air raid wardens bellow senseless orders and brandish their service revolvers. Above the roar of the fire stoked by every puff of wind, a constant murmuring and whispering can be heard: "Here you are, Herr Professor!"—"Thank you very much, Herr Professor!"—"Here you are, Herr Councilor!"—"Thank you very much, Herr Councilor!"—every time a bucket passes from one hand to the next—"Here you are, Herr Doctor!"—"Thank you very much, Herr Doctor!"—A bomb falls nearby with a mighty crash and a woman's voice screams, "My God, that was more bad than the last one!" A male voice corrects her, "In the first place, it's 'worse,' and in the second place, that's no reason to interrupt the bucket brigade!"

—and then there's the opposite type: the buddies from the primal community—yes indeed, we always circle back to the laughable, pitiful, wonderful, primal community in the Nagel-Witte garden house, a pack of repeat survivors, wan from hunger, scruffy in worn-out clothes, eyes bright with childish confidence and cheeks flushed with turnip schnapps and enthusiasm for the good, the true, and the beautiful after the hell they'd been through, inflamed by the sacred will for the new, the better, purer, greedy for everything intellectual . . . and their beautiful utopias: We set up a kolkhoz, get them to allocate us a former parade ground, work together digging unexploded ordnance out of the ground, and plant carrots and cabbages and potatoes in its place. In the evenings we come together with clammy, numbed hands and bent, aching backs for a Hegel colloquium or to listen to Pachelbel and Hindemith on the radio while the womenfolk weave our home-grown flax into diapers for the collective brood, the germ cells of a new, natural society dedicated to culture, a German model won from the bitterest experience of defeat, humiliation, insight into our guilt, and self-recrimination ... (to be sure, the womenfolk—right, Niemöller old friend?—the womenfolk, who live solely through and for their uterus ...)

(Quote from a 1942 speech by Hitler, speaking about the times of struggle at the beginning of the movement: "... and, my comrades in the Party, whenever you were almost convinced by the arguments of our opponents and felt yourselves starting to waver, it was the German Woman who sprang up and simply shouted them down ...")

The womenfolk, right Willy? They wanted to get down to brass tacks! (Christa: "You'd do better to find me some bacon grease instead of guzzling schnapps with your crazy friends!")—soon, ah so soon we had to thank them, the womenfolk, for the insight that the chance for the kind of unblemished new beginning we were imagining was lost, untenable from the get-go, the childish, sweet, foolish plan of our naiveté, the battle against the termite power of the philistines lost a priori, the perseverance of the myrmidons in their eat-in kitchens and allotment gardens, our visions laughably anemic compared to the tenacious vitality and swaggering pretension of the petit bourgeois and the petit bourgeois narrow-mindedness of the upper and middle classes, compared to the burgeoning life in the pelvises of their womenfolk—

Although they're all tattered and underprivileged, they're equipped with the invincible energy of eternal strivers, constantly clambering over one another, eagerly struggling up the chicken coop ramp of traditional hierarchies—If you would be so kind, Herr Head Official, many thanks, Frau Head Official, if you would be so kind, Herr Assessor, many thanks, Frau Assessor, if you would be so kind, Dr. So-and-so, Many thanks, Frau Doctor, if you would be so kind, Herr Professor, your devoted servant, Herr von Krautjunker. Frau von Hinterstossen, *Küss die Hand*, Frau Baroness, an honor to meet you, Count So-and-so, Countess So-and-so, if I may be allowed, Your Serene Highness...

all of it the precipitate of the spirit of schoolmasters, the essence of their promulgations, slicing with ice-crystal hardness into our visionary Ice Age, our naive Christmas at the crèche of the promised future, the spirit of schoolmasters a gift from the Byzantine East, conveyed by Professor Hertzog ("Hertzog with tee-zee, if you please!"), first of all to make us aware how unseemly our behavior was: disheveled hicks just barely liberated from the army and the prison camps, roughnecks tramping—so to speak—with bare feet (although some, like our dear amputee Wilhelm Niemöller, with only one) into the salon of higher education—yes indeed!—in order to clap the titans of Western thought on the shoulder with rough-hewn familiarity, feed ravenously from their golden plates and drink from their crystal glassware and mingle our cowherds' voices in their grandiose monologues and dialogues—

shouldn't our women be ashamed of themselves right down to their fallopian tubes? Especially Christa...

Willi Niemöller, yes, the very one. Naturally, he drew the conclusions and simply took off. Of course, he had nothing constructive to suggest for the problem of the "new" societal order we were seeking, but he represents at any rate a lovely example of individualistic independence. He did put down on paper his insight into the genealogy of the schoolmasters, if not in the form of a novel like Nagel. Years later, around 1950, a postcard from Vienna arrived with a picture of the restored St. Stephen's Cathedral. On the other side, it read—

> My landlady also had a swine
> who got along with Freud just fine;
> for all sorts of reasons—
> in vaginal and anal seasons—
> now it snuffles psyches.
> Cordially, W. N.

A folk poet, a genuine German...

A. is surprised when Witte takes him aside after dinner. "Very interesting, what you had to say about problems of social structures. Could give a new direction to my advertising department, as Herr von Rönnekamp suggested. What we need are young people with ideas. Why not drop by day after tomorrow, Thursday the ninth—okay? Thursday is the ninth, isn't it?—so drop by my office at eleven sharp."

He's my opposite in every respect: light-footed where I'm lumbering, elegant where I'm dull and average, suave where I'm awkward, nimble where I'm clumsy. He's at home in any milieu but identifies with none, speaks every language, puts a good face on everything, isn't intimidated by anything, and is always relaxed, with the *nil admirari* attitude of a sophisticate. Where I'm cold, he's fiery; where I get excited, he stays cool. He's indifferent where I'm sentimental, and soulful where I'm apathetic... He's also proud, but from a sort of humbleness, not from hubris—

in a word, he's the spitting image of the me I dream up in literature.

Painfully awkward argument with Scherping: All of a sudden he finds our expectation of having made a literary discovery in A. if not unfounded, then at least exaggerated. "Take for example that treatment—right?—the one that I, uh, you know..." (suggestive bleat of laughter), "...what I mean is, it may well be that in an—emotively speaking—somewhat overheated environment, it struck me as something extraordinary—and you felt the same way, you've got to admit—anyway, on a second or third reading, it seems a bit thin to justify the assumption we've discovered some goddamn genius." His gaze becomes restless as it always does when he senses an occasion to expose his real or imagined weaknesses (a strange sort of exhibitionism not mentioned by Sacher-Masoch). "Once again, of course, proving myself the lowbrow you rightly think I am, but I'd like to stress that I became a publisher—and not a potato dealer—from a certain higher aspiration. And although I may be below par intellectually, at least I don't want all my motives to be seen as simply those of a business type focused solely on profits, even if I don't neglect the financial part. With all due respect to great literature, it seems to me we shouldn't invest blindly in something that at best holds promise of talent but with a fairly uncertain ending..."

The objection I raise (morosely, I admit) is that in the meantime, I've had the opportunity on several occasions to become convinced of A.'s brilliant mind and extraordinary powers of observation—moreover, A. himself doesn't regard the treatment that fell into our hands by such a peculiar accident as a sample of his talent. He says it was a playful attempt to present the producer Stoffel with something reminiscent of the era of Expressionist film ("National-Socialist Ufa Studios Star Astrid von Bürger as the Bride of Dr. Caligari"), a joke he played to see how the spanking new mogul of the silver screen would react. Besides, we have other examples of his linguistic agility and after all, the sum I suggested as an advance is not exactly earth-shaking—in short, all my bubbly efforts to defend my plan to lure A. into writing a book (which I'm very vexed at my obvious difficulties articulating, due to a heavy dose of gin and tonic on top of too much Allonal) is only water for Scherping's mill. Not without sardonic asides about my condition ("Do you think it's wise to smooth out your psychic ups and downs with self-administered substances? Or should I put in a good word for you with Professor Hertzog? The fellow has a great deal of sympathy for alcoholics") he gives me a lecture "about the new situation in the publishing trade—in case all of us who still believe in the book as a means of education and communication—but also as the noblest of pastimes—don't want to go miserably belly-up."

Namely, the situation has changed drastically. ("You see that even I am following your fellow poet Gottfried Benn by recognizing it.") We are approaching the dawn of a new age of bookselling, "in which belles lettres, what the Anglo-Saxons call 'fiction"—you follow?—so, mainly novels, will to a great extent take a back seat to nonfiction, reportage, political analyses, celebrity memoirs—even literary criticism, philosophical essays, and similar kinds of what may strike you as bullshit from your seat astride Pegasus's saddle." (I have to struggle to conceal my trembling hands; what's especially embarrassing is that in a "situation" like mine, my thirst becomes unbearable in the face of his hectoring. He seems to notice and gets even more lathered up.) "Don't be blinded by the current fad for reading. You've got to cater to people's need to make up for emotional lost time—are you with me?—especially vis-à-vis that old standby, love as the axis of the novel—with special circumstances, for example, the experience of war, as confirmed by the success of Nagel's books. But in the long run that'll probably also turn out to be old hat—actually, it's already been old hat for ages." (Suddenly, he lowers his voice.) "Unless of course—" (his face assumes an expression of vulpine cunning) "one approaches the subject from a somewhat more interesting point of view—I mean, love as a primal experience of pain." (Another explosive bleat of billy-goat laughter.) "Because there's one thing you'll be good enough to concede: I may be a bumbler in Logos, but I've earned my spurs in Eros."

(The only thing I suffer from anymore is his language, the slipshod, unkempt words swept up from all the dusty corners of what's possible to express, the practically sleepwalking semantic assurance with which he nearly but not quite hits the nail on the nose—it's almost seductive, insinuating itself into my thinking and corrupting my language. Involuntarily I imitate him and have no idea how to express myself better.)

I stopped listening quite a while ago. Together with a furious increase in my need for another long drink (I'm dying of thirst. It's eleven o'clock in the morning, so still two hours to go till I can get out of here and into the nearest bar), I'm bowled over by the truth: Scherping is right that in fact, there is no guarantee that A. is capable of writing a serious book—or even intends to write one at all. I realize what drove me to suggest that Scherping give him an advance—and an unusually big one too. I am moved by Christa's fear. She's no longer up to living from one day to the next without the least prospect of even a minimal regular income; she's sold the last pitiful remnants of the girlhood jewelry she saved from the Russians and her relatives are impoverished themselves. She would be too proud to ask them for money anyway when she already has trouble deflecting their mistrust and unconcealed dislike of A. She defends him with less and less conviction, her arguments sounding increasingly lame. She regards his scriptwriting as a frivolous game and so does he. Aside from the fact that it always involves so-called "projects" that never come to fruition, the amounts that the producer Stoffel pays for a treatment are laughably measly and slip through A's fingers before he has time to recall that Christa doesn't live in the same "holy frivolity" as him. It never occurs to him to think about tomorrow. ("Don't expect me to perform the same collective somersault this nation carried out after the currency reform of 1948: yesterday, still shaken to the core of their souls by the terrors of the apocalypse and as a result compassionate, sympathetic with the sufferings of others, and self-sacrificing in the hope that from the ruins could arise something utterly new, rational, and humane; today, driven by insatiable greed, ruthlessly clawing their way over one another like crabs in a basket, and prepared to commit mayhem and murder if their jobs and pensions are threatened...") What Christa fears—and I along with her—is his incorruptibility, his penchant for sarcasm. Sooner or later, Stoffel will discover that with A., he's got a louse in his fur that he can't get rid of without a good scratch.

For the time being, of course, A. is enjoying his role as the prankster Till Eulenspiegel, surely partly out of a schoolboyish spirit of revenge against his one-time friend Nagel who has turned his back on him in order—as A. believes—"to no longer be disturbed in his endeavor to participate literarily in what everyone else is doing: namely, chasing after the illusion of success on all fours, with hands and feet, by whatever means and in whatever ways necessary." If I try to use his overt critique of Nagel as an opportunity to get him to discuss his own ideas about literature, he mounts a frontal offense against me (Clausewitz: the most effective defense). "I hope you're not spending your time trying to answer the question of what literature is—that's taboo for editors. If you deviate even a millimeter from the notion that literature is simply anything that can be sold as such, you're sawing off the branch you sit on. Your Protestant ethic requires the conviction that any aesthetic measure of the protean character of the subject will end in boundless relativity, ergo all that's left is what can be concretely read from the sales figures. Literature is what readers regard and consume as such, and your job as middleman is to evaluate the various kinds of demand."

I'm caught in a double bind between him and Scherping. His writing me off so disdainfully could be irritating, but curiously enough, it animates me. I even find it enjoyable. (Is Scherping's hunt for a sublime increase in pleasure rubbing off on me? Rönnekamp claims that any relationship between two men is in the end homoerotic and sadomasochistic.) "What should I write about?" A. asks me. "What is there left to say these days? After Beckett. The same thing, only more banal. I grant you, a wordier, watered-down, muddied version makes it more comprehensible for the average reader. It bolsters his resistance to perceiving his essential self by a gradual approach to the shock of recognition. All well and good. But am I supposed to stoop to interpreting for idiots? Or be a miserable epigone of yesterday's colossal mediators of reality—Proust, Joyce, Musil, Broch? We kneel before them, but should we strive to imitate them? With a bush jacket over our hairy chest like Ernest Hemingway? Goes down like butter—*et ça passe le temps*, as my legendary patron Uncle Ferdinand would have said. It's well known that reading is the best pastime. It can even become a vice. In the years between 1939 and 1945, while your kind were forced to carry out mass murder, this malingerer was doing nothing but reading, day and night, in and out of bomb shelters, whence my modest knowledge of the subject. In any event, it's brought me to the insight that a person with even a half-developed feeling of modesty isn't permitted to pinkle his own, personal contribution into the already existing oceans of fountain-pen and printer's ink. Am I not expressing exactly what you think and feel? You're also a world sailor on that murky sea. Would you venture to increase it with even a half bottle of Johannes-Schwab-Trocken-Letter-Auslese?"—

Nothing makes me more convinced that he will write. He'll have to, so as not to kill himself. I tell that to Scherping and curiously enough, he understands and agrees with me.

Draft:
He goes to Witte's office at the appointed hour. The headquarters of Witte Laundromats ("Wittewash Washes Whiter than White!"), a brand new high-rise put up on the rubble heap of the old building from the turn of the century, replacing that hybrid of neo-Gothic fortified villa and barracks, with glass and concrete in Le Corbusier style. The windows of Witte's office (he sometimes refers to it with the old-fashioned term "countinghouse") on the fifteenth floor look out across churned-up construction sites populated—for now!—by backhoes and cranes, all the way to the duty-free port which also still displays the unhealed wounds of the bombing.

A. tells the assistant secretary (Carlotta is with Witte, taking dictation) that he was asked to come by "at eleven sharp." Half an hour passes, then Witte appears at the door, turns, and recognizes him. "Ah yes, of course—just a moment and I'll be right back!" And he bends down to the secretary and whispers something in her ear.

She nods, gets up, and disappears behind the door to his office that closes silently but smartly. A. is alone. Another twenty minutes pass. It's a sunny day, clear and pale except for the unceasing trickle of vehicles along a stretch of street visible from so high up, tiny beetles in loud, synthetic colors.

The door of the "countinghouse" opens, Carlotta sticks her head out and announces loudly, "You may come in now." She remains standing in the door, holding it open for him with the doorknob in her hand. As he goes past, their bodies almost brush against each other before she lets go of the handle. She doesn't need to close it because it closes automatically. The look they exchange confirms a sort of genetic agreement.

Behind his mammoth desk, Witte barely looks up. "Afternoon, my friend. What was it you wanted from me?"

A. looks at Carlotta but at the thought of the shameless way Christa and Astrid von Bürger play games with their glances, he lowers his eyes and gently points out that it was Witte himself who asked him to come by.

"Ah yes, yes, now I remember. You suggested introducing a little more aristocratic nonchalance into our advertising. Sounds interesting, but overlooks the fact that our job is first and foremost to educate the public. Once that task is accomplished, we can contemplate the next step into the aesthetics of advertising. The average housewife can't keep up with the advancements of science. Detergents like Wittewash-Whiter-than-White are based on avant-garde formulas that eclipse all previous detergents. Have you ever had the chance to convince yourself of the effectiveness of our detergent?"

A. must admit he hasn't and avoids looking at Carlotta whose eyes—he can sense it—are riveted on him.

"You see!" Witte exults. "Although it's safe to assume you're no housewife and so don't need to know the first thing about fine laundry detergents, nevertheless, as you so rightly remarked at dinner at my house the day before yesterday, if I remember correctly—that was when it was, right?—the social structure has changed. There's an increasing development in the direction of including the husband in housework to a much greater extent than was previously the case. Though we mustn't exaggerate in this regard, and it will still be quite some time before the German husband ties on an apron, or rather, until the German wife surrenders the scepter of the household regime, in the meantime it's our duty as farsighted, future-oriented entrepreneurs to sniff out future trends and adapt to them. Meanwhile, even in the present sociological situation, our mission is basically didactic: how do I educate my customers about the quality I'm offering them? You, my friend, are a prime example—I won't say, of ignorance, for I can't assume that you ought to be familiar with our products already—but of our own failure to inform the public. Have you ever observed your charming young wife doing the wash? As it is, it's a crying shame that such a well-born creature has to contend with such menial housework when that is truly not what she was brought up for. Well, that's precisely where we can help her out. I'm going to demonstrate how for you." He turns to Carlotta. "Carlotta, child, be so good and have the secretarial pool call the advertising director. And please tell Fräulein Busse to put calls directly through to my office."

Carlotta rises languidly from the visitor's armchair where she had seated herself collegially next to Aristides and walks to the door in all her corporeality to relay Witte's wish to the secretary in the outer office. A. can't figure out what her role is here. The leisureliness of her movements is provocative, with a slatternly elegance, animalistic and unwholesome, a demonstration of erotic power. The way Aristides watches her does not escape Witte. With a little edge he says, "Frau Schwab is my personal assistant." (Schwab? A. swiftly weighs the possibility that she is S.'s former wife. S. has never mentioned her, in fact, but Rönnekamp has said something about an ex-wife named Charlotte. As she comes back, A. regards her with new eyes.)

Witte uses the time that passes until the advertising director arrives to continue his lecture. "My principle is to give my people complete independence to do their jobs—assuming a certain minimum of control, of course. But I myself determine the course of the company, which requires a strictly centralized organization. If you will, we're the brain cells in the organism of our affiliates. If you don't look after every shitty little detail personally, you go broke. Only unambiguously clear leadership determines the profile of our brand and makes it resistant to the crushing competition of the big national firms—Henkel, for instance—and also from abroad. Of course, our advertising is crucial to the struggle, especially its . . ." He's interrupted by a knock on the door. "Ah, here he is already!" With a jovial wave of his arm, "Come in, come in . . ." (his good mood increases with the possibility of favorable self-presentation) ". . . May I introduce the director of our advertising department, Dr. Fiebig? Herr—what was your name again? Subicz, of course!—Herr, or rather, Baron von Subicz."

Neither the one nor the other, A. assures him.

"The Subiczes were a Bosnian royal family," A. says mischievously, "who died out in the fourteenth century." Now he can't help stealing a glance at Carlotta and reaps ironical agreement in return.

For a moment, Witte is struck dumb. Then he clears his throat lightly and continues: "The idea of raising the aesthetic level of our advertising already occurred to me quite some time ago—but here's Dr. Fiebig. Show us what we've been doing up to now."

He's interrupted by the purring of his phone. He picks up, says several times "Yes? Yes? Yes! Wait a sec," then presses the button for the outer office and says, "Frau Busse, connect this guy to sales and don't bother me with such stuff for the next half an hour!" He turns to A.: "A former admiral with connections in the navy—pure bullshit, but what can you do? These guys need to make a living too" and to the advertising director: "Well, Dr. Fiebig, fire away."—"With what?" asks Dr. Fiebig.

"With what we've been doing in advertising. Herr von Subicz wants to be informed about it."

The director of advertising doesn't try to hide the fact that he has more important things to do than spread out the entire advertising material for a visitor. At the moment, he says, they're concentrating on the campaign "Wittewash Washes Whiter than White" initiated by the head of the company, Herr Witte himself. "Yes, yes, of course," Witte interrupts him, "but I just had the idea that we are basically doing nothing concrete to illustrate that slogan. Have you ever considered the possibility that we could put on a sort of public washing demonstration, not as a big event before a big audience, of course, but with in-house demos from door to door?"

Dr. Fiebig stares wide-eyed at him. Witte gets impatient. "Remind me of the subtitle to our slogan?"

"The up-to-the-minute detergent with modern suds: not too much, not too little—just right!" Dr. Fiebig intones.

"There you have it! You can't just make the claim, you've got to demonstrate it. The housewife has to see it with her own eyes."

With a glance at his watch, the advertising director replies dryly that such a plan—or rather, the possibility of putting it into operation—could not be managed within his budget. It would need an organization that would have to be discussed first with the director of sales, and only then could the details of the campaign be contemplated.

"Okay then, let's get the sales director in here—what? He's on the road at the moment? In the provinces? Well then, his representative—he's got to have a representative, doesn't he?" Dr. Fiebig declares himself prepared to seek out his representative and speedily takes his leave. Witte turns to A. "You can see how things function around here. It just eats up all my time."And in fact, the telephone purrs again. Witte picks up and hisses into the receiver, "Didn't I tell you . . . What's that? Aha, yes, put me through." After a short pause, "Yes, Witte speaking—I'm honored, dear lady! Yes of course—yes—with pleasure—what was that? Do I recommend it? I certainly do! The castle itself is first-rate—a fairy-tale building—yes indeed, the former Empress Friedrich—excellent, really, the cuisine is A-1—that's right, all-inclusive, we all got an egg for breakfast—oh, my sister and I, of course, ha ha, no one else—" shoots a look at Carlotta—"as I said, a stupendous atmosphere, very pretty rooms, very cozy, large lounges—but of course, happy to do it—hope to see you soon, dear lady!" He makes a little bow while still holding the receiver, presses the button to the outer office, "Bussekins, take down this lady's number. That's all." And turning back to A.: "You can see, not a free minute!"

As if on cue, Carlotta lazily heaves her body out of the chair: "Apropos free minutes, it's almost noon. Isn't it time for a little pick-me-up?"

Witte distractedly concurs. "Yes, of course, Carlotta, child." And to A.: "Let's try to concentrate in this monkey house. What I'd like to demonstrate to you is the brilliantly effective action of our detergent. It's the same thing I'd like to get across to the housewife. Just as you will soon be able to convince yourself of it, the German housewife will be able to see concretely that our advertising is not hollow phrase mongering (although our slogan is neat, isn't it? Wittewash Washes Whiter than White—alliteration, right? Richard Wagner uses it too..." Carlotta brings a bottle of champagne and glasses from the outer office. "What? A whole bottle?!" says Witte. Carlotta shrugs. "For three people..." She starts to open the bottle. A. jumps up to help her. Their hands touch—the most banal form of bodily contact. Witte accepts a full glass. "All right then, cheers! A little champagne's always good for what ails you. Loosens up the coronary arteries!"

As they clink glasses—"Prosit! Cheers!"—a stooped fellow, the representative of the sales director, appears. "A glass for you too, Colonel?" asks Carlotta.

The person addressed declines with a morose "Thank you, no."

"Herr Kunzelmann is a retired colonel," Witte explains. "Spent three years in a Russian POW camp."

The man thus apostrophized shows no reaction.

"Well, dear Kunzelmann, have a seat, won't you? You're Schröder's representative?"

"Yes sir, Herr Witte," rumbles the retired soldier, ignoring the offer of a chair.

"All right then. Here's an order straight from the general staff. Our guest here, Herr von Subicz from Romania, is interested in our products. The two of us have decided it's necessary to present their advantages to the customer in a concrete way—"

"That's the business of the advertising department," rasps the retired colonel.

"I'm quite aware of that," Witte replies sharply. "But I said 'in a concrete way,' and I meant it literally: demonstrated to the housewife in a genuine act of laundering—"

"That may be necessary in Romania," rasps the retired colonel again. "But the German housewife is already amply familiar with the use of contemporary laundry products."

"You say that, dear Kunzelmann, and I understand: thinking otherwise would offend your patriotism. 'Reit or rong, mei Köntri,' as the Tommies say. But just ask Schröder—you're in telephone contact with him, right?—Okay then, just ask your superior if he'd reject my idea out of hand. You see? Even with a glorious past you've got to be open to new things. You really do. Are we able to give Herr von Subicz here—a descendant of the former royal family, by the way—can we give him a concrete demonstration of the fact that Wittewash washes whiter than white?"

"What, now? Here?" The retired colonel lapses into a nervous shaking of the head.

"Of course. When and where else? We must have a dose of Wittewash somewhere in the building."

"Probably. In fact, yes, certainly."

"You see? And probably a bucket too."

"You'd have to ask building services about that."

"So get in touch with the super. Or, wait a sec! Hang on!" Witte presses the button to the outer office and says to A., "I've got to do everything myself!" Then into the receiver: "Bussekins, call building services, would you? It's urgent. I need a bucket and some washable rag, as dirty as possible, right away, okay?—What? Nobody's there in building services? Well what about the cleaning staff? What's that? The ladies only work from seven to nine?! What ladies are we talking about? That's what it's come to, that the dames who do the cleaning call themselves ladies! So at nine o'clock on the dot, their ladyships take all the buckets and mops home with them? Well it seems impossible to me too. So please see to this matter yourself, Frau Busse." Hangs up with a heavy sigh: "This outfit needs a thorough reorganization from the ground up."

Carlotta to the retired colonel: "Won't you take a little glass to loosen up your coronary arteries?" "No thanks! Already turned it down," hisses the burned-out military man venomously. To Witte: "Might I ask to be represented at the pending demonstration by someone less busy at the moment? Personally, I'm awaiting a visit from Admiral Neuner—"

"Sure, sure ! Another reunion of the old guard. Ain't there a chief prosecutor in the group too? Please accept my application to make it a foursome!—"

"In the name of the supply office of the Ministry of Naval Affairs, Herr Admiral Neuner has suggested provisioning the new fleet currently under development with our products," says the retired colonel with great dignity. "We are in the process of working out our offer."

"Excellent! Don't be too stingy about the percentage. See you later and thanks, Kunzelmann!" He gives an affable nod to the punctiliously withdrawing colonel. "But I could do with another drop of liquid refreshment, Lottiekins—and one for our guest too, of course—I don't have to tell you not to neglect yourself." With a nod toward the door, he says to A., "Typical how much the good fellow was impressed by your royal origins." (A. starts to tell him it was meant as a joke, an ironic rise in his social level, but it doesn't come to that since Witte drones on.) "These people have blind obedience in their bones. You saw it for yourself: the little formal bows and clicking heels. They're not free Hanseatic citizens like us: civil pride before the thrones of power. And we have at least as much sense of tradition, but it's Hanseatic tradition: connection to the wide world, not fixated on a single point. You can see it in our eyes; they gaze into the distance, the open, the future. I never knew my father; he died before I was born. My sister, whom you've met, was just two years old. But we were able to have a clear image of the old gentleman from the stories of our mother, God rest her soul. You wouldn't believe it, but as a young man he walked all over the place as a Hamburg carpenter even though he wasn't one. He was a swabbie, a seaman, but the sea wasn't enough for him. He wanted to learn about dry land too—he hoofed it all the way to Morocco via Spain in the traditional garb of the Hamburg carpenters: velvet bell-bottoms, a velvet jacket with white buttons, a black, broad-brimmed hat, and a stick with a bundle over his shoulder. You can still buy 'em today: 'We suit you up swell at Arthur Capelle'—good slogan, right? Could've written it myself. And he was so modest he smeared black shoe polish on his ankles so they wouldn't notice he didn't have any socks... By the way, Lottie girl, you could think of me too if you're gonna pour another glass." The telephone purrs and he picks up. "What? It's already one thirty? Where was I supposed to be? The Regatta Club? We'll have to cancel it!... Whaddya mean, not possible? Why's it impossible when we've got this washing demonstration going... oh, our people are on lunch break?—now listen here: if I'm working through lunch myself, maybe the little apprentice who's s'pposed to fetch a bucket can... Where the hell is he, by the way? We've been waiting here for hours... Okay, just have some sausage sandwiches brought up for us—and—Bussekins, we got another bottle of champagne in the fridge? Good. Carlotta'll be right out t'get it..."

Out beyond the glass of the big windows, the day was brightening.

—does it seem so glassy because it follows so many icy nights? The star-spangled winter nights beyond the frost flower–encrusted windows of Uncle Ferdinand's konak in Bessarabia, the ornamentation on the Saracen arches, topped with rustling palm fronds. When the reflections from the open fireplace dance on them they sparkle as if displayed on black basalt. The flames are also reflected in my operetta-ready cavalry boots. The old servant who claims to have known me as a child has polished them to a shine, for only thus am I allowed to present myself to Uncle Ferdinand. He treats me like family (just as he would any guest in his house, by the way). In his salon he receives only guests he can treat like family. He counts me, the son of a whore, as a member of his household like his dogs, his horses, and his long-established staff of servants. His sharp eyes would notice if instead of wearing shiny boots I had painted my ankles with shoe polish—

—and the nights in Bucharest under a fleece of snow, Stella and me on the Şoseaua Kiseleff, in the car with the motor running and clinched in a kiss as desperate as if it were the last before parting forever... (and before long it would be so: soon we would never see each other again)—

—and suddenly, there's a hard rap on the window, a flashlight beam stabs into the car—and I panic. Thank God I'm not in uniform. I know it's the police. They lie in wait to ambush couples and can only be dissuaded from charging you with a public display of immorality with much pleading and more baksheesh—as a soldier, I'd be in for it and if they ask to see our papers, Stella's reputation would hang in the balance. The wife of a diplomat is easy to blackmail...

—And the nights of thin snow in Berlin with the wind whistling through the gaps between buildings and in the evaporating darkness, the sirens began their angry howl and soon the pale tentacles of the searchlights probed the black sky, crisscrossing and joining together at a single point and the clattering salvos of antiaircraft fire and the first bombs exploding and the edge of the sky beginning to redden—

and the nights of biting frost in Witte's bombed-out villa on the Elbchaussee and me holding Christa in my arms to warm her up—Christa, whom I loved and who couldn't make much of my love because she was so cold and hungry—

many, many such nights have clarified the day out there and cleared the lots so the city might rise anew in concrete and steel and glass...

"... all of that used to be residential neighborhoods, mostly working class, you know?—so to that extent, just between you and me, the Allies did us a favor—I mean, as our friend Baron von Rönnekamp so rightly put it, if we hadn't been able to start over again with a *tabula rasa*, we'd never have been able to carry out reconstruction so successfully—well, here you are at last! Man, is it possible that half a day has to pass before somebody scares up a pail in this cathouse? Carlotta, child, take down a memo right now that sales should send around a note to all our affiliates to always have a bucket and a washable piece of material on hand for the laundering demonstration—apropos: have you got a piece of material on you too?"

The young man who arrived with the bucket produces an unspeakably greasy rag—

"—Where'd you get that thing, in the garage? Well, dear friend, by all that's right and fair, Wittewash is too top-shelf to clean off lubricating oil—"

—while Frau Busse from the outer office helps to fill the bucket and get the laundry powder ready ("Didja remember t'get out another bottle too, Bussekins?"), they go searching for an acceptable object to launder (Carlotta: "Perhaps one of the younger employees would lend us an undergarment ... !").

Meanwhile a waiter, obviously summoned from a nearby restaurant, is standing at the door with a tray of sandwiches, causing some confusion. Witte gives instructions to the secretary. "See to it he's paid, Bussekins. Yep, from the postage money. Book it 'For food and drink' as usual." Then he turns—at last!—to the bucket: "'Course, we gotta put some water in first."

A. doesn't dare look at Carlotta. He can sense the danger that a look between them might trigger an uncontrollable fit of laughter.

Frau Busse, who'd gone looking for something washable, reappears with something balled up in her fist: "It's a hankie from a temp in bookkeeping who just had a nosebleed—" She unrolls the little piece of reddish brown, leopard-spotted cloth and offers it between thumb and forefinger to Carlotta, who waves it off in disgust. Witte gallantly takes it from her. "Outstanding. Blood is especially hard to wash out." Frau Busse nods in agreement: "Hopefully it's really from her nose."

That has an effect. A.'s laughter dies in his throat and hatred bubbles up—

> Cousin Wolfgang shared it with me—that hatred. He never admitted it. Unlike mine, his hatred was not directed at a class, at a particular kind of person shaped by society, at the type of person represented by this philistine Witte. When Wolfgang's hatred broke out, it was always against Uncle Helmuth, his father; he loved his mother, Aunt Hertha, with an angry idolatry and suffered because she was "in thrall" to Uncle Helmuth. ("That bovine look! I can't stand how she looks at him: as if nothing else in the world is happening in her field of vision except him. As if nothing is as desirable as suckling at the warm, comfortable udder of their togetherness . . .")
>
> But he courted her, continually gave her signs of his love: all sorts of attentions, little presents, proofs of his devotion. And yet she was the essence of everything I hated and he hated too, but without extending it to her class: soulful stupidity, the certainty that she and her kind were the omphalos, the navel of the world, contempt for everyone who wasn't her kind, innate suspicion, envy, malice . . .
>
> The characteristics of the middle class. Aunt Selma had none of them except anger, gnawing anger directed against herself, the anger of someone fallen in social status, which drove her to work like a indentured servant, "slave away," deny herself—and to dream in secret: the nixie from the millpond bewitched into a cart horse—
>
> and her love for me, the bastard washed up on her shore, her silent admiration of the other, dead sister, the beautiful Maud who strayed onto the path of shiny, golden intoxication—

—and her indifference to Cousin Wolfgang, which hurt him. He too could see that she was not of the same middle-class ilk as his parents—

Sunday evenings they come home from one of their spiritist séances, hand in hand like a pair of siblings ("Hansel and Gretel in astral league," hisses Cousin Wolfgang), their faces transfigured by supernatural gentleness as they lower them in thanks over their supper of sour pickles and kippers (prepared by Aunt Selma with an especially generous portion of Liptauer cheese for me). They close their eyes for the blessing; they've given up trying to persuade the three of us—Aunt Selma, Cousin Wolfgang, and me—to participate. Wolfgang always ostentatiously clears his throat during the "psychologically intrusive ceremony that begins so discreetly." They don't talk at table. Their experience is too valuable, their insights into the beyond too ineffable and harrowing, their encounters with those who have already cast off their mortal husk to enter into the pure transcendental element too revelatory to tell us about them. Only in passing do we learn what's really happening to us—("Of course sometimes, a soul voluntarily accepts the trial of rebirth although it's already purified; but it does so to assist a dual who has incurred guilt and is condemned to be reborn—which is the case with Uncle Helmuth and me . . .").—

—and so he assembles electrical appliances in a big factory for starvation wages, which don't suffice to spare the other half of the dual soulless drudgery as a bookkeeper for a moth-eaten little music publisher. They too "slave away," those lofty souls, to support us, feed us poorly and dress us even worse, and provide us boys the worst possible education in the public schools—:

The products cranked out by head teachers: cannon- and office-fodder, effortlessly manipulable by Podunk politicians, pettifoggers, snake-oil salesmen, and charlatans of every stripe—

("The leader of our séances, a spirit of the highest rank who has voluntarily returned to this cosmic form of existence, reports that a potentialization of our planet is imminent—i.e., that our earthly existence will dematerialize and thereby enter a higher stage of universal order—and that the spirit destined to fulfill this messianic mission, although in the opposite sense, has already been born—" Wolfgang stares at his father, flabbergasted, and can't believe his ears: "And who's that supposed to be? Adolf Hitler?!"—"Yes indeed, the same Adolf Hitler you illegally tag along after, one of the many brutal men summoned up by the evil counterprinciple while the pure spirit of National Socialism, as enunciated by Lanz von Liebenfels, is nonviolent, a purely spiritual power...")—

—and in the end, he's right: the brutal men summoned up by the evil counterprinciple will kill one another and destroy the world along the way, but the spirit of the stigmatized philistines will triumph—

John is right about them, the "bloody fucking middle classes" of every nation. They will rise phoenix-like from the rubble, the victors, the makers of the new world...

All those in attendance take part in the act of laundering: Witte's very own pudgy fingers stir the detergent powder to foam—not too much, not too little—just right!—in the bucket and Carlotta kneads the blood-spattered handkerchief in it until the red spots turn pale pink and at last disappear entirely. The result is convincing, but Witte isn't satisfied yet. The red, white, and blue cockade of his burgher's face is afire as he calls for more objects to launder. A. offers a snow-white cambric handkerchief (Jermyn Street, from John's supply) and without hesitation pours ink on it before Witte can intervene. The detergent foam and the water in the bucket turn brownish-blue and have to be replaced. Frau Busse takes over the washing with a second dose of Wittewash-Whiter-than-White, and after four acts of laundering pulls the handkerchief, now perfectly sky-blue, from the suds. She refuses to continue, says she's got to protect her hands, and Carlotta opens the fourth bottle of champagne.

Despite a "not yet hundred-and-fifty-percent demonstration," Witte is in high spirits, his ruddy face aglow, his sea-blue eyes twinkling: the champagne is having its effect. It's five in the afternoon and the sandwiches haven't filled them up. Witte orders lobster sent in ("Let lobster be our lodestar, eh? See, I can make puns too. Our mutual friend Baron von Rönnekamp even thinks me capable of better things. He says in English, 'Za pun iss za wurst form uff Witt.' Get it? Pun is the least of Witte's talents.") But the name Rönnekamp opens up a piquant field in which Witte whiffs the possibility of gamboling about and showing he's familiar with "the intellectual principles to which I owe your visit, dear friend. I know you were angling at an opportunity to enter my firm. And why not? There's always need for new blood. I wouldn't entrust the cash box to you, but as I said, in advertising, why not, even if you may have a penchant for drastic measures, as you showed with your lovely handkerchief. But there were a few things that interested me in your remarks at dinner the other evening at my house, to which you were brought by your charming wife. I mean, what you had to say about the multiplicity of the social structure of postwar Germany. It's true that the main emphasis of our current form of government and economy is on the bourgeoisie, and the old upper classes just have to fall in line with that, however much sympathy I may have for Baron von Rönnekamp—not to mention his outstanding talents as broker and financial advisor—but take that other gentleman he brought along, Count Lentzau-Wilmersbüttel: I mean *really*, not my cup of tea at all! That's truly a kind of decadence you would seek in vain in solid middle-class circles—here in Hamburg, I mean. Or can you imagine Hans Albers as a homo? Mind you, a democracy should have a place for all kinds of eccentricities, and it does. Not being from here, you'd be astonished if I told you, for example, the rumors that circulate about one of our most renowned publishers whose name I'd rather not mention, and while such things don't take place in public, they do in municipal establishments that are a testimony to our Hanseatic open-mindedness —we've seen just about every curiosity our globe has to offer and we swear by the well-known Bible verse 'Let him who is without sin cast the first stone.' Deviations such as those of the gentlemen in question may not be exactly rare in general. I'm not gonna get hot under the collar about it and I can even see it from a humorous point of view to a certain extent—I mean, those affected gestures just kill me—but as I said, their whole class is rotten to the core. Nowadays we have nothing more to expect from the aristocracy, especially us Hamburgers. Our best families proudly refused to be ennobled and it was likely our straightforward modesty that persuaded the Iron Chancellor to settle so near our gates, in Friedrichsruh—I understand your spouse is a regular guest there—no? Not yet. But given her family ties, it won't be long..."

He's interrupted by the lobsters, three brick-red monsters on meadow-green lettuce leaves, surrounded by green wedges of lime and white-bordered yellow wedges of lemon ("Book it 'For food and drink,' Bussekins—and here, have a piece yourself. It's easier with these shears!")

and while they fall to with plastic cups and paper plates scared up from somewhere or other—the lobster flesh is elastic and tender and conjures up images of anthropophagy; our fingers fishing it out of the shell smell of vaginal manipulations. We devour what we're offered, and since Frau Busse's gone home, Carlotta opens the God-knows-how-manyeth bottle of Söhnlein Dry. And Witte talks, keeps talking, and talks and talks and talks—

—the sky in the large windows turns a dusty turquoise green and the light in the room is completely dematerialized, the lighting conditions of an abstract world,

abstract as the presence of the woman lounging next to him in an armchair—no, she's lying diagonally in leisurely siesta mode, legs stretched out and crossed. She barely moves, raising her arm only now and then to reach for her glass, fish a cigarette from her case, or support herself as she leans forward to have him light it—

abstract as the condition of inebriation whose successive phases of euphoria I observe in myself and measure in Witte's increasingly confused talk while outside the sky turns inky, first as pale as the final washing of his handkerchief and then, as if being run backwards, a deeper and deeper sepia—

—and far below on the road, the motley trickle of tinny vehicles is embellished with a dance of white and red stars, the tail lights of the tinny vehicles trickling up and down, semiological signs for the presence of—what? of human beings?—in this abstract world—people I can't see, people who have been absorbed by their shiny, motley, drivable crustacean shells

and while windows light up "like crossword puzzles" on the stelae of high-rises here and in the distance across fields of rubble, construction excavations, factory sites

—blue and red light begins to pulse through a tangle of neon tubes as if showing the blood vessels of the resurrected city...

But the nights, the nights... they were dark and gloomy and weighed on my chest. I had trouble breathing all night long. It didn't help that I crept from the wall of boards that separated our miserably furnished rooms and the collapsed part of Witte's villa on the Elbchaussee out across the bomb crater to the nettles among the crumbled bricks where no one would look for me—not Christa in any case, and Nagel couldn't see me from his garden house either—and sat down there and stared up at the sky as if expecting deliverance. I couldn't see any stars. Thick clouds pressed on my eyes. The nights were in league with my nightmare and left me no way out of my torment. Wherever I fled, the old woman was with me, even there in my hideout among the ruins of the Hanseatic past. The old woman herself came from the ruins of the past, even if not the Hanseatic past, but who could say for sure? She evaded all my questions. I never could discover what corner she arose from. I've been a night owl all my life, in the cynicism of my badly disguised Romanticism. Too often kept awake by daytime adventures, by too many people and events, by waiting for Mommy, who I knew was with one of her beaus (my "uncles"), by Cousin Wolfgang's panting curiosity, and soon too by the scream of air raid sirens. The nights were never my enemies. I was never afraid of them then, as I was of these now. The nights of the pre–Ice Age were transparent all the way to the stars. I loved their stillness, feeling solitary in their immensity, alone in the world. I added my ambition to their vastness. We cobbled together what was my secret treasure: freedom from guilt and the pride of being—despite everything that might confront me—indisputably well born. I was never closer to my true self than at night in Uncle Bully Olivera's villa on the Cap d'Ail. I slept with the windows wide open to the sea, and of course I didn't sleep. Miss Fern was gone. I lay with my eyes open, looking down onto the restless, splintering silver on the black velvet of the lazy waves that rocked the fishing boats and caused their naked masts to scribble confused hieroglyphics in the violet sky. And I knew I wasn't like my occasional playmates and wouldn't become like the adults around me and had been granted a special path I would tread, head held high, to the amazement of all the others. And I still knew it when I returned to Bessarabia and, half-numb from exhaustion after Uncle Ferdinand's tales of his crumbling Middle Kingdom, threw myself onto the bed, knowing that beyond the sparkle of frost flowers on the windowpanes was my friend, the lofty night, keeper of my secrets—the night that generously left it to the moon to spill its milky light over the humps of snow-covered willows in the Dniester meadows while it filled the vastness above with cosmic frost and the rustling light of its showers of stars. But already in Berlin, the nights defected. They no longer belonged to me alone. The mournful howl of sirens tore the sleepers from their beds and pillows and drove them into the cellars where they huddled together like a herd of animals in a thunderstorm, while outside the anemic tentacles of the searchlights probed the sky, crisscrossing and joining together and sometimes capturing a thing pale as a moth, and the clatter of the flak swelled to a thunder and flames billowed up where the bombs went down. All that fierce action robbed the nights of their grandeur, constricted their spaces, and made the darkness dense and ominous, the night air choking. Turning away from the sunlit sky was not an invitation to contemplation, I said, it did not make us conscious of the isolation of the planets in space as it was revealed to the desert prophets when they had eaten their grasshoppers and gazed in unison up into the firmament. Night was the lightless part of a twenty-four-hour cowering under a deadly, humiliating assault, a daily recurring extension of the sentence for our guilty existence, and the nights remained so up to the last painful bite of the Ice Age in Hamburg, and even later. I don't know how Christa came to terms with it. She slept like a statue in our marital lair, her curves and concavities a confirmation of Canova's art. Her regular breathing calmed the world around her—except for me. I started up from a sleep haunted by wild nightmares and had to force myself not to flail about. I lay there panting, and the old hag lay next to me, her gray stringy hair smeared with blood and brains and pasted across her staring eyes. And although I knew it was nothing more than a dream—a nightmare vision that repeatedly haunted me—there was no trace of relief in knowing I was awake. She would not let go of me, that terrible old woman, it all surrounded me in a dreadful, timeless present: the office building devoid of people with its paternoster elevators whirring endlessly up and down. At any moment their empty cabins could be followed by one from which my pursuers would spring. The clammy clinker-brick walls of the cellar I had lured her into. She saw the pile of coal and a shovel and looked at me at the same time and didn't take her eyes off me as I struck, transforming her face into a portrait by Bacon.

Letter to a Son

Dear little man,
I call you that because you've been born with the curse of being a man and being raised to be a man. I can't spare you that, even if I wanted to. It's your destiny to be a man one day, whatever I may tell you about it. I'm not very skilled at writing declarations of love. Ask your mother: she got only a few from me in writing, although I stammered countless ones into her ear, some in embraces from which she expected more concrete proofs of my love, some in the encoded form of monologues in which, in my masculine extremity, I tried to explain myself to her. Only in my youth was I able to give my love voluble expression on paper—if one can speak of youth in the case of a mixture of nostalgically retarded child and precocious misanthrope, which is what I was in those days. Mind you, a misanthrope from the noble line of a Karl Kraus (about whom I would have known little if Stella hadn't hammered him into me, line by line and sentence by sentence). But you've only just been born and have no idea what I'm talking about. Talking too much, as usual. This letter is meant as a declaration of love.

Back in the days of Stella I was capable of writing love letters. Manly ceasefire agreements, declarations of devotion to a feminine creature who was everything to me: lover, mother, deliverer from ignorance, midwife and wet nurse of my awakening intellect, teacher, doorkeeper to the world, comrade, and proprietor proud to display her pupil. Was it not imperative for me to be grateful to her? So grateful that even then, long—very, very long—before you were born, I wished you would meet someone like her before you were spoiled by the bias of having to prove yourself a man by excelling, unless it be intellectually.

I bestowed upon Stella what my turbulent emotional life was boiling over with. I wrote and thanked her for showing me the way back to myself. Yes: to myself as a child, as a human being, a *child of man*. Still in a condition of innocence—innocent also of the offenses others had committed against me, not yet grown into the conflict between the son of a whore raised like an aristocrat and the poor boy condemned to live among philistines, still in possession of what everyone born of woman ought to be granted: an unfettered mind. Unfettered enough to be receptive to the virtues of humanity: freedom from prejudice; courage to be oneself; and above all, disengagement from oneself, insight into oneself, and the recognition that one is part of a great game—and the serene pleasure of watching the game even when it's shitty, and laughing at it—laughing in the cheerful comfort of cynicism and including yourself in this liberating laughter.

You will grow up, my son, and will come upon these pieces of wisdom from your father and find them to be annoying, tedious clichés more likely to hinder than help you be yourself. I don't have to tell you that this situation is repeated from generation to generation. It's not just resistance to fathers that is repeated, but rather resistance through them and beyond them, to the natural order of things in life and in the world. Resistance to life's awkwardnesses, with which the fathers couldn't cope either. Sons don't grant fathers the right to speak wisely about things they themselves—the fathers—couldn't cope with.

And so, little man, I won't pester you with the things that weigh me down, the insoluble problems of this world, one of which is the relationship of fathers and sons. I love you and want you to know that none of my loves—and there were many—was purer, more unselfish, more heartfelt than my love for you. When you were born, I picked you up and looked you in the eye so that in you I could see my resurrected self. Myself, cleansed of all the blemishes clinging to me. Should I enumerate them for you? It would be not just the story of a life with everything that made it understandable and perhaps also forgivable—the story of unfulfilled and falsely fulfilled dreams; the story too of chance occurrences, of circumstances inextricably tangled together over which the person caught in their net has no influence; the story of an era—and how could I explain all that to you except in a book? A book that would burst the bounds of all literary categories and be untellable in its diversity, complexity, and confusion. A book that could explain to you not just me, but also—in order to explain myself—the quicksilver spirit of the times into which I was born, in which I lived, live, and shall live, thousands of days of drawn breaths and breaths yet to be drawn, days that lend the contents of their predecessors kaleidoscopically new and varied significance, overlapping like the lenses of a telescope through which you can simultaneously see far away and up close, both magically abstracted from yourself.

Must I confess to you, my son, that I've carried this book within myself from the beginning. That I live as if my existence was not real unless I *said* it—that is, narrated it in my book. What is it that forces me, allows me to hope, drives me to the certainty that I am only *real* when I abstract—subtract—myself from myself and go—where? Onto a few hundred printed pages? Will you be able, my son, to respect this form of existence for your father? Especially if it too becomes unreal? If he carries his book—his self!—within himself as nothing but a beautiful intention—worse yet, as a promise he doesn't keep because he's too weak to keep it. Not enough of a man?—or rather: too much of a man?

You're barely born and I already know I'm going to disappoint you, my beloved child. You won't grow up like other sons whose fathers are not myths but rather stand before them, chock-full of reality: real men. Dynamic. Reliable. Honest and modest. No fibbers; no bullshitters. The son of a cabinetmaker, a locksmith, a lathe operator sees his father doing useful things at his workbench. Happy the son of a farmer, a fisherman, a businessman, a mason. He sees his father in the realization of what he does, even if that activity obviously isn't completely fulfilling and something ineffable urges him to another, utterly useless activity—breeding pigeons, for instance, or spending years meticulously building a scale model of the Eiffel Tower out of toothpicks. It's as if he's creating something beyond himself, beyond the shoemaker, mason, lathe operator. Nothing useful, perhaps, just something playful, but even so, a worshipful accomplishment. Mind you, in the worship of a dubious god.

Consider one thing, my son: even the sons of clerks and bureaucrats know that although their fathers produce nothing visible or tangible, they are—as my patron Witte would say—"plugged into the work process that keeps the whole shebang afloat." It's unfair of a son not to take any pride in the knowledge that his father is a postal clerk—without a doubt an honorable profession, but looked down upon out of class arrogance. At any rate, he—the son—sees his father leaving home with his briefcase and mid-morning snack, anxiously hurrying for fear of being late for "work." And what are the feelings of the son as he sees his honorable progenitor off? Pride and deep respect, I would hope. Whatever form it takes, it's well known that work ennobles and is—however badly—rewarded: it is the father whose work guarantees the existence of the family; even after his working life is through, his widow will continue to live off his work. Ask your mother: she's in a position to describe it more convincingly than I can. She respects the myth of work well done and will try to plant it in you as well, thereby seeing to it that your father will not partake of the respect other sons show their fathers. But do they really show it? Or do they show it only when they watch their father building an Eiffel Tower from toothpicks in his spare time? When he's worshiping the dubious god of idle play.

You've been born into a thorny conflict, my poor son. Even at the tenderest age, you'll already be suspicious of your father because he's been pumped up by a false myth. He is a high priest of that untrustworthy deity of idle play and will be shown the respect the clergy of all churches receive. But only as long as and to the extent that he is also plugged into the work process that keeps the whole shebang going. If he isn't plugged in with some visible, tangible accomplishment—and you need good eyes to see it and good senses to grasp it—every post office clerk can look down on him as a pariah. God—not the god of idle play but the god of the upright, the REAL, TRUE God who keeps the whole shebang going—will spit him from HIS mouth.

So you see, my child, you were born into a divine conflict. Although you'll be raised to think you live in a monotheistic community of faith, it isn't so. There are countless other gods besides HIM, the ONLY god who keeps the whole shebang going, among them the god of the toothpick Eiffel Tower builders. And his clergy is also supported by the community; he too is given credit. Above all, you yourself will give your father credit. He is a high priest of the idle deity PLAY, one of those who invent their world in play: a WRITER. Now, how shall he present himself to you as such? You'll have to tiptoe so as not to disturb him in his sacred "work." And if you peek through the keyhole into the room where he has withdrawn as if into the holy of holies of his high priesthood, you'll see him lying on the couch, smoking and staring at the ceiling if he hasn't already closed his eyes and fallen asleep. It can also happen that you'll hear him pounding on his typewriter like a wild man, and then—alas!—that all too rare flow of words will be dismayingly interrupted by the grinding sound of the page being torn from the roller and the crunch as it's balled up and tossed on the floor. You'll fear the stillness that follows, fear your pretty mother's pallor. Haggard and disheveled, he—your father—will appear at the door, make a beeline for the bottle of cognac in the liquor cabinet, pour himself a drinking glass full, and down it in one swallow—

and although your mother will roll her eyes to the Savior above the ceiling, she's so much under the spell of the myth of the work ethic, she'll take just such a ostentatious performance of a so-called creative crisis as the occasion to compensate her for her disappointment in a husband without a steady income and benefits with the hope she places in his power as a creative artist. She will doubt him, but she's too proud to admit that she was mistaken about him. But you're going to feel like throwing up. You're going to see through the false myth. Your father is nothing but a swindler. A confidence man. He may court you as other fathers court their sons. He may hold your hand and take you to Hagenbeck Zoo or rent a rowboat and go rowing on the Alster with you like a cabinetmaker locksmith carpenter lathe operator father with his son. You'll take it as your due and know that your father is a parasite on the world by making a promise he can't keep. (Why, oh why aren't you Karl Nagel's son!) You will see it in the eyes of your parents' friends, relatives, and acquaintances that they don't believe in his creative power any more than you do, although they also pretend that if—against all expectations—his promise should actually be realized, they will see therein the culmination and fulfillment of the myth of creativity: mythic, although useless. It would be the birth of a book! (Of which there are a few hundred thousand a year.) But you would know that your father is a swindler. And if they said, "What a great man!" an inner voice would say to you, "Yes, but unfortunately all too much a man!" Especially when he falls short.

I love you, little man, and I don't like to think about the immediate future, where humiliations unavoidably await you given your unfortunate choice of a father: creditors pounding on the door (the rent is overdue); the bailiff's sympathy with your mother's troubles, which doesn't stop him from doing his duty; the neighbors' malicious gossip ("—'cause these have-nots from out of town think they're better than us—"). The false myths that circulate about your father ("Artists and writers are always part of the bohemian scene") will make him seem—and this will particularly disgust you—sleazy and Romantic. Rumors will circulate branding him an irresistible seducer of young ladies from the best families and recently married wives of German men with steady incomes and benefits, and at the same time a shameless whoremonger. He's often spotted in the bordellos on the Reeperbahn. He appears in public with a prostitute named Gisela who's known all over town. One can't help wondering if he's her pimp, because he can't afford her price, so he probably is. You'll look at your mother and admire her good breeding, her slim figure, the girlish blond of her hair, the magical enchantment of her blue eyes, and her haughty little mouth, and your love for her will tie up your heart, along with your hatred for the man who's inflicted such abuse on her in the name of his inflated myth as artist and high priest of one of our lesser gods.

I don't like to think how bitter it will be for you, since for a while in your childhood, before you begin to see through me, you will love me too. Your little hand will take hold of my big one with fervent trust. You'll listen with bated breath to the fairy tales I tell you—and they certainly won't be the ones I tell everyone else to their incredulous astonishment—no, they'll be fairy tales from the forests of the country I was born in: legends of kings' sons, of herdsmen and hajduks and beautiful women, not of the millionaire whoremongers of the Côte d'Azur, from whose number you can select you own progenitor. I'm going to hide from you the box with the dubious photographic evidence. You'll do very well without it. You're going to be plagued with enough ominous suspicions as it is: you're my son, whether you like it or not. You'll recognize yourself in me by our common blood, our common penchant for play, anger, and laughter, sharply mocking observations, our contemptuous shrug for everything petty, our brooding, indolence, innate sadness—in a word, by all the characteristics you will later strive manfully to overcome in order to correspond to your genetic material from the distaff side by being upright, unambiguous, reliable, trustworthy, and in compliance with the general rules of etiquette. You'll still love me as I am because you'll sense that a part of you is exactly the same. But that won't last long. You are your mother's son too. You'll grow up to be a German man, my little man. And you'll succumb to another dubious myth: what is a man?

And I will always love you and love you all the more painfully, *unselfishly*—how do you say that in German? And not just for the sake of the short span of a few years in which you love me too and think I'm upright, unambiguous, reliable, and creditworthy (as far as you're concerned, I probably will be), but rather because you're something I created, even more abstract than the book I'll have to write to keep the promise I go around conning people with. A promise not to others and not to myself, but—as Uncle Helmuth would have said—decreed by my karma. And to that extent, a maternal product, conceived in pleasure and languorously incubated, nourished by my mind and brought into the world amid torments and joys. Must I explain the paradox? While you, my son, flesh of my flesh, are not really my child no matter how many of my genes are kicking around inside you, my very own most personal creation would be my book—if I ever write it. And while I, as your biological progenitor, am permitted to call myself your father—i.e., a man who has produced another man—I would be the mother of my book, and therefore all the more a man. Do you understand? You are your mother's child and my contribution to your begetting was one moment of death-like oblivion, while she did everything else: carried you inside her in all your vital reality, nourished you along with herself, let you mature and then released you amid pain, brought you from her womb into the light of day.

Soon, my son, the faster you grow into a man, you may forget that it was she (almost) alone who made you in nine months of speeded-up recapitulation of the development from tadpole to stereotypical example of the zoological species *Homo sapiens*. (If only there was a puddle left in the concrete desert we live in where I could show you some tadpoles! How many hours I spent at a pond in Bessarabia, under the guidance of my pompous prince of an uncle, Ferdinand, looking at the frogs' eggs and the swarming tadpoles, nimbly sliding past one another—"like sperm," Uncle Ferdinand said—their mysterious development, limb by limb, into frogs that the kiss of a princess could transform into a handsome prince... If only there were a chance here to show you such things, little man. Until recently, there were plenty of tiny bodies of water in the bomb craters, but they were dull and barren and got buried in the rush to rebuild: life which began in the waters will come to an end in concrete.) Forgive the digression. I was speaking man-to-man about your parentage. With all the great love you bear your mother, little man, you won't thank her for making you (almost) by herself—or for needing a contribution from your father and thus making you into a man who's inherited the curse of the fathers of men: to be a DRONE, incapable of bringing forth a human being out of your own body the way every mother can. May Father Freud rest in peace in the spermatozoal swarm of his adepts and disciples.

Women's supposed penis envy for your little willy is nothing compared to your primeval envy because you cannot REALLY BEGET. You are condemned to abstract begetting: to replaying the world in its eternal self-renewal. Condemned to imitating and aping in eternally insatiable insufficiency. Everything you produce—abstract. Never life itself, but only an imitation of life, a destruction of life. And however much you curse this legacy from your father (I fear it will be the only one!) and hate me for it, you won't be able to sever your connection to me. You too will feel the urge to play men's abstract game of re-creating the world. Even if as the dutiful son of your mother you choose the honest path from desk chair to pension plan, nothing will keep you from building the Eiffel Tower with toothpicks in your spare time. And it may even be that your male inheritance has made you daring enough to lead you to the applied art of a potter or even to self-realization on canvas or in clay, plaster, or marble—or even on paper. Sometime someone will say admiringly behind your back and sotto voce, "He has it from his father. An excellent man."—

—Just don't forget the curse of being a man as well: a man who's unaware of the curse remains at best someone who keeps the whole shebang going. It's up to you to reinvent it completely.

But perhaps you'll be too weak and lazy for that and remain an unfulfilled promise. I'll still be enormously proud of you, and although it will be too late to tell you how much I love you, I always will—

namely, as
Your Father

Uncle Ferdinand's thoughts on literature:

"... So, take Goethe for example—you had a German upbringing, I mean, even in Vienna they shared the attitudes that were circulating in Germany, not in society of course, where with very few exceptions they read nothing at all, not in my day at any rate, and in the schools my sort attended they set more store by homegrown talents: Grillparzer, etc., but with nothing like the emphasis bourgeois circles placed on literature, I know because I have a lot of Austrian friends, and of course also relatives both on the Lobkowitz and the Rohan sides—I mean the Czech Rohans who belong to the five Bohemian dukes, and then the Clarys etc., we have relatives all over Europe, including Russia back then, and so as children and adolescents we were often together when our parents visited one another to go hunting, etc., and I was able to compare what they tried to teach us, only briefly in public schools, most of us had private tutors before they ever got to those institutions to prepare for their final examinations, but even in the private lessons it was apparent what would be dispensed in general, the tutors were all bourgeois intellectuals and of course wanted to teach us their conception of things, that wasn't the case just in Austria, but in general and everywhere, my friend John Fox—you know him—and an Englishman himself, even claims that the decline of the aristocracy stems from the fact that all of us, including the non-English, had English nannies and tutors in the Victorian era inculcating us with their bourgeois ideas, among them naturally the unbelievable overvaluation of novels, an influence so strong that many people took them as a guide to life, we know that when Goethe's *Werther* was published dozens of young people committed suicide, you were taught that too, but it's a big misunderstanding that's never been cleared up, on the contrary, it became all the more entrenched, namely, that young Werther shot himself out of love for Charlotte, it ain't so, I've read *Werther* very carefully because I was curious to see what could bring a person in the bloom of youth to put a bullet through his head if it isn't a case of gambling debts his family can't or won't pay, or simply boredom or because he was told he has syphilis—which was, by the way, quite frequent in my day—and sooner or later is going to go soft in the head despite Salvarsan and such treatments, but nobody shot themselves out of love and if they did it was extremely rare, you'd really have to be a housemaid to believe that Archduke Rudolf, the heir apparent, shot himself with Baroness Vetsera in Mayerling, that's pure nonsense and I'm not even going to discuss it, I'll leave that to the journalists, I'm talking about something else entirely, because if you read *Werther* closely, you'll discover that the troubles caused by his unfulfillable love affair weren't his real motive for killing himself at all, of course they constantly preoccupied him, but that was because he was young, at that age you don't think about anything else and so naturally, it can happen that a guy who's got a certain girl in his sights and she doesn't let him get nearer, that he's going to go crazy even though he knows that once he's slept with her most of the fascination will be gone, at the end of the great majority of love affairs you can't explain what drove you into the necessary mental state and that is exactly what I'm saying: it's the influence of reading novels that put so much store in love, but as I said, if you read *Werther* again all the way through and carefully—you can read it here, there's a nice first edition in the library, and one of the Cotta ur-*Faust* as well and the first English translation with engravings by Retzsch—if you give *Werther* a thorough reading you'll see that he shot himself because he wasn't admitted to an aristocratic party, they turned him away at the door and for a young person with an exalted opinion of himself and perhaps the intention to be a private tutor in a great house, that's a real insult, but strangely enough, precisely the people who could have been in the same situation couldn't empathize with it, no, they all stubbornly insisted that it was love that made him kill himself, although shortly after him—after Goethe, I mean—novels still had a love interest but it wasn't their main focus anymore, which was society, especially the French with Balzac and Stendhal, one in a more bourgeois milieu and the other in aristocratic circles, but always the tension of the individual who somehow is askew in society, as for instance Madame Bovary. She's a particularly graphic example, not to mention the great Russians, of course, Tolstoy and then especially that stigmatized idiot Dostoevsky and whoever else you can think of, the English with Thackeray and Dickens, that's where it starts to get interesting again, who cares anyway how much Monsieur Dupont loves Mademoiselle Legrand—at least, that's what one would think, but the great reading public is just extraordinarily slow on the uptake, and once it finally realizes there's something it needs to understand, you can bet your life that it misunderstands, it's been that way since the world began: all great ideas get immediately corrupted and it's the same with discoveries, you've got to shove people's noses into something and even then they misunderstand it and turn it into something they're familiar with, Goethe knew that very well or he wouldn't have written *Elective Affinities* so close to his end, a novel that takes the theme of love ad absurdum, I mean, why do you have to bring metaphysics—or rather, metaphysiology—into play to have two healthy and attractive couples discover they're not just attracted to their respective partners, but also crossways, nowadays that's positively become a sport, only people aren't as discreet about it as we used to be in our circles, but then, there used to be a lot more urbanity back then, people knew that if you invited a friend to be a houseguest, don't tell me you didn't know what you were doing, especially if you loved your wife and wanted to have a free hand yourself, just take Putzi Schrempff—you know, from the Schrempffs in Auffenberg who went to Hungary and had the most fabulous stags in the Danube meadows—he always said '*Je veux bien être embêté par les femmes, mais pas tout le temps par la même,*' and burst out laughing at himself, especially when his wife was present when he said it, but she was so good-natured, dear old Tina, if she hadn't porked up so much in her last years there are quite a few who would have gladly been guests in her house, of course, it takes a sedentary nature to do that and there weren't many of those among Putzi's friends, and that's why he didn't share the same fate as Edoard and Carlotta (I call them that because I read *Elective Affinities* in Italian, where the house guest is called Ottone, which unfortunately loses the piquant similarity of Otto and Ottilie, not completely, but still) but that's just one of Goethe's ironical artifices and you know, the irony in *Werther* is even more subtle. It's not true that young Werther is hopelessly in love with Charlotte, not at all, she's constantly offering herself in the most shameless way, just read it once through and pay attention, it's very interesting, even as a married woman she's still making innuendos and you've got to be a dope to misunderstand them, take the scene with the bird she wants to get to 'peck' her, for example—couldn't be much clearer than that! But no, the jackass acts like he doesn't get it. He just doesn't dare go for it. That's the real suffering of young Werther, and then he gets turned away from the party and that's enough for him to doubt himself and reach for his pistol. But that's a nonissue in *Elective Affinities*. They've completed the sex act long since in their minds, what's at issue is just that one shouldn't think love is the only power that makes the world go round, people like Putzi and Tina were much too well brought up to think that, they understood the irony, but for others—the great crowd of readers that can get drunk on novels—it was for them that he wrote that story of the lovers attracted crisscross to one another and had a good laugh at people for thinking it unbelievable that, for example, Charlotte bore a child with the red hair of one man and the mole on his cheek of the other and God knows what other personal characteristics from the other two members of the quartet, and the gruesome outcome of the whole calamity, like in Greek tragedy, where everyone knows there are more serious things involved than love, Goethe ironized the whole thing with colossal delicacy and I consider *Elective Affinities* at least as important a book as *Don Quixote*, it's totally in Cervantes's spirit, who would want to write a chivalric romance after *Don Quixote* and who'd have a word to say about erotic attraction after *Elective Affinities*, and I'm not just talking about sex life, but the illusion of spiritual connections spun back and forth between us when we're in the condition of physical attraction. Especially when you've lived too long in the country and haven't been out in the world for a long time—but I can see you aren't interested in what I'm rattling on about, you can't keep your eyes open anymore—no no, no need to apologize, I know at your age you need twice as much sleep as me, it's one of nature's injustices: you could get more out of life if was the other way round—at least when you're young, it's of no use to me now..."

Back then I'd known Schwab a fairly short time and only spoke to him about Nagel because I assumed that, if only for professional reasons, he would be just as interested in him (the newly minted author) as I was for the personal reason of our friendship (was friendship my only reason?). And I wasn't mistaken. Schwab listened very closely to me. His massive face remained impassive. As usual, his sensitive mouth lay like a haughty pasha between the soft cushions of his cheeks, and above it the pale blue carp eyes of a man bespectacled since early childhood (and a regularly relapsing dipsomaniac) stared without expression through his thick lenses. And then all the more unexpected was the malice of his quiet interruptions, questions of perfidious personal provocation, for example, "Was it Nagel the storyteller who disappointed you or Nagel the lover?"

I admit that in those days, my place in the bourgeois order was not easy to determine. I had no profession, wrote occasional treatments for the successors of the late lamented STELLA FILMS (Stoffel has disappeared, Astrid von Bürger grows gracefully older, and the industrious little movie piglets I work for confine themselves to making plans). My free-time activities also left something to be desired. I didn't play soccer or tennis in a fancy club, to say nothing of golf, not even hockey and not bridge in any case. I was ignorant of soccer pools and didn't watch TV or play skat at the kitchen table with buddies in shirtsleeves. I didn't fish, bowl, ride, hunt, row, box, or do gymnastics. I didn't sing in a men's chorus, collect donations for the Red Cross—not even for thalidomide cripples or wheelchair polo players—didn't read a newspaper and wasn't interested in politics. I couldn't tell the CDU from NATO, the Monroe Doctrine from the Hallstein Doctrine, state capitalism from the Comintern, and hopelessly confused the EEC, FDP, SPD, and SED. Whenever I said something about current events, Christa blushed liked I'd felt her up. I couldn't care less about German universities or space travel, didn't give a shit about the Oder–Neisse line. The Wall of Shame in Berlin was okay with me (it's only logical that if the Jews have a Wailing Wall, the Germans have a Wall of Shame). I thought being a manager was great: it absolved me of the responsibility no one had asked me to shoulder in the first place. Engagé art, literature, radio, film, and theater left me cold. I had no past to come to terms with except my own, and it was spurious anyway. I left the topic of the kibbutzim to Nagel, compensation for the Arab states to Rönnekamp and his business associates, and the question of rearmament to the chancellor, Pope John XXIII, de Gaulle, President John Fitzgerald Kennedy and his wife Jackie, Khrushchev, the Lorelei, Willy Brandt, the neo-Nazis, Dr. Albert Schweitzer, and Edith Piaf. I hoped to survive the Cold War just as I had the hot one (and this time, my chances were considerably better). Both intra- and extramaritally, I shoved the birth control pill in with my middle finger. There were already enough people preoccupied with the Red Army Faction as well as with the victims of the Twentieth of July plot, even though they had nothing to do with either one. I hadn't had the pleasure of hearing Pastor Thielicke's sermons. I'd already read most of the novels Rowohlt started reissuing as cheap paperbacks after the war. I hadn't seen the DOKUMENTA exhibition. Like so many other things in life, the results of the Ecumenical Council would be made clear simply by the passage of time. Had water polo already been accepted into the Olympic Games, or when and how and by whom would that be decided (and would the teams from the GDR and the Federal Republic—i.e., the anticapitalistic and capitalistic, anti-imperialistic and imperialistic aquatic acrobats—splash around in the pool together or separately)? Whatever the answer, it didn't move me a hair's breadth from the conviction that it was utterly unimportant. Philosophically and politically and athletically I wasn't on the left or the right or the middle (I hadn't noticed the disappearance of the latter, by the way), not even on the right wing or left wing of the right, to say nothing of being on one or the other extremes—so I lacked any sort of spatial orientation, so to speak.

"Tell me, do you actually exist at all?"—Yes, alas, you'll be surprised to hear that you can exist despite all that, one can exist. I can, for one, although I leave the question of deciding between Romain Gary and Robbe-Grillet, or who's to blame for the First World War, up to King Solomon, while the question of whether the Protestant hymn has a future is best left up to the infallible wisdom of the pope or Marilyn Monroe—what do I care—WHAT DO I CARE?!...

Of course, this attitude comes with a certain loneliness: it has an isolating effect if you have nothing to say about the Hamburg Derby or the Formula One races on the Nuremburg Ring, much less the Berlin Festival or the launch of Sputnik I, II, III—

Incidentally, nowadays such events problems scandals threats are delivered abstractly right to our door by the press, radio, and TV. Their emotional effect is almost identical, their informational value in fact is even greater than when you're an eyewitness, so why should I exert myself? There's a few things I can even admit ingenuously, for example, that culturally I'm a philistine, I don't travel, and so I've never been to Baalbek or Samarkand or Angkor Wat, or—to my shame—even Crete, although that shows up prominently in organized tours, but on the other hand, it's strange that as a rule, in museums I only look at objects I'd like to steal and have no intention of following the traces of the Hittites or learning about the creators of Cycladic sculpture or pre-Columbian pottery. That's odd for a so-called intellectual.

—but what is that anyway? A profession? What does "an intellectual" mean? Basically, it means I can't come home with the housekeeping money on the first of the month, taxes already deducted and accident, life, retirement, and health insurance as well as burial fund all paid up; rent, telephone, light, and gas bills all automatically deducted from my bank account; installments laid aside for the new car, patio furniture, Mom's fur coat, the dentist, the Klepper kayak, refrigerator, TV set, floor polisher, and electric iron. I was shamelessly delinquent on all that, left it up to the repo man. If I ever happened to have some money, it ran through my fingers like water, which led to terribly embarrassing scenes. ("The child asked me in front of everybody why the man had put seals on our furniture—he said you told him it was a trademark like his teddy bears with the button in their ears—what kind of nonsense is that? You're giving him the wrong ideas...")

to whom could I possibly explain that all that didn't count, that I expected something else from myself, required it—as an intellectual, if you will—even if it was the book Schwab was demanding from me like an existential debt...

Note:
The volatility of his intellect. He is hypersensitive to all impressions, most of which are lasting: he is surrounded by immediately available memories and is constantly in search of connections, of what he calls their *meaning*. What has kept him from writing up to now is

the obsessive notion that he can only begin when he has found this meaning.

Sometimes he reveals himself. In drunken dialogue with S.: "And so you're trying to persuade me to write a book—would it floor you to learn that in mortal terror I think of nothing else, dream of nothing else, wish for and expect nothing else..."

On the subject of Nagel: "He may well be destined for something great, good old Nagel, namely, for something not even remotely connected to writing—what do I know? Maybe as a leader of men, a politician. Just imagine what an immensely valuable role he could play at a party convention, a hobgoblin of the categorical imperative who puts the fear of God into the pilots of our state. Back in the days of our primal community, he often played that role in his notebook. But he's not destined to be an artist. For that, he would have had to experience fewer bloody spectacles and more quiet, would have to see less and listen more—like the blind Homer, for instance. We all know that the *Iliad* includes not just the immediate reality of the battle for Troy, but also the core that partakes of the stillness of eternity: the discord of the gods... An artist needs ears to hear that, not GOD THE FATHER'S all-embracing love for mankind..."

And he added: "Your subtle smile tells me you think you know very well why I get so riled up—but believe me, it's out of pure sympathy for our friend. Whoever wishes Nagel well ought to keep him from writing for the very reason that he probably has some talent for it and has the best intentions to do good. That's exactly what will prevent him from fulfilling his greatest aspirations. He'll remain a middling scribbler suffering the disastrous effects of success. For if there's one thing that from the get-go stamps people who set out to write as second-rate and parasites on humanity, it's their good intentions to uplift it—humanity—morally. Nagel's an ethicist, that's all there is to it, and he won't be able to resist beating his readers over the head with it. Admittedly, he's a mighty good pal, a most foursquare fellow with a crystal-clear character, the stoutest, most upright person, striving to do the impossible. He accomplishes things even with only a left hand. In person, sitting across from you with his white-toothed smile and his chesty drone, marvelously vital yet with a manly, gallant sensitivity—and all that in a compact format: five foot three in his socks, size seven shoes—he's a jewel of a human being, a gem of the finest water. But on paper, alas, a character in a book for young readers ..."

Imperious, indolent, voluptuous, they filled the rows of mirroring windows flowing into one another along the half-timbered facades of the sagging, gabled little houses with the trumpery of their tawdry coiffures, feather boas, fringed bras, and froufrou; filled to overflowing the silk receptacles of their bodices stretched tightly over wire and whalebone forms with a gaudy bounty of female flesh, pushed-up breasts, rolls of fat, powdered shoulders and arms, burst out of them with powerful thighs that funneled into obscenely crossed legs in black net stockings. They filled the glassed-in, dollhouse interiors of the humble cottages with the trumpery of their female scent, the smell of powder and cheap perfume, filled the vitrines shining in the darkness of Whores' Alley with the shrill trumpery of their make-up, false eyelashes, locks of hair pasted to their forehead like a flamenco dancer's, and hennaed quiffs: duenna, matriarch, and mousie, child bride, tomboy, giant baby, she-werewolf, spider, wasp—each one the overly sharp copy of some woman once desired, loved, never possessed, the shamelessly revealed ur-image of a female type, the brazen mask of an anima—

thus they filled the short Whores' Alley, screened off at either end by a wall of corrugated iron, with light and color, with the pattering rain of the keys they tapped against the window panes to entice customers, those magnificent augurs of happiness—

and all around, the concrete desert sprung from bomb craters, the faceless crowds, the lava of tinny vehicles rolling through the streets, the icy light of the arc lamps reflected in glass and steel and enamel, the trumpery consumer products filling the wasteland of department store windows

---

I knew I was drunk, but I stubbornly kept talking all the more. I said, "Try to express that in a comprehensible way—in images, I mean. You intend to write about that yourself sometime, right? Okay then, you won't rise to the bait—I'm not going to either, no matter how hard you try—by the way, did you ever try offering cash? A check signed by your employer Scherping—given the right circumstances that might tempt me to take up my pen. Go ahead! Do as my swinish film bosses do: they get me to write with false promises too . . . But I mean, just for the fun of it: where would you find the images for a gripping novel of the present day? I mean, a present that's not decoupled from the past. Where would you begin? Probably in the death camps, where guilt and enslaved innocence, terror, fear and deprivation and insanity, the madness inherent in human beings were raised to such a monstrous level that they assumed the character of a dream; where they had metastasized into a surrealistic nightmare; where hundreds of thousands died senseless deaths without the slightest chance for a litmus test to prove their will to live and a consideration of the murderers' motives had become almost laughable. How does a potential author provide a vivid image of all that? Those who survived don't like to talk about it, and if they do, then quite inadequately, for language can't cope with that telling. Especially not with the encounter with GOD. He wasn't much in evidence there behind the barbed wire. For the great majority of others however—namely, the ones who strung the barbed wire around the camps—the spectacular thunder, lightning, and fire of their experiences at the front and in the nights of air raids in the cities obscured this core reality of the past. The benevolent Veil of Maya, right? Fitfully illuminated by exploding bombs. The terror bombing of German cities, the wild escapes, the loss of the Homeland, the rapes of German women and girls by Asiatic subhumans, etc., such are the novelistic themes that obscure the essence. This incursion of physical ur-reality into metaphysics had a positively cleansing, liberating effect: the horror latent in the epoch was happening at last, quite widely recognized although not yet as directly experienced as inside the barbed wire. But that still was not enough to leave one stone upon another. Not enough to avoid anything of what followed: the reconstruction of the possibility it would happen again. Peace—you'll protest—a cleansing of conscience, democracy, etc.—those were nothing to sneeze at, were they? Granted. But what about the guilt that continues to grow in the background? The catharsis that never happened! Still charitably veiled by Maya? And you intend to continue to weave that veil and with GOD's help give a leg up to tomorrow's reality? So that it doesn't see? So that the future discovers it's as blind as ever! Is that what we writers are destined to do? Never to speak the truth! Always weaving the veil of Maya—and all the tighter, the more vividly we depict the terrors of the world of men . . . Many thanks, dear sir, but count me out!"

Scherping was in America and has returned with plans for countless books, among them a translation of a recently published biography of Sonja Henie. Purely out of spite, Schwab refuses to support the plan, declares absolutely that if Scherping Publishing is moving in the direction of athletes' biographies, he cannot remain as lead editor. Scherping, who enjoys torturing him, calls Sonja Henie "a genius." Schwab ironically quotes Robert Musil's "genius of a racehorse" from *The Man without Qualities*, which Scherping doesn't get at first and then—after it's been explained to him—he takes painful pleasure in his own philistinism. Aristides, bored to tears, stops listening to them. His thoughts stray: Sonja Henie, spinning like a top on the toes of her skates, takes on the shape of Uncle Ferdinand. The scene is the park in Bessarabia in the depths of winter. The pond is frozen, the ice swept clean and smooth as a mirror. Under their load of snow, the weeping willows on its banks are as bent as peddler women. The rowboat with its ornamental cast-iron seat back is stuck in the icy reeds and covered with snow. Uncle Ferdinand in a belted Norfolk jacket, knee britches, and woolen stockings and, like an adolescent, a fur cap on his head and his hands in a muff, has strapped ice skates onto his high lace-up boots. His left leg raised and gracefully bent at the knee, his hands in the muff in front of his chest, he executes a rapid spin on the toe of the other skate. His high cheekbones are burning with frost, the centrifugal force of his rotation combs his mustache in the direction of the spin. The image is so vivid that A. has the impression of a "manifestation" (as Uncle Helmuth described them from his spiritist séances). He clearly hears his mother's ironical voice: "Isn't he unspeakably ridiculous? He's trying to bore his way through the ice to poor me. He always had to come to me through the ice, always on tiptoe . . ."

A sudden insight whose absurdity strikes his innermost being connects this image of Uncle Ferdinand with Schwab. His mother's words seem to apply to Schwab and himself. He has to shake himself awake.

OTHER NEW YORK REVIEW CLASSICS

For a complete list of titles, visit www.nyrb.com or write to:
Catalog Requests, NYRB, 435 Hudson Street, New York, NY 10014

J.R. ACKERLEY My Dog Tulip*
RENATA ADLER Speedboat*
LEOPOLDO ALAS His Only Son *with* Doña Berta*
CÉLESTE ALBARET Monsieur Proust
JEAN AMÉRY Charles Bovary, Country Doctor*
KINGSLEY AMIS Lucky Jim*
U.R. ANANTHAMURTHY Samskara: A Rite for a Dead Man*
IVO ANDRIĆ Omer Pasha Latas*
EVE BABITZ Slow Days, Fast Company: The World, the Flesh, and L.A.*
DOROTHY BAKER Cassandra at the Wedding*
J.A. BAKER The Peregrine
HONORÉ DE BALZAC The Memoirs of Two Young Wives*
VICKI BAUM Grand Hotel*
SYBILLE BEDFORD A Legacy*
MAX BEERBOHM The Prince of Minor Writers: The Selected Essays of Max Beerbohm*
STEPHEN BENATAR Wish Her Safe at Home*
MIRON BIAŁOSZEWSKI A Memoir of the Warsaw Uprising*
ADOLFO BIOY CASARES The Invention of Morel
PAUL BLACKBURN (TRANSLATOR) Proensa*
CAROLINE BLACKWOOD Great Granny Webster*
LESLEY BLANCH Journey into the Mind's Eye: Fragments of an Autobiography*
NICOLAS BOUVIER The Way of the World
EMMANUEL BOVE My Friends*
ROBERT BRESSON Notes on the Cinematograph*
SIR THOMAS BROWNE Religio Medici and Urne-Buriall*
DAVID R. BUNCH Moderan*
JOHN HORNE BURNS The Gallery
ROBERT BURTON The Anatomy of Melancholy
MATEI CALINESCU The Life and Opinions of Zacharias Lichter*
J.L. CARR A Month in the Country*
LEONORA CARRINGTON Down Below*
BLAISE CENDRARS Moravagine
EILEEN CHANG Love in a Fallen City*
JOAN CHASE During the Reign of the Queen of Persia*
ELLIOTT CHAZE Black Wings Has My Angel*
UPAMANYU CHATTERJEE English, August: An Indian Story
FRANÇOIS-RENÉ DE CHATEAUBRIAND Memoirs from Beyond the Grave, 1768–1800
ANTON CHEKHOV Peasants and Other Stories
GABRIEL CHEVALLIER Fear: A Novel of World War I*
JEAN-PAUL CLÉBERT Paris Vagabond*
RICHARD COBB Paris and Elsewhere
COLETTE The Pure and the Impure
JOHN COLLIER Fancies and Goodnights
CARLO COLLODI The Adventures of Pinocchio*
IVY COMPTON-BURNETT Manservant and Maidservant
BARBARA COMYNS Our Spoons Came from Woolworths*
ALBERT COSSERY Proud Beggars*

* *Also available as an electronic book.*

ASTOLPHE DE CUSTINE Letters from Russia*
JÓZEF CZAPSKI Inhuman Land: A Wartime Journey through the USSR*
JÓZEF CZAPSKI Lost Time: Lectures on Proust in a Soviet Prison Camp*
LORENZO DA PONTE Memoirs
ELIZABETH DAVID Summer Cooking
AGNES DE MILLE Dance to the Piper*
VIVANT DENON No Tomorrow/Point de lendemain
ANTONIO DI BENEDETTO Zama*
ALFRED DÖBLIN Berlin Alexanderplatz*
JEAN D'ORMESSON The Glory of the Empire: A Novel, A History*
ARTHUR CONAN DOYLE The Exploits and Adventures of Brigadier Gerard
BRUCE DUFFY The World As I Found It*
DAPHNE DU MAURIER Don't Look Now: Stories
ELAINE DUNDY The Dud Avocado*
G.B. EDWARDS The Book of Ebenezer Le Page*
JOHN EHLE The Land Breakers*
MARCELLUS EMANTS A Posthumous Confession
J.G. FARRELL The Singapore Grip*
KENNETH FEARING The Big Clock
FÉLIX FÉNÉON Novels in Three Lines*
M.I. FINLEY The World of Odysseus
THOMAS FLANAGAN The Year of the French*
BENJAMIN FONDANE Existential Monday: Philosophical Essays*
SANFORD FRIEDMAN Conversations with Beethoven*
MARC FUMAROLI When the World Spoke French
CARLO EMILIO GADDA That Awful Mess on the Via Merulana
BENITO PÉREZ GÁLDOS Tristana*
MAVIS GALLANT The Cost of Living: Early and Uncollected Stories*
MAVIS GALLANT A Fairly Good Time *with* Green Water, Green Sky*
LEONARD GARDNER Fat City*
WILLIAM H. GASS On Being Blue: A Philosophical Inquiry*
THÉOPHILE GAUTIER My Fantoms
GE FEI The Invisibility Cloak
JEAN GENET Prisoner of Love
ÉLISABETH GILLE The Mirador: Dreamed Memories of Irène Némirovsky by Her Daughter*
NATALIA GINZBURG Family Lexicon*
JEAN GIONO Hill*
JEAN GIONO Melville: A Novel*
JOHN GLASSCO Memoirs of Montparnasse*
NIKOLAI GOGOL Dead Souls*
EDMOND AND JULES DE GONCOURT Pages from the Goncourt Journals
ALICE GOODMAN History Is Our Mother: Three Libretti*
PAUL GOODMAN Growing Up Absurd: Problems of Youth in the Organized Society*
JULIEN GRACQ Balcony in the Forest*
HENRY GREEN Living*
HENRY GREEN Loving*
VASILY GROSSMAN Life and Fate*
VASILY GROSSMAN The Road*
LOUIS GUILLOUX Blood Dark*
PETER HANDKE Slow Homecoming
THORKILD HANSEN Arabia Felix: The Danish Expedition of 1761–1767*
ELIZABETH HARDWICK The Collected Essays of Elizabeth Hardwick*
ELIZABETH HARDWICK Sleepless Nights*

L.P. HARTLEY The Go-Between*
ALFRED HAYES My Face for the World to See*
PAUL HAZARD The Crisis of the European Mind: 1680–1715*
ALICE HERDAN-ZUCKMAYER The Farm in the Green Mountains*
YOEL HOFFMANN The Sound of the One Hand: 281 Zen Koans with Answers*
HUGO VON HOFMANNSTHAL The Lord Chandos Letter*
RICHARD HOLMES Shelley: The Pursuit*
ALISTAIR HORNE A Savage War of Peace: Algeria 1954–1962*
GEOFFREY HOUSEHOLD Rogue Male*
DOROTHY B. HUGHES In a Lonely Place*
RICHARD HUGHES A High Wind in Jamaica*
INTIZAR HUSAIN Basti*
DARIUS JAMES Negrophobia: An Urban Parable
HENRY JAMES The New York Stories of Henry James*
TOVE JANSSON The Summer Book*
UWE JOHNSON Anniversaries*
JOSEPH JOUBERT The Notebooks of Joseph Joubert; translated by Paul Auster
KABIR Songs of Kabir; translated by Arvind Krishna Mehrotra*
FRIGYES KARINTHY A Journey Round My Skull
ERICH KÄSTNER Going to the Dogs: The Story of a Moralist*
YASHAR KEMAL Memed, My Hawk
YASHAR KEMAL They Burn the Thistles
WALTER KEMPOWSKI All for Nothing
TOM KRISTENSEN Havoc*
GYULA KRÚDY The Adventures of Sindbad*
SIGIZMUND KRZHIZHANOVSKY Autobiography of a Corpse*
K'UNG SHANG-JEN The Peach Blossom Fan*
PATRICK LEIGH FERMOR A Time of Gifts*
PATRICK LEIGH FERMOR The Violins of Saint-Jacques*
SIMON LEYS The Hall of Uselessness: Collected Essays*
GEORG CHRISTOPH LICHTENBERG The Waste Books
CURZIO MALAPARTE The Kremlin Ball
JEAN-PATRICK MANCHETTE The Mad and the Bad*
OSIP MANDELSTAM The Selected Poems of Osip Mandelstam
OLIVIA MANNING Fortunes of War: The Balkan Trilogy*
GUY DE MAUPASSANT Like Death*
JAMES McCOURT Mawrdew Czgowchwz*
WILLIAM McPHERSON Testing the Current*
JESSICA MITFORD Hons and Rebels
NANCY MITFORD Voltaire in Love*
KENJI MIYAZAWA Once and Forever: The Tales of Kenji Miyazawa*
PATRICK MODIANO Young Once*
MICHEL DE MONTAIGNE Shakespeare's Montaigne; translated by John Florio*
ALBERTO MORAVIA Agostino*
IRIS ORIGO A Chill in the Air: An Italian War Diary, 1939–1940*
MAXIM OSIPOV Rock, Paper, Scissors and Other Stories*
LEV OZEROV Portraits Without Frames*
CESARE PAVESE The Selected Works of Cesare Pavese
ELEANOR PERÉNYI More Was Lost: A Memoir*
LUIGI PIRANDELLO The Late Mattia Pascal
DAVID PLANTE Difficult Women: A Memoir of Three*
ANDREY PLATONOV Soul and Other Stories
J.F. POWERS The Stories of J.F. Powers*

QIU MIAOJIN Notes of a Crocodile*
JEAN RENOIR Renoir, My Father
GREGOR VON REZZORI An Ermine in Czernopol*
GREGOR VON REZZORI Memoirs of an Anti-Semite*
GREGOR VON REZZORI The Snows of Yesteryear: Portraits for an Autobiography*
TIM ROBINSON Stones of Aran: Labyrinth
LILLIAN ROSS Picture*
UMBERTO SABA Ernesto*
JOAN SALES Uncertain Glory*
TAYEB SALIH Season of Migration to the North
JEAN-PAUL SARTRE We Have Only This Life to Live: Selected Essays. 1939–1975
ARTHUR SCHNITZLER Late Fame*
GERSHOM SCHOLEM Walter Benjamin: The Story of a Friendship*
LEONARDO SCIASCIA The Wine-Dark Sea
ANNA SEGHERS Transit*
VICTOR SERGE Notebooks, 1936–1947*
VICTOR SERGE Unforgiving Years
VARLAM SHALAMOV Kolyma Stories*
SASHA SOKOLOV A School for Fools*
VLADIMIR SOROKIN The Queue
NATSUME SŌSEKI The Gate*
RICHARD STERN Other Men's Daughters
JEAN STROUSE Alice James: A Biography*
MAGDA SZABÓ The Door*
MAGDA SZABÓ Katalin Street*
ANTAL SZERB Journey by Moonlight*
ELIZABETH TAYLOR Angel*
TEFFI Tolstoy, Rasputin, Others, and Me: The Best of Teffi*
TATYANA TOLSTAYA White Walls: Collected Stories
MARINA TSVETAEVA Earthly Signs: Moscow Diaries, 1917–1922*
KURT TUCHOLSKY Castle Gripsholm*
SALKA VIERTEL The Kindness of Strangers*
EDWARD LEWIS WALLANT The Tenants of Moonbloom
ROBERT WALSER A Schoolboy's Diary and Other Stories*
MICHAEL WALZER Political Action: A Practical Guide to Movement Politics*
SYLVIA TOWNSEND WARNER Lolly Willowes*
JAKOB WASSERMANN My Marriage*
ALEKSANDER WAT My Century*
C.V. WEDGWOOD The Thirty Years War
SIMONE WEIL On the Abolition of All Political Parties*
HELEN WEINZWEIG Basic Black with Pearls*
GLENWAY WESCOTT The Pilgrim Hawk*
REBECCA WEST The Fountain Overflows
EDITH WHARTON The New York Stories of Edith Wharton*
T. H. WHITE The Goshawk*
JOHN WILLIAMS Nothing but the Night*
JOHN WILLIAMS Stoner*
RUDOLF AND MARGARET WITTKOWER Born Under Saturn
GEOFFREY WOLFF Black Sun*
FRANCIS WYNDHAM The Complete Fiction
BÉLA ZOMBORY-MOLDOVÁN The Burning of the World: A Memoir of 1914*
STEFAN ZWEIG Chess Story*
STEFAN ZWEIG The Post-Office Girl*